UNSURE SHOT

Longarm's fingers twitched as Cahill spurred forward, and Hollister twisted around, not sure who to shoot at. He must have decided Cahill was the greater threat, because he jerked the barrels of the shotgun toward the onrushing rider.

Longarm's Colt seemed to leap into his hand from the cross-draw rig on his left hip. Even if Cahill gunned down Hollister, the man would probably be able to fire both barrels of the shotgun. And at this range, they would cut both Cahill and his horse to ribbons. Longarm brought the Colt up. The light was bad and he only had a fraction of a heartbeat to aim, but he knew he had to make the shot.

The revolver bucked in his hand as he fired . . .

DON'T MISS THESE ALL-ACTION WESTERN SERIES FROM THE BERKLEY PUBLISHING GROUP

THE GUNSMITH by J. R. Roberts

Clint Adams was a legend among lawmen, outlaws, and ladies. They called him . . . the Gunsmith.

LONGARM by Tabor Evans

The popular long-running series about Deputy U.S. Marshal Long—his life, his loves, his fight for justice.

SLOCUM by Jake Logan

Today's longest-running action Western. John Slocum rides a deadly trail of hot blood and cold steel.

BUSHWHACKERS by B. J. Lanagan

An action-packed series by the creators of Longarm! The rousing adventures of the most brutal gang of cutthroats ever assembled—Quantrill's Raiders.

DIAMONDBACK by Guy Brewer

Dex Yancey is Diamondback, a Southern gentleman turned con man when his brother cheats him out of the family fortune. Ladies love him. Gamblers hate him. But nobody pulls one over on Dex . . .

WILDGUN by Jack Hanson

Will Barlow's continuing search for his daughter, kidnapped by the Blackfeet Indians who slaughtered the rest of his family.

TABOR EVANS

J

JOVE BOOKS, NEW YORK

LONGARM AND THE OZARK ANGEL

A Jove Book / published by arrangement with the author

PRINTING HISTORY
Jove edition / June 2002

For information address: The Berkley Publishing Group, a division of Penguin Putnam Inc.,
375 Hudson Street, New York, New York 10014.

Visit our website at
www.penguinputnam.com

ISBN: 0-515-13311-6

A JOVE BOOK®
Jove Books are published by The Berkley Publishing Group, a division of Penguin Putnam Inc.,
375 Hudson Street, New York, New York 10014.
JOVE and the "J" design are trademarks belonging to Penguin Putnam Inc.

PRINTED IN THE UNITED STATES OF AMERICA

10 9 8 7 6 5 4 3 2 1

Chapter 1

Despite his reputation as a ladies' man, Longarm didn't really make a habit of taking gals to bed right after he met them.

In Libby's case, he was going to make an exception.

She stood in the center of the room, next to the scarred bedstead with its feather mattress, and reached down to grasp the hem of her homespun dress. With a lithe motion, she pulled the dress up and peeled it off over her head. As she tossed it aside, Longarm saw that she was naked underneath it, just as he had thought when he first saw her in the roadhouse.

She was eighteen, fresh and ripe, rounded in all the right places and slender in the others. Her hair was a cloud of sable around her face as she tossed her head. The triangle between her muscular thighs was the same color. Her large breasts were full and firm, barely bouncing as she came toward Longarm. The dark brown nipples were the size of silver dollars.

Boldly, she reached out and pressed the palm of her hand against the front of his trousers. His shaft was already stiffening into an erection. She smiled as she felt it growing.

"Lordy, you got a big one," she said. "Let's take a look at it."

Standing there fully dressed while a naked young woman fondled him through his trousers was pretty damned arousing, thought Longarm. His pants were getting tight around his erect manhood. He didn't object as Libby started unfastening his buttons. Instead, he stood there and puffed on the cheroot he'd been smoking when she led him through the woods from the roadhouse over to this one-room log cabin.

When she had his fly unbuttoned, she delved inside it, wrapped her fingers as far around the thick, fleshy pole as they would go, and tugged it free. She stepped back as Longarm's organ jutted proudly from his groin. A low whistle of appreciation came from her pursed lips.

"I wouldn't be surprised if that was the biggest talleywhacker I ever saw," she said. "You mind if I suck on it for a while?"

"Be my guest," Longarm said hoarsely.

Libby went to her knees before him and used both hands to steady his shaft as she leaned toward it. Her mouth opened, then a second later her soft, warm lips closed around the head of his manhood. She went, "Mmmm," as she started to suck on it.

Longarm had to close his eyes for a moment and think about the time a longhorn steer had stepped on his foot in Abilene, Kansas. That was back in the days when he'd been cowboying, not long after he'd come west following the end of the war that he thought of as the Late Unpleasantness. It had hurt like hell when that steer stepped on him, and although no bones were broken, he was laid up for a week while the foot healed. The rest of the outfit, having already delivered the herd, had drawn their pay, blown most of it in a couple of days of sin and debauchery along Abilene's Front Street, then started back to Texas. Longarm wasn't able to go with them, so when he'd recuperated enough to get around, he signed on as a skinner with a bunch of buffalo hunters. That was the dirtiest, nastiest job he'd ever had in his life, and when the hunting party got back to Abilene he swore he'd never do anything like that ever again. It wasn't long after that when he'd pinned on a lawman's badge for the first time.

Lot of water under the bridge since then, thought Longarm. Yes, sir, a whole lot of water.

While he was thinking that, Libby suddenly swallowed a good half of his shaft, and Longarm couldn't hold back any longer. He gritted his teeth on the cheroot, put his hands on Libby's head, and started emptying himself into her mouth. His shaft swelled and throbbed and sent spurt after spurt of thick white cream over her tongue and down her throat. Libby swallowed fast, trying to keep up with Longarm's erupting seed.

In the back of Longarm's mind, part of his brain was cursing in frustration. He hadn't meant for that to happen so fast. Not enough time had passed since he left the roadhouse with Libby. He didn't want to go back just yet.

His head was thrown back and his eyes were closed as he finished pumping the last of his climax into Libby's mouth. He lowered his head, opened his eyes, and took a deep breath. Libby lifted her head from his shaft, milked the last couple of drops from it, and licked them off the head. "That was mighty good, Custis," she said, "but I ain't done with you yet."

Longarm was glad to hear that. He needed to spend more time with her.

He put his hands under her arms and lifted her to her feet. She was petite, coming only to his chin. She smiled up at him, and he said, "It's your turn now."

Her smile stretched into an excited grin. "You mean it? Hot damn! These ol' boys around here never seem to think that turnabout's fair play."

With that, she threw herself onto the feather mattress and spread her legs as far as she could. The pink, pouting lips of her femininity were clearly visible in the thicket of dark, finespun hair between her thighs. She reached down and plunged a finger into herself. "See how wet I am already?" she asked.

Longarm saw, all right. "Just let me get out of some of

these clothes," he said as he tugged on the string tie around his neck.

"Don't be too long about it." Libby kept playing with herself, adding a second finger to the first one as Longarm undressed.

He didn't strip down to the buff but left the bottom half of his long underwear on. He was careful to coil the shell belt with its holstered Colt and place it on the small table beside the bed, in easy reach. If Libby thought there was anything unusual about that, she gave no sign. Instead, she reached for him eagerly as he knelt between her wide-spread thighs. She pressed his head down so that his lips and tongue could find her hot, slippery core.

Longarm went to work on her, licking and tonguing and thrusting, and Libby cried out several times as her hips bucked up off the mattress. This little gal pure-dee liked what he was doing, thought Longarm. He had seen soiled doves who could fake such enthusiasm, but he didn't believe Libby was one of them. Her reaction to what he was doing to her was genuine.

He continued teasing and licking, and after a few minutes Libby yelled again and clamped her thighs tightly around his head. The yell gave Longarm a second's warning of what was about to happen, so he was able to grab a quick breath before she trapped him there. It would have been damned embarrassing to suffocate with his face buried in a gal's private parts. As it was, he was able to hold his breath until Libby went limp and her thighs fell away from his ears. She sprawled on the bed like a rag doll as she gave a long, shuddery sigh.

"Custis, you plumb wear a girl out," she said when she had caught her breath and was able to talk again. "Come spoon with me for a spell."

Longarm slid onto the bed next to her as she turned onto her left side with her back toward him. He snuggled up against her, with her rump tucked firmly into his groin. He was erect again, his manhood poking out the opening in his long underwear. Libby opened her legs enough so that the shaft went between her thighs, then she closed them on it. The pole rubbed against her wet furrow.

Longarm slipped his left arm underneath her so that he could fill his palm with her breast. He kneaded the warm, fleshy globe and toyed with the hard nipple that crowned it. Libby wiggled her rump against him and made a sound of satisfaction.

It would have been easy to doze off like this, with his arms full of warm woman. But Longarm knew he couldn't afford to fall asleep. He was expecting company pretty soon, and he had to be ready. The hand he was playing was a risky one. It could backfire on him and ruin everything. But if it succeeded, it was the quickest way to accomplish his goal.

After a while, Libby began to move her hips again, rocking them backward and forward. That made his shaft slide along the lips of her sex. The sensation that caused was exquisite torment for both of them. Finally, she said in a half-whisper, "Put it in me, Custis. Please. I need you inside me."

Longarm grasped her hips, adjusted his angle a little, and surged forward so that his shaft sheathed itself in her. The hot, slick walls of her femaleness closed around him. He launched into a slow but powerful rhythm, driving himself in and out of her.

He knew that pacing himself like this, he could keep going for quite a while. He wanted to give Libby all the pleasure he could, since in a way he was doing this under false pretenses and he felt a mite guilty. When the idea had occurred to him, bedding her was just a means to an end. Now that he had seen how wholeheartedly she gave herself to her work, he felt that he owed her something besides the usual payment she received from her customers. Maybe that was foolish, but that was the sort of hombre he was. He liked to do right by folks.

So he was going to give Libby the best ride that he possibly could.

After a while she rolled onto her belly and pulled her knees up. Longarm went with her, keeping his manhood embedded deeply within her. He began thrusting in and out of her again as he knelt behind her. She clutched at the homespun sheets on the mattress and made little panting noises.

"Do me, Custis!" she gasped. "Do me good!"

Longarm went at it then, no longer holding back anything. He held tightly to her hips as he drove into her. As her sex began to spasm around him, he tipped over the edge into his own climax. Once again his seed boiled out into her in scalding spurts. Libby screamed with her mouth against the mattress.

Covered with a fine sheet of sweat, Longarm felt lassitude stealing over him as his organ gave a final little twitch inside Libby. He pulled back so that it slid wetly out of her. She collapsed onto her belly, breathing heavily. Longarm lay beside her, trying to catch his own breath. Maybe he *had* used Libby for his own purposes, but he didn't think she was going to have any complaints.

When she could speak again, she lifted her head and said, "Custis, I don't know where you're from or where you're headed, but I hope you're going to be around here for a while. You can come see me *any* time you want to."

"I might just take you up on that," said Longarm.

"Right now, though . . ." She frowned slightly. "You wouldn't happen to know what time it is, would you?"

"We can find out." He swung his legs off the bed and went to the chair where he had left his clothes. He picked up his vest and slipped a large, turnip-shaped pocket watch from one of the pockets. The heavy gold chain attached to the watch dipped into the vest's other pocket, and welded to that end of it was a two-shot, .41 caliber derringer. Longarm kept the derringer out of sight as he flipped open the turnip and checked the time. "It's a little after eight o'clock."

"Eight o'clock?" Libby echoed, alarm in her voice as she sat up sharply. Her breasts bounced a little more this time. "Damn it, I didn't know it was so late. You made me lose all track of time, Custis."

"What's wrong with that?" Longarm asked mildly as he replaced the watch in the vest pocket and lowered the garment to the chair.

"Wrong? Just that—"

Libby broke off and gave a little scream as somebody kicked open the cabin door. A large male shape bulked in the doorway, and an angry voice demanded harshly, "What the hell's goin' on here?"

"Roney!" Libby cried.

It was damned well about time, Longarm thought fleetingly as the newcomer swung toward him and roared, "I'm goin' to kill you, you son of a bitch!"

Chapter 2

Nobody had been threatening to kill Longarm when it all started a few days earlier. Instead, Chief Marshal Billy Vail had said in a voice that was fairly mild for him, "I think I'm going to send you to Arkansas again, Custis."

Deputy United States Marshal Custis Long leaned back in the red leather chair in front of Vail's desk, slipped a cheroot from his vest pocket, and said, "The hangin' judge got another problem that needs taken care of, Billy?"

Vail frowned. "I wouldn't call Isaac Parker the hanging judge where he can hear it. He's just enforcing the law the best way he knows how."

"Which usually involves a noose and a gallows," Longarm pointed out.

Vail shrugged shoulders that had grown pudgy through inaction. A former Texas Ranger and a real hell-roarer in his time, he had been riding the chief marshal's desk in the Denver office for a good many years. For most of that time, Longarm had been the deputy Vail turned to first when he had a hard, dangerous assignment to hand out.

"We've received an official request from Judge Parker for the loan of one of our deputies," Vail said. "That's going to be you, Custis."

Longarm took out a lucifer, snapped it into life with an iron-hard thumbnail, and held the flame of the sulfur match to the tip of the cheroot. When he had the tightly rolled cylinder of tobacco burning to suit him, he dropped the match on the floor next to the chair and ground it out with his boot heel. Henry, the four-eyed gent who played the typewriter in Vail's outer office, would see that later and start foaming at the mouth like a dog with hydrophobia. Longarm hoped so, anyway.

"The Ozarks are mighty pretty this time of year," he said. "What's Judge Parker want, anyway?"

"He needs a man who won't be recognized. All of his regular deputies are too well-known in Arkansas."

"I've been there before, you know," Longarm pointed out. In truth, several of his assignments had taken him to Arkansas in the past.

"It's been a while," Vail replied with another shrug. "Besides, most of the fellas you met up with while you were there wound up dead, didn't they?"

It was Longarm's turn to shrug. "Sometimes things work out that way."

Vail cleared his throat, then picked up a sheet of paper from his desk and held it out toward Longarm. "Anyway, this is what the judge has on his plate right now. He's hoping you can give him a hand with it."

Longarm took the report and read it as he puffed on his cheroot. According to the document in his hand, a wave of lawlessness was sweeping over the northwestern part of Arkansas. Quite a few stagecoaches and trains had been robbed, and banks had been hit in Dardenelles, Fayetteville, and other settlements scattered throughout the Ozark Mountains. The robberies seemed to be the work of a large, well-organized gang.

"Judge Parker has some suspects in mind," Vail said when Longarm had finished reading the report. "He'll tell you all about them when you get to Fort Smith."

Longarm shifted the cheroot from one side of his mouth

to the other, then said around it, "Why don't he just send out a big ol' posse to round up these boys?"

"He would if he was sure who to go after. That's where you come in."

"How's that?"

"He wants you to infiltrate the gang and find out exactly who's responsible for all that lawbreaking."

Longarm grimaced. He had been afraid of that when he heard that Judge Parker wanted someone who wasn't well-known in the area, and now his suspicions had been proven right. Putting a man inside a gang of owlhoots was a time-honored technique on the part of lawmen, and when it worked, it usually worked spectacularly. The only problem was, a lot of the time the only result of such a plan was a dead star-packer. Most outlaws weren't overly smart, but they were a damned suspicious lot and it was hard to pull off a masquerade that was convincing enough to win them over.

"This is out of our bailiwick, Custis," Vail went on, "so I'm not going to order you to do it . . ."

"I'll give 'er a try," Longarm said, and tried not to sound bitter. Billy Vail had known damned good and well that he wasn't going to turn down an assignment. It would have taken extraordinary circumstances to make Longarm do that.

"All right," Vail said with a nod. "I'm sure you'll do just fine, Custis."

"I reckon I'd better not be too convincing as an owlhoot," Longarm said. "The judge might up and decide to hang *me*."

Vail gave a short bark of laughter. He said, "Henry has your travel vouchers. You can catch a train this evening for Kansas City and transfer there to one that'll take you to Fort Smith. I'll wire Judge Parker to expect you. He'll want you to avoid the courthouse, so I reckon he'll have somebody meet you and give you all the details." Vail hesitated. "Be careful, Custis."

"I intend to, Billy."

Longarm remembered, though, the old saying about good intentions and the road to hell . . .

• • •

Fort Smith was built on a bluff overlooking the Arkansas River. It was a good-sized city, with several brick buildings that were three and four stories tall. The view was dominated by the large, redbrick federal courthouse that sat almost at the very edge of the bluff. The depot was down by the river itself, and to reach the rest of the town, visitors had to walk up a winding path or take a horse-drawn trolley.

Longarm didn't figure he'd have to make that walk. If his identity as a deputy U.S. marshal was going to remain a secret, he couldn't very well go traipsing into Judge Isaac Parker's office in the courthouse and ask what the judge wanted done. Billy Vail had said that Parker would have someone meet him here at the station.

But as he looked up and down the platform, Longarm didn't see anybody paying attention to him. Folks were coming and going, some getting on the train and some getting off, but none of them spared a second look at the tall, rangy figure in a brown tweed suit and snuff-brown, flat-crowned Stetson. He strolled along the platform to the baggage car, intending to reclaim his warbag, McClellan saddle, and Winchester.

"Mistuh Jones? This heah yo' bag, Mistuh Jones?"

Longarm looked around and saw that an elderly black porter was coming toward him, lugging his warbag and saddle. The Winchester was tucked under the porter's arm.

Frowning, Longarm wondered how the man had known who he was. A possible answer came to him. He nodded and said, "Yes, those are my things. I can take them." He reached out.

"No, suh, I got 'em. You just let me carry 'em out front, an' you can get a trolley there to take you up the hill."

"I'm much obliged," Longarm said.

"No trouble, Mistuh Jones. No trouble a'tall."

A lot of the time when he was on a job where he didn't want his real identity known, Longarm used his middle name, Parker, as an alias. In this case, though, calling himself Parker would have just drawn unwanted attention to him in the famous hanging judge's own backyard. Pretending to be somebody named Custis Jones was unoriginal, but as long as it worked, Longarm didn't care.

As he walked through the depot with the elderly porter beside him, the man said to Longarm, "Stayin' long in Fort Smith?"

"I don't rightly know yet," Longarm replied honestly.

"If'n I was you, I'd get me a room at the Danvers House. Yes, suh, best place in town to stay. You just go to the Danvers House and ask the fella at the desk for the best room in the house."

"Wouldn't that be expensive?"

"Oh, not so much as you'd think, suh. That's sure what I'd do, if'n I was you."

"Well, I'm much obliged for the advice," Longarm said. "I think I'll do that."

"You won't be disappointed, suh."

Longarm didn't think he would be, either. If he was right and Judge Parker had given the porter his description and asked the man to meet him, somebody else would probably be waiting for him when he got to the Danvers House.

In front of the depot, Longarm took his gear from the porter and pressed a coin into the man's hand. "Thanks."

"Thank *you*, suh!"

A trolley was waiting with several passengers already on it. Longarm stepped up and took a seat. The vehicle was open on the sides to let in a cool spring breeze. Later in the summer, Fort Smith would be miserably hot and sultry, Longarm recalled from previous visits, with swarms of mosquitoes that could drive a man mad. At this time of year, however, the weather was quite pleasant.

A few more passengers came out of the depot and boarded the trolley, then the driver got the team of horses moving. The path wound back and forth up the bluff so that it wouldn't be as steep as the ones pedestrians used. After a few minutes, it reached the top, clattered past the big courthouse, and rolled along a cobblestone street into downtown Fort Smith.

Longarm got off at the trolley's second stop, which was across the street from the Danvers House. It was a decent-looking, two-story hotel, hardly the palace that the porter had made it sound like. Longarm thought that probably he would be comfortable there for however long he would be staying. He didn't figure that would be very long.

He went up a couple of steps and through a door into the hotel lobby. It was decorated by a couple of dusty potted plants and several overstuffed armchairs. A couple of the chairs were occupied by bowler-hatted men who had to be drummers of some sort. Longarm had seen thousands of similar figures in his travels through the West, men garbed in cheap suits, with an air of desperation. He walked past them to the desk and said to the slick-haired gent behind it, "I was told by one of the porters at the train station that this is the best hotel in town and that I should ask for your best room."

The clerk grinned, revealing a gold tooth in the front of his mouth. "Well, ain't that just fine an' dandy?" he said. "I'll bet it was ol' Mose who told you that."

"Could've been," Longarm said. "I didn't catch his name."

The clerk turned the register around, plucked a pen from an inkwell, and held it out toward Longarm. "If you'll just put your name down right here, sir, we'll get you all fixed up."

Longarm signed *Custis Jones*, and for his address he put *Albuquerque*. He knew that New Mexico town more than well enough to answer any questions about it if anyone got suspicious and asked.

"Thank you, Mr. Jones," the clerk said. He reached to the board behind him and snagged a key. "You'll be in Room Seven. It's the best, just like you said you wanted. First floor, rear, so you won't be disturbed. I'll get a boy to take your bags."

"No need," Longarm said. "I can handle my gear myself."

"You're sure?"

"Positive."

"Well, then, you can go right on up. Room's clean, and there's fresh linen on the bed."

Longarm nodded his thanks and went to the stairs. He climbed to the first floor and turned down the hallway toward the rear. It took him only a moment to find Room Seven. He set his saddle down, tried the knob, and found it locked. The key turned smoothly and unlocked it.

Longarm bent, picked up his saddle, stepped into the room, and pushed the door shut behind him with the heel of his right boot. The room was dim because the shades had been drawn, but enough light came around them for Longarm to be able to see the short, slender man who stood there. The man reached up, tugged on his beard, and nodded. "Hello, Marshal Long."

"Howdy, Judge," Longarm said to Isaac Parker. "I reckoned you might be waiting for me."

Chapter 3

"How are you, Marshal Long?" Parker asked.

Longarm tossed his warbag on the bed, dropped his saddle in a corner, and leaned the Winchester beside it. "Fair to middlin', Judge, fair to middlin'," he said. "Yourself?"

"I'm fine," Parker replied curtly. He was a man who had little time for pleasantries. "You were met at the train station, I assume?"

"Yep. Don't reckon I'd be here otherwise."

A thin smile touched Parker's mouth. "Mose is a good man. He keeps me abreast of the comings and goings in Fort Smith and helps me out on other matters from time to time."

"What about the fella down at the desk?"

"Burt?" Parker shook his head. "He's not in my confidence. He knows only that he gets occasional instructions from an anonymous source, along with a modest payment."

"Sounds like you know how to be careful, Judge."

"Discretion is frequently important in my job, as I'm sure it is in yours, Marshal." Parker clasped his hands behind his back and got further down to business. "I trust you've read the report I sent to Chief Marshal Vail?"

Longarm nodded. "I did. Sounds like you've got trouble here."

"Policing Indian Territory is a difficult enough task. Having desperadoes roaming unchecked through Arkansas itself just makes things worse. There have been more than a dozen robberies of various kinds in the past month. I want to put a stop to this lawlessness."

"Sounds like these owlhoots have been busy, all right," Longarm agreed. "Marshal Vail said you had some suspects in mind . . . ?"

"Two, actually. I'm not sure which of these men is heading up the gang, but the rumors I hear from my informants tell me that it's one of them."

"You got names?"

"Cahill," said Parker. "Roney Cahill. He's from one of these fierce mountain clans that populate the Ozarks. He has quite a reputation as a gunman and a brawler."

"But not as an outlaw?"

Parker frowned. "He hasn't really been connected to any crimes, but I'm certain he'd have no trouble gathering a gang around him. He's said to have killed several men in fair fights, some of them with his bare hands."

"What about the other suspect?"

"A man named Deuce Thaxton."

That took Longarm by surprise. "The same Thaxton who was a jayhawker during the war?"

"That's right."

"I thought he was still raising hell up in Kansas somewhere."

"Rumor has it that he's drifted down here. I'm hoping you can confirm that one way or the other, Marshal."

Longarm raked a thumbnail along the line of his jaw as he frowned in thought. "I don't know Cahill, but I've heard plenty about Thaxton. He's been mixed up in a heap of robberies and killings in Kansas and Nebraska, and he's a slippery son of a bitch. The law's never been able to lay hands on him."

"Yes, well, if he's responsible for the wave of terror that's been going through the state, I intend to see that he's brought to justice," Parker declared. "However, I don't know where to suggest that you start looking for him. Cahill is a different story."

"Where do I find him?"

"His stomping grounds are the mountains between here and Fayetteville. He's said to frequent a roadhouse called Strickland's Tavern. That's where I'd start looking for him if I were you." Parker paused, then went on, "Perhaps Cahill knows something about Thaxton. These mountain people have their own telegraph, I suppose you could call it. They know practically everything that goes on in the Ozarks."

Longarm nodded. It was a place to start, all right. "They don't take to outsiders, either," he mused. "I'll have to figure out a way to get Cahill to talk to me."

"That may prove difficult. But I have confidence in you, Marshal. If anyone can work his way into Cahill's good graces, it's you." Parker hesitated. "There's one more thing I haven't told you yet, something that wasn't in the report I sent to Marshal Vail and wasn't mentioned in my letter to him."

That took Longarm by surprise. It wasn't like Judge Parker to be secretive with other lawmen. He was nearly always straightforward, even blunt. "What would that be, Judge?" Longarm asked.

"I haven't said anything about the murders."

Longarm's eyebrows rose. "Murders?" he repeated. "You mean shootings during those robberies?"

Parker made a brusque gesture and said, "No, although there have been some of those. I'm talking about the assassinations that have taken place here in recent weeks."

Assassinations? This was turning strange in a hurry, thought Longarm. He said, "Maybe you better tell me a little more, Judge."

Parker sighed. "A month ago, one of the federal land commissioners for this district was shot in an ambush as he drove his buggy along a road north of here. He was killed. A short time after that, a clerk from the land office was ambushed under similar circumstances, also fatally. Then, last week, the director of the local office of the Bureau of Indian Affairs was killed. Three bushwhackings in the space of a month, three federal officials dead."

"You think they've got something to do with Cahill or Thaxton or whoever's behind the robberies?"

"The ambushes started about the same time," Parker said. "It seems to be a reasonable assumption that they're related."

"Two victims from the land office and one from the BIA. Don't hardly seem like they'd have anything to do with a bunch of robberies."

"Not on the surface of it. I'm counting on you, Marshal, to uncover the connection, if there is one, and put a stop to these bushwhackings as well."

That made his job considerably more complicated, thought Longarm, but he didn't say anything. He had traveled all the way to Fort Smith; he damned sure wasn't going to back out of the assignment now just because Judge Parker had thrown an unexpected new wrinkle into it.

"I'll do my best, Judge," Longarm said.

"Excellent." Parker extended his hand and as Longarm shook with him, he went on, "You can get word to me through Mose. Otherwise I don't expect to see you or hear from you until you have the evidence we need to put a stop to all the depredations."

Longarm nodded. "How do I find this Strickland's Tavern?"

"Ask Burt downstairs. He can give you better directions than I can."

"I'll do that. I'll ride up there first thing in the morning, Judge."

"I knew you wouldn't waste any time."

Longarm grinned. "Nope, that's me, always in a hurry to get myself killed . . ."

In the morning, Longarm rented a horse at a livery stable down the street from the Danvers House. It was a bay gelding with shorter legs than the mounts Longarm usually chose. Long-legged horses had more trouble in the mountains. The bay was more suited to the sort of traveling that Longarm would be doing.

The clerk told him to follow the Fayetteville road for about fifteen miles, then turn right on a smaller road that would intersect the main route. From there it was seven miles to Strickland's Tavern, which was one of only three main buildings in a community called Skunk Hollow.

"There's really a place called Skunk Hollow?" Longarm asked with a grin.

Burt frowned. "What's wrong with that? I got cousins who live up around there."

Longarm held up his hands and said, "No offense, old son. Hell, I've been lots of places with stranger names than that." He couldn't think of any right off the top of his head, but he was sure that he had.

Burt looked a little mollified. "Best be careful up there, Mr. Jones. I've heard tell that Strickland's is a rough place."

"I'll keep my eyes open," Longarm promised.

Burt went on to warn him that it would probably take most of the day to get there, since the mountainous terrain would slow him down considerably. Longarm went into the hotel dining room and got the cook to pack a lunch for him. That way he wouldn't have to worry about finding a place to stop and eat.

He had already saddled the bay. He tied the burlap sack containing his lunch to the saddlebags and swung up onto the horse. Finding his way out of Fort Smith wasn't difficult. A spur rail line ran up to Fayetteville, and the road paralleled it for the most part. Longarm rode north into the Ozarks.

It was beautiful country. The pine-covered slopes stayed green all year 'round, but now in the spring, the meadows were full of wildflowers and lush green grass. Creeks bubbled and laughed, adding their music to the songs of the birds that flitted from branch to branch in the pines. Squirrels lurked in the trees, too, chattering amongst themselves and scolding Longarm when he rode past. He just grinned at them and restrained the impulse to wave. "You go ahead and tell it, old son," he called to a particularly noisy squirrel.

Now he was talking to critters, he thought with a wry shake of his head. If Henry could see him now, the clerk would say that he'd lost his mind. What Henry wouldn't know was how much those fussy little squirrels reminded Longarm of a certain four-eyed typewriter pounder back in Denver.

At midday, he stopped and sat under the shade of a tree to eat his lunch, then dozed for a little while before mounting up and riding on. He hadn't seen many people since leaving Fort Smith. A few wagons on the road, a handful of men riding horses or mules, once a woman and a pack of dirty-faced kids walking along—that was about it. He saw frequent tendrils of smoke rising from the woods, however, and knew they came from the chimneys of shacks and cabins that he couldn't see from the road. From time to time, he passed narrow footpaths, and he knew they led to those hidden cabins.

It was past the middle of the afternoon when he came to the turnoff for Skunk Hollow. At this rate, it would be almost nightfall before he reached the tiny settlement where Strickland's Tavern was located. That was all right, he reflected. He'd halfway planned to spend the night there anyway. There was no guarantee he would make contact with Roney Cahill today. It might even take him several days.

Dusk was indeed settling down over the rugged landscape when Longarm rode down a long slope into the village. A few lights burned yellow to mark the location of the buildings. As he came closer, he saw a large plank structure with a sign in front that read JEPPSON'S TRADING POST. Diagonally across the road was a church with a crude cross on its roof in place of a regular steeple. Farther along, on the same side of the trail as the trading post, was a long building made of logs. That had to be Strickland's Tavern. Several horses were tied to the hitch rack in front, he noted.

The way the buildings were laid out, they formed a rough triangle, Longarm thought. Trading post, church, and tavern formed the points. Business, salvation, and sin, all working together to form the community of Skunk Hollow. Wasn't that always the way? Longarm asked himself with a grin.

He rode past the trading post and the church to the tavern. Leaving the bay tied to the rack, he went to the door and pulled the latch string.

The roadhouse backed up to a hill, and it was built on two levels. As Longarm went inside, he saw a crude bar to his right, made from thick planks laid across whiskey barrels. Several rough-hewn tables and chairs were scattered across the floor in front of the bar. The floor was made of puncheons, pine trunks peeled of their bark and split in half, then laid side by side with the relatively flat sides turned up. To Longarm's left, looking somewhat out of place in this backwoods tavern, was a billiard table. Halfway back, the second level rose three feet from the floor, with a short flight of steps leading up to it. It was an open area, probably used for dancing.

No one was up there cutting a rug at the moment. Several men stood at the bar, and others occupied some of the tables. A poker game was going on at one of the tables. Two men were shooting pool, the click of the balls providing a counterpoint to the conversation and laughter elsewhere in the room.

The bartender was skinny as a rail, with a shock of white hair. He wore a soiled apron over a pair of overalls and seemed pretty spry despite his age. He glanced toward Longarm but didn't seem overly curious about the newcomer. No one else paid any attention to him at all.

There was only one female in the place, as far as Longarm could see. She was a young woman with thick dark hair that fell around her shoulders and down her back. She wore a simple homespun dress that was cut square in the front and low enough so that he could see the upper slopes of large, firm breasts. The way the dress clung to her body, Longarm had a pretty good idea it was the only thing she had on. She carried a tray and was delivering drinks from the bar to the tables. She placed a bottle on one of the tables, and one of the men sitting there reached over and squeezed her rump. She laughed and swatted him playfully with the tray.

Somebody to Longarm's left laughed and said, "Damn, Corby, you're the worst billy-ard player I ever did see."

Longarm looked over at the felt-covered table. One of the men who had been playing was grinning, while the other scowled at the balls remaining on the table. "Hell, you didn't give me a chance, Jim."

"You had your chance," Jim replied with a chuckle. He picked up a piece of chalk and began to rub it against the tip of the cue stick in his hand. "I give you the first shot."

"And nary another one!"

"Got to make your shots count," Jim advised in mock solemnity.

Still grumbling, the man called Corby pulled a coin from his pocket and flipped it to Jim, who caught it deftly. Corby tossed his stick on the table and turned away.

Jim looked at Longarm, who had watched the exchange with interest. "You play billy-ards, stranger?" he asked.

Without hesitation, Longarm nodded. "A little."

"How about a game, then? We mostly play for five bucks a game."

Longarm pretended to think about it. In reality, he was more than ready to seize this opportunity. Some men preferred silence when they were shooting pool, but he sensed that Jim was the garrulous sort. Chances were, he could get Jim talking while they were playing, maybe even find out something about Roney Cahill.

"Sure," Longarm said with a nod. "Why not?"

Jim extended a hand. "What do they call you, mister? I'm Jim. Jim Cahill."

Chapter 4

With a skill born of years of practice, Longarm kept his surprise from showing on his face. "Jones," he said as he shook hands with Jim Cahill. "Custis Jones."

"Mighty glad to meet you, Custis. I'll rack 'em, and you can break."

Jim was giving him the first shot, just as he had Corby. He wouldn't find Longarm quite as easy a victim as Corby had been, however.

While he waited for Jim to rack the balls, Longarm studied his opponent. Jim was tall and slender, with a battered white Stetson shoved to the back of his head, revealing bright red hair. He wore a cowhide vest over a work shirt, whipcord trousers, and high-topped black boots. A gunbelt rode around his narrow hips, with the fancy pearl grips of a Remington revolver jutting up from the holster. He had the look of a hardcase about him, but his quick grin dispelled that somewhat.

When he lifted the triangle from around the balls, he said, "There you go. Any time you're ready, Custis."

Longarm took his time lining up the break. He said, "Cahill, Cahill . . . seems like I know that name from somewhere. We haven't ever met, have we?"

"I don't recollect it, and I think I would, a big Indian-lookin' galoot like you. No offense."

Longarm shook his head. "None taken." He knew that his high cheekbones and skin tanned to the color of old saddle leather gave him something of the appearance of an Indian.

"There's lots of Cahills in these parts," Jim went on. "Maybe you've run into my cousin Roney. I reckon he's the best known of us all."

"Could be," Longarm said vaguely. "I don't really know." Now that he knew Jim Cahill was Roney's cousin, he wanted more than ever to keep the man talking. He drew back the stick and hit the cue ball with a smooth, strong stroke.

With a series of loud, sharp clicks, the gathered balls broke apart and rolled around the table. Two of them dropped in the side pockets. Jim raised his bushy eyebrows in surprise. "Nice break."

"Thanks," Longarm said as he began to line up his next shot. "Come to think of it, I believe I have heard of Roney Cahill."

"If you've been around the Ozarks much, you have," Jim said. He gave a hoot of laughter. "Don't believe ever'thing you hear, though. Roney's even more of a ring-tailed roarer than he's made out to be."

"Seems there was something about some shootings . . ."

The grin dropped off Jim's face, and for a second Longarm thought he had made a mistake. But then Jim said, "Ever' one of those killin's was in a fair fight, and I'll whip any man who says different."

"Not me," Longarm said. "That's just what I heard, that Roney Cahill is a fair man and always gives a fella an even break." He pointed the cue stick at the table. "Sort of like here."

That brought the smile back to Jim's face. "Yeah, but billy-ards ain't like goin' up against another fella with a gun. Even though I *do* take the game pretty serious-like."

Longarm shot again, sank another ball. Jim whistled and went on, "You ain't a-gonna run the table on me, are you?"

Longarm grinned. "We'll see."

He missed his next shot, though not deliberately. Jim chuckled as the ball almost fell, then bounced back from the fender. "Now you gave me an openin'. You'll be sorry, Custis."

"Maybe, maybe not."

"A man with confidence. I like that." Barely seeming to aim, Jim shot, and one of the balls fell.

He sank two more before barely missing his next shot, which involved a complicated, difficult bank. As he straightened from the table, he said, "Looks like we're pretty evenly matched."

"I'd say so," agreed Longarm. He bent to the task. "I wouldn't mind meeting your cousin. He around these parts now?"

"Roney's always around where you least expect him." Jim paused, then continued, "Now don't get me wrong, Custis, but I never seen you until today. You wouldn't happen to be a lawman, would you?"

Longarm had left his badge and bona fides with Judge Parker back in Fort Smith. No one who searched him would find anything to indicate that he worked for Uncle Sam. He laughed and said, "If I was toting a badge, likely I wouldn't tell you, now would I?"

"Likely not." Longarm made a difficult shot, and Jim went on, "I never saw a lawman who could play billy-ards like that, though. Shows you had what the preachers call a misspent youth."

Longarm's laugh was genuine. "Maybe so, but it wasn't for lack of my mama trying to raise me right."

"Where were you raised up?"

"West-by-God Virginia."

"A mountain boy like us around here. I should've knowed." Jim's eyes narrowed. "Say, you didn't fight for the Yankees, did you?"

"Was there a war here lately? I disremember." Longarm stroked the cue ball, sent it spinning across the table to barely clip one of the other balls. That one rolled a foot straight to the side and plunked into a pocket.

"I was just a younker back then, myself. Hell, I can't hold no grudges against anybody who can shoot pool like you, Custis, even if you did happen to wear the blue."

"Never said I did," Longarm said blandly.

"That's right, you didn't. Anyway, you asked about Roney. I reckon he's around. He's sweet on ol' Libby over yonder." Jim pointed with his chin toward the bar, where the young woman was getting another bottle from the white-haired bartender.

Longarm straightened from the table and pretended to notice her for the first time. "Nice looking gal," he commented. "She spoken for?"

"Yeah, by anybody who's got a silver dollar. Don't get me wrong—Libby's as sweet as sorghum. But she's still a whore."

"Not necessarily a dishonorable profession."

"You sound like you've had some schoolin'."

"Mostly just what I've read," Longarm said. A few more shots and he would win the game. But he missed the next one, grimacing as he did so.

"Reckon I'd better pounce whilst I got the chance," Jim said. He grew solemn as he lined up his shot. He made it and moved around the table to the next one.

"When we're done I might buy Miss Libby a drink," Longarm said.

Jim sank one of the balls, then straightened and said, "No offense, Custis, but you ain't from around here. Now, us hill folks are more tolerable than people make us out to be, but we still don't cotton much to outsiders takin' a shine to our women."

"I can understand that. It was the same where I come from."

"Just so you know. Prob'ly nobody in here right now would be too upset if you was to buy Libby a drink, but if Roney came in and found you makin' eyes at her, he'd be plenty mad. Might even try to give you a whippin'."

"Likes to brawl, does he?" An idea was forming in Longarm's brain.

"Shoot, there's nothin' Roney likes more than a good ol' bare knuckles, knock-down, drag-out fight. He says it gets the blood to pumpin'."

"Well, then, I'd better steer clear of him."

Jim started lining up another shot. "Just consider it a friendly piece of advice, from one billy-ard player to another."

A moment later, he cursed as the shot he needed to win failed to fall by a fraction of an inch. That left Longarm with an opening.

He knocked two balls down, one each into the corner pockets at the end of the table. That left him needing just one more to win, and it was lined up fairly well for a shot. Still, it would be tricky. . . .

Longarm made his best shot of the game so far. He missed.

Jim let out a whoop of relief, clearly unaware that Longarm had deliberately sent the ball an eighth of an inch too far to the right. "You should've made that one, Custis. You ain't gettin' another shot."

Sure enough, a moment later, with a click and a thump, the final ball fell home for Jim. Longarm shook his head and sighed in mock disappointment. He dug out a five-dollar gold piece and handed it to Jim. "Least you can do is give me a rematch sometime."

"Sure, but not tonight," Jim said. "I don't want to press my luck against a fella who can shoot like you do, Custis."

"How about you buy me a beer, then?"

"Don't mind if I do. Come on." Jim set his stick aside, as did Longarm. They went over to one of the tables, and Jim signalled to the young woman. "Two beers over here, Libby!"

She nodded and took the mugs from the bartender after the old man had filled them from one of the barrels. As she brought the beers over to the table, Longarm looked frankly at her, appreciating the thrust of her breasts against the homespun fabric of her dress. She saw him looking and smiled, obviously not minding his appraisal.

"Here you go, Jim," she said as she set the mugs on the table. "Who's your friend?"

"He's the fella who just lost five dollars to me at billyards. Name's Custis."

She looked at Longarm and said, "I'm Libby." Her tongue darted out and played wetly over her lips for a second.

"Mighty pleased to meet you, Miss Libby," Longarm said.

"I saw you playing pool. You're a mighty big gent, aren't you?"

"Now, Libby," Jim said in an amused but warning tone, "ain't no point in you flirtin' with Custis here. He knows he's an outsider and ain't supposed to mess with our women."

"Says who?" Libby shot back at him. "You just hush your mouth, Jim Cahill. Ain't you or anybody else goin' to tell me who I can talk to . . . or do anything else I want to."

"What about Roney? You better watch what you're sayin', girl."

Libby tossed her head defiantly, making the long dark hair swirl around her shoulders. "Roney ain't the boss of me."

Jim grunted. "That's easy to say while he ain't here."

"I'd say it to his face if he was here," Libby snapped. She turned back to Longarm with a sweet smile, but the look in her eyes was hot and smoldering with passion. "Don't you pay a lick of attention to what this ol' boy says, Custis. I'm a grown woman and I do what I want, with whoever I want."

"Well, that's mighty nice to know, Miss Libby," Longarm told her. So far he'd been lucky, but he wanted to push things even further. "This Roney Cahill, though, I've heard he's a dangerous man."

"Don't you worry about Roney." Libby reached down and caught hold of Longarm's hand. "I've got a cabin not far from here. Why don't you come over there with me?"

Longarm glanced at Jim, who was starting to look worried and angry. "Listen here, Libby," Jim said. "You know Roney will be here in a little while—"

"Roney doesn't care who I take back to the cabin with me."

"Maybe when he's not around, but if he comes in and finds out you're over there rompin' with a stranger, he'll be fit to be tied!"

"I'm not afraid of him." Libby looked at Longarm. "Are you afraid of him, Custis?"

"I never met the man," Longarm replied honestly. "I'll admit that I'm mighty taken with you, though, Miss Libby."

She squeezed his hand. "You're so polite—not like the rest of these razorback hogs around here. You just come on with me, Custis. I'll show you a mighty good time, and it'll only cost you a silver dollar."

Longarm came to his feet. "I don't reckon I can turn down such a nice invite from a lady."

Jim scowled at both of them. "Don't say I didn't warn you," he said. "Roney'll bust ever' bone in your body, Custis, and you, Libby, he'll beat that butt of yours 'til it shines like the sun."

Libby tossed her head again and sniffed in contempt. "Come on, Custis," she said to Longarm as she tugged him toward the door of the roadhouse.

Longarm went with her, not looking back at Jim. He could feel eyes boring into his back, however. Not just Jim's, he judged. Probably every man in the place was staring daggers at him for daring to go off with Libby. But they were willing to leave it to Roney Cahill to deal with him, which was exactly what Longarm wanted. Luck had presented him with an opportunity, and he didn't want to waste it.

Of course, he was betting on his ability to hold his own in a fight with Cahill and maybe, just maybe, win the man's respect. If he could do that, if he could fight Cahill to a standstill, it would be the quickest—though not the least painful—way of gaining the man's friendship.

Some of Libby's bravado deserted her as she led Longarm along a narrow path through the woods. "It might be best if we get back to the tavern before Roney gets there, Custis. It ain't that I'm scared of him, mind you, I just—"

"No sense in borrowing trouble," Longarm said. "When do you expect him?"

"He never shows up before about eight o'clock." She slipped an arm around his waist. "I'll show you a mighty good time before then."

Longarm put his arm around her and felt it brush against the side of her full breast. "You know, Miss Libby, I think you're right."

But it hadn't worked out that way, as Longarm had deliberately drawn out their lovemaking until it was after eight o'clock. He suspected that as soon as Roney Cahill arrived at Strickland's Tavern, his cousin Jim would tell him all about how Libby had sassed him and gone to her cabin with an outsider. Longarm hoped that would bring Roney on the run, outraged and looking for a fight.

Now, as he stood there in his long underwear, looking at the flushed, furious face of the man who stood just inside the cabin door, Longarm knew that his hastily-formed plan had come together perfectly.

All he had to do was keep Roney Cahill from beating him to death.

Chapter 5

Roney Cahill was tall, with heavy, powerful shoulders. Like his cousin Jim, he had red hair, but Roney's was a darker shade, more like copper. His features were too rugged to be called handsome. He wore a black, high-crowned hat, plaid shirt, and denim trousers tucked into brown boots. He didn't have a gunbelt on, but a .36 Colt Navy was stuck behind the broad black belt around his waist, butt forward just ahead of his left hip. Both hands were clenched into big, knobby-knuckled fists.

Libby scooted all the way to the head of the bed and was cowered there. Obviously, she was terrified of Cahill. "R-Roney, I'm sorry!" she said. "I don't know what got into me—"

"That'd be me," Longarm drawled, adding fuel to the fire.

Cahill flushed an even darker shade of red than his hair. "Who in blazes are you?" he thundered at Longarm.

"Name's Custis Jones. You'd be Roney Cahill. I've heard of you."

Cahill took a step toward him. "Then you know I'm gonna give you the worst thrashin' you ever took in your life."

"You may try to give it, but I'm not taking," Longarm said. "There's no need to fight, Cahill."

Longarm knew better. Cahill wasn't going to be talked out of this battle. Longarm didn't *want* to talk him out of it. But he had to try, because that was what Cahill would expect. Even a man who wasn't afraid of him, as Longarm obviously wasn't, would normally try to persuade him not to fight.

Another step forward by Cahill. He took the gun out of his belt and set it aside on the table. "You been messin' with my girl!"

"I thought she was anybody's girl who had a silver dollar."

Libby exclaimed, "Oh!" and glared at Longarm in shame and anger. "You don't have to be so . . . so damn crass about it."

"Highfalutin talk for a whore."

"That's it!" Cahill rushed him, fist cocked back to strike. "I'm gonna knock your head clean off!"

The punch came at him faster than Longarm expected it to. He barely moved his head aside in time. As it was, Cahill's fist raked his left ear and made it sting.

But Cahill was off-balance and close enough for Longarm to hit him in the belly. Longarm sank his right fist in Cahill's midsection. The punch didn't travel far, only about a foot, but it had most of Longarm's considerable power behind it. Cahill's breath burst out of his lungs and his face turned white as he started to double over.

Longarm was ready for that, too. His left came up and smashed into Cahill's jaw. The second part of the dandy combination sent Cahill flying backward to crash against the door jamb.

He caught himself there and kept himself from falling through the open door. As he straightened, he grinned and reached up to take hold of his chin and work his jaw back and forth. "Damn, that was a nice one," he said to Longarm. "This might be fun after all."

Oh, shit, thought Longarm.

Libby screamed as Cahill threw himself across the room at Longarm. Longarm didn't know why she was hollering. She had two big, powerful men fighting over her, and one of them was only half-dressed. Most gals would consider that not too shabby a situation.

That was all he had time to think before he had his hands full with Cahill. Longarm blocked the man's first punch but couldn't get out of the way of the second. Cahill's fist caught him on the jaw and flung him back against the wall. The rough bark of the logs out of which the cabin was constructed scraped Longarm's back. He ignored that pain and concentrated on Cahill, who was closing in on him from the front. Again Longarm parried a blow, and this time he was able to land a punch of his own—a hard, straight right to the sternum that rocked Cahill back a step. Longarm jabbed with a left, then hit Cahill with a right cross. Cahill shrugged it off and threw a left that knocked Longarm down and sent him rolling across the floor toward the bed.

Cahill rushed him. Longarm knew that if he let Cahill trap him on the floor against the bed, Cahill could stomp and kick the life out of him. Acting quickly, Longarm pulled himself onto the bed and rolled across it, colliding with Libby as he did so. The impact knocked her off the bed. She squealed as she fell, a sound that ended with an "Ooof!" as her pretty rump hit the floor.

Longarm landed on his feet beside the bed, facing Cahill across the mattress. Cahill glanced worriedly at Libby. "You all right, girl?" he asked.

"I'm f-fine," she sniffled. "Pound him, Roney! Pound the big bastard!"

Cahill flexed his fists. "That's just what I intend to do." With a shout, he leaped onto the bed, planting a foot right in the middle of the mattress, and threw himself at Longarm.

The simple thing was often the best. Longarm got out of the way.

Cahill sailed past him and crashed to the floor, landing so hard that the whole cabin seemed to shake. Longarm could have stepped in then, kicked Cahill in the head while he was still groggy, and put an end to this, but he didn't want to. For one thing, it wouldn't have been fair. For another, Longarm didn't want Cahill unconscious. For yet another, he thought he might break a toe on the man's hard skull.

Instead, he stepped back and waited while Cahill pushed himself onto his hands and knees, shook his head a time or two, then lumbered to his feet. Blood was leaking from Cahill's nose where he'd smacked it on the floor. Cahill pointed a finger at Longarm and said hoarsely, "You should've lit out while you had the chance, mister."

"Then I'd have missed the rest of this *fun*," Longarm jibed.

Cahill growled and came at him again, swinging wildly. Longarm ducked some of the punches, blocked others, and absorbed the punishment from still others. He jabbed at Cahill, maneuvering him around toward the bed. When Longarm had Cahill standing where he wanted him, he crouched so that one of Cahill's wild swings went over his head. Then he tackled the big redhead. Cahill went over backward, taking Longarm with him. Both men landed on the bed. With the sharp crack of splintering wood, the bedstead broke in half under their weight, dumping the mattress and both men on the floor.

Longarm got his knees in Cahill's belly and pinned him there. He hit Cahill with a right, a left, and another right. Cahill was almost out. Longarm didn't have to let up on him on purpose, however. With an angry roar, Cahill summoned up the strength to throw Longarm off of him.

Longarm landed on the floor, rolled over, and came up on his feet. He was tired, and he had taken a lot of punishment. His heart slugged heavily in his chest and his pulse pounded loudly in his head. Cahill looked to be in just as bad shape, though, as he staggered to his feet.

Cahill rushed him again. Longarm met him with a right. Cahill almost went down but stayed upright somehow. He swung a right of his own that Longarm couldn't turn aside. It knocked Longarm back a step. One of Longarm's feet slipped, and he thought for an awful second that he was going to fall. If he did, he might not have the strength to get back up again, and his gamble would have failed. His instincts told him that he had to fight Cahill to a draw. That would win the man's respect and possibly even his friendship, whereas a loss would just earn Cahill's scorn. And if he defeated Cahill, the man would be his enemy forever, unless and until he evened the score. No, thought Longarm as he desperately caught his balance and stayed on his feet, this had to be a standoff.

He and Cahill both threw punches at the same time. Both missed. Longarm stumbled forward and bumped into Cahill. He grabbed Cahill's shirt to keep from falling. At the same time, Cahill caught hold of Longarm's shoulder to steady himself. They wound up staring into each other's face, bleeding and sweating and panting for breath.

"Damned if you ain't . . . a scrapper!" Cahill said.

"You . . . too," Longarm said. He grinned, though his lips were swollen from some of Cahill's punches and the expression hurt.

Cahill grinned back at him. "Sorry I . . . flew off the handle."

"And I'm sorry I . . . messed with your woman," Longarm replied.

"Ah, hell." Cahill waved a hand vaguely toward Libby, who sat in a corner of the room with her arms hugged tightly around herself and her knees drawn up, trying to stay out of the way of the two men as they fought. "She ain't really my girl."

"Am so!" Libby piped up, sounding offended.

Cahill turned his head to look at her. "When I ain't around, you're not. And I wasn't here when you met this fella . . . What was your name again?"

"Custis," Longarm said. "Custis Jones."

"When you met ol' Custis, I wasn't here," Cahill went on to Libby. "I had no call to get so mad."

"That's mighty kindly of you to look at it that way," Longarm told him.

Cahill straightened and took a step back. "Sometimes this Irish temper of mine gets the best of me." He stuck out his hand. "No hard feelin's, Custis?"

"No hard feelings." Longarm shook hands with Cahill, matching the man's powerful grip with his own.

Libby looked disgusted. "Why don't you two just kiss each other if you're so damned fond of each other?"

"Shut up, gal," Cahill said carelessly. "Custis, why don't you get dressed and go on back over to the tavern? I'd like to buy you a drink in a little while."

"Sounds fine, Roney." Longarm reached for his trousers.

Cahill turned and went over to where Libby crouched in the corner. He reached down, caught hold of her arms, and lifted her. Her feet came off the floor and her legs wrapped around Cahill's hips. He put one arm under her rump to support her as he kissed her. Both of Libby's arms went around his neck and held on tight.

Longarm had his trousers, shirt, and boots on by the time Cahill broke the kiss and turned his head to grin over his shoulder at him. "See you in a spell, Custis."

"Sure," Longarm replied as he draped his coat and gunbelt over his arm. He stuffed his string tie into his pocket, picked up his hat, and cocked it jauntily on his head as he went out.

It was dark in the woods, but he didn't have any trouble following the footpath back to the tavern. He paused long enough to buckle on his gunbelt and tie down the holster, then stepped inside. The buzz of conversation halted abruptly as everyone in the place looked around and saw him standing there, battered and bruised but apparently undefeated.

Jim Cahill was back at the pool table, practicing some shots. He lowered the cue stick and stared openly at Longarm. "Damn!" he exclaimed. "I figured Roney'd give you such a beatin' you wouldn't wake up until the middle of next week!" Judging from the startled expressions of everyone else in the tavern, he seemed to be speaking for them, too.

Longarm chuckled. "Didn't quite work out that way."

Jim suddenly dropped the stick and put his hand on the butt of his Remington revolver. "Where's Roney?" His voice was hard and dangerous now.

Longarm's voice was icy as he snapped, "Take it easy. Your cousin's fine. He asked me to come over here and wait for him while he, ah, pays a visit to Miss Libby. Said he wanted to buy me a drink."

Jim frowned suspiciously at him. "No foolin'?"

"No fooling," said Longarm. "Now, I'd take it kindly if you was to remove your hand from the butt of that Remington, Jim. Seeing you standing there like that sort of makes me want to reach for my own gun."

Jim hesitated, then a grin suddenly broke out on his face again. "Sure, Custis," he said. "What did you and Roney do, pound each other until neither one of you could throw another punch?"

"Something like that," Longarm admitted.

Jim gestured at one of the tables. "Come on over and sit down. I knew you was a talented gent from the way you played billy-ards, but I never ran into anybody who could fight Roney to a draw before."

Longarm sank gratefully into one of the chairs as talk welled up again and the tavern's customers went back to what they were doing when he came in. He smiled tiredly at Jim, who sat down across from him, and said, "To tell you the truth, I'm glad your cousin didn't have one more punch in him, because I was about done in."

"I can see why he took a likin' to you. Ain't very many people around who can give ol' Roney a good tussle, and like I told you, he sure enjoys a good fight." Jim leaned forward. "Say, are you just passin' through these parts, or do you think you might stay a spell?"

Longarm shrugged. "I'm open to anything that might be worth my while."

"Now that's a good thing to hear. Could be that Roney an' me, we can put you onto something. That is, if you ain't a stickler for the law."

Longarm just grinned and didn't say anything, letting Jim draw his own conclusions. What Jim was saying was music to Longarm's ears.

Or maybe that was just his head still ringing from being clouted by Roney Cahill's big fists. Longarm wasn't sure.

Chapter 6

By the time Roney Cahill came into the roadhouse a little later, Longarm and Jim had already had a couple of beers. It was too much to hope that this little Ozark Mountain tavern would have any Maryland rye, so Longarm settled for beer instead of the home-brewed panther piss that passed for whiskey around here.

The white-haired bartender had to deliver drinks to the tables now, since Libby had gone off to her cabin with Longarm and didn't return when he did. Strickland, if that was indeed who he was, grumbled about the added work, but grinned when Cahill came in and hollered for a fresh bucket of beer. For a man who'd had such an exhausting fight not long before, Cahill had a little extra spring in his step as he came over to the table where Longarm and Jim sat. Longarm figured that Libby must have some pretty potent restorative powers.

"How are you, Custis?" Cahill asked as he pulled out a chair and sat down.

"Same as I was last time you saw me, pounded half to death by those hams you call fists."

Cahill threw back his head and laughed. "Shoot, that wasn't nothin'. We just waltzed around a mite. If it had been a real fight, you'd have needed to bring a couple of extra fellas and pack a lunch, 'cause it would've lasted all day."

Longarm grinned. He couldn't help it. He felt an instinctive liking for Cahill.

It would be a damned shame when it came time to arrest the man, or worse yet, kill him.

Maybe it wouldn't come to that. Cahill was only a suspect in the wave of robberies to hit western Arkansas, after all. Judge Parker hadn't said for certain that Cahill was mixed up in the lawlessness.

But judging from the way Jim had been talking earlier, he and Cahill were involved in *something* that was at least borderline illegal, and lucrative to boot. To Longarm, that sure sounded like they were outlaws.

Strickland brought over the bucket of beer and a mug for Cahill. The big redhead dipped the mug in the bucket and motioned for Longarm and Jim to refill theirs. Longarm did so, taking a long swallow of the warm, bitter brew. He licked foam off his longhorn mustache, then said, "Jim here was telling me about something you and him are up to that I might be interested in."

Cahill's throat worked as he swallowed beer, then he lowered the mug and glanced at his cousin. "That's what Jim was sayin', is it?"

Jim suddenly looked a little nervous. "I didn't mean to talk out of turn, Roney," he said. "I just knew that Custis seems like a pretty tough gent, and I knew you an' him were gettin' along now . . ."

"He ain't a bad fella, but he ain't one of us," Cahill said. He looked over at Longarm. "Jim spoke out of turn. Hope you'll accept that with no hard feelin's."

Longarm shrugged, hiding his disappointment. It certainly would have made his job easier if Cahill had invited him to join the gang—assuming there was a gang—but that was probably too much good luck to hope for. He said, "I've always got plenty to occupy my time, Roney. No hard feelings."

Cahill grunted. "Good. Drink up."

Longarm downed the rest of his beer and refilled the mug again. The beer wasn't making him drunk, but he was starting to feel a little sluggish. He said, "I'm a mite curious, though. Whatever it was, it sounded like a hell of a deal."

Cahill's mouth thinned. These mountain folk were literally tight-lipped when it came to spilling secrets to outsiders. Longarm drank beer and didn't push the issue.

He still didn't know anything more a short time later when the door of the roadhouse slammed open and an old man half-ran, half-fell through it. He caught his balance and looked around, wild-eyed. His gaze lit on Roney Cahill, and he started across the room toward the table where Cahill sat with Longarm and Jim.

"Roney!" the old man exclaimed. "Roney, ye got to come quick! Sary Jane's in trouble!"

Cahill had tensed as soon as he saw the old man come into the tavern. "What's wrong?" he asked.

"Ed Hollister's up there at Sary Jane's place, and he's drunk and he's mad. He says he's gonna get even with her for what happened to Bertie!"

Cahill set his mug on the table with a hard thump and muttered, "Son of a bitch! And you went off and left her up there by herself, Gyp?"

The old man jerked his battered hat from his head and nervously ran his fingers through tangled gray hair. "I'm sorry, Roney. She said for me to run down here and get help." Tears began to run down his leathery cheeks. "I . . . I think maybe she was just tryin' to get me away from Ed, though, so's nothin' would happen to me."

"That's probably it," Cahill said as he came to his feet. "Come on, Jim."

Longarm stood up, too. "If there's trouble, Cahill, I'd admire to go with you."

Cahill paused long enough to grin at him. "Ain't had enough fun for one night, Custis?" Without waiting for an answer, he went on, "Well, come on, if you're of a mind to. But we got to hurry, so don't slow us down."

"I'll be right behind you," Longarm said.

The four men left the tavern. The old man called Gyp wiped his eyes and nodded when Cahill said, "You ride with Jim, Gyp. You two are the lightest."

Longarm jerked the bay's reins loose from the hitch rack and swung up into the saddle. Jim and Gyp climbed onto a chestnut, and Cahill was mounted on a big black with a white blaze on its face and white stockings. From what Longarm could see in the light that spilled through the open roadhouse door, it was a fine-looking horse.

Cahill took the lead, urging his mount into an easy lope. There was a sense of urgency about him, but on these winding mountain trails, a horse couldn't really work up to a gallop. Longarm, Jim, and Gyp followed close behind.

Obviously, Cahill knew where he was going and had no trouble following the path in the darkness. He veered off the Fayetteville road onto a smaller trail, then onto one that was even smaller. The men had to ride single file because the pine forest pressed in closely on both sides. Longarm brought up the rear, keeping a close eye on Jim's horse just ahead of him. If he got separated from the others in this stygian wilderness, he wouldn't be able to keep up. He probably wouldn't even be able to find his way out until morning.

They were climbing, the trail zigzagging back and forth up the side of a mountain that loomed darkly above them, blotting out some of the stars. After a while, Longarm saw a flicker of light through the trees up ahead, and a few moments later the riders came out on a small bench of land that shouldered out from the mountain slope. There was a clearing ahead of them with a log cabin in it. The cabin door was open; that was where the light came from. A slender figure stood there, facing out into the night. In front of the cabin, a burly man paced back and forth, waving something in the air. As Longarm and the others drew closer, he could tell that the thing the man was brandishing was a double-barreled shotgun.

Cahill reined in as the man with the scattergun wheeled toward the newcomers. "Take it easy, Ed!" he called. "It's Roney Cahill!"

"Roney?" The shotgunner's voice was thick with drink and something else. "Roney, you just stay back! I don't wanna kill you, but I swear I will if I have to!"

Cahill leaned forward in the saddle, at the same time motioning for Longarm, Jim, and Gyp to stay back. "Now, Ed, I know you don't want to kill nobody," he said. "Why don't you just put that shotgun down and come along with me to Strickland's for a drink?"

Ed shook his head. Hollister was his last name, Longarm recalled Gyp saying. He trembled, and emotion clogged his throat as he said, "I got to settle things for the old woman, Roney. You understand, don't you? This . . . this gal's got to pay for what she done!"

"All I did was try to save Bertie's life, Ed," said the woman who stood in the doorway of the cabin. With the light behind her, Longarm couldn't tell much about her, but her voice sounded young. "She was just too sick. There was nothing anyone could have done."

Hollister swung back toward her. The woman didn't flinch as the barrels of the shotgun lined up on her again. "I brung her here 'cause you're supposed to be so damned smart!" he shouted. "You've saved other folks! Why the hell couldn't you save my wife?"

"Because the consumption had progressed too far," the woman said, still sounding calm. She couldn't really be that calm, Longarm thought, not with a shotgun in the hands of a drunken, grief-stricken man pointing at her. "I'm truly sorry," she went on. "There was nothing I could do."

"You could've saved her!"

"Ed!" Cahill snapped. "That's enough. You listen to me now. You know me. You know I won't stand for this. You want to make an enemy out of me, Ed Hollister? You want a feud between your family and mine? Lots of innocent folks'll get hurt that way."

"I don't give a damn!" Hollister raged. "I don't care 'bout nothin' with Bertie gone!"

"She wouldn't have wanted you to do this, Ed," Cahill said. "You know she wouldn't."

"Go to hell! You don't know nothin' 'bout my Bertie!"

Jim said quietly, "You're goin' to have to shoot the dumb son of a buck, Roney."

"Hush up, damn it!" Cahill hissed.

Longarm was afraid Jim was right. Hollister was out of his head. The man was so overcome with grief at his wife's death that he wasn't going to listen to reason. And the longer this standoff went on, the more likely it was that he would fire that shotgun, even if it was accidentally. Longarm knew that a lot of the scatterguns used by these mountaineers had hair-triggers.

Cahill must have realized the same thing. Longarm saw him put his hand on the butt of his gun. "Ed, I'm warnin' you," Cahill said. "Put that shotgun down and get out of here, or there'll be blood spilled tonight."

"No!"

The cry came from an unexpected source. The woman in the doorway stepped forward, walking straight toward Hollister. She went on, "If anyone has to die tonight, let it be me. I won't have anyone else's blood on my hands!"

From where he sat on the back of the chestnut behind Jim, Gyp let out a whimper.

"Damn it, get back, Sarah Jane!" Cahill called. "You little fool—!"

He spurred forward suddenly. Hollister twisted around, not sure who to shoot at. He must have decided that Cahill was the greater threat, because he jerked the barrels of the greener toward the onrushing rider.

Longarm's Colt seemed to leap into his hand from the cross-draw rig on his left hip. Even if Cahill gunned down Hollister, the man would probably be able to fire both barrels of the greener. And at this range, they would cut both Cahill and his horse to ribbons. Longarm brought the Colt up. The light was bad and he had only a fraction of a heartbeat to aim, but he knew he had to make the shot.

The revolver bucked in his hand as he fired.

Jim yelped as the bullet whipped past his ear, sizzled through the air less than a foot to the left of Cahill's shoulder, then smacked into the breech of the shotgun Hollister was holding. The impact jolted the weapon out of Hollister's suddenly numb fingers and made him cry out in surprise and pain. The bullet deflected down from the shotgun's breech and cut a shallow groove in his right hip. He twisted around in agony, and that saved his life as Cahill fired, missing narrowly as the slug cut through the space where Hollister's head had been less than a second earlier and bored into the ground between Hollister and the woman. The whole thing had taken bare instants of time.

Hollister crumpled to the ground. The woman hurried forward and knelt beside him, obviously bent on helping him. Cahill wheeled the black around and exclaimed, "What the hell!"

"He like to shot my ear off!" Jim said.

Longarm lowered the Colt and slid it back into its holster. "Seemed like the only way to keep anybody from getting killed," he said.

"Includin' me," Cahill said. "At that range, Ed would've gotten me, no matter what I did."

Longarm nodded. "That's what I thought."

Jim glared at him suspiciously and asked, "Are you *sure* you weren't shootin' at me?"

"I reckon if Custis had meant to shoot you, you'd be dead now, Jim. I got the feelin' he generally hits what he aims at." Cahill regarded Longarm intently for a moment, then turned his horse back toward the cabin. He dismounted and walked over to where the woman was still kneeling beside the fallen Hollister.

"I think he'll be all right," she said to Cahill. "It's just a minor wound."

Cahill laughed humorlessly. "You're the only person I know who'd tend to a man's hurts after he was tryin' to kill you just a minute or two earlier."

"He was out of his head," the woman said. "I can't hold a man's grief against him. I just wish I could have helped Bertie." She stood and looked at the men who were still on horseback. "Jim, why don't you and Gyp carry Ed into the cabin. I'll come in and clean up that wound in a minute."

"Sure thing, Sary Jane," Gyp said as he slid down from the horse. Jim followed him. The two of them got hold of Hollister's shoulders and feet and started lugging him into the cabin.

"Who's that?" the woman asked Cahill as she looked at Longarm.

Cahill motioned to him. "Come on over here, Custis," he said. "I want you to meet somebody."

Longarm swung down from the saddle and led the bay over to Cahill and the woman. He reached up with his other hand and took off his hat. "Ma'am," he said, as he nodded to the woman.

"Custis Jones," Cahill said, "this here is another of my cousins, Sarah Jane Masterson. Sarah Jane, this is Custis Jones."

Sarah Jane Masterson held out a hand to Longarm. "You're not from the mountains, are you, Mr. Jones?"

"Not these," Longarm replied as he shook hands with her. Her fingers were cool and slender, like the rest of her. The light from the cabin reflected on blond hair so pale that it was almost white. Longarm doubted if the woman was much more than twenty years old.

"I'm pleased to meet you," she said. "Thank you for stepping in to prevent any more bloodshed than was necessary."

"Seemed like the thing to do at the time."

"It's *always* the thing to do," Sarah Jane Masterson said. With a meaningful glance at Cahill, she added, "That's something that *some* people around here don't seem able to grasp."

Cahill scuffed his boot toe in the dirt like a little boy. "Aw, Sarah Jane . . ."

"I've got a patient to tend to." With that, Sarah Jane turned and walked into the cabin, leaving Longarm and Cahill standing there.

"She seems a mite, ah, unusual," Longarm said. "Are you sure she's *your* cousin?"

"Oh, shut up," Cahill said.

Chapter 7

Longarm and Cahill went into the cabin, which was brightly lit by several lanterns. It was partitioned off into two sections by hanging blankets. To the left was an area with several benches facing a little platform with a slate chalkboard behind it. Longarm frowned. He had been in enough country schools to recognize one when he saw it. The other side of the log cabin was set up more like a doctor's office, with a sheet-draped table, a couple of chairs, and a double-doored cabinet full of medical instruments and pill bottles. Was Sarah Jane Masterson a doctor or a teacher—or both?

Judging by the way she bent over the table to clean the blood away from the wound on Ed Hollister's hip, she was a doctor or at least had some medical training. Or maybe she was just experienced at patching up bullet holes. Longarm had never been to medical school, but he was a pretty fair hand at such things, having learned from experience.

Hollister's drunkenness had reached the maudlin stage, aggravated by the pain he was in from his wound. He was blubbering now as he tried to apologize to Sarah Jane. "I never would've h-hurt you," he said. "N-not r-really."

"I know that," she said. "Now just lay there quietly, Ed, and let me get a dressing on this bullet crease."

Jim and Gyp walked around the blankets to the other side of the cabin and sat down on one of the benches. Jim took out the makin's and started to roll a quirly, while Gyp pulled a pipe from his pocket and clamped the stem of it—unlit—between strong yellow teeth.

Jim licked the cigarette paper, then said to Longarm, "Next time you're fixin' to shoot off a gun next to a fella's ear, give him a little warnin', will you? I reckon I'll be half-deef for a week."

"Maybe not," Longarm said with a grin. "Anyway, I didn't figure there was a whole lot of time for discussion."

"That's the damned truth," said Cahill. "If not for Custis here, I reckon I'd be blown in half about now. It would've been worth it, though . . ." He glanced toward the other side of the cabin, where Sarah Jane was still tending to the wounded Hollister. "She means a hell of a lot more to the folks around here than I do."

"I was just joshing out there," Longarm said, keeping his voice pitched low, "but Miss Sarah Jane don't really seem like your ordinary mountain girl."

"She ain't," Jim said. "She's done been to college."

Longarm had been able to tell that Sarah Jane was an educated young woman. He wasn't surprised to hear that she had attended college, probably back east somewhere.

"She grew up just like the rest of us around here," Cahill said, "dirt poor and not knowin' much. When she left a few years ago, none of us knew where she'd got off to. She just up and vanished one day. We didn't expect to ever see her again." He glanced fondly toward the blanket partition. "But then, about six months ago, she showed up out of the blue, dressed nice and sayin' she had come back to help us if she could. Me and Jim and some of the other boys built this place for her, so she could start a school. She's been teachin' the young'uns around here to read and write and cipher. Wasn't long before we figured out that she knew enough about doctorin' to help with that, too."

"Nearest regular sawbones is in Fayetteville or Fort Smith," Jim put in. "When you're walkin', or ridin' on an old mule, that's too far away sometimes if somebody's hurt bad and needs doctorin' right away."

Longarm nodded as he thought over what he was hearing. To the people who lived in these mountains, Sarah Jane Masterson must seem like an angel sent down from heaven.

With that pale blond hair and those lovely features, she sure *looked* like an angel, he told himself. Sarah Jane was as pretty a woman as he had seen in a long time.

Longarm heard snoring coming from the other side of the cabin. Sarah Jane walked around the partition, a smile on her face. "Ed will be all right," she announced. "He's dozed off. He can sleep it off here, then go home in the morning."

"All right," Cahill said. "I'm stayin', though, just in case he wakes up and goes crazy again."

Sarah Jane shook her head. "That's not necessary. Ed will have such a headache when he wakes up that he won't want to cause any trouble and make it worse. Besides, Gyp will be here with me."

The old man grinned and bobbed his head. Longarm wasn't sure if he was a half-wit or not, but he didn't seem to have all his faculties.

Evidently, Jim agreed with Longarm. He snorted and said, "That old geezer ain't any help in a tight spot."

"I ain't that old!" Gyp protested.

"Hell, you're older'n dirt!" Jim shot a contrite glance at Sarah Jane. "Pardon my language, Sarah Jane."

She smiled and made shooing motions with her hands. "All of you just go on about your business, whatever that is. Mr. Jones, I'm glad to have met you."

Longarm tugged on the brim of his Stetson. "Same here, ma'am."

"Are you going to be around these parts for long?"

Longarm glanced at Cahill and Jim. "Well, I don't rightly know . . ."

"As long as you are, feel free to stop by any time. The children and I always enjoy having visitors during school hours."

"Thank you, ma'am."

Sarah Jane looked at Jim. "By the way, how are you coming along with that book I gave you?"

Jim looked at the floor and shuffled his feet. "Ah, not too bad, Sarah Jane. I'm, ah, on the second page now, and I'm pretty sure I know most of the words on the first page."

She smiled. "That's fine. Keep up the good work, Jim, and you'll be reading everything before you know it."

"Yes'm. But it surely does seem like some o' them fellas who write books sure are long-winded sons o'—"

"Come on, Jim," Cahill said, taking his cousin's arm and tugging him toward the door of the cabin. "Night, Sarah Jane."

"Good night."

Longarm gave her one last nod, then followed Cahill and Jim out of the cabin. They walked over to their horses, and as they mounted up, Cahill said to Longarm, "Come on back down to Strickland's with us, Custis. There's something I want to talk to you about."

"What we talked about earlier?" Longarm ventured.

Cahill settled himself in the saddle and shrugged. "Maybe. Things are different now. I reckon you saved my life tonight."

"You don't owe me anything for that."

"The hell I don't," Cahill said. "Come on."

They started down the mountain, Cahill taking the lead again, Longarm following behind him, grinning in the darkness because it looked like fate had turned in his favor tonight after all.

"It's pretty damned simple," Cahill said later as he and Longarm and Jim sat at a corner table in Strickland's Tavern. Smoke hung in a haze above the table. Jim had rolled another quirly, Longarm had one of his cheroots going, and Cahill had packed a briar pipe and lit up. Cahill went on, "If you can trust a man to save your life, you can trust him with just about anything else."

"Even an outsider?" Longarm asked.

Cahill nodded solemnly. "Even an outsider."

Jim put in, "See, I told you right from the start that ol' Custis here was a good fella, didn't I, Roney?"

"You still jumped the gun a mite," Cahill said. "But I reckon in the end you were right, Jim." He looked at Longarm. "Custis, if you're goin' to be in these parts for a while, I've got a proposition for you. Jim and me and a few of the other boys do a little job from time to time that makes some decent money. How'd you like to go along with us next time?"

"Just what sort of job are you talking about?" Longarm asked cautiously.

Cahill shrugged. "Whatever comes along."

"I'm not sure I understand . . ."

Cahill's face hardened. "I ain't in the mood to spell it out. You're either in or you're not, and you'll find out the details when the time comes."

Longarm hesitated just long enough to make his indecision seem real, then said, "I'm in. I sort of like the country around here, and I'm not in a hurry to get to anywhere else as long as I'm out of Texas." That made it sound like he was on the dodge from the law, which was exactly the impression he wanted to create.

Cahill nodded in satisfaction. "All right, then. You got a place to stay?"

"Nope."

"Talk to Strickland," Cahill said, nodding toward the bar. "There's a couple of rooms in back here that he rents out sometimes. Not very often, though, because not many travelers pass through here."

"Skunk Hollow ain't really on the way to anywhere else," Jim added, with a laugh.

Cahill lifted a hand and motioned to Strickland, and when the white-haired proprietor came over, Cahill said, "Bring us that bottle I had you hold for me. And three glasses. *Clean* glasses."

"Sure thing, Roney," Strickland replied. He hustled off.

Everyone around here seemed to know and like Roney Cahill, Longarm reflected. But the man had to have at least some enemies. Judge Parker had mentioned that Cahill had been involved in several shooting scrapes. The men who had wound up dead following those corpse-and-cartridge sessions must have had relatives who would hold a grudge against Cahill. Joining the man's gang would have its hazards. Longarm would have to worry not only about running afoul of the local law but also about eagle-eyed feudists who might not be above a little backshooting. He would be walking a tightrope, that was for danged sure.

Yet he felt very good about what had happened tonight. He had gotten a foothold in Cahill's gang, had gained the man's respect and even some of his trust. He thought about asking Cahill what he knew about Deuce Thaxton but decided to wait on that. He didn't need to get in a hurry.

The thing that had him worried was that he liked Roney Cahill. For that matter, he liked Jim, too, and evidently Jim was mixed up in the gang right along with his cousin. Were they both thieves and murderers? They didn't seem like it to Longarm, but in his career as a lawman, he had run across more than one cold-blooded killer who was just as pleasant as could be most of the time.

Emotions didn't really have anything to do with anything, Longarm reminded himself. He was here in the Ozarks to do a job, and that job involved gathering evidence and bringing criminals to justice. When you got down to the nub, that was all he could worry about.

Strickland came over to the table carrying a tray with a bottle and three glasses on it. Longarm's eyes widened a little as he saw the label on the bottle. "Is that really what it looks like?" he asked.

"Genuine Tom Moore Maryland Rye," Cahill said as he snagged the neck of the bottle and began working loose the cork. "I ran across it a while back and had Strickland set it aside for me. Savin' it for a special occasion, you understand. I figure nearly dyin' and havin' my life saved by a new friend counts."

"I'm honored," Longarm said as the cork popped free and

Cahill began pouring the whiskey in the glasses, a couple of fingers in each one.

The three men lifted the glasses, clinked them together above the center of the table. "Here's mud in your eye," Jim said.

Longarm tossed back the drink, then sighed in satisfaction as he felt the warmth from it go through him. The whiskey was the real thing, all right. He'd been afraid that Strickland might have emptied the bottle and then refilled it with some home-brewed who-hit-John. But he knew the taste of genuine Tom Moore, and this was it.

"Nectar of the gods," he said.

"Now you're talkin' all educated-like, the way Sarah Jane does," Cahill said. He splashed more rye into Longarm's glass.

"You're a man after my own heart, old son," Longarm said, then knocked back the second drink.

He hoped more than ever that the day wouldn't come when he had to shoot Roney Cahill.

Chapter 8

Strickland agreed to rent one of the spare rooms to Longarm and seemed quite happy to get the four bits per night he was charging. Longarm thought the price was a mite high for a dirt-floored room barely big enough to swing a cat in, but he'd let Henry worry about the expense account when he got back to Denver. And Henry *would* worry, Longarm was sure of that. He sort of looked forward to the argument.

The narrow bunk had a thin mattress stuffed with corn shucks. Longarm stripped to his underwear, stretched out on the bunk, and went to sleep immediately. He'd had enough beer during the evening, followed by several shots of the Maryland rye he'd shared with Cahill and Jim, so that he slept soundly and woke up the next morning with a fuzzy taste in his mouth.

He pulled on his trousers and boots, then went out back to the pump to douse his head and shave. When that was done, he finished dressing, then the smell of coffee drew him into the tavern's main room. Strickland had a pot of coffee on the stove at the end of the bar and was cooking flapjacks as well.

"Breakfast ain't included in the price of the room," the tavernkeeper informed Longarm. "It'll cost you extra."

Longarm wasn't hungry, but the idea of coffee appealed to him. Without asking the price, he poured himself a cup and carried it over to a table. He sat down, stretched out his long legs, and sipped the hot black brew. Each sip cleared away a few of the cobwebs in his brain, until the thought of a stack of flapjacks didn't sound so bad after all. He said as much to Strickland, who brought over a platter piled high with food.

Longarm dug in. Strickland sat down at the table and ate with him. Idly curious, Longarm asked, "Been around these parts long?"

"All my life. There's Stricklands all over these mountains."

"Let me guess: You're cousin to the Cahills, too."

Strickland shook his head. "Nope, I ain't any relation to Roney or Jim or any of them other Cahills."

"You seem pretty friendly toward them, though."

"Why wouldn't I be?" Strickland asked. "Roney Cahill's as fine a feller as you'd ever want to meet. Jim's a mite on the flighty side, but he's all right, too. Them boys grew up together, you know. They's more like brothers than cousins."

"What about the Masterson side of the family? You know them, too?"

"Of course I do. I know pert near everybody in these parts." Strickland's mouth thinned in disapproval. "Mastersons like to put on airs, but to my way of thinkin', they ain't as good as the Cahills. Why, Sarah Jane's ma and pa didn't hardly seem to care when she disappeared. Roney was the one who was upset. He always set a lot of store by Sarah Jane."

Longarm grinned. "Sweet on her, is he?"

"Well, they're kin, sort of. Roney calls her his cousin, but it ain't quite the same as him and Jim. Sarah Jane's Uncle Lonzo was married to the brother of a gal who was married to Roney's Uncle Fordyce. But one of Fordyce's brother-in-laws was the nephew of Sarah Jane's granddaddy . . . no, wait, that ain't right . . . Sarah Jane's daddy was cousin to Fordyce . . . or was that Tom Pinch, who was Roney's grandma's third husband . . ." Strickland shook his head. "I forget. Anyway, Roney and Sarah Jane always called theirselves cousins, but it ain't like they're close kin. Roney always looked out for her when she was little, and she follered him around like a puppy dog. He was sure broke up about it when she went off wherever she went off to."

"I've heard tell that Roney's been in some trouble with the law," Longarm ventured, since Strickland seemed to be in a talkative mood.

"Where in blazes did you hear that?" Strickland snorted in indignation. "Roney's been in a few scrapes, but it weren't never his fault. Usually Jim's the one who gets hisself in some sort of bind, and then Roney has to help him out of it. I can tell you this right now: Roney Cahill never shot nobody who weren't in serious need o' bein' shot." Strickland's eyes narrowed in suspicion. "Say, you're a mighty curious feller, especially considerin' that you and Roney are supposed to be friends."

"We are friends," Longarm insisted. "But he asked me to get mixed up in some business dealings with him, and I like to know who I'm doing business with."

Strickland's mouth snapped shut almost like a steel trap. "Roney's business is Roney's business and none of mine," he said. He stood up and carried his empty plate and coffee cup back to the bar, adding over his shoulder, "Breakfast is an extra two bits."

"Does that include a second cup of coffee?"

Reluctantly, Strickland shrugged and then nodded.

Longarm was at loose ends this morning. Cahill had told Longarm to wait here at the roadhouse, to take it easy for a few days and then he would contact Longarm again when the time was near for whatever job he had in mind. Longarm had a hunch it was going to be another in the series of robberies he was investigating. In the meantime, though, he didn't much care for the idea of sitting in the tavern doing nothing, so when he'd finished that second cup of coffee, he told Strickland he'd be back later, then went out to the small shed behind the tavern where he'd left the rented bay horse.

He saddled up and rode along the twisting trail that led east from Skunk Hollow. This was the way he and Cahill and Jim had gone the night before, and Longarm thought he stood a pretty good chance of being able to find the smaller trail they had turned onto. Despite the darkness of the night, he had been able to pick out a few landmarks during the hurried ride up to Sarah Jane's place, such as a dead, lightning-blasted tree just to the right of the road not far from the cutoff. When he passed the tree and came to a smaller trail not a hundred yards farther on, he knew he was heading in the right direction.

He studied the thickly wooded slopes rising all around him. That bench where Sarah Jane's cabin was located had a pretty steep slope directly behind it. Longarm thought he knew which one it was. As he came closer, however, he found himself getting confused. The trees closed in around him and blocked his view. He hadn't come across the second turn yet, the one that would put him on a still narrower trail. Maybe he was getting lost, he thought. He was confident he could find his way back out as long as he could see the sun. Even that, though, was becoming more difficult as the foliage overhead grew thicker. He felt himself growing disoriented, unsure which direction he was going. He frowned. Passing the time by paying a visit to Sarah Jane might not have been such a good idea after all. He reined in and rubbed his jaw, trying to decide what to do next.

"Hello!"

The lilting voice startled him, made his head jerk up. He turned in the saddle and saw Sarah Jane herself stepping out of the woods. She wore a dark green dress and a bonnet of the same shade over her pale hair, and Longarm would have been willing to bet that if she moved back among the trees, she would vanish within seconds. Just like a wood nymph, he thought.

He nodded, tugged on the brim of his Stetson, and said, "Mornin', Miss Sarah Jane."

"Mr. Jones. What are you doing up here on the mountain? Are you alone?"

"Yes, ma'am. And you might say it's your fault that I'm here."

She smiled. "My fault?"

"Yep. I thought it might be a good idea to ride up and make sure that Hollister fella didn't cause any more trouble for you."

"Oh, no," Sarah Jane said with a shake of her head. "Ed was very contrite this morning, just as I expected him to be, as well as quite hung over. He was just out of his head with grief last night. I can't hold that against him. I gave him some breakfast and sent him home."

"Well, ma'am, you're quicker than I would be to forgive somebody who'd pointed a loaded shotgun at me."

"There's no point in holding grudges. That's one thing that has held back the people in these mountains. They're too quick to anger and too slow to forgive."

Longarm leaned forward in the saddle. "You talk like you're not one of them anymore."

"Oh, but I am. I still have a mountaineer's temper. It's just that I've learned to control it."

Longarm wanted to ask her where and how she had learned that, but he didn't want to pry too much into her personal life. Besides, it was curiosity about Roney Cahill that had really led him to come up here, along with some genuine concern about Sarah Jane. He hadn't been lying when he said he wanted to make sure Ed Hollister hadn't bothered her anymore.

"Why don't you come on up to the cabin with me, if you're not in a hurry to be anywhere else?" Sarah Jane suggested. "The children will be there soon, and I'm sure they'd be thrilled to have a visitor."

Longarm wasn't exactly thrilled about the prospect of sitting in on the day's school session, but he didn't see any graceful way of refusing. He said, "Sure. I'd like that. But, uh, how do we get there?"

Sarah Jane laughed, a sound as pretty as the music of any brook Longarm had ever heard. "I thought when I first saw you that you had a lost look on your face."

"I just got a mite turned around."

"That's easy to do up here. Come on. Why don't you lead your horse, so we can walk together?"

Longarm thought that was a good suggestion. He swung down from the saddle and led the bay by the reins. Falling in step alongside Sarah Jane, he asked, "Why were you out here wandering around the woods this morning?"

"I go for a walk nearly every morning before school starts, especially when the weather is as beautiful as it is today. The walk helps me clear my head and get my thoughts in order for the day."

Longarm got the same effect from a healthy dollop of Maryland rye in a cup of strong black coffee—which he hadn't gotten this morning because Cahill had taken what was left of the bottle of Tom Moore with him when he left the roadhouse the night before—but he didn't say as much to Sarah Jane.

"They tell me you've been back east to college," he said.

"Yes." That was all Sarah Jane said in reply, and the unexpected curtness of it told Longarm that it wasn't a subject she wanted to discuss.

He moved on instead, saying, "Roney and Jim seem like pretty good fellas."

Sarah Jane relaxed, the quick tension that had come into her shoulders disappearing. "Yes, they are. Jim's something of a character, but deep down he's a fine man. And Roney is as solid as these mountains."

Longarm heard the admiration in her voice. She and Cahill seemed to care for each other a lot. Whether there was anything more to it, Longarm didn't know yet.

"I may be doing some business with them."

"Really?" Sarah Jane sounded surprised. "I mean no offense, Mr. Jones, but it strikes me as strange that Roney would become too involved with someone who's not from around here."

"It was Jim's idea at first," Longarm admitted. "Roney didn't care for it. Then we came up here to lend you a hand with Hollister, and there was that shooting . . ."

"So since you saved his life, Roney decided he could trust you after all," Sarah Jane finished.

"Something close to that, I reckon."

"Once Roney decides to trust someone, not much can change his mind." She glanced over at Longarm. "A man like that can be easily hurt. I wouldn't like it if anyone hurt Roney, Mr. Jones."

"Neither would I, ma'am," Longarm said with as much sincerity as he could muster.

Inside, Longarm felt a little uneasy. There were times he didn't like this part of his job, and this was one of them. He had never minded lying to owlhoots and killers and the sort of human varmints he mostly ran into in his line of work, but sometimes he had to lie to honest folks, and that went against the grain for him.

Of course, it might turn out that Cahill *was* a killer and an outlaw. Longarm recalled those federal officials who had been bushwhacked in recent weeks. If Cahill was responsible for those murders, he didn't deserve any sympathy. Sarah Jane didn't have anything to do with the killings, but she was connected with Cahill, and so Longarm would do what he had to in order to carry out his job, even if it was unpleasant at times.

Sarah Jane led him onto a smaller trail, and after they had followed it for a few minutes, Longarm heard a bell ringing somewhere close by. "What's that?" he asked with a frown.

"Why, it's the school bell," Sarah Jane replied. "Gyp's ringing it to let any children who aren't there yet know that it's time to come on to class."

"That's the old man? Gyp?"

Sarah Jane nodded. "His name is Egypt Foster, but everyone has called him Gyp as far back as I can remember. He helps me out around the school, and I give him a place to stay."

"He's not quite right in the head, is he?"

"Gyp's suffered a great deal in his life," Sarah Jane said, her voice becoming solemn. "All five of his sons were killed in the war, and his wife and daughters all died from a fever.

He had a large, happy family, and then suddenly he was alone. It probably did affect his mind. But he's sweet and very helpful. I do what I can for him."

"I get the idea you try to help out all these folks up here in the mountains," Longarm said.

She stopped and looked up at him, brushing her bonnet back so that the sunlight slanting through the trees shone on her pale blond hair. "Some people have a . . . a calling, Mr. Jones. I'm not nearly that noble. I'm just trying to do what I can to make life a little better for the people where I grew up." She waved a slender hand at the mountains around them. "I know I can't really make that much of a difference, but I do what I can."

"Reckon that's all anybody can do," Longarm told her.

She smiled brightly at him, then turned and started along the path again. "We'd better hurry," she said. "It wouldn't do for the teacher—or her guest—to be late for school."

Chapter 9

Sarah Jane proved to be correct—the children who attended her school were happy to have a visitor. They stared up at Longarm with wide eyes and open mouths. Their scrutiny was so intense, in fact, that it made him a mite nervous.

A dozen children were waiting in the cabin when Longarm and Sarah Jane got there, seven boys and five girls. They were typical mountain youngsters, boys in tattered overalls, girls in threadbare dresses. None of them wore any shoes. Their faces were clean, even if the rest of them wasn't particularly. They were all between the ages of six and ten.

"Who's this galoot, Miss Sary Jane?" one of the boys asked. He was a carrot top and squinted up at Longarm as if he were a bit near-sighted. His voice was unusually deep for a child.

"Why, George, this is my friend Mr. Jones," Sarah Jane explained with a smile.

"Is he your beau?"

Sarah Jane glanced at Longarm, a blush spreading prettily over her face. "No, like I said, he's just a friend. Why don't you say hello to him?"

Without an ounce of fear at meeting a strange adult,

George came up to Longarm and stuck out his hand. "Howdy," he boomed in his deep voice.

"Howdy your own self," Longarm said with a grin as he shook hands with the boy. "I'm pleased to meet you."

"Likewise." George jerked a thumb over his shoulder at Sarah Jane. "Are you sweet on Miss Sary Jane?"

"George!" she exclaimed.

Still grinning, Longarm said, "Well, George, I think Miss Sarah Jane's mighty nice, and any fella with eyes in his head can see that she's as pretty as a peach. What I'm wondering is if *you're* sweet on her?"

"Me?" George croaked in alarm. "But she . . . she's a *girl*!"

"Yep," Longarm said solemnly. "And you didn't answer my question."

George turned and hurried off to the front of the room, scuffing his feet and muttering under his breath. Longarm managed not to laugh at the youngster's discomfiture.

Sarah Jane came up to him and touched him lightly on the arm. "That was very wicked," she said quietly, so that the children couldn't overhear.

"Yes, ma'am, I reckon it was," Longarm agreed.

"And *you* never answered George's question, either," Sarah Jane pointed out, mischief flashing in her eyes.

Longarm didn't know what to say to that, but Sarah Jane saved him from having to answer by turning back to the youngsters and saying, "Everyone take your seats, and we'll get started on today's lessons." She threw a smile over her shoulder at Longarm. "Mr. Jones, why don't you sit there in the back? Feel free to join in any time you want to."

Longarm turned around a ladder-back chair and straddled it. Sarah Jane started writing words on the chalk board and asking the children to read them. When they finished with that lesson, she started in on addition and subtraction.

It had been a lot of years since Longarm had been in a classroom as a student. The schooling he'd received as a child back in the mountains of West Virginia had been fairly rudimentary. Since then, he had learned a great deal on his own, mostly by reading and by listening to the old-timers who had been the first ones to settle the frontier a generation earlier. Some of those men had been quite educated, though you'd never guess it to look at them. Longarm had known buffalo-robe-wearing mountain men who could quote extensively from Shakespeare and Milton and discuss Archimedes and the Pythagorean theorem. If a fella lived long enough and kept his ears open, that was an education in itself.

After a while he got bored and took out a cheroot. Before he could light it, he caught the look of disapproval on Sarah Jane's face and put the cigar away with a grimace of apology. He was glad when it got to be the middle of the day and the youngsters went outside to eat the lunches they had brought with them.

Longarm stood up as Sarah Jane came over to him. "You don't have to stay, Mr. Jones," she said. "I'm sure you have other things to do. Thank you for visiting us."

"I enjoyed it," Longarm said.

"Come back any time."

"Thanks. I might just do that." Longarm started to turn away, then something made him pause. "By the way, the answer to what that little fella George asked me is . . . I could be."

Sarah Jane looked confused. "You could be what?" Suddenly, her hand went to her mouth as she remembered the discussion between Longarm and George. "Oh!"

Longarm reached up, took hold of her wrist, and gently moved her hand down so that her fingers no longer covered her lips. Then he leaned toward her and kissed her. It was sweet at first, but then Sarah Jane's lips clung to his with surprising tenacity. The kiss grew more intense. She put her other hand on the back of his neck.

Then she broke away and gasped a little. "Why, Mr. Jones! I . . . I had no idea . . ."

Neither had Longarm. He'd acted on impulse, kissing her simply because the urge to do so had struck him. It had been a foolish thing to do, and he knew it. She was, perhaps, romantically involved with Roney Cahill, the man who might well be to blame for the lawlessness that had brought Longarm here to the Ozarks. Getting mixed up with Sarah Jane couldn't help but complicate things unnecessarily.

But with the sweet taste of her mouth still on his lips, Longarm couldn't really bring himself to care right now.

"Sorry—" he started to say.

"I knowed it! I knowed he was sweet on her the first time I seen him!"

The excited, deep-voiced words came from the doorway of the cabin. Longarm and Sarah Jane looked in that direction and saw George standing there, a big grin on his freckled face. He turned and ran off, whooping and shouting about how the stranger was in the classroom sparking with Miss Sary Jane.

"Damn it!" Sarah Jane burst out angrily. "Now everyone in the mountains will know."

Including Roney Cahill, thought Longarm. That could ruin everything.

Sarah Jane took a deep breath. "But I don't really care," she went on. "If anyone doesn't like it, that's just too bad."

"Anyone meaning Roney." Longarm's words were a statement, not a question.

Sarah Jane flushed. "Sometimes men just expect a woman to wait until they're good and ready to make up their minds about something. Well, sometimes a woman gets tired of waiting." She came up on her toes, put a hand on each side of his face, and kissed him again, hard and urgent this time. Longarm put his arms around her waist and felt her body mold against his. She was tense at first but then relaxed, softening in his embrace.

Just the opposite was happening to Longarm. He was getting hard.

She had to feel the rising at his groin as it prodded against her belly, but she didn't pull away. When she finally broke the kiss and slipped out of his arms, she murmured, "You come back to see me anytime, Mr. Jones. Anytime."

Longarm swallowed. "Why don't you call me Custis?"

"All right, Custis," Sarah Jane said with a smile. She

glanced down at the front of his trousers. "Why don't you, ah, go over on the other side of the cabin and wait a few minutes before you leave? You wouldn't want to parade out past the children in that condition."

"No, ma'am," Longarm agreed. He took out a cheroot and clamped it unlit between his teeth.

This visit to school had been educational, that was for damned sure. He just wasn't quite certain yet what he had learned.

Longarm rode back down the mountain and followed the twisting trails to Skunk Hollow. Now that he had covered the ground during the daylight, the route was imprinted on his brain and he wouldn't have any trouble finding his way back to Sarah Jane's cabin again.

He wasn't sure it would be a good idea to return there, however. He had already jeopardized his assignment by giving in to the impulse to kiss Sarah Jane. If Roney Cahill really was interested in her, Longarm's actions might cause Cahill to turn on him. Hell, thought Longarm, even if Cahill didn't want Sarah Jane for himself, he'd made it plain that he looked out for her best interests. He might think it was a bad idea for her to be involved with Longarm. He might even try to run Longarm out of the mountains.

This wasn't the first time a pretty gal had thrown a kink into his plans, Longarm reflected with a sigh. *You'd think that you would learn sooner or later, old son,* he told himself.

When he reached Strickland's place, several horses and a mule were tied at the hitch rack outside. Longarm didn't see the mounts Cahill and Jim had been riding the night before, so he figured they weren't there. He glanced around the room as he went in and saw that his assumption was correct. There was no sign of the two Cahill cousins.

Libby was back, though. She sat at one of the tables talking to a couple of men in overalls. As soon as she saw Longarm, she stood up and came over to him, leaving the men at the table to look disappointed.

"Mr. Strickland told me you were staying here," she said

as she put a hand on Longarm's sleeve. She tugged on his arm. "Come on back to my place with me."

"Wait a minute," Longarm said. "I just got here."

"I don't care. I woke up this mornin' wantin' that big ol' pecker of yours inside me, and I'm tired of waitin' for it."

Longarm couldn't argue with that. He let her pull him out the door of the roadhouse and onto the narrow path that led to her cabin.

"You don't have to pay this time," she said as she led him into the cabin. As Longarm closed the door behind him with his boot heel, Libby started unbuttoning her dress. In what seemed like less than a heartbeat, she was naked and kneeling on the bed on her hands and knees, with her pretty round rump stuck up in the air behind her. "I like it from behind," she went on. "Stick it in me, Custis."

"Lordy, gal, I've barely had time to take my hat off," he protested.

"I don't care if you leave your hat on. Just get inside me."

Longarm rolled his eyes, shook his head, and started stripping off his clothes. He didn't have to worry about them being interrupted this time, so he figured he could take off everything, down to the skin. While he was doing that, Libby wiggled her rump and moaned in frustration.

"If you don't hurry up, Custis, I'm liable to start by myself," she warned him.

"You do that," muttered Longarm as he set his trousers aside. He pushed the long underwear down over his hips and legs, stepped out of them, and kicked them aside. Naked now, with the long, thick shaft sticking out straight in front of him, he moved to the edge of the bed where Libby waited.

The folds of her femininity were already glistening with moisture. She was wet and ready for him. Longarm grasped her hips, brought the head of his organ to her portal, and shoved it in. Libby wasn't interested in romance, just rutting. That certainly had its place, Longarm thought as he drove in and out of her and she bucked back at him. Soft little cries escaped from her lips with each thrust he made. Her hands clawed at the mattress, and she shook her head from side to side, the long dark hair falling around her face.

Longarm let go of her hips, leaned forward, and reached under her to cup her breasts. "Yes!" she exclaimed as he roughly caressed the globes of flesh. He lifted her, squeezing and kneading her breasts as he continued to drive into her from behind. She balanced on her knees at the edge of the bed, with some of her weight resting on Longarm's shaft where it spiked into her.

Neither of them wanted to postpone their climax. Longarm drove as deeply into her as he could and began to erupt. Libby cried out and whipped her head back and forth as her own culmination rolled through her. Longarm pumped his seed into her until she was full to overflowing.

Both of them fell forward onto the bed as they crested the peak of their lovemaking and started down the far side. Longarm rolled off of her. Libby twisted around and draped herself over him, finding his mouth with hers and raining kisses on him.

"That's what I've been wantin' all day," she said breathlessly. "Oh, Custis, I'm so glad you're goin' to be around here for a while. I'm gonna plumb wear you out!"

As he lay there with his chest heaving and his pulse pounding, Longarm couldn't help but wonder if maybe she was right.

He sure wished, though, that he could stop thinking about Sarah Jane Masterson.

Chapter 10

Over the next couple of days, Libby did her best to make good on her prediction, but somehow Longarm was able to keep up with her. He spent more time at her cabin than he did in his rented room at the roadhouse. Strickland's other customers were getting a mite impatient with him, he thought every time he went into the place and saw the resentful glances they gave him. He was taking up all of Libby's time and energy, instead of her passing around her favors freely as she usually did.

So he was glad when Cahill and Jim came into the roadhouse late in the afternoon while he was sitting at a table nursing a beer. He had left Libby in the cabin a short time earlier. She'd been sprawled out naked on the bed, a contented smile on her face. "You hurry back now, Custis, you hear?" she'd said as Longarm went out the door. He had just grunted noncommittally.

The presence of Cahill and Jim would give him an excuse not to go back to Libby's cabin right away. It might also give him a chance to see if Cahill had heard about those kisses he'd shared with Sarah Jane, Longarm thought.

If Cahill was upset, he didn't show it. In fact, he was grinning as he sat down at the table with Longarm. He signaled to Strickland for a drink, then asked, "How are you, Custis?"

"Pretty good," Longarm replied. *If you don't count being worn to a frazzle by romping with that Libby gal,* he added to himself. "How about you two?"

Jim straddled one of the other chairs and smirked at Cahill. "We're fine, ain't we, Roney?"

Cahill nodded solemnly. "Yep. Fine."

The two of them were up to something, Longarm realized. They both looked quite pleased with themselves. He said, "You two look like a couple of tomcats with a bowlful of cream in front of you."

That struck Jim as funny. He laughed and pounded the table. "That's a good'un!" he gasped between gales of laughter.

Cahill's attitude changed abruptly. "That's enough," he said, a note of warning coming into his voice. "Settle down, Jim. This is serious business."

That was what Longarm wanted to hear, especially if robbery was the business Cahill was talking about. He said, "I'm ready to listen, if you want to fill me in on it."

Strickland brought mugs of beer over to the table for Cahill and Jim. Cahill waited until the proprietor had returned to his position behind the bar, then he leaned forward and said, "How about takin' a ride with us this evening, Custis?"

Longarm nodded. "Sure."

Cahill drained half his mug, then wiped the back of his other hand across his mouth. "Don't get too excited. We're just takin' a look-see. Won't be any trouble."

"Whatever you say, Roney."

Cahill drank the rest of his beer, then motioned to his cousin. "Finish that up, Jim, then go saddle Custis's horse for him."

"Sure thing," Jim agreed, before Longarm could protest that it wasn't necessary for somebody else to saddle his horse. Jim made gulping noises as he drank his beer, then said, "Ah," as he set down the empty mug. He stood up and left the tavern.

"We'll be takin' a ride over to the Fayetteville road," Cahill said to Longarm. "Won't be back until after dark. I hope that won't cause a problem for you."

Longarm shook his head. "Nope. Like I told you starting out, there's no particular place I have to be."

"Except in Libby's bed," Cahill said with a grin. "I've heard about how you and her have been goin' at it like a couple of rabbits these past few days. Hell, you're probably glad to get a little break this evenin'."

"She *is* a right friendly girl," Longarm allowed.

Cahill laughed. "Come on. Jim'll have your horse ready to ride by now."

The three of them left the roadhouse and headed west on the trail that led to the Fayetteville road. When they got there, Cahill swung to the north and led the way for several miles.

The road twisted and turned, following the valleys between the mountains in a serpentine course. From time to time, the road climbed to a pass and then dipped down on the far side. Longarm had been all over the Rockies, from Canada down south of the border to Mexico. The Ozarks weren't a patch on those towering peaks that formed the spine of the continent, but some of them were pretty good-sized hills, he thought. And they were rugged in their own way because once you got off the road, the steep slopes were covered with trees and underbrush.

Finally, Cahill reined in and motioned for his companions to follow suit. "Look up yonder," he said to Longarm, pointing ahead of them. "See where the valley pinches down?"

Longarm saw the place Cahill indicated. The road dipped and twisted and went through a narrow cut in the mountains. The opening was the width of the road, no more, and the slopes on each side went almost straight up. The passage created thusly ran for about seventy or eighty yards, Longarm estimated.

"That's Buzzard's Notch," Cahill said.

Something about the name evoked a tingle of recognition in Longarm's brain. He cast his memory back and suddenly recalled where he had read about Buzzard's Notch. It had been in the report that Billy Vail had handed to him, back in the chief marshal's Denver office. Several of the stagecoach robberies that had taken place in the past couple of months had occurred right here.

"There'll be a southbound stage coming through there tomorrow afternoon," Cahill went on.

Longarm nodded, feeling his spirits sink. A part of him had hoped that Judge Parker was wrong about Cahill, but it was certainly looking like that wasn't going to be the case. Unless Longarm missed his guess, Cahill was about to convict himself with his own words.

"Jim and me and some of the boys plan to be here to stop it," Cahill went on. "You can get in on it, too, if you want, Custis."

"Stagecoach holdup, eh?" Longarm said, stalling for time as he thought about his options.

"That's right. You bothered by that?"

Longarm shrugged. "Not especially. I never knew the pickings to be very good on a stagecoach, though. There's usually just a few drummers and storekeepers on board as passengers. All the mail and express shipments go by train now."

"Yeah, and they've got express guards on those trains, too," Cahill said. "That means shootin'."

"I heard you were handy with a gun."

Cahill looked slit-eyed at him. "I don't hanker to get in any battles with a bunch of express messengers armed with scatterguns. You stop a stage, you don't have to worry about anybody except the driver most of the time. Sometimes there's a shotgun guard, but he's usually an old-timer who's got enough sense not to put up a fight."

Longarm tried not to show the thoughts that were racing through his mind. What was Cahill saying? The report Longarm had read had detailed not only stagecoach holdups but also train and bank robberies. The assumption had been that one well-organized gang was responsible for all the crimes. But from the way Cahill was talking, it sounded like he was admitting to the stagecoach robberies but not the other crimes.

"Well, what's it going to be?" Cahill prodded. "Are you in or not?"

"I'm in," Longarm said. He had to play along for now, until he had a chance to figure out more of the puzzle that presented itself to him.

Jim said, "I'm mighty glad to hear you say that, Custis. I told Roney you'd jump at the chance to join up with a bunch like us."

"Regular desperadoes, are you?" Longarm asked with a grin.

"You wouldn't want to cross us, know what I mean?"

Cahill said, "Stop trying to make out like we're Frank and Jesse James. We're just tryin' to do right by the folks who live up here in the mountains."

"How do you figure that?" Longarm asked.

Cahill leaned forward in the saddle and thumbed his high-crowned Stetson to the back of his head. "Think about it," he said. "People travel through here all the time, goin' from Fort Smith or Little Rock on up to Fayetteville or Kansas City. But they don't stop. They don't have any use for us mountain folks. Hell, when they pass us on the road, they won't even look at us. They think they're so much better'n us. So what the boys and me do is sort of like . . . collectin' a toll, I guess you could say. If you travel through the Ozarks, you got to pay."

"And the loot goes to the poor folks hereabouts?"

"Well . . . not all of it," Jim replied with a grin.

"We help out where we can," Cahill added, more serious than his cousin. "If you ride with us, we'll expect you to chip in, too, Custis."

Longarm thought about it, then said, "I never played Robin Hood before."

"Who?" Jim asked.

"A fella in a story from over in England. An outlaw who claimed he robbed from the rich to give to the poor."

"Yep, that's what we do, all right. 'Course, we keep some for our ownselves, too."

Cahill said, "Now you know the whole story, Custis. You still want to be part of it?"

"I don't mind helping folks out," Longarm said. "Sure, I'll ride with you."

Cahill turned his horse. "Come on, then. We'll go back to Strickland's and have a drink to seal the deal."

Longarm wheeled the bay around and fell in alongside Cahill. Jim brought up the rear. The sun was low in the sky, and as it slid behind the mountains to the west, dusky shadows gathered quickly. By the time they reached the turnoff to Skunk Hollow, it was almost completely dark.

The horses turned onto the smaller trail, moving at a brisk walk. Up ahead, birds cried out in the thick woods that bordered the trail, and over the clopping of their mounts' hooves, Longarm heard a loud flutter of wings.

Cahill heard it, too, and stiffened in his saddle just as Longarm did. He muttered, "What the hell—"

"Down!" Longarm shouted, bending forward over the neck of his horse. "Light a shuck, boys!" He jammed his boot heels into the bay's flanks and sent it leaping forward into a gallop.

Even as the horse lunged into a run, fireflies winked brightly in the dark shadows under the trees alongside the trail. Only they weren't fireflies, Longarm knew, but muzzle flashes instead. Shots slammed out, strangely muffled by the thick vegetation but still plenty ominous.

Something burned past Longarm's ear. Somewhere behind him, a man let out a yell of pain. Cahill shouted, "Jim!" and reined in.

Longarm bit back a curse and hauled on the bay's reins, jerking it to a stop. His right hand flashed across his body and palmed out the Colt. He fired, triggering three times in the direction of the muzzle flashes he had seen. He didn't have any real hope of hitting the bushwhackers, but maybe by throwing some lead at them he could distract them long enough for him and his companions to get away.

He heard the thunder of hoofbeats and looked over his shoulder to see Cahill and Jim galloping toward him. Cahill rode close beside his cousin, one hand reaching out to steady Jim in the saddle.

"Jim's hit!" Cahill shouted to Longarm as they approached.

"Keep going!" Longarm called back. "I'll cover you!"

Cahill and Jim swept past him on the trail as Longarm snapped two more shots into the woods. Bullets clawed the air around him as he kicked his own horse into a run again. The Colt was empty. Longarm guided the bay with his knees as he thumbed out the empty rounds and replaced them with fresh cartridges from his coat pocket.

He snapped the revolver's loading gate closed, twisted in the hull, and emptied the Colt into the woods again. More of those deadly fireflies winked at him. He was suddenly thrown forward over the bay's neck as something struck him hard on the outside of his upper left arm.

Longarm managed to stay in the saddle and didn't pass out from the pain that coursed from his arm through his entire body. He jammed the empty Colt back in its holster. He'd dropped the reins when he was hit. Now he caught them up in his right hand. His left arm hung uselessly at his side. Since he was already hunched over, making himself a smaller target, he stayed that way.

Half-stunned, Longarm guided the horse by instinct as much as anything else. He heard the clatter of hooves ahead of him and knew that Cahill and Jim were still up there. He tried to listen for sounds of pursuit but didn't hear any. Maybe the bushwhackers weren't coming after them.

Longarm wondered how badly Jim was hit. The part of his brain that was still functioning logically told him that his own wound probably wasn't serious, despite the pain and shock he was experiencing. He gritted his teeth and forced his left arm to move. He could tell that the bullet hadn't broken any bones. Likely it had just clipped a hunk of meat from his arm.

The wound was bleeding, though. Longarm could feel the

warm wetness spreading down his arm. He needed medical attention, and chances were Jim did, too. Up here in these mountains, there was only one place for them to go.

Sarah Jane's.

Chapter 11

By the time he reached Skunk Hollow, Longarm was sure no one was chasing them. He could still hear Cahill and Jim riding ahead of him, but there had been no more shots and no sound of hoofbeats from behind. The pain in his arm had receded to a dull ache, confirming his guess that the wound wasn't too bad, but it was still bleeding. That had to be stopped, and the wound would need to be cleaned and bandaged.

He was glad now that he had learned the trails to Sarah Jane's place, because Cahill and Jim weren't waiting around to show him the way. He slowed the bay to a walk when he reached the smaller path that worked its winding way up the side of the mountain to the bench where the cabin was located.

The yellow glow of lamplight through an open door was a welcome sight. Longarm steered by that beacon until he had crossed the bench to the cabin. Cahill's and Jim's horses stood outside, their reins dangling where they had been dropped. Longarm pulled the bay to a halt and slid awkwardly out of the saddle, reaching across his body to hold his wounded arm tight against his side so that it wouldn't flop around. He stumbled as his feet hit the ground and might have fallen if a strong hand had not gripped his right shoulder.

"Steady there," Cahill said. "You look like you're hit, too, Custis."

"Drilled through the left arm," Longarm said through clenched teeth.

"Let me help you inside. I thought I heard you ride up." Cahill steered Longarm toward the door of the cabin. "Leastways, I was hopin' it was you, and not that damned Deuce Thaxton."

Longarm stopped and muttered, "Thaxton?"

"Yeah. I've got a pretty good idea it was him who bushwhacked us, him and that bunch of damned jayhawkers who ride with him. But we'll worry about that later. Come on inside so Sarah Jane can take a look at your arm when she finishes patching up Jim."

Longarm let Cahill help him into the cabin and onto a chair on the side of the room where Sarah Jane practiced her medical skills. He took his mind off the pain in his arm by thinking about what Cahill had just said about Deuce Thaxton. Clearly, Thaxton *was* here in the Ozarks, confirming the rumors that Judge Parker had heard from his informants. Equally clear was the fact that there was some connection between Cahill and Thaxton, which was something that the judge *hadn't* suspected. Cahill and Thaxton weren't friends, that was for sure, otherwise Cahill wouldn't have suspected immediately that Thaxton might have been in charge of the ambush.

Longarm looked at the table where Jim lay while Sarah Jane bent to her task of doctoring him. She had cut away his shirt, and her face was grimly intent as she leaned over him and explored the wound in his chest. Blood was splashed all over his torso. Sarah Jane had cleaned most of the gore from around the wound itself, and she had a thin metal probe inserted in the bullet hole. "Hang on, Jim," she said quietly as she searched for the slug that had imbedded itself in his chest. "You're doing just fine."

Jim had a thick leather belt clenched between his teeth.

He bit down hard on it to keep from crying out as Sarah Jane probed the wound. Longarm saw an open bottle of whiskey sitting on a smaller table off to the side. Sarah Jane had probably used the liquor to help clean the wound. Longarm hoped she'd given Jim a slug or two from the bottle as well, to help deaden the pain.

Cahill moved up on the other side of the table. "Is there anything I can do to help?" he asked.

"No," Sarah Jane gritted. "I just have to get . . . this . . . uh . . . bullet!"

Jim flinched and moaned around the belt in his mouth as fresh pain hit him. Sarah Jane went on, "I've found it now. I'm sure it missed his heart, and it doesn't seem to have hit a lung, either." She picked up a pair of narrow forceps. "Hang on, Jim, this is going to hurt even worse."

She used the probe to guide the forceps. The instrument spread the bullet hole open even wider as Sarah Jane delved for the slug. Jim whimpered. Sarah Jane gnawed at her bottom lip, and beads of sweat appeared on her forehead.

"I've got it," she breathed after a moment. Carefully, she withdrew the forceps, keeping them clamped tight on the bullet. It came free of Jim's body, and Sarah Jane turned and dropped the misshapen bit of lead into a basin. It rattled as it rolled from one side to the other.

Jim was breathing heavily from the agony he had just endured. Sarah Jane leaned over and put her ear close to the wound in his chest. Longarm knew she was listening for the whistle of air from a perforated lung.

"Nothing," she said after a few seconds.

"Is that good?" Cahill asked.

"Very good," she told him. "As I suspected, Jim's lungs weren't hit. The bullet lodged against his breastbone and probably cracked it, but that will heal. I'll clean the wound and bandage it, and he should be all right as long as he doesn't get blood poisoning. He'll be flat on his back for several weeks, though."

"Damn it!" Cahill bit out. "I count on Jim ridin' with me."

"He won't be doing any riding for a long time," Sarah

Jane said, and her tone of voice made it clear there would be no argument with her diagnosis. "You'll have to find someone else to ride with you."

Longarm met Cahill's gaze as the big redheaded mountaineer glanced at him. "Maybe I already have," Cahill muttered.

Sarah Jane looked in the same direction and exclaimed, "Oh!" Her eyes widened as if she were noticing Longarm's presence in the cabin for the first time. That might well be the case, Longarm thought. Sarah Jane had been concentrating so hard on treating Jim's injury that it was possible she hadn't known Longarm was there.

Now she came toward him, concern on her face as she said, "You're hurt, Custis!"

"Yes, ma'am, a little." Longarm moved his ventilated arm and tried not to wince. "Shot through the meaty part of this here left wing of mine."

"Who did this?"

Longarm inclined his head toward Cahill. "You'd better ask Roney."

"Somebody bushwhacked us at the turnoff from the Fayetteville road," Cahill said, scowling. "They were up in the trees, so we didn't get a look at them, but I'd bet my bottom dollar it was Deuce Thaxton and his bunch."

"Thaxton." Sarah Jane said the word like it tasted bad in her mouth. "I wouldn't be a bit surprised." She stood in front of Longarm and ordered, "Take off your coat and shirt while I'm bandaging Jim's wound."

"Yes, ma'am."

Jim had passed out. Cahill lifted him into a sitting position and held him there while Sarah Jane wound strips of cloth tightly around his chest. When she was finished, she said, "Ease him back down now and let him sleep. The rest will do him good."

She turned to Longarm, who had managed to get his coat off but was struggling with his shirt. The sleeve had to be cut away; it was soaked with blood and already beginning to dry and stick to the pair of wounds in his arm, one in the front and one in the back. Sarah Jane wielded a pair of scissors calmly and efficiently, then used a cloth saturated with whiskey to soak off the last shreds of fabric. Longarm's face whitened as he felt the fiery bite of the liquor on the open wounds.

The bullet hole in the front of his arm was slightly larger, since it was the exit wound. Sarah Jane cleaned both holes, then said, "It doesn't look like the bone is broken."

"I'm pretty sure it's not," Longarm agreed, making an effort to keep his voice normal. At least it seemed normal to his ears. He couldn't have sworn what it sounded like to the others.

"You've lost a lot of blood." Sarah Jane sounded worried about that. "Are you feeling light-headed?"

"Maybe a mite. A little bracer from that bottle wouldn't hurt, I reckon."

She shook her head. "No, you don't need any whiskey right now. The bleeding seems to have stopped. I'm going to clean these wounds a little better, then bandage them. Then you're going to get some rest, and after that, some solid food."

"I don't feel too awful hungry right now—"

"You will. Now, just sit quietly while I take care of this . . ."

Longarm knew she was right. Rest, then food and maybe some coffee. This wasn't the first time he'd been shot. He knew he was going to be fine.

But why was the cabin spinning around so crazily all of a sudden?

As if from far away, he heard Sarah Jane's voice as she cried out, "Roney! Help me!"

Then Longarm went flying off into a darkness so deep it must have been at the very center of the universe.

"Welcome back to the land of the living."

Longarm wasn't sure about that. From the way his arm felt, a dozen of ol' Beelzebub's imps were jabbing it with their pitchforks. It hurt so bad he wondered if he was waking up in Hades.

That voice hadn't sounded like the Devil's, though. In fact, it had been soft and musical, like water trickling over the rocks in the bottom of a brook.

He shivered, realizing that he was cold. That was another reason he couldn't be in hell, he told himself. Unless it had finally frozen over.

"C-cold," he mumbled.

"Of course you are," that pretty voice said again. "You've got a fever. But I expect it's going to break soon. The infection's not really that bad."

Longarm pried his eyes open and looked up at the face of the person leaning over him. Nope, not hell. He was in heaven instead, because he had an angel looking at him. A beautiful angel, with a halo like pale gold . . .

"Sarah Jane," he whispered.

"I'm right here." She took his right hand where it lay on his chest and squeezed it. "Just rest, Custis. You've been unconscious for a while. You lost too much blood too fast. But you're going to be fine."

The memories came swirling back into Longarm's head. The ambush where the Skunk Hollow trail turned off from the Fayetteville road; the wild ride through the woods and up the mountain; the warmly lit cabin where Sarah Jane had been tending to him . . .

"How's . . . Jim?" he croaked.

"He's fine," Sarah Jane replied as she patted his shoulder. "Actually, he's not in much worse shape than you right now. His wound is more serious, but he hasn't developed an infection."

"Cahill . . . ?"

"You mean Roney? He's here. Well, actually, he's outside seeing to the horses. It's morning, Custis. You were unconscious all night."

"The bushwhackers?" Longarm said. "They didn't come here?"

Sarah Jane shook her head. "It was a quiet night, except when you were raving."

Longarm realized he was lying on a bunk of some sort. He let his head sag back against the pillow that was propped under it. So he'd been out of his head and raving during the night, he thought. He wondered if he had said anything to give away his true identity as a deputy United States marshal. From the way Sarah Jane was acting, he didn't think he had, but he couldn't be sure of that until he talked to Cahill.

And if he had slipped up and Cahill knew he was a lawman, Cahill might just up and shoot him.

A door banged, and a voice said loudly, "The horses are fine. You got any chores you need done, Sarah Jane?"

She turned away from Longarm and shushed Cahill. "For goodness sake, Roney, we have a couple of wounded men here. They need their rest."

Cahill came over where Longarm could see him and peered down at the wounded deputy. Longarm summoned up a grin. Cahill returned it, with no sign on his rugged face of suspicion or anger.

Longarm could breathe a little easier now. Cahill didn't know who he really was.

"This one's awake," Cahill said to Sarah Jane, gesturing toward Longarm.

"Yes, but Jim's not," she said crisply. "Please keep your voice down."

"Yeah, yeah." Cahill took off his hat. He seemed to be in a surprisingly good mood this morning, Longarm thought. "How's the arm, Custis?"

"Hurts like blazes."

Cahill nodded. "I'm not surprised. I've been drilled like that before. The arm'll be stiff for a week or so, but you'll be all right."

Longarm was beginning to agree with that diagnosis. With his right hand, he motioned to a chair that was close beside the bunk. "Sit down," he said to Cahill. "Tell me about what happened last night."

"We got bushwhacked, that's what happened," Cahill said

grimly, his good mood disappearing as he swung the chair around and straddled it. "They were layin' for us in the woods, right there at the Skunk Hollow cut-off."

"I remember that," Longarm said. "I heard some birds fly up all of a sudden and knew something had disturbed them."

"Yeah, I noticed that, too. You're an observant cuss."

Longarm managed a weak smile. "It's kept me alive this long." He paused, then went on, "You said you thought somebody named Thaxton was behind the ambush. You mean the outlaw Deuce Thaxton, from Kansas?"

"You know him?"

"I know of him," Longarm said. "He's supposed to be a bad man."

"Bad enough," Cahill said flatly. "Him and all that bunch of his who hang out at the Bloody Holler."

"The . . . Bloody Holler?" Longarm repeated. "What's that?"

"Just a shack off in the woods east of here. I wouldn't even call it a tavern like Strickland's. Nobody ever goes there except outlaws like Thaxton."

"Why would he want to ambush us?"

"Thaxton and me don't get along. We got crossways with each other not long after he drifted into these parts. He asked me to ride with him, and I turned him down. Then, later, somebody took a shot at me and I shot back. Killed the son of a buck. It turned out he was one of Thaxton's men. Thaxton said he didn't know anything about it, but I know better."

Longarm closed his eyes for a moment and thought. The situation was becoming clearer now. Instead of one gang of bandits operating in these mountains, there were two. And while Cahill had evidently been willing to live and let live, Thaxton hadn't seen things that way. He wanted to be bull of the woods, and that meant getting rid of Roney Cahill.

"Sounds like . . . you've got your hands full," he murmured.

"Don't you worry about me," Cahill said. "I can take care of mysel—"

He stopped short, his head coming up as he listened intently to something outside. "Horses," he muttered. "Somebody's coming." He stood up, his hand going to the butt of his gun.

Longarm grimaced in frustration. Trouble was on the way, and he was too weak to do anything except lie here helplessly.

If he lived through this, he would have a score of his own to settle with Deuce Thaxton.

Chapter 12

Longarm tried to push himself into a sitting position, but Sarah Jane hurried over from the other side of the room and put a hand on his shoulder, gently urging him back down. "Be careful, Custis," she said. "You don't want to start that wound bleeding again."

Cahill stepped to the door, his gun out now, held ready in his hand.

"Roney!" Sarah Jane's voice was sharp. "What are you doing?"

"Somebody's comin'," he hissed over his shoulder. "Could be trouble."

"Yes, and it could be some of my students, too. More than one of them ride over here on mules. Or had you forgotten that I have a school here?" She brushed past him and stepped to the door and opened it, ignoring his low-voiced warning.

A familiar deep voice came from outside. "Good mornin', Miss Sary Jane."

"Good morning, George," she told the little boy, then hissed over her shoulder to Cahill, "Put that gun away! Do you want to scare the children?"

Muttering under his breath, Cahill holstered his revolver.

He looked over at Longarm and shrugged. "Could've been Thaxton."

Longarm nodded in agreement. If Thaxton knew enough about Cahill to be his enemy, chances were Thaxton also knew about Cahill's connection to Sarah Jane. The bushwhackers must have known they had at least wounded some of their targets the night before; it made sense that they would come looking for the wounded men at Sarah Jane's cabin.

So far, though, that hadn't happened. Longarm wondered why Thaxton was giving them this break. He intended to find out, sooner or later. He intended to get answers to all the questions he had.

Sarah Jane drew the blanket partition up so that Longarm and Jim weren't visible from the doorway. Longarm could hear the children trooping in for the day's lessons. Their voices were excited and happy as they talked among themselves and with Sarah Jane. Cahill came over and sat down on the chair beside Longarm's bunk again. He got out his pipe and chewed on the stem without lighting it.

"She won't let me smoke in here, claims it stinks the place up," he said quietly.

Longarm nodded in sympathy. His mouth was too dry and he felt too bad to want a cheroot right now, but later, when he got to feeling better, he was sure the craving for one would hit him.

Sarah Jane stuck her head around the partition. "Roney, there's a pot of stew on the stove, as well as some coffee. Will you see to it that Custis gets fed, and Jim, too, when he wakes up?"

"Sure," Cahill said as he got to his feet. He went through a door in the rear of the makeshift surgery. Longarm hadn't been back there. He supposed that was where the kitchen was located, as well as Sarah Jane's sleeping quarters.

Cahill came back a few minutes later carrying a cup and a bowl. He drew the chair closer to the bed with his foot, then sat down and said, "I reckon I'm goin' to have to feed you."

"The hell with that," Longarm muttered. "Just help me sit up." He wouldn't have minded all that much if Sarah Jane had fed him, but he was damned if he was going to sit still for a big galoot like Roney Cahill sticking a spoon in his mouth.

"All right, but be careful," Cahill said. He put the bowl and the cup on the floor next to the bunk. "If you get those bullet holes to bleedin' again, she'll take it out of my hide."

Longarm started to grin, but it turned into a grimace as Cahill took hold of his shoulders and helped him into a sitting position. His head spun wildly for a few seconds before settling down. When he figured he wasn't going to go flying off into space again, he heaved a sigh.

Cahill put the back of his hand against Longarm's forehead. Longarm jerked away and said, "What the hell are you doing?"

"Sarah Jane's right, you've got a fever. Better eat anyway. You know what they say: starve the grippe, feed a fever."

"I thought it was the other way around."

Cahill frowned. "Is it? Hell, I don't know. But she said eat, so you're goin' to eat."

Longarm took the coffee cup first, wrapping both hands around it and lifting it carefully to his mouth. He felt a little better right away after he'd sipped some of the strong black brew. Cahill gave him the bowl of stew. The spoon rattled against the bowl as Longarm tried to lift it. He took a deep breath to steady himself and managed to get a bite to his mouth. The stew was good, savory with herbs. He chewed on a hunk of meat that had been boiled in it. Probably squirrel, Longarm decided. Right now it could have been 'possum and he wouldn't have cared. The more he ate, the more he realized how ravenously hungry he was.

By the time he'd cleaned the bowl and drained all the coffee from the cup, he was sweating. Cahill gave him a cool, wet cloth to wipe his face. "Looks like the fever's broken," Cahill commented. "You'll be all right, Custis."

"Yeah." Longarm eased back onto the pillow. "But I'm sure mighty tired all of a sudden."

"Nothing wrong with that. You just go ahead and sleep."

Longarm felt himself slipping away. "You'll . . . keep an eye out?"

"Don't you worry 'bout a thing," Cahill assured him. "Sarah Jane and me, we're not going anywhere."

Longarm dozed off, listening to the soft, sweet sound of Sarah Jane's voice as she taught the children their lessons on the other side of the blankets.

He was hungry again when he woke up late in the afternoon. Jim Cahill was awake then, too, and propped up in the bunk on the other side of the room. Jim was very pale and lines were etched in his lean face, but he summoned up a grin for Longarm as he said, "Howdy, Custis. Looks like we're both back in the land of the livin', know what I mean?"

"That's right," Longarm agreed. "Where are Sarah Jane and Roney?"

"Roney's out splittin' some wood for the stove, and Sary Jane's gone up the hill to pick huckleberries."

Longarm frowned. He had already heard the solid *thunk!* of an ax blade biting deeply into wood and figured that was Cahill's work. But he didn't like the idea of Sarah Jane wandering off very far from the cabin. With Deuce Thaxton lurking around the area, she might be in danger.

Cahill came into the cabin a moment later with his arms full of short lengths of split wood. He carried the load into the kitchen, then came back into the room where Longarm and Jim sat.

"Do you think Sarah Jane ought to be off by herself just now?" Longarm asked without preamble.

Cahill looked at him. "What are you talkin' about?"

"Jim said she's gone up the hill to pick huckleberries. How do you know Thaxton won't grab her or try to harm her?"

"For one thing, she's got that little redheaded kid and several more of her students with her, and for another, she's got her rifle. Sarah Jane's as good a shot with a long gun as I am, and I'm just about the best in the Ozarks. And not even

Thaxton would try anything with half a dozen kids hanging around as witnesses."

Longarm wasn't so sure of that. From what he had heard of Deuce Thaxton, the man was ruthless and didn't care who got hurt if they got in his way. But he had to admit it was unlikely anything would happen under the circumstances Cahill described.

Unlikely, but not impossible . . . Longarm knew he would feel better when Sarah Jane returned safely to the cabin.

That happened less than a quarter of an hour later. She waved from the doorway to her departing students, then came into the cabin carrying a basket full of huckleberries. It was a little early in the season, but the fruit looked ripe anyway.

"Well, looks like both my patients are awake," she said with a smile. "How do you feel?"

"Fit as a fiddle, Sary Jane," Jim replied. "I'm ready to jump on a horse and go a-roarin' out of here."

"I hardly think so," she said. "You'll be doing good to get out of that bunk for a few minutes at a time in a week. Until then, you'll do nothing but rest. Speaking of which, I think you should go ahead and lie down now. It's too soon for you to be sitting up."

"You're just underestimatin' my iron constitution, that's all," Jim muttered. But he laid down again with Cahill's help.

Sarah Jane turned to Longarm. "What about you, Custis?"

He had a dull ache in his tightly bandaged left arm. He moved it experimentally and felt the ache become a little sharper, but not unbearably so by any means. "Not too bad. Like Roney said, the arm's just a little stiff."

Sarah Jane came over to him and placed the back of her hand against his forehead, as Cahill had done that morning. "The fever hasn't come back," she judged. "The red streaks lower down on your arm are gone, too. You've beaten the infection." She glanced at Jim and chuckled. "You really do appear to have an iron constitution."

"Hey!" Jim protested. "That's me!"

"Both of you still need rest," Sarah Jane declared. "And I'm going to see that you get it."

Longarm didn't doubt for a moment that she would enforce that rule.

They had more stew for supper that night, along with huckleberry pie. Longarm complimented Sarah Jane on her cooking. There seemed to be no end to her talents. Teaching, doctoring, cooking . . . Longarm wondered what else she was good at.

That thought made him follow her around the room with his eyes for a moment. He liked the way her pale blond hair framed her face, and her white shirt and long, dark blue skirt looked good on her slender but amply curved body. He recalled the sweetness of her lips and the warmth of her embrace, and he felt himself reacting to those memories. As his arousal grew, he looked away from her and sternly told himself to think about something else. He didn't want her coming over to the bunk and finding the sheet tented up over his groin.

Cahill came back inside a short time later. Longarm wasn't sure where he'd been, but he suspected Cahill had prowled around outside, making certain that Thaxton and the gang he had brought with him from Kansas weren't skulking in the vicinity of the cabin.

"Roney," Jim said from the bunk on the other side of the room, "it's time you and me had a talk 'bout Thaxton. What're we goin' to do about this here ambush? We can't just let it pass. Thaxton'll think he's got us hoorawed."

"*You're* not goin' to do anything about it," Cahill replied. "Didn't you hear Sarah Jane? You're not goin' to do anything except rest for the next few weeks."

"Dadgum it, Roney—"

"Don't argue with me," Cahill said. "Take it up with her, if you're of a mind to."

Jim's protests subsided. Obviously, arguing with Sarah Jane wasn't anything he cared to do, no matter how badly he was frustrated by the current situation.

"What about me?" Longarm said. "I've got a pair of bullet holes in my arm courtesy of that rannihan. I'd say that's a score that needs some settling, too."

Cahill straddled the chair next to Longarm's bunk and cast a glance toward the door into the rear of the cabin. Sarah Jane had gone in there a short time earlier and hadn't returned. Quietly, so that she wouldn't overhear him, he said, "You know, I've been thinkin' about that, Custis. You'll be up and around in a day or two, and that's not your gun arm you got plugged in. I was wonderin' if you and me ought to take a ride over to Bloody Holler."

"Beard Thaxton in his own den, huh?" Longarm grunted. "Sounds like a good way to wind up dead."

"Maybe. But some of the other boys could go with us. They could hang back and surround the place, then cover it with their rifles. We'd call Thaxton outside and have it out with him."

"How do you know he'd come out?"

"Because he's a proud son of a bitch. Thinks he's got to be cock of the walk. Otherwise he wouldn't have got so damned mad when I told him I didn't want to ride with him. With me backing his play, he could have lorded it over the Ozarks like he was a king. With me opposin' him, though, he'll never be anything more than another outlaw to the folks around here."

What Cahill was saying made sense in its own way. Thaxton might indeed be the sort of man who would risk a showdown just for the chance to defeat an enemy. If Thaxton was behind the train and bank holdups in the area, getting rid of him would accomplish a significant part of Longarm's job. He would still have the problem of bringing Cahill and Jim and the men who rode with them to justice for the stagecoach robberies, but apples always tasted better eaten one bite at a time, Longarm reflected.

Thaxton first, he thought as he came to a decision, then he would deal with the problem of Cahill.

"All right," he said. "I'll go with you to Bloody Holler and we'll see what Thaxton has to say for himself."

"He's so brazen he probably won't even deny bein' behind that bushwhacking." Cahill inclined his head toward the rear of the cabin. "We'll have to be careful, though. If Sarah Jane finds out what we're plannin' to do, she'll pitch a conniption cow."

"We'll keep it to ourselves," Longarm promised. "Won't we, Jim?"

Jim frowned at them from across the room. "I'll be damned if I like the idea of you goin' up against Thaxton without me, Roney. But I won't say anything if that's the way you want it."

"That's the way I want it," Cahill said with a nod. "I want to see Deuce Thaxton lined up over the sights of my gun."

Chapter 13

Though his job often required great patience, deep down Longarm was not the patient sort and never had been. He knew that about himself. So it came as no great surprise when a strong feeling of restlessness grew inside him during the next couple of days he spent at Sarah Jane Masterson's cabin.

The desire to be out and doing something wasn't the only thing gnawing at Longarm. He spent a lot of hours sitting and talking with Cahill and Jim, and when they weren't talking, they were playing dominoes or cards. The instinctive liking Longarm felt for both men grew stronger as they talked about their families and their lives. The Cahill family was large and scattered all over the Ozarks, but despite the distances involved, the family members maintained close emotional ties. As Longarm had been told, Cahill and Jim were more like brothers than cousins, having been raised so that they spent as much time at each other's cabin as they did at their own. The bond between them was obviously strong.

Sooner or later, Longarm knew, he would have to take action against the two men. It might mean arresting them, or, if they resisted arrest, gunplay wasn't out of the question.

Longarm had no doubt he would be able to pull the trigger on either of them. His job came first and always had. But it would be hard, Lord, it would be hard to kill Roney Cahill or his cousin, Jim.

By the evening of the third day after the bushwhacking, Longarm could flex his left arm without much pain. "Nearly good as new," he announced with a grin as Sarah Jane looked on, frowning in disapproval. They were standing in the cabin's kitchen, talking quietly while Cahill and Jim were in the other room.

"I seriously doubt that," she said, her voice tart. "You need more rest, Custis."

"I ain't saying that I don't appreciate your hospitality," Longarm said, "but as pleasant as it's been, I reckon it's time I moved on."

"Where? Back to Strickland's?" Sarah Jane came closer to him. "Back to that girl?"

Longarm's eyebrows lifted in surprise. If he hadn't known better, he would have said that Sarah Jane had heard about the time he'd spent with Libby and was jealous. Come to think of it, he *didn't* know better. Sarah Jane knew almost everything that went on in the mountains; the children who attended her classes kept her informed of all the gossip they heard. And maybe she *was* jealous of Libby. There had certainly been a spark between them when Longarm kissed her.

"There are things I need to do, Sarah Jane," Longarm said. "Things that don't have anything to do with Libby."

"Is that her name?" Sarah Jane asked testily.

Longarm felt a flash of irritation. "You know danged well it's her name. You've probably known her all her life, just like you know everybody else around here. For all I know, her little brothers and sisters go to school here with you."

"That doesn't have anything to do with your wound," Sarah Jane said, changing the subject. "You're not ready to . . . to go off and face Deuce Thaxton in a gunfight!"

"Oh," Longarm said slowly. "So you heard about that, did you?"

"I didn't have to hear about it. As soon as Roney brought

you and Jim here and I saw that you were wounded, I knew he'd have to try to settle the score. No one else around here would have done such a thing other than Thaxton or some of his men." She shook her head. "When you know Roney as well as I do, it's not hard to know what he's planning."

Longarm couldn't argue with that. Sarah Jane was right about Cahill wanting to confront Thaxton. And Longarm couldn't let Cahill ride up to the Bloody Holler alone.

"We're just going to talk to Thaxton," he said. "We have to find out what happened. Maybe there won't be any shooting."

She looked at him with scorn and hurt in her eyes. "You don't really believe that, do you?"

Longarm didn't believe it, but he was too stubborn to say so. "Never can tell what'll happen," he insisted.

"All right, then," Sarah Jane snapped. "Go on and get yourself killed. Make sure all my hard work on your arm goes to waste. I won't cry over you, Custis."

"Don't recall asking you to," Longarm replied, his voice taut. He didn't blame Sarah Jane for being upset, but she sure as hell wasn't making this any easier.

Cahill appeared in the doorway. "Whatever you two are jawin' about, it can wait. Jim wants to play forty-two, so we need two more players. Come on."

Sarah Jane brushed past Longarm. "All right. That sounds like fun," she said. Her voice was still strained, however.

Longarm followed her. Cahill stopped him by putting a hand on his arm. "Sarah Jane got her dander up about something?" he asked in a half-whisper.

"Nothing important," Longarm replied. "Tomorrow, I reckon you and me will go see Deuce Thaxton, if you still want to."

A fierce light burned in Cahill's eyes. "Damn right I want to. This is the best news I've heard since that bushwhackin'. We'd better keep it to ourselves, though, or Jim's liable to start complainin' again about bein' left out."

Longarm nodded. He wanted to spend one more nice, peaceful evening—before things got deadly again.

• • •

The underbrush along both sides of the trail grew thicker and more tangled as Longarm and Roney Cahill rode east along the meandering path. A fella who got lost in there would have a real chore hacking his way back out, Longarm thought as he eyed the bushes and brambles. Pine trees towered above them, blocking the sun, creating a world that was permanently in shadow except for narrow rays of light that slanted down through small gaps in the roof of the forest. The trail twisted and turned, following the rugged terrain. The slopes were too steep for farming. It had been over an hour since Longarm had seen any cabins.

"Is this country good for anything?" he asked.

Cahill shrugged. "Not much. There's been talk of companies comin' in and cuttin' down the trees for lumber, but there are too many places where loggin' is easier. They may get to it sooner or later, but I don't reckon it'll be anytime soon. There's plenty of game hereabouts, though. If a man's a good shot with a rifle, he can put meat on the table for his family. And a stubborn woman can grow a few vegetables in small plots. But it's rough country, that's for sure. There are people up here, folks who want to live as far back in the mountains away from other people as they can get."

"And Thaxton," Longarm said.

"And Thaxton," Cahill agreed. "He figures he's safe up here, away from any deputies the law down in Fort Smith might send out."

"Is he?" asked Longarm.

Cahill grinned. "Not many lawmen in these parts. When we started stickin' up those stagecoaches, Jim and me figured it might bring the law down on us. So far, though, they've left us alone."

Cahill didn't know it, Longarm thought grimly, but that had changed.

"I've heard that Thaxton is wanted for a bunch of killin's up in Kansas and Nebraska," Cahill went on. "Arkansas might sent him back up there if they could catch him. The man who brought Thaxton in could write his own ticket with the law, I reckon." Cahill gave a little shake of his head. "Of course, that'll never happen. Nobody will have the chance to arrest Thaxton, because I intend to kill him."

Longarm wondered if there was some way to prevent that. Ideally, he'd like to take Thaxton into custody, see him stand trial for the crimes he'd committed in Arkansas, then see him sent back to the other states where he was wanted to answer for those crimes, too. Chances were, Cahill was right and that would never happen. Justice might have to settle for a bullet in Deuce Thaxton's heart.

Longarm and Cahill rounded a bend, and Cahill reined in sharply at the sight of several men on horseback sitting in the trail up ahead. Longarm jerked the bay's reins, his other hand moving toward the butt of his Colt.

"No, it's all right," Cahill said with a quick gesture. "They're friends of mine, the boys who ride with me and Jim. Come on, I'll introduce you."

He rode forward, grinning and answering the greetings that the men called to him. Longarm followed along.

"Boys, meet Custis Jones," Cahill said as he and Longarm came up to the other riders. "You've heard me talk about him. He's got a couple of bullet holes in his arm courtesy of Deuce Thaxton."

The men nodded to Longarm. Not surprisingly, they were a rough-looking bunch. Of the six of them, five were bearded, and the other wore a thick mustache that drooped over his mouth. His name was Linus Sanderson, Cahill said. The other five were Seamus Cahill—another distant cousin—Mitch Duncan, Fred McHaney, Lonzo Pearson, and Bill Fowley. Fowley was the most fierce-looking of the bunch, with bushy dark hair, a tangled beard, and a savage, gap-toothed grin that made Longarm think Fowley had probably pulled the wings off a heap of flies when he was a youngster.

Cahill vouched for all of them, though, and for now, that would have to be good enough. Longarm said his howdies and nodded pleasantly to the men. Fowley leaned over in the saddle, spat on the ground, and rasped, "This is the feller who's takin' over for Jim?"

"That's the way it's worked out," Cahill replied. "I figured to just have Custis ride with us as another of the bunch, but with Jim laid up, I guess you could say that Custis is takin' his place."

"He ain't from around here," Fowley said ominously.

"No, I ain't," Longarm said. "I'm from West-by-God Virginia. Got anything to say about that, Fowley?" His tone was sharp, almost challenging. He didn't intend to take a lot of shit from this ridge-runner.

Fowley glared at him for a few seconds, then burst out laughing. "I reckon he'll do, Roney. Want me to fight him, just so's you'll know he's tough enough to ride with us?"

"No, that ain't necessary." Cahill heeled his horse into a walk. "Come on, boys, we're on our way to Bloody Holler."

The group couldn't ride side by side on the narrow trail. They stretched out, Cahill taking the lead, followed by Longarm, and then the rest of the men. Longarm glanced over his shoulder and saw that Fowley was bringing up the rear.

In a quiet voice, Longarm said to Cahill, "I don't think Fowley much likes the idea of me joining up with you."

"Don't worry about Bill," Cahill said over his shoulder. "He's rough as a cob, but he's a good man."

Longarm was willing to believe the part about the cob. He was going to reserve judgment on the rest of it.

Another half-hour's ride took them around the bulky shoulder of a mountain, then down a steep trail toward a depression in the slope. A rocky promontory jutted out above the depression, forming a hollow in the mountainside that seemed to be in perpetual shadow. A squat, sturdy-looking log cabin was built under the beetling bluff. Longarm knew without being told that he was looking at Bloody Holler.

Cahill reined in and nodded toward the cabin. "There it is. Looks like Thaxton is home, too." He pointed toward several horses stabled in a crude, lean-to shed at the end of the cabin.

Longarm was about to agree when a voice called suddenly from somewhere, "You boys just sit your saddles and don't move! I'll blow your damned heads off if you try anything funny!"

So Thaxton had at least one sentry posted up here, Longarm thought. That came as no surprise. Desperadoes like Thaxton were usually cautious men, suspicious of every little thing.

With a rustling of brush, a man in a floppy-brimmed felt hat stepped out into the trail. He carried a shotgun in his hands and wore a revolver on his hip. Leveling the greener at Longarm and Cahill, he demanded in a flat, midwestern voice, "What do you two want here?"

Longarm's eyes narrowed. *Two?* He glanced over his shoulder. He and Cahill were alone, all right. The other men had faded off into the tangled wilderness without Longarm even being aware they were gone. That told him how good they were at their business, because his senses were much keener than those of the average man.

"We want to see Deuce Thaxton," Cahill said to the guard.

The man glared at him. "Don't I know you?"

"I've been here before. The name's Roney Cahill."

"Cahill! That's right. You're the hillbilly Deuce wanted to ride with us. But no, you're too damned good for the likes of us. You damn backwoods trash."

Cahill's back stiffened. He restrained his anger with a visible effort. He had little choice in the matter; at this range, the shotgun could blow both him and Longarm out of their saddles.

"Just let Thaxton know that I want to talk to him," Cahill said.

"Oh, I'll let him know you're here, all right." The sentry shifted the greener into his left hand but kept the barrels level, even holding the weapon one-handed. He drew his pistol with his right hand, pointed it into the air, and fired three evenly spaced shots. Longarm looked down at the cabin and saw rifle barrels poke out from firing slits cut between the logs.

The guard gave them an ugly grin and said, "Go on down, if you're of a mind to." He holstered his revolver and stepped back. "I won't stand in your way."

A muscle jumped in Cahill's jaw as it clenched. "Come on, Custis," he said through gritted teeth.

Longarm didn't cotton to the idea of having that shotgunner at his back, but there was nothing he could do about it. He lifted the bay's reins and heeled the horse forward, following Cahill down into Bloody Holler.

He could feel eyes watching him as he rode toward the cabin. He became aware that his muscles were tensed, as if in expectation of a bullet, and he tried to force himself to relax. Cahill's men were up there in the woods somewhere, surrounding the place and training their rifles on it. At least, Longarm hoped so. That was the plan, anyway. If Thaxton started any shooting, Cahill's men could keep him bottled up in the cabin indefinitely.

The problem with that was that Longarm and Cahill might already be dead if that happened, and the log walls of that cabin were thick enough to stop just about anything short of a cannonball. Cahill's men could lay siege to the place, but if Thaxton had enough food and water in there, he might be able to wait them out.

Maybe it wouldn't come to that, Longarm thought. Cahill was counting on Thaxton's pride forcing him out into a showdown. It could happen that way, Longarm supposed.

The ground leveled out a short distance in front of the cabin. Cahill brought his mount to a stop there, and Longarm did likewise. They sat side by side, facing the cabin twenty feet away. "Thaxton!" Cahill called. "This is Roney Cahill! You in there? Come on out and talk!"

For a moment, the cabin sat there, squat, ugly, and silent. Then a voice came from inside. "What the hell do you want, Cahill? I thought you was too good to have anything to do with us!"

"I want to know why you thought you could bushwhack me and my friends and get away with it!" Cahill shot back.

Suddenly, to Longarm's surprise, the door of the cabin was jerked open, and a man stalked out, bristling with weapons.

It looked like Cahill had been right about Deuce Thaxton's pride.

Longarm wondered how many men were about to get killed because of that pride.

Chapter 14

Thaxton was a wiry man of medium height. He was hatless, had thinning dark hair, and several days' worth of dark beard stubble gave his face a muddy look. He carried a Winchester and wore crossed cartridge belts that supported a holstered pistol on each hip. The one on the right was worn normally; the one on the left had its butt turned forward for a cross-draw, like Longarm's Colt. Just behind the left-hand pistol was a sheathed Bowie knife, and Longarm spotted the handle of a dagger sticking up from the top of Thaxton's right boot. The badman from Kansas was armed for bear, that was for sure.

"What the hell are you talkin' about, Cahill?" Thaxton demanded. "I don't know anything about any bushwhackin'."

Cahill glared right back at him. "Four evenings ago, right at dusk, me and my cousin Jim and our friend Custis here were turnin' onto the trail to Skunk Hollow from the Fayetteville road when somebody opened up on us from the woods. Jim and Custis were wounded."

Thaxton shook his head and said, "I don't know a damned thing about it. This is the first I've heard of it, Cahill. You can believe me, or you can go to hell. I don't care which."

Oddly enough, Longarm realized abruptly that he *did* believe Thaxton. The outlaw's words carried the ring of truth.

Cahill wasn't so accepting, though. He snapped, "If you didn't do it, then who the hell did?"

"I don't know and I don't care. I ain't your keeper. I offered you the chance to ride with me, remember? If you'd taken me up on it, chances are nobody would've risked takin' any potshots at you."

"I'd rather dodge lead than have to smell a snake like you all the time," Cahill said.

Obviously, diplomacy wasn't Cahill's strongest skill, thought Longarm. He said, "Hold on here. Maybe Thaxton's got a point."

Cahill looked angrily at Longarm. "What?"

"Who in blazes are you?" asked Thaxton.

"Custis Jones," Longarm said to him. To Cahill, he went on, "You've got other enemies up in these mountains besides Thaxton, Roney. Maybe one of them ambushed us, thinking that you'd likely blame Thaxton for it."

"Do I know you?" Thaxton said.

Longarm shook his head. "Nope. I just rode into these parts not long ago."

"Ever been up in Kansas?"

Longarm had worried a little about that very thing. As far as he knew, he had never crossed paths with Deuce Thaxton. But it was possible he had tangled with one of the men in Thaxton's gang. Longarm had run up against a lot of lawbreakers in his time.

"I've been a lot of places," he said coolly, in reply to Thaxton's question.

Thaxton's squinty eyes narrowed even more. "I *do* know you. You held up a bank in Topeka and then gunned down Jack Graham in Wichita."

Longarm shrugged but didn't deny the allegations. If Thaxton wanted to believe he was an outlaw, that was fine with Longarm. That was the guise he was cultivating with Cahill, after all.

Cahill had been pondering what Longarm had said earlier.

Now he declared, "I don't believe it, Custis. Thaxton was behind that ambush."

"I don't cotton to bein' called a liar, Cahill," Thaxton said. With his left hand, he let go of the rifle and reached up to rub his beard-stubbled jaw. "Howsomever, I reckon it's possible some of the boys who ride with me might've decided to throw down on you. On their own, you understand."

Longarm hadn't considered that possibility. Would any of Thaxton's men act on their own like that, perhaps in hopes of currying favor with the boss outlaw by killing the man who had turned down Thaxton's offer of a partnership? Longarm couldn't rule it out. Desperadoes were often ruthless, ambitious men, otherwise they wouldn't be criminals.

Thaxton turned his head and bellowed at the cabin, "You boys get out here!"

One by one, eight men emerged from the cabin, all of them heavily armed and almost as dangerous-looking as Thaxton himself. Every one of them looked like he could have the blood of a dozen murders on his hands.

"Any of you gents take some shots at Cahill and his pards the other night?" Thaxton asked. His tone was conversational now, as if he were merely curious.

Three of the outlaws glanced at each other, and Longarm knew immediately that they were the guilty parties. His instincts made him sure of it. After a moment, the three men stepped forward, and one of them said proudly, "We done it, Deuce. We figgered it was time somebody showed that dumb hillbilly who's boss around here."

"Why didn't you say anything about it?"

The spokesman for the three outlaws grimaced. "We, uh, was waitin' until we heard whether or not any of 'em died. The light weren't real good, Deuce. We were afraid we didn't put any of 'em under after all."

The barrel of Thaxton's rifle had been pointing in the general direction of Longarm and Cahill. Now it lowered toward the ground. In fact, Thaxton tucked the Winchester under his arm and nodded to Cahill. "I reckon you were almost right, Cahill," he said. "It was some of my boys who bushwhacked you. But I didn't know a thing about it. You heard that for yourself."

That muscle in Cahill's jaw was jumping again, Longarm noted. Cahill didn't want to believe that Thaxton hadn't had anything to do with the ambush. He had worked himself up into a killing rage over the shooting, a rage directed at Thaxton, and now it had been thwarted.

Cahill glanced toward the darkly wooded slopes looming above the hollow, and as he did so, Thaxton laughed. "Got riflemen up there in the trees, do you?" Thaxton asked. "I can tell what you're thinkin', Cahill. You yell out for them to shoot, and maybe they could cut me and my boys down 'fore we can get back in the cabin. But if you start the ball, you and your pard there will get shot to doll rags, and you know it. You're weighin' whether the chance of killin' me is worth it."

Longarm knew that Thaxton was right. Cahill's hatred for the man was so powerful, he might be willing to sacrifice himself if it meant Thaxton and his gang would be wiped out. But there could be no guarantee of that. He and Longarm might die for nothing.

"Looks like I don't have any score to settle with you after all, Thaxton," Cahill said tightly.

"That's what I told you all along," Thaxton said with a smirk.

"But those three—" Cahill jerked his chin toward the three outlaws who had admitted to the ambush. "That's a different story."

"You're right about that," Thaxton said. "Cramer, you and Hardesty and Quince stay where you are. Me and the other boys are goin' back inside the cabin."

Cramer, the spokesman for the trio, stared at Thaxton. "Deuce, what do you mean?" he asked, an edge of desperation creeping into his voice.

"I mean you three are stayin' out here, and Cahill and what's his name, Jones, can settle things with you however they please."

Cahill straightened in the saddle. Longarm could tell he

was thinking that he might get to satisfy his wounded pride after all.

One of the other men said, "Deuce, you can't do that. We ride with you. Everybody backs the other fella's play."

Thaxton shook his head. "Not when you go off and do something stupid on your own. You know I'm supposed to do the thinkin' for this bunch. When I want Cahill bushwhacked, I'll tell you so. Until then . . ." Thaxton shrugged. "You're on your own."

So it was to be an object lesson to the rest of Thaxton's gang, Longarm thought. Of course, the odds were three to two. Thaxton was probably hoping that he could teach his men a lesson and rid himself of two enemies at the same time. He had to be thinking that his men would prevail over Cahill and Longarm, even though one or two of them might be wounded or even killed. That was a trade Thaxton was willing to make.

Thaxton looked up the hill and waved, letting the sentry know that everything was all right. Then he jerked the barrel of the rifle in a curt gesture and said to the other outlaws, "Get inside. Now."

Slowly, they began to withdraw, leaving behind the unlucky trio of Cramer, Hardesty, and Quince. Cramer was a burly man wearing a filthy buckskin shirt. A reddish-brown beard came down over his chest. Hardesty was thin and sallow, his face pockmarked. Quince was the youngest of the three and visibly nervous.

Thaxton waited until all his other men were inside the cabin. Then he said, "We won't interfere, Cahill. Neither will your boys, right?"

"That's right," Cahill replied. He made a slashing gesture with his left hand, indicating to the watching gunmen on the slopes that they should stay out of whatever happened.

Thaxton smiled thinly. "All right, then. You have fun now, hear?" He backed through the open door of the cabin and closed it behind him.

Cahill looked at the three bushwhackers and said, "You—"

Whatever he meant to say, he didn't get the rest of it out.

Cramer's hand flew toward his pistol, and he yelled, "Gun 'em!"

In the few moments he'd had to study the three men, Longarm had formed some definite impressions. Hardesty's pockmarked face was calm and expressionless, so Longarm had him figured as the most dangerous of the bunch. It was a toss-up between Cramer and Quince who was next. Cramer was big, which meant he might be a little slow, but Quince was nervous, never a good quality for a shootist to have. But there was no time to ponder the situation further, because guns were leaping into hands.

Longarm took Hardesty first, palming out his Colt and snapping off a shot that smacked into Hardesty's chest. Hardesty was fast, all right. He had gotten his gun out and almost brought it into line by the time Longarm fired. Hardesty's Colt boomed, but the impact of Longarm's slug driving into his body made the shot go wild. The bullet whined harmlessly past Longarm's head.

At the same instant as Hardesty's shot, Cahill fired at Cramer. The bullet caught Cramer in the shoulder and staggered him, but he didn't go down. He pulled his gun and was trying to bring it up when Cahill shot him again, this time in the belly. Cramer folded up and pitched forward, his pistol falling unfired from his hand.

As soon as Longarm saw Hardesty go down, he switched his aim to Quince. The bay skittered a step to the side, however, spooked by the sudden burst of gunfire. That threw off Longarm's aim just as he triggered. The shot missed Quince. The young man got off a shot of his own. It passed between Longarm and Cahill. The two of them fired at the same time, so close together the two shots sounded like one. Both slugs punched into Quince's body, lifting him from the ground and flinging him backward. He landed on his back in a loose-limbed sprawl, dead before he hit the ground.

Echoes of gunfire rolled back from the hills around Bloody Holler, which had certainly lived up to its name today. Clouds of acrid powder smoke hung in the air. There wasn't any breeze down here to blow away the smoke. It would have to settle and disperse on its own.

The smoke stung Longarm's eyes a little. He squinted against it and saw that all three of the outlaws were down, lying motionless on the ground. He was confident that Hardesty and Quince were dead. If Cramer wasn't, he soon would be with a bullet in his belly. The gunfight was over. Longarm and Cahill had won.

But only if they could make it out of here alive. Would Thaxton keep his part of the bargain? Or would he order his men to open up on Longarm and Cahill, now that they were safely inside the cabin again?

The echoes gradually died away, and silence reigned. The gunshots had driven away all the birds and small animals in the area. Longarm holstered his Colt and said, "Let's get out of here."

Cahill looked at the cabin, and Longarm knew that a part of his mind was hoping Thaxton would start something else. But nothing happened, and after a moment Cahill holstered his weapon as well.

"Yeah," Cahill said thickly. "It stinks here."

He turned his horse and urged it up the hill. Longarm followed. Despite all the indications that Thaxton was going to let them leave unmolested, the skin in the middle of his back crawled, as if a target were painted on it.

The woods closed in around them as they reached the top of the slope. They were relatively safe now. Cahill reined in for a second and heaved a sigh. He looked over at Longarm and asked, "Do you reckon Thaxton really didn't know anything about that ambush?"

"Whether he did or not, the ones who wounded me and Jim are dead. I'd say that's all that matters today."

"Yeah." Cahill wiped the back of his hand across his mouth. "But there's always tomorrow."

Yep, thought Longarm, *that was the catch, all right . . .*

Chapter 15

Bill Fowley and the rest of Cahill's men came out of the woods to rejoin Longarm and Cahill as they rode away from Bloody Holler. They emerged from the brush as noiselessly as they had disappeared into it.

Fowley's savage grin was in place as he said, "I sure thought Thaxton was gonna try to smoke you, Roney."

"I reckon the thought crossed my mind, too," Cahill admitted dryly.

"If he had, we'd 'a shot the shit out of him."

"I appreciate that, but I'd have still been dead, wouldn't I?"

Fowley frowned in confusion. "You was the one who went down there bold as brass."

"Yeah, I don't reckon I can argue with that."

Longarm listened to the conversation with half an ear. He was thinking about what he had accomplished today. First and foremost, he had survived a gun battle that could have easily gotten him killed. Second, he had not only confirmed with his own eyes that the fugitive Deuce Thaxton was now operating in the Ozarks, he had located the man's hideout. And third, he had made his position in Cahill's gang that much more secure. Now that he had fought alongside Cahill, no one could say that he didn't belong, even if he was an outsider.

After the group had ridden along for a few minutes, Fowley said, "Now that we got Thaxton buffaloed, when are we goin' to pull a job again, Roney? I was countin' on stoppin' that stagecoach the other day, but we didn't get to after that bushwhackin'."

"There'll be another coach day after tomorrow," Cahill said. "We'll hit it. You're wrong, though, Bill, if you think Deuce Thaxton's buffaloed. He's not scared of us or anything else."

"Hell, he chopped the legs out from under them boys of his, rather than have us cut loose our wolf on him."

Cahill shook his head. "He just wanted the rest of his gang to see that it wasn't safe to do anything behind his back. That's all."

Longarm knew Cahill was right. Fowley didn't want to think so, though. The burly, bearded outlaw shook his shaggy head. "We don't have to worry about Thaxton no more. You just wait and see, Roney. We're the top dogs 'round here now. It's time we started thinkin' bigger."

Cahill reined in and turned to Fowley with a frown. "You're not talkin' about banks and trains again, are you, Bill?"

"There'd be a lot more loot than what's on those danged stagecoaches we been stoppin'," Fowley said truculently.

"And a lot more chance of us gettin' shot up, not to mention that we'd probably have to shoot some of the guards."

"What's wrong with that? We're outlaws, ain't we?"

"We're not murderers," Cahill said.

"Damn it, Roney, you've killed men before!"

"In fair fights, when they were tryin' to kill me for no good reason." Cahill shook his head. "I'm not goin' to shoot down a man who's only doin' his job."

"Anybody who'd work for a bank or a railroad or an express company has got it comin'," Fowley argued. "They're all a bunch of damn Yankees anyway!"

Again, Cahill shook his head. "We rob stagecoaches, and

we don't kill anybody." He heeled his horse into motion. "I'm done talkin'."

Longarm followed, riding past the darkly scowling Bill Fowley. The other five men came along, too, and finally Fowley started after them.

Despite what Cahill had said earlier about Fowley being a good man, alarm bells were ringing in Longarm's head. Fowley could be a problem. Cahill would be well advised to watch his back while Bill Fowley was around, thought Longarm.

One by one, the other members of the gang veered off into the woods, drifting back toward their homes, until Longarm and Cahill were riding by themselves. "How's that arm of yours, Custis?" Cahill asked idly.

"Just fine," Longarm replied. "That little fracas doesn't seem to have hurt it at all."

"Good. I'm glad you decided to come through the mountains on your way to wherever you were goin'."

"I think I found where I was going, Roney," Longarm said. "I just didn't know it until I got here."

When they got back to Sarah Jane's place, she wasn't there. Jim was sitting up in bed when Longarm and Cahill came in. The classroom side of the cabin was empty.

"What happened?" Jim asked eagerly. "Damn, I'm glad to see you two boys got back safe from Bloody Holler."

Cahill frowned. "How do you know that's where we went?"

"You think I'm a damned fool? I knew you'd have to have it out with Thaxton. When you and Custis rode off this mornin', it didn't take no genius to figure out where you was goin'."

"We're all right," Cahill said, "but three of Thaxton's boys ain't."

"You put 'em under?"

Cahill nodded.

"And I missed it! Damn! I reckon it's too much to hope that Thaxton was one of 'em?"

"He claimed he didn't know anything about the bushwhacking," Longarm said. "Three of his men admitted to it, though. They were just trying to get in better with Thaxton by getting rid of you and Roney."

"How'd you manage to shoot it out with 'em?"

Longarm smiled humorlessly. "It was Thaxton's idea."

Jim let out a low whistle. "I reckon I *did* miss something. I'll be better by the next time you tangle with that son of a bitch."

"Where's Sarah Jane?" Cahill asked.

"Gone up to Fayetteville. Said she needed some things she can't get at the tradin' post in Skunk Holler."

"She went by herself?"

Jim shook his head and said, "Naw, that crazy ol' coot Gyp drove the wagon for her. Sary Jane said they'd be back tomorrow sometime."

Cahill looked at Longarm. Sarah Jane had had a pretty good idea where they were going today, and she hadn't been pleased about it. Longarm wondered if she had left so she wouldn't be there if he and Cahill had gotten themselves killed? He figured Cahill was wondering the same thing.

"I reckon we're supposed to take care of you," Cahill said to Jim.

"I can take care of myself!"

"No, you can't. Sarah Jane said you still have to rest for a long time, remember? You just take it easy, and I'll cook up some stew in a little while for supper."

Jim leaned back against the pillow, frowning and muttering, "Gal goes off and leaves me with a fella whose cookin' will probably kill me deader'n any bullet ever could."

Cahill said, "I heard that. I can let you starve, if you want."

"I ain't sure that wouldn't be a more pleasant way to go."

Longarm chuckled and went outside to smoke a cheroot, leaving the two of them wrangling.

Longarm thought the stew Cahill cooked up was rather tasty, despite Jim's complaints. He noticed that Jim put away two big bowls of the stew, too.

After supper, Longarm went out to the shed to tend to the horses. His arm was better now, and as long as he took it easy and didn't try to do too much, he didn't see any reason why he couldn't start pitching in to help with the chores. He could use a pitchfork one-handed and fork up some hay into the feeding trough for the horses.

That's what he was doing when a step sounded behind him and a voice said, "Custis Jones."

Longarm had heard the voice only a few times, but he recognized it. He turned around, not too fast because he didn't want to spook this nocturnal visitor. The pitchfork was still gripped tightly in his right hand. He figured he could use it as a weapon if he had to—if Deuce Thaxton was within reach.

"Take it easy, Jones," Thaxton said with a chuckle. "I'm not lookin' for trouble."

"What are you looking for, then?" Longarm asked.

Thaxton stood about five feet away from him, a blur of shadow in the night topped by a black hat. "I just want to talk to you."

"If Cahill knew you were out here, there'd be shooting."

"I didn't come to see Cahill, now did I?" Thaxton snapped.

Longarm hesitated, then said, "Speak your piece."

"You didn't go by the name Jones up in Kansas, did you?"

"A man can have a lot of names in a lifetime."

"It don't really matter. I know what you can do. I know what kind of man you are."

Longarm doubted that, very much.

"A gent like you don't need to be ridin' with a bunch of dirty-necked ridge runners like Cahill and his gang," Thaxton went on. "They think they're badmen, but hell, they don't amount to nothin'. All they've done is pull a few penny-ante stagecoach holdups. You ride with me, Jones, and the payoff will be a hell of a lot bigger for you."

This was an unexpected development, thought Longarm. When he and Cahill rode away from Bloody Holler that afternoon, he hadn't dreamed that Thaxton would follow and try to recruit him for his gang.

"Well, what do you say?" Thaxton prodded.

"I'll have to think about it," Longarm replied slowly. "I gunned down one of your men today and helped kill another. I ain't sure how the rest of your bunch would feel about me riding with them."

"My men feel what I damned well tell them to feel," Thaxton said. "I'm the boss. I make the decisions. Ain't none of them goin' to forget that again."

Longarm knew what he meant. None of the outlaws would forget that thinking for themselves had cost Cramer, Hardesty, and Quince their lives.

"I'll mull it over," Longarm said. "That's all I can promise."

"Don't mull for too long," Thaxton said. "The offer ain't good forever. Sooner or later I figure a man who ain't with me is against me."

"Well, we'll just have to wait and see what happens, won't we?"

Thaxton didn't say anything else. He just grunted and slid off into the darkness, gliding noiselessly out of sight.

When Longarm went back into the cabin a few minutes later, he found Cahill and Jim playing dominoes. Cahill glanced up at him and said, "Thought I heard you talkin' to somebody out there." He left the question of who it was unspoken, but Longarm heard it anyway.

"The horses were a mite skittish tonight," Longarm said. "I talked to them for a while to calm them down. Could be they smelled a cougar or something out in the woods."

"We call 'em painters," Jim said, "and there ain't been one seen in these parts for quite a spell."

Longarm shrugged. "You never know." He glanced toward the door, which he had pulled shut behind him. "Could be all kinds of bad things hiding out there in the dark."

Chapter 16

About the middle of the next day, the sound of wagon wheels outside drew Longarm and Roney Cahill out of the cabin. A spring wagon was making its laborious way up the narrow, twisting trail. Sarah Jane was perched on the seat with Gyp Foster beside her handling the reins. The pair of mules pulling the wagon strained against their harness as they hauled the vehicle up the slope.

Gyp brought the wagon to a stop in front of the cabin and hopped down from the seat. He turned back as if to help Sarah Jane down, but Cahill was already there, shouldering him aside and reaching up to take Sarah Jane's hands. "Hey! Watch it!" Gyp protested, but Cahill ignored him.

Changing his mind, Cahill put his hands on Sarah Jane's waist instead of taking her hands. She gave a startled little cry as he lifted her down from the wagon seat. "Roney?" she said. "You're . . . all right?"

"Fit as a fiddle," Cahill told her with a grin.

Sarah Jane looked over at Longarm, who was lounging in the doorway of the cabin with a smile on his face. "Hello, Custis. How's your arm?"

"Not even stiff today," Longarm told her. He moved the limb back and forth to demonstrate. "I reckon those bandages wrapped around it are ready to come off and stay off."

"I'll be the judge of that," Sarah Jane said severely, but her smile took any sting out of the words. She turned to the old man and asked him, "Gyp, could you unload the supplies?"

"I loaded 'em in Fayetteville, didn't I?" Gyp said. "Reckon I can unload 'em, too." He fell to the task, muttering as he did so about having to do all the work around here.

Cahill pitched in to help with the unloading, but when Longarm offered, Sarah Jane told him not to. "You don't want to strain that arm and reopen those wounds, just when you've made so much progress."

She took off her bonnet and supervised the unloading and putting away of the supplies she had bought in Fayetteville, and Longarm heard her humming a pretty little tune several times as she did so. She was in a good mood. He supposed that coming home and finding both him and Cahill alive was responsible for that.

He wondered if she had heard about the gunfight with Thaxton's men. Judging by her reaction when she came up to the cabin and saw the two of them, Longarm figured she probably hadn't. Otherwise she would have known that they had come through the shoot-out alive. She had been worried that there would be trouble with Thaxton, though, which explained her relief.

Longarm hadn't said a word to Cahill about Thaxton's visit the night before. He hadn't quite figured out how he wanted to proceed, but he knew he wasn't going to be joining up with Thaxton's gang. Since he knew Thaxton was responsible for the bank and train robberies in the area, he could ride down to Fort Smith, gather up a posse of Judge Parker's deputies, and come back up here to lay siege to Bloody Holler. Cahill would find out about that, however, and he and the other men who had been in on the stagecoach robberies would take off for the tall and uncut and vanish in the mountains.

And what was wrong with that? Longarm asked himself as he sat down on a three-legged stool just outside the cabin door. Cahill and his bunch hadn't killed anybody in those robberies. Next to Thaxton's gang they were wooly little lambs.

Even as that thought went through his head, Longarm knew he couldn't convince himself of it. Holding up stagecoaches was still a crime, even if no one had been injured in the robberies. Besides, if Cahill and the others were left alone to continue what they were doing, chances were that sooner or later somebody *would* be hurt, maybe even killed. Longarm didn't trust Bill Fowley to continue controlling indefinitely the violence that seemed to seethe inside him.

No, what he had to do, he told himself, was to figure out some way to bring Cahill and the others to justice, then go after Deuce Thaxton's gang. When he started the outlaw roundup, though, he would have to move quickly. Once he revealed that he was a lawman, news of his true identity would travel like wildfire through the mountains.

Sarah Jane came outside, breaking into Longarm's reverie. She had a bucket in her hand and announced, "I'm going to pick some more berries. I'll bake another pie for supper tonight."

"Roney know you're going up the hill?"

Sarah Jane gave a defiant toss of her head, making the long pale hair swirl around her face. "I don't have to have Mr. Roney Cahill approve of all my comings and goings," she said. "And I won't take it kindly if you go in there tattling on me like one of my students, either."

Longarm grinned. "Wasn't intending to." He put his hands on his knees and pushed himself to his feet, reaching out to take the wooden bucket from her. "I'll go with you, though. Carryin' a bucket of berries can get to be hard work."

She looked at him for a second as if she were going to argue with him, then laughed and shook her head instead. "Come along, then," she said. "To tell you the truth, I'll be glad for the company. Gyp's an old dear, but he's not much of a conversationalist."

The two of them walked around to the back of the cabin and started up the steep hill. Sarah Jane knew all the trails that wound in and out of the brush, so the going wasn't really as hard as Longarm had thought it would be. He had come along to keep Sarah Jane safe, since she didn't have her rifle and wasn't accompanied by the children today, but he also enjoyed being with her.

"How was Fayetteville?" he asked.

"Fine. Busy, of course. The town's really grown since the state university was founded there a few years ago. It's not nearly as peaceful there as it is up here in the mountains."

"I reckon it's the biggest town you've ever been in?"

"Oh, no, St. Louis is much large—"

She stopped short and broke off her words in mid-sentence. Longarm stopped as well and turned to look at her. She had brought her hand to her mouth and pressed her fingers against her lips in horror.

"I don't care that you've been to St. Louis, Sarah Jane," Longarm said quietly. "I know it's a big mystery how you up and disappeared from the Ozarks a few years ago, but to tell you the truth, it ain't none of my business."

She slowly lowered her hand. "Custis, I . . . I don't know what to say."

"Then don't say anything," he told her with a shrug.

"No, I . . . I want to talk." She looked around. They were standing in a small clearing surrounded by trees and brush. The cabin wasn't visible from where they were, but Longarm could smell a faint tang of woodsmoke in the air from the chimney down below. Sarah Jane reached over and took hold of his left hand, the one that wasn't carrying the bucket. "Custis, I hadn't realized until this very minute how much I want to talk, to tell someone about it. I can't . . . no one from up here would understand . . . I've been carrying it all around with me . . ."

"And I'm pretty much a stranger," Longarm said, "a fella you've never seen before and once I ride away from here won't ever see again. I reckon if you want to talk, Sarah Jane, I don't mind listening."

"Come over here," she said, tugging him toward a fallen tree. "Let's sit down."

They sat on the thick log, and without looking at Longarm, Sarah Jane took a deep breath and began, "I left the mountains with a man. I was walking down the road one day, and he came along in a buggy."

"He kidnapped you?"

"Oh, no. I went with him of my own free will." She closed her eyes for a second and pressed her fingertips to her forehead, then went on, "He stopped to ask me something. I don't even remember what it was now. Anyway, it was just an excuse to stop and talk to me. He was older, you see, a businessman from Missouri, and I was . . . I was a mountain girl in a thin little dress with nothing under it. I knew he was looking at me . . . looking at my body. Men had looked at me like that before. I didn't really mind." She stopped again for a moment, then resumed, "His name was Daniel, he said. He told me . . . he told me if I would go to Fayetteville with him for the night, he'd give me twenty dollars." Finally, she turned to look at Longarm. "Custis, I'd never even *seen* twenty dollars in my life, let alone had that much money to myself."

"I reckon not," he said softly, because she seemed to be waiting for him to say something.

"I told him I'd come with him. My folks . . ." She shook her head. "My folks didn't really care about me. I knew that. I was just another mouth to feed. So I went with Daniel to Fayetteville, and he snuck me into his hotel room, and the next morning he gave me a twenty-dollar gold piece. I knew by then he was from St. Louis, that he owned a lumber company there. So I gave him the gold piece back and told him that I'd go to St. Louis and stay with him for as long as he wanted me to as long as he took care of me." She looked away again. "You must think I'm horrible."

"Nope. Just human."

"Thank you," Sarah Jane whispered. She swallowed, gathered herself, blew out a breath, and went on, "Daniel had a wife, so he found a place for me to stay where he could come see me. He told me his wife was ill, and I found out later it wasn't just the sort of story that a married man always tells to a woman he . . . he's keeping. She really *was* sick. In fact, she died a few months after Daniel brought me to St. Louis. That was when Daniel came up with his idea."

Longarm didn't ask what that idea was. He was sure she would tell him.

"He sent me back east, to the best finishing school for young ladies that he could find. He was a fine gentleman and had already started teaching me about music and art and literature and how to act like a lady. I know you probably think he was a monster for taking a young girl and . . . and doing the things he did, and at first I suppose that was all he was interested in, but then . . . then things changed. He sent me to school, and when I wrote to him and told him I wanted more than just a finishing school education, he arranged for me to go to college. He came to visit me sometimes, but there was never anything improper. Not once, even though I told him it would be all right. I think . . . I think he was sorry for the way he had taken me from the mountains, from my family. He was trying to make it up to me."

"I can see why you thought he wasn't such a bad fella," Longarm said.

Sarah Jane nodded. "After I graduated from college, he brought me back to St. Louis and moved me into his house. He told everyone I was his niece, and that's the way he treated me. He never touched me again except to pat my hand or kiss me on the forehead. He said . . ." Her voice broke, and she had to fight back a sob. "He said just having me around was joy enough for him."

Longarm didn't say anything. Silence settled down over the clearing, but it wasn't an uncomfortable one. After a while, Sarah Jane said, "He died last year. He left me some money—not a lot, you understand, and I was glad that he didn't—but enough so that I was able to come back here to the mountains. I'd run away from here once before because I knew there was nothing here for me. Now I . . . I want to do something to help the people here who may feel the same way."

"I reckon you're doing that, all right," Longarm told her.

"But you're a mite young to be appointing yourself guardian angel to so many folks."

"I haven't felt young for a long time, Custis," she said with a solemn smile. "Not since that day when I hiked up my dress and climbed into Daniel's buggy."

"If you're waiting for me to tell you that you done something wrong or that you're the world's worst sinner, you're going to have a long wait." Longarm shook his head. "I don't pass judgment on nobody. The old hymn's good enough for me, where it says that further along we'll know more about it."

"Custis, you are . . . an unusual man."

He grinned. "I been told that a time or two."

She laughed, and suddenly she was leaning against him, her blond head resting easily on his shoulder. Longarm's arm went around her shoulders sort of natural-like, and she snuggled closer. It felt mighty good holding her like that, Longarm thought.

Then she lifted her head and whispered, "Custis," and he turned to look down at her and saw her lips, red and full and parted slightly, and he seemed to fall into those big blue eyes of hers. He leaned over and kissed her, and his other arm went around her and drew her tight against him. She didn't pull away. Her lips were soft and sweet and opened invitingly under his kiss. When she finally eased her head back, breaking the kiss, she said urgently, "It's been so long . . ."

"I won't make you wait any longer," he said.

Chapter 17

This was what Sarah Jane really wanted. Longarm could tell that by the urgency in her kiss and the way she reached down to caress his stiffening shaft through the fabric of his trousers. Her long, slender fingers found the buttons of his fly and deftly unfastened them. She slid her hand inside and closed it around his manhood. She worked it through the opening so that the long, thick pole of male flesh sprang free.

"Oh, my goodness," Sarah Jane breathed. "Custis, I . . . I've never seen anything quite so beautiful."

Longarm wouldn't have gone so far as to describe it as beautiful, but if Sarah Jane wanted to think so, that was fine with him. She ran her fingertip around the crown, then toyed with the little slit in the head where clear fluid was already pearling out. She put both hands around the shaft and squeezed lightly, milking out more of Longarm's juices. The warmth and pressure of her grip made him close his eyes for a moment in pure pleasure. She leaned over, her lips parting, and took him into her mouth. Her tongue swirled around the crown, spreading the slick wetness.

Longarm rested a hand on the back of her head as she continued the French lesson for long, delicious minutes. She sucked lightly, teasingly, maddeningly. Longarm had to restrain himself from thrusting deeper into her mouth and letting his climax wash over him. He wanted to wait, for Sarah Jane's sake. She needed this moment, needed for what passed between them to be special. Longarm wanted to give that to her.

While she was doing what she was doing, he caressed her breasts through her dress with his other hand. He could feel her hard nipples poking against the dress and the shift she wore under it. He strummed them with his thumb, playing the hard little buds of flesh with an expert's touch. Sarah Jane's sucking took a renewed intensity as her arousal built up under Longarm's fondling.

Finally she lifted her head, threw her hair back, and said breathlessly, "I need you inside me, Custis. Now!"

Longarm was glad to oblige. He lifted her from the log and stood her in front of him. She raised her skirt and reached underneath it to pull her bloomers off. The triangle of hair between her legs was almost as fair as that on her head. She spread her thighs and moved closer so that she was straddling his legs. He gripped her under the arms to steady her as she lowered herself onto him. The fact that both of them were almost fully dressed didn't hamper their joining. Sarah Jane poised her feminine opening against the tip of his shaft, then sank down slowly, engulfing him. The hot, wet sensation as he penetrated her made both of them shudder with desire.

In a matter of seconds, his organ was fully inside her. Longarm's hips flexed as he thrust slowly and powerfully into her. His feet were planted firmly on the ground to help him balance on the log. He put his arms around Sarah Jane's waist and held her. She wrapped her arms around his neck and leaned closer so that his face was in the hollow of her throat. He began to kiss her there, sucking lightly on her soft skin.

She threw her head back and ground her pelvis against his. "Oh, Custis," she said. "Oh, my God. I needed this so much . . ."

She found his mouth again and kissed him with a searing intensity. Longarm tightened his grip around her waist. Sarah

Jane had too much pent-up passion inside her. Longarm could tell that it would be only moments before her culmination swept over her. His shaft worked in and out of her like a piston. She was drenched with moisture.

As Sarah Jane began to shudder and spasm, Longarm drove into her as far as he could go and surrendered himself to his own climax. His seed boiled up from the heavy sacs and erupted into her. Burst after burst filled her. Sarah Jane's mouth was still plastered to Longarm's. She cried out and then thrust her tongue deeply into his mouth. Longarm's hips jerked as he poured more of himself into her.

He wasn't even aware he was falling backward off the log until his back thumped heavily against the ground, knocking the breath out of him.

Sarah Jane was still locked to him, so she fell on top of him. "Oh!" she gasped. "Custis! Custis, are you all right? Your arm—"

"It's . . . fine," Longarm assured her. Catching his breath wasn't easy with Sarah Jane lying on top of him. She might look like a little slip of a girl, but she was more solid than she appeared to be. Finally, Longarm was able to drag a full breath into his lungs, and he said, "It twinged a mite when we landed, but it's all right, Sarah Jane."

"I'll need to remove the bandages and check the wounds to make sure they didn't open up again."

"I can tell they're not bleeding," Longarm assured her. He grinned up at her. "Even if they were, I reckon it would have been worth it."

She smiled and pushed back some of the fair hair that had fallen over her face. "You sweet, sweet man." She leaned down and brushed her lips over his. "Custis, I can't thank you enough."

"Most folks would say I was the one who ought to be thanking you."

His shaft was still sheathed inside her and was still fairly hard. She wiggled her hips, creating a delicious sensation for both of them. "I wasn't thanking you for this, even though it was wonderful. I was thanking you for listening to me and letting me get everything off my chest."

"It was my pleasure," Longarm told her.

Sarah Jane wiggled her hips again. "Mine, too. I suppose we'd better get up off the ground, though."

Longarm was about to agree with her when both of them heard someone moving through the brush not too far away. "Sarah Jane?" Roney Cahill called. "Are you up here? Custis?"

Sarah Jane's eyes widened. She rolled off of Longarm and sprang to her feet, letting her dress fall around her hips again. She snatched up the underwear she had discarded a few minutes earlier. Meanwhile, Longarm was getting to his feet as well. He buttoned up his trousers and found his hat, which had fallen off his head when the two of them toppled from the log.

By the time Cahill pushed through the brush into the clearing a few minutes later, Longarm and Sarah Jane were nowhere to be seen. He grunted and went on up the hill, finding them at the patch of wild huckleberries that spread across the slope. Sarah Jane was picking the berries and putting them in the bucket she carried while Longarm stood nearby chewing on an unlit cheroot.

"Jim said you came to get some berries, Sarah Jane," Cahill said. "When I saw that Custis was gone, too, I figured he'd come with you."

"Thought it might be a good idea," Longarm said around the cheroot. "I don't trust Thaxton."

"Neither do I," agreed Cahill. "I appreciate you lookin' out for Sarah Jane, Custis."

Longarm's teeth clenched a little tighter on the cheroot. He wished Cahill hadn't said that. It wasn't like Cahill had any claim on Sarah Jane's affections. And the fooling around had been Sarah Jane's idea, though Longarm definitely hadn't objected. So there was no real reason for him to feel guilty. But that knowledge didn't stop him from feeling a twinge of it anyway.

"Nobody makes a better huckleberry pie than you do, Sarah Jane," Cahill went on.

"Why, thank you, Roney," she said. "Just for that, I'm going to let you carry this bucket back down the hill when I'm finished filling it. Custis was going to, but I think you deserve that honor."

Cahill looked a little confused, but he said, "Well, uh, sure. I'll be glad to carry the bucket." He glanced over at Longarm. "I guess that means you can go on about your business, Custis, if there's anything else you want to do."

"Mighty obliging of you, Roney," Longarm said. "I'll go see what Jim's up to."

"He and Gyp were about to play some checkers."

Longarm grinned. "Sounds mighty exciting."

He walked down the hill, leaving Sarah Jane and Cahill in the huckleberry patch. He knew that Cahill had been hinting for him to leave the two of them alone. Obviously, Cahill wasn't aware of what Longarm and Sarah Jane had been doing just a few minutes earlier. He probably planned to do a little wooing of his own.

Even if Longarm and Cahill hadn't been on opposite sides of the law, there might have been trouble between them sooner or later, Longarm mused as he walked toward the cabin. A beautiful woman like Sarah Jane could do that. But, he reminded himself, he likely never would have met Sarah Jane if his job hadn't brought him here to the Ozarks, so in the end it all came down to the law, as usual.

He fished out a match, snapped it into life on his thumbnail, and held the flame to the tip of the cheroot. When he had the cigar burning properly, Longarm shook out the lucifer, dropped it on the ground, and stepped on it with his boot heel to make sure it was extinguished. He paused, drawing deeply on the cheroot, and as the smoke settled in his lungs he thought about the people he had met and everything that had happened since he came to Arkansas. This case was murkier than some, with plenty of shades of gray. What it came down to, though, was that sooner or later he was going to have to bring Roney Cahill and the others to justice, and he didn't like the idea. Longarm had never turned his back on his job. He had bent the law on many occasions, but he had never really broken it, not so badly that he couldn't sleep at night. He told himself that this job would be no different. He would do his duty.

He went on down the hill to the cabin, hoping that his resolve would hold out when the time came for action.

Otherwise he might hesitate at just the wrong moment and wind up dead.

Sarah Jane's good mood lasted through the evening and was infectious. After supper, she, Longarm, Cahill, and Jim played forty-two until quite late, laughing and talking as they did so. Gyp Foster had eaten with them, but then the old man went out to the shed to bed down with the horses, as he usually did, muttering that he preferred the company of horses to humans. Sarah Jane assured Longarm it was nothing to worry about. That was just the way Gyp was.

Longarm slept well that night. The next morning, Sarah Jane inspected the wounds on his arm and pronounced them healed enough so that he could stop wearing bandages around them. Longarm was glad to hear that.

While Sarah Jane was leaning close to him, he caught a whiff of her fragrance, a blend of clean female flesh and soap. That brought back memories of how she had felt in his arms the day before, and for a moment he felt desire rising inside him. He suppressed the urge. That incident might turn out to be the only time they would be together like that. It wouldn't do for a man in his line of work to start getting fancy ideas.

In fact, he decided, it might not be a bad idea to get out of the cabin and away from Sarah Jane for a while. When she was finished checking his arm, he said, "I think I'll ride over to Strickland's for a spell."

Sarah Jane gave him a severe look. "I know what you're after," she said.

"You do?"

"Of course I do." She glanced over her shoulder at Jim,

who was engrossed in a yellowback novel at the moment. "And if you'll bring a bottle back with you, I don't think it would hurt for Jim to have a little nip every now and then. He's much stronger now than he was right after he was shot."

Longarm nodded and squeezed her arm. "That's a mighty fine idea. I'll be back later."

"Be careful. There could still be trouble."

He wasn't sure how much she knew about what had happened over at Bloody Holler, but she was right that the uneasy truce with Deuce Thaxton might be over at any time, with no warning. Longarm nodded and said, "Don't worry. I'll keep a close eye out."

He wasn't sure where Cahill was this morning. The stagecoach robbery was planned for the next day at Buzzard's Notch, so he might be off going over the details with the rest of the gang. Longarm saddled the bay and rode toward Skunk Hollow, thinking it was possible he might run into Cahill at Strickland's Tavern.

When he got there, though, he didn't see Cahill's horse. He dismounted, looped the bay's reins over the hitch rack, and went inside. At mid-morning like this, the roadhouse wasn't very busy, but several men were at the bar nursing drinks. One of them, who wore a garish tweed suit and a bowler hat and had a carpetbag at his feet, was unmistakably a drummer of some sort. As Longarm came in, he was saying, "The whole town's abuzz about it."

Strickland stood behind the bar, polishing it idly with a cloth. "I ain't surprised, what with the fella gettin' shot down in broad daylight like that."

Longarm's senses perked up, but he tried not to show his interest as he sidled up to the bar and gave Strickland a friendly nod. "Beer," Longarm said.

Strickland drew the beer and slid the mug over to Longarm, then motioned to the drummer. "Go on. What happened then?"

"Well, the city marshal and his deputies spent the rest of the day searching for the killer, of course, but they didn't find any sign of him." The drummer shook his head. "It was quite a daring crime, gunning down a government official right on the steps of the county courthouse."

"What's that?" Longarm asked, attempting to sound idly curious and not betray his intense concern. "Who got killed, a country commissioner or something like that?"

The drummer looked at him and shook his head. "Oh, no, it was a federal man. Deputy assistant secretary of land management from the Department of the Interior, or something like that. Down here checking logging permits on file at the courthouse in Fayetteville. A nobody, really." The drummer shrugged and laughed nervously. "Of course, the same could be said of me, I suppose, and I don't want some mysterious rifleman bushwhacking me."

"Me, neither," Longarm muttered. He drank some of his beer to hide the worried frown that he couldn't keep off his face. He hadn't forgotten about the murders of federal officials, but in his concentration on the outlaw gangs being ramrodded by Roney Cahill and Deuce Thaxton, that part of the case had sort of gotten shoved aside in his brain. He asked the drummer, "When did this killing happen?"

"Early yesterday morning, right after the courthouse opened."

That meant it was impossible for Cahill to have had anything to do with the murder, thought Longarm. Cahill had been at Sarah Jane's cabin at the time the deputy assistant secretary was being gunned down on the steps of the courthouse. As for Thaxton, Longarm had no idea where the man had been at that time. Thaxton was slick enough to have carried out the murder and gotten away—but why? What motive could Thaxton have had for murdering a minor federal official? Not to mention the other officials who had been killed in recent weeks. Thaxton had been holed up at Bloody Holler during that time, although he and his gang had ventured out to rob a few trains and hold up a few banks, there was no doubt about that. Thaxton could have left the hideout in order to commit those murders. But Longarm still came back to the question of motive.

He drained the rest of the beer, then set the empty mug

on the bar. Judge Parker hadn't necessarily ordered him to solve the killings, just to find out if whoever was behind the rest of the crime spree in the Ozarks had anything to do with them. Longarm had eliminated Cahill as a suspect, but not Thaxton. So he couldn't move against either of them just yet, but had to continue playing his cards close to the vest.

That meant he would definitely have to go along with the others for that stagecoach robbery the next day. He had to keep up the masquerade.

"I need a bottle to take with me," he said to Strickland.

The proprietor grinned. "I'll bet it's for Jim Cahill, ain't it? I heard he was laid up and staying at Sarah Jane's place. She stopped by here to say howdy on her way back from Fayetteville yesterday."

The drummer said, "Why'd you let me tell you all about that killing if you already knew about it?"

Strickland shook his head. "I didn't know a thing about it," he said. "Nobody mentioned a word until you came in and started talking about it."

"I'm surprised. It's big news."

"To some folks, maybe," Strickland said as he turned away from the bar to get a bottle off the back bar for Longarm.

Longarm's hands pressed down hard on the bar. His mind was racing. Why *hadn't* Sarah Jane said anything to Strickland about the killing? Why hadn't she mentioned it to Longarm and Cahill and Jim? If Fayetteville was in such an uproar about it, wouldn't the normal thing been to have at least mentioned it when she got back home?

Maybe the bushwhacking of the government man had happened after she and Gyp left town, thought Longarm. That would explain why she hadn't said anything about it. She wouldn't have known. That made a whole hell of a lot more sense than what he had been thinking for a second there, Longarm told himself.

He had been remembering what Cahill had told him about Sarah Jane, about how she was a crack shot with a rifle . . .

Chapter 18

By the time he got back to the cabin, Longarm had put that ridiculous theory completely out of his head. It made no sense at all to think that Sarah Jane had had anything to do with the murders of federal officials in the area. Sure, she had been in Fayetteville at the time of the killing the day before, but so had several thousand other people. Longarm had no reason to think she would have done such a thing.

But that afternoon he found himself asking her what time she had left Fayetteville.

"I think it was about ten o'clock," Sarah Jane replied. "Maybe a little later. Why do you ask?"

"Oh, just curious how long it takes to get from there to here."

Longarm couldn't be certain how it was in Fayetteville, but in most places, courthouses opened for business at nine o'clock in the morning. If that was the case here—and Longarm didn't doubt that it was—then Sarah Jane had still been in Fayetteville at the time of the murder.

He would have felt better if he had found out that she'd left town earlier.

She didn't need an alibi, he reminded himself. She wasn't a suspect. And right now he had other things with which to concern himself, namely that stagecoach robbery that Roney Cahill was planning for the next day.

Cahill rode up to the cabin late that afternoon. Longarm was sitting on the stool just outside the door. Cahill greeted him with a curt nod, then asked in a low voice, "Is Sarah Jane inside?"

Longarm nodded. "She's tending to Jim, changing the dressing on his wound."

Cahill jerked his head toward the woods and said, "Let's take a walk."

Longarm stood up and went with him, thinking that from Cahill's demeanor, he wanted to talk about the stagecoach holdup. That proved to be correct. As soon as they were out of easy earshot of the cabin, Cahill said, "I've talked to all the boys today. Everything's set for tomorrow."

"What time does the coach come through Buzzard's Notch?" Longarm asked.

"Two o'clock. We'll be there, ready to stop it."

Longarm nodded. "Everybody going along with the plan?"

"Why wouldn't they?" Cahill bristled.

"That fella Fowley didn't seem satisfied to be sticking up stagecoaches."

"Bill will do what I say," snapped Cahill. "Don't worry about him."

"All right," Longarm said, but he added silently to himself, *I'm going to be keeping an eye on that old son anyway.*

Longarm slept a little restlessly that night. His thoughts kept whirling around so that his brain could never quite relax. What to do about Cahill, and Thaxton, and Sarah Jane . . . ? Longarm had plenty of questions but not nearly enough answers.

He was tired the next morning and evidently looked like it, because Sarah Jane asked him at breakfast, "Are you all right, Custis? Your arm's not bothering you again, is it?"

"No, my arm's fine," Longarm replied, and he moved it around without any pain to demonstrate. "I reckon I'm just a mite weary. Didn't sleep too well last night."

Jim said, "You should've had a drink with me, Custis. I slept like a baby."

"I never heard a baby snore like you do," Longarm said dryly.

"Snore? What are you talkin' about? I never snored a lick in my life!"

"I'm afraid Custis is right, Jim," Sarah Jane said with a smile. "You were sawing logs last night."

"Well, I never!"

Longarm was glad the subject had gotten changed. He didn't want Sarah Jane exploring the topic of why he had been so restless. No good could come of that.

Not long after breakfast, the children began arriving for school. Little redheaded George greeted Longarm in his deep, rumbling voice. "Howdy, Mr. Jones. How are you today?"

"I'm just fine," Longarm told him with a smile. "How about you, George?"

"Reckon I'm dandy. You stayin' for school today?"

Longarm shook his head. "No, I'm afraid I have some things to do."

"Well, you take care," George said solemnly. Longarm had never seen the boy when he *wasn't* solemn.

Before Longarm could leave the cabin, Sarah Jane caught a moment alone with him. Quietly, she said, "You be careful today, Custis." Something in her voice and the serious expression on her face told him that she knew exactly what he was going to be doing. "I've gotten used to having you around here."

"You know what Roney and me are up to, don't you?"

"Of course." A smile flickered over her face. "Whose idea do you think it was?"

She turned quickly and went into the classroom, leaving Longarm to stare after her in astonishment. *Sarah Jane* was the one who'd come up with the idea of robbing travelers on the stagecoaches that came through the Ozarks?

Jim was dozing and hadn't overheard the exchange. Gyp was nowhere around, having disappeared as usual. That left

Longarm to stand there and feel foolish as he considered what he had just learned. He stepped out of the cabin and lit a cheroot, puffing furiously on it.

Sarah Jane?

That put a whole new face on things. Since she had as much as admitted masterminding the stagecoach robberies, now he was going to have to arrest her, too, when he rounded up the gang. After all she'd been through in her life, after all the good she had done for the people of the mountains, now in the eyes of the law she was nothing more than a common criminal.

"Damn it!" Longarm said out loud. He wished Billy Vail and Judge Parker had given this job to somebody else.

But he was stuck with it now. He had to see it through.

Cahill rode up at mid-morning. "Ready to go?" he asked Longarm.

The big lawman nodded and said, "My horse is already saddled. Where are the rest of the boys?"

"They'll meet us not far from there."

Longarm went around to the shed and led the bay to the front of the cabin. He swung up into the saddle. He and Cahill rode along the twisting trails to the Skunk Hollow road, then passed through the little settlement and reached the road from Fort Smith to Fayetteville a little after noon.

"You're not very talkative today," Cahill commented as they rode north. "Not worried about what we're fixin' to do, are you?"

"Not particularly. There shouldn't be much to it." Longarm decided to risk telling some of the truth. "Sarah Jane hinted pretty strongly to me that holding up the stagecoaches was her idea."

Cahill reined in abruptly. "Damn it!" he burst out. "She was supposed to keep that to herself! If the law ever comes lookin' for us, I don't want her gettin' into trouble."

"So it *was* her idea?"

Cahill grimaced. "I reckon you could say she had somethin' to do with it. We were just talkin' one day, and I said it was a damned shame the way people from outside look down on us, and she said they ought to have to pay for the way they feel about us. She brought up that Robin Hood fella, the one you mentioned before. Said there was even a book about him by some Englishman named Sir Walter Scott. I said maybe I ought to be the Robin Hood of the Ozarks, and that was how it all got started. But damn it, Custis, nobody was supposed to know about that!"

"You either trust me by now or you don't, Roney," Longarm said tightly. "It's as simple as that."

"Yeah." Cahill relaxed a little. "I reckon you're right. You sure ain't given me any reason not to trust you." He shook his head. "Still, I wish Sarah Jane had kept quiet about that. When nobody but me and her knew, I could be sure her part in it would never get out."

"She hasn't been in on any of the actual holdups, has she?"

"Hell, no! She didn't even know about all of them ahead of time. Really, all she did was give me the idea."

Which made her an accomplice both before and after the fact, Longarm mused. Still, it could have been worse. She might be able to get by without serving any time in prison. He would do everything in his power to see that was the way it worked out.

Assuming, of course, that she didn't have anything to do with murdering those government men. . . .

That thought popped unbidden into his head as he and Cahill began riding toward Buzzard's Notch again. He let a little time pass in silence, then said, "Does Sarah Jane ever get down to Fort Smith?"

"What?"

"Fort Smith," Longarm repeated. "I was just wondering if Sarah Jane ever goes down there."

"Sure she does, sometimes. Fact is, she's been there several times lately, fetching medical supplies that she can't get anywhere else."

"In the past month, do you mean?"

Cahill nodded. "That's right. She usually goes on the weekends, so she doesn't have to close school. She can drive down on Saturday and come back on Sunday." A frown etched deep lines in the redhead's brow. "Seems to me like a damned strange question to ask."

"I was just curious," Longarm said. "She mentioned something about going to Fort Smith, and I didn't know if she meant to go in the future, or if she had already been there."

"Oh." That answer seemed to satisfy Cahill. "I reckon that makes sense."

Cahill's mind might have been eased, but not Longarm's. He was going to have to find out the exact dates of those bushwhackings, then try to discover if Sarah Jane had been away from the cabin on those dates. Once this stagecoach robbery was behind him, he would have to risk a quick trip to Fort Smith so that he could get in touch with Judge Parker.

For now, he forced his attention back to the task at hand. Buzzard's Notch became visible in the distance, and not long after that, they were met by Bill Fowley and the other members of Cahill's gang.

"This time we're goin' to get that loot, aren't we, Roney?" Fowley asked with a grin of anticipation. "Anybody gets in our way, we'll make 'em wish they hadn't!"

"Take it easy, Bill," Cahill ordered. "You know we're not lookin' for any trouble."

Fowley slapped the butt of his pistol. "Maybe not, but I'm damned sure ready for it if it comes lookin' for us!"

Longarm's misgivings grew with every word out of the burly outlaw's mouth. Fowley seemed especially primed for violence today. Cahill was convinced he could keep Fowley under control, but Longarm wasn't so sure of that.

When the seven men reached Buzzard's Notch, they fanned out into the woods on either side of the trail, taking up positions that Cahill assigned to them. "You'll be with me," he said to Longarm as they withdrew a short distance off the road into the brush. "We'll ride out and stop the stage. The other boys will cover the passengers, the driver, and the guard, if there is one, from the woods."

Longarm nodded. The plan ought to work smoothly, but there could always be unforeseen circumstances that might make the best plan go all to hell.

A short time later, Cahill said, "Better pull your bandanna up. I think I hear the stage."

Both men raised the bandannas around their necks so that the bottom halves of their faces were covered. Longarm made the knot behind his head a little tighter, just to be sure the bandanna wouldn't slip during the robbery. He and Cahill pulled their hats down over their eyes, shielding even more of their features.

Longarm saw the stagecoach pass through the notch, silhouetted for a second against the sky behind it. Then it came barreling down the road toward them, the jehu urging his team on to greater speed. The drivers who worked this run had to be aware that Buzzard's Notch was the most likely place for bandits to strike.

"Come on!" Cahill said tautly, spurring his horse out of the brush and onto the road. He pulled his gun.

Longarm followed, palming out the Colt on his left hip. He and Cahill positioned their horses in the middle of the road and lifted their guns. The driver of the stagecoach saw them and hauled back on the reins while kicking the brake lever with his foot. The coach skidded and shuddered to a halt about twenty feet from Longarm and Cahill.

"Take the left," Cahill said tersely. He spurred to the right. Longarm went the other way. They kept their guns trained on the coach. The driver had his hands up and appeared to be intent on not causing any trouble.

"Go easy on them trigger fingers, boys!" he called to them. "I don't want nobody shot, 'specially me!"

"That's fine, old-timer," Cahill said. "We're not here to hurt anybody. Everybody in the coach, pile out!"

The doors opened on both sides of the stagecoach. Longarm's jaw was clenched tightly under the bandanna as the passengers began to climb out. He was glad Billy Vail couldn't see him now. Robbing a damned stagecoach! Even if it *was* in the line of duty, Longarm felt like hell doing this.

The passengers included a couple of well-dressed businessmen, a traveling salesman, a preacher, and a young woman with a baby. The woman looked scared to death as she climbed out of the coach on Longarm's side, holding the infant. Longarm edged his horse a little closer to her and said quietly, "Don't worry, ma'am. No one's going to be hurt."

"You . . . you can take all the money I have," she told him. "It's not much, but you're welcome to it. Just . . . just don't hurt me or my baby." The child fretted and wiggled in the woman's arms as she spoke.

"Go around behind the coach and line up with the folks on the other side," Longarm said. "Nobody's going to hurt you or the young'un, ma'am."

When Longarm and Cahill had all the passengers and the driver lined up beside the stagecoach, Cahill said to the businessmen and the drummer, "You gents empty your pockets. I want your wallets, watches, anything else that has any value. Parson, we'll take a pass on you and the lady."

One of the businessmen blustered, "See here, you can't—"

"Sure I can," Cahill said with a chuckle. "I got half a dozen riflemen in the woods who say I can do just about anything I want to, hoss."

Fuming, the businessmen and the drummer began to comply with Cahill's orders. Longarm went to the boot on the rear of the coach and pulled back the canvas cover over it. Inside were several carpetbags. He said, "Ma'am, which one of these belongs to you?"

She pointed a trembling finger. "That one right there."

"All right." Longarm leaned over in the saddle, took hold of the other bags, and tossed them out onto the ground one by one.

"Empty those bags of valuables when you're done with your pockets," Cahill ordered.

Longarm rode to the front of the coach and pulled the express box from under the driver's seat. It was locked, but a bullet from his six-gun took care of that, shattering the lock. He dismounted and looked inside the box, finding a packet of letters with a string tied around it and a small canvas pouch that jingled when he hefted it. He opened the drawstring and saw the gleam of gold coins inside. Longarm tightened the string and tossed the pouch to Cahill, who caught it deftly.

Just at that moment, a rifle blasted from the woods. The preacher cried out as he was flung back against the coach by a bullet. Longarm and Cahill whirled around, trying to see what the hell was going on. Their guns were held ready for instant use.

Instead of more shots, Bill Fowley came out of the trees. He had pulled his bandanna up, but it did little to disguise his bushy face. Smoke still drifted from the barrel of his rifle. "Did I get him?" he called. "Did I get the son of a bitch?"

"What in blazes are you doin'?" Cahill raged at him. "I said no shootin' unless you had to!"

"But I saw the little bastard reachin' for a gun!" Fowley protested.

Longarm knelt beside the preacher, who was only half-conscious and even more pale-faced than he had been starting out. The bullet had hit the man in the right shoulder. There was a considerable amount of blood, but Longarm figured the wound wasn't a mortal one, especially if it was tied up good and tight and the preacher got to a doctor within a reasonable amount of time.

Longarm looked up at Cahill and nodded. "He'll live."

"Good," Cahill grated. He swung back to Fowley. "You damned fool!"

"But . . . but he was about to shoot you! When you took your eyes off him to catch that pouch, he reached for a gun."

Longarm slipped his hand inside the preacher's coat and came out with a small, leather-bound New Testament. "Reckon this was what he was reaching for. He was so scared of us big bad robbers that he needed a little strength from the Good Book."

"You men are nothing but filthy thieves!" one of the businessmen burst out.

Cahill looked coldly at him. "Better watch your mouth, mister. I'm sorry the sky pilot got shot. I wouldn't feel near as bad about pluggin' the likes of you."

The man paled and swallowed and backed off a step.

Longarm said to the woman, "Do you reckon you can take care of the preacher, ma'am?"

She nodded. "I'll tend to him, don't worry."

"We're much obliged."

Longarm and Cahill finished gathering up the loot, then Cahill said, "We'll be leavin' now. If anybody comes after us, whatever happens will be on their head."

Longarm looked at the passengers and the driver. None of this timid bunch was going to mount any pursuit. He was fairly certain of that.

They galloped away from the stagecoach as the others gathered around the wounded preacher. Cahill led the way off the road into the woods, taking a narrow trail that twisted and turned so much no one could follow it without knowing where they were going. The other members of the gang joined them as they rode. Cahill kept up a fast pace until Longarm judged they had traveled at least three miles from where they had stopped the stagecoach. Then Cahill reined in and turned toward Bill Fowley. "You damned fool!" he said again. "You could've ruined everything! I didn't want anybody hurt."

Fowley still had his bandanna over his face. He jerked it down and glowered at Cahill. "You know, Roney, I'm gettin' mighty tired of you talkin' to me like that. I'm gettin' tired of you ridin' roughshod over the rest of us, too."

"I'm the boss of this bunch," Cahill growled.

Fowley rubbed his bearded jaw. "Yeah . . . and I'm thinkin' maybe it's time to change that."

Longarm saw what was about to happen, but before he could call a warning, Fowley launched himself out of his saddle at Cahill, tackling him. Both men fell hard to the ground.

Chapter 19

The impact as they landed broke them apart. They rolled in different directions. The other men were shouting curses and questions as both Cahill and Fowley came to their feet.

Longarm caused silence to fall over the woods by earing back the hammer of the Colt in his hand. The metallic ratcheting of the action cut through the hubbub and quieted it.

"Take it easy, Fowley," he ordered as he trained the revolver on the burly outlaw. Fowley glared at him, fairly quivering with rage.

"Damn it, no!" The exclamation came from Cahill. "Custis, put up that gun!"

Longarm hesitated. "Roney, are you sure . . . ?"

Cahill unbuckled his gunbelt and let it fall at his feet. He clenched both hands into fists. "I been makin' excuses for Fowley for a long time now," he said. "It's time I whipped him so he'll know who's boss."

Fowley's savage grin stretched across his face. "That's just what I wanted to hear you say, Cahill." He took off his own gunbelt and dropped it, then spit in his hands and rubbed them together. "Come on, if you think you're man enough."

Cahill glanced at Longarm again and said, "Stay out of it, Custis. I mean it."

Longarm nodded and let down the hammer of his gun. As he holstered the Colt, he said, "All right, Roney. It's your show."

The men still on horseback moved their mounts into a rough circle. Cahill and Fowley faced each other in the middle of that circle. Each man had his fists poised for the first punch.

Fowley threw that punch, rushing forward and swinging an arm that was like the trunk of a young tree. The blow had enough power behind it to have taken off Cahill's head if it had landed. Instead, Cahill was able to dart aside with surprising speed for a man of his size. Fowley's slow-moving punch slid harmlessly past Cahill's shoulder. Cahill stepped closer and pounded a blow into Fowley's midsection.

The punch staggered Fowley, but he didn't go down or even double over. He swung a left that caught Cahill on the chest. Cahill went back a step. Fowley brought up his other fist in an uppercut. Cahill jerked his chin out of the way just in time, but Fowley's fist still scraped along the side of his head. Blood began to drip from Cahill's ear.

Cahill jabbed a left into Fowley's face, followed it with a right cross, then hooked a left into Fowley's belly again. Watching from horseback, Longarm questioned Cahill's strategy. From the looks of Fowley, he could absorb those punches to the body all day long without suffering much punishment. He had been hit in the mouth before; those gaps in his teeth were proof of that. There had to be a reason previous opponents had gone after his mouth.

Longarm wanted to yell out some advice to Cahill, but Cahill was already busy slugging punch after punch into Fowley's midsection. Just as Longarm had thought, Fowley shrugged off those blows to the breadbasket. Finally, with a roar of anger, Fowley threw himself forward and wrapped his arms around Cahill in a bear hug. Both of them toppled to the ground again, but this time Fowley hung on for dear life, crushing Cahill in his monstrous grip.

Longarm's instincts urged him forward, but he remembered Cahill's warning to stay out of it. If he interfered now,

Cahill would likely never forgive him. That could ruin the trust Longarm had built up with him.

Of course, that trust was going to be shattered sooner or later anyway, when Longarm arrested Cahill, but Longarm wasn't ready for that yet.

With a grunt of effort, Cahill worked one arm free and brought his cupped hand around in a stinging slap to Fowley's ear. Fowley yelled in pain. His grip loosened, and Cahill was able to get his other hand free. He smashed a punch into Fowley's mouth.

Blood spurted from Fowley's pulped lips. Cahill hit him again and sent him rolling to the side. Free at last, Cahill rolled over, too, and came up on hands and knees. His back heaved as he drew precious air back into his lungs. Fowley had almost squeezed the life out of him.

They were slower getting up this time, but both men made it to their feet. Fowley weaved back and forth, blood all over his mouth and beard. But he was still grinning, and his voice was strong as he said, "Had enough, Cahill?"

"On your best day you couldn't whip me," Cahill rasped. "Come on."

Fowley lunged again, sweeping both arms around. Cahill dodged the punches and peppered Fowley's face with stinging blows. Cahill had caught on, thought Longarm. He knew now where he had to hit Fowley in order to hurt him. Cahill's fists were covered with blood, but most of it was Fowley's.

Not fast to start with, Fowley was slowing down even more. He stumbled back and forth, trying to close with Cahill, who managed to stay out of his way. Fowley threw ponderous punches that failed to connect, and after each one, Cahill hit him at least twice in the face. Fowley's head jerked back with each blow. Fat drops of blood flew through the air, so much blood that a red mist seemed to float around his head. He roared incoherently, trying to form curses with his ruined mouth.

Cahill launched a hard right that caught Fowley on the left cheekbone, just below the eye. While Fowley was still staggering from that, Cahill clipped him with a left. A hard right and left to the mouth sent Fowley staggering backward. His feet went out from under him and he fell heavily, landing on his back. He sprawled there, his face awash in crimson, his chest rising and falling rapidly. He made bubbling sounds as he breathed.

Cahill was breathing hard, too, but he was still on his feet. He said, "Had enough, Bill?"

Fowley made no response. Cahill turned to walk away.

That was when Fowley surged up from the ground gripping a broken branch that his hand had landed on when he fell. The limb was thick and sturdy and would crush Cahill's skull when it landed. One of the other men yelled, "Look out, Roney!"

Though Cahill was victorious, the fight had taken a lot out of him. He started to turn, but too slowly. He wasn't going to be able to get out of the way of the branch whipping toward his head.

Longarm's gun cracked, and the makeshift club was blasted in two and torn out of Fowley's hand by the bullet. Fowley stumbled, thrown off balance, and fell to his knees. Cahill met him with a brutal kick that sent him onto his back again. This time Fowley didn't budge.

"I don't know if you can hear me or not," Cahill said, "but we're done, Fowley. You don't ride with this bunch anymore. If you know what's good for you, you'll get the hell out of the Ozarks."

Fowley rolled onto his side and muttered something, his voice so thick that it was incomprehensible. Cahill took a few bills from the cache of loot he had stored in his saddlebags and threw them toward Fowley. "There's your cut for today's job. You won't ever get any more from me."

The other men were silent as Cahill bent down, picked up his gunbelt, and buckled it on. As he was putting on his hat, McHaney said, "You did what you had to do, Roney. None of us hold it against you."

"I appreciate that," Cahill said. "I know Fowley was friends with all of you. Hell, I thought of him as a friend, too." Cahill shook his head and swung up into the saddle.

"Not any more." He hitched his horse into motion. "Let's ride."

The gang pulled out silently, leaving the battered Fowley lying on the forest floor behind them.

The group drifted apart as they rode back through the woods toward Skunk Hollow, the other men veering off one by one to head back to their own homes. They would meet at Strickland's later to divvy up the loot, Cahill explained. He stopped at the tavern on the way past it, picked up a bottle, then took a swig from it after he had swung back into the saddle. He grimaced as the fiery liquor stung the cuts inside his mouth.

When he was finished drinking, he took off his bandanna, poured whiskey on it, and used it to clean dried blood off his ear and the side of his face. He winced as he did that, too. After working at it for a minute, he said to Longarm, "How does it look?"

"Better," Longarm said. "You don't have blood all over your face anymore. But Sarah Jane's still going to know something happened. She's not blind."

"Yeah, I guess so." Cahill took another drink, then held out the bottle to Longarm, who shook his head. Cahill went on, "I didn't want her seeing all the blood and getting upset."

"That ear of yours could use some stitches where Fowley tore it loose," Longarm pointed out.

Cahill shrugged. "It's still better than walking in there looking the way I did."

Longarm couldn't argue with that. As they set off toward Sarah Jane's cabin, he said, "What do you reckon Fowley will do now?"

"If he's smart, he'll get the hell out of the Ozarks, like I told him," Cahill said with a snort of disgust. "I knew he wasn't happy all the time with the way I've been runnin' things, but I never thought he'd jump me like that."

"Man gets ambitious, he's liable to do 'most anything."

"I suppose so."

"What I was asking was if you think he's liable to take a potshot at you?"

Cahill frowned. "Somehow I can't see Bill being a bushwhacker."

"Then you and me see him a heap different," Longarm said. "I'd sure keep a close eye on my back for a while, if I was you."

"I do that anyway. Fowley ain't the only enemy I've got in these mountains, not to mention the law could come snoopin' around any time."

Longarm didn't say anything to that. In fact, both of them were quiet the rest of the way.

Sarah Jane must have heard them coming. She appeared in the doorway of the cabin as they rode up onto the bench and waited there for them. Her expression was anxious, Longarm saw as he and Cahill drew closer. Finally, Sarah Jane couldn't stand it any longer and ran out to meet them when they were still about forty feet from the cabin.

"Roney," she said, "are you all right?"

"I'm fine, Sarah Jane," he assured her. He reined in, stepped down off his horse, and took her in his arms to hug her. While Cahill was doing that, Longarm dismounted, and Sarah Jane turned to him after a moment, embracing him as well.

"What about you, Custis?" she asked.

"Fine as frog hair," Longarm said with a grin.

Sarah Jane looked at Cahill again and said, "You're hurt, Roney. What happened to your ear?"

"It's not a gunshot wound, if that's what you're worried about," Cahill assured her. "I got in a little fracas with Bill Fowley. He clouted me on the ear while we were scuffling."

Sarah Jane's mouth tightened. "I don't like Fowley," she said with a frown. "Is he still riding with you?"

Cahill shook his head. "Not any more. Not after what he did today."

"There was some trouble?"

Cahill glanced at Longarm, then said, "Might as well speak frankly, since we all know what's goin' on anyway. Fowley shot one of the stagecoach passengers."

"Oh, no!" Sarah Jane exclaimed.

Longarm said, “Don’t worry, he’ll be all right. Fowley plugged him in the shoulder when he thought the fella was about to pull a gun on Roney.”

“That’s what he said,” Cahill commented. “I think Bill was just lookin’ for an excuse to shoot somebody.”

Sarah Jane nodded. “I don’t doubt that for a second. All the other men are all right, but I always thought there was just too much of a brute inside Bill Fowley.”

“Well, he’s out of the bunch now, so we don’t have to worry about him anymore,” Cahill said. “Are all the kids gone?”

“Yes, I sent them home a little early today, because I was expecting you back.”

“Why don’t we go see if you can tend to this ear, then?” Cahill made a face. “I got to admit, it’s startin’ to hurt a mite.”

The three of them went inside, where Longarm had to tell Jim all about the stagecoach robbery while Sarah Jane did a better job of cleaning Cahill’s ear and then took a couple of stitches in the lobe to reattach it to the side of Cahill’s head. Cahill gritted his teeth but didn’t yelp while Sarah Jane was doing her sewing.

Longarm glanced several times at Sarah Jane while he was talking to Jim. He hadn’t forgotten what he’d found out about Sarah Jane’s visits to Fort Smith. Coupled with what had happened when she went to Fayetteville a few days earlier, it was enough to make him curious, but he still thought suspecting her of killing those government officials was quite a stretch.

He knew, though, that there was enough of the Ozark mountain girl in her to have prompted the idea of holding up stagecoaches because they carried outsiders. She might have spent several years in St. Louis, but she still carried within her the clannishness and distrust and outright dislike of anyone she perceived as taking advantage of “her people.” Could that attitude have extended to the federal government?

A long shot, he told himself again. But if that was the case, then why did all his lawman’s instincts kick in every time he thought about Sarah Jane's trips to Fayetteville and Fort Smith?

"Good thing I wasn't there," Jim was saying as Longarm came out of his reverie. "I'd've ventilated the son of a bitch, that's for damned sure."

Longarm realized Jim was talking about Bill Fowley. Longarm had been telling him about the robbery and about the fight between Cahill and Fowley afterward.

"No, you wouldn't have," Cahill said from the other side of the room, where Sarah Jane was covering his stitched-up ear with a bandage. "That ruckus was strictly between Fowley and me."

"I thought Custis said he had to shoot a branch out of Fowley's hand when he tried to brain you with it," Jim protested.

"Well, there was that. And I'm obliged for the help, Custis, you know that."

Longarm nodded.

"That's at least twice you've saved my bacon," Cahill went on. "You may not be from the Ozarks, Custis, but you'll do to ride the river with."

"I appreciate that, Roney," Longarm said, and meant it.

And even as he spoke, he felt once again the unease his deception was causing him.

The law, he thought, *could be a damned harsh mistress sometimes. . . .*

Chapter 20

For the next several days, the mountains were quiet. Sarah Jane held school every day, Jim continued to recuperate from his wound, and old Gyp Foster did chores around the place and spent long hours hunting in the woods. Longarm and Roney Cahill spent a lot of time at Strickland's playing billiards and drinking beer. Sometimes some of the men from Cahill's gang of stagecoach robbers joined them.

There was no sign of Bill Fowley. He seemed to have dropped off the face of the earth.

Strickland had heard a rumor that Fowley had gone north to Missouri. He had relatives up there, or so the gossip said. After the beating Cahill had handed him, it made sense that he wouldn't want to stay around a place where everybody had heard about his defeat less than twelve hours after it occurred. News of such things traveled around the Ozarks quite rapidly.

Bad news traveled fast—that was how Fowley would see it.

Longarm tried to find some time to ask Sarah Jane about her trips to Fort Smith and Fayetteville. He made it all sound casual and found out the dates she had traveled to Fort Smith. To make it seem like a normal conversation, he said, "I was thinking that next time you needed anything from down yonder, I could go get it for you. That way you wouldn't have to miss any school days at all." He grinned. "I reckon that little redheaded rascal has a crush on you."

Sarah Jane blushed prettily. "Are you talking about George? For goodness sake, don't let him hear you say a thing like that, Custis! At his age, boys don't want to have anything to do with girls."

"I'm mighty glad that changes later on."

Sarah Jane's blush deepened, and Longarm knew she was probably remembering their tryst in the woods, up by the huckleberry patch. He wouldn't have minded going to pick huckleberries with Sarah Jane again, but that opportunity hadn't come up.

The fact of the matter was, Sarah Jane had been spending a lot of her free time with Cahill. They went for walks and rode horses and generally acted like a couple who were courting. Longarm didn't know whether to be jealous or not. There couldn't ever be anything serious between him and Sarah Jane—and if anything like that grew up between her and Cahill, Longarm was going to ruin that when he finally arrested both of them for their part in the series of stagecoach robberies.

He had been in the Ozarks for more than two weeks now. Some folks would probably say he was doing mighty good to be in so solidly with Cahill in such a short time, but Longarm was impatient. He wanted to get down to Fort Smith so that he could meet secretly with Judge Parker and find out the exact dates of those murders. Until he did that, he had to string these people along . . . these people who had become his friends.

When he once again brought up the subject of picking up medicines for her in Fort Smith, Sarah Jane waved off the offer. "Roney would be glad to go any time I wanted him to," she explained, "but I like making the trip myself. I have to get away from this cabin every so often."

Longarm nodded as if in understanding, while he was actually masking his disappointment. He would have to come up with some other excuse for riding down to Fort Smith.

Before he could do that, Cahill came up to him while Longarm was chopping wood. It was almost sundown, a peaceful time in the mountains. Another day was making its lazy way to a close.

"Time for us to be ridin' up to Buzzard's Notch again," Cahill said.

Longarm paused and rested the ax head on the ground, leaning on the handle. "Another stagecoach?"

"That's right. Northbound, this time, but we'll hit it on this side of the notch anyway. Take 'em by surprise that way."

"You think the driver will be expecting trouble?"

"I know he will," Cahill said. "And there'll be a guard on this coach, too. You see, Custis, I got word that the stagecoach will be carryin' a special cargo."

"And what might that be?"

"Money for the banks in Fayetteville."

Longarm frowned. "I thought all the bank money around here traveled by train now, in special cars guarded by express messengers."

"That's what the banks want everybody to think," Cahill said. "But several of those trains have been held up, and now the bankers are startin' to get tricky. Tryin' to, anyhow."

"Thaxton's responsible for those train robberies," Longarm commented.

"Of course he is. And as long as he's hidin' at the Bloody Holler, no posse of deputies will ever get him. It'd take the army to root him out of that place."

Longarm wasn't as convinced of that as Cahill seemed to be. Given some good men to back his play, he thought he could capture or kill Deuce Thaxton and wipe out his gang. But the time still hadn't come for that, and when it did, if the army was what it took, then that's what Longarm would throw at Thaxton.

"Anyway," Cahill went on, "I got a tip that coach will be carryin' plenty of cash because the bankers all think it'll be safer goin' that way. Nobody would expect it."

Longarm nodded slowly. "Makes sense, I reckon. Those bank officials who have been losing money shipments to Thaxton are probably willing to try just about anything."

"Yep. That's why you and me and the boys will be at Buzzard's Notch tomorrow."

Longarm inclined his head toward the cabin. "Does Sarah Jane know about this one?"

Cahill's expression grew more solemn. "Nope, and I don't want her to. The way she's been worryin' lately every time we pull a job, I'd just as soon she didn't know any more than she has to. We'll tell her we're goin' to Strickland's to play pool."

"Jim will complain," Longarm said with a chuckle. "He misses his billy-ards."

"Sarah Jane says he'll be up and around in another week. He can play billy-ards then."

Longarm nodded and hefted the ax to go back to his wood-chopping.

"We'll meet at Strickland's around two and ride up to get in position," Cahill added.

"You're not coming by here?"

"Naw. Got somethin' else to do first."

Cahill didn't offer an explanation of what that something else was, and Longarm didn't press for one.

He had hoped to be able to wrap up this case before another stagecoach robbery took place, he thought as he drove the ax blade deep in a chunk of wood, splitting so that it could be burned in the fireplace. Obviously that wasn't going to happen. It was more important than ever that he go along on this holdup, he realized. The coach would have a driver and a guard and possibly even another guard riding inside. This might be the perfect opportunity to turn the tables on Cahill and capture the entire gang without a shot being fired. Of course, once he did that, the die would be cast, Longarm told himself. He would have to go ahead and move against Thaxton immediately. That would leave the question of the murders of the federal officials up in the air, but there was nothing he could do about that. Not every case wrapped up as neatly as the law might have liked. The fellas who packed a badge, like Longarm, just did the best they could to bring law and order to the frontier. It was, at times, an ugly and unsatisfying business.

But after all these years, it was the only one Longarm knew.

If Sarah Jane had any suspicions that Longarm and Cahill were up to something, she gave no sign of it the next day when Longarm left the cabin not long after lunch. He had finally given in to the children's coaxing and spent the morning in class with them, listening to them recite their lessons and watching them do ciphering problems on the blackboard. Some of them were pretty smart, he decided, especially George. Sarah Jane would probably deny it, but Longarm could tell that George was her pet, and deservedly so.

It was another beautiful spring day as he rode toward Skunk Hollow and his appointment at Strickland's with Cahill. But the sun was a bit warmer now than it had been at the same time of day a couple of weeks earlier, an indication that summer was on its way. Longarm hoped to be out of the Ozarks before the real heat set in, bringing with it an uncomfortable stickiness and swarms of mosquitoes that would drive a fella plumb mad. He wanted to be back in the high, cool Colorado country by then.

He was thinking about how pretty the Rockies were early in the morning, when several men suddenly spurred their horses out of the brush alongside the trail, closing in around him. Longarm stiffened and his hand started toward the butt of his Colt, but he stopped the motion when he realized that the men already had their guns drawn and leveled at him.

"What the hell is this?" Longarm asked harshly. He looked around at his captors—and he *was* a prisoner, no getting around it—and recognized them from the visit he and Cahill had paid to the Bloody Holler. These were some of Deuce Thaxton's men.

"Take it easy, Jones," one of them advised him. Longarm recognized the man as the sentry who had been standing guard above the hideout. He wore the same floppy-brimmed felt hat, and his voice had a Kansas twang. "Deuce said for us not to kill you, but he never said we couldn't bust you up a mite if you give us any trouble. You're comin' with us."

"To see Thaxton?"

The outlaw's bony shoulders rose and fell in a shrug. "Ain't nobody else gives the orders."

"What does he want with me?"

"I reckon that's Deuce's business, and if he wants to, he'll tell you when he sees you. Now come on. We ain't got time to sit around jawin'."

There were five of them. Longarm knew unbeatable odds when he saw them. He could resist, but the spokesman had made it plain that wouldn't get him anything except a beating.

But Cahill was waiting for him at Strickland's tavern. And in a couple of hours that stagecoach carrying the shipment of bank money would be rolling up to Buzzard's Notch. Cahill would be upset if Longarm didn't show up at Strickland's, but he would go ahead with the holdup. Longarm was certain of that.

"Come on," Thaxton's flunky said impatiently. "Let's go."

Longarm nodded and heeled his horse into motion. There was nothing else he could do.

The five bandits fell in around him, blocking him so that he couldn't try to make a run for it. He was being herded like a steer, Longarm realized, and the thought made him even more angry.

The outlaws took some trails Longarm hadn't been on yet, but he knew enough landmarks now to have a pretty good idea where they were headed. They were circling around north of the mountain where Sarah Jane's cabin was located. If they did what Longarm expected, they would then swing back to the south and head toward Bloody Holler.

But then they surprised him by turning west instead of east. Longarm was lost for a while as they followed a series of twisting backwoods trails, but then he spotted a physical feature in the distance that was familiar: Buzzard's Notch.

Good Lord! thought Longarm. Was Thaxton planning to hit that stagecoach himself? If that was the case, there could be a battle royal between the two bands of outlaws. They might even wipe each other out and do his job for him.

The possibility of that didn't sit well in his gut, Longarm discovered. Roney Cahill and his friends had to face justice for what they had done, but Longarm didn't want to see them shot up by Thaxton's gang.

The outlaws pushed on, and Longarm had no choice but to go with them. They rode to the top of a rugged hogback ridge that overlooked the Fayetteville road and Buzzard's Notch. A man on horseback was waiting there for them. Longarm recognized him as soon as he came into view.

Deuce Thaxton.

An ugly grin stretched across Thaxton's face as Longarm and the others rode up to him. "Howdy, Jones," he greeted Longarm. "Glad you could accept my little invite."

Longarm glanced at the gunmen surrounding him. "I didn't have a hell of a lot of choice."

Thaxton rested his hands on his saddle horn and leaned forward as he said, "Everybody's got choices. Sometimes they just don't know about 'em and don't realize they're makin' 'em. Once before I asked you to ride with us, and you turned me down. You didn't realize you were choosin' to have Cahill and his other boys die."

Longarm felt cold fingers tickling along his spine. "What're you talking about, Thaxton? Roney and the others are fine."

"For now," Thaxton said. He pointed to Buzzard's Notch. "But in a little while, they're goin' to stop a stagecoach goin' through there, and they're goin' to get one hell of a surprise."

The coldness invaded Longarm's belly. "It's a trap." The words were jolted out of him.

Thaxton nodded, a self-satisfied smirk on his face. "That ain't the coach Cahill thinks it is, and it sure ain't got no bank money on it. What it's got is half a dozen of my best men, and another half-dozen are up on the cliffs of the Notch, ready to blow Cahill and his pards right into hell." Thaxton chuckled. "Just think about it, Jones. You'd be right there with 'em, shot to pieces, if I hadn't sent some of my boys to fetch you. You know why I did that?"

"No." Longarm's voice sounded hollow and strange to his ears, strained as it was with emotion.

"Because I knew as soon as I saw you that you're too good to be ridin' with a bunch of hillbillies. You're a top gunhand, Jones, and that's the kind of man I want sidin' me. I got big plans, and I want you to be part of 'em."

"So this is your way of recruiting me?"

Thaxton laughed again. "I reckon you could put it like that."

"Go to hell."

Thaxton pulled out a pocket watch and flipped it open. "We'll see if you still feel like that about fifteen minutes from now."

That quarter of an hour dragged by like a week to Longarm. He was thinking desperately, trying to come up with some way of warning Cahill about the trap Thaxton had set for him. Thaxton had figured everything nice and tight, though. Longarm stood little or no chance of getting away, and the distance to Buzzard's Notch was too great for him to shout a warning.

He spotted movement in the woods along the road and knew that was probably Cahill and the others moving into position to stop the stage. Tension made Longarm lean forward. A question occurred to him, and he asked Thaxton, "How'd you manage to get Cahill to believe that phony story about the bank money?"

"Wasn't hard," Thaxton said. "You know how word gets passed around these mountains. All I needed was somebody to start the rumor. Fact of the matter is, he's the one who came to me with the idea." Thaxton jerked his head to the side. "Here he comes now. Reckon he wants to watch the show."

Longarm turned his head and saw a burly, bearded figure on horseback riding toward them.

He didn't have to see the brutal, gap-toothed grin to know that Bill Fowley had come back to the Ozarks for his revenge on Roney Cahill.

Chapter 21

If in fact Fowley had ever really left, Longarm amended to himself. It was possible that Fowley had simply been lying low in the mountains ever since his defeat at Cahill's hands.

Either way, Fowley was here now, and from what Thaxton had just said, it was obvious that Fowley was actually the one who had set the trap for Cahill.

"Howdy, Jones," Fowley said as he reined in next to Longarm and Thaxton. "Fancy meetin' you here." The grin dropped off his face to be replaced by a savage glower. "Last time I saw you, you were shootin' at me."

"I was shooting at that club you were swinging at Cahill's head," Longarm said. "Too bad I didn't put the bullet through your head instead."

Fowley growled and shifted his horse toward Longarm's, but Thaxton said, "That's enough. The show's down there, not up here."

Longarm turned his attention back to Buzzard's Notch. More movement caught his eye, and he spotted the stagecoach rolling toward the Notch. Sickness roiled in his stomach. That was actually death rolling toward Cahill and the others, and there wasn't anything he could do to stop it.

The sound of gunshots would carry that far, Longarm realized. A sudden flurry of shots might alert Cahill that something was wrong, that not everything was as it seemed. Thaxton's men hadn't taken Longarm's Colt. It still rode in the cross-draw rig on his left hip. His captors had assumed that he wouldn't try to use it against such overwhelming odds, that he had more sense than that. If he started shooting, they would have to fire back, and the fusillade would warn Cahill.

Longarm knew he couldn't sit there and think about it. His hand moved.

But his fingers had just touched the butt of the revolver when Fowley sent his horse crashing into Longarm's mount. "Look out!" Fowley yelled. "He's goin' for his gun!"

Longarm bit back a curse as he struggled to bring the spooked bay under control. Fowley must have been watching him like a hawk, fearful that he would try something like that. Fowley had his gun out now, and he slashed with it at Longarm's head.

Longarm tried to avoid the blow, but it clipped him on the side of the head, knocking his hat off and opening up a shallow cut that stung like blazes. Half-stunned, Longarm still tried to get his own gun out of its holster. Before he could do so, Thaxton pistol-whipped him from the other side, and the boss outlaw's blow landed solidly. Longarm slumped forward in the saddle. His Colt, half-drawn, slipped from his fingers and thudded to the ground. Longarm followed it a second later as he toppled from the saddle.

At that moment, guns began to bark in the distance. Longarm groaned as he heard the rattle and crash of rifle fire. He knew what that meant. The trap had sprung closed, and Roney Cahill and his men were running into an unexpected hailstorm of lead.

Thaxton dismounted and grabbed Longarm under his left arm. Thaxton hauled the lawman to his feet and thrust him toward the edge of the ridge. "Look at that," Thaxton said triumphantly. "Look what's happenin' to your pards, Jones."

The distance was too great for Longarm to see much other than muzzle flashes and drifting clouds of powdersmoke. It was like watching some of the skirmishes he had seen from a distance during the war. He knew men were fighting and dying over there, but there was nothing he could do about it, nothing except feel a little hollow and empty inside.

"You son of a bitch," he grated at Thaxton.

Thaxton laughed. "You say that now, but I reckon you're a pretty smart fella. You'll see that the only thing you can do now is join up with me. Ride with us and you'll be a rich man, Jones."

Longarm turned his head and looked at Fowley. "Ride with the same bunch as *him*?"

"Hell, he's got a grudge against you, too," Thaxton pointed out. "I figure if Fowley can get over it, you can, too. Think about it, Jones. What the hell does any of it mean if you're rich?"

Down around Buzzard's Notch, the firing was dying away now. The ambush was just about over. Cahill and his friends had been wiped out.

But Longarm still had half of his original assignment to carry out. He lifted a hand, wiped the back of it across his mouth, and said, "I reckon you're right, old son. What's done is done."

Thaxton slapped him on the back. "Now you're talkin'! Of course, you realize I ain't gonna trust you right away. No offense, Jones, but I don't want you thinkin' that you can gun me down and even the score for Cahill. So don't expect to be seein' my back anytime soon."

Longarm bent over and picked up his fallen hat and gun. He holstered the Colt and settled the hat on his head, wincing slightly at the pain that caused. The valley in front of Buzzard's Notch was silent now, and the clouds of smoke were breaking up and blowing away on the breeze.

Making his voice sound as pragmatic as possible, Longarm said, "I ain't a fool, Thaxton. Give me a chance and you'll see that you can trust me."

"That's just what I aim to do." Thaxton grasped his saddle horn and swung up onto his horse. "Come on, let's head back to the Holler. The rest of the boys will meet us there."

Longarm exchanged a hostile glance with Fowley, then mounted up. He wasn't going to pretend to like the big, gap-toothed man. Not even Thaxton, who was anxious to have Longarm in his gang, would believe that transformation.

Turning his back on Buzzard's Notch, Longarm rode away with the outlaws.

The Bloody Holler still looked as impregnable as Longarm remembered it. Maybe it *would* take the army to pry Thaxton out of this hidey-hole.

The rest of the gang was waiting for them, over a dozen men. They were all grinning broadly, and one of them reported to Thaxton, "Everything went just like you said, Deuce. Cahill wasn't expectin' a thing!"

Thaxton laughed as he dismounted. "Looked a mite surprised when the bullets started rippin' into him, did he?"

"That's right. Him and one of the other hillbillies stopped the coach and told the passengers to get out. We opened up on him then, and the fellas on top of the Notch had spotted the rest of 'em when they were gettin' into position, so they started shootin' at 'em. The plan worked mighty fine. Cahill and his boys tried to fight back, but they didn't have no chance in hell. None of us got so much as a scratch."

"And they were all dead?"

The outlaw nodded. "Damn right."

Thaxton looked at Longarm, who had dismounted and kept his face carefully expressionless during the gruesome recital of how the trap had caught Cahill and the others.

"Let's go inside and have a drink to celebrate," Thaxton said.

The cabin was crudely furnished with bunks, a rough-hewn table, and some rickety chairs. Thaxton sat down at the table with a bottle and motioned for Longarm to take a seat opposite him.

"I've been thinkin' about what you said up on that hog-back," Thaxton began as the other outlaws spread out through the big cabin. Fowley stood over by the fireplace, his arms folded across his powerful chest and a glare on his face as he stared at Longarm. Thaxton continued, "You said to give you a chance, Jones, and I reckon I know what I'm goin' to ask you to do to prove yourself." He took a swig from the bottle, then passed it across the table to Longarm. "I want you to bring me that girl."

Longarm hesitated for just an instant, then took a healthy swallow from the bottle. The raw whiskey burned like fire on the way down his gullet. He lowered the bottle and said, "What girl?"

"You know damned well who I mean. The Masterson girl."

Longarm frowned. "What do you want with her?" He was struggling not to show the horror that was creeping around in the back of his mind at the thought of Sarah Jane in the hands of Thaxton, Fowley, and the rest of these owlhoots.

"She was Cahill's girl, wasn't she? I reckon if these hillbillies see that she's mine now, they'll know I've taken Cahill's place and they won't put up such a ruckus about me takin' over."

Thaxton had a point there, thought Longarm. Taking Sarah Jane for his own would complete his triumph over Roney Cahill and demonstrate to the mountain folks the futility of trying to stand up to Thaxton. It would be an effective, if ruthless, move.

"Bring her here to the Holler, you mean?" Longarm said. He was stalling for time, and he hoped that wasn't obvious.

"That's right."

"You want me to go to her cabin and get her?"

Thaxton nodded. "Yep. You won't be goin' alone, though."

That scotched some of Longarm's hopes. He had thought that he might get Sarah Jane and make a run for Fort Smith with her.

"I plan to send a couple of my best sharpshooters with you," Thaxton went on. "They'll stay back and let you go into the girl's cabin by yourself. When you come out with her, if you do anything except head straight back here, they'll kill both of you."

"Sounds like you've got the whole thing figured out," Longarm drawled. He took another pull on the bottle.

"Gimme that." Thaxton took a drink. "Of course I got it figured out. If you're tryin' to double-cross me, you wind up dead. If you do like you're told, I'll know you really do want to be part of the gang."

"All right. When do you figure on me doing this?"

Thaxton grinned. "No time like the present."

Longarm had been afraid he would say that. Thaxton wasn't going to give him a chance to come up with any sort of tricky scheme. He had to ride over to Sarah Jane's right now and make it look like he was kidnapping her.

Hell, that was what it amounted to, he thought bitterly. She would never come willingly to the Bloody Holler, and he didn't blame her for that.

"And don't get any ideas about fortin' up inside the girl's cabin," Thaxton added. "We'll burn it down around your ears if you do."

Blast it! The man had thought of everything.

"All right." Longarm put his hands flat on the table and pushed himself to his feet. "Let's go."

"That's what I like," Thaxton said with a grin, "a man who don't waste no time."

From the fireplace, Fowley said, "Don't you trust him, Thaxton. Don't you trust that bastard an inch."

"I don't. Not yet. But I gave you a chance to prove yourself to me, Fowley, and Jones deserves the same chance, whether you and him get along or not."

Longarm started toward the door, saying over his shoulder, "Are we riding or jawing?"

His head still ached where he'd been hit with the pistols. He hoped that before the day was over he wouldn't have some hurts that were a lot worse.

Thaxton remained at the Bloody Holler, sending two men with Longarm as he had said. One of them was the twangy-voiced Kansan, whose name was Spillman, Longarm learned during the ride. The other was a stocky gunman called Brock.

Spillman had a heavy-caliber Sharps, while Brock toted a Winchester. Both of them were deadly shots with the rifles, they assured Longarm.

"I figure if you try to double-cross Deuce, I'll put a bullet in you whilst Brock does for the girl," Spillman said cheerfully. "Be a shame to kill such a nice-lookin' gal, but that's what Deuce said to do."

"You don't have to worry about that," Longarm said. "I'll go along with what Thaxton wants. I'd be a fool not to, now."

"You just remember that," Spillman warned.

They veered off the trail before reaching Sarah Jane's cabin, and Spillman warned Longarm again that they would be watching over the sights of their weapons. Longarm rode on toward the cabin, feeling a mixture of despair and anger rising in him. There had to be *something* he could do to turn the tables on Thaxton.

He was damned, though, if he could see what it was.

He rode up onto the bench and saw the cabin sitting there peacefully, smoke curling from the rock chimney. As he came closer, he saw Gyp Foster walk from the shed into the cabin. The old-timer would probably tell Sarah Jane he was coming.

Sarah Jane had no idea Cahill was dead, Longarm thought bleakly. He wasn't looking forward to telling her and Jim about the trap. Nor did he relish the idea of explaining to them that he was actually a deputy United States marshal and had been lying to them for more than two weeks now, deceiving them and playing on their friendship. But that had to be done, too. An idea was scurrying around in the back of Longarm's brain, but it required telling the truth for a change.

It also required relying on the old half-wit, Gyp, and that might be a dangerous thing to do. Longarm didn't see that he had any choice, however.

He reined to a stop in front of the cabin, dismounted, and looped the bay's reins over the rack. The door stood open, but Sarah Jane hadn't come there to greet him. He didn't hear the voices of the children inside. It was late enough in the day that all of them had probably gone home. Sarah Jane would be alone in there with Jim and Gyp.

Longarm took a deep breath and started toward the door. No point in postponing the inevitable. As he walked up to the cabin, he was acutely conscious that Thaxton's sharpshooters were watching him over the barrels of their rifles.

He stepped in the door, said, "Sarah Jane—"

Then froze as a gun barrel was pressed against the back of his head, and a dead man's voice said, "You son of a bitch."

Chapter 22

"Cahill?" Longarm breathed. His heart pounded heavily in his chest as surprise and disbelief coursed through him.

"That's right," Roney Cahill said. "And I oughta blow your brains out where you stand, you damned dirty double-crosser."

Longarm looked around the cabin. He saw that Cahill wasn't the only one with a gun trained on him. Jim sat up in bed, a pistol in his hand, and the revolver's barrel was steady as a rock. In the kitchen doorway, Sarah Jane stood with her rifle, and off to the side, near the partition that divided the cabin, Gyp had his single-shot rifle trained on Longarm. He had walked into a hornet's nest, sure enough, reflected Longarm.

"Roney," he said, "you don't know how glad I am that you're alive."

"Shut your damned mouth," Cahill grated. "I don't want to hear any more of your lies."

"It's the truth, old son," Longarm said. "I—"

"Roney!" Sarah Jane cried out.

She must have seen something that Longarm couldn't, because a second later the gun barrel went away from Longarm's head and he heard a thud as Cahill collapsed. He started to turn, but Jim barked, "Don't move, Custis! I'll shoot you sure as Roney would have."

Longarm stayed where he was, hands slightly lifted, as Sarah Jane rushed past him and dropped to her knees beside Cahill. Longarm turned his head enough to look at the fallen outlaw and saw that Cahill had his shirt off and a lot of bandages wrapped around his torso. Those bandages had red stains blossoming on them like crimson flowers.

"He's bleeding again," Sarah Jane said anxiously. "Gyp, help me get him onto the bunk."

"I'll lend you a hand," Longarm said.

She cast an icy glance at him. "You think we'd accept help from you, after what you did?"

"Whatever you think happened today, Sarah Jane, you've got it wrong," Longarm told her.

From the bunk, Jim snorted in disbelief and contempt while Sarah Jane and Gyp wrestled Cahill's unconscious form onto the bunk that Longarm had occupied when he was wounded. "Roney told us all about how you never showed up at Strickland's to meet him," Jim said. "That stagecoach holdup was nothin' but a damned trap you set up with that bastard Thaxton."

Slowly, Longarm shook his head. "It was a trap, all right, but I didn't have anything to do with it. It was all Bill Fowley's idea."

"Fowley?" Sarah Jane looked up sharply. "What are you talking about?"

Longarm sensed that he still had a chance to set things right. While Sarah Jane unwrapped the bandages and tried to stop the bleeding from the bullet holes in Cahill's riddled body, Longarm explained how Thaxton's men had grabbed him and taken him to the hogback ridge overlooking Buzzard's Notch. "Fowley was there, too. Thaxton even admitted it was Fowley's idea to start a rumor about a fake money shipment to get Roney to stop that stagecoach. Thaxton's men were inside waiting for him, and there were riflemen up on top of the Notch to take care of the other boys."

"They're all dead," Jim said, a catch in his voice. "Ever'

blessed one of 'em. Roney's the only one who got out alive, and he barely made it back here to tell us what happened."

"He's going to be all right," Sarah Jane said. "He's going to live." Her voice carried plenty of determination, but Longarm thought he detected a hint of uncertainty in it, too, as if she were trying to *will* Roney Cahill to survive his wounds.

Jim kept the pistol trained on Longarm, but he used his other hand to rub his jaw as he frowned in thought. "I ain't sure whether to believe you or not, Custis," he said. "I reckon it could've happened the way you say it did. Hell, I *want* to believe you. But you know how it looked to us when you didn't show up and then Roney rode into a trap."

Longarm nodded. "I understand. You must've thought I'd gone over to Thaxton's side."

"That's exactly what we thought," Sarah Jane said. She straightened from the bunk and sighed. "I think I've got the bleeding stopped again. I hope so, because Roney can't stand to lose much more."

"How badly is he hit?" Longarm asked.

"He was shot four times through the body. It'll be a miracle if all the bullets missed any vital organs. Even if they did, shock and the loss of blood may still kill him." Sarah Jane took a deep breath. "But I won't let it. He's going to be fine."

"There's a couple of things I don't understand," Jim put in. "You said Thaxton's men told him Roney was dead."

Longarm nodded. "That's what they claimed. Maybe they just didn't want to admit to Thaxton that he'd gotten away. They saw he was hit real bad and figured he was going to die anyway, so it didn't matter if he did it there or fell off his horse and died a mile down the road."

"Yeah, maybe. But how come Thaxton let you go?"

Longarm smiled humorlessly. "He thinks I'm one of his gang now."

"You told him that, and he just up and believed you?"

"Not exactly. He sent me here to prove it."

Sarah Jane asked, "How are you supposed to do that?"

Longarm looked at her and said, "I'm supposed to take you back to him."

For a long moment that seemed even lengthier than it was, no one said anything. Then Jim hissed, "You bastard," and brought up the pistol, his finger tightening on the trigger.

"Jim, wait!" Sarah Jane exclaimed. "Custis said that was what Thaxton wants him to do. He didn't say he was going to do it."

"Reckon I don't have a lot of choice in the matter," Longarm said. "Thaxton sent a couple of his men with me. They're outside somewhere with rifles. When we leave, if we don't head straight for Thaxton's hideout, they'll kill us."

"When you leave?" Jim repeated. "Hell, you're not goin' anywhere!"

"If I don't come out with Sarah Jane in a reasonable amount of time, I reckon one of Thaxton's men will go back for the rest of the bunch. Then they'll come here and burn down the cabin and kill us all. Thaxton made that mighty plain."

Sarah Jane looked calm, but her voice was strained as she said, "So you do plan to turn me over to that monster?"

"Well . . . yes and no."

"Dadgum it!" Jim burst out in frustration. "I don't understand this at all!"

"I have to take Sarah Jane to Bloody Holler. That's the only chance we have." Longarm turned to look at Gyp. "But I'm going to send the old-timer here for help."

Gyp's eyes widened. "Me? Send me where?"

"Gyp's right, Custis," Jim said. "The only fellas we could count on are all dead now, wiped out in Thaxton's trap. Where are we gonna get enough help to take on Thaxton's gang?"

"I reckon a posse of federal marshals from Fort Smith might have a chance," Longarm said.

They all stared at him, then Jim said, "Judge Parker would have to send out a posse like that. Why would the hangin' judge listen to anything Gyp had to say?"

"Parker will believe Gyp because he'll be carrying a note from me."

Sarah Jane caught on before Jim did, but it was only a second before Jim exclaimed, "Son of a bitch! You're a lawman!"

"Deputy U.S. Marshal Custis Long. I was sent here to find out who's responsible for all the holdups in the Ozarks lately." For some reason, Longarm didn't say anything about the murders of federal officials. That could wait until later, if ever.

Jim grimaced. "I oughta—"

"Leave him alone."

The words came from the other bunk. Cahill's eyes were open, and he had propped himself up on an elbow to look intently at Longarm.

Sarah Jane turned quickly toward him. "Roney, lie back down. You have to rest—"

"No time for that," Cahill cut in. "I heard most of what Custis had to say." He laughed without so much as a hint of humor. "So you're a star-packer. I thought at first there was something off about you, Custis, but I figured it was just my imagination."

"For what it's worth," Longarm said, "I wound up being sorry I had to lie to all of you. You can believe that or not, but it's the truth."

"Goin' to arrest us?" Cahill asked mockingly.

"Nope. I figure it's more important to round up Thaxton's bunch." Longarm paused, thinking about the men who had been killed in the trap set by Thaxton and Fowley. "Your boys have paid enough for their crimes."

Pain that didn't come from his wounds flickered across Cahill's face. "I got a score to settle," he said. "If you can help me do that, I don't care that you're a lawman. I don't care what happens later on. I just want Thaxton—and Fowley."

"You're in no shape to do anything, Roney," Sarah Jane said firmly. "You're shot up worse than Jim was in that other ambush, and he's been in bed for two weeks now, recuperating."

"I can get up and about," Jim protested. "I'll ride to Fort Smith with Gyp—"

"No," Gyp said. His mind seemed clearer now, and he had drawn himself up with a new-found dignity. "You'd just slow me down. I'll fetch help, don't you worry."

"That's what I wanted to hear," Longarm said. He looked around for pencil and paper. "I'll write that note to Judge Parker—"

"Wait a minute," Cahill said. "You can't take Sarah Jane to Thaxton."

"I have to. That's the only way I can stall until Gyp gets back with the marshals."

"But that son of a bitch . . . there's no tellin' what he's liable to do. He could . . . could . . ."

"It's all right, Roney," Sarah Jane said. "Custis is right. We have to play for time now." She smiled. "And I'm the trump card."

"I don't like it," Longarm said honestly, "but I don't see no other way. I'll do my best to keep you safe, Sarah Jane."

"I know." She took a deep breath. "Well, I guess I'd better get ready to ride."

"Damn it—" Cahill began.

"Roney, I'm sorry," she said. "But you're not giving the orders now. The Ozarks will never be safe for the common folks or anyone else until Thaxton is taken care of."

"Blast it, nobody made you the guardian of the whole damned Ozarks—"

Sarah Jane pressed a hand on his shoulder, gently urging him back on the bunk. "You just rest," she told him. "I want you alive when I get back, Roney." She straightened and turned to Longarm. "I'll be ready in a few minutes."

"Better make it fast," Longarm said, thinking of Spillman and Brock. "We don't want Thaxton's boys getting impatient and deciding I've pulled a double-cross."

Sarah Jane hurried into the back of the cabin, where her living quarters were. While she was gone, Cahill looked coldly at Longarm and said, "When this is all over . . ."

"We'll settle it any way you want," Longarm said. "That's a promise."

Longarm wrote the note to Judge Parker explaining the situation and giving directions to the Bloody Holler. Gyp knew the way there as well and promised that he would lead the posse personally.

"Don't hardly see how we can get there before tomorrow mornin'," he said worriedly. "And that's ridin' all night."

"Just get there as soon as you can," Longarm told him.

Gyp would leave after Longarm and Sarah Jane, and he would take Cahill's horse, which was hidden in the shed. It was the fastest mount in the mountains, Cahill said.

Sarah Jane came back wearing a pair of man's trousers and a shirt. Her long, fair hair was tied back in a ponytail. Longarm thought she looked beautiful.

She pulled the shirt aside enough to reveal the butt of a small pistol tucked behind her belt. "I've got this if I need it," she said.

Longarm nodded. "Good idea. I just hope you don't need it."

Left unspoken was the thought that he and Sarah Jane would likely be inside the cabin with the outlaws when the posse arrived. They would probably have to shoot their way out.

As they rode away and turned toward Bloody Holler, Longarm felt the eyes of Spillman and Brock watching them. Sarah Jane must have experienced the same sensation, because she shivered. "It's going to get a lot worse before it gets better, isn't it?" she said.

"We'll keep our fingers crossed for luck," Longarm said.

"Luck." Her voice was hollow. "I never had much of that in my life until lately. I must have used it up."

Longarm didn't know what to say to that. Sarah Jane's normally fiery spirit seemed to be flickering.

Since they might well be riding to their deaths, Longarm decided it didn't make sense to wait on the other question gnawing at him. He said, "Sarah Jane, is there anything about those trips to Fort Smith and Fayetteville you made in the last month or so that you want to tell me about, now that you know I'm a lawman?"

"What?" She turned her head to look at him. "What are you talking about, Custis?"

He heaved a sigh of relief. He had known some fine actresses in his time, but none of them had been good enough to convey the sense of sheer surprise and confusion Sarah Jane displayed at his question. He knew now she hadn't had anything to do with the murders. If he didn't make it through the next twelve hours or so alive, somebody else would have to solve that case—if it ever got solved.

"Never mind," he said. "Just a crazy idea."

"It must have been."

They rode on. Dusk was gathering. Spillman and Brock came out of the woods to join them on the trail, and Sarah Jane looked nervously at the two outlaws. They leered at her, causing Longarm's temper to rise, but he made an effort to control it. From here on out, he would be walking a very thin line.

Light showed through the chinks in the cabin walls as the little group rode up to it a short time later. The cabin was in thick shadow because of the rocky bluff that hung over it. The door opened, and Deuce Thaxton stepped outside to greet them.

"By golly, I reckon you were tellin' the truth after all, Custis," he said to Longarm. "I didn't really figure you'd bring the little lady to see me."

Longarm swung down from the saddle, then turned to help Sarah Jane dismount. "You said you wanted her," he said to Thaxton. "Well, here she is." He paused, then went on, "The thing of it is, she's mine tonight."

Thaxton stiffened. "What?"

"You heard me, Deuce. I did just like you said. I went to the gal's cabin and brought her back. But I want first crack at her. I figure I've got it coming, the way she's been flaunting herself around and teasing me the past couple of weeks."

"You bastard," Sarah Jane said coldly.

Thaxton's hand was hovering over the butt of his gun, and Longarm could tell from the tension in the boss outlaw's body that he was thinking about slapping leather. But then, abruptly, Thaxton seemed to relax. He even chuckled.

"Hell, you're right," he said to Longarm. "I reckon I can wait. It ain't like I'd be the first for her, anyway. None of these hillbilly girls are virgins after they're about twelve years old. Their pas and their brothers see to that."

Anger blazed in Sarah Jane's eyes as she turned to him. "You filthy—"

Longarm's palm cracked across her face in a slap. "Shut up, bitch." He grabbed her arm and jerked her roughly toward him. "You got a place around here where we can have some privacy, Deuce?"

"As a matter of fact, there's a little cave in the side of the bluff, behind the cabin," Thaxton said with a grin, enjoying the way Longarm was manhandling Sarah Jane. "You could take a lantern and a bedroll back there, and you'd be all set. Of course, I'd have to put a guard outside—"

"That's all right, as long as he don't get too nosy."

"Come on," Thaxton said. "I'll show the place to you."

He fetched a lantern from inside, then led the way behind the cabin. Longarm followed, tugging Sarah Jane along with him. She cried and struggled, but he kept his tight grip on her arm and didn't let her go.

The light from the lantern showed the entrance to the cave in the side of the bluff. It reminded Longarm of a dark, gaping maw. But then the light washed over the interior of the cave, and he saw that it was just a plain, empty chamber with irregular walls, about twenty feet deep. The entrance was only four feet across, but the cave widened out to twelve feet or so.

Spillman brought a bedroll from the cabin and flung it on the stone floor of the cave. "There you go," he said to Longarm with a grin. "Have fun." To Sarah Jane, he added, "One o' these days soon, it'll be you and me, missy."

"Go to hell," she told him.

Thaxton laughed again. "This one's goin' to take some tamin', Custis. You sure you're up to the job?"

"I'll make a good start on it, anyway," Longarm replied with the same sort of smarmy grin the others were giving him and Sarah Jane.

"All right, then," Thaxton said. "There'll be a man right outside with a greener. If you need to take a leak or somethin', Custis, you'd better sing out before you set one foot outside, or you'll get a load of buckshot."

Longarm nodded in understanding. "I expect I'll find plenty to keep me busy."

"I expect," Thaxton agreed. He and the other outlaws filed out of the cave, leaving the lantern sitting on the floor.

Longarm looked at Sarah Jane, then leaned over and blew out the flame. Stygian darkness fell in the cave. He reached over and found her arm, drew her toward him again. She didn't resist, and he knew she understood.

He put his mouth next to her ear. "I'm sorry about all that," he breathed. "It was the only way to keep Thaxton away from you tonight." No one more than a foot away could have heard the words.

"It's all right," she told him, her voice equally quiet, her breath warm and soft against his ear. "I figured out what you were doing." She moved back a step then but kept her hands on his arms. "No!" she cried. "Oh, God, don't! Please, don't—" A scream ripped from her mouth.

Then she was in his arms again, and she whispered, "How was that?"

"Mighty convincing," he told her. "Hang on." He slapped his own thigh, hard, once and then again. "Shut up!" he growled loudly.

Sarah Jane shook in his arms, and he realized after a second that she was laughing. The absurdity of the whole situation was a little funny in a grim way, Longarm supposed. He felt himself grinning.

He put a hand under her chin and tipped her head back, leaned closer and brushed his lips across hers. "Now we wait," he murmured. "We wait for morning, and hope that Gyp didn't get lost."

Chapter 23

Longarm figured he wouldn't sleep during the long, tense night ahead of them, but he surprised himself by dozing off. So did Sarah Jane as she lay huddled against him on the bedroll. Even with it for padding, the rocky floor of the cave wasn't very comfortable.

When Longarm awoke, the mouth of the cave was visible as a rough oval of lighter gray against the blackness of the fading night. He figured it was about an hour until dawn. He reached over, touched Sarah Jane on the shoulder, and said her name.

She stirred a little, then rolled onto her side and pressed herself more closely against him. "Custis," she murmured. Her hand slid down over his stomach to his groin and caressed him through his trousers. The gesture took Longarm by surprise.

He didn't object, though, nor did he stop her as she unbuttoned his trousers and freed his stiffening manhood. She pumped her hand up and down the shaft, bringing it to a full erection, then skinned quickly out of her own clothes and swung a leg across him, straddling his hips. Longarm grasped the cheeks of her bottom and guided her down onto him. His organ slid into her, sheathing its thick length in her hot, wet core.

They made love in silence, mouths locked together in an intense kiss, hips moving in perfect counterpoint to each other. Longarm felt his climax building rapidly but didn't try to hold it back. Neither of them were holding back anything now. This moment in time had been given to them, a present from fate, but there might never be another. They gave their all to each other, Longarm's hips rising from the bedroll as he began to empty himself into her, Sarah Jane clutching him with a strength born of incredible passion. She rode him frenziedly as their culmination played itself out, then they both sagged onto the bedroll, her head resting on his chest.

Longarm was so sated, his senses so dulled by the languor that inevitably followed lovemaking, that he almost didn't hear the sudden sounds of a scuffle outside the cave.

Then he heard an unmistakable gurgling rattle and knew that somebody had just died out there. He rolled away from Sarah Jane, hissing, "Stay here!" and came to his feet. He still had his gun, so he slipped it from the holster, ready for whatever might happen next.

Or so he thought. He really wasn't ready for what he heard next.

"Sarah Jane? Custis? You in there?"

For the second time in less than twenty-four hours, Longarm was shocked to hear Roney Cahill's voice. "Roney?" he whispered. Sarah Jane hurried up behind him, fastening the trousers she had quickly pulled back on.

The sky was growing lighter. Longarm saw the figure silhouetted against the grayness as Cahill stepped into the mouth of the cave. "Come on," Cahill said. "Let's get out of here."

"Roney, what are you doing here?" Sarah Jane asked as she pushed past Longarm. "You're hurt! You need to be in bed—"

"Shoot, Jim and me, we're the walkin' wounded, I reckon," Cahill said. "He's up on top of the bluff, at the other end of the rope I used to get down here. He'll cover us while we climb back up."

"What about the guard?" Longarm asked.

"He won't bother nobody, not after my Arkansas toothpick carved his gullet open. It's a good thing he was there, though. If we hadn't spotted him, we might not have figured out there was somebody in this cave. Figured it had to be one or both of you."

Longarm stepped out of the cave and looked up at the beetling bluff. Getting up there must have been hard, especially for a couple of wounded men like Cahill and Jim, but climbing down on a rope would have been even more difficult. Yet Cahill had done it, even with four bullet holes in his body. Longarm saw dark stains on Cahill's shirt and knew that he was bleeding again.

Sarah Jane saw the stains, too. "Oh, Roney . . ." she said, putting out a hand to him.

He took her hand, squeezed it for a second, and said, "You can fuss at us all you want after we get out of here, Sarah Jane, but Jim and me couldn't just sit there and wait. We had to come do what we could to help you and Custis."

"We're obliged," Longarm said. "Sarah Jane, you shinny up that rope first, then Roney, then I'll bring up the rear."

"I don't—"

"You heard him, Sarah Jane," Cahill said. "Go ahead, it'll be—"

Longarm saw movement in the fading shadows around the cabin, saw a man step around the corner and stop short at the sight of them. He recognized Spillman's tall, lanky figure and knew that in a split second, Spillman would yell a warning.

Before that could happen, a rifle cracked from the top of the bluff, and Spillman was thrown backward by the bullet striking him. Longarm grimaced. Spillman hadn't had a chance to yell, but the shot was just as good a warning to Thaxton and the other outlaws.

He and Sarah Jane and Cahill could never climb that rope now before Thaxton and the others poured out of the cabin and riddled them with bullets. "Back into the cave!" he said. At least there they could make a stand.

Cahill turned, then let out a groan and started to collapse. Sarah Jane cried out and grabbed him, steadying him until he could lurch into the cave. Longarm backed into the opening after them. Someone came running around the corner of the cabin. Longarm snapped a shot at him and was gratified to see the man go spinning off his feet.

Sarah Jane helped Cahill all the way to the back end of the cave. Longarm stayed near the mouth. He heard shouts and curses from the cabin. A minute later, Thaxton yelled, "Custis? What's goin' on out there?"

With three of Thaxton's men dead or wounded, there was no longer any point in deception. Longarm shouted back, "Looks like I won't be riding with you after all, Deuce! In fact, you're under arrest!"

"Arrest!" Thaxton bellowed. "You're a goddamn lawman?"

"Deputy U.S. marshal," Longarm called back.

Thaxton spewed obscenities for a couple of seconds, then ordered, "Pour it in there, boys!"

"Get your heads down!" Longarm warned Sarah Jane and Cahill. He ducked behind a small outcropping of rock near the cave mouth.

It sounded like a battle as the outlaws opened fire on the cave. Bullets poured through the opening in a deadly storm of lead. The whine of ricochets filled the air. Longarm knew their luck couldn't last very long.

The shots from the cabin suddenly fell silent, but a rifle was still cracking up above them somewhere. That would be Jim, trying to distract Thaxton, Longarm guessed. A moment later that was confirmed, as Jim whooped and called down, "Why don't you come and get me, you damn Yankee owlhoot?"

Longarm heard Thaxton barking orders. "Harbin, take Tompkins and Coffman and get that damned hillbilly! The rest of us are gonna rush that cave!"

Thaxton was too furious to be thinking straight, Longarm

realized. Rushing the cave would cost him at least a few men. But in the end, the result would be the same: he and Sarah Jane and Cahill would be dead. He supposed Thaxton didn't mind spending the lives of a few men, as long as he got what he wanted.

Before that could happen, more shots rang out, but these weren't directed at the cave. Longarm heard men cry out in pain, then a new voice shouted, "Thaxton! Deuce Thaxton! This is Deputy Marshal Jack Pierce from Fort Smith! I got a whole posse of deputies out here, so you and your boys better throw down your guns and come out with your hands up!"

Longarm felt a surge of excitement go through him. Gyp had come through! The old man had made it to Fort Smith and brought back a posse of lawmen.

"Go to hell!" Thaxton bellowed back. "Come and get us if you think you can!"

Once again, the sounds of battle rolled over the Ozarks as the posse and the outlaws forted up inside the cabin began shooting at each other. Longarm was grateful that the deputies had arrived in time to distract Thaxton from him and his two companions, but they still weren't out of the woods. They were trapped in the cave with no food or water, and a stray bullet could come bouncing around in here any time and wound or kill one of them. Longarm tried to think of something he could do to tip the odds in the posse's favor . . .

His eyes fell on the lantern that had been left in the cave by Thaxton the night before. He scooped it up and shook it, listening to the kerosene sloshing around inside it. The lantern was almost full, he judged. He holstered his gun and felt inside his shirt pocket, looking for a match.

"Custis, what are you doing?" Sarah Jane asked from the rear of the cave.

"Going to give Thaxton a little surprise," Longarm said. He found a lucifer, snapped it into life, then lit the lantern, waiting until the wick was burning good before he lowered the chimney.

Then he stepped just outside the mouth of the cave and

let fly with the lantern, throwing it at the roof of the cabin.

Thaxton must have told at least one man to keep an eye on the cave, because flame and lead spat from a gun slit in the rear wall of the cabin. The bullet spanged off the bluff a few feet to Longarm's left. He threw himself back into the cave, but even as he did, he saw the lantern land on the roof and shatter. The kerosene splashed across the logs and caught fire, a sheet of flame whooshing up into the air.

Longarm rolled over on the rocky floor of the cave and came to rest on his belly. His gun was back in his hand. He listened to the popping and crackling as the fire on the roof of the cabin took hold and began to spread. Smoke filled the hollow and started to drift into the cave. "Stay close to the floor," Longarm called back to Sarah Jane and Cahill. "It's liable to get hard to breathe in here."

Men were shouting in alarm inside the cabin now. They knew it was on fire, and they knew as well that since the roof was burning, it might collapse at any moment. They had to get out or risk being crushed and burned to death. The outlaws' only chance for survival now lay in surrendering to the posse.

Thaxton's bloody-handed crew knew they would only be postponing their ends, however. Hangropes waited for all of them. So, Longarm wasn't surprised when he heard the sudden burst of firing from the front of the cabin. The outlaws were coming out, but they were coming out shooting.

Not all of them, though. As Longarm peered through the thickening smoke, a couple of logs were kicked out of the back wall of the cabin, and Deuce Thaxton squirmed through the opening he had created. Longarm came up onto his feet as Thaxton started toward the bluff, obviously intending to try to climb up it to safety. The rope Cahill had used earlier was still there. With the thick smoke covering him, Thaxton might have even made it.

Longarm stepped out of the cave and called, "Hold it, Thaxton!"

The boss outlaw whirled toward Longarm, his face contorted now with insane hatred. The gun in his hand jumped up and belched fire. Flame geysered from the muzzle of Longarm's Colt as he triggered twice. Thaxton fired again, and Longarm felt the bullet tear across the outside of his left thigh. The impact turned him halfway around. Longarm fired again as his leg gave out and he went toppling to the side. Thaxton's head jerked back as Longarm's last bullet drilled into his forehead and burst through his brain. He folded onto the ground, lifeless.

Longarm was about to pass out from the pain of his leg wound. He lifted his head and saw a bulky figure striding through the smoke toward him. The smoke cleared for a second, revealing Bill Fowley's battered face. Fowley's hand came up with a gun in it. Longarm tried to lift his own Colt but knew he was going to be too late to stop Fowley from getting off at least one shot.

That was when Roney Cahill stepped over Longarm and called, "Fowley!"

Fowley was so startled to see the man he had thought was dead that he hesitated, and that gave Cahill time to fire. The gun in Cahill's hand blasted. Fowley staggered, and Cahill fired again. A third shot knocked out even more of Fowley's teeth as it entered through his mouth and bored out the back of his skull in a shower of blood and bone shards. Fowley went over backward, dead before he hit the ground.

Cahill dropped beside Longarm, unable to stand up any longer. He grinned over at the lawman and said, "We're . . . a fine pair . . . ain't we? Shot all to pieces."

Longarm chuckled. "Yeah, but we're still alive."

Sarah Jane hurriedly came out of the cave and knelt between them. "My God," she said. "You're crazy, both of you. But I love you."

"Well, now," Longarm said, "looks like we got us another problem."

Chapter 24

Judge Isaac Parker looked coldly across the desk in his office at Longarm and asked, "What did you say, Marshal Long?"

Longarm glanced at the man sitting beside him and said, "That I deputized Mr. Cahill here as soon as I got to the mountains. He was working with me the whole time I was up in the Ozarks, helping me get the goods on Thaxton's bunch."

"You lack the authority to officially deputize anyone," Parker pointed out.

"Well, then, I done it unofficially," Longarm said, returning Parker's stare with one of his own that was every bit as intense. "As far as Mr. Cahill was concerned, I was acting on behalf of the United States Justice Department, and I reckon the only fair thing is to honor what I told him."

"You want me to make him one of my deputies? A man who is well-known as an outlaw?"

Cahill cleared his throat. "Beggin' your pardon, Judge, but I ain't never been convicted of a crime, no matter what folks have said about me. I've got sort of a rough reputation, I won't deny that, but so have some of the other fellas who pack a badge for you."

Parker leaned back against his leather chair and frowned.

"That's true enough, I suppose. But still . . ." He stopped and shook his head. "All right. A vicious gang of killers has been wiped out, and I'm confident that their reign of terror is over. According to Marshal Long, you helped make that possible, Mr. Cahill, so I suppose I will honor his request. If you'd like to go to work for this office as a deputy—once you have fully recovered from your wounds, that is—then you can consider yourself hired."

Cahill grinned. "You won't be sorry, Judge. I'll make a good lawman, just you wait and see."

"Yes, I suppose I'll have to," Parker said with a sigh.

When Longarm and Cahill emerged from Parker's office a few minutes later, Sarah Jane and Jim stood up from the bench in the corridor where they had been waiting. Longarm was walking with a cane, and Cahill carried himself with the stiffness of a man whose entire torso was wrapped tightly in bandages. But both of them were grinning.

"It went all right?" Sarah Jane asked anxiously.

Cahill nodded. "I'm goin' to be a deputy marshal, just like Custis figured out."

"Never thought I'd see the day," Jim said in disgust. "A Cahill packin' a badge. It's plumb disgraceful. You realize that sooner or later you'll probably wind up arrestin' half your own family?"

"Not if you start stayin' on the straight and narrow," Cahill said, poking Jim in the chest with a finger. "I know you're the biggest troublemaker in the Ozarks."

"Me?" Jim yelped. "Hell, I was just tryin' to be like you!"

"Then maybe we can get you a deputy's job, too," Longarm suggested wryly.

Jim looked horrified.

Sarah Jane took Cahill's arm. "Come on, let's get you back to the hotel. You still need a lot of rest. You shouldn't even be up yet."

"Wait just a minute," Cahill said. "There's one more thing . . ." He reached inside the pocket of his coat. "Custis, you remember when I said I had something else to do, that morning before everything that happened at Buzzard's Notch?"

"I remember," Longarm said.

"Well, this is it. I had to hunt up a fella and buy this ring." Cahill turned to Sarah Jane, a gold ring in his fingers, and said, "Sarah Jane, now that I'm, uh, an honest man . . . I reckon . . . would you do me the honor of bein' my wife?"

She put her hand to her mouth. "Oh, my," she said softly. She looked at Longarm. He nodded slowly. He had jobs waiting for him back in Denver. His leg was going to be all right, so he was sure it wouldn't be long before Billy Vail had him out on the trail again, hunting down all sorts of owlhoots. Cahill would face many of the same dangers, but at least working for Judge Parker he would get to stay closer to home.

"Well?" Cahill said. "I'm a wounded man, Sarah Jane, don't do this to me."

"Of course I'll marry you," she said. She put her arms around his neck. "I've always loved you, ever since we were kids."

Longarm caught Jim's eye and inclined his head toward the courthouse doors. They went outside, giving Cahill and Sarah Jane a moment alone.

Gyp Foster was waiting with the wagon that had brought them all to Fort Smith. Longarm and Jim were walking toward the old man when Longarm saw Gyp reach into the back of the wagon and pick up his rifle. "There's one of the bastards now," Longarm heard Gyp say.

Amazingly, Gyp brought the rifle to his shoulder and began to aim at someone down the street.

Longarm lunged forward, the cane in his hand sweeping up and then down to smack into the barrel of Gyp's rifle and knock the weapon down just as the old-timer pulled the trigger. The bullet plowed harmlessly into the street. Longarm grabbed the rifle and wrenched it out of Gyp's hands.

"What the hell do you think you're doing?" Longarm demanded. Jim hurried up right behind him, breathing hard.

Gyp looked at Longarm and frowned in confusion.

"Shootin' Yankees," he said. "I seen one down the street just now. I always shoot Yankees when I see 'em. They killed my boys, you know. All five of my boys gone. Damned war took my wife and my girls away from me, too. Now I don't have anybody." He shrugged. "So I shoot Yankees."

"My God," Jim said. "The crazy old man must think the war's still goin' on."

"Oh, no," Gyp said. "The war's over. But I shoot Yankees anyway. They got it comin'."

Longarm swallowed hard. His mind was spinning. He handed the rifle to Jim, then put a hand on Gyp's arm. "Gyp, why don't you come on in the courthouse with me? I reckon we need to go have a talk with Judge Parker."

Gyp looked suspicious. "He's a Yankee, ain't he?"

"Yeah, but you can't shoot him. You can't shoot anybody else, you hear?"

"Don't know what I'll do if I can't shoot Yankees." Gyp sounded a little like a lost child as he spoke the words.

Longarm led him toward the courthouse steps and started up them toward the big, red-brick building. He knew now why his instincts had made him suspicious of Sarah Jane's visits to Fayetteville and Fort Smith. Gyp had driven her on those trips. Gyp was the one Longarm's gut had been warning him about.

Sarah Jane and Cahill came out of the building and paused at the top of the steps, arm in arm. They looked down at Longarm and Gyp climbing toward them, and Sarah Jane's face went solemn. Did she suspect? Had she known all along what the old man was doing? Longarm didn't believe that, but he didn't want to ask.

"Custis . . . ?" she said as he went by.

"I'll be back out in a little while," Longarm said. "Gyp and me got something to do."

Watch for

LONGARM AND HAUNTED WHOREHOUSE

284th novel in the exciting LONGARM series
from Jove

Coming in July!

Preface to the second edition

This is the second edition of the POPULAR NORTHERN SOTHO – ENGLISH DICTIONARY which was published for the first time in 1971 as the outcome of a wish expressed by my sincere friend the Rev. J. M. Louw, esteemed missionary in the Northern Transvaal and a man who campaigned for the recognition of Northern Sotho in the evangelical field. This book is also meant to serve as a bridge between the different language groups and especially to further the scientific study of Northern Sotho (Sepedi) in our schools. For the same reason the compiler has also compiled two other dictionaries. May these books serve to bring about a better understanding between the various races of South Africa and a love for one another's language!

T. J. KRIEL

N. SOTHO – ENGLISH

A

aatšhi, no!
aba, divide, distribute.
abaganya, distribute.
abela, allocate to, offer, designate, dedicate.
abja, be offered.
abo! oh!
abokato, avocado pear.
abula, crawl.
adibetša, take with both hands.
adile, spread out.
adima, lend, borrow.
adimiša, mortgage, money lending.
adingwa, be lent/borrowed.
adiwa, be spread out.
aena, iron clothes.
aene, iron.
afa? interr., is it? is it so?
afaye? see **afa.**
afe? which? what?
Afrika-Borwa, South Africa.
Afrika-Gare, Central Africa.
aga, build, construct, live.
agaa! yes! I told you so!
agathe, agate.
age! yes!
agee! hail! greetings!
agelela, build (well) up, edify.
ageletša, catch up, fence in.
agente, lawyer.
agiša, cause (help) to build.
agišana, be neighbours; live peacefully together.
agola, catch fire.
agolla, break down, demolish.
agwa lefsa, be rebuilt.
ahlaahlwa, receive attention.
ahlama, become open.
ahlola, to judge.
aka, to tell a lie, prevaricate, hook.
akadibetša, take with both hands.
akalala, to soar, hover.
akalalela, look down upon.
akama, marvel, wonder.
akametša, exclaim in wonder.
akanya, mediate, think, have in mind.
akanyetša, plan, devise, design.
akarela, embrace.
akaretša, sum up, generalize, incude.
akela, tell lies, prevaricate.
akere, acre.
aketša, tell a lie.
akga, throw, swing, sling, hurl.
akga-akgwa, be tossed.
akga diatla, gesticulate; – **dikobo,** pull off clothes.
akga dinao, run, make haste.
akgamala, astonish.
akgatha, boil, simmer, carry on the shoulder.
akgela, lasso, catch.
akgofa, make haste, hurry, hasten.
akgola, catch quickly.
akgoletša, catch for/at.
akhiolotši, archaeology.
ak'o, will you, please.
akoma, hint at, allude to.
akomela, look down upon, be above, peep over.
akwareamo, acquarium.
ala, spread out; – **mabata,** flee.
ala, those.
alafa, cure, attend medically.
alama, hatch, brood.
albamo, album.
ale, those.
alegile, extended.
alemanaka, almanac, calendar.
aletare, altar.
alfabeta, alphabet.
alkoholo, alcohol.
aloga, dismiss, be finished and go home.
alola, spread, roll up.
aloša, dismiss, wean.
altare, altar.
aluminiamo, aluminium.
ama, touch, concern.
amana, connected with.

amandele, almond.
amere, be pregnant.
Amerika, America.
amethiste, amethyst.
amfiteatara, amphitheatre.
aminoesiti, aminoacid.
amoga, take away, deprive of, take by force.
amogela, receive, accept.
amogelwa, be received/accepted.
amole, hammer.
amologa, become divided.
amonia, ammonia.
ampolose, ambulance.
amule, has sucked.
amuša, suckle.
ana? what? now?
ana, swear, venerate or treat as sacred.
ana-anela, speak well of, praise.
ananya, barter.
anathema, curse.
anatomi, anatomy.
anega, spread out in order to dry, to hang out in the sun, to air, tell.
anela, be sufficient for.
anemia, anaemia.
angwa, be touched, involved, concerned.
anise, anise.
a nke, please.
ano, these.
Antatiki, Antarctic.
anolla, select.
anthe, whereas, however, yet.
anthere, anther.
antikriste, antichrist.
antšha, suckle.
anuse, anus, arse.
anya, to suck.
ao! fie, oh.
ao, (aowe), those.
aowa, no, not at all.
aowi! fie, dear me! oh!
apara, dress, wear, put on clothes.
aparata, apparatus.
aparela, cover totally.
apea, cook; – **bjalwa,** to brew beer.
apere, be dressed.
apeša, clothe, cause to dress.
apodiša, cause to undress.
apoga, become undressed, (open) clear.
apola, undress.
apola, apple.
apolekose, apricot
Aporele, April.
apotše, naked, undressed.
araba, answer, reply.
aramela, steam.
areka, ark.
arena, arena.
a-re-tse, we do not know.
aroga, part, become separated, separate.
aroganya, separate.
arola, divide, distribute.
aroša, cause to stray, seduce, mislead.
arubela, inhale.
asbestose, asbestos.
ase, axle.
aše, No, I refuse!
asene, vinegar.
aši, no!
asma, asthma.
aspurini, aspirin.
ata, increase, multiply.
atafala, increase, multiply.
atafetše, has increased.
atemosfere, atmosphere.
atenoite, adenoid.
atha, sling over the shoulder.
athe, whereas, however, yet.
atiša, multiply, aux, v., often.
atla, kiss, make prosperous.
atlafala, become prosperous.
atlase, atlas.
atlatša, stretch out, spread out, make prosperous.
atlega, prosper, become prosperous, make progress, be successful.
atmosfere, atmosphere.

atrese, address.
Australia, Australia.
awela, lie on the back, rest.
ayotine, iodine.

B

ba, these (men, people . . .).
ba, even.
ba, be, become; **go – le,** be with, have, possess.
baa, be!
baagi, builders.
baagišani, neighbours.
baahlodi, judges.
baapei, cooks.
baapostola, apostles.
baasa, master.
baba, be bitter, itch, smart, burn.
babadi, readers.
babaila, walk painfully.
babalela, care for, provide for.
babapadi, players.
babapatši, traders.
Babaso (ba Baso), Africans.
babeakanyi, composers, compilers.
babedi, two (people).
babegi, accusers, plaintiffs.
babela, dehorn, do poker-work.
babelegi, they who give birth.
babelegiši, midwives.
babeodi, shearers, barbers, shavers.
babeši, they who roast, fry or bake.
babetli, carpenters.
babini, dancers, who venerate.
babja, be ill, be indisposed.
babo, theirs.
babohlale, wise men, philosophers.
babola, dehorn, burn, scorch.
babolai, murderers, killers.
baboledi, speakers.
baboleta, the gentle, friendly people.
babolodi, initiates (in the circumcision school).
baboloki, keepers, preservers.
babomotho, relatives.
baboni, seers.
babotegi, trustworthy people.
babotlana, lonely/needy people, the humble.
babotse, handsome (ba-class).
babui, skinners.
babuni, reapers.
babuši, rulers.
badiidi/badiitšana, needy/poor people.
badile, has read.
badima, glisten.
badimo, spirits of the ancestors.
badirabobe, malefactors.
badiradibe, sinners.
badiredi, deacons, servants.
badiša, cause to (read) count.
badiša, herdboys, herds.
baditi, initiated young men who serve at the initiation.
badudi, inhabitants, tenants.
baeng, guests, strangers.
baesa: *baisa.*
baeti, travellers.
bafaladi, emigrants.
bafalaledi, squatters.
bafe, which people.
bafeti, passers-by.
bagolegwa, prisoners.
bagolo, parents, elders.
bagwera, friends.
baheitene, heathens.
bahlabani, soldiers.
bahlale, the wise, wise men.
bahlanka, servants, **-na,** young men.
bahlano, five people.
bahu, the dead (people.)
bahumagadi, ladies.
bai, flash as lightning.
baikaketši, hypocrites.
baipuši, people who govern themselves, who practise self-control.
baisa, chaps, fellows.
Baisrael, Israelites.

baithaopi, volunteers.
baithati, selfish people, egoists.
baithuti, learners, students.
bajalefa, heirs.
baji, eaters.
baka, contend, excite, aspire.
baka, repent, regret.
baka, bake (bread, etc.).
baka, time, reason.
bakgethwa, saints.
bakgomana, nobility, peers, elite.
bakgopo, evil-doers.
bakgotse, friends.
bakhwi, these people.
baki, coat, jacket.
bala, count, read, reckon, include.
bala or **bale,** those (people).
balabala, babble, chatter, complain, mediate.
balahlegi, lost people.
balama, wax (of the moon).
balaledi, people lying in ambush.
balamile, new moon.
balamiša, dry in order to preserve, embalm.
balaodi, directors.
balata, followers, retinue, entourage.
balatedi, followers.
bale, those (people) yonder.
bale, girls in the cicumcision school.
balega, be counted.
balege, go se –, innumerable.
balekane, mates.
balekgetho, publicans.
balekwa, candidates for an exam.
balela, bind round the edges of a thatched roof.
balela, put laths on a roof; v. to choke (as by food).
balemi, ploughmen, hoers.
balephera, lepers.
baleti, guards.
baloki, the righteous.
balola, recount, be nice.
balomatsebe, people who inform quietly or secretly.
balwa le, including.
balwetši; sick people.
bammušo, government, authorities.
bana, children.
bana ba phefo, goose-flesh; **banabešo,** my or our brothers or relatives; **banabeno,** your kinsmen; **banabo,** their kinsmen or people, his brothers.
banamedi, riders, horsemen.
bane, four (people).
banenyana, girls.
bang, some, other.
bangangišani, squabblers, thwarters.
bangwe, some (people).
bakana, (bankane), mates.
banna, men.
bantle, outsiders.
bantši, many, many people.
banyana, little girls.
banyane, small, little ones.
banyatši, despisers.
bao, (baowe), those people.
baokamedi, supervisors.
baopa, barren women.
baopedi, singers.
bapa, stretch, peg a skin on the ground.
bapa, to be parallel, be side by side.
bapadiša, cause to play.
bapaditše, has traded.
bapala, to play; – **ka motho,** to make fun of a person.
bapaletša, exchange for.
bapantšha, (bapanya), compare two things lying next to each other.
bapateletši, oppressors.
bapatša, trade, exchange, barter.
bapela, be parallel or next to each other.
bapetša, compare things (which are next to each other).
baphološwa, redeemed (people).
bapola, crucify, stretch out and peg down.
baprista, priests.

baraloki, players.
barapedi, supplicants.
baratiwa, beloved ones.
baratwa, beloved ones.
barena, gentlemen, chiefs.
baromi, senders.
barongwa, angels.
barudi, smiths.
barukhuhli, conspirators.
baruti, missionaries, parsons, clergy, ministers.
barutiwa, (barutwa), scholars, students or disciples.
barutwana, scholars.
barwa, sons.
barwadi, bearers.
Barwana, Bushmen.
barwedi, daughters.
barwetšana, little daughters.
baša, scoundrels, vagabonds, rogues.
bašabi, traders.
basadi, women.
bašaledi, remainder, rest.
basekiši, prosecutors.
bašele, strangers.
baselina, vaseline.
basenyi, evil-doers, culprits.
basepedi, travellers.
basepediši, directors.
basetsana, girls.
bašimane, boys.
baso, black (people).
basokologi, converts.
bašomi, workers.
bašomi-ka-nna, my colleagues.
bašomišani, staff.
bašoro, fierce (people).
bašwahledi, invaders.
Baswana, Africans.
Bašweu, Europeans.
bata, slap, smite, strike on the ground, plaster.
batabatela, plaster up.
batagana, be next to, close to.
batala, old people.
batalala, crouch, lie flat.
batalatša, cause to lie down.
batamela, approach, come nearer or closer; **ka go batamela,** approximately.
batanya, throw flat on the ground.
batega, plaster roughly, be plastered.
baterepase, spirit-level.
batho, people, public.
batho, middle class.
batho bešo, exclam., good gracious!
bathobi, robbers, masseurs.
bathopi, kidnappers.
bathudi, smiths, repairers.
batimedi, strayers, wanderers.
batlaiši, oppressors, tyrants.
batlaišwa, oppressed.
batola, forge by hammering, sharpen a grinding stone.
batolla, dig up a floor.
batsebalegi, famous people.
batsebi, experts, knowers, authorities.
batswadi, parents.
be, adj., bad, ugly.
be, to be; **e se be mohlomong,** lest.
bea, to quiet, subside, abate.
bea, put, place, lay eggs, bear fruit, appoint, install; – **pelo,** be patient; – **molao,** make a law; – **thapelo,** to offer a prayer; – **molato,** accuse.
beakanya, put in order, arrange, assemble.
beanya, dress (hair); arrange.
beba, esteem, discriminate.
bebefatša, make lighter, reduce weight.
bebenya, glitter, shine, shiver.
bedi, two.
bedile, has boiled.
bediša, boil, foment.
bee, re bêê, stink.
beega, placeable.
beegile, be well placed.
beela, put aside for, put by, allot.
beeleditše, has betrothed, reserved for.
beelela, guarantee.

beeletša, betroth (a woman), give as security.
beetša, pawn, race, cause to compete.
befa, be ugly, be bad or sorrowful.
befediša, enrage.
befela, be angry with.
befelwa, become angry; **befediša,** enrage; **befetša,** enrage.
befile, be ugly or bad.
bega, notify, report, accuse; – **kamogelo,** acknowledge receipt.
bega, weigh.
begela, report to/for.
bego, which was.
beine, wine.
beiša, race, cause to run a race.
beka, cut (meat), split, cleave.
beka, marry.
beke, week, seven days.
bekenya, reflect, glitter, sparkle.
beketla, enchant.
bekiwa, be married.
bela, boil; – **oga,** foam; – **belega,** insist.
bela, insist, insist on payment.
belabela, v., be dissatisfied; n., hot spring.
Belabela, Warmbaths.
belaela, belaetše (pft.), doubt, be uncertain, be anxious about; be displeased with; **belaetša,** displease, make uneasy, cause to doubt; – **lela,** wish for.
belefe, valve.
belega, carry a burden, give birth to.
belege, has carried, has given birth to.
belegiša, act as a midwife.
belegolola, unburden.
beleka, angry.
beletša, hurl, throw for, shoot at.
bene, van, panel van.
beng, masters, owners.
benggadi, lords, masters.
beno, your people.
bentšha, cause to shine.
benya, glisten, glitter, sparkle.
benye, see: **beng.**
beola, shave.
bera, sprinkle, **(bere),** bear.
berebela, bolt a door.
bereka, work (espec. for white people).
beša, make a fire, roast, bake.
beša, keep ahead of, be successful.
bešo, our parents, our people.
bešola, take off the fire.
beta, choke, grasp by the throat.
betana, wrestle, grapple with.
beta pelo, take courage, dare.
betha, hit, strike.
betla, chisel, cut, carve, dress a stone or a piece of wood.
betoga, belch, breathe freely.
betša, throw, shoot, hit, strike.
betši, n. pl., of **ngwetši,** brides, daughters-in-law.
Bibele, Bible.
bidietša, hide, shield.
bidika, roll over.
bile, aux., even.
bileditše, has summoned to.
biletša, call (for) to, summon.
biloga, be agitated, bubble up, become muddy or turbid.
bina, dance, acknowledge an animal, as a totem; – **kela,** dance for.
binabina, dance, hop, frolic.
binika, vinegar.
binne, has danced.
bipa, cover, smother, veil; **bipa taba,** keep secret.
bipela, hide (cover) for, **bipela/bipetšwe,** have indigestion.
bipologa, uncover.
birase, virus.
biro, bureau.
bitia, patch, besmear.
bitiela, put a patch on, cover up.
bitoga, emerge.
bitša, call, name.
bja, of, belonging to.
bjabjara, chatter.

bjabjaretša, crush with the teeth.
bjabjatla, crush.
bjadile, has planted.
bjai (bjang), grass.
bjako, adv., quickly, speedily; n., speed, haste.
bjala, plant.
bjalapeu, robinchat, cuckoo.
bjale, now, then; n., initiation school for girls.
bjalo, thus, so, in this way; **go** –, it is so; **ga go bjalo,** it is not –.
bjalolla, transplant.
bjalwa, beer; – **bja sekgowa,** liquor.
bjana, youth, childhood, infancy.
bjang, n., pl., **ma-,** grass.
bjang? how?
bjebjera, jabber, speak, gibberish.
bjelele, sello se llwe ke –, something has vanished into thin air.
bjera, (bera), sprinkle.
bjetše, has planted; – **tšwe,** is planted.
bjo, this
bjoba, honest, true, good.
bjoko, brains.
bjokhwi, this . . .
bjola, that yonder.
bjona, it.
bjoo, that.
bjouwe, bjowe, that.
boa, come back, return; – **boela,** return repeatedly.
boagi, citizenship.
boaparelo, dressing room.
boapeelo, cookery centre.
boatla, carelessness.
boba, swallow greedily, gulp food down.
boba, decrease, lessen, wane.
bobama, lie flat, hide by stooping.
bobapalelo, playground.
bobare, rumour.
bobe, evil, badness, wickedness.
bobebe, lightness, easiness.
bobedi, second; **la** –, the second day or the second time.
bobedi, pair.
bobeelo, nest.
bobela, abate, subside.
bobete, blood when cooked; coagulated blood.
bobi, a spider's web.
boboana, care, distress.
bobodu, laziness, rottenness.
boboela, spoil.
bobogelo, pavilion, stand.
boboi, fear, timid.
bobola, moan, buzz, hum.
bobolai, murderousness.
bobolokelo, store-room, treasury, garner.
bobona, their (nature), **ya-,** theirs.
bobono, handsomeness, beauty.
bobora, murmur, speak low.
boborana, dread, hide.
bobotlana, smallness, lowliness, modesty.
bobotse, beauty.
bobui, surgery.
bobušakapatla, tyranny.
bobuši, reign.
bodiabolo, devilish.
bodiba, a pool of water, deep hole in a river; abyss.
bodiegi, habit of tarrying, hesitancy.
bodiidi, poverty.
bodika, initiation school.
bodikadiki, hesitancy.
bodikane, circumcision school.
bodikela, west.
bodila, sourness, sour.
bodile, be rotten/bad.
bodilo, wall or floor that has been plastered, plastering.
bodimo, cannibalism.
bodiradibe, sinfulness, sinful nature.
bodiša, caûse to rot.
boditse, hair of the tail, tuft, tassel.
boditše, has told.
boditsi, wild asparagus.
bodufula, become lazy.
bodufatša, make indolent.

bodulabahu, realm of the dead.
bodulo, sitting place, dwelling place, seat.
boduma, rotten, bad, languor.
bodupe, magic, augury.
bodutu, feeling of loneliness, boredom.
boela, come back to, renturn to; **–na,** be reconciled.
boelanya, reconcile.
boelela, repeat.
boeletša, repeat.
boelwa ke, profit by.
boemasekepe, dock.
boemelafofane, airport.
boemo, stature, standing position.
boeng, tšholla –, go on a honeymoon.
boetapele, leadership.
boetelo, visiting place.
boetsana, office of a bridesmaid or bestman, a little wool or hair.
bofa, tie, bind, inspan oxen, heal.
bofa poriki, apply the brake(s).
bofase, lowness.
bofasese, facism.
bofe, which.
bofebe, immorality, prostitution.
bofejana, last child in the family.
bofelo, end, termination.
bofepi, office of one who feeds others.
boferekanyi, distortion.
bofetwa, state of an old maid.
bofetodi, habit of changing.
bofetogi, changeableness.
bofoa, deafness.
bofofane, aviation.
bofofu, blindness.
bofokodi, weakness.
bofolla, untie, loosen; – **mala,** cause the bowels to move.
bofora, falsity, falseness.
bofoši, tendency to err.
bofsa, again, anew.
bofša, be tied.
bofšega, fear, cowardice.
boga, look at, watch.
bogadi, home of one's husband.
bogafa, madness; – **bja mpša,** hydrophobia, rabies.
bogalaka, bitterness.
bogale, blade, sharpness, wrath, bravery, adj., angry, sharp brave, harsh.
bogare, middle, midst.
bogaregare, centre.
bogarigari, deceit, sham.
bogašu, cramp.
bogata, tripe.
bogateledi, oppression.
bogato, step.
bogatsekana, timidness.
bogatšu, cramp.
bogega, worthy to be looked at, beautiful.
bogela, look at/for.
bogobe, porridge, bread.
bogodimo, the top, height.
bogogoma, apparent death.
bogoko, gravy, sauce.
bogola, bark.
bogole, deformity, physical defect.
bogolelo, place where one grows up.
bogolo, size, age, greatness, superannuation.
bogologolo, bygone days, past.
bogolopedi, double-sized.
bogoma, stick-grass.
bogoma, arrogance, arrogant.
bogomo, cattle, end.
bogompana, a beetle that simulates death; **go hwa-,** simulate death.
bogona, presence.
bogopše, species of weed.
bogori, gluttony.
bogorogelo, place of arrival.
bogoši, rule, kingdom, dominion.
bogoši, birth-mark, beauty-spot.
bogošonya, heap of money.
bogotše, has barked.
bogwanta, impudence.
bogwata, roughness.
bogwera, circumcision or initiation

ceremony for boys, friendship.
bohla, brackishness, tastelessness; adv., brackish, tasteless.
bohla, blech.
bohlabapshio, treachery.
bohlabatšatši, east.
bohlabela, east.
bohlagahlaga, adventure.
bohlajana, little wisdom.
bohlale, wisdom, cunning, wise.
bohlanka, office of a servant, servitude.
bohlankana, youth.
bohlano, fifth, fifth part.
bohlanogi, heresy.
bohlapelo, swimming/bathing place.
bohlaswa, imprudence, debauchery, filth, licence.
bohlatse, proof, evidence, testimony.
bohlayatumelo, lack of faith.
bohle, all men, everybody, public.
bohlofo, easy, ease, easily.
bohloki, poverty, want.
bohloko, pain, grief, suffering.
bohloko, poison, venom.
bohlokwa, scarcity, preciousness; adv., scarce, precious, rare.
bohlola, bad conduct, immorality, vice.
bohlologadi, state of a widow or widower.
bohlomogi, sadness.
bohlomphegi, respectability.
bohlonami, sadness.
bohlotlolo, adultery, immorality.
bohlwekišetšo, refinery.
bohlwele, clot of blood; vomiting of gall.
bohlwelo, sojourn.
bohodu, theft, thieving.
bohubedu, red, redness.
bohumanegi, poverty.
bohunamatolo (-maoto), grave.
bohwa, inheritance.
bohwefe, lightness in weight.
bohwirihwiri, roguery, knavery, deceit.
boi, timidity, timid, fearful.
boifa, fear; **boifile,** be afraid of.
boifiša, frighten, cause to fear.
boijane, hopper (locust).
boikaketši, hypocrisy.
boikanyo, confidence, trust.
boikanyologo, mistrust, distrust.
boikarabelo, responsibility.
boiketlo, ease, leisure.
boiketšišo, make-believe.
boikgafo, devotion.
boikgakanyo, disguise; **lebitšo la boikgakanyo,** nom-de-plume.
boikganelo, refusal.
boikgantšho, pride, self-exaltation, vaunting, arrogance.
boikgodišo, self-exaltation, pride.
boikgogomošo, pride, self-exaltation.
boikhutšo, rest, holiday.
boikgafo, devotion.
boikono, fasting.
boile, has returned; **boilwe,** be drunk.
boima, weight, heaviness, hardship.
boimahwefo, light-weight.
boimaima, heavy-weight.
boimaimahwefo, lightheavy-weight.
boimperialeseme, imperialism.
boinyatšo, self-contempt, inferiority.
boiphagamišo, act of raising oneself.
boiphedišo, providing for one's own life, career.
boiphihlo, act of hiding oneself.
boipiletšo, appeal to a higher court.
boipobolo, confession.
boipolao, suicide, self-murder.
boipolelo, confession.
boipoloko, self-preservation, act of keeping oneself.
boipušo, self-government, independence, liberty.
boitaodišaphelo, autobiography.
boitaolo, self-control, independence.
boitapišo, self-trouble.
boitatolo, act of excusing oneself, apology.
boitebalo, act of forgetting oneself.

boitefeletšo, retaliation, requittal, vengeance.
boitekanyo, act of judging one's own value.
boitekolo, self-examination, introspection.
boitemogelo, experience.
boitemogo, self-consciousness.
boithaopo, freewill.
boithapo, a volunteering.
boithatafatšo, act of hardening oneself.
boithatelo, self-will, free will, caprice.
boithato, self-love.
boithomelo, lavatory, W.C., urinal.
boithušo, self-help.
boitišo, keeping watch over oneself.
boitlhabollo, self-development.
boitlhaganelo, haste.
boitlhalošo, act of explaining oneself.
boitlhokomologo, neglect.
boitlhompho, self-respect.
boitlotlo, self-esteem.
boitokafatšo, self-justification, act of pretending to be just.
boitokollo, act of unbinding or freeing oneself.
boitopollo, self-redeeming.
boitsebišo, act of making known what one is.
boitsebo, self-knowledge.
boitshedišo, self-consolation.
boitshepo, self-confident.
boitšhidillo, physical exercise.
boitšhilafatšo, act of defiling oneself.
boitšhireletšo, act of protecting oneself.
boitsholo, self-b!ame, regret.
boitshwarelo, apology, excuse.
boitshwaro, self-control, self-restraint.
boitumelo, joy, gladness.
boitumišo, pride.
boitwelo, self-defence.
boiwa, be drunk.
bojalefa, quality and rights of an heir.
bojato, stinginess, gluttony.
bojelo, dining-saloon, diningroom.
bojeo, flesh (of fruit).
boka, chase, chase away (flies).
boka, gather.
boka, so much, so big.
bokaakaa, quantity, size.
bokae, amount, price.
bokae, whereabouts.
bokagare, inner, inside, interior.
bokala, nicotine.
bokalala, sit quiet and erect.
bokamoso, future – **bjo bo botse,** glorious –.
bokangwana, childlike.
bokantle, the outside, the outer layer or covering.
bokanya, bring together.
bokaone, improvement, recovery; adv., adj., better.
bokapele, the front.
bokapitaliseme, capitalism.
bokatlase, the bottom, lowness.
bo-kea-tseba, those who pretend to know, witch-doctors.
bokebekwa, brigandage.
bokete, somewhere.
bokga, lie flat, lie low.
bokgabane, virtue, artistic beauty.
bokgabo, art.
bokgaetšedi, younger sisters, brothers.
bokgahlo, freezing point.
bokgakala, distance.
bokgalabje, old age (of a man).
Bokgalaka, Rhodesia.
bokgalemo, act of scolding.
bokgalwa, rust.
bokgama, lie down flat.
bokgarakgara, hustling.
bokgarebe, maidenhood, virginity.
bokgekema, petulance, wilfulness.
bokgauswi, nearness.
bokgelogi, heresy.
bokgethego, holiness, sanctity.
bokgethwa, holiness.
bokgobadingwalo, archive(s).
bokgobapuku, library.

bokgogo, fowls.
bokgokgosane, detribalisation.
bokgole, distnace.
bokgomo, cattle.
bokgoni, mastery, skill, know-how.
bokgopo, crookedness, perversity.
bokgosela, sleep like a hare.
bokgwara, roughness.
bokgwari, skill, neatness.
bokhuparele, avarice, miserliness.
bokhutšasetimela, siding, halt.
bokhutšo, place of rest, rest, holiday.
bokhutšwana, brevity, breathing-space, pause, breather; **ka** –, briefly.
bokidi, numbness.
bokobo, ugliness.
bokoka, illness.
bokokolohutwe, herons.
bokokotelo, hairdressing-saloon.
bokokwana, foolishness, obstinate.
bokolla, howl, cry, roar.
bokoma, roasted corn or mealies.
bokominisi, communism.
bokomo, limit.
bokopana, shortness; **ka** –, briefly.
bokosegi, cutworm.
bokosei, silkworm.
bokoti, (a game), touch.
bokoto, thickness.
bokriste, Christianity.
bokubu, hippopotami.
bokwala, clearness.
bokwatla, strength.
bokwefa, smuggling.
bola, let out a secret, report, throw bones, divine.
bola, rot, mould, putrify, decay.
bolabola, chatter, babble.
boladu, pus, matter.
bolaela, kill for; – **ruri,** exterminate, destroy.
bolaeta, brigandage.
bolaile, has killed.
bolaiša, help (cause) to kill, cause to suffer.
bolao, bed, sleeping place.
bolapologelo, place of rest, haven.
bolata, state of being a layman.
bolatla, stinging nettle, "brandboontjie".
bolatswa, cracked lips.
bolawa, be killed, suffer.
bolaya, kill, grieve, injure, hurt badly; – **mabele,** have a large crop.
bolebadi, forgetfulness, absentmindedness.
bolebana, opposite.
bolebe, such and such a person or place.
bolediša, cause to speak.
boledišana, converse, talk.
bolekana, can, small tin.
bolekane, friendship.
boleke, tin, can.
bolela, speak, say, tell; – **tša,** report.
bolele, water moss, seaweed, alga.
bolela, tell to; plead for.
bolema, habit, custoom./**bolemadi,** habit, custom.
bolemi, agricuture.
boleng, existence.
bolepa, spider's web, cobweb, birdlime.
bolepu, cobweb, spider's web, birdlime.
bolesome, tenth.
boleta, soft, smooth.
boletiana, little, soft.
boletla, stinging nettle.
boletše, spoken, proclaimed, told.
boletswa, bird-lime.
bolkano, volcano.
bolla, get circumcised, **se bolle,** be uncircumcised.
bollo, hot.
bollonyana, little hot.
bolo, ball, football.
boloi, witchcraft.
boloka, save, preserve, bury.
bolokega, become saved, preserved.
bolokegile, be saved, preserved, secure.

bolokiša, cause to preserve.
bolokišetšo, workshop.
boloko, dung, cow-dung.
bolokwane, necklace made of grass.
bololla, reveal, disclose (secret).
bololo, lukewarm.
bolomo, flower.
bolongwane, sores on the mouth.
bolosaka, woolsack.
boloto, bare-back, volt.
bolotša, circumcise, let out cattle.
bolotsana, wickedness, fraud.
bolotšwe, be circumcised.
bolumo, volume.
bolwetši, disease, sickness, illness.
bomadimabe, bad luck, fate, ill luck, misfortune.
bomalome, uncles.
bomaminana, kids, toddlers, tiny tots.
bomang, who, whom.
bomang-le-mang, everybody.
bomapimpane, kids, toddlers.
boMarkseseme, Marxism.
bomašianoke, hammer-heads, mudlarks (birds).
bomedišetšo, nursery.
bommankgaganyane, bats.
bommaseletswane, mantes.
bommatswale, mothers-in-law.
bomme, mothers, mother.
bomodimo, godhead, divinity.
bomoloko, descendants, relatives.
bomorwarra, brothers.
bomoswe, polecats.
bomotswala, cousins.
bomotswalagwe, his/her relatives.
bomumu, dumbness, muteness.
bona, they, them.
bona, see, look, get, find.
bonabo, enmity.
bonagala, visible, evident.
bonagatša, expose, reveal.
bonako, the proper time, in time.
bonana, see each other.
bonang! look! behold!
bonatla, courage, vigour.
bone, have seen, experienced.
bone, fourth.
bonegela, give light, shine for.
bonela, see for.
bonepi, marksmanship.
bong, gender.
bongaka, medical (practice).
bonganga, obstinancy, stubbornness.
bonggohle, common gender.
bongtona, masculine gender.
bongwana, childishness.
bongwe, other.
bongwetši, pertaining to a bride or daughter-in-law.
bonkane, friendship.
bonna, I myself.
bonna, manliness, manhood; **nna ka** –, I myself.
bonno, dwelling place, seat, sitting place.
bonoge, divining art, divination.
bonokwane, cheating, roquery; **go sepediša** –, cheat and rob.
bonolo, softness, meekness, easiness.
bonong, depraved appetite like a vulture's.
bonono, fatness.
bontle, the outside.
bontšha, show, prove.
bontši, majority, multitude.
bontšintši, great multitude.
bonwelo, drinking-place.
bonya, slowness; adj., slow; v., wink.
bonyane, smallness, littleness; adj., small.
bonyefodi, habit of swearing.
bonyelele, rheumatism, numbness, arthritis.
bonyenyane, smallness, adj., little.
bonyonyo, small black ant.
bookamedi, superintendence.
bookelo, nursing home.
boola, cut off their hair as a sign of mourning.
boologa, turn back.

boomo, on purpose, **ka** –, purposely, deliberately.
boona, ka –, by itself.
boopa, stinging-nettle, barrenness, sterility.
boore = **boori.**
boori, withchweed, mildew.
booswa, (boušwa), porridge.
bootswa, adultery.
bopa, bellow, roar, sulk.
bopa, sulk, be peevish.
bopa, mould, create, fashion, model.
bopaki, proof, testimony.
bopama, grow thin (lean).
bopapetla, flatness, level.
bopele, forefront, penis.
bopelela, follow in line, walk in single file.
bopelonolo, meekness, tenderness.
bopelontsho, sadness.
bopelopedi, double-mindedness.
bopelotelele, patience, endurance.
bopelothata, hardness of heart.
bopelotshehla, jealousy.
bopelotšhweu, goodness, kindness.
bophaiphai, folly, stupidity.
bophale, magic, witchcraft, sorcery.
bophaphathi, flatness, breadth.
bophara, breadth, width, detail.
bophaswa, black and white colour in males.
bophatlalatša, obviousness.
bophelephethe, cunning.
bophelo, life, health.
bophiri, wolfishness.
bophirima, west.
bophirimatšatši, west, sunset.
bophirimela, west.
bophodisa, police service.
bopholo, oxen.
bophukubje, jackals.
bopitla, narrowness.
bopolola, undo.
bopologa, become undone, sulk.
boponopono, nakedness.
bopontšheng, obviousness, in public.
boprista, priesthood.
bopša, be moulded.
bopudi, goats.
bopula, carry on the back.
boputlatšatši, a line north-south.
boputswa, greyness, grey colour.
bora, bow; – **le mosebe,** bow and arrow, v., bore̹ (a hole).
bora, poison (on an arrow-head).
borabora, mumble, mutter.
borabele, rebelliousness.
boradia, cunning, underhandedness, perfidy.
borakgadi, aunt(s), sisters of one's father.
borakgolo, grandfathers, grandpa.
borakgolokhukhu, ancestors.
borala, shelf, shelf on top of a wall.
borale, iron ore.
borama, lie flat on the ground, crumple up.
boramaaka, liers.
borangwane, uncle, uncles.
boranyana, vague, faint.
borapedi, prayerfulness, piety.
borara, father, our fathers.
borare, father(s), ancestors; **bošego bja** –, early in the morning.
boraro, third; – **bja,** the three of.
boreatseba, witch-doctors, people who pretend to know everything.
boreba, cheeck, impudence.
boreelo, leina la –, nickname.
borekereke, trembling, shaking.
borekhu, gum, juice of tree.
boreledi, smoothness, slipperiness; adj., smooth, slippery.
borena, chieftainship, kingship, authority.
borere, jelly.
borethe, smooth, slippery.
boretse, mud, clay.
bori, mildew, blight, withchweed.
boriba, plateau, escarpment, moss.
borifi, letter.

borile (ditsebe), put the ears backwards, flatten the ears.
boripa, adv., shortly; n., shortness, brevity.
boripana, ka –, shortly, briefly.
borite, smoothness.
boro, drill, auger.
borobalelo, sleeping place.
borobalo, accommodation.
borobedi, eight.
borobong, nine.
borofa, paw; **borofa bja tau,** the plant "vingerpol".
borofo, rough play.
boroga, curse.
borogata, borehole.
Boroka, Low Veld in Tvl.
borokgo, trousers; – **bja phupha,** wide trousers, Oxford bags.
borokgwana, knicker.
borokhu, gum, juice of a tree.
boroki, tailoring.
boroko, sleepy, drowsiness, drowsy.
boroku, gum, juice.
bororo, drowsy, heap (beads).
borotho, bread.
borotlolo, carrot.
borotsogo, handdrill.
borui, animal husbandry.
boruma (borume), soft, tender.
borumulano, strife, annoyance.
borutho, heat.
boruti, ministry.
borutiwa, discipleship.
borwa, south, south wind.
borwana, small drill, bit.
borwerwe, go kwa –, hear indistinctly.
bošaedi, carelessness, negligence.
bosafeleng, eternity, everlasting.
bošakašaka, cheating, intrigue.
bosana, nice.
bosasa, tomorrow morning, in the morning, dawn.
bosatsebjeng, the unknown.
bosatšhabego, fearless(ness).
bose, n., sweetness; adj., adv., sweet, nice.
bosea, infancy.
bosebi, gossip.
bosebokae, few.
bosegi, dressmaking.
bošego, n., night; adv., at night; – **gare,** midnight.
bosehla, yellow(ness).
boseka, bangle.
bosele, softly, slowly.
boselela, sixth.
bosemangmang, some people.
bosenyane, ninth.
boselo, place where food is found.
bosenyi, mischief.
bosesane, thinness, narrowness, fineness.
boseswai, eight.
bosetsana, girlhood.
bošidi, moist(ure), damp(ness).
bošilo, folly, foolishness.
bošimane, boyhood.
boširelo, shelter.
bošiwana, state of being an orphan.
boso, n., blackness; adj., black, dark.
boso, weather.
bosobatšatši, west.
bosobela, west.
bosodi, blame, blot, stain, want, defect.
bosogana, youth.
bosole, military service.
bošolopudi, folly.
bosome, tenth part.
bošoro, violence, violent, cruel(ty).
bosošiale, socialism.
bošuana, state of being an orphan.
bošula, evil, insipidity; adj., bad, tasteless.
bošupa, seven, seventh.
boswa, porridge.
bošwata, a craving for meat.
bošweu, white(ness).
bota, trust.
bota, plaster.

botagwa, drunkenness.
botala, old age, greenness, blue (colour); – **bja legodimo,** blue.
botalanyana, vendure, greenness.
botatabo, their fathers.
botatarena, botatago rena, our fathers.
botate, our fathers, father.
botebo, depth.
botee, unity, singular, one(ness).
botega, be trustworthy.
botegela, be loyal.
boteketeke, shakiness, looseness.
botelele, length; adj., long.
boteme, stammering, stuttering.
botemepedi, double-tonguedness.
boteng, interior, inside.
botengteng, innermost, interior.
botengwa, lottery, gamble.
botetema, shakiness, wavering.
botha, gather.
botha, lie down, subside.
bothaka, children of the same age, friends.
bothakga, cleanliness, neatness; adj., refined, tidy.
bothama, squat down.
bothata, hardness, difficulty; adj., hard, difficult; – **nyana,** a little difficult.
bothega, gather.
bothegela, gather at/for.
bothepa, girlhood, maidenhood.
bothiša, cause to lie down/gather.
bothitho, heat, warmth; adj., hot.
botho, kindness.
bothokgo, compulsory service in the chief's garden.
botholo, poison, deafness.
bothôlô, herd of kudu.
bothologa, rise and depart.
bothopša, captivity.
bothotho, stupidity, dull(ness), opaque.
bothulatšhipi, metal-work.
bothumaša, girlhood.
bothwaadi, championship.
bothwadi, state of being a hireling.
bothwethwelo, runway.
botile, plastered, trusted.
botimedi, state of being lost.
botla, antidote against witchcraft.
botla, bellow, roar.
botlaela, folly.
botlalo, fullness, abundance.
botlamegi, guardianship.
botlana, humble.
botlase, lowness, bottom.
botlatla, foolishness.
botlemetleme, idiocy.
botlepetlepe, idiocy.
botlolo, bottle.
botlwaollong, reformatory.
botoga, arrive, go up.
botogela, go up to.
botona, masculinity, state of being a councillor.
botoro, butter.
botša, tell, ask.
botsana, dim., somewhat beautiful.
botšana, tell one another.
botse, beauty, beautiful, graceful.
botsebitsebi, polytechnical.
botsebotse, very beautiful.
botsefatša, beautify.
botseno, entry, entrance.
botšhabelo, place of refuge.
botšheba, jealousy, envy.
botshephegi, fairness, integrity.
botšhepi, grandeur.
botšididi, cold.
botšikiri, abundance of money.
botšiša, question, ask.
botšišiša, inquire carefully.
botšofadi, old age.
botsororo, crying (of birds).
botsorwana, a stringed instrument.
botšwa, laziness; be told.
botswadi, parenthood.
botšwafa, laziness.
botumo, fame, renown.
boušwa, porridge.

bouta, v., vote.
bouto, n., vote.
bowena, you yourself.
boyena, himself, herself.
boyo, destination.
boyona, ka –, by itself.
bua, skin, flay, operate.
budula, blow; – **tše,** has blown.
budulala, become shut (of the eyes).
budule, has ripened, is cooked.
budulela, blow into.
budulla (mahlo), open the eyes.
buduloga, swell out, become inflated, become opened of the eyes.
budulola, open the eyes.
budutša, glean.
buela, skin for/at.
buka, book; see: **puku.**
bula, open.
buna, harvest.
bupi, meal, flour.
buša, reign, govern.
buša, send back, return; – **šetša,** restore to; – **šetšwe,** be restored to.
buša moya, breathe.
bušeletša, repeat, repay.
butšwa, ripen, get cooked.
butšwela, blow the fire.
butšwetša, blow the fire, aspirate.
butšwitše, be ripe or cooked.

D

Dafida, David.
dahlia, dahlia.
depot, depot.
diabolo, devil; **bo** –, devilish.
diadia, delay.
diagente, agents.
diakaboi, handcuffs, shackles.
diako, ears of corn wheat.
diala, plumes, **rweša** –, praise.
dialetare, altars.
dialoga, girls from the initiation school.
diamandele, almonds.
diamuši, mammals.
diano, tribal totems, objects of veneration.
diaparo, clothes.
diapola, (diapole), apples.
diase, axles.
diatla, hands; **go rwala** –, cry, despair; **bodile** –, be lazy.
diba, stop; see: **thiba.**
dibabo, rash.
dibakete, buckets.
dibano, incense.
dibarwana, detours, mischief.
dibatana, beasts of prey.
Dibatsela, November.
dibe, sins.
dibego, tribute.
dibenyabje, jewellery.
dibere, bears.
dibešo, hearths, grates.
dibešwa, fuel.
dibetša, weapons, ammunition.
dibja, jugs, crockery, cutlery.
dibjalo, plants.
dibjana, crockery.
dibo, fortresses, castles, ramparts.
diboba, large flies, gad-flies.
dibodu, lazy people.
dibofša, prisoners.
diboga, capsize, topple
Dibokwane, February.
dibolang, organic matter.
dibolao, weapons.
dibolawa, prey, spoil.
dibopiwa, creatures.
dibothwana, clusters.
dibotse, beautiful (things).
didiba, wells.
didietša, shriek, trill, jubilate.
didile, has smeared (the floor).
didimo, sacrificial animals for idols.
didimoša, cause to shudder.
didirišwa, apparatus, equipment.
didulo, stools.
didupe, magicians, witch-doctors.

diega, delay.
dieie, onions.
diela, liquids.
diemere, buckets.
dienywa, fruit.
diesela, (diesele), donkeys.
dieta, shoes.
dietša, lights.
difahlogo, faces.
difaka, fore-arms.
difaro, lap.
dife? which?
difepammele, nourishment, nutrition.
difero, passages, entrances.
difilimi, films
difiwa, data, gifts.
difoa, deaf people.
difofu, blind people.
difola, tobacco.
diforeime, frames.
difoto, photographs.
diga, cast down.
digafe, mad people.
digafing, mental hospital.
digagabi, reptiles.
diganka, valiant men.
diganetšwa, things prohibited.
digantšatša, food prepared by chief's wife for a guest.
digarafo, spades.
digayo, incisions, engravings.
digela, thrown down, praise, – **fase,** dash to the ground.
digempe, shirts.
digoboga, thugs, rogues, hooligans.
digogobi, reptiles.
digogoropo, felloes of a wheel.
digokgo, spiders.
digoro, bow-legged person(s), leggings.
digwagwa, frogs.
digwai, spirits.
digwe, loops.
digwebakamarago, prostitutes.
digwete, edible roots.
digwetla, loose-hanging horns.
dihempe, shirts.
dihla, seasons.
dihlabelo, sacrifices.
dihlano, five.
dihlakahlaka, islands.
dihlapelo, basins, baths.
dihlare, trees, medicine.
dihlašana, small trees, shrubs.
dihlatse, witnesses.
dihlaya, drawers.
dihlodi, peas, a small Native variety.
dihlong, shame, modesty; **go welwa ke** –, be shy.
dihlopha, groups.
dihlora, tops, summits.
dihuba, chests, cough.
dihuswane, small livestock.
dihwahwa, epileptic fits.
dihwirihwiri, rogues, rascals.
diila, be poor, be in need or want.
diila, taboo, things not permitted.
diiri, hours.
dijagobe, gluttons.
dijesi, jerseys.
diji, eaters.
dijo, food; **-nyana,** a little food.
dika, surround, tarry: n., signs, metaphor.
dikabelo, alms, offering.
dikae? how many?
dikagare, contents.
dikago, building material.
dikakabalo, perplexities.
dikakanyo, thoughts, meditations.
dikala, boughs, branches, council of the chief.
dikalana, small branches, umbilical cords.
dikamase, leggings.
dikamela, camels.
dikamora, rooms.
dikampa, camps.
dikanela, encircle, besiege, surround.
dikanetša, surround, besiege.
dikanono, cannon.
dikapa, shades, hoods, capes.

dikapilari, capillary tubes.
dikapolelo, second-hand clothes.
dikapukapu, big ears, long ears.
dikariki, carts.
dikarogo, transgressions, deviations.
dikarolo, parts.
dikata, wild hemp, lots.
dikatana, luggage, pack, rags.
dikateng, entrails, bowels.
dikatlo, kisses.
dikaušo, socks, stockings.
dike, rad., **re** –, surround, set.
dikebeka, brigands, highwaymen.
dikei, yoke-skeys.
dikeketane, stubble.
dikela, go round, set (sun.)
dikelela, go round to.
dikeledi, tears.
dikeleketlana, small things, mannerisms.
dikeletšo, advice.
dikeloboima, weights.
dikemola, pimples.
dikeno, aoths, vows.
dikenywa, fruit.
dikepe, boats, ships.
dikete, thousands.
diketlele, kettles.
diketo, five-stones (a game).
diketše, has set/gone round.
diketswana, little boats.
dikgabišo, ornaments, decorations.
dikgabo, monkeys, flames.
dikgadika, greaves, cracklings.
dikgadima, flashes of lightning.
dikgaetšedi, younger sisters/ brothers.
dikgaga, caves.
dikgaga, pangolins.
dikgagara, knuckle-bones.
dikgaka, guineafowl.
dikgaketla, sheets of ice.
dikgakgamatšo, wonders.
dikgakgara, knuckle-bones.
dikgala, spaces.
dikgalabje, old men.
dikgalefo, anger.
dikgalo, berries of the wait-a-bit thron(tree).
dikgamathi, bark (of a tree).
dikgampane, cocopans.
dikgampi, total darkness; **mahlo ke** –, eyes that reveal age and suffering.
dikgang, strife.
dikganyogo, desires.
dikgaokgaotša, staccato.
dikgaola, young initiates.
dikgapa, calabashes, sockets, bows, rams.
dikgapetla, shells, shards, scales.
dikgara, breast, chests.
dikgata, skulls.
dikgati, sticks, beating, punishment.
dikgatlo, confluence.
dikgato, steps.
dikgekolo, old women.
dikgepetla, scales, shards.
dikgepetlana, fragments, shall shards.
dikgerekgere, tools.
dikgero, nutshells, nuts, chips.
dikgeru, nutshells.
dikgetla, shells.
dikgetlo, edged, toothed.
dikgoba, spaces, opening.
dikgobadi, injured people.
dikgobe, tears, boiled cereals.
dikgobe, fish.
dikgobedi, injured people.
dikgobjana, small fish, peppercorn hair.
dikgobololo, insults.
dikgodišo, praises.
dikgofa, ticks.
dikgofe, palms of the hands.
dikgoge, hooks, clasps.
dikgogetša, hooks.
dikgogo, fowls.
dikgogo, crusts, scabs.
dikgogodi, washings-up, flotsam.
dikgokabadiša, games for herdboys.
dikgokelo, hinges.
dikgokgoilane, ankles.

dikgokgokgo, sweet-potatoes; **go ntšha,** –, curry flavour.
dikgokolo, discs, quarters of an orange.
dikgokong, gnu, wildebeest.
dikgolo, big.
dikgolokgothwane, wild grapes.
dikgolomelo, sighs.
dikgomo, cattle; – **tshadi,** cows.
dikgong, wood, timber, firewood.
dikgoni, professionals.
dikgono, broken pieces.
dikgonye, firewood.
dikgopa, snails.
dikgopelo, petitions, requests.
dikgopišo, offences, stumbling-blocks.
dikgopo, ribs.
dikgora, hedges.
dikgorane, rich people.
dikgoro, entrances, gateways, clans, tribes.
dikgorogoro, rattletrap, ramshackles.
dikgoroto, bullies, champions.
dikgošana, petty chiefs.
dikgoši, chiefs, kings.
dikgothalo, encouragement.
dikgotho, male dogs.
dikgotswana, cutlets.
dikgotšwana, small-rib.
dikgwa, forests, thickets.
dikgwama, purses.
dikgwana, small forests, black and white fem. animals.
dikgwara, pangolins.
dikgwari, neat persons.
dikgweng, in the bushveld.
dikhamera, cameras.
dikhamphani, companies.
dikhanakhana, chilli (cayenne) pepper.
dikhastamo, custom-house.
dikhokho, togs.
dikholofedišo, promises.
dikholofelo, expectations.
dikholofetšo, promises.
dikhomotšo, consolations.
dikhouni, coniferous trees, cones.
dikhuba, chests, breasts, expectorations.
dikhunkhwane, insects.
dikhupamarama, secrets.
dikhuru, knees.
dikhunwane, toes, (dial).
dikhutlo, corners, stops.
dikhutlopewa, fixed points.
dikhwama, purses.
dikhwiri, quails.
dikilokramo, kilogrammes.
dikiša, cause to go round/surround.
diko, sense-organs.
dikobi, hooks.
dikobo, blankets, clothes.
dikodi, spots, stains.
dikojaba, guavas.
dikokobele, flying-ants.
dikokoilane, ankles.
dikokolohute, herons.
dikokontwane, pegs.
dikokwane, pillars, posts.
dikologa, revolve, go round, roll.
dikoloi, waggons.
dikolomelo, grief, mourning.
dikološa, turn, cause to turn.
dikoloto, debts.
dikoma, secrets, ceremonial images.
dikomana, ceremonial drums.
dikomokomo, gooseberries.
dikomoto, shackles, fetters.
dikompase, compasses.
dikompo, compounds.
dikomporomai, swings.
dikopelo, songs
dikoro, weeds.
dikoša, songs, dances.
dikota, timber, poles, posts.
dikoti, holes.
dikotlelo, basins, dishes.
dikotlopo, quivers for arrows.
dikotse, shields.
dikotsi, dangers.
dikoto, thick ones.
dikoto, sections.
dikotwane, epilepsy.

dikrosari, groceries.
dikudumela, sweat, perspiration.
dikuntwana, epilepsy.
dikuranta, newspapers.
dikuswana, small-stock.
dikutla, hooks, pegs.
dikutu, stems, trunks.
dikwala, neat people.
dikwana, lambs.
dikwankwetla, giants, strong men.
dikwapi, dried fruit.
dikwata, poles.
dikwelemi, spoil-sports, wet blankets.
dikwena, crocodiles.
dikwete, group-leaders.
dikwi, sense-organs, sensory nerves.
dila, smear a floor (or wall) with dung.
dilaesense, licences.
dilahlwa, excretion, night-soil.
diledu, chins.
dilei, sledges.
dileketlana, trinkets.
dilepe, axes.
dilete, regions.
diletšo, musical instruments.
dilewa, edible things.
diliki, leeks.
dilitara, litres.
dillo, weeping, tears.
dilo, things.
diloba, tribute.
dilofo, di lô fô, loaves of bread.
dilogwa, textiles.
diloka, stick-grass.
dilokwata, loquats.
dilola, look round.
dilomi, things that bite.
diloro, dreams.
dilotelo, keys.
dilwana, small things.
dimaake, ground-nuts.
dimaekorofone, microphones.
dimaele, miles.
dimakatšo, wonders.
dimapolo, pegs.
dimaswi, dairy-products.
dimatla, pancakes.
dimedi, flora.
dimeko, rinds of sugar-cane.
dimela, plants, vegetation.
dimpa, bellies.
dimola, snatch away;
dimpe, bad(things).
dimpho, gifts.
dimpša, dogs.
dimpsha, new (things).
dimuma, the dumb or mute.
dinaelone, nylon goods.
dinaga, lands, countries.
dinaka, horns, flutes, whistles, orchestra; – **na,** feelers, small horns.
dinakaladi, small edible bulbs, "uintjies, euntjies".
dinako, times.
dinala, nails; many-coloured animals.
dinalana, little nails/holes.
dinalete, needles.
dinama, meat.
dinamane, calves.
dinamelwa, vehicles, carriages.
dinana, the pubes, rain-frogs.
dinanahla, tiptoes; adv., on tiptoe.
dinanana, small things.
dinao, feet.
dinare, buffaloes.
dinatla, strong men, the mighty, heroes.
dinawa, beans.
dine, four.
dingalo, bruises.
dingame, sponges.
dingangele, obstinate people.
dingope, gutters, furrows.
dingwalelo, stationery.
dingwathi, cutlery.
dingwe, other.
dinkeketane, stubble.
dinkgwa, loaves of bread.
dinko, nose, noses, nostrils.
dinku, sheep.
dino, drink; – **fufula,** mineral waters.

dinobi, otters.
dinoka, rivers; – **na,** rivulets.
dinoka, loins.
dinoko, spices, hedgehogs.
dinokwane, rogues, rascals.
dinolofatši, facilities, amenities.
dinone, blesbuck.
dinong, vultures; **iphoša** –, arrive.
dinonnori, surprises.
dinonwane, fables, stories related in chant or dialogue.
dinonyana, birds.
dinopodi, select.
dinose, honey (bees).
dinošo, wedding gift (drink).
dinote, notes, synods.
dinotlelo, keys.
dinta, lice.
dintasteri, industries.
dinte, strings.
dinteo, stripes.
dintepa, skirts, aprons.
dinthe, shafts.
dintho, sores, wounds; **ntšha** –, wound.
dinthoba, holes.
dinti, strings.
dintlanya, bicycle.
dintlha, ends, peaks, sharp points.
dintlho, berries of the waterbessieboom.
dintlhwa, ants, termites.
dintotoma, dumps.
dintšhi, shores, flies, eyebrows.
dintšhu, eagles.
dintšhwe, sugar-cane.
dintši, many.
dintwa, wars, battles.
dinwamadi, bloodthirsty people.
dinwelo, cups.
dinyakwa, demand, things wanted.
dinyane, small (things/animals).
dinyatši, paramours.
dinyebu, boiled beans.
dinyepo, riddles.
dinyeunya, swarms.
dio, just, only.
dioka, huge animals, big men.
diokobatši, drugs, narcotics.
diolo, ant-hills.
diopedi, singers, vocalists (of fame).
diorelo, spices.
diorisi, horrors, delirium tremens.
diota, fools, idiots.
diotswa, adulterers.
dipabe, (dipabi), pop-corn.
dipadi, scars.
dipadišo, readers.
dipaka, (dipaki), witnesses.
dipala, goal-posts, marks on the body made by fire, scalds.
dipale, marks on the body made by fire.
dipale, mealies cracked by roasting.
dipalelo, bindings round the tops of hedges, laths.
dipalo, sums, arithmetic, numbers.
dipampiri, papers.
dipanana, bananas.
dipanka, banks, benches.
dipantetše, bandages.
dipapadi, plays, games, sports.
dipapatšo, merchandise.
dipara, bars, pubs.
dipasa, passes.
dipataka, mosaic.
dipatla, sticks.
dipatlabokwana, handcuffs.
dipatlelo, open spaces, market places.
dipato, sticks used for threshing, spattles.
dipatolo, anvils, hard stones used for sharpening millstones.
dipatso, spots, stains.
dipego, see: **dipeo.**
dipejama, pyjamas.
dipeke, picks.
dipeketsane, spectacles, glasses.
dipela, rock rabbits, xylophones.
dipeo, twigs or grass placed in a pot to prevent the water from spilling.
dipeolwane, swallows.

dipetlo, adzes, scrapers.
dipeu, seeds.
dipeudi, style or fashion or wearing the hair.
diphafana, calabashes, beer, liquor; jars.
diphahlo, goods, luggage.
diphaka, fore-arms.
diphala, impala, rooibuck.
Diphalana, October.
diphao, hives, holes in a tree, fence-poles.
diphapano, disputes, quarrels.
diphaphatha, flat cakes.
diphaphati, tablets.
diphara, division between the nates, bitter melons.
dipharelankong, lizards, S.A. rock-lizards.
dipharo, clefts in a rock fissures.
dipharoganyo, opposites.
diphasela, parcels.
diphata, forked, divided as branches.
diphate, sticks, hides.
diphatla, foreheads.
diphatša, chips.
diphedi, living animals.
diphefo, winds.
diphegelo, panting, sighs.
diphegišano, competitions.
diphego, wings.
dipheko, charms.
diphepheng, scorpions.
diphetogo, changes.
diphihlo, secrets.
diphikoko, peacocks.
diphilisi, pills.
dihiri, hyenas, wolves.
diphogo, fontanelles.
diphohla, groups.
diphoko, strong drink.
diphone, blisters.
diphoofolo, game, wild animals.
diphopho, pawpaws.
diphororo, waterfalls.
diphošo, mistakes, faults, misses.
diphoto, gate-posts.
diphukubje, jackals, foxes.
diphuphu, eyelids.
dipikiri, nails.
dipilisi (diphilisi), pills.
dipitša, pots.
dipitsi, horses, zebra.
dipitšo, gatherings, meetings.
dipoamoše, old men.
dipolai, tusks.
dipolelo, talk, assertions.
dipolokelo, barns, granaries.
dipompong, sweets.
dipong, sore eyes.
diporiki, brakes.
diporing, springs, (steel-).
diporo, railway lines, rails.
diporogwana, baggage.
diporompeta, trumpets.
dipositi, deposit.
dipotšišo, questions.
dipoudi, style of wearing the hair.
dipounama, lips.
dipowana, small/young bulls.
diprofeto, (diporofeto), prophecies.
dipshio, kidneys.
dipudi, goats.
dipudi, ringworm.
dipududu, grey, old people.
dipuno, harvests.
diputšane, kids.
dira, make, do, work, do to.
di'ra, a hostile army, troops.
diragala, happen.
diraka, shelves.
diramphašane, sandals.
diranta, rand (money).
dirantabola, round huts.
dirapa, gardens, graveyards.
diraro, three.
direga, be done.
direkhoto, records.
direla, do for, serve, minister to; **direla boroko,** work (for love) without receiving pay.
direthe, heels.

direti, poets.
diretlo, entrails.
direto, praises, poems.
diripa, pieces.
diriša, cause (help) to do.
dirite, stubble.
dirithene, quarterly returns.
dirolla, undo.
dirope, thighs, hind legs.
diroto, baskets.
diroto, big baboons, industrious people.
dirotwana, small baskets.
diruiwa, domestic animals.
dirukguhli, rebels.
dirulelo, thatch.
dirumola, firebrands.
diruo, possessions.
dirupu, tloga ka –, run away.
dirurubele, butterflies.
diruthamatswalo, fearful things.
dirwalo, coverings for head or feet, load, pack.
diša, herd, watch over.
disala, saddles.
disasedi, whirlwinds.
disaweleng, ja –, have a hard time.
disebi, tell-tales
dišebo, titbits.
disegi, cutworms.
disegišabaeng, dimples.
dišego, large grain baskets.
disego, laughter.
dišego, grain-baskets, grainaries.
diseila, sails.
disekele, sickles.
disekerete, cigarettes.
disele, celles.
diselo, food, grain.
Disemere, December.
disenyi, evildoers.
diseto, carvings.
dišikara, poles for carrying.
disilibera, silver pieces.
dięiro, curtains, veils, blinds.
diso, black.
dišo, sores, ulcers.
disohlo, cuds.
disokisi, socks.
disola, food served up, soles.
dišoro, fearful things.
dišothi, shorts.
dišotšhweu, diphtheria.
dišu, dry cow-dung.
dišuana, orphans.
disutu, suits.
diswantšho/betlwa, images, statues.
diswanyane, news, rumours.
diswaro, money.
diswikiri, sugar.
diswiri, lemons.
dita, teach at an initiation school.
ditaamane, diamonds.
ditaba, matters, affairs.
ditaeledi, messages.
ditaelo, instructions, commandments.
ditaese, dice cube.
ditaetšo, message(s).
ditafola, tables.
dita'la, green or blue (things).
di'tala, old (things).
ditalente, talents.
ditamati, tomatoes.
ditanka, tanks.
ditao, commands, statutes, footsteps.
ditaola, divination, knuckle-bones.
ditaolo, commandments.
ditapola, potatoes.
ditasi, mission stations.
ditatlele, dates.
ditau, lions; – **tona,** lions, cabinet ministers.
ditebane, by rights, things one deserves.
ditebogo, thanks.
ditedu, beard, beards.
ditee, ones; – **someng,** tenths.
ditefa, remuneration, ransom, fees.
ditefišo, fine.
ditela, wait for, delay.
ditelele, lone things.
diteme, rolling of "r", lisp.

ditempe, postage-stamps.
diterebe, grapes.
diterekere, tractors.
diteselepomo, shafts, beams.
ditete, spittle.
dithaba, mountains.
dithabe, branches, tributaries, hiccoughs, subordinate clauses.
dithabišaphelo, that which gladdens the heart, joy in the heart.
dithaele, tiles.
dithaere, tyres.
dithafelo, honey jars, quarries.
dithaka, mates, comrades.
dithaka, pips, glands, seeds of the **leraka,** eye-balls, tonsils.
dithakangwaga, first-fruit.
dithakola, fruit of the guarri-tree.
dithala, scaffolding, galleries.
dithalo, berries, drawings, sketches.
dithaloko, games.
dithama, cheeks.
dithapa, sides.
dithapelo, prayers.
dithapo, cords, stones, kernels.
ditharaang, encumbrances.
ditharane, climbers (plants).
dithata, (dithate), poles, firm things; adj., hard.
dithathanyana, crumbs.
dithapelo, prayers.
dithebele, medicine bags.
dithebola, booty, loot.
ditheka, loins.
dithekgo, snuff-boxes.
dithekniki, techniques.
dithele, udders.
dithemo, choppings.
dithepa, calabashes, gourds.
ditherabolare, travellers.
dithete, cutworms, caterpillars.
dithethenkgwane, sticks, – for traps.
dithetlwa, berries of the Grewia Occidentalis, fourcorners.
dithibo, stoppers.
dithipa, knives, gripes.
dithito, tree-trunks, sweat.
ditho, members, limbs.
dithobe, fruits of the morobe bush.
dithobo, strong beer.
dithobollo, gymnastics.
dithogako, (dithogo), curses.
dithogorogo, rubbish.
dithojana, heifers.
dithokgwa, forests.
dithoko, sides, directions.
dithoko, pus in the eye.
dithokolo, berries of the morokolo tree, "noemnoem".
dithokolo, dung of sheep, buck or goats.
dithole, heifers.
dithole, (marole), dust.
dithopa, secret thoughts.
dithopelegi, genital organs.
dithoro, grains.
dithoromo, trembling.
dithota, humps, heaps, mounds.
dithotho, fools.
dithoto, goods, luggage.
dithotswala, genital organs.
dithunya, guns.
dithuo, possessions.
dithupa, hiding, lashes.
dithušathuto, teaching aids.
dithušo, aid, help.
dithuthupe, pop-corn, roasted grain.
dithutla, a game.
dithutlwa, giraffes, the Southern cross.
dithwadi, bearers, champions.
dithwai, game played by herdboys.
dithwalo, pack, burden, load.
dithwaša, press-studs.
ditiego, delays.
ditimela, trains, wandering or stray animals.
ditiragalo, happenings.
ditiro, deeds.
ditlabakelo, equipment, fittings, furnishings.

ditlabele, equipment.
ditlakala, leaves, rubbish.
ditlamo, bindings, bands, bonds.
ditlankane, counterfoils.
ditlao, tongs, snuffers.
ditlapirwa, wild dogs.
ditlase, the vulva.
ditlatla, fools.
ditleloko, bells, clocks.
ditlemo, bindings, bonds, obligations.
ditlhaka, letters, marks.
ditlhako, hoofs; – **tša mapharo,** cloven-hoofed.
ditlhakore, sides.
ditlhalošišo, explanations.
ditlhamo, armour, equipment, inventions.
ditlhase, (dihlase), sparks.
ditlhathollo, explanations.
ditlhodi, spies.
ditlhokofalo, tortures.
ditlholo, rock hares, creations.
ditlhono, scrapings of a hide.
ditlogolo, grandchildren, offspring, descendants.
ditlolo, transgressions.
ditlolo, ointments.
ditloo, ground-nuts, lentils.
ditloomake, ground-nuts.
ditloomarapo, n'jugo-beans.
ditlopo, crests, tufts.
ditloro, prickly-pears.
ditlou, elephants.
ditlwaedi, practises.
ditlwaelo, customs, habits.
ditoba, tribute.
ditokelo, rights.
ditokišetšo, preparations.
ditokišo, corrections.
ditokololo, joints.
ditokomane, peanuts.
ditomega, cuppings.
ditona, male animals, cabinet ministers.
ditone, tons.
ditonele, tunnels.
ditonki, donkeys.
ditoro, prickly-pears.
ditoro, dreams.
ditoropo, yoke-straps, towns.
ditoto, carcases, corpses.
ditotolo, ash-heaps.
ditotomana, sand-dunes.
ditotonya, boiled mealies.
ditrompeta, trumpets.
ditše, smeared.
ditsebe, ears; **sepela ka** –, be attentive.
ditsebi, (ditsebitsebi), authorities.
ditsela, roads.
ditsepu, tail(s).
ditsetselo, sobs.
ditshego, laughter.
ditšhegofatšo, blessings.
ditshehla, adj., yellow; n., white people.
ditshehlo, devil's throns.
ditsheka, armlets.
ditsheko, actions, differences, law-suits.
ditshela, tail-feathers.
ditshele, quarrels.
ditšhelete, money.
ditshelo, hunting for food.
ditshenyegelo, damages, expences.
ditshetlana, pieces.
ditšhidi, pips of wild plums.
ditšhika, sinews, generations, blood-vessels.
ditšhikarelo, staves for carrying.
ditšhila, dirt.
ditšhipi, iron(s).
ditšhipisi, chips.
ditšhitšhidi, bugs.
ditšhitšhiripa, giants.
ditshola, food dished out.
ditsholo, blame.
ditšhomo, works.
ditšhošane, (ditšhoši), ants.
ditšhuana, orphans.
ditšhumamelomo, coffee, tea, hotdrink.
ditšhupo, signs, examples.

ditšhwana, seeds of the camel-thorn tree.
ditshwanelo, rights, duties.
ditšhweu, Europeans, di-class, white.
ditsiba, cruppers.
ditšie, locusts, – **badimo,** trash.
ditsikiditlane, spurs.
ditsiritsiri, crickets.
ditšitširipa, giants.
ditšo, germs.
ditsopa, pottery, crockery.
ditšu, elbows.
ditšwantle, imports.
ditšwapelong, thoughts.
ditšwaphoofolong, animal products.
ditšwaro, clothes.
ditswetši, cows that have just calved.
ditswetswe, dutše ka –, squat.
ditswitswitswi, altogether wrong.
dutulo, stools, chairs.
ditumanoši, vowels.
ditumo, rumours, desires.
ditwatši, germs.
diyamaleng, food.
diyantle, export.
duba, knead; incite, stir.
dubagana, be mixed up.
dudiša, cause to sit.
duduetša, carol, trill, shriek.
dukula, pick one's teeth, pick out.
dula, sit down, stay, dwell.
duma, rumble, boom, thunder.
duma, covet, wish for, desire.
dumaela, roar, groan.
dumala, fail in one's aims.
dumediša, greet.
dumela, agree, greet, believe, admit.
dumela khwele, b. fickle, credulous.
dumelang, affirmative, greetings.
dumeletšwe, be permitted.
dumologa, loose faith.
dupa, scent, sniff.
duša, be with calf.
duta, lower, carry in the hand.
dutla, leak, drip.
dutula, shave off the hair as a token of mourning.

E

e, it, this; – **ke,** perhaps.
eba, swing, rock.
ebago, namely.
ebangedi, gospel.
ebela, wave to and fro.
ebenyu, avenue.
ebile, then, even.
ebo, yes.
ebodiša, cause to pair/peel.
eboga, peel off.
ebola, pare, peel.
ebolusi, evolution.
edimola, yawn, gape.
ediša, radiate, help to measure, enlighten.
ediša, megokgo, cry.
edišitswego, enlightened.
ee, yes.
efa, ward off, dodge, evade.
efe, which?
efela, indeed, after all.
efoga, avoid, escape, dodge.
efola, remove.
ega, harrow.
ege, n. harrow.
ehula, aid, lighten.
ehwa, die.
eie, onion.
eike, acorn.
eile; e ile, happened, when.
eisteddfod, eisteddfod.
eitše, when, as if.
eja, eat.
eka, betray, lure.
eka, brandish a weapon.
eka, as if, it seems.
eke, gate.
eke, it seems as if, possibly.
ekelela, spoil, pamper.
ekeletša, add, add to.

ekesetra, extra.
eketša, add, increase.
ekhweita, equator.
ekiša, imitate.
ekonomi, economy.
eksponente, index.
Eksrei, X-rays.
ekwa, hear.
ela, those, that yonder.
ela, flow.
ela, measure, weigh.
ela hloko, note, observe, heed.
eleletša, think, consider.
elelwa, remember.
elemente, element.
elese, awl.
eletša, remind, advise.
eletšega, advisable.
elwa, fight, be measured.
ema, stand, stop; – **engwa,** be waited for.
emaema, tarry, delay; – **ela,** wait for/on.
emara, conceive (of animals only)
eme, stand, b. standing, stopped.
emela, stand for, support, wait for.
emelela, stand up.
emerale, emerald
emiša, cause to stand, set.
emule, has borne fruit.
ena, take an oath, vow.
ena (yena), he, she.
ena, have.
enamele, enamel.
enela, be sufficient, swear for.
enfelopo, envelope.
eng, what?
Engelane, England.
engelesoutu, epsom salt.
eng le eng, whatever.
eniša, eniše, cause to take an oath/swear.
enke, ink.
enne, has sworn, taken an oath.
ensime, enzyme.
enta, vaccinate.
entšene, engine.
entšha, cause to take an oath.
enwa! drink!
enya, bear fruit.
enywa, bear fruit or seed.
epa dig, – **dira,** call together, stir up war.
epela, bury, dig on behalf of; – **ditsepu,** flee.
Epistola, Epistle.
epolola, dig up or out.
eponi, ebony.
era, speak of, mention.
ere, when, whereas.
erekisi, pea.
erile, when.
esa, see: **sa,** dawn, become clear (of the sky).
e sa le, since, just then; adv., when last.
e se ya selo, unimportant.
e sego, not.
esela, ass.
ešima, even.
ešita, even.
esiti, acid.
ešo, not yet.
eswa, burn.
eta, journey, travel.
etela, travel to, or for, visit.
etelela, grow (worse), proceed.
ethimola, sneeze.
e tla re, it will happen.
e tle e re, whenever.
etla, come!
etša, be like.
etše, has flowed.
etsela, sleep, slumber.
etšiša, copy.
etshwa, spit.
etšwa! come out!
etšwe, whereas, even so.
eupša, but.
Europa, Europe.
eya, yes, really?
eya, go!

F

fa, give, grant, bestow.
fa, here; **a fa,** indeed?
fadiša, cause (help) to scrape, boast.
faele, file.
fafama, flutter, quiver.
fafanyega, glow, glitter.
fafatla, be delirious.
fafetla, toss about.
faga, pour flour into a pot, put in.
fagola, take out, castrate, geld.
fagolla, take out, diminish the contents.
fahla, dazzle, blind, ward off, eat tripe.
fahlela, shield, parry.
fahlogela, look at closely, study.
fahlologa, be opened (of the eye or ear).
Fahrenheit, Fahrenheit.
faka, put in.
faki, barrel, vat.
fala, scrape.
fala, stand fast, be determined.
fala, there.
falala, overflow, emigrate.
falatša, cause to overflow, spill.
fale, there, yonder.
falola, escape when hemmed in or surrounded, raise an alarm.
famoga, become enlarged.
famola, open (the nostrils) the eyes wide, push the hair back from the forehead.
fana, give to one another.
fankase, fungus.
fano, here.
fantisa, sell, auction.
fantisi, sale.
fantšha, see indistinctly.
fanyafanya, be weak-sighted, wanton.
fao, there, yonder.
faola, castrate.
fapa, wrap up, wind round.
fapana, differ, clash.
fapanya, cause to differ.
fapha, chop or cut lengthwise, put a ribbon across the head.
faphola, slap.
fapoga, turn (branch) off, deviate.
faporiki, factory.
fapoša, mislead, cause to deviate.
fara, hold a child on the lap.
fara, bring forth ears of corn, form an obstruction.
farafara, spread all over.
farakana, wrestle, be mixed up, stir up.
Farao, King of Egypt.
farasa, disperse.
farinkisi, pharynx.
farola, divide, split.
farologana, differ.
farologanya, cause a difference.
fase, down.
fase-molepo, flat on the ground.
fata, burrow, scratch.
fatoga, be rent asunder, be split.
fatoganya, cut lengthwise, split.
fatokana, split.
fatokanya, cause to split.
fatola, split, cleave.
fatologa, crack.
fatša, split by cutting, chip.
fatuku, dish-cloth.
fe, which?
feba, commit adultery.
Feberware, February.
fedile, is done, has come to an end.
fediša, finish, cause to cease; – **wa,** be destroyed.
feditše, has finished, has completed.
fefera, winnow, chatter.
fefetha, speak foolishly.
fefola, make lighter or easier.
fega, hang up, suspend.
fegedišwa, cause to sigh.
fegela, suspend for.
fegelwa, pant, be out of breath.
fegelwana, comma.

fegola, raise.
fegolla, take down from.
fehla, churn, stir, perforate.
feila, file; – **kgwakgwa,** rasp.
feisi, fist.
fekeetša, conquer.
fekemela, go under, disappear.
fekemetša, throw down, cast down.
feketori, (fektri), factory.
fela, come to an end, perish.
fela, but, only, just.
felegetša, accompany.
feleletša, complete, finish, destroy.
felemašale, field-marshal.
felesetša, accompany.
felo, place; **felo gongwe/felotsoko,** somewhere.
fema, avoid blows, escape, breathe, parry, fob, grease.
fengere, thimble.
fengwa, be overcome.
fenišara, (fenitšhara), furniture.
fenoga, be thrown over.
fenola, lift up and throw over.
fentše, has conquered.
fentšha, cause to win or conquer.
fenya, conquer, overcome, vanquish.
fepa, feed, nourish, nurse.
fepeletša, implore, coax.
fera, put on rafters, cross; – **seseka,** cross the legs.
fera, bend the finger when counting.
ferea, court (a girl).
ferefa, v., paint.
ferefe, n., paint.
ferehla, stir, speak foolishly, incite.
ferehlega, be disturbed.
fereka, become agitated.
ferekana, become disturbed.
ferekanya, embroil, disturb.
ferelela, run round, interfere.
ferella, whirl round.
feroga, have nausea.
ferola, stir up.
feroša, stir up.
feta, pass (by), exceed, die.
fetela, pass on to.
feterasi, federation.
fetiša, cause to pass, go beyond.
fetišetša, transfer to/for.
fetla, open up, avoid a blow.
fetleka, analyse.
fetoga, become changed.
fetola, change, translate, answer.
fetolela, translate (into).
fetša, finish, exterminate.
fi, re-, become dark.
fifala, become dark.
fifatša, darken.
fifalela, mourn over.
fihla, arrive.
fihla, hide, bury.
fihlela, until, reach.
fihliša, cause to (arrive) hide.
fihlola, eat breakfast.
fihlolla, reveal.
fikela, have a cold (influenza).
filamente, filament.
filimi, film.
filo, merely.
filologi, (filolotši), philology.
filosofare, philosopher.
filosofi, philosophy.
fina, bind.
fiolo, violin.
fioto, fjord.
fiša, burn, be ill, be hot, brand (cattle).
fiša, lend out cattle; **go fišafiša,** ailment.
fišegela, disire urgently, yearn for.
fisiolotši, physiology.
fiusa, fuse.
fiuse, fuse wire.
fiwa, be given.
fo, merely, just.
foa, listen; **foafoa,** deaf, hear indistinctly.
fodile, be well, has become cool.
fodiša, heal, cure, cool down.
fofa, fly, jump.
fofo, hot drink.

fofoma, burst forth.
fofomoga, rise up in bulk.
fofona, finger, feel.
fofonela, scent, sniff, smell.
fofora, brush off, shake off, break off.
foforega, crumble, fall off, shed teeth.
fogamo, hot tea.
fogohla, scrub, scour.
fohla, chop off twigs, cut one's way through.
foka, blow, make a noise, sprinkle.
foka, sprinkle (medicine).
fokaela, waddle.
fokela, sprinkle with medicine.
fokiša, cause to blow or sprinkle.
fokodiša, cause to be weak.
fokoditše, lessened.
fokola, be weak, be (ill) feeble.
fokotša, diminish, lessen.
fokotšega, become diminished.
fola, thresh corn.
fola, recover from a disease, become cool.
fola, smoke (tobacco), take snuff.
fola, n., tobacco.
folakese, flax.
folenana, flannel(ette).
folene, flannel.
folete, flat (quarters).
follela, string beads, lace in, tack.
folletša, rejoice.
folodiša, cause to abort.
fologa, descend, come down.
fologela, descend to, for or on account of.
foloko, (A.,), folk, people.
folomente, foundation.
folorini, florin.
fološa, let down, take down, lower.
folotša, abort, miscarry (of an animal), – **go,** abortive.
foma, fat and full.
fomaline, formalin.
fomo, form.
fomoliri, formulary.
fomula, formula.
fonetiki, phonetics.
fong, re –, smell badly.
fonkodiša, cause to search well.
fonolotši, phonology.
foofoo, hot drink (tea, coffee).
fopha, strike, smite.
fora, deceive, hoax.
Fora, France.
fora, dress or curl the hair.
foraforetša, deceive, hoax.
foraga, (A.,), wagon-load.
foreime, frame.
foro, water, furrow.
forohla, rub, polish.
foroko, fork.
foroma, (A.,), mould (bricks).
foromane, foreman.
foromo, mould.
foromo, ingot.
forosela, run out slowly (as maize).
foša, miss, make a mistake, blunder.
foša, hurl, throw.
fosfate, phosphate.
fosforo, phosphor.
fošišago nako, abortive, premature.
fotha, swoop down, skim.
fotlela, snub, rate, chide.
foto, photo (graph), armlet of beads.
fotša, cure, caress.
fotšha, caress, stroke.
fotšholo, shovel.
foufala, become blind.
foufatša, make blind, to blind.
foufetše, be blind.
foufologa, recover sight.
France, France.
Freistata, Orange Free State.
fšega, be afraid.
fudiša, cause to graze, cause to pluck or pick.
fufula, (fufulelwa), transpire, bubble; – **letšwe,** enraged, cross.
fufuletša, cause to transpire.
fukuletša, throw a stick so as to make a noise.

fula, graze, pluck flowers and fruit.
fulela ntwa, pick a quarrel, start a fight.
fulara, turn one's back on, depart.
fularela, turn the back upon, turn away from.
fulere, has turned the back, has departed.
fuputša, gather ears of corn after the harvest, search.
furalela, (fularela), turn one's back upon, abandon.
furalla, turn one's back upon.
furu, forage.
furung, lining.
futu, foot, (measure).
futupolo, football.

G

ga, not, not to, if, when.
ga, at, to.
ga, –thwe, it is (was) said.
ga, draw water, pluck, pick fruit.
gaba, scoop out, hollow out.
gaba, desire, want, need.
gabalala, become arched, lean forward.
gabea, enchant.
gabedi, twice.
gabela, scoop or hollow out for.
gabo, at their home; **–bona,** their home/family.
gaboi, di-, banns.
gaboima, heavily, with difficulty.
gabohloko, painfully.
gabolena, at your home.
gabotša, grind carelessly, state coarsely.
gabotse, nicely, well, carefully.
gabosebotse, very well.
gadikega, become roasted, have stomach-ache.
gadima, flash, glance.
gadimola, beat, strike.
gae, home, residence; adv., at home.
gaediša, cause to cry.
gaela, cry.
gafa, be mad.
gafa, renounce, repudiate, deliver.
gafela, deliver, hand over to, entrust.
gagaba, creep, crawl, drag.
gagabiša mahlo, be ashamed.
gagabo, at their home; **se** –, their language/customs.
gagalala, dry up.
gagama, adhere, stick to.
gagamala, dry up, strive; **– ela,** strive after.
gagamela, enforce.
gagametše, be strict.
gagapa, persevere, strong, obdurate.
gagara, gather up.
gagautla, tear to pieces.
gageno, at your home.
gagešo, at our home.
gago, yours.
gagoga, tear, become torn.
gagoganya, tear asunder, rend.
gagola, tear, rend.
gagolo, greatly, specially, mostly.
gagwe, his, hers.
gahla, coagulate, curdle.
gahlana, meet (with).
gahlanetša, cause to meet, meet.
gahlano, five times.
gahlola, speak loudly, rejoice.
gaila, crush, grind coarsely.
gaiwa, be scarified.
gaka, forget, puzzle.
gakaa(ka), so much.
gakaalo, so much.
gakala, crystallize, be zealous/angry.
gakalo, so much.
gakanega, be astonished.
gakantšha, confuse, confound.
gakanya, disguise, confuse.
gakatša, incite to anger.
gaketla, hack, cut up.

gaketše, determined.
gakgamala, wonder, be surprised.
gakgamatša, cause to wonder.
gakgamatšago, fantastic.
gakilwe, has slipped one's memory.
gakiša, cause to forget.
gakolla, remind.
gakologa, thaw, be reminded.
gala, resound, scream, echo.
galagadiša, cause to resound.
galaka, be (bitter) brackish, acrid.
galala, despise, disdain.
galalega, be unsufficient.
galapatša, palatalise, (-ze).
galase, glass.
galefa, become angry.
galoga, fade.
galone, gallon.
gama, milk.
gamelela, squeeze out.
gammalwa, often.
gammogo, together.
gamola, take in, squeeze (wring) out, drain.
gampa, be pregnant (dog or sow).
gampe, badly.
gamputša, wield, brandish.
gana, refuse, object.
gane, four times.
ganeditše, has contradicted.
ganela, refuse, dispute, resist.
ganelela, refuse utterly.
ganetša, contradict, resist.
ganka, swagger.
gangwa, be milked.
gankafala, become bold.
ganne, refused, objected.
gannyane, little; **le** –, not at all.
gantši, often, frequently.
gantšintši, very often.
ganyane, little, sparingly; **le** – not at all, never.
ganyetša, contest, oppose.
gaogela, have mercy.
gapa, drive, seize; – **bogoši,** coup.
gape, again, once more; conj., moreover.
gapela, take by force.
gapeletša, compel, force, urge.
gapoša, drain.
gapša, be driven.
gara, coil, wind.
garafo, spade.
garama, dance for joy.
garanate, pomegranate.
gararo, three times, thrice.
garagaša, deceive, defraud.
garane, thread, cotton.
garase, barley.
garaswana, small spade.
garateine, curtain.
gare, middle, halfway; **ka** –! come in!
garenate, pomegranate.
garese, barley.
garetene, curtain.
garetse, we don't know.
garima, criss-cross.
garola, tear to pieces.
garuma, snarl.
gaša, broadcast, scatter, sprinkle.
gašanya, scatter.
gase, gas.
gasele, slowly.
gaselela, six times.
gaseswai, eight times.
gasoga, fade.
gašupa, seven times.
gataka, trample.
gatee, once; – **tee,** suddenly.
gatelela, tread (press) down.
gatelele, for some length.
gatholela (mahlo), look with an evil eye.
gatla, strike, beat, clout, slap.
gatlela, wean before the time.
gatlola, grind coarsely.
gatoga, remove, retrace.
gatolla, remove the foot.
gatoša, cause to remove.
gaugela, have mercy on.

gauta, gold.
Gauteng, Johannesburg.
gaya, scarify.
ge, if, when; now; as for.
gebela, belabour.
gee, now, so then.
gega, walk sideways.
gegea, mock at, fool.
gegera, annihilate.
gela, draw (pluck) for.
gemere, ginger beer.
gemotša, hurry.
gempe, shirt.
geno, your. (A.,)
genosekapa, (A.,) society.
geologi, geology.
geometri, geometry.
geotropi, geotropism.
gera, gnaw; – **ega,** crumble.
gereisi, mealie rice.
gerema, run towards; – **ela,** flock towards.
Gerike, Greece.
geripi, influenza.
gerula, look askance, peep.
gešo, our; **ga** –, at our home.
getla, cut, look askance, despise.
getlola, look askance at.
gitla, strike, slap.
go, indef. pron., it.
go, obj. pron., you.
go, prep., to, which, in.
goa, shout, rumble.
goba, or, that, whether.
goba, bark, hum, jubilate.
gobagoba, wander.
gobagobiša, hurry, cause to wander.
gobala, get (hurt) wounded.
gobalala, drive, wander around.
gobane, because, that.
gobatha, gather.
gobatša, hurt, wound.
gobe, bad.
gobedi, dual.
gobeetša, ill-treat.
gobela, hum, dance and sing.
gobelana, mix, amass, heap-up.
gobelane, mixed, crowded together.
gobelela, over-fill.
gobetše, be injured.
gobja, splash.
goboga, become defamed, reviled or tasteless.
goboga, disgrace.
gobola, strip plaster.
gobolola, revile, defame.
gobośa, defame, revile, desecrate.
gobotla, curse; – **mapele,** masturbate.
godile, has grown, be full-grown.
godimo, high, above, up.
Godimodimo, yo –, the Most High.
godiša, cause to grow, honour, rear, praise.
godišega, be praiseworthy.
goela, shout for, copulate (animals).
goela, shout at/to.
goeletša, shout.
gofejane, youngest child.
gofiša, purge.
goga, pull, draw, smoke.
gogagoga, pull, draw.
gogela, pull for/towards.
gogoba, drag along, crawl along (as a lizard).
gogoba, gather up and remove.
gogoila, draw.
gogola, remove rubbish, carry away.
gogoma, project.
gogomoga, swell out.
gogomoša, exalt, make proud.
gogona, snore.
gogongwe, perhaps.
gogorela, scrape together.
gogoropa, (gogorupa), be curved.
gogotša, smuggle.
gohla rub, scour, file.
gohle, everywhere.
gohlo, id., re –, dive.
gohlola, cough.
gohlomela, decline, fall in.
gohlometša, swallow.
goiša, cause to shout.

gokae, where?
gokaganya, fasten together.
gokara, entice, carry/hold in the arms.
gokarela, embrace.
gokela, entice.
goketša, entice, draw.
gokga, grieve, rattle in the throat.
gokgama, surprised.
gokola, scrape coals from the fire.
gola, earn, receive pay.
gola, grow, gather.
gola, when, formerly.
golagolega, crave for.
golega, imprison.
golela, grow up at, multiply for.
golo, big, important.
golofala, become disabled, crippled.
golofatša, cripple.
gologa, become free, sag, b. eager.
goloka, cry out, roll into a ball.
golola, deliver, unbind.
golola, cry, bewail.
goloma, roam about.
golopa, scold.
goma, turn back, – **tseleng,** have a miscarriage.
goma, adhere to, adorn.
gomara, adhere to, stick to.
gomarela, adhere to, stick to.
gomela, go back to.
gomela, n., shorts.
gomme, and.
gomotša, comfort.
gompana, tapping beetle.
gona, there, hence, therefore, then; **e be** –, then; **ka** –, and so; **se be** –, absent.
gona, snore, draw in, purr.
gonega, be drawn back.
gongwe, perhaps, at another place.
gonoga, lengthen (shadows).
gonoka, lose courage.
gonona, suspect, become suspicious.
gonontšha, make suspicious.
gontše, has (plucked) hooked out.
gontši, often.
gonya, pluck (hook) out.
gonyane, little, slightly.
gopa, dry (suck) up.
gopa, scrape, scoop out.
gopagopela, eat cutlets of meat.
gopalala, wander.
gopane, field iguana.
gopela, accept cutlets of meat.
gopodiša, remind, cause to think.
gopodišiša, memorise.
gopola, have an attitude.
gopola, think, remember.
gopolela, suspect.
gopotša, remind.
gopša, be scraped.
gora, scrape, lick.
goramela, adhere (stick) to.
gore, (in order) that.
gorega, mouth becomes dry.
gorela, scrape out, lick the finger.
goroga, arrive (go) home.
gorogoša mahlo, stare at.
gorogoša, probe.
gorola, gaze at.
goromela, gush out.
gorometša, push.
goroša, cause to go home.
gorulla, evacuate.
gosa, abuse.
gosasa, in the morning, to-morrow.
gosela, sip.
gošele, somewhere else.
gosenene, slightly.
goseng, in the morning.
gošoro, awful, cruelly.
gošwama, jingle.
gota, couple, have sexual relations with an animal.
gotediša, kindle, light.
gotee, together (with).
gotela, burn.
gotetša, kindle, light, inflame.
gotla, roar, bellow.
gotola, glare.
gotša, light, kindle.

gouta, gold, (dial.) see: **gauta.**
gwa, (– ba), it was.
gwaba, be (cheeky) insolent.
gwabela, link up.
gwaela, incriminate, accuse falsely.
gwahla, be an invalid.
gwahlafala, become an invalid.
gwahlafatša, cripple, disable, impuir.
gwaila, walk briskly.
gwalala, be tough or hard.
gwaletša, prevail upon.
gwama, become dry.
gwamela, dry up.
gwametše, be thin or lean.
gwanta, strut.
gwaragwara, show signs of birth.
gwaša, rustle.
gwatalala, stand defiantly.
gwatalatša, stretch.
gwatelana, wrestle.
gwaya, scoop out, itch.
gweba, trade.
gwebehla, be pregnant, be with young (of a dog or sow).
gwebiša, import.
gwela, climb fast.
gwelea, gather.
gwelega, tie, handcuff.
gweleka, swallow.
gwera, or **gwerana,** make friends, be friends.
gwetea, muddle up.
gwetetša, pull tight.
gwidii, glutton.

H

ha!, exclam. of surprise.
habalala, make haste.
habore, oats.
haeroklifiki, hieroglyph.
haetrotšene, hydrogen.
hafo, half.
haka, clasp, hook on.
hakisi, hook.
hakolola, unhook, let loose.
hale, shot, shotgun.
halleluya, halleluyah.
hamola, hammer, sit improperly.
hapo (hapu), nave, hub.
haralala, stand legs astride.
hareka, rake.
harepa, harp.
hautša, drizzle, lie.
hebehebetša, whisper.
hele, hell.
helikoptere, helicopter.
hema, sigh, take a deep breath.
hempe, shirt, dial., see: **gempe.**
hiatuse, hiatus (gram.).
hidihitša, cry.
hidinya, cry.
hira, hire.
hiriša, lease.
hiroklifi, hieroglyph.
Hispania, Spain.
histori, history.
hlaba, illegitimate child, crupper.
hlaba, stab, plant, slaughter, quote, strike.
hlaba mokgoši, make a noise, give an alarm, advertise. – **ka mahlo,** look fixedly at.
hlaba, rise (sun); – **ela,** dawn for; – **etše,** has dawned for.
hlaba, dark brown with yellow patches about the nose (of a domestic animal).
hlabana, fight.
hlabanela, fight for, defend.
hlabela, vaccinate, inject, sacrifice, offer.
hlabelela, set a tune for singing.
hlabeletša, set a tune for singing.
hlabiša dihlong, put to shame, make ashamed.
hlabja, be stabbed.
hlabola, speak loudly.
hlabolla, excite, change, renew.

hlaboša, refresh, speak loudly, renew.
hlabošega, be nice.
hladia, put the pot on the fire.
hladile, has divorced.
hlaela, come short of, be in want.
hlaetša, (– mahlo), despise.
hlafa, lose (hair) power, slough, be tasteless.
hlafile, tasteless.
hlaga, dense undergrowth, wild.
hlaga, appear; – **elwa ke kotsi,** meet with an accident.
hlagahlagane, siskin (bird).
hlagala, become old and worn.
hlaganela, make haste.
hlagatša, wear out.
hlageletše, tattered and torn.
hlagiša, cause to appear.
hlagola, cultivate, weed.
hlagolela, weed (for), cultivate.
hlahla, lead (the blind).
hlahlafinya, scrawl.
hlahlama, follow, come after.
hlahlamolla, unravel.
hlahlamphela, overdress.
hlahlamuši, dense smoke, fumes.
hlahlareele, noisy, excited person.
hlahlara, wake up.
hlahlarega, wake up.
hlahlariela, troublesome.
hlahlatha, roam about, speak nonsense.
hlahlawe, noisy person, excited person; speak noisely.
hlahlela, drive animals into a kraal or camp, string beads, load a gun.
hlahloba, examine, inspect.
hlahlobišiša, examine carefully.
hlahuna, chew.
hlaka, worry, be wanting, be bright, improvise, invent.
hlaka, begin (a song or a play).
hlakana, meet, mix.
hlakahlakana, become mixed.
hlakana hlogo, be mad, be off one's head.
hlakanetša, cause to meet.
hlakantšha, mix, add to.
hlakantšuku, mixture of things, cosmopolitan.
hlakanya, mix, add to.
hlakela, rejoice, be happy and playful.
hlakhuna, chew.
hlakiša, worry.
hlakodiša, redeem, save.
hlakoga, be wiped, deprived of.
hlakola, rob, wipe.
Hlakola, February.
hlakolega, be robbed.
hlala, divorce, give up, forsake.
hlalala, rejoice.
hlalefa, become wise or clever.
hlalefetša, cheat, defraud.
hlalefile, be clever.
hlaleswa, blame falsely.
hlaletša, rock/amuse a child.
hlalla, ask, request.
hlalela, invite to a meal, share.
hlaloganya, understand, grasp, comprehend.
hlaloša, explain, interpret.
hlalošago, explanatory.
hlalošetša, explain to.
hlama, dress well, compose, invent, fit, n., beer (yeast).
hlamalala, become stiff, be straight.
hlamalatša, straighten out.
hlamatšega, become improved, be beautiful, perfect.
hlame (tlhame), secretary bird.
hlamuka, eat greedily.
hlamukela, besmear one's mouth.
hlamula, narrate, tell.
hlana, go re –, eddy, roll, turn around.
hlanama, turn upside-down, change your mind, be fickle, **hlanamela,** turn against.
hlanasela, move from side to side.
hlanhlagane, linnet, siskin.
hlankela, serve.

hlankiša, enslave.
hlano, five.
hlanoga, be turned inside out, change one's mind.
hlanogela, turn against.
hlanogetše, turned away from, rejected.
hlanola, turn inside out, alter.
hlanoša, cause to turn inside out.
hlantha, roam about.
hlanya, be mad.
hlaola, select, distinguish, separate.
hlaologanya, understand, differentiate.
hlaološa, dilute, add to, explain.
hlapa, wash the body, bathe, menstruate.
hlapaola, curse, swear at.
hlapetša, care for, look after, herd; – **ditše,** cared for.
hlaphoga, get well, get clear.
hlaphola, batter, pound, splash.
hlaphu, splash.
hlapi, fish.
hlaphuhla, shamble.
hlapi-jeli, jelly-fish.
hlapiša, wash (someone else).
hlapologa, urinate, melt.
hlaputla, lap up.
hlarakana, make a rattling noise.
hlarakanya, cause a rattling noise.
hlaramolla, flutter, flap, display.
hlarolla, ravel out.
hlarologa, stand on end.
hlasa, chase away.
hlasela, assault, raid, attack; – **na,** attack each other.
hlasima, teem with, abound.
hlaswa, abhor, become tasteless, renounce; – **itše,** rejected.
hlatha, chop off, understand.
hlathi, unbroken boiled grain.
hlatholla, explain, interpet.
hlatlagana, be in layers.
hlatlama, follow, succeed.
hlatlea, put a pot on the fire.
hlatlega, be put on the fire.
hlatlegelang! beware!
hlatloga, ascend, rise.
hlatlola, relieve, raise, ascend.
hlatlologa, move in order of succession.
hlatlologanya, remove one thing off another.
hlatloša, raise.
hlatša, vomit, eject, reject.
hlatša, bring forth young (a sow or cat).
hlatsa, testify, give evidence.
hlatse, witness.
hlatsela, give evidence.
hlatsetša, give evidence in favour of.
hlatšiša, cause to vomit.
hlatswa, wash anything except the body; – **dinoka,** purify a woman that gives birth to girls only; – **dirope,** concubine.
hlatswadiatla, commission.
hlatswana, small fish.
hlatswega, washable.
hlatswetša, wash for/in.
hlaya, lack, n., drawer.
hle, please, do!
hlegere, senya –, do by trial and error, experiment.
hlehla, walk alongside.
hleka, spoil, pamper, respect.
hlekesetša, pamper, fondle, handle carefully.
hleng, next to.
hleng! if you please! upon my word!
hlepha, become loose, become slack.
hlephiša, slacken.
hloba, pluck off.
hlobaela, be sleepless.
hlobaetša, hinder, worry.
hlobega, become plucked.
hlobodiša, cause to undress, deprive of.
hloboga, despair.
hlobola, undress, strip.
hlodi = **tlhodi,** spy.
hlodia, annoy, howl.

hlodiega, be annoyed.
hlodile, has created, has spied.
hlodimela, peep, spy.
hloega, be despised, be hateful.
hloela, loathe, hate for.
hloga, sprout, germinate.
hlogo, head, prefix, heading, principal; **ja** –, ponder, think.
hlogofala, become cruel/fierce.
hlogonolofala, be or become blessed.
hlogonolofatša, bless, make prosperous.
hlogosetimela, engine, locomotive.
hlogwana, small head; item, knob.
hlohla, probe, stuff, challenge.
hlohleletša, incite, provoke.
hlohletša, incite, stir up.
hlohlomiša, investigate.
hlohlona, itch.
hlohlonwa ke ditsebe, be curious, inquisitive.
hlohlora, dust, shed.
hlohlorega, become shaken off.
hloile, has hated.
hloka, cover, (of an animal).
hloka, lack, miss; – **tšhelete,** impecunius.
hlokafala, be rare of wanting.
hlokafetše, has died, be missing.
hlokagala, be (no more) lacking.
hlokega, be lacking, be scarce.
hlokgosela, be shaken in; – **setša,** shake in (a bag).
hlokiša, cause to lack.
hloko, ela –, be observant.
hlokofala, become painful, be grieved.
hlokofala, get hurt; – **fetše,** be heartsore, complain bitterly.
hlokofatša, cause (pain) grief, torment.
hlokoga, mourn, have pity on.
hlokola, winnow, jolt, wobble.
hlokomela, observe, guard, mind.
hlokometše, observed, guarded, were responsible.
hlokomologa, neglect, disregard, overlook.
hlokosetša, hush, lull.
hlokotša, sharpen, (as a stick).
hlokwa, be lacking, be rare.
hlola, create, spy, sojourn; start (a war), find out.
hlola, spell, forebode, be wont, forecast, predict evil.
hlola, overcome, conquer.
hlolega, be conquered, be overcome.
hlolega, be or become created.
hlolela, predict, forebode, evil curse.
hlologela, yearn, long for.
hlologetšwe, yearn.
hlolosela, yearn for.
hloma, pitch, plant, fix in upright.
hloma, imagine, suppose.
hlomagana, imagine, become fastened together.
hlomaganya, link up, join.
hlomalala, stand erect.
hlomama, stand upright, be firm.
hlomamiša, confirm, affirm, establish.
hlomara, encompass, pursue, persecute.
hlomarela, persecute.
hlomatiša, affix.
hlomela, plant in, establish.
hlomelela, add to, lengthen.
hlomeletša, add on, lengthen.
hlomere, pursued.
hlomesetša, affix.
hlometša, peep over.
hlomoga, mourn, be sad.
hlomogela, have pity on, be merciful to.
hlomogelwa, be treated with compassion.
hlomola, (hlomolla), pull out, uproot.
hlompha, respect, honour, be polite, observe.
hlomphega, be respectable, be honourable.
hlompholla, dishonour, disrespect.
hlompšha, be respected/observed.

hlonama, sulk.
hlong, hedge-hog, shame.
hlonka, gnaw, have gripes.
hlonya, pull faces.
hlopha, tease, annoy, worry.
hlopha, heap up, group, assort; – **gane,** be heaped up.
hlophara, set up properly.
hlophega, be grouped, b. worried.
hlophiša, cause to stack.
hlopholla, take apart, analyse, straighten.
hlophologa, be straight, stand up straight.
hlora, strike down, head-dress; – **hlora,** be restive.
hlorega, become emaciated.
hloriša, worry.
hlosa, eat as a titbit.
hlotha, pluck or cut off, snatch away.
hlothola, snatch away.
hlotla, filter, strain, probe.
hlotlega, be filtered, percolate.
hlotlela, walk with a stick.
hlotša, limp.
hlotšiša, cause to limp.
hloya, hate, detest. n., whey
hluduwee! Time!
hlwa, tarry, remain for a time, spend the day. **go – maabane,** the day before yesterday.
hlwaela, drive in.
hlware, python.
hlwaya, prick the ears.
hlweka, be clean.
hlwekiša, cleanse.
hlwekišaoma, dry-cleaning.
hlwela, endure.
hoi-hoi, drive cattle to the yoke.
hola, benefit; – **ega,** profit by.
holla, choose and cast away.
holofela, trust, hope.
holofetša, promise; – **ditše,** has promised.
holofologa, lose hope, despair.
homoditše, has silenced.
homola, be silent.
homotša, silence, calm, comfort.
hoo, be (empty) bare.
hopane, mountain leguan, iguana.
horiša, satisfy hunger.
hoša, satisfy hunger.
hoše, satisfied.
hosphuephe, hose.
huba, hiss, seethe, rustle.
hubaa! red.
hubaka, strut.
hubala, become red.
hubata, strut.
hubedu, red.
hubee, be very red.
hudua, agitate, stir up.
huduega, be stirred, become (be) agitated.
huduga, depart, trek, move, migrate.
huduša, remove, cause to move.
huela, blow, blow into, hiss.
huetša, blow into, hiss, exhale; – **ana,** assimilate.
hufega, be envious, be jealous.
hufula, snatch away.
huhuhu, id., cold.
huhumela, creep under.
huhumetša, cause to go under or creep through.
huka, give a hooked blow (fist).
huku, hook, corner.
hula, rob, draw.
huma, become rich.
humana, find.
humanega, be or become poor.
humase, humus.
humela, mediate.
humile, be rich.
humiša, make rich, enrich.
huna, tie a knot; – **ela,** tie for; – **letswele,** clench the fist.
hunagana, become tied together.
hunaganya, tie together.
hunolla, untie, free.
hunologa, become untied; – **ile,** be free.

hunolola, untie, undo a knot.
hunya, shrink.
hunyapana, be crooked, be shrunk up, b. troubled.
hunyela, shrink, draw together.
hunyelela, shrink away, disappear.
huyetšetsa, cause to shrink.
hupa, put in the mouth, absorb; – **lenala,** hold thumbs.
hupara, clasp, hold on to.
huparela, hold in the hand, clasp.
hupeditšwe, be out of breath.
hupela, – **moya,** keep your breath.
hupere, has clasped, be thrifty.
hupetša, suffocate, choke.
hupologa, recover breath.
hupulo, hoop iron.
huputša, search well.
hura, gnaw.
huruga, migrate.
huswane, small livestock.
huta, shift, move.
hutagana, become bowed or cramped up.
hutaganya, cause to bend.
hutama, squat, lie down.
hutela, move, shove.
hutere, hooter.
hutša, trust, bellow.
hutše, has robbed.
hutšwela, make a mash.
hutšwetša, make a mash.
hwa, die, pass away; – **kgaba,** enthusiastic.
hwafoga, become light in weight.
hwahwaela, be dejected.
hwanyolla, draw out as a sword or a purse.
hweditše, has found.
hwela, die on behalf of.
hwelela, die out, become extinct.
hweletša, find for.
hwenahwena, whisper.
hwetša, find.
hwetše, has died for.
hwibidu, red.
hwibifala, become red, redden.
hwibila, become red, n., rain-bird.
hwibitšwana, reddish.
hwidietšega, whirl, wind.
hwidihwitša, whirl, hurl.
hwidinya, wag, sling, whisk.
hwiditša, brandish, swagger, sling.
hwile, has (died) passed away.
hwirihwitša, deceive.

I

idibala, faint
idibana, faint.
idibatša, cause of faint.
idibetše, has fainted.
idibologa, recover after fainting.
idile, has dreaded, has hated.
idimola, yawn, gape.
ifala, become dark.
ifatša, darken.
ihula, remove from danger.
ikaba, stop one's ears.
ikabela, devote oneself to, consecrate to oneself
ikabetše, claim, devoted – self to.
ikadile, be extensive.
ikagela, build (for oneself).
ikagiša, establish – self, pretend to build.
ikahlola, judge oneself.
ikahlolela, judge (for oneself).
ikala, spread.
ikakela, feign, tell lies.
ikakatša, deceive oneself, feign.
ikakgela, throw oneself into.
ikalafa, cure oneself.
ikama, comb one's own hair, be confederate.
ikamoga, deprive oneself of.
ikamogela, receive (for oneself).
ikana, take an oath.
ikanya, trust (confide) in, rely on.

ikapara, put on second hand clothes.
ikapere, be tattered.
ikapeela, cook, do one's own cooking.
ikapola, undress oneself.
ikarabela, answer (for oneself).
ikeka, betray oneself.
ikekeletša, increase for oneself.
ikela, go (away).
ikemela, defend oneself, stand (alone).
ikemiša, pretend to stand, set oneself.
ikemišetša, intentionally.
ikepela, dig (for oneself).
ikepolla, dig out oneself.
iketla, be at ease, relax, comfortable.
iketlela, take time for.
iketliša, put at ease.
iketlologa, be uneasy, become unrestful.
ikgabiša, decorate oneself.
ikgadikela, roast (for oneself).
ikgafa, surrender.
ikgafela, surrender to or for.
ikgagola, tear one's own clothes.
ikgahla, please oneself; – **hletšwe,** be pleased.
ikgakantšha, disguise oneself, pretend not to know.
ikgakanya, disguise oneself, simulate.
ikgakolla, remind oneself.
ikgakolola, remind oneself.
ikgakgaretša, wrap oneself up.
ikgama, stifle (choke) oneself.
ikgamela, milk (for oneself).
ikganela, refuse.
ikgantšha, exalt oneself, be proud.
ikganyogela, desire, covet.
ikgaoganya, separate oneself from others.
ikgapa, be idle, be at leisure.
ikgapeletša, force oneself to.
ikgara, coil oneself up, meander.
ikgatela, tread.
ikgediša, pretend to (draw water) pick.
ikgela, draw, pluck for oneself.
ikgelela, draw water for oneself.
ikgelola, wipe perspiration.
ikgethela, select (for oneself).
ikgobokeletša, gather (for oneself).
ikgoboša, dishonour oneself.
ikgodiša, exalt oneself, be proud.
ikgodišitše, convinced oneself.
ikgoga, drag oneself.
ikgogiša, pretend to smoke.
ikgogomoša, be proud, pride oneself.
ikgoka, bind oneself.
ikgokela, draw upon oneself.
ikgokela, gather (for oneself).
ikgolela, grow, grow up.
ikgolofatša, cripple oneself.
ikgoloka, curl up into a ball.
ikgolola, free oneself, deliver oneself.
ikgonara, be poor/destitute.
ikgopola, think of oneself.
ikgopolela, think.
ikgopotša, remind oneself.
ikgotlela, disgrace oneself.
ikgotletše, defiled oneself.
ikgweranya, be friends.
ikhola, benefit oneself.
ikholofetša, depend upon.
ikhomolela, keep quiet, stop crying.
ikhomotša, console oneself.
ikhuditše, reposed, rested.
ikhula, rob oneself.
ikhumiša, enrich oneself, pretend to be rich.
ikhunela, draw oneself up for, menstruate.
ikhunolola, untie (free) oneself.
ikhutša, rest oneself.
ikhutšiša, give oneself rest.
ikhwela, die.
ikhwetše, died (a natural death)
ikhwiša, simulate death.
ikilela, take care of oneself.
ikiletša, shun.
ikimeletša, be reluctant.
ikimetša, burden oneself.
ikimolla, unburden oneself.

ikiša, go (willingly, by oneself).
ikitimela, run.
ikoba, bow.
ikobela, bow down to; – **molato,** transgress, trespass.
ikokobetša, humble oneself.
ikokotlela, lean against.
ikomanya, scold oneself.
ikomelela, dry up.
ikomoša, warm oneself.
ikona, fast.
ikopanya, join oneself to.
ikopantše, has joined oneself.
ikotamela, squat.
ikotla, strike or punish oneself.
ikotlela, bring up for oneself (as an adopted child), provide for oneself.
ikotlolla, stretch oneself.
ikotlolola, stretch oneself.
ikubuela, scatter over oneself.
ikuša, throw oneself down.
ikušetša, (godimo) throw oneself upon.
ikuta, hide (oneself).
ikutiša, pretend to hide.
ikutlwa, feel, be conscious.
ikutlwela, hear or feel.
ikutswa, steal away, leave secretly.
ikwa, feel, sense, experience.
ikwanela, come to an agreement.
ikwaralatša, harden oneself.
ikwetša, cast oneself into.
ila, avoid regard with superstition, abhor.
ilalo, say so, say thus.
ile, has gone.
ilega, be avoided, be regarded with superstition.
ilela, avoid, abstain from, mourn over.
iletša, forbid.
iletše, avoided, mourned.
ilola, revive by medicine, render harmless, rescue, aid, save.
ima, become pregnant.
imakaletše, be amazed.
imela, burden, be heavy upon.
imelelago ka noši, grow by itself.
imetša, overload.
imilwe, be pregnant.
imola, unburden.
imollwa, be relieved of one's burden.
imphi, army.
ina, put in water.
inama, bow down, bend.
inamologa, come erect.
inela, intervene.
ineela, submit to, give in to; **go** –, dedication.
inflasi, inflation.
infleisene, inflation.
inšora, insure.
insense, incense.
inyawela, foul/besmirch oneself.
inyorolla, quench the thirst.
ipala, count (include) oneself.
ipalela, read, count.
ipapetša, compare oneself.
iparametša, sit down.
ipata, hide oneself, go –, along.
ipatametša, draw near, appraoch.
ipatolla, reveal/help oneself, prove oneself.
ipea, place oneself, pose.
ipega, report oneself.
ipeola, shave onself.
ipha, give oneself; – **naga,** run away.
iphahla, dazzle oneself.
iphahlolla, remove what duzzles oneself.
iphara, sit with folded legs.
iphediša, sustain oneself, support oneself.
iphega, hang oneself.
iphelela, live (for oneself), be selfish.
iphemela, defend oneself.
iphenyetša, prevail upon.
iphepa, feed oneself.
iphepentšha, pretend.
iphera, sit with crossed legs.
ipherela, – **seseka,** sit with the legs crossed.

ipherogela, abhor.
iphetela, pass by.
iphetša, full-grown.
iphihla, hide oneself.
iphihlile, has hidden oneself.
iphile, given to oneself.
iphodiša, cure oneself.
iphokodiša, pretend to be weak.
iphološa, free oneself.
iphora, deceive oneself.
iphoromela, make bricks.
iphoufatša, blind oneself.
iphulela, graze.
iphuralla (or) **iphuralela,** turn one's back.
iphutha, enwrap oneself.
iphuthela, gather (for oneself).
ipikitla, rub one's eyes.
ipiletša, appeal to.
ipinela, sing, dance.
ipipa, cover oneself.
ipitša, call oneself, name oneself.
ipoba, crouch, lie low.
ipobola, confess.
ipoela, come back, go back; **ipoetše,** returned.
ipoelanya, reconcile oneself.
ipoeletša, repeat itself.
ipofa, bind (harness) oneself.
ipofela, bind.
ipofolla, free oneself, untie oneself.
ipokelela, gather, collect.
ipolaela, kill (for oneself).
ipolaiša, injure oneself.
ipolaya, injure oneself, commit suicide.
ipolediša, pretend to speak.
ipolela, confess, speak of oneself.
ipoloka, take care of oneself.
ipona, see oneself; – **molato,** admit one's guilt.
iponagatša, show oneself, appear.
iponela, see for oneself, bear the consequences.
ipontšha, show – self, reveal.
ipoola, shave oneself.
ipopa, mould, develop oneself.
ipopela, mould, grumble.
ipotela, plaster (for oneself).
ipshina, feel well, enjoy (oneself)
ipuša, govern (control) oneself.
ipušeletša, avenge oneself.
iri, hour.
iša, take to, convey.
išago, next year.
iše, greetings.
išitše, has taken to.
išiwa, be taken to.
itaeditše, has revealed oneself.
itahla, throw oneself away.
itahlela, throw (oneself upon).
Italia, Italy.
itanya, strike.
itapiša, trouble or exert oneself.
itapološa, give oneself rest.
itatola, prove an alibi, excuse oneself.
itatswa, lick oneself.
itebala, forget oneself.
itebelela, look at oneself.
itebetše, unaware, be surprised.
iteboga, thank oneself.
itebogela, thank, congratulate.
itefela, pay (for oneself).
iteile, beaten, given a hiding; – **motato,** telephoned.
iteiwa, be beaten, struck.
iteka, try (oneself).
itekanela, be self-sufficient, fit.
itekanya, compare oneself.
itekela, try (for oneself).
itekola, examine oneself.
itelela, weep, complain.
itemela, plough or cultivate (for oneself).
itemoga, discover; – **ela,** experience.
itemolla, disaccustom.
itesa, let oneself go.
iteseletša, let oneself go.
iteta, strike one's own breast.
ithabiša, rejoice.
ithafela, take out for oneself (as honey), delve.

ithagaraga, struggle.
ithakgafatša, beautify oneself.
ithakgaletše, rejoice.
ithalega, menstruate for the first time.
ithaopa, volunteer.
ithapa, volunteer.
ithapalatša, throw oneself flat on the ground.
ithapediša, pretend to pray.
ithapelela, pray (for oneself), curry favour.
itharetša, entangle oneself.
itharolla, loosen oneself.
ithata, love oneself, be selfish.
ithatela, love, like, desire.
ithatiša, make oneself beloved, curry favour.
ithea, give oneself a name.
itheela, give a name.
ithekela, buy (for oneself).
itheketše, has bought (for oneself).
ithekiša, be worthy its price; pretend to sell, sell oneself.
ithekga, support oneself.
ithekola, cure (ransom) oneself.
ithema, chop oneself.
ithemiša, pretend to chop.
ithera, make plans about oneself.
itherela, plan.
ithiba, restrain oneself.
ithoba, break oneself; – **leoto,** break one's leg.
ithobalela, sleep.
ithobatša, pretend to sleep.
ithobela, break.
ithoga, cure oneself.
ithokela, sew (for oneself).
ithokola, keep aloof.
ithola, remove one's own burden.
ithoma, go to stool, relieve oneself.
ithomela, begin, make a start.
ithonkga, hurt one's sore.
ithoriša, boast.
ithuela, earn (for oneself).
ithuiša, enrich oneself, pretend to be rich.
ithulela, mend, do one's own blacksmithing.
ithuntšha, shoot oneself.
ithunya, shoot oneself.
ithurugela, swell up.
ithuša, help oneself; – **semeetseng,** improvise.
ithuta, teach oneself, study, learn.
ithutela, study for, learn for.
ithwadiša, take up one's own burden.
ithwalela, carry (for oneself).
ithwele dikgono, place the arms acroos the head when crying, be sad.
ithweša, take up one's burden.
itia, beat, strike.
itiegela, delay.
itiga, cast oneself down.
itigela, precipitate (praise) oneself.
itiiša, strengthen oneself.
itikološa, turn automatically, pretend to turn.
itima, deny oneself something.
itimetša, cause oneself to stray.
itimola, quench the thirst.
itira, pretend to be, do to oneself.
itirela, make for oneself, serve oneself.
itiriša, cause oneself to do, simulate.
itiša, take care of oneself, while away the time, idle.
ititia, strike oneself often or many times.
itiwa, be beaten.
itladika, besmear oneself.
itlama, bind oneself, resolve.
itlamolla, untie oneself.
itlema, bind oneself.
itlemolla, free oneself.
itlhaba, stab oneself.
itlhabanela, fight (for oneself), defend (oneself).
itlhabela, stab.
itlhabiša, pretend to stab.
itlhabolla, rest one's body.

itlhaganediša, cause (pretend) to make haste.
itlhaganela, hasten, make haste.
itlhagatša, wear out.
itlhagela, appear.
itlhagolela, weed (for oneself).
itlhahloba, examine oneself.
itlhakiša, trouble oneself.
itlhakola, rob oneself, wipe oneself.
itlhalefela, be clever.
itlhalefiša, educate oneself, pretend to be wise.
itlhalela, divorce.
itlhaloša, explain oneself.
itlhama, arm, decorate oneself.
itlhametše (-ntwa), ready for battle.
itlhantšha, pretend to be mad.
itlhaola, exclude oneself.
itlhaotše, excelled.
itlhatsela, give evidence.
itlhatšiša, cause oneself to or pretend to vomit.
itlhatswa, pardon (excuse) oneself.
itlhoba, moult.
itlhobodiša, pretend to undress.
itlhobola, undress.
itlhobotše, be undressed, be naked, be penniless.
itlhobogela, lose hope.
itlhoiša, make oneself hateful.
itlhokela, be wanting.
itlhokiša, deprive oneself.
itlhokofatša, torture oneself.
itlhokofaletša, torture oneself for.
itlhokomela, take heed of oneself, be careful.
itlhola, conquer oneself.
itlholela, invent, fabricate.
itlhoma, suppose, settle, establish oneself.
itlhomogela, be sorry.
itlhompha, respect oneself.
itlhompholla, dishonour oneself.
itlhopha, bother oneself.
itlhotšiša, pretend to limp.
itlhwekiša, purify oneself.
itlhwekišetša, purify oneself for.
itlhwela, sojourn.
itliša, come (of one's own accord).
itlomoka, enjoy.
itlopela, be too full, exaggerate.
itloša, go away, leave.
itlotša, anoint oneself.
itlwaetša, accustom oneself to.
itogela, plait, plait for oneself.
itoiša, pretend to bewitch.
itokafalela, become righteous.
itokafatša, pretend to be righteous.
itokiša, prepare onself.
itokišeditše, has prepared for, be ready.
itokišetša, prepare oneself for.
itokolla, free oneself.
itokollela, free oneself for.
itoma, bite oneself; – **(setšu),** – **seokgola,** bite one's elbow, try to do the impossible.
itomiša, pretend to bite.
itomolola, wean oneself.
itora, dream about oneself.
itorela, dream.
itota, take care of oneself, be careful.
itše, has said; – **tuu,** be silent.
itseba, know oneself.
itšeela, take, take for oneself.
itšeetše, has taken for oneself.
itšego, certain, specified.
itšela, eat.
itsenela, enter (by oneself).
itšeng, special.
itsenya, cause oneself to enter, intrude.
itseparela, stick to.
itsetsepela, stand firm.
itšhadiša, leave oneself (out).
itšhadišetša, reserve oneself for.
itšhalela, remain behind.
itshama, lean against.
itshamela, rest one's head on a pillow.
itšhatšhara, cry sadly.
itshega, laugh at oneself, cut oneself.

itshegela, cut, laugh.
itshegiša, pretend to cut (laugh).
itshegiša, make oneself rediculous.
itsheka, shed tears, be clean.
itshekamela, be slanting.
itshekamiša, incline oneself.
itshekamolla, come erect, put oneself right.
itshekile, be clear, pure or clean, has shed tears.
itshelekela, spoil (one's own).
itshelela, cross over.
itshelela, buy food, hunt for food.
itšhelela, pour in (for oneself).
itshema, consider oneself, feign, assume, pretend.
itshenkela, choose for oneself.
itshenola, reveal oneself.
itshenya, spoil oneself.
itshenyetša, spoil one's (future) chances.
itshepelela, walk (by oneself).
itshepha, trust oneself, have selfconfidence.
itšhetše (ka meetse), poured water over/on oneself.
itshetshengwa, have a guilty conscience.
itshetshewa, feel guilty.
itshetla, strike oneself.
itšhia, leave oneself out.
itšhidila, do physical exercise.
itšhilela, grind (for oneself).
itšhilafatša, defile oneself.
itšhira, veil oneself, shade oneself.
itšhireletša, protect oneself.
itshoba, pinch oneself.
itšhoga, be frightened.
itshola, blame oneself, repent.
itsholela, dish up (for oneself), be egoistic.
itshoma, accuse oneself.
itshomela, accuse, report.
itshomiša, cause others to accuse one, pretend to accuse.
itšhonela, be without clothes.
itšhupa, point at oneself, disclose oneself.
itšhuthela, stand aside, draw back.
itshwara, behave, hold oneself; – **etše,** hold on to.
itshwarelela, hold on to.
itšibola, have the first born child.
itšibula, see: **itšibola.**
itšimeletša, neglect your duty.
itšua, condemn oneself.
itswala, give birth to a child or young resembling the parent in all respects.
itswalanya, associated with.
itšwela, go out (one one's own).
itubela, knead (for oneself).
itudiša, settle; – **itše,** settled.
itulela, sit.
itumela, rejoice.
itumiša, make oneself famous; boast.
itwanela, fight for oneself.
itwatša, pretend to be sick.
itwela, fight for oneself.
iwa, be gone; **go** – **kae?** whither are you going.

J

ja, eat, cost, despoil; **ja botšeka,** b. foolish, unskilled; **ja boloko,** poor; – **tša fase,** be poor; – **di sa wele (theogelego),** have a hard time.
jabajabetša, cheat.
jabetša, cheat.
jae, exlam. of admiration.
jaka, live in a foreign country for a time.
jakalase, fox.
jamo, jam.
jana, eat (cheat one another).
Janaware, January.
jarata, yard.

jase, overcoat.
jeba, to jab,
jefreu, madam.
jega, wear out; **jegilwego,** which is worn out.
jeile, gaol.
jekepoto, jackpot.
jeletša, take from one by cunning, take advantage of.
jeli, jelly.
jeme, jam.
jenale, journal, gazette.
jeresi, jersey.
jesa, give to eat, espec. poison, bewitch by putting drugs in one's food.
jesi, jersey.
jewa, be eaten.
jo! alas!
joko, yoke.
Julae, July.
June, June.
juri, jury.
jute, jute.

K

ka, my, mine.
ka, aux. v., can, may.
ka, like, according to, by, with, in, fellow.
kaa, as big, as many.
kaaka, so big.
kaate, wild melon.
kaba, catch, plug up (close) a hole.
kaba, whisk made of the tail of an animal.
kabaganyo, distribution.
ka baka la, on account of.
kabata, romp, gambol.
kabelela, close anything against.
kabelo, share, part, portion, offering, contribution.
kabetla, fragment, piece.
kabetša, eat greedily, milk to the last drop.
kabetša, drive gently.
kabo, part, portion.
kabola, break off a piece.
kabolla, open, uncork.
kabologa, become opened.
kabolola, open, uncork.
kadi, plume, tassel.
kadiana, totter, stagger.
kadiela, suspend, hand up, dangle.
kadietša, cause to waver, dangle.
kadija, old veteran, whopper/stunner.
kadimo, a loan.
kadipotšana, wrestle.
kadiša, cause to weigh, herded.
kadula, perch.
kae, where, whither, whence.
kaela, direct, speak figuratively.
ka ga, relative to.
kagišano, neighbourly intercourse, fellowship.
kago, building, habitation.
kagodikgwa, afforestation.
kahlolo, judgement.
kaiša, grind, mill.
kaka, as big as, such; v., boast, be proud.
kakabala, be stretched, obstinate.
kakabalo, headstrong, headstrongness.
kakabolla, cause to part, tear asunder, overcharge.
kakadia, struggle.
kakabologa, become torn apart.
kakabolola, cause to part, tear asunder.
kakaila, limp.
kakalla, fall backwards.
kakama, carry with both hands.
kakamala, pause in wonder, be constipated.
kakamara, carry in the arms.
kakana, clay pipe.
kaka'ng? (kakang), adv., how great?

kakanyatshenyegelo, costing.
kakanyo, reasoning, thought, estimation.
kakapolla, uproot, pull out.
kakara, take with both hands.
kakaretšo, summary, precis.
kakata, strike hard, enjoy.
kakatlela, pull tight, pull hard, strain.
kaketšo, lying, deception.
kakgofišo, acceleration.
kakgofo, haste.
kakola, pick up, take a portion.
kala, branch, navel string, v., weight.
kalafi, a doctoring.
kalafo, cure.
kalaka, lime.
kalakata, worry, disturb.
kalakatiša, pursue.
kalakatlega, run hither and thither.
kalakune, turkey.
kalana, navel-string, little branch, perch, umbilical cord.
kalapa, hop, skip.
kalasiamo, calcium.
kalatiša, make a show of.
kalatša, be fickle, dangle, make a show of, recruit, deceive, entice.
kalatšane, fickle person, flirt, recruiter.
kalekisi, calyx.
kalela, weigh for, hang on a branch.
kalema, prance.
kalentara, calendar, almanac.
kaliko, calico.
kalo, as great.
kaloga, become dim, disappear.
kalogo, end of the circumcision ceremony.
kalokana, trade, work for a living.
kalola, to dim.
kalolla, unhook.
kaloma, pretend to bite.
kalošo, dismissal of the initiated.
kama, comb the hair, catch.
kamakama, fill one's arm.
kamalala, be obstinate.
kamanyo, making contact.
kamela, camel.
kamo, n. comb.
kamoga, get broken, deprive of.
kamogelo, reception, hospitality.
kamogo, depriving.
kamola, break.
kamora, (kamore), room.
kampa, camp.
kampana, wrestle.
kampetša, swallow, drink quickly.
kampiamo, cambium.
kamute, gamut, scale.
Kanada, Canada.
kanale, channel.
kanama, lie on one's back.
Kanana, Canaan.
kanamiša, cause to lie o/t back.
kananyo, barter, trade, commerce.
kanapa, knapsack.
kanari, canary.
kanase, canna.
kandelare, candlestick.
kanegelo, story.
kanegelo-kopana, short-story.
kanego, a hanging up to dry.
kang, such as, by means of what.
kankaru, kangaroo.
kangwa, be combed.
kankere, cancer.
kano, oath.
kanono, cannon.
kanthe, whereas.
kantoro, office.
kanyakanya, collection of things, joy, activity.
kanya, fold, roll up.
kanyo, sucking.
kaologa, part.
kaolola, separate, part.
kaone, better; **kaonekaone,** best.
kaonefatša, improve, improvement.
Kapa, Cape Town.
kapa, hood, rafter.

kaparelo, covering for.
kaparo, dressing.
kapeo, cooking, cookery.
kapetla, fragment.
kapetlele, capital (money).
kapetša, lap up water.
kapi, hood.
kapilari, capillary.
kapogo, clearing up.
kapoko, snow.
kalopedi, second-hand clothes.
kapolo, opening, unveiling, undressing.
kapotene, captain.
kapuetša, feed an infant.
kapusela, flutter, gallop slowly.
kara, buttermilk, churn.
karabane, caravan.
karabo, answer, reply.
karabole, gravel.
karalala, stand astride.
karamafone, gramophone.
karanta, guarantee.
karanti, security, guarantee.
karapa, (A.), scrape.
karata, chart, card.
karatšhe, garage.
kariki, cart.
karodi, divisor.
karogano, parting.
karogo, exception.
karolelo, setting apart for.
karolo, division, part, portion.
karolwa, dividend.
Karu, Karoo.
kase, cheese.
kasino, casino.
kasteroli, caster oil.
kata, trot, tramp, make haste.
kata, fell, strike down, rape.
kata, hard-working person, hemp.
katakata, retreat.
katakelwa ke, be under the power of, be suppressed by.
katana, struggle, fight, do-best.
katapa, wilt.
katapulela, jump upon.
katara, guitar.
katekisema, catechism, confirmation (classes).
katela, press down.
katelelo, pressure, throng.
kathe, whereas.
kati, go itia –, hop, rejoice.
katiela, prop up, stay, stem.
katika, trample down.
katišanetšwa, mutliple.
katišani, divisor.
katišo, increasing, multiplication.
katla, stretch.
katlego, prosperity, success.
katlelela, pull tight.
katliša, bully.
katlo, kiss; **– phedišo,** kiss of life.
katlolola, stretch out.
kato, rape.
katoga, move away, withdraw.
katologa, withdraw, stand apart.
katologane, be separated.
katologo, expansion, lengthening.
katološa, expand, lengthen.
katološo, lengthening.
katoša, move away; **– ka sa nthago,** move backwards.
katrolo, pulley.
katša, rest, lie down.
katse, cat.
kaušu, sock, stocking.
kaya, sew together, grind, (coarsely), mince.
ke, I.
ke, it is.
ke, by.
kea, frolic, dance.
keatseba, witchdoctor.
keba, slumber.
kebama, droop.
kebeka, rob, cheat.
kebja, spotted (animal).
kebola, peal.
kebolo, pealing,
kedimolo, yawning, yawn.

kedišo, enlightement.
kefa, hat, cap, v., speak much, prate.
kefo, dodging.
keiti, gate.
keka, spread, increase.
kekela, spread.
kekeletšo, increase, supplement.
kekema, slant.
kekenene, very big ox.
kekeretša, cackle.
keketa, strike, beat, gnaw, enjoy.
keketane, stubble.
keketla, become notched or dented.
keketlega, go to pieces, get worn-out.
keketlolla, cut out a piece.
keketo, striking.
keketšo, increase, increment.
kekišo, copying, imitation.
keko, treason.
kelapula, rain-gauge.
keledi, tear.
kelee, go re –! fall (of tears, water).
keleketa, keep on spreaking.
keleketla, lengthen the story.
kelelelo, thought.
keleletšo, consideration.
kelelo, remembrance.
kelello, understanding, memory.
kelepiša, chatter, yap, jaw.
keletšo, advice.
kelo, measure.
kelotlhoko, attention.
kemakgale, of long standing.
kemaro, pregnancy.
kemelo, support, waiting for.
kemišo, causing to stand.
kemo, standing, stand.
kemola, pimple, acne.
kemotia, stability.
keng, strange; what? foreign.
keno, vow, oath.
kenywa, fruit.
kepelo, burial.
kepi, crowbar.
kepu, digging.
kepu, crowbar.
kera, smile.
kerafite, graphite.
keremafomo, gramophone.
kerese, candle.
keretla, prattle.
keta, play at five-stones.
ketaketa, active.
ketane, chain.
ketapele, leader, forerunner.
keteka, rejoice, play (mokete).
ketela, end off, cut (ears of corn).
ketla, punch.
ketla, shard, fragment.
ketlaketla, walk quickly.
ketlele, kettle.
ketletša, knock a thing against another.
keto, re –! fall.
ketoga, appear.
ketola, break off.
ketšišo, imitation.
ketwane, chain.
kga, pick, draw water, pluck, exude.
kgaba, ornate, adorn, dress well, dig; **ehwa** –, be terribly ashamed.
kgabagare, middle, centre, midst.
kgabakgabetša, stammer.
kgabakgabiša, decorate, boil.
kgabane, shoot, offspring.
kgabela, cut up, carve into.
kgabelela, cut to pieces.
kgabetla, chop to pieces, hack.
kgabetlela, mince.
kgabiša, adorn, beautify.
kgabišang, ornamental.
kgabišitše, adorned.
kgabišo, ornament, adorning.
kgabja, adorned.
kgabo, monkey, flame.
kgabola, take a short cut, pass by quickly.
kgabutla, cut asunder, eat greedily.
kgabutlana, small hare, baby hare.
kgadi, go re –! glance, appear for an instant, feminine, female, father's sister.

kgadibete, top-dog.
kgadibetša, bully.
kgadika, roasted fat, greave.
kgadimola, reprimand, scold.
kgadimolo, reflection, scolding.
kgadiša, cause to reprimand.
kgaetšedi, younger brother, younger sister; – **agwe,** his younger sister.
kgafa, brush aside, drive away.
kgafelo, surrendering to.
kgafetša, time and again.
kgafetšo, concession.
kgafo, rejection.
kgaga, scaly ant-eater, armadillo, pangolin.
kgagabi, reptile or creeping animal.
kgagabo, creeping or crawling.
kgagamala, b. atsonished.
kgagamalo, stretching.
kgagamatša, surprise, astonish.
kgagamela, v. glitter; n., lantern.
kgagamologo, slackening.
kgagapa, bully.
kgagara, knuckle-bone.
kgagaripa, scratch (the ground when ploughing).
kgagoga, snap, break off.
kgagogo, rent, tear, breach.
kgagola, break off, tear devour.
kgahla, curdle, solidify.
kgahlano, meeting, encounter, rendezvous.
kgahlantšho, joining.
kgahlega, be pleasing, be desirable; adv., **ka go** – voluntarily.
kgahlega, be charmed, be delighted.
kgahlego, desirability, choice.
kgahliša, –go, attractive, charming, be admirable.
kgahlišo, pleasing.
kgahlo, pleasure, curdling, solidification.
kgahlo, big ox.
kgahlolla, melt.
kgahlologa, melt as ice.
kgaitšadi, (kgaitšedi), younger brother of a female, (younger) sister of a male, cousin.
kgaka, n., guinea-fowl; v., arrange, mix, join; **ja** –, transgress.
kgakajana, little distance.
kgakala, far, distant; outside; **ya** –, go far away, go to stool.
kgakanego, dilemma, confusion, crisis.
kgakantšho, confusion.
kgakanyo, confusion.
kgakatšo, provocation.
kgaketla, n., shell, shard; v.t., cut fringes in the edge of a cloth.
kgakga, desire (something one can never get), scratch.
kgakgamala, be astonished, wonder.
kgakgamalo, wonder, astonishment.
kgakgamolla, pull apart.
kgakgamotša, tear asunder.
kgakgamuši, flames.
kgakgangwe, forked stick.
kgakgapa, robust person.
kgakgaphega, peel off.
kgakgara, rustle, crackle, startle.
kgakgarapa, big and strong man, giant.
kgakgarega, dash away.
kgakgaripa, scrape the topsoil.
kgakgasa, hurry, be diligent.
kgakgatha, beat repeatedly, simmer.
kgakgathega, bubble, simmer, fizz.
kgakgathi, tussle, beating, rustling.
kgakola, initiate, use for the first time.
kgala, scold, reprimand, abuse, revile.
kgalagapa, palate; **iša,** palatalize.
kgalakega, crave for food.
kgalakgathela, boil, yearn for.
kgalakišo, provocation, embitterment.
kgalako, bitterness.
kgalalo, despising a gift.
kgalapatša, palatize.
kgalapatšo, palatalisation.
kgale, long ago, formerly, of old.
kgalefo, anger, wrath.

kgalega, be scoldable, become abused, dried up, thirsty.
kgalegile, be thirsty.
kgalema, scold, reprimand.
kgalemelo, scolding.
kgama, strangle, stick in the throat, choke.
kgama, antelope, hartebeest, deer; **thari ya** –, care, protection.
kgamaka, stammer, crowbar.
kgamakanya, be undecided.
kgamathela, stick to.
kgamathetše, be dirty or smudged.
kgamathi, bark (of a tree).
kgamelo, pail, bucket.
kgamilwe, drowned, strangled, throttled.
kgamo, milking, strangulation.
kgamogo, drainage.
kgamola, divide into two parts, fasten in the middle.
kgamolo, the squeezing out, drainage.
kgamolola, pull asunder.
kgampane, small calabash, cocopan.
kgampi, hollow, cave.
kgampi, leswiswi la –, pitch dark.
kgamutha, besmear the mouth.
kgana, hop, skip, display, boast.
kganatha, become smeared or smudged, n. darkness.
kgane, perhaps.
kganela, stop, restrain, bridle.
kganetši, anti-thesis.
kganelo, prohibition.
kganetšo, refusal, prohibition, negative, denial, contradiction.
kgang, debate, talk, impudence.
kgankga, struggle.
kgankgathi, conflict, dispute, bustle.
kgankgerepe, crab, lobster.
kgano, refusal, denial.
kgano, wildcat, bush-cat, serval.
kgantele, presently, by and by.
kganthe, however yet, whereas, perhaps.
kganthola, game of skipping.
kgantšha, tantalize.
kganya, detest, abhor, cry.
kganya, be bright, shine, proud.
kganyana, a little argument/talk.
kganyela, run, make haste.
kganyelela, hurry to/for.
kganyoga, desire, please, covet.
kganyogo, desire, pleasing.
kgao, opening; **phula** –, pave a way.
kgaoga, break, be divided, snap.
kgaogana, part.
kgaogano, parting, division.
kgaoganya, divide, separate.
kgaoganyo, separation.
kgaola, divide, cut through, break off; – **setho,** amputate.
kgaolaka, divide completely.
kgaoletša, cut off, precede, abbreviate.
kgaolo, division, chapter.
kgaotša, cause to break off, cease.
kgaotšo, breaking off, stopping.
kgapa, gourd, calabash.
kgapa, ram, male sheep.
kgapeletšo, coercion, constraint.
kgapetla, scale, shard, shell.
kgapha, scoop, wipe (perspiration).
kgaphakgapha, splash, flap.
kgaphasa, dangle, flutter.
kgaphasela, dash, splash, flutter.
kgaphaselo, flutter, splashing.
kgaphatša, spill.
kgaphatšega, overflow.
kgaphatšo, spilling.
kgaphea, half-fill, hang over.
kgaphela, pour water (on) out for.
kgaphela ka thoko, push aside.
kgaphetša, drape, lasso, lap up water.
kgaphola, drain.
kgaphoša, drain.
kgaphošo, draining, drainage.
kgaphunya, break away.
kgapo, loot, spoil, booty, coup.
kgapolotša, peel.
kgapolotšega, peel off, scale.

kgapotša, feed a baby (in African style).
kgapuru, re –; break away.
kgapurutša, break away, dislocate.
kgara, chest, breast.
kgarakgaša, crackle, croak, screech.
kgarama, hop, skip.
kgaramatšega, be parted, open up.
kgarametša, push, shove, force.
kgarametšo, pushing, shoving.
kgarankana, wrestle.
kgare, crown, ring made of grass, bobbin.
kgarebe, virgin, maiden.
kgareetša = **kgarietša.**
kgariet[1]sa, rouse, incite, instigate.
kgarietšo, instigation, urge.
kgarihla, (kgaritla), empty.
kgaripa, empty.
kgaritsa, scratch, sharpen.
kgaro, coil, tress.
kgaroga, be startled.
kgarola, frighten.
kgarološa, expand.
kgaruma, growl.
kgarumo, snarl, growl.
kgaruru, unrest, quarrel.
kgasa, encircle.
kgašana, small crown, ring made of grass.
kgašo, broadcasting.
kgatelelo, accent, pressure.
kgatha, chop off twigs, break up new soil, crush.
kgathala, be weary, careless.
kgathalo, fatigue, carelessness.
kgathatša, weary, tire.
kgathe, whereas.
kgathola, take a draught, breathe in cold air, rest, punctuate, experience.
kgatholela, gulp down.
kgathologa, rest.
kgati, cane, skipping-rope; **tia** –, skip.
kgatikanya, brandish, slash, wield.
kgatišo, printing.
kgatla, sheath, handle of a knife.
kgatla, strike, stone, crush; – **motswiri,** make a click.
kgatlametša, push in.
kgatlampi, shallow hole.
kgato, step, footprint, yard.
kgatogo, a stepping-off.
kgatsele, beestings.
kgaugelo, pity, mercy.
kgauswana, near by.
kgauswane, vicinity.
kgauswi, near.
kgaya, mob, humiliate.
kgeba, belch, break a wind.
kgebotša, remove the bark of a tree.
kgefola, chip, break the neck or brim.
kgegeo, irony.
kgehlenke, a tinkling sound.
kgeiga, tear.
kgeila, tear.
kgeke, concubine, mistress, paramour.
kgeketla, cut unevenly.
kgekga, walk hurriedly.
kgekgeša, perforate.
kgeko, prostitution.
kgelekgetha, deceive, cheat.
kgelepua, skip.
kgelešwa, gland disease.
kgeloga, turn aside, backslide.
kgelogo, breaking away from, heresy.
kgelola, turn from.
kgeloša, mislead, avert.
kgema, bite off.
kgemetha, bite off, cut off, smite.
kgenkgerepe, crab, lobster.
kgepetla, scale, shell.
kgephola, break off a piece.
kgera, nibble, gnaw.
kgeramatona, hermaphrodite.
kgerehla, rattle, snore.
kgerehlwa, worn-out and useless thing.
kgerekgere, tool, garden tool.
kgerekgetša, cackle.
kgereša, demolish.
kgeretla, tear.

kgero, shell, chip, nutshell.
kgeroga, chip off.
kgeru, kernel, nutshell, nut, chip.
kgeruga, have a dry cough.
kgesa, turn back, catch red-handed, throng.
kgetha, choose, elect, pick.
kgethego, consecration, holiness.
kgethela pele, predestine.
kgethelo, consecration, dedication.
kgethelwa, be chosen for.
kgetho, choice, election.
kgetholla, be partial.
kgethollo ya mmala, colour-bar.
kgethula, pull down, bite off.
kgethwa, holy; – **falo,** sanctification.
kgetlane, collarbone.
kgetloga, fall off, chip off.
kgetsi, bag, knapsack.
kgetwane, lizard.
kgina, kneehalter.
kgiripa, cut too short.
kgiritla, roar, bellow, snore.
kgitla, strike jaw with the elbow.
kgitlela, strike for, heap up (wood on the fire).
kgo, re –, sleep.
kgoa, provoke, tease, screaming of many people.
kgoane, rumour.
kgoba, reproach, rail at, be sarcastic.
kgoba, collect, gather.
kgobaboloko, tumble-bug, dung-beetle.
kgobadi, wounded person or animal.
kgobakgoba, chisel out.
kgobalo, getting hurt.
kgobe, fish, boiled grain, prosperous, fortunate.
kgobe, pan, puddle.
kgobea, move excitedly.
kgobela, gather up, put away.
kgobelela, gather for.
kgobja, be gathered.
kgobo, gathering, injury.
kgobo, sarcasm, reproach, railing.
kgoboga, become frayed, disgusted, degeneration.
kgobogo, shame, disgust, abuse, offence.
kgobokana, come together, meet; – **nywa,** be brought together.
kgobokanela, gather for/at, gather against.
kgobokano, gathering, meeting.
kgobokantše, has gathered.
kgobokanya, gather, collect.
kgobokela, gather.
kgoboketša, gather, collect.
kgobola, scold, cut off (hair).
kgobošo, shame, disgust; – **ya mapele,** masturbation.
kgobotla, taunt, corrode.
kgodi, fog.
kgodi-a-kgokgo, a real gentleman.
kgodiša, satisfy.
kgodišo, praise, honour, bringing-up.
kgodu, pumpkin broth.
kgodukoma, Adam's apple.
kgodumodumo, a fabulous monster.
kgoelelo, calling, shouting.
kgoeletšo, a call, a shouting.
kgoetša, hook on.
kgofa, tick.
kgofa, shovel away, drive out.
kgoga, smoke a pipe or cigarette, take snuff.
kgoga, shaft, bone used for inhaling snuff, dragon-fly.
kgogamašego, evening star.
kgogelo, attraction.
kgogetša, hook (hang) on, link up.
kgogo, fowl, domestic fowl.
kgogo, rattle, (Cape) badger.
kgogobadimo, cattle-egret.
kgogodi, washing-up, flotsam.
kgogola, wash away, drag along.
kgogolamoko, winter rain.
kgogoropo, the horn-bill bird, adj., curved.
kgohlagane, joined together.
kgohlano, friction.

kgohletša, add wood to the fire, encourage.
kgohlo, kloof, yellow copper.
kgohlo, white clay.
kgohlola, cough.
kgohlolo, coughing, cough.
kgohlomela, fall into, get discouraged.
kgohlopo, quiver.
kgohu, snail.
kgoima, hundredweight, central, quintal.
kgojana, a small distance away.
kgoka, bind, tie, try hard.
kgoka, eel.
kgokafalo, fornication, adultery.
kgokedi, buckle.
kgoketša, catch with a hook, entice.
kgokgo, crown of the watermelon.
kgokgoba, stoop.
kgokgoetša, hook together, drag along, drive.
kgokgofane, dwarf.
kgokgoilane, ankle.
kgokgokgo, larynx.
kgokgola, crown of water-melon.
kgokgola, wipe away.
kgokgoma, move about (in the dark).
kgokgomela, force.
kgokgometša, take indecent liberties with a woman.
kgokgomothi, woodpecker.
kgokgontšha, offend.
kgokgoša, shell mealies.
kgokgotha, knock, shake out, trail.
kgokgothela, strike, hammer, knock in.
kgokgothi, stalk, core of the mealie cob.
kgokgotša, even up thatch, knock stones against each other.
kgokolla, untie, loosen.
kgokolo, circle, ball.
kgokolodumo, a fabulous monster.
kgokologa, roll down.
kgokološane, tumble bug.
kgokolwana, small circle or ball.
kgokomodumo, fabulous monster.
kgokong, gnu, blue wildebeest; **–e ntsho,** victim of the initiation ritual.
kgokola, rusk.
kgola, cut away, clear up, shed the milk teeth, n., bunch, cluster.
kgolaboloko, tumble-bug.
kgolane, tuft of grass.
kgolawa, big animal.
kgole, rope, string.
kgole, far, distant.
kgolegelo, imprisonment (for or at).
kgolego, prison, goal.
kgolla, unfasten, cut away.
kgolo, big, important, full-grown.
kgolo, satisfaction, contentment.
kgolofatšo, crippling.
kgologolo, larynx, gullet, oesophagus.
kgolokela, make a ball of.
kgolokgohla, be loose, be hipshot rickety.
kgolokgotha, make round, be rickety.
kgolokgothega, roll down, be loose.
kgolokgotla, shake, be loose.
kgolokwe, ball.
kgolong, percentage, per cent.
kgololo, deliverance.
kgolwa, be satisfied, believe, be convinced.
kgclwanyane, fairly big.
kgoma, touch.
kgomagana, stick together, join.
kgomaganya, stick on, paste togehter.
kgomano, contact.
kgomarela, cling to, adhere to, hang on to.
kgomaretša, stick on.
kgomarologa, come loose.
kgomaswantšho, flannel board.
kgome, black scorpion.
kgometše, be sleepy.
kgomo, a head of cattle.
kgomobolekana, tinned milk.
kgomogadi, cow.
kgomomolongwane, bull-frog.

kgona, be able, overcome; aux. verb and then.
kgonagatšo, facility.
kgonama, bend down.
kgone, serves you right.
kgonega, be possible.
kgonego, possibility, potential.
kgong, wood, firewood.
kgonoga, be or become broken off.
kgonono, grumbling.
kgonosela, break off as a thorn.
kgonthiša, ascertain, verify.
kgonthe, true, truly, genuine.
kgonya, lock, bolt, bar.
kgoo, shout, cry.
kgoo, go re –! snore.
kgopa, trip up, n., heap.
kgopa, snail, ball, one body.
kgopafala, become crooked, bad or immoral.
kgopama, become crooked, distorted, warped.
kgopamiša, make crooked, twist:
kgopamolla, straighten.
kgopana, small snail, dwarf.
kgoparara, leswiswi la –, pitch dark night.
kgope, bachelor.
kgopega, become offended.
kgopela, ask, beg.
kgopela tsela, ask leave to go.
kgopha, smear with dung, scrape together.
kgophaboloko, tumble-bug.
kgophane, polecat, aloe.
kgophela, gather the nectar of the aloe.
kgophetša, put the blame on someone.
kgophola, upset, raise dust, scape out.
kgopilwe, be offended, be tripped up.
kgopiša, offend, cause to stumble, worry, tease.
kgopišo, stumbling-block, offence, scandal.
kgopo, adj., crooked, perverse; n., rib.
kgopolla, straighten, recitfy.
kgopolo, thought, idea.
kgopolola, straighten, recitfy.
kgopotšo, reminder, souvenir.
kgopša, stumble, be tripped.
kgopu, joining hands, stalk of a pumpkin leaf.
kgora, sufficient, sufficiency (of food).
kgora, scoop out, clear.
kgoramela, adhere to, cling to.
kgoramolla, remove.
kgori, bustard, paauw.
kgoriša, satisfy hunger.
kgoro, entrance, department, enclosure, tribe.
kgorogela, attack, fall upon.
kgorogelabaeng, guest house.
kgorogelo, arrival at.
kgorogo, going home.
kgorogoro, calabash for holding seed.
kgorokgoro, rustling.
kgorokgotša, shake, shake up.
kgorola, press on, push on.
kgorometša, push forward, push, shove; – **na,** push one another.
kgoromolla, detach.
kgoromolotša, detach.
kgoropana, become crooked, shrivelled up, bent.
kgororwane, species of very small bird, a trifle.
kgorošo, bringing home.
kgoroto, champion, leader.
kgošana, petty chief.
kgosane, drowsiness.
kgošetša, shut a door by bolting.
kgoši, di –, **magoši,** chief king.
kgošigadi, queen, chieftainess.
kgosoka, walk with effort.
kgosoma, walk, dejectedly.
kgoteledi, go swa –, be burnt by a live coal.
kgotelo, burning.
kgotha, prune, chop off.
kgothala, take courage.

kgothatša, exhort, encourage.
kgothatšo, exhortation, encouragement.
kgothego, denudation.
kgothela, strip off.
kgothi, stalk, handle of calabash.
kgotho, male dog, chine.
kgothola, dump.
kgothula, bow, bend.
kgothwane, juice of the aloe.
kgotla, poke, push with the finger, mash; – **-o-mone,** syrup.
kgotla, court.
kgotlakgotla, poke.
kgotlela, v., mash, defile, disgrace, dishonour.
kgotlelela, endure, persevere.
kgotlelelo, perseverance.
kgotleletša, excite, exhort, stir a fire.
kgotletša, stir a fire, stoke, poke.
kgotlopo, quiver.
kgoto, chine, backbone.
kgotsa, be astonished, conj., whether, lest.
kgotšana, little mist or fog.
kgotše, be satisfied, have had enough.
kgotswana, small rib.
kgotswane, playing at dolls.
kgoula, pounce; – **ela,** upon.
kgwa, spit, expectorate.
kgwadi, spotted animal, long knife, exemplary, white-backed ox or bull; clever person.
kgwadira, variety of eagle, "berghaan".
kgwaediša, cause to put food in one's bag, share the spoil.
kgwaetša, share the hunter's spoil.
kgwagetša, hang up, hook on.
kgwahla, become strong or firm.
kgwahla, re –! rustle.
kgwahlišitše dinao, run faster, double up.
kgwaila, strike match, etch, tattoo.
kgwakgwa, whooping cough.
kgwakgwaripa, scratch, plough shallow.
kgwakgwathi, something hard and coarse, bark of a tree.
kgwale, partridge.
kgwamola, take out.
kgwana, white-backed cow or heifer.
kgwankgati, a duel (fight) between girls.
kgwanya, tap.
kgwao, craving for meat.
kgwaphela, draw in the feet.
kgwapho! re –! rise suddenly.
kgwaphoga, be startled, be roused.
kgwapsi, cry; **ološa** –! raise a cry.
kgwara, armadilo, scaly ant-eater, rust, unlikeable character.
kgwarahla, rustle.
kgwaralala, stiffen, harden.
kgwarapetša, hold on to.
kgwarinya, strike a match.
kgwaripa, scratch; adj., roan (coloured).
kgwaritša, strike a match, scratch, write.
kgwaša, rustle.
kgwašo, rustling.
kgwatha, touch with the finger, touch lightly, silent.
kgwathaa, rad., silence.
kgwathetša, beckon, prune.
kgwathi, re –! be silent.
kgwathile, be strong.
kgwebanoši, monopoly.
kgwebo, barter, trade, commerce.
kgwebola, pluck, peal.
kgwedi, moon, month; **bona** –, have monthly period.
kgwele, thigh, a game resembling hockey.
kgweloga, snap, break off.
kgwerano, league, covenant, friendship.
kgweša, hook on.
kgwii, re –! be straight, be fast alseep.
khabareitha, carburetter.

khabetšhe, cabbage.
khabole, esiti ya –, carbolic acid.
khalenta, calender.
khamera, camera.
khamphase, compass.
khansela, cancel.
khapohaetrete, carbohydrate.
khapone, carbon.
khaponemonoksaete, carbon monoxide.
khaponetaoksaete, carbon dioxide.
khastate, custard.
khastamo, customs.
khatepokisi, cardboard box.
khatepoto, cardboard.
khefi, tea-room.
khemišo, artificial respiration.
khemo, breathing, respiration.
kheše, cash.
khii, quay, key, clef.
khile, keel.
khina, knee-halter.
khinne, has knee-haltered.
khinolla, loosen the drag.
khiro, hire, rent.
khitši, kitchen.
khoile, (khoele), coil.
khokhase, caucus.
kholetšhe, college.
kholifolawa, cauliflower.
kholofedišo, promise.
kholofelo, hope, expectation.
kholofologo, despair.
kholomo, column.
kholomodumo, legendary dragon.
kholoro, collar.
khomolo, silence, doldrum.
khona, v., go round the corner; n., corner.
khora, have plenty, be satisfied: – **mpa,** become pregnant.
khoriša, satisfy.
khoro, plenty, satisfaction.
khoše, appeased, satisfied.
khosetšhumo, costume.
khotoletone, cotyledon.
khoukhou, cocoa, coco.
khouni, cone.
khouta, quote.
khretšhe, creche.
khrikethe, cricket.
khubama, kneel, be in labour.
khubamela, kneel to.
khubedu, red.
khubidu, red.
khubu, a navel.
khudu, tortoise.
khuduego, agitation, commotion, emotion.
khuduga, move, migrate.
khudugo, trek, migration.
khuduthamaga, executive.
khuduo, stirring.
khudutlou, elephant-tortoise.
khuela, fill up and swell, (as an abscess).
khukhuna, creep, crawl.
khukhunela, creep to, stalk.
khukhunetša, stalk; – **tše,** slipped into.
khukhurapa, fleshy (hardy) person.
khukhuša, bud, blossom.
khukhutha, walk slowly.
khula, subside, abate, cease.
khulo, abating, subsiding, termination, robbery.
khulong, brown (red), ox or bull.
khulou, brown (red) ox or bull.
khulwana, brown (red) cow.
khuma, remove the bark or skin, fray.
khumanego, poverty.
khumedi, intercessor, mediator.
khumela, mediate, intercede, curry favour.
khumela, n., **pudi ya –,** goat paid as compensation.
khumelo, intercesion, mediation.
khumišo, enrichment, a making rich.
khumo, wealth.
khumoga, be removed (of the skin), abrasion.
khumola, pull out, abrade.
khuna, bind.

khunama, kneel down.
khunamela, kneel down to, worship.
khunamologa, rise, stand.
khunelo, a tying, binding.
khunkhwane, insect, beetle.
khunola, liberate, undo, untie.
khunologo, becoming liberated, confinement.
khunou, red ox or bull.
khunwana, red cow or heifer.
khunyane, small dog, puppy.
khupa, hold in the closed hand or mouth; – **dinala,** hold thumbs.
khupa, secret, private affair; – **marama,** secret.
khuparela, grasp, hold in the hand.
khupe, ant-lion.
khupei, coupe.
khupela moya, keep your breath.
khupetša, cover up, conceal.
khupetšega, be covered up.
khupolotše, has stripped, laid bare.
khupone, coupon.
khuru, knee.
khurumela, put a lid on.
khurumetša, cover up.
khurumolla, uncover.
khuša, cook, or boil insufficiently.
khušwane, knee-cap, patella.
khuta, hide, take shelter.
khutela, hide for, hide in.
khuti, river bank, shore, mole.
khutla, return, butt.
khutlana, knock against each other.
khutlo, corner; – **tharo,** triangle.
khutlo, full-stop.
khutlola, protrude, project.
khutlwana, semicolon.
khuto, hiding, concealing.
khutša, rest, repose.
khutše, subsided, abated, ceased.
khutšiša, give rest.
khutšo, rest, peace.
khutsofatša, shorten, abbreviate.
khwaere, choir.
khwamela, insert, put in.
khwamoga, come out or off.
khwamola, take out, open a purse.
khwaphetša, crestfallen.
khwelatumelo, martyr.
khwele, partiality, bias.
khwephane, polecat.
khwetšo, n., find.
khwibidu, red.
khwibiletša, (mahlo), stare angrily.
khwinine, quinine.
khwiti, bank, river-bank, shore, mole.
kiba, beat time, plug, stamp.
kibja, be pushed in, be stuffed.
kididii, thunder.
kiiti, bitter melon.
kikitlela, draw, make an effort.
kilana, gizzard.
kile, once, ever.
kilelo, hatred, taboo.
kiletšo, interdict, prohibition.
kilibana, display strength, health or swiftness.
kilo, ban, hatred.
kilokramo, kilogramme.
kilometara, kilometre.
kinamo, a bending.
kinata, knee-halter.
kinipitane, pliers.
kinipitang, pincers, pliers.
kioseke, kiosk.
kiribana, wheelbarrow.
kirietša, thunder, throw, pacify.
kišo, act of taking to.
kišontle, export.
kišopele, advance.
kitela, ram down, strike down.
kiti, mob-psychology, esprit de corps.
kitikiti, re –, trot, run.
kitima, run.
kitimela, run to or for.
kitimiša, chase.
kitla, strike.
kitlagane, be dense.
kitlano, density.
kitletša, strike, give a blow.
klase, class.

klasekamore class-room.
klasiki, classic.
klereke, clerk.
kliente, client.
klimate, climate.
klosari, glossary.
koakoetša, stammer.
koba, drive away, scare away.
koba, bend, look round.
kobama, bend forward.
kobamelo, a bowing down to.
kobela, earn a cutlet, set, mount.
kobi, book.
kobile, chased.
kobo, blanket, coat, clothes.
kobolá, peck, pick, bite (of a snake).
kobolela, peck or pick for, allot a task.
kobotela, peck, pick and plant.
kobotetša, bend the face downwards.
kodi, stain, blot, defect.
kodimela, bow down low, bend under.
kodimpitsane, tadpole.
kodintsane, tadpole.
kodu, skin under the chin of an animal, dewlap.
koduma, jump off, climb down, descend.
kodumela, bend the back, descend, fall head foremost.
kofi, coffee.
kofuto, crowbar.
kojaba, guava.
kokamelo, overseeing.
kokoletšo, addition, increase.
koketšo, an adding, addition.
koko, grandmother, grandfather.
koko, nut.
koko, nursing.
ko-ko, re –, knock (at a door).
kokobaditšweng, embossed.
kokobala, float, be bouyant, press lightly upon, wait upon.
kokobana, squat, sit on the haunches.
kokobanya, double up.
kokobatša, emboss.
kokobeditše, has humbled; – **ditšwe,** be humbled.
kokobela, become humble, decrease, settle down quietly, become assauged, sink, drop.
kokobele, flying ant.
kokobetša, humble, diminish.
kokobetšo, humbling, diminishing.
kokobolla, raise up.
kokoilane, ankle.
kokola, swell with hope.
kokolohuto, heron.
kokoma, swell, protrude; n., lump.
kokomala, squat, crouch down.
kokomalela, keep watch over a patient.
kokomatša, place in a sitting position.
kokomo, swelling.
kokomoga, rise, swell, swell up.
kokona, nibble, chew.
kokonata, coco(a)nut.
kokoni, rodent.
kokokono, strong thing.
kokopa, give a small bit (of food), give less than one's due.
kokopane, cocopan.
kokopela, give a small bit.
kokorala, be arched.
kokoretša, cluck.
kokorietša, handle carefully.
kokoropa, become arched, crooked.
kokoropana, arched, crooked.
kokoropo, curved.
kokota, knock, hammer.
kokotela, knock in a nail, lean upon.
kokotlela, lean upon, increase.
kokotletša, support.
kokoto, giant, male baboon.
kokotša, wood-pecker.
kokwane, pillar, post.
kola, n., plume; cup, trophy, prize; v., catch with the hand, strip.
kole, cabbage.
kolege, college.

koleka, collect.
kolela, catch with the hand, throw food into the mouth (by hand).
kolo, bullet.
koloba, become wet, soak.
kolobe, pig.
kolobetša, baptise, baptize.
kolobetšo, baptism.
kolobile, be wet or soaked.
kolobiša, wet, soak, moisten; – **šitšwe,** moistened.
kolohutwe, heron.
koloi, waggon, wagon.
kolokota, turn somersault.
kololo, small antelope, klipspringer.
kolomelo, lamentation.
koloni, colony.
kolopetša, add to.
kolota, owe.
koma, eat, eat something soft.
koma, circumcision school, secret, truth, song of triumph.
komakoma, turn somersault.
komakomana, silence.
komakometša, tantalize.
komakomiša, cause to (turn somersault), topple.
komang, scolding.
kome, re –, throw into one's mouth to eat.
kome, klipspringer, antelope.
komeditše, swallowed whole.
komela, slander.
komelelo, drought, dryness.
komello, drought, dryness.
komelo, yeast, fermentation.
kometša, swallow at once.
komiki, cup.
komokomo, gooseberry.
komola, break off.
komolla, uproot, pull out.
komota, hit the forehead.
kompo(ne), compound, company.
kona, give sparingly, eat dainties secretly, be stingy.
konalo, a growing old and useless.
kongkonetša, re –, tantalize.
kong-kong, re –! tantalize.
konketša, tantalize.
konofele, garlic.
konope, (konpi), button.
konopela, button, fasten your buttons.
konopolla, unbutton, undo the buttons.
konota, be stingy.
konotela, stick to, strive, insist, pursue.
kontae, conductor.
kontira, tar, macadamize.
kontraka, agreement, contract.
konya, failure, miscarriage.
koo koo, re –, knock, rap, knock at the door.
kootse, probably, perhaps.
kopana, meet, join, come together, be united, have sex. intercourse.
kopantšha, join.
kopanya, join.
kopela, plant in between, plant for the second time, lock, encircle.
kopelo, song, hymn.
kopi, cup, copy.
kopilwe, be bitten (by a snake).
kopiša, copy.
kopo, a hare's tail.
koporasi, co-operation.
koporo, copper.
kora, score.
korakoretša, stammer.
koreka, correct.
korola, aim (with a gun).
korolo, sight of a gun.
korone, crown (coin).
korong, wheat.
koropa, scrub.
koropagana, become bent or doubled up.
koropane, bent.
korosari, groceries.
korosetina, concertina.
koroso, gross.

korotla, talk in a low voice, sing low.
koša, song, dance, troupe.
kosene, frame, sill.
kota, stick, beam, wood, mast, wooden, post, timber.
kota, clip the hair, prune.
kotama, sit on the haunches, squat.
kotangwa, be sat on.
kotara, quarter.
kotela, drive away a calf whilst its mother is milked.
kotelo, stick for driving a calf.
kotelwa, be driven off/pruned.
koti, id., descend.
koti, serval tiger, bush-cat.
kotimela, go under, disappear.
kotla, press in.
kotlo, beating, punishment, plague.
kotlo, feeding, nourishment.
kotlobana, become shrivelled up.
kotlollo, stretching.
kotlologo, extension, uprightness.
kotlomela, disappear below the horizon.
koto, bulky.
kotolana, bulb.
kotse, perhaps.
kotse, shield.
kotselo, sleep, slumber.
kotsi, danger, misfortune, accident, disaster.
kotsiela, limp.
kotswa, speckled.
kotwa, be shaved, (shorn), clipped.
kou, bay.
kowa, be heard, be felt, be sensed.
krayone, crayon.
krekere, cracker.
krikete, cricket.
Krisemose, Christmas.
kristale, crystal.
Kriste, Christ.
kua, there, yonder.
kuane, hat.
kuba, rise up (as smoke); strike against without penetrating.
kubega, become (slightly depressed) blunt.
kubela, force the skin off a slaughtered animal by pressing it with a stick; shake forcibly.
kubelela, hang up to dry, or to be smoked as bacon.
kubetsa, burn medicine, incense, disinfect.
kubu, hippopotamus, sjambok.
kubuela, throw up, scatter, sprinkle.
kudu, much, greatly.
kudukudu, very much, greatly.
kudumela, perspire, sweat.
kudupana, be bent as with pain, shrink, curl, bend, clutch.
kuela, proclaim to.
kuelela, rise (as smoke).
kuiša, cause to proclaim.
kuka, lift, pick up.
kukega, can be lifted.
kukegela, be lifted to.
kuku, cake.
kukubane, huddled up.
kukuntšha, cause to bud.
kukusota, bicarbonate of soda.
kukutana, tassel.
kuma, bite off a bit, chew, tear up.
kumako, a mentioning.
kuna, refuse, eat dainties secretly, be stingy.
kunkubetša, fondle, pamper, rock.
kunkuretša, fondle, pamper, rock.
kunya, move (out and in) as a mole.
kunyelela, pine away, burn dimly (as a candle).
kunyola, lift up with a lever.
kupela, choke, fester.
kupo, protection against birds.
kuranta, newspaper.
kuruetša, coo (as a dove), play with a baby of two months old, fondle, pamper.
kuruetšo, a lullaby, a cooing.
kurumane, injection.
kurutla, growl, rumble, boom.

kutamo, hiding.
kutla, poke, rub with a hard object.
kutletša, poke, hurt, bump.
kutlola (mahlo), open die eyes wide.
kutlwano, agreement, concord.
kutollo, revelation.
kutso, theft.
kutšwane, rather much.
kutu, trunk, stump, noise.
kutu, principal clause.
kutubana, become blunt.
kutuloga, turn round.
kwa, (kwele), hear, feel, taste, smell, sense.
kwabela, mount.
kwadi, musical instrument.
kwaela, lie on the back, shelter anything by holding it behind your back.
kwagala, be audible, be clear.
kwakwalala, stiffen the neck, become stiff, stand firm.
kwakwaretša, quack, croak.
kwakwetša, stammer, stutter.
kwala, be heard, be understood.
kwalagala, be well-known.
kwale, may be heard, yonder.
kwametša, fill the mouth, put into the mouth.
kwana, lamb.
kwana, v., agree.
kwano, agreement, concord, friendship.
kwanyana, lambskin.
kwapiša, dry fruit, meat, etc.
kwara, put on clothes.
kwarantini, quarantine.
kwata, a stick; v., beat drive away; – **na,** little stick.
kwata, pole; **sa** –, wooden.
kwatabolotša, strip off bark.
kwatalala, become stiff, pine away.
kwatama, squat.
kwatla, be strong.
kwatša, announce, proclaim.
kwe, se –, not to hear, feel, smell, etc. **gore-,** may hear/feel.
kweba, sentence, parry, fence; – **ja,** be sentenced.
kweba, roan (animal).
kwefa, bootlegger, bootlegging.
kwela, overhear, eavesdrop.
kwele, neat person; heard, felt.
kwele, water-buck.
kwelela, investigate; – **tše,** investigated.
kwelema, cause to (desert) be disloyal.
kweletše, appeared, arrived.
kwelo, a falling into.
kwena, crocodile.
kwepere, quince.
kwera, mock, be sarcastic.
kwere, dressed.
kweša, cause to feel or to sense.
kwete, group-leader, champion.
kwetše, be understood.
kwidinya, ring, wag the tail, neigh.
kwinya, swallow whole, cheat.
kwiša, cause to feel, to hear, to taste or to sense.
kwišiša, understand, appreciate.
kwišišega, be clear, be understandable.
kwišišo, comprehension.
kwotela, drive away a calf (when milking).

L

laba, set a trap.
laba, desire.
laba, take anything out of an eye with the tongue, move.
labalabela, yearn for, long for.
Labobedi, Tuesday.
Labohlano, Friday.
Labone, Thursday.

laboraro, tenor.
Laboraro, Wednesday.
ladiša, let the land lie fallow, help to watch the whole night through.
laeditše, has shown, directed.
laela, instruct, direct, control.
laelana, bid farewell.
laelela, instruct or direct for, put in charge of.
laeletša, send a message.
laesense, licence.
laetša, send a message, direct, show.
laetše, has ordered.
lafentere, lavender.
lahla, discard, lose, reject.
lahlega, become lost.
lahlegile, be lost.
lahletša, deceive, mislead.
lai, re –! dazzle, destroy.
lai-lai, glitter, shine.
laile, has directed.
laiša, load.
laišitše, has loaded.
laiwa, be ordered.
laka, control, direct.
lakaletša, wish good luck, congratulate.
lakana, agree, make an appointment.
lakane, sheet.
lakatša, desire, wish, covet.
lakatšega, be desirable.
laksense, licence.
lala, lie down, abide, spend the night.
lalela, lie in ambush, sup.
laletša, invite for or to.
laloma, tarry.
lalomela, interfere, tarry for.
Lamodimo, Sunday.
lamola, rescue, deliver, settle a dispute.
lamolela, deliver, rescue, interfere on behalf of.
lamolla, see: **lamolela.**
Lamorena, Sunday.
lampi, lamp.
lantšhogohlo, left hand, left.
laodiša, explain, expound, cause to rule, ordain, narrate.
loala, command, direct, administer, manage, divine; **itaola,** be independent.
laola, throw the divining bones; **laola ka bola,** decide by drawing lots.
laolla, unload.
laolola, annul a law or command.
laotše, has commanded, directed, determined, appointed, divined.
lapa, court-yard, household family.
lapa, become tired or weary.
lapile, be tired or weary.
lapiša, tire out.
lapologa, become refreshed or rested.
lapološa, refresh, cause to rest.
lata, follow, look for, fetch a bride.
latela, follow (after).
latofatša, blame.
latola, disavow, renounce, give the opposite, deny.
latša, lay a person down, give rest to, – **badimo,** make an offering of peace to the spirits of the ancestors.
latswa, lick, taste; – **ka lerumo,** conquer; – **ka leleme,** flatter.
lau, id., crackle.
lawa, be ordered, be commanded, directed.
laya, order, direct, instruct, lay down the rule or law.
laya, bind, tie (without straining or using force).
le, also too, together with, you; – **bjale,** even now.
lea, bind, tie.
leago, neighbourship, neighbourly intercourse, dwelling.
leaka, stork, locust-bird.
leakabosane, locust-bird.
leakgamotsana, lancet.
leako, stretcher.
lealea, peep round.
leamanyi, relative (gram.)
leana, squint, overlap, devise.

leano, overlapping, scheme.
leanya, cause to overlap.
leaparankwe, chief.
learogi, exception.
leatla, fool; **sekhuba sa** –, asthma.
leba, aim, face, go towards.
leba, copulative formative.
lebadi, numeral, mark, scar.
lebagana, be opposite to; – **nya,** cause to face.
lebaka, cause, reason, opportunity, space of time, place.
lebake, wild hemp, dagga.
lebala, forget.
lebala, plain, open place.
lebalafela, indefinite numeral.
lebalatatelano, ordinal numeral.
lebaleba, be alert.
lebalebanya, even up, level.
lebalela, forgive.
lebalelo, rafter, lath.
leballo, lath.
lebana, be opposite to, deserve, face one another.
lebantšha, place opposite each other, cause to look at each other, cause to aim; – **tšhitše,** fase in the direction of.
lebanya, aim at, direct.
lebara, lever.
lebatama, heat of the sun.
lebatha, foot turned outwards.
lebati, door; see: **lemati.**
lebatla, public assembly.
lebato, floor
lebebe, cream.
lebebetšididi, ice-cream.
lebeko, nose-cleaner, handkerchief, spatula.
lebele, breast of a woman.
ebele, grain.
ebelebele, millet.
ebeledіša, (lebeledišiša), look well, note well.
ebelela, look, look at, expect.
ebelelega, be (beautiful) handsome.
lebeleša, stare at.
lebelete, wild person or animal.
lebeletše, looked at, expect(ed).
lebelo, speed, agility, velocity.
lebenkele, shop.
lebenyabje, jewel.
Lebepe, Limpopo.
lebese, milk.
lebete, spleen, anthrax.
lebetše, has forgotten.
lebei, levy.
lebedi, cud (of an animal).
lebikiri, n., mug.
lebila, an old path, an old track.
lebila, footpath.
lebilo, the fruit of the medlar tree.
lebiša, direct towards; **lebišitše,** has directed towards, facing.
lebitla, grave, tomb.
lebitsi, beetle.
lebitšo, name, nomenclature.
lebjale, (lebjalo), present tense.
lebje, stone.
leboa, north.
Lebodi, dewlap, apron worn by little girls, a species of field rat.
lebodu, dewlap, double chin.
leboelela, repetition, repeatedly.
leboga, thank, give thanks.
lebogo, arm, hand.
lebokoboko, plumpy.
lebola, n., sting.
lebole, apron of beads worn by little girls.
lebolela, sting.
lebollo, circumcision, initiation.
lebolobolo, puff-adder.
lebone, candle, light, principal wife of the chief.
lebopi leba, copulative formative.
lebopo, coast, shore, seaside, bank.
lebota, wall, brim, margin.
lebotla, calf; – **na,** small calf.
lebotlelo, bottle.
lebotlolo, bottle.
leboto, wall, brim, margin.

lebotšiši, interrogative.
leboya, fruit of the baobab tree.
lebue, flower.
lebupudu, fruit of the red milkwood.
Leburu, Dutch South African, Boer.
lebutšwapele, first-fruit.
lebutšwedi, blow-lamp.
ledi, blood corpuscle.
lediba, pool, fountain.
ledibogo, drift, ford.
ledietšane, dizziness, giddiness.
lediga, branch, symbol.
ledimo, storm, hurricane, cyclone.
ledimo, cannibal, avaricious person.
ledingwadingwa, the early morning, dawn.
ledingwana, circumcised boy.
ledinyane, baby animal.
lediri, verb.
lediriši, causative (verb).
ledirolli, inversive (verb).
lediša, cause to cry, cause to weep.
ledubalela, thin grass, tender grass.
ledumaedi, a young lion.
ledutla, crack in a container. (pot).
ledutšwe, cataract (on the eye).
lee, egg.
leeba, dove, pigeon.
leebakgorwane, turtle-dove.
leebarope, rock-pigeon.
leekiši, onomatopoeia, ideophone.
leeto, journey, voyage.
leetse, lock of hair.
lefa, inheritance.
lefaaphefo, windbreak.
lefa, pay, pay a fine, pay a debt.
lefahla, one of twins.
lefao, fence made of reeds, a screen.
lefasana, continent.
lefase, earth, country, a land, the world.
lefastere, window.
lefata, pole, wooden pole or post, a reliable old person.
lefatla, a bald head.
lefato, scratch.
lefatša, splint, splinter, chip.
lefe, which, what?
lefegelwana, comma.
lefego, wing, fin, pinion.
lefehlo, ladle, stick used for kindling fire by friction, churning stick, spattle.
lefekefeke, panic.
lefela, pay for, atone for.
lefela, useless, worthless, for nothing.
lefela, mealie, maize.
lefele, cockroach.
lefeletša, avenge.
lefelo, locative.
lefene, cockroach.
lefenefene, busy-body.
lefera, side-room, passage, pantry.
lefetša, avenge.
lefetwa, old maid, spinster.
lefiša, cause to pay, fine.
lefišwa, pass., be fined.
lefodi, pumpkin.
lefofa, feather, quill.
lefoka, weeds, plot of grass and weeds, thicket.
lefokisi, detective, trap.
lefoko, sentence.
lefokofokwana, complex sentence.
lefokonngwe, simple sentence.
lefokonolo, simple sentence.
lefokontši, compound sentence.
lefokwana, clause.
lefolotšana, stillborn.
lefonokwane, stump.
Lefora, Frenchman.
lefora, deceiver, rogue, cheat, hoaxer.
leforafora, cheat, rogue.
lefoto, young of a bird, chicken.
lefsa, new.
lefša, pass., be paid.
lefšega, coward.
legaba, bulbous plant, jade, tuber.
legaba, empty stomach.
legabe, apron made of beads and worn by uninitiated girls.
legabea, love potion, charm, spell.

legadima, lightning, flash of lightning.
leage, home.
legai, nit, egg of louse.
legafa, madman, lunatic, maniac.
legaga, cliff, crevasse, cave, precipice, snake skin.
legakabje, crystal.
legakadima, stone knife, quartz.
legakgala, grub, constellation.
legala, porridge cooked with fresh milk.
legala, coal, cinder.
legalapa, palate.
leganata, desert.
legano, mouth cavity.
leganse, goose.
legaola, initiated or circumcised young man.
legapa, calabash, gourd.
legapi, shell, peel, husk, scale.
lekgapikgetla, shell of an oyster.
legapu, watermelon.
legare, razor (blade), blade of a knife.
legaro, zone, region.
legarorutho, temperate zone.
legarotšididi, frigid zone.
legata, skull, cranium.
legato, step; – **ng,** instead of, vicarious.
Legerike, Greek.
legetla, shoulder.
lego, wild fig.
lego, rel., which (that) is; **mo go –,** where there is.
legoa, shouting.
legodi, starling (bird).
legodimo, sky, heaven.
legofe, palm of the hand.
legofejana, youngest (last) child.
legogo, crust of porridge or bread, mat.
legogodi, washing-up, flotsam.
legogomedi, lizard.
legogwa, mat, sleeping mat.
legogwana, small mat.
legohle, universe, world.
legohlola, cough.
legokgolana, youngster.
legokobu, crow.
legola, plain, veld, steppe.
legomotša, careless person.
legong, wood, timber.
legonyana, piece of wood.
legôpô, curve, winding.
legopo, manger, tray, trough.
legopo, rib, rafter.
legopo, a spoon (scraper) for wiping perspiration.
legora, fence, hedge.
legoro, clan.
legoroina, class (of nouns).
legorwana, small clan.
legoswi, applause, clapping of hands.
legoswi, handful.
legotlo, mouse, rat.
legoto, stooge.
legukubu, crow.
legwale, partridge, pheasant.
legwara, armdillo, ant-eater.
legwere, green tree snake.
legwete, lack of hair.
lehaahaa, brown ibis.
lehlabathe, sand.
lehlabo, wooden needle for thatching a roof.
lehlabula, summer; **go bolawa ke –,** have a good harvest.
lehlagamonna, attractive girl.
lehlagare, jaw bone.
lehlaka, reed, stalk.
lehlakanoka, reed, cane, rush.
lehlakore, side, railing.
lehlaku, perch.
lehlalerwa, Cape hunting-dog.
lehlanya, mad person.
lehlaodi, adjective.
lehlaodipotšiši, interrogative adjective.
lehlapa, swear-word, invective.
lehlapagadi, one of the divining bones.
lehlapelo, basin, tub.
lehlapo, menstruation.

lehlare, branch (with twigs on), twig.
lehlasedi, ray, sunbeam.
lehlaswa, careless person, untidy person.
lehlathafelo, locative.
lehlathi, adverb.
lehlatšo, vomiting.
lehlatswa, edible berry, "stamvrug".
lehlaya, drawer.
lehlayana, drawer.
lehlogedi, sprout, shoot, sucker.
lehlogonno, blessing.
lehlogonolo, blessing.
lehlokwa, bit of dry grass, gras stalk, match.
lehloma, cutting, slip.
lehlono, dandruff.
lehlotlo, staff, walking-stick.
lehloyo, hatred.
lehlwa, snow.
lehlwapula, sleet.
lehlwele, clot.
leho, ladle, spoon.
lehodu, thief.
lehono, today, to-day.
lehotswanyana, little thief.
lehu, death.
lehubedu, le-class, red.
lehudu, pounding-block, wooden mortar.
lehuduo, ladle.
lehufa, jealousy.
lehuhu, pheasant.
lehuhumedi, legaun.
lehulapša, ulcer on dogs.
lehulo, foam, froth.
lehumagadi, wealthy person.
lehumo, wealth, riches.
lehutla, hump, hunch, hunchback.
lehuto, knot, knob.
lehwafa, armpit, poor soil.
lehwama, bulbous plant.
lehwana, teaspoon.
lehwefe, albino.
lehwiti, new soil.
leifo, hearth, fireplace.
leihlo, eye.
leihlwana, small eye.
leina, name, Christian name, noun substantive, – **ina,** proper noun.
leinago, verbal noun, infinitive.
leinagohle, common noun.
leinakgoboka, collective noun.
leino, tooth.
leipei, free and independent person.
leisi, lace.
leisiisi, mounted policeman.
Leisimane, Englishman.
leitšibulo, first-born.
Lejahlapi, Englishman.
lejakane, Native convert.
lejatšhelete, spendthrift.
lejelakgareng, greyhound, whippet.
leka, try, attempt, test, tempt.
lekaba, pack-ox.
lekaka, green fruit.
lekako, porridge dished out in lumps, a loaf (of bread).
lekala, branch, tributary.
lekalakune, turkey.
lekaleka, try a bit.
lekalekana, be equal.
lekana, be equal, be sufficient for, be enough.
lekanego, sufficient.
lekanetše, be suitable or good for.
lekanti, tin, paraffin-tin.
lekantšha, measure.
lekanya, compare, weigh, estimate, measure, asses, equate.
lekanyetša, estimate.
lekarapa, youth that comes home from work (abroad).
lekase, n., coffin, box.
lekata, egg, uninitiated girl.
lekatane, Kaffir-melon.
lekatse, colly.
lekau, a young man, a muscovy.
leke, go re –! hang down.
lekebu, foam, froth on milk.
lekeke, termite, slant.
lekelela, hang down.

lekelelanya, smoothen, even.
lekeletša, cause to hang down.
lekêsê, home-made knife.
leketla, hang down, be loose.
leketša, hoe, pick.
lekga, league, approx. 3 km.
lekga, case, instance.
lekgaba, plant of corn before the ear is formed.
lekgabi, piece of a bulb, chip.
lekgaga, rush, bulrush.
lekgai, nit (of a louse).
lekgantlele, candle.
lekgaolane, dicision, conclusion.
lekgapetla, scale, peel.
lekgapšakgapša; nwa ka –, scoop up water.
lekgaša, uninitiated girl.
lekgata, peal.
lekgarebe, virgin, maid.
lekgema, cannibal.
lekgero, one having some teeth missing.
lekgeswa, crupper.
lekgetho, tax, duty.
lekgetla, bestman, bridesmaid.
lekgetlo, stage of a journey, period, time.
lekgoba, slave.
lekgohlo, cough.
lekgokaleamanyi, relative concord.
lekgokamong, possessive concord.
lekgokasediri, sub., concord.
lekgokasedirwa, objectival concord.
lekgokathui, possessive concord.
lekgokedi, concord.
lekgokgoro, dry hide.
lekgolo, hundred, century.
lekgolwa, a satisfied person.
lekgonono, doubt, grumbling.
lekgonthe, genuine.
lekgookgoo, whooping-cough.
lekgotla, court, tribunal, council, board.
lekgotlataolo, board of control.
lekgowa, European, gentleman.
lekgwa, frost, snow, ice.
lekgwahla, single (unmarried) person.
lekgwekgwe, scab, scabies.
lekhoro, lean animal.
lekhura, a piece of hard fat.
lekhwekhwe, scab, itch.
lekidimetša, thundering.
lekirikiri, haste.
lekitikiti, rush, haste.
lekobakobane, tramp, wanderer, vagabond.
lekodišiša, examine carefully.
lekokgwana, life-boat.
lekoko, group, co., followers, band.
lekokoro, boiled grain.
lekokwana, rising ground, slope.
lekola, supervise, survey, explore.
lekola, tuft (on the head).
lekoma, roast corn.
lekonko, pock-mark.
lekopano, conjunction.
lekopantšhi, conjunctive.
lekopanyane, subordinate conjunction.
lekopanyi, conjunction.
lekopathaka, co-ordinate conjunction.
lekope, musical instrument having one string.
lekopelo, broken piece of pottery, potsherd, – **la magala,** firepan.
lekoriba, bank of a river.
lekoro, horn bent forward.
lekota, sod, brick, lump.
lekote, sod, brick, lump.
lekoto, adj., thick, big; n., leg, dial., see: **leoto.**
lekotše, explored, supervised.
lekubana, summer-house.
lekudula, "tampan", a fowl-tick.
lekuka, milk-sack.
lekukumo, ridge, swelling, rugged place.
Lekula, Indian.
lekunutu, secret, secret matter.
lukutukutu, rustling noise, struggle.

lekwala, brackish soil, barren country.
Lekwapa, member of the Tsonga tribe.
lekwapi, dried fruit.
lekwate, sod, lump of clay.
Lekwe, Vaal River.
lekwekwe, partridge; adj., uninitiated, uncircumcised boy.
lela, weep, cry, ring.
lela, demons., that, n., intestine.
lela, bring up (a child); v.i., be very hot of the sun.
lelaeta, gangster.
lelahla, a coal.
lelahlelwa, interjection.
lelakgolo, colon.
lelala, look upwards.
lelalela, look up to.
lelalome, seer, prophet.
lelana, appendix.
lelapi, rag, piece of cloth.
lelata, layman, follower.
lelatša, cause to look up.
lele, long.
leledu, beard, plume of a reed, beard of wheat or maize.
lelefa, extend, become long or longer; become tall.
lelefatša, lengthen.
lelefiša, lengthen.
leleka, drive away, chase.
leleke, a slender person, a tall and thin person.
lelekiša, cause to drive away, chase, help to drive away.
lelelo, lengthy.
leleme, tongue, language, tenon joint; – **la semmušo,** official language.
lelengwana, epiglottis, small tongue.
lelera, roam about.
lelia, lily.
leloba, flower.
leloko, sib, tribe, race, clan, lineage member of a tribe, relation; **leloko la kgomo,** relatives in-law.
lelokollo, joint.
lelopo, witch doctor, evil spirit.
leloto, the leader of a swarm of locusts, the forerunner, a stray locust.
lema, plough, hoe, till the soil, cultivate.
lema, accustom to, adapt, to.
lema dinaka, have outstretched horns.
lemala, form a habit, spoil, become accustomed.
lemala, be ruttish, on heat.
lemalela, become ruttish.
lemao, needle.
lemati, door.
lematša, accustom to, spoil.
lemeko, bark of the sugar-cane.
lemena, pit-fall, cistern.
lemeno, fold, plait, hem.
lemila, mucus, snot.
lemina, mucus, snot.
lemipi, peritoneum.
lemoga, understand, find out, notice.
lemoko, species of wild pome (fruit).
lemolla, unaccustom, unlearn, rectify a bad habit.
lemolla, turn over the soil.
lemoša, cause to observe or to understand, advise.
lempatekgomo, devil's thorn.
lena, pers, pron., you.
lena, young bee, larva.
lenaba, enemy, friend, the devil.
lenaga, blanket made of skins, kaross.
lenaka, horn, flute.
lenakaila, wrist, joint.
lenala, nail (of the finger or toe).
lenamola, first layer of thatch on a roof.
lenana, young, soft, tender (le-class).
lenane, index, inventory, list, table.
lenaneo, index, syllabus, inventory, list.
lenaneporeisi, price-list.
lenaneroto, price-list.
lenanetheko, price-list.

lenanethero, agenda.
lenanethuto, curriculum.
lenano, quickness, diligence.
lenao, foot.
leng, what is, which is; adv., when?
lenga, crack.
lengalatsepa, spot, spotted animal.
lengamu, groin.
lengana, South African worm-wood.
lengangale, dried pumpkin.
lengau, cheetah.
lengeta, piece of broken pot.
lengetana, dim. of **lengeta.**
lengina, ear-ring, nose-ring.
lengopa, sterile cow.
lengope, ditch, donga.
lengotlo, the comb (of a bird), the crest.
lengwalo, latter, (document), – **la tumelo,** credential.
lengwane, flute made of bone.
lengwe, one.
lenketane, dove, (namaqua).
lenkwane, "ouklip", pudding stone.
leno, this.
lenoko, slow.
lenong, vulture.
lenoni, fat, fertile (place).
lenono, stalk, stamen.
lenonya, variety of herb.
lenotlo, skin, shin-bone, talon, toe of a bird.
lente, ribbon.
lentha, click.
lenti, string, ribbon.
lentlwane, toy-house.
lentopodi, locust bird, stork.
lentšana, little string.
lentšu, word, voice.
lentšwana, soft voice, small word.
lentswe, stone, rock.
lentswiana, chicken.
lenyaga, this year.
lenyalo, marriage, wedding.
lenyatšo, contempt.
lenywenywe, small red ant.
leo, dem., that.
leobo, garage, cellar.
leobu, chameleon, a stupid person.
leodi, flax.
leoka, mimosa bush, a place where mimosa trees grow.
leokgo, one of the poles of a "rondawel" hut.
leokgwe, pole of a hut.
leokodi, cotton.
leolo, wrinkle, fold.
Leolo, The Lulu Mountains.
leonyane, go ja motho –, to shadow a person, follow stealthily.
leope, ditch.
leoto, leg.
leotša, manna, millet.
leotwana, small leg or wheel, bicycle, quarter evil.
lepa, observe the stars.
lepa, be correct.
lepai, cotton blanket.
lepaka, panga.
lepalapala, bare field.
lepanta, tyre, band, tape.
lepapata, trumpet.
lepara, stick, cane, stretcher, wheelbarrow, carrying-pole.
leparapatla, flute, trumpet (made of horn).
lepaša, bee, forced labour.
lepastere, bastard, half-caste, mulatto.
lepatata, trumpet (made of horn).
lapatlaoko, bare space.
lepatlelo, market place, public place.
lepayana, small cotton blanket.
lepelela, hang down, be worn-out, be sulky, droop, overlap.
lepelepele, duck.
lepeliti, pleat, fold.
Lepelle, Olifants River.
lepepe, cry-baby, brat.
lepetleke, apart, wide.
lepetu, seam.
lephaka, hurry, haste, speed.
lephakaphaka, great hurry.

lephakga, slit, flap.
lephako, hollow between thigh and ribs, flank, empty belly.
lephala, witch-doctor, sorcerer.
lephale, see: **lephala.**
lephama, embarkment, slope, rampart.
lephao, a fence made of reeds, reed enclosure.
lepharwa, cake of dung.
lephatakalala, edible locust.
lephefo, greyhound.
lephego, wing, fin, pinion.
lephegwana, fin.
lephekgophekgo, rout, flight, panic.
lepheko, bar, barrier, shutter.
lephene, cockroach.
lephephe, paper, watcher's hut in the fields.
lephepheupheu, windy.
lephera, leprosy.
lephethephethe, haste.
lephilo, foam.
lephodisa, policeman.
lephone, horny skin, blister.
lephoto, wave.
lepidibidi, duck.
lepidipidi, duck.
lepogo, leopard; – **nyana,** small leopard.
lepokisi, box.
lepolanka, plank, board, deal.
lepologa, trickle down, hang down, be viscous.
lepolola, solve a mystery, untie.
lepono, nudist.
leponono, dragon-fly.
lepotlana, young of an animal.
Lepotokisi, Portuguese.
lepudutšwana, grey (old man).
leputlaputla, one who traverses, hasty person.
leputswa, grey-haired person, old person.
lera, thin membrane, web, film, cuticle.
leraba, snare, ambush.
leraga, mud.
leragane, finch.
lerago, hind part, buttock, rump.
leraka, vegetable marrow, gourd.
lerako, wall, stone wall.
lerala, rope, thong.
lerama, cheek.
lerapamela, slant; **go tsena ditabeng ka** –, to interfere with another's business.
lerapo, thong, strap, tendril.
lerapo, bone.
lereratua, the plant Asparagus africanus.
lerata, noise.
leratadimo, firmament.
leratano, mutual love.
leratetšo, tripod.
leratha, piece of bread.
lerathana, crumb.
lerato, love, passion.
leratorato, great love.
leratšhika, neuralgia.
leri, denominator.
lereo, term.
lerephu, lobe, lappet.
lerete, testicle.
lerethe, cinder.
leriba, overhanging ledge, bank, peak, brow.
leribiši, owl.
lerinini, gum.
leroba, hole.
lerobana, small hole, pore.
lerobanare, tambookie (grass).
lerobo, place full of the holes of mice or other burrowing animals.
leroborobo, id., **go hwa** –, die in large humbers.
lerofa, claw, paw.
lerojana, a little dust.
lerole, dust.
lerole, last year's calf or foal.
leroo, claw, paw.
lerope, ruin.

leropotlane, gooseberry.
lerotho, spinach, dusk, twilight.
lerothodi, drop.
lerothwe, species of spinach.
lerotse, pumpkin, bitter melon.
leru, cloud.
leruarua, whale.
lerula, fruit of the "morula" tree.
lerumo, assegai, spear, lance.
leruo, possession, wealth.
leruputla, pulverised soil.
lerutla, wild pome.
lerwa, crack.
lesa, let alone, leave off, let go.
leša, cause to eat, poison.
lešaba, crowd.
lešabašaba, sand, sandy plain.
lesaeboko, angora goat.
lešaedi, careless person, untidy person, rude person, uncouth person.
lešaetšana, a girl.
lešago, buttock, seat, fundament.
lesaka, bag, sack.
lešaka, cattle kraal, fold, flock.
lešako, country, veld, land.
lešala, pronoun.
lešalaba, shouting, noise.
lešalapadi, quantitative, pronoun.
lešalatho, personal pronoun.
lešalatšhupi, demonstrative pronoun.
lešama, cheek.
lešapa, curse.
lešapelo, basin.
lešaphu, tassel.
lešapo, bone.
lešaša, branch.
lešašano, panic.
lešata, noise.
lesea, infant, baby, babe.
lesedi, light.
lešee, colly, coly.
lešego, blessing.
lesego, laughter.
leseka, bracelet, bangle, child born with teeth.
lesela, spur-toed frog, boiled water (given to infants).
lešela, cloth, linen, patch.
leselaga, butcher's shop, butchery.
lešelagohlo, emery cloth.
leselaphala, patch of mimosa trees.
lešelathekgo, sling (for support).
leselawatle, boat, ship.
lešele, foreign, strange.
lesele, species of frog.
leselo, winnowing fan, crop.
leselo, pitchfork, prong.
leselo, tribute paid in grain to the chief.
leselwana, small (basket), winnowing fan.
lesenke, galvanized iron.
lesepa, excrement, dung.
lešere, sour milk, whey.
lesese, thin.
lešeše, thistle.
lesetafase, longitude.
lešetla, sort bone, spongy bone, cartilage.
lesetša, forgive, leave for, cease.
leši, brim, edge, shore.
lešianoka, hammerhead (the bird).
lešika, sinew, vein, artery, tributary.
lešika, family, kin, genealogical table.
lešikahlaba, sand.
lešikišiki, brown scorpion.
lešilo, stupid, idiot, fool.
lešimelatadi, lad, boy.
lešimelo, fork, forked stick.
lešinkwane, convulsion.
lešintlwane, convulsion.
lešira, veil, screen, net.
lešiši, tambookie-veld.
lešiši, scorpion.
lešitaphiri, bone of the nape.
lešitši, want, poverty, destitution.
lešo, ours.
leso, black.
lešoba, hole, tunnel; – **na,** little hole, pore.
lešobe, albino.

lešoboro, uninitiated boy.
lesobosobo, type of locust.
lesodi, plantation, forest.
lesoga, bachelor.
lesogana, young man.
lešohlo, cud.
lešoka, wilderness, desert.
lešoko, compassion, pity, labour.
lesokolela, heartburn.
lesokolodi, millepede.
lešokotšo, second drawing of milk.
lesokwana, oar.
lešole, soldier.
lesolo, hunting party, tribal hunt, action.
lešolopudi, boy that refuses to heard the stock.
lesome, ten.
lesomehlano, fifteen.
lesomenne, fourteen.
lesomepedi, twelve.
lesometee, eleven.
lesometharo, thirteen.
lesomila, mucus, snot.
lešoo, claw, paw.
lešope, ruin.
lesoro, gate, pass.
lesoro, third stomach, paunch.
lešoro, cruel, fierce.
lešošo, fold.
Lesotho, Basutoland.
lesothwana, paunch, omasum, manyplies.
lešotlo, contempt, mockery.
lešoto, luck, good fortune.
lešoto, band, apron-string.
lešotša, grub (eaten by Natives).
lesotwana, young of a bird.
lesufi, dark, darkness.
lešuhu, femur, thigh-bone.
lešukhu, femur, humerus.
lešukhuhlaba, sand.
lesuko, penis of a bull.
lešula, temple of the head.
lešupafa, proximate dem.
lešupafale, remote dem.
lešupafao, mediate dem.
lešupi, demonstrative adjective.
lešuputšane, pig, hog.
lešwa, be given poison.
leswafo, lung, **-hlapi,** gill.
lešwana, "oudoring-veld", a place where mimosa trees grow.
leswao, mark, sign, token, brand.
Leswatsi, Swazi.
lešwefe, albino.
leswela, snow.
leswete, wrinkle, wrigglilng, writhing.
lešweu, adj., white.
leswielo, broom.
leswika, stone, rock.
leswiswi, dark, darkness.
leta, wait, wait for, guard; letela, wait for, expect.
letadi, malaria, fever; – **la mohlapo o moso,** black water fever.
letadi, burweed.
letago, lustre, gloss, glory.
letagwa, drunkard.
letakataka, bushbaby.
letala, adj., green, blue.
letala, adj., old.
letamo, dam.
letanka, tank.
letata, kaross, skin blanket.
letata, a blade of grass besmeared with bird-lime, a cobweb.
letata, green fruit.
letaya, Cape hunting-dog, wild dog, notorious thief.
Letebele, a member of the Amandebele tribe.
letee, adj., one.
letee, species of green grasshopper (locust).
letete, a blade of grass besmeared with bird-lime.
lethabo, joy, happiness.
lethakgo, whooping cough.
lethaolana, slender girl.
lethapišwa, young animal being broken in.

lethari, married young woman, young mother.
letheba, spot, mark, stain.
lethebo, kaross, skin blanket.
letheka, hip, waist.
lethekga, prop, support, stay.
lethole, heifer.
lethologatse, heifer, pullet.
lethopo, bowel, hose.
lethudi, verandah.
lethumaša, young girl, uninitiated young girl.
lethuši, aux. verb.
letimela, lost animal homeless person.
letita, unmarried mother.
letla, become long, be long.
letlabo, rhebuck, roe.
letlagapi, scale.
letlago, (lebaka-), future tense.
letlaka, vulture, mark.
letalakala, leaf, page, peal.
letlalo, skin, leather.
letlapa, flat stone, flag-stone, slate, blackboard.
letlapele, antecedent.
letlega, be prosperous, be fortunate.
letlema, ruin, roofless house.
letlepetlepe, idiot, fool.
letlere, split, crack.
letletsela, parting (hair).
letloboro, bundle.
letlole, box.
letlopo, crest, coxcomb.
letlotlo, house in bad repair.
letlotlo, capital, fund.
letobe, mist, fog, haze.
Letoitšhi, German.
letoko, greyhound.
letolo, knee.
letona, masculine, right (hand).
letopanta, bright moonlight.
letša, ring, cause to cry, play an instrument; **go – wa nko,** be pleased, laugh up your sleeve.
lêtša, ledger.
letšaba, burrow (animal).
letšae, egg.
letšapa, fatigue, hunger, labour.
letsatsa, place where animals have dug many holes.
letsatsarapana, cunning little fellow.
letšatši, sun, day.
letše, has lain down, tarried.
letšeka, earth-snake.
letseka, detective, space between two front teeth.
letsekere, side, edge, sideways.
letšema, company of workers, bee.
letsenela, intruder.
letšepe, hoe.
letsetlela, parting (hair).
letsetse, flea, agile person.
letsha, lake, rhebuck, roe.
letshadi, feminine.
letšheta, last ox in a team; the hindmost one.
letšhidi, wild plum.
letšhoba, ox tail fastened on to a stick and used by witch-doctors; a fly swat.
letšhogo, fright, fear.
letšhologo, (letšhollo), diarrhoea.
letšhošo, alarm.
letshwenyo, worry.
letši, forest, wood.
letšibogo, a ford, a drift.
letšididi, cold.
letšimane, flea.
letšioko, colly, coly.
letšoba, flower.
letsogo, arm, aid, assistant, a shoulder of meat, rank of second wife of the chief.
letšoka, butcher-bird.
letsoku, red ochre, red clay, haematite.
letsolo, sharp weapon, javelin.
letšolobolo, puff-adder.
letsopa, clay.
letšwa, be sounded.
letswa, (dial.), thong.
letšwabadi, bruise.

letswai, salt; **ke** –! it is well!
letswalo, diaphragm, conscience, remorse.
letswapo, flank of a mountain.
letswata, group of workers, bee.
letswatha, blaze, pellagra.
letswele, fist.
letswele, breast, teat, nipple; **ngwana wa** – infant; **bana** –, children of one mother.
letswiababa, colly, coly.
letswidi, a cane-rat.
letswienyana, chicken, baby baboon.
letswiobaba, colly, coly.
letutu, ear of corn without any grains, an undeveloped ear of corn.
letwašatwaša, sound of running.
leuba, epidemic, depression, shanty.
leubaubane, nightjar, screech owl.
leubelo, forge, furnace.
leumo, thorax, breast.
leutu, mist, fog.
lewa, boiled grain.
lewa, cave, cavern.
lewa, v., be eaten, be edible.
lewatle, sea.
Lewedi, September.
leyakgatišong, manuscript.
liberale, liberal.
liki, league.
likwiteišene, liquidation.
lili, lily.
linsiti, (makhura a-), linseed oil.
litara, litre.
litemase, litmus.
lla, cry, weep, yelp, howl, whine.
llase, consolation prize, last.
lle, has eaten.
llela, cry out to/for, complain.
llere, ladder.
lletša, play instrument for or to.
lletše, cried to.
llifi, leave.
llile, has cried.
lliša, cause to cry.
loa, bewitch.
loba, lose, conceal, suppress.
loba, pay tribute, ransom.
lobiša, cause loss or damage, suppress.
lodi, cambium layer, twine.
loetše, has bewitched for.
loga, plait, weave; – **maano,** devise a plan.
logaganya, weave, intertwine.
logetša, put (pour) in drops.
logolla, undo the plaiting or weaving.
lohlanya, cause to fight, stir up.
loile, has bewitched, has become thick (or porridge).
loiša, add meal to a boiling pot, cause to bewitch.
loiwa, be bewitched.
loka, be or become (straight) just.
loka, season, flavour with salt.
loka, put in.
lokafala, become (straight) righteous.
lokafatša, straighten.
lokasi, location.
lokela, put in, put inside.
lokela, be fit for.
lokeletša, lace.
lokiša, prepare, straighten.
lokišitše, prepared.
lokodiša, speak at length.
lokolla, untie, deliver, analyse.
lokologa, become free.
lokologana, be in order of succession, be in single file.
lokologile, be file.
lokolola, loosen, put out of joint.
lokosela, move in the eye.
lokotša, sweeten the mouth.
lokwa, (lelokwa), net.
lokwata, loquat.
loma, bite, sting; **go** –, eat the first-fruits; – **tsebe,** tell a secret.
lomagana, stick to.
lomaganya, unite.
lomega, be dry-cupped, sup.

lomela, fix on a handle.
lomeletša, incite, instigate, rouse.
lomella, let in, dovetail, mortise.
lomola, wean.
lomolla, wean, remove from somebody's mouth.
lona, le-class, it.
lone, lawn.
lonteri, laundry.
lontše, lounge.
lonya, lazy, harshness, spite, malice.
lootša, sharpen, whet, grind.
lootšegile, be sharpened.
lopa, pray for, ask a favour.
lopa, hook, draw.
lope, sterile cow.
lopo, barrel (of a gun).
lopolla, redeem.
lopologa, become free, be redeemed or rescued.
lopološa, redeem, set free.
lora, dream (of).
lore, id., burnt to ashes.
lorela, burn to ashes, destroy completely.
lori, lorry.
loša, court, woo.
lota, lead.
lota, look after, attend, trace.
lotega, be attended to; **lotegile,** be looked after.
lotolola, unlock.
lotšha, greet, salute, pay tribute.
loutša, sharpen, whet.
lousela, v., blue.
lowa, be fought.
loya, bewitch.
lwala, be sick, ill.
lwala, mill(-stone).
lwana, quarrel.
lwantšha, cause to fight, oppose.
lwao, (dial.), foot, sole of the foot.
lwatša, cause illness or disease.
lwele, has fought.
lweša, cause to fight.

M

maabane, yesterday.
maaka, lies.
maaka(bosane), locust-birds.
maamane, calves.
maano, plan, plans, scheme, strategy.
maarogano, parting.
maarogi, exceptions.
maaswa, porridge.
maatla, power, strength.
maatlakgogedi, gravitation, magnetism.
Maatlaohle, yo –, the Almighty.
mabadi, numerals, scars.
mabaibai, glittering.
mabaka, periods, reasons.
mabala, plains.
mabala, many colours, spots.
mabalaphiri, spotted.
mabapi, parallel, opposite, concerning.
mabarebare, n., talk, hearsay.
mabatha, feet turned outwards.
mabe, bad, evil.
mabedi, two.
mabekana, enemies.
mabele, breasts, sorghum, Kaffir corn, salary, grain.
mabele, measles (in a pig).
mabelebetlwa, divining bones.
mabelethoro, red sorghum.
mabeo, things placed.
mabete, games for boys and girls.
mabetlela, chips, shavings.
mabilo, fruit of the medlar tree.
mabilobilo, jumble.
mabitsi, patterns, type of beetle, horses.
mabjalwa, beer, liquor.
mabjang, grass.
mabje, stones.
mabjoko, brains.
maboelela, repetitions.
maboeletša, repetition(s).

mabofe, drugs.
mabogato, bases.
mabohlale, wisdom.
mabogo, arms, hands.
mabokoboko, soft: (articles).
mabole, skirts made of string.
mabolela, (bees') stings.
mabollo, circumcision.
mabolokelo, store-rooms.
mabolotšo, circumcision.
mabone, candles.
maboo, return.
mabora, chickenpox.
maboroko, sleepiness.
mabota, walls.
mabothakga, neatness.
mabothata, hardship, difficulties, adversity, problems.
mabotla, calves; – **na,** small calves.
mabotša, marriage feast.
maboya, wool, mohair, fur.
mabu, soil; **tšhabile** –, a tall person.
mabudi, goats.
mabudutšwa, gleanings.
mabue, flowers.
mabutšwamorago, late (last) – fruits.
mabutšwapele, first-fruits.
madi, blood.
madiampa, pulsations in the stomach.
madiba, fountains, wells.
madibogo, fords, drifts.
madiga, branches.
madiilelo, alienship.
madika, exercises and songs at the initiation school.
madikana, pupils (from the initiation school).
madikela, sunset.
madila, beer.
madimabe, bad luck, misfortune, woe.
madimo, hurricanes, cyclones, storms.
madimo (ma-ja-batho), cannibals.
madingwana, ceremonies (at the initiation school).
madinyana, baby baboons.
madira, soldiers, the army.
madirasefapano, crusaders.
madireng, news.
madiri, verbs.
madišakgomo, (cattle) egrets.
madišo, grazing grounds, pastures.
madubedube, confusion, boggy, confused.
madulagae, the season that follows the harvest.
madulo, dwelling place(s), seats.
madume, greetings.
mae, eggs.
maeba, pigeons, doves.
maebeebe, epilepsy.
maekiši, ideophones.
maekropaele, micropyle.
maekropo, (maekrope), microbe.
maekrosekopo, microscope.
maele, proverbs, maxims.
maele, mile.
maemo, standing position, contention.
maene, mine.
mafahla, pneumonia; twins.
mafarafara, things scattered about.
mafarasa, things scattered about.
mafase, worlds, countries.
mafasetere, windows.
mafastere, windows.
mafata, poles in a fence.
mafatla, bald-headed person.
mafato, scratchings.
mafatša, chips, splinters.
mafee! exclam., rogue!
mafego, tripod, trivit.
mafela, mealies.
mafela, useless, vain.
mafele, cockroaches.
mafeledi, intr. verbs.
mafelelo, end(s).
mafelo, places; – **felwana,** small places.
mafetla, the smell of an animal.
mafiša, animals (cattle) placed under the care of other people.
mafodi, pumpkins.
mafofa, feathers.

mafofonyane, hysteria, express train.
mafokisi, detectives.
mafoko, sentences.
mafolofolo, eagerness, zeal, pep.
mafoto, young of birds, chickens.
mafotwana, young birds.
mafsa, new, fresh.
mafula, floods.
mafulo, grazing grounds, pastures.
mafuri, back-yard.
magabe, fringe of strings worn in front by girls.
magabea, a love potion, a charm.
magadi, dowry.
magadima, lightning.
magae, homes.
magaga, caves.
magagabo, (at) their homes.
magagana, battle-axe.
magageno, (at) your homes.
magagešo, (at) our homes.
magahlano, meeting, junction.
magai, nits.
magaila, mealie rice.
magakadima, flint stone, crystals.
magakga, young corn nearing the earing stage.
magakgala, grub, caterpillar.
magakwa, crystals, flints.
magala, live coals.
magalagapa, palate; **letša** –, snore.
magalapa, the palate; – **thata,** hard palate; – **leta,** soft palate.
magale, blades, edges.
maganagodiša, a herd-funk.
magang, disputes, conversation.
magano, insides of the mouths.
maganse, geese.
magapu, watermelons.
magareng a, in the midst of.
magata, head and trotters.
magato, steps.
magetla, shoulders.
mageu, light beer, "suurpap".
magistrata, magistrate.
mago, wild figs.
magobe, porridge, food.
magodimo, heavens, the sky.
magogo, crustation(s).
magagodi, washings-up.
magokobu, crows.
magol(l)ela, things scraped together.
magolo, great, old.
magologelo, slopes.
magomo, herds of cattle.
magong, much wood.
magopa, scrapings.
magopelo, cutlets.
magopo, dishes, troughs.
magora, fences, reed enclosures.
magoro, entrances; (noun) classes, clans.
magorogelo, place(s) of arrival, home.
magorometšo, medicine used to stimulate childbirth.
magorogo, arrivals.
magorwana, dim. small entrances, clans.
magošana, petty chiefs.
magoši, chiefs.
magoswi, applause, royal salute.
magotlo, mice.
magotšana, chilblains.
magwata, rough, coarse.
mahaahaa, the brown ibis birds.
mahea, mealies, maize.
mahlabišadihlong, shame, disgrace.
mahlafarara, mixed, flurried, dishevelled, unkempt, uncombed.
mahlagahlaga, wildness.
mahlahla, excitement; adj., active, wild.
mahlahlakgoma, uncombed hair, matted hair.
mahlahlo, excitement; adj., active, spirited.
mahlajana, shrewd.
mahlaka, reeds, stalks.
mahlakanano, junction.
mahlakanoka, reeds.
mahlakansela, disorder, confusion.
mahlakore, sides.

mahlale, wisdom, cunning; **lahliša** –, cause to leave tricks.
mahlalerwa, wild dogs.
mahlalosetšagotee, synonyms.
mahlano, five.
mahlanohlano, capricious, changeable.
mahlapa, curses.
mahlapelo, bathrooms.
mahlapholane, the morning star.
mahlare, twigs, leaves.
mahlasedi, sunbeams, rays.
mahlathi, adverbs.
mahlatlo, food prepared for an expected visitor.
mahlatša, vomiting, vomited matter.
mahlatse, good fortune, good luck.
mahlatswa, type of edible berry (magalismontanum chrysophyllum).
mahlayana, shelves.
mahlo, eyes; **hwibila (iletša)** –, be cross.
mahlobogo, mourning.
mahlogedi, shoots, buds.
mahlogela, shoots, buds.
mahlogonolo, blessings.
mahlokapopo, shapeless things.
mahloko, sorrows, pain, sufferings.
mahlokwa, dry sticks, matches.
mahlola, omens; – **kotsi,** ill omen.
mahlomo, frames.
mahlophaasenya (pula ke –), said of rain which may be harmful (excessive).
mahlwana, little (small) eyes, buds.
mahlwele, coagulated blood.
Maholanere, Dutchmen.
mahu, deaths.
mahube, dawn; – **a basadi,** early dawn.
mahubedu, red.
mahuduo, spattles, ladles, oars.
mahulo, foam, forth.
mahumo, riches.
mahuto, knots.
mahwafa, armpits.
mahwana, spoons, small spoons or ladles.
mahwibi, dawn.
maidi, a swoon.
maikapolelo, second-hand clothes, old clothes.
maikarabelo, responsibilities.
maikemišetšo, intention, aim.
maikutlo, feeling.
mailwa, things avoided, things feared.
maina, names, nouns.
mainago, verbal nouns.
mainaina, proper nouns
mainagohle, common nouns.
mainakgopolo, abstract nouns.
mainamabopša, derived nouns.
mainasebele, proper names.
mainelwa, grain steeped in water, malt.
mainyakelo, fabrication.
maitekelo, exercise, experiment, trial.
maitirelo, home-made, self-made.
maitiši, loungers.
maitišo, leisure, recreation.
maitshwarelo, excuse, pardon.
maithswaro, behaviour, conduct, character.
maitšibolo, first-born.
maja, eaters of, those who eat.
ma-ja-a-itlhakola, one who denies what he has done.
majadikenywa, eaters of fruit (birds, insects).
majahlapi, Europeans.
majakane, Africans who have become Christians.
Majapane, Japanese.
majaseuta, people who do not forget (forgive).
majathoro, grain-eaters.
makaa, so big.
makaba, pack-oxen.
makae, how many.
makako, heaps of porridge.
makala, branches.
makala, be astonished, be surprised.

makalo, exclamation.
makarapa, young men from the town.
makatane, large species of bitter melon.
makatika, capers, antics.
makatša, surprise.
makatšgo, fantastic.
makau, young men.
makawe, rafts.
makeke, white-ants, termites.
makesemamo, maximum.
makga, times, occasions.
makgaba, green plants of sorghum.
makgabetla, thin slices, chips.
makgabetlela, chops, minced meat.
makgahla, curd.
makgabi, chips.
makgahlano, junction(s).
makgahlo, junction.
makgalwa, rust.
makgamatha, bark of a tree.
makgao, regiments.
makgaogo, division, split.
makgaolakgang, conclusion.
makgapha, an abomination, adj., dirty, sinful, abominable.
makgarebe, virgins, young women.
makgata, peals.
makgatheng, in the midst of.
makgema, cannibals.
makgere, beer made of prickly pears.
makgeretla, tatters.
makgethe, choice, pick, pure.
makgoba, slaves.
makgolela, an awkward position.
makgolo, hundreds.
makgolo, patterns.
makgolonne, four hundred.
makgolopedi, two hundred.
makgolotharo, three hundred.
makgonatšohle, handy person, handyman; adj., skilful.
makgone, success, mastery.
makgonthe, true, real, genuine.
makgopa, eggs.
makgopo, sins, evil, injustice; adj., crooked.
makgotla, courts, councils.
makgotlo, owl.
makgotlwe, owl.
makgwahla, single (unmarried) people, dehydrated greens.
makgwai, engravings, rock paintings, patterns.
makgwakgwa, rough.
makgwara, hard, rough.
makgwathi, twigs, sticks, strips of bark.
makhanekhe, mechanic.
makhura, fat, oil; butter.
makisimamo, maximum.
maknisiamo, magnesium.
mako, eggs (fat) inside a female locust.
makobakobana, wanderers.
makokekobe, large quantities.
makobela, cutlets.
makoko, pranks, impudence; adj., impudent.
makokote, sods.
makokwana, impudent.
makoloi, wa(g)gons.
makoma, roasted grain.
makonka, pock marks.
makopanelo, junction(s), meeting places.
makopelo, potsherds; – **a magala,** firepans.
makopo, eye ridges.
makota, mortuary.
makote, lumps of earth.
makubu, the wrong side (when milking a cow).
makudula, tampans.
makukuno, uneven, lumpy.
Makula, Indians, Coolies.
makwapi, dried fruit or vegetables.
makwate, lumps of earth, sods.
makwati, bark of trees.
makwele, bulbul, tiptol.
mala, bowels, tripe; – **a mahubedu,**

dysentery; – **-a-dibe** n., gonorrhoea.
malabulabu, tatters.
maludu, matter, pus.
malahla, coal (coals).
malakabe, conflagration.
malalakwaetša, devil's thorn.
malao, bed(s), bedding; **malaomabe,** insomnia.
malaodišo, explanation(s).
malapa, yard(s), homes, families.
malapane, play of children, nursery school.
malatši, days.
malealea, squint.
maleba, opposite to, **tšea** –, aim.
malebana, opposite to, with regard to.
malebelebe, odds and ends.
malebiša, hints.
malebo, aiming, thanks.
malebogo, thanks, thanksgivings.
maledu, beard(s).
maleiri, napkins, swaddling clothes.
maleisele, reins.
maleka, trials.
maleke, tins.
malekere, sweets.
malele, sea weeds.
malengwana, small tongues, tenons.
malepa, puzzle(s), riddle.
maloba, flowers.
maloba, the day before yesterday, lately, the other day.
maloi, withchcraft.
maloka, – **le,** in connection with.
malokelo, privilege, prerogative.
maloko, fresh cow-dung, members of a tribe.
malokollo, joints.
malokwa, nets.
malokwane, leader at a dance.
malome, my maternal uncle.
malomo, flowers.
malopi, flowers of the aloe.
malopo, (evil) spirits.
maloro, (troublesome) dreams.
malwetši, diseases.
mama, suck, patch.
mamane, calves.
mamapu, honeycombs.
mamarela, adhere to, stick to.
mamati, doors, bark, planks.
mamatlela, cling to, adhere to.
mamediša, upshot (crop).
mameko, peel of the sugar-cane.
mamelela, cling to.
mamello, patience, submission.
mamenemene, tricks, deceit.
mamila, mucus.
mamiša, give suck, suckle.
mamoga, turn asunder.
mamokgadi, house cricket.
mamola, tear, strike.
mamoratwe, beloved.
mamoso, the day after tomorrow, some time in the future.
mampate, devil's thorn.
mamphašane, sandal, toeless shoe.
mampša, dogs.
mana, honeycomb (with larvae).
manaba, enemies, foe.
managa, skin clothes.
manaka, thorns.
manakane, horned species, (animals).
manamelo, ladder, stairs.
mane, four.
manega, overlay, inlay.
manele, dress-coat.
manelo, the time for giving young animals to their dams.
manetša, paste on.
mang? who? what kind, – **le** – whosoever, anyone, everybody.
manga, cracks.
manganga, obstinary.
mangangahlaa, the animal paid by the accused and slaughtered for the jurymen.
mangangala, dried pumpkin.
mangina, earrings.
mangotlo, combs, crests.
mangwalo, letters, writing(s), writ, documents.

mangwe, other.
manka, capers.
mankadile, swing.
mankanese, manganese.
mankapele, quickly.
mankekišane, imitator.
mankgapela, presently, soon.
mankgeledi, water marks.
mankgeretla, rags, tatters, torn clothes.
mankgwari, box of matches.
manko, mango.
mankotane, namaqua pigeon.
manku, many sheep.
mankutukutu, the secretary bird.
mankwane, pudding stone, "ouklip".
mankwetlana, namaqua pigeon.
manna, millet, manna.
manno, seats.
manolla, unglue, tear off.
manologa, come off.
manolola, take off, remove.
manong, vultures.
manoni, fat (animals).
manopi, nectar.
manotlo, shins, legs or toes (of a bird), talons.
mante, ribbons.
mantha, clicks.
manthaladi, rounds.
manthapama, afternoon.
manthau, kgoka –, shackle.
Manthole, December.
manti, strings, ribbons.
mantiko, giddiness, dizziness, a turning.
mantlalekgeru, thistle.
mantle, human excrements.
mantlwantlwane, play with dolls.
mantoline, mandoline.
mantona, chiefs.
mantserere, dinala tša, –, long nails.
mantshegele, song of old men.
mantshwantshwane, play with dolls.
mantšiboa, (in the) evening.
mantswantswane, children's play.
manya, excreta, patchwork, scallops.
manya-a-tšhipi, dross of iron.
manyala, evil.
manyalo, marriages.
manyami, sorrow, pity.
manyenyema, small black ants.
manyokenyoke, turns, winding, crooked (ness).
manyomonyomo, swarms.
maodi, washings-up.
maoko, top grain in a pot; **go tšea** –, to do the preliminary.
maolo, wrinkles, folds.
maope, trenches.
maopšana, small dongas.
maorahlolo, spots of sunlight.
maora-o-tuka, chancer.
maotwanahunyela, the grave.
mapaila, robin red-breast (bird).
mapapata, trumpets.
mapega, price (cattle) paid for a wife.
mapele, genital organs.
mapara, sticks, carrying-poles.
maperepere, colon and anus.
maphaaphaa, abundant food.
maphaga, forked stick, gibbet.
maphakela, early morning.
maphala, (maphale), witch-doctors.
maphampha, pools.
maphara, widely distended.
maphata, forked, cloven.
maphatakalala, edible locusts.
maphefo, greyhounds.
mapheko, hurdles, crossbars.
maphelo, health, hygiene.
maphetho, trimmings, finishing-off.
maphodisa, police.
mapholo, many oxen.
maphone, blisters.
maphoto, waves.
maphušuphušu, moth-eaten.
maphutse, pumpkins.
mapidipidi, (mapidibidi), ducks.
mapimpane, kid, toddler, tot.
mapogo, leopards.
mapolanka, planks, boards.

mapono, nudists, naked people.
Mapono, the Matabele, Swazis or Zulu people.
maporogo, bridges.
Mapotokisi, Portuguese.
mapudi, the many goats of the village.
mapupureše, round and soft.
mara, bows, films, webs, cuticles.
mara, stain, distort, misrepresent.
marabe, puff-adder.
maradu, lean old cattle.
maraga, mud.
maragane, finches.
marago, hinder parts, buttocks.
maraka, cattle posts, gourds, vegetable-marrow.
marakanele, junction.
marakodu, vocal cords.
marama, cheeks.
maramanyane, lizard.
marangrang, complications, confusion.
marapo, bones, reins.
marara, mess, muddled up.
maratetšo, tripod, trivet.
maratha, crumbs, fragments.
maratone, marathon.
mare, spittle, expectoration, saliva.
marega, winter.
mareka-a-rekiša, speculator.
marekereke, jelly.
marela(rela), asbestos.
maremela, chips.
maremo, cutting, chopping, hewing.
marena, kings, lords, masters.
mareo, terms.
marepherephe, wide.
marete, testicles.
marethe, ash and cinders.
maretho, swinging, wielding, starting.
mariba, overhanging ledges, peaks of caps.
marinini, gums, alveolar.
mariri, mane, slowness.
maririmoga, sad.
maroba, pieces of firewood, holes; – **na,** pores.
marobalelo, accommodation.
marobapheka, pieces of wood.
marobapoo, pieces of wood (in a cattle kraal).
maroboko, spots.
marofa, paws, claws.
maroga, curses.
marole, heifers.
marolo, slow dog.
maroo, paws.
marope, ruins.
maropotlane, gooseberries.
marota, humps.
marotho, bread, loaves.
marothorothwana, spotted, freckles.
marotobolo, ash heaps.
marotse, pumpkins.
maru, clouds; – **a thibile,** overcast, cloudy.
marula, fruit of the (morula) tree.
marulelo, thatch, roof.
marumo, arms, weapons, spears.
maruo, property, possessions.
marwa, cracks, cracked skin.
masa, dawn, the early morning.
mašaba, crowds.
mašaka, (cattle) kraals, pens.
mašakana, brackets, small pens/kraals.
mašalakgokong, stick-in-the mud.
mašaledi, (mašaletšana), survivors, rest.
mašaphu, tassels.
mašarakane, mixed up, muddle(d).
mašarašara, muddled, confused.
mašaša, branches.
mašata, noises.
masea, infants, babes.
masedi, lights.
masegelo, marks left by a saw.
masegišane, joker.
masego, tripod, trivet.
mašego, blessings, nights.

maseka, bangles, bracelets.
masekama, slanting position(s).
masekanta, musician.
mašela, clothing material, washing.
maseme, suspicion.
mašemo, gardens, lands.
masenamelo, eaves.
masenke, sheets of galvanized iron or zinc.
masepa, excrements, faeces.
maseterata, magistrate.
masetlana, distress.
masetlaoka, white-ants.
masetlapelo, tragedy, distress.
mašiagodiša, herd-funk.
mašianoke, hammerhead (the bird).
mašika, sinews, clans, tribes.
mašilone, compulsion.
mašilwane, tick-birds, cattle egrets.
mašiši, tambookie grass.
masisi, scorpions.
mašišimalo, serenity.
Mašišing, Lydenburg.
mašoba, holes.
masodi, bush, forests.
masogana, young men; **-tia,** strong young men.
mašogedi, washings-up, flotsam.
mašoko, labour, travail.
mašokotšo, second drawing of milk, interest, arrears.
masole, soldiers.
mašolopudi, herd-funk.
masome, tens.
mašope, ruins.
mašoto, favour, fortune.
mašoto, strings.
mašukhu, thigh bones.
mašumatho, deceit, fraud.
mašupšane, a drum used at the initiation ceremony for girls.
mašuputšane, pigs, hogs.
maswabi, grief, sadness.
maswabiša, that which causes grief/sadness.
maswafo, lungs; **rwalela – godimo,** be afraid.
maswanedi, proper.
maswaiša, haul, spoil.
maswena, enemy.
maswete, wrinkles.
mašweu, white, good.
maswika, rocks, stones.
matagwa, drunkards.
matakataka, bush-baby, lemur.
matamišwa, cutlets given to one who assists in slaughtering an animal.
matamo, dams.
matanyetša, bangles.
mataya, (mataa), Cape hunting dogs.
matekwane, dagga, hemp.
matena, dinner.
mateng, content(s).
matepe, sulkiness, capriciousness.
matete, wonders.
mathai, riddles.
mathaka, comrades.
mathapama, afternoon(s).
mathari, young mothers.
mathata, difficulty, adversity.
mathe, (dial.), spittle, saliva.
mathebo, skin-rugs, karosses.
mathedithedi, slippery (things).
matheka, hips, waist.
matheti, tattoo, tattooing.
mathinthedi, things shaken out or off.
mathobela, the butcher-bird.
mathoko, sides, directions.
mathologatse, beifers.
mathomo, beginning; – **thomo,** very (first) beginning.
mathopša, slaves, exiles.
mathudi, veranda(h), porch(es).
mathume, fine.
mathumiša, fine meal, flour.
mathutšana, small veranda(h).
mathwalwane, foundings.
matikireng, diggings, diamond fields.
Matikiring, Lichtenburg.
matilwane, sorrel.

matimela, people or animals that are lost.
matipane, dip inspector, cattle guard.
matla, thresh, thrash, beat.
matladima, dizziness.
matlafala, become strong.
matlafatša, strengthen, empower.
matlafatšo, strengthening.
matlafatšwa, be empowered.
matlagosa, dawn.
matlaka, vultures, eagles.
matlakala, leaves, pages, refuse, sweeping.
matlalo, skins.
matlametlo, bullfrogs.
matlao, forceps, pincers.
matlapa, flat stones, blackboards, slates.
matlapulele, splashing.
matlawa, dilapidated.
matlere, cracks.
matlobotlobo, shower/drops of rain.
matlole, boxes, chests.
matlorotloro, deluge, shower of rain.
matlotla, ruins, old huts.
matoka, chips, pieces.
matokwane, dagga, Indian hemp.
matola, plaster.
matologa, come off.
matolo, knees.
matolola, loosen, tear off.
matome, second son.
matona, officers, generals.
matong, grain stored in a basket under the dung.
matonki, donkeys.
matrikale, n., madrigal.
matsae, (dial.), eggs.
matsaka, luxuries.
matšarene, margarine.
matšarete, majorette.
matšatši, days, suns.
matšegetšege, big species of scorpion.
matseno, entrance(s).
matšerwana, meno a –, sharp little teeth.
matsetse, fleas.
matsha, lakes.
matšha, march.
matšhaotšhele, semen.
matšhedi, semen.
matshedišo, consolation.
matshego, cruet-stand.
matšhogo, fear.
matšhotšhobo, downpour of rain.
matšhotšhoro, drops of rain, downpour.
matshwenyego, difficulty, troubles.
matshwete, wrinkles, writhing.
matši, forests, woods.
matšibogo, fords, drifts.
matsikiri, tambookie grass.
matšimane, fleas.
matsioko, colly, coly.
matšoba, flowers.
matsogo, arms.
matsolwane, spurs, pricks.
matšwa, dowry.
matswa, thongs.
ma(t)swafo, lungs.
matšwagodimo, beestings, colostrum.
matswai, salt.
matswale, mother-in-law.
matswalo, birth.
matswamati, bark (of a tree).
matswedintsweke, zig-zag.
matswele, teats, nipples.
matswele, fists, stacks, heaps.
matswiana, chickens, young of birds.
matswianyana, chicken, young of birds.
matswinyane, the young of birds or snakes.
matute, nectar, sap.
matwa, partly soft (a skin).
maudi, washings-up, scum.
maumo, fruit (of the womb).
maupi, much mealie meal.
mawa, precipices, caves.
mawatle, seas, oceans.
mawelakgahlano, by chance.
mawelewele, talk, chattering.

meago, buildings.
meakanyetšo, designs.
mebala, colours.
mebanki, baskets.
mebila, footpaths, roads.
mebolelo, speeches, sayings.
meboto, hills.
mebotoro, motor-cars.
mebotša, species of wild fruit.
meboya, (meoya), souls, wool, spirits.
mebu, earth, ground.
meburu, nuts (of a bolt).
mebušo, governments, realms, kingdoms.
mebutele, manure.
mebutla, hares, rabbits.
medi, roots.
medile, has grown.
medimo, gods.
medša, cause to sprout, germinate; – **šitše,** made to grow.
mediti, teachers at a circumcision school.
medu, roots.
medumaedi, sounds, howling.
medumaolo, noises, sounds, howling.
medumo, noises, sounds.
medupe, gentle rain, long continued rain.
mee, (mêê), re –, bleat.
meedi, watercourses, valleys.
meeike, oaktrees.
meela, watercourses.
meepeletšane, songs of triumph.
meepo, mines, diggings.
meetlwa, thorns.
meetse, manes.
meetse, water, juice.
Meetsefula, The Flood.
mefafa, sweet grass, "buffelsgras".
mefago, provisions for the road.
mefaka, knives, mealie cobs.
mefarafara, things scattered about.
mefaratšhweng, four-corners, "kruisbessie".
mefatša, crevices.
mefeng, handles.
mefiri, bangles made of copper, copper bracelets.
mefoka, grainless ears of corn, weeds.
mefolo, poisons.
mefoma, caves, caverns.
mefsiri, copper bracelets.
megabaru, greed.
megala, nose-bands, cords, telegrams.
megalatšhika, nerves.
megano, muscles of the neck, gristle.
megaranafase, latitudes.
megobe, pools of water, pans.
megobelo, rejoicing.
megobo, rejoicing by men, songs of triumph, **kgomo e letše le** –, said of a cow which was not milked in the evening.
megodu, stomachs, paunches.
megokgo, tears.
megolo, big.
megolo, throats.
megolodi, cranes.
megono, bea diatla –, place the hands behind the neck.
megopo, bowls, dishes.
megopolo, thoughts.
megorogoro, ravines.
megwang, leaves of the mealie, corn or millet plants, stalks.
megwapa, biltong, dried meat, fruit or vegetables.
megwaša, rustling.
mehla, times, days; **ka** –, always; **ka** – **le** –, for ever, evermore; **ya mehleng,** daily.
mehlaba, sands.
mehlaka, vleys, marches.
mehlako, troubles.
mehlamo, (mehlamu), news.
mehlantšho, strings of the crupper.
mehlobo, races, tribes.
mehloko, type of grass used for thatching roofs.
mehlonyo, curses.
mehola, uses.

mehuta, kinds, sorts, species.
Mei, May.
meila, mule.
meila, mile.
mejakaranda, jacaranda trees.
mejako, entrances, doorways.
mekae, how many, few.
mekaa, so many.
mekgabišo, ornaments.
mekgaditswana, lizards.
mekganya, go bea –, to shade the eyes.
mekgatlo, associations, societies, groups.
mekgato, mother's milk; **bana ba nkgago** –, mere children.
mekgatša, food for pigs.
mekgerane, scrub cattle.
mekgobo, heaps.
mekgolokwane, shouts of joy, rejoicing by women.
mekgopho, the patterns on a floor smeared with cow-dung.
mekgoro, leggings; **pere ya** –, white-footed horse.
mekgoši, shouts of alarm.
mekgotha, streets.
mekhuri, mercury.
mekodua, lean animals.
mekokotlo, backs, the spine.
mekoto, thick.
mekubego ya meuši, fumes of smoke.
mekuru, pigeons.
mekurwana, young pigeons.
mela, germinate, grow, n. lines.
melaba, traps, snares, runners, suckers, tendrils, creepers.
melaka, pus, matter in the eye.
melao, laws.
melapo, river-beds, vales.
melato, debts, cases, transgressions.
melatša, cold porridge.
melatšatši, tropics.
melatwana, small debts, transgressions.
melawana, regulations.
melebo, runners, tendrils.
meleko, temptations, examinations.
melela meno (dinaka), turn against.
melete, holes, pits.
meletlo, feasts.
meletša, girdles of beads; v., endure.
mellwane, boundaries.
melodi, whistles, tunes, songs of birds.
melogelelo; mašela a –, embroidered pieces.
meloko, relatives.
melomo, mouths, lips.
melora, ashes.
mema, invite.
memeru, gravid animal(s).
mena, fold, hem, bend.
menagana, be folded.
menagano, meditations.
menaganya, fold.
menakwe, skipping game.
menamune, orange trees.
menang, mosquitoes.
menasi, mess.
mene, four.
menga, cracks, crevices.
mengena, "boekenhout" trees.
mengwaga, years.
mengwako, houses.
mengwakwana, small houses.
mengwe, some, other.
menkgenkge, bad-smelling weeds.
menkgo, smells, odours.
menko, mango.
meno, teeth.
menola, turn back.
menolla, unfold.
menollo, unfolding.
menono, riches, fertility.
menopo, oval.
menotlo, feet of birds, talons, toes of birds.
mentši, many; **-ntši,** very many.
menwana, little teeth.
menwana, fingers.
menwana ya maoto, toes.

menya, v., squeeze; n., excrement, dung.
menyana, small.
menyane, small.
menyanya, feasts, festivals.
meoba, sugar-canes.
meobu, wasps.
meoka, mimosa trees.
meomo, shins, shin-bones.
meono, snoring.
meopelo, songs.
meoya, spirits.
mepalema, palm-trees.
meperekisi, peach-trees.
mepete, beds.
mephagana, pullets.
mephako, cross-bars.
mephato, classes, Native regiments.
mepiere, pear trees.
mepšere, pear trees.
mepu, wasps, hornets.
meputso, marks, points.
merafe, tribes, nations.
merafo, handfuls.
meraka, cattle-ranches.
merako, stone walls.
merakwana, small stone walls.
meraladi, stripes.
meralala, wanderings.
meralo, lines.
meraloko, games, plays.
merapelo, prayers.
merapelelo, intercessory prayers.
merara, creeping plants, climbers.
meraro, three.
meratha, porridge eaten without any extras.
mere, trees, forests.
mereba, insolence, impudence, cheek.
merepa, sweet-potatoes.
merethetho, pulsation.
mereto, stripes; adj., striped.
mereto, pet names, praise names.
meriri, hair.
merithi = **meriti.**
meriti, shadows, **ka** –, afternoon.
meritšhana, little hair.
merogano, curses.
merogo, vegetables.
meroko, bran.
meropa, drums.
meropana, timbrels.
meropotlane, gooseberry trees.
meroro, roars, bellowing.
meruba, a game like draughts.
meruka, stringed beads, bangles.
merutlo, calabashes for beer.
merwalo, burdens.
mesamo, (mesamelo), pillows, cushions.
mešaša, shelters, huts made of branches.
meše, sides; **ya go fela,** both sides.
mese, crushers, pestles.
mesc, mcss.
mesebe, arrows.
mesela ya mahlo, corners of the eyes.
meselane, mason.
mesehla, yellow.
mesehumulo, gasping.
mesepelo, journeys.
mesese, skirts.
mesibihla, mimosa trees.
mešidi, soot, gun powder, charcoal.
mešifa, muscles, fibres.
mešima, holes.
mešito, tramping, footsteps.
meso, dawn.
mešoro, cruel.
mešunkwane, herbs, medicine.
mešutša, sniffing.
mešutšo, snorting.
metala, blue, green, old.
metale, n., metal.
metamofose, metamorphosis.
metara, metre.
methaladi, stripes, lines, rows.
methama, cheeks.
methape, runners, ranks.
methapo, runners, ranks.
metheo, foundations.
methepa, young girls.

methopo, fountains, springs.
methopothušo, resources.
metlae, jokes.
metlang, stalks.
metlwae, customs.
metša, swallow (whole), devour, absorb.
metsana, small villages.
metse, towns, villages.
metše, has sprouted, grown or germinated.
metšega, clay pots; v., be swallowed.
metsetlo, sobs, sobbing.
metšhelo, taxes.
metšhene, machines.
metšhokga, debt.
metšo, units.
metsoko, tobacco.
metswako, mixtures.
metswala, relatives, relations.
metswalle, friends.
meuba, bellows.
meuwane, mists, fogs.
mimila, blow the nose.
mimisa, cry (as a baby).
mina, strain, filter.
minega, trickle out.
minerala, (minerale), mineral.
minimamo, minimum.
minola, blow the nose.
minte, (minti), mint.
minyuete, minuet.
mira, myrrh.
mitere, mitre.
mma, mother.
mmaba, an enemy.
mmabaledi, caretaker.
mmaballa, take care of him/her.
mmabasadi, a ladies' man.
mmabi, species of wild cotton bush.
mmabišetša, embitter for one.
mmabo, essen-wood, their mother.
mmabole, marble.
mmaborokwane, sleepy head.
mmadi, reader, counter.
mmaditsela, go-between, messenger.
mmago, your mother.
mmagoje, right.
mmagojeng, ka –, right (turn).
mmagomanke, repetition of the game.
mmago yona, its mother.
mmagwe, his (her) mother.
mmakapušo, pretender, claimant.
mmakgere, beer from prickly pears.
mmakgomathe, the real thing; adj., real true.
mmakgonthe, truth; adj., true, real.
mmaki, claimant.
mmakiši, opponent.
mmako, claim, demand.
mmala, colour; **ba** –, coloured people.
mmalabadi, babbler, chatterbox.
mmalatšhelete, cashier, teller.
mmale, the Kaffir tree.
mmalehufane, a jealous woman.
mmaletlotlo, cashier (woman).
mmaletswai, species of locust.
mmalewaneng, fern.
mmalo! Oh, dear me!
mmalo, manner of reading.
mmamaphengwana, fairy.
mmamati, species of locust.
mmami, mummy.
mmamogolo, maternal aunt.
mmamogašwa, legendary water snake.
mmamohlake, storm, cloudburst.
mmamokebe, species of water snake.
mmamokgadi, the belle of the ball.
mmamolangwane, secretary bird.
mmamolatela, the second wife.
mmamolema, bat.
mmamongwe, another mother.
mmamonotswana, sugar-bird, sunbird.
mmamoratwa/-e, beloved one.
mmane, maternal aunt.
mmane, mother.
mmangwane, maternal aunt.
mmankgonyane, magic wand, stethoscope.
mmanki, basket.
mmankoko, species of locust.
mmankokonono, mantis.

mmankoting, mine-worker, miner.
mmanoke, widow-bird, bishop-bird.
mmanthaladi, wanderer, tramp.
mmantlhakane, wasp.
mmantlhwa, queen ant.
mmantopi (selo sa ka), dabs! claim a thing that is seen or picked up.
mmapa, together, side by side.
mmapa, map, trinket.
mmapadi, player.
mmapala, true, real.
mmapale, good.
mmapalo, manner of playing.
mmapatšadiokobatši, drug peddler.
mmapatši, trader.
mmaphaka, days of yore.
mmaphateng, flirt.
mmapo, necklace of beads.
mmapola, crucify him.
mmapoo (boroko bja) –, sound sleep.
mmaraka, market.
mmaruri, sa –, truly.
mmasa, dye.
mmasebotsane, fair lady.
mmasekanta, musician.
mmaseletswane, bo –, the mantis.
mmasepala, municipality.
mmasona, its mother.
mmatamela, approach him/her.
mmatlafatši, invigorator.
mmatšo, their mother (animals).
mmatswale, mother-in-law.
mmayo, its mother.
mmawešo, our mother.
mme, mother, my mother.
mme, and, furthermore.
mmea, place him.
mmeakanyi, organiser.
mmee, the bleating of a sheep.
mmeela, place him/her.
mmeeletši, a man who gets engaged.
mmeeletšwa, the woman who is (engaged) betrothed.
mmefelo, anger, wrath.
mmegi, reporter.
mmegiwa, accused, one reported.
mmela, malt.
mmelaedi, complainant, plaintiff.
mmelaetša, cause someone to doubt.
mmele, body.
mmelegi, a bearer, one who (is confined)., gives birth.
mmelegiši, midwife.
mmelego, burden.
mmelo, germination, growth.
mmemogolo, grandmother.
mmeno, a fold.
mmenyana, an abject thing.
mmeodi, a barber.
mmereki, labourer.
mmereko, labour, work.
mmese, cap, beret.
mmeši, roaster, baker.
mmešola, remove him/her from the fire.
mmetela, adv., by storm; **ka** –, in waves, forcibly.
mmetha, beat/strike him/her.
mmethe, muid.
mmetli, carpenter, mason, stone-cutter.
mmetši, marksman.
mmidi, mealies, maize.
mmidiwa, one called.
mmila, footpath, road.
mmilo, medlar tree.
mmini, dancer.
mmino, totem, dance.
mminotetšo, orchestra, band.
mmipe, panting, maise-cricket.
mmitši, crier, one who calls.
mmoelanya, reconcile him/her.
mmoelanyi, mediator.
mmofiwa, prisoner.
mmogedi, spectator.
mmogelwa, one who is looked at.
mmogo, the trunk of an elephant, proboscis.
mmogo, together with.
mmoi, timid person.
mmola, species of tree, sandapple.
mmolabolo, noisy conversation.

mmolai, killer, murderer.
mmolao, murder.
mmolaya, kill him (her).
mmoledi, narrator, preacher, first person.
mmoleledi, intercessor, advocate.
mmolelo, language, manner of speaking.
mmolelwa, the one talked about, third person.
mmolodi, initiate.
mmoloki, saviour, keeper.
mmoni, seer, the one who sees.
mmopa, clay, plasticine.
mmopi, creator, moulder, potter.
mmopo, manner of creating or moulding.
mmopo, the bridge of the nose, the muzzle of an animal.
mmopu, spatula, oar, club, bat.
mmorogo, morgen.
mmotegela, be faithful to him/her.
mmotlana, solitary/helpless person.
mmoto, hill.
mmoto, moth.
mmotoro, motorcar.
mmotša, tell him/her.
mmotšiši, questioner.
mmotwana, small hill, mound.
mmu, soil, earth, ground.
mmula, species of tree, "grys-appelboom".
mmulo, the opening.
mmupudu, a species of tree, the wild apple.
mmurupei, mulberry tree.
mmuši, governor, ruler.
mmušiši, the one who helps to govern.
mmušo, (ba –), the government, empire.
mmutedi, (mmutele), manure.
mmutla, hare, rabbit; **go robatša,** –, pacify, coax, **lomilwe ke** –, be sterile.
moabedi, distributor.
moabi, divider, one who allots.
moadi, one who spreads.
moadimi, borrower, lender.
moadimiši, money-lender.
moadingwa, debtor.
moagi, builder, mason, dweller.
moagišani, neighbour.
moagiši, assistant builder.
moago, building, manner (style) of building.
moahlodi, judge.
moahloledi, arbiter, referee.
moahlolelo, judgment.
moahlolwa, accused.
moakedi, (moaketši), liar.
moakgo, gesticulation.
moakgofi, one who works in a hurry.
moalafi, healer, doctor.
moalo, bed, bedding.
moamandele, almond tree.
moamogedi, receiver.
moamogi, expropriator, depossessor.
moamogwabonna, eunuch.
moamuši, dam, mother.
moanegi, one who hangs out to dry.
moani, one who takes an oath.
moano, totem, totemic animal.
moanyesi, one who suckles, wet-nurse.
moanyi, one who sucks.
moanyo, period of infancy.
moanywi, one who sucks.
moapari, one who puts on clothes.
moaparo, fashion, dress.
moapei, cook.
moapeiši, assistant cook.
moapeo, way of cooking, decoction.
moapeši, one who (covers) dresses someone else.
moapostola, apostle.
moarabi, one who answers.
moarodi, one who divides.
moaroganyi, one who separates.
moarogi, transgressor.
moaroledi, distributor.
moaroši, tempter, deceiver, seducer.

moatiši, one who increases.
moatletiki, athlete.
moatli, one who kisses.
moato, manner of increasing, increase.
mobja, riem, thong.
mobjadi, planter, sower.
mobjang, what (kind) manner.
mobjalo, such.
mobu, soil, earth, wasp.
mobugodimo, top soil.
mobupewa, sedimentary soil.
mobutlase, subsoil.
modi, root, plant used for making ropes.
modiadie, hesitator.
modiidi, poor (man).
modiiledi, squatter.
modiitšana, poor man.
modika, perimeter.
modikadiki, hesitator, waverer.
modikadiko, hesitation.
modikana, initiate, boy in circumcision school.
modiko, a surrounding, perimeter.
modikologa, slow person.
modikutu, adventitious root.
modikwa, one who is besieged (surrounded).
Modimo, God.
modimo, ancestral spirit.
Modimolle, Nylstroom.
modimotsela, mirage, a name used to frighten children.
modingwana, idol, fetish.
modira, worker of, **mo-dira-dibe,** sinner; **mo-dira-khutšo,** peacemaker; **mo-dira-mehlolo,** one who does wonders.
modiredi, servant, deacon.
modiri, worker, labourer, doer.
modirišani, partner, co-worker.
modiriši, assistant.
modirišo, mood.
modirišogo, infinitive.
modirišogore, subjunctive.
modirišohlaodi, participial.
modirišokgonego, potential.
modirišopego, indicative.
modirišotaelo, imperative.
modiro, task, work, function.
modiša, shepherd, herd, watchman, keeper, pastor, penis.
modiši, teacher at an initiation school.
moditšhaba, heathen, pagan.
modu, root.
modubadubi, bustler, fidget.
modubi, one who mixes.
moduboyana, hair-root.
modudi, one who (sits) is seated.
moduduetši, one who (shrieks) applauds.
moduduetšo, rejoicing, applause.
moduhlare, kaffir wait-a-bit thorn.
modula, pollen, species of grass.
modula, one who lives or inhabits; – **noši,** hermit; – **setulo,** chairman; – **thoko,** outsider.
modulakgogo, wild quince tree.
modulatore, modulator.
moduledi, squatter.
modumedi, believer, Christian.
modumela, species of tree, “bergsering”.
modumi, one who desires.
modumo, sound, rumbling, booming.
modupe, (modupi), standing rain.
modutama, slope.
modutona, tap-root.
modutu, white stinkwood, Camdeboo stinkwood.
moebangedi, evangelist.
moedi, water-course, vlei, valley.
moeike, oak-tree.
moeketši, one who adds to.
moeki, traitor, deceiver.
moela, water course, stream, current.
moelamoya, current of air.
moelawatle, gulf-stream.
moeledi, surveyor.
moelelo, thought.

moeletši, adviser, counsellor.
moeletšwi, one who is advised.
moelo, measure.
moemedi, representative, surety, vicar, comforter, intercessor, mediator.
moemi, one who is standing.
moeng, stranger, guest.
moeniši, commissioner of oaths.
moeno, totem, coat of arms.
moenti, vaccinator, inoculator.
moento, vaccination.
moenyana, harbinger.
moepa, digger of.
moepapitšo, convenor.
moepathutse, digger of the plant baboon's tail.
moepedi, one who buries.
moepela, trench.
moepi, digger.
moepo, digging, mine.
moepolodi, one who digs out.
moepšana, small mine.
moesa, lad.
moeta, vessel, clay pot, earthen pot.
moetapele, leader, captain (team).
moetelwa, host.
moethimolo, sneezing, sneeze.
moeti, traveller, visitor, pilgrim.
moetšana, bridesmaid, bestman.
moetse, mane, ridge.
moetšiši, imitator.
mofadi, scraper of skins.
mofagi, one who pours meal into a pot.
mofahloši, educator.
mofaladi, emigrant, foreigner.
mofantisi, auctioneer.
mofapahlogo, crown.
mofapogi, stray person.
mofarisei, pharisee.
mofati, digger.
mofato, digging.
mofediši, one who finishes.
mofefere, shotgun.
mofeferi, winnower.
mofegi, hangman.
mofehli, one who (strikes fire).
mofehlo, buttermilk.
mofeie, fig tree.
mofelegetši, one who accompanies.
mofenyi, conqueror.
mofepalapa, bread-winner.
mofepi, one who feeds others, caterer.
moferefere, riot, tumult, fracas.
moferefi, painter.
moferekanyi, instigator.
mofero, weeds.
mofetakatsela, passer-by, traveller.
mofeti, one who passes (by).
mofetodi, one who replies.
mofetoledi, interpreter, translator.
mofetolo, way of answering.
mofi, giver, donor, mitten.
mofifadi, mourner.
mofihli, one who (arrives) hides.
mofodiši, a healer.
mofofakakota, pole-jumper.
mofofane, pilot.
mofofi, one who flies, airman, jumper.
mofoki, one that sprinkles medicine.
mofokodi, weak person, sick person, stick-in-the-mud.
mofokotši, one who diminishes.
mofolo, parade.
mofoma, cave.
Mofonesia, Phoenecian.
Mofora, Frenchman.
moforani, cheat, fraud.
mofori, cheat, fraud.
moforomi, brick-maker.
mofoši, one who (throws) makes mistakes.
mofudi, one who (plucks) threshes.
mofuraledi, one who turns his back on.
mogaba, species of wild lilac, "bergsering, slaploot".
mogadibo, sister-in-law, daughter-in-law.
mogadika, rival.

mogadikane, one of the two wives of a man.
mogadiki, one who roasts.
mogaditšong, co-wife.
mogagabo, relative, relation.
mogageno, one of your relatives.
mogagešo, one of our (people) relatives.
mogahlana, apron.
mogajana, brave little fellow.
mogala, cord, rope, nose-band, bit, bridle, telegraph wire; **tiela** –, send a telegram.
mogaladi, species of Protea, "suikerbos".
Mogalakwena, tributary of the Limpopo River.
mogalantšu, telephone.
mogalatladi, boekenhout, beech.
mogalatšhika, nerve.
mogale, hero.
mogalefi, quick-tempered person.
mogami, milker.
moganedi, one who refuses.
moganetšamodimo, atheist.
moganetši, opponent, one who denies.
mogani, one who refuses.
mogano, gristle, neck-sinew.
mogapa, species of thorn-tree, "Apiesdoring".
mogapa, eye-socket.
mogapagare, centre-forward.
mogapi, driver, capturer.
mogapu, stalk of the watermelon.
mogarafase, equator.
mogarogo, rash.
mogaši, disperser.
mogašwa, blanket of oxhide.
mogateledi, oppressor.
mogati, one who treads on.
mogatiši, printer.
mogatišo, script.
mogato, footstep.
mogatša, spouse.
mogatšanoga, earth-snake.
mogau, a poisonous herb, gifblaar.
mogau, thirst, mercy, pity.
mogaugedi, merciful one.
mogaugelo, mercy, compassion.
mogaugelwa, object of (mercy), compassion, blessed one.
mogauwane, garden nightshade.
mogaya, grapple-plant.
mogeledi, drawer of water (for).
mogeologi, geologist.
mogo, wild fig, sycamore.
mogobagoba, yellowwood tree.
mogobe, a pan, a pool.
mogobelo, song of triumph (sung by men).
mogobo, war-cry, song of triumph, cry.
mogoboši, slanderer.
mogodi, mist, fog.
mogodišo, way of increasing one's salary.
mogodu, belly, stomach, paunch.
mogofe, go gapša, ke –, go with the stream.
mogopa, trail, head of cattle killed at a burial.
mogogadi, wife's father or mother.
mogogedi, one who attracts.
mogogi, one who pulls, leader.
mogogolwa, aluvial soil.
mogogoma, wound (caused by a beating).
mogogonope, cock.
mogogorupa, crooked.
mogogorupo, thumb.
mogogotši, smuggler.
mogohlo, mimosa, (kameeldoring).
mogokare, the willow.
mogokgo, tear.
mogokolodi, millepede.
mogokong, army-worm.
Mogokotlou, Pietermaritzburg.
mogola, land lying fallow.
mogole, deformed person.
mogole, crane, heron.
mogolegwa, prisoner, captive.
mogolle, elder brother or sister.

mogolo, elder, elder (brother) sister.
mogolo, throat, oesophagus.
mogolodi, crane, deliverer, stork.
mogololwa, a person who is set free.
mogolwane, elder (brother) sister.
mogoma, hoe, plough.
mogoma, stick-grass.
mogomarakgapana, burdock, burr.
mogomi, one who returns.
mogong, perhaps.
mogongwe, perhaps.
mogoo, shout, outcry.
mogopane, species of "kanniedood" tree.
mogope, cutlet, "karmenaadjie".
mogope, drinking calabash, beetle.
mogopo, a wooden bowl.
mogopodi, thinker, meditator.
mogopolo, idea, thought, opinion.
mogopotši, one who reminds.
mogoriri, "taaibos".
mogorogo, rash.
mogorogoro, mixture of things.
mogorogoro, "kanniedood" tree, a ravine.
mogoti, black-jacks.
mogoturi, tree-snake.
mogudi, mist, fog.
mogwa, brother-in-law, son-in-law.
mogwa, species of thorn-tree.
mogwagadi, mother-in-law, sister-in-law.
mogwagwe, his (her) brother-in-law.
mogwana, four-corners, stick, "kruisbessie".
mogwang, leaf of the maize or millet plant, blade or leaf of a reed.
mogwapa, biltong, dried fruit.
mogwaripa, "knoppiesdoring, haakdoring".
mogwaša, rustling.
mogwe, brother-in-law, son-in-law.
mogwegadi, mother-in-law.
mogwanyana, son-in-law.
mogwera, friend, boy in the circumcision school.
moheitene, heathen.
mohla, day, time, season.
mohlaba, malt.
mohlabanedi, one who fights for, defender.
mohlábáni, soldier, warrior.
mohlabeledi, conductor, psalmist.
mohlabelo, vaccine.
mohlabetšana, spot behind the shoulder or neck where an animal is easily killed.
mohlabi, butcher, planter.
mohladi, one who divorces.
mohlaeledi, one who lacks something.
mohlagare, jaw.
mohlagase, electricity.
mohlahla, rush, reed, hut.
mohlahlaiša, bush-tea.
mohlahli, leader, guide.
mohlahlobi, inspector.
mohlahlobiši, assistant inspector.
mohlaka, marsh, vlei.
mohlaka, white (collar) neck, smooth part of a quill.
mohlakase, electricity.
mohlaki, composer, inventor, wretch.
mohlako, trouble, worry, protea.
mohlakodi, robber.
mohlakodiši, saviour, redeemer.
mohlakola, quarri-tree.
mohlakolane, garden nightshade.
mohlala, footstep, track, example.
mohlalefi, wise person.
mohlalefo, intelligence.
mohlaloši, one who explains.
mohlalwa, divorcee.
mohlamaru, time of danger, when the sky is clouded (grey).
mohlami, composer, inventor.
mohlamonene, formerly, in olden times.
mohlamong, perhaps.
mohlana, afterbirth of an animal.
mohlanare, species of hardwood, yellow wood.
mohlanka, servant.

mohlankana, young man.
mohlankedi, official, civil servant.
mohlanogi, unfaithful, deserter.
mohlantšho, string of the crupper.
mohlaope, perhaps.
mohlapanyi, one who swears.
mohlape, flock, herd, pack.
mohlapetši, foreman, manager, director.
mohlapi, bather, washer.
mohlapo, urine, periods, medicine for making rain.
mohlapokhubedu, bilharzia.
mohlapologo, urine.
mohlare, tree.
mohlašána, small tree.
mohlase, egg of an insect.
mohlasedi, attacker.
mohlatholodi, expositor.
mohlatša, species of wild fig-tree.
mohlatšiša, a plant that causes people to vomit, an emetic.
mohlatswa, the sisal, Chrysophyllum Magalismontanum.
mohlatswana, dim. small flock/herd.
mohlatswe, see: **mohlatswa.**
mohlatswi, one who does the washing.
mohlekwa, spoilt person.
mohlo, waterberry tree.
mohlobo, race, clan, tribe.
mohlobodi, one who undresses, naked (poor) person.
mohlobogedi, consoler, sympathiser.
mohlobogi, despairer.
mohlobolo, side-piece (meat).
mohlodi, creator, spy.
mohlodi, flavour, (sweet) juice.
mohlogo, cupping horn.
mohlogotsi, must, beer that is still fermenting.
mohlohleletši, instigator, agitator, insurgent.
mohlohli, challenger.
mohlohlomiši, explorer.
mohlohlono, itch(ing).
mohloi, one who hates.
mohloki, one who is in want, a needy person.
mohloko, species of euphorbia.
mohlokofadi, tormented, persecuted, tortured person.
mohlokofatši, tormentor, persecutor.
mohlokomedi, caretaker, guardian, trustee.
mohlokomelo, care.
mohlolo, wonder, miracle.
mohlologadi, widow, widower.
mohlolwa, one who is conquered.
mohlomaredi, persecutor.
mohlomi, one who plants, planter.
mohlomo, manner of (planting) founding.
mohlomogi, one who is sad.
mohlomong, perhaps, maybe.
mohlomphegi, honourable person.
mohlomphi, one who respects.
mohlompholli, disrespectful person.
mohlonami, sulky person.
mohlono, wild apricot-tree.
mohlonyo, curse, malediction.
mohlopa, bulge.
mohlopi, "witgatboom", Capparis albitrunca.
mohloriši, tormentor.
mohloro, the green grasshopper.
mohlosa, an ear of corn destroyed by birds.
mohlose, see: **mohlosa.**
mohlotlo, strainer.
mohlotši, one who limps, a lame person.
mohlwa, the white-ant, termite.
mohlwa, quick-grass.
mohlwaelá, series.
mohlwaremmipe, cricket.
mohlwekišaoma, dry-cleaner.
mohlwekiši, cleaner.
mohokani, mahogany.
mohola, use, advantage.
mohu, deceased.
mohudu, tortoise.
mohuetšo, exhaled breath.

mohuhu, (mohuhwane), drizzle.
mohumagadi, lady, queen.
mohumagatšana, princess.
mohumanegi, poor (needy) person.
mohumi, rich person.
mohunolodi, deliverer, liberator, redeemer.
mohuta, kind, species, variety.
mohwahwa, epileptic.
mohwana, person whose relative has died.
mohwelere, red-bush (species of Borbonia).
mohwelwa, widower.
mohwelwagadi, widow.
mohwetši, finder.
mohwidinyane, skittles.
mohwidiri, see: **mohwelere.**
moihlo, one-eyed person.
moilhlwe, one-eyed person.
moikahlodi, one who judges himself.
moikaketši, hypocrite.
moikemiši, one who raises himself, pretends to stand.
moikepi, a person who brings about his own downfall.
moiketli, one who is at ease.
moikgantšhi, proud person.
moikgodiši, boaster, conceited person.
moikgogomoši, proud person.
moikgolofatši, person who cripples himself.
moikiši, one who goes of his own accord.
moikoki, one who nurses himself.
moikokobetši, one who humbles himself.
moikomoši, one who warms himself.
moikotli, one who strikes or punishes himself.
moikotlolli, one who stretches himself.
moila, one who (hates) despises.
moilabasadi, woman-hater.
moiladitagi, total abstainer, teetotaller.
moilwa, hated one.
moima, pregnant woman.
moimana, pregnant woman.
Moindia, Indian.
moipati, one who hides himself.
moipegi, one who reports himself.
moipei, one who places himself.
moiphagamiši, one who exalts himself.
moiphediši, independent person.
moiphepi, one who feeds himself.
moiphodiši, one who heals himself.
moipolai, one who kills himself, one who commits suicide.
moipoloki, one who takes care of himself.
moiponi, one who sees himself.
moipontšhi, one who reveals himself.
moipoti, one who trusts (relies on) himself.
moipuši, one who governs himself, who practices self-control.
moisa, chap, fellow.
moiša, one who takes anything to.
moiši, he who takes to.
moitaodi, who is his own master.
moitaodišaphelo, autobiographer.
moitatodi, one who excuses himself.
moitebadi, one who forgets himself.
moitekodi, who examines himself.
moithapi, volunteer.
moithati, selfish, egoistical person.
moithutafika, geologist.
moithuti, student.
moitimi, one who deprives himself.
moitiredi, one who works for himself, one who makes things for himself.
moitiši, one who minds himself.
moitlami, monk, nun.
moitlhokofatši, self-torturer.
moitlhomphi, one who respects himself or who has self-respect.
moitlhompholli, one who has no self-respect.
moitsebi, person who knows himself.
moitshenyetši, one who spoils his own affairs.

moitshepi, one who has self-confidence.
moitšhireletši, one who protects himself.
moituledi, one who sits idle.
mojagobedi, funnel.
mojako, doorway, entrance.
mojatswetswetswe, epicure.
moji, eater, consumer.
Mojuda, Jew.
mojuri, juryman.
moka, all; **ke** –, then, it is all.
mokadi, tassel.
mokadikadi, a flirt, a fickle person.
mokae, ke – of what nationality is he?
mokaka, udder, protuberance of the vent of a bird when she starts laying eggs.
mokakamalo, dysentery.
mokakatlelo, strain, stress.
mokakenomokakua, neutral (person).
mokalametara, meter-reader.
mokalatšane, flirt, coquette.
mokamo, manner of dressing the hair.
mokaola, concubine, burweed.
mokatala, rash person.
mokataphase, caterpillar-tractor.
mokatiši, a jockey.
mokato, races.
mokekolo, old woman.
mokero, furrow, channel.
mokerubi, cherub.
mokete, festival.
mokete, someone, so and so.
moketla, green wood, damp wood.
moketwana, belt.
moketwane, small gourd.
mokga, kind, sort, species.
mokgabišo, ornament.
mokgadi, one who scolds, remonstrator.
mokgaditswana, lizard.
mokgahlo, interlude.
mokgakgapitsi, wild asparagus.
mokgaki, one who strings beads.
mokgako, new clay-pot, something new and clean.
mokgalabjana, little old man.
mokgalabje, old man.
mokgalemi, censor, proctor.
mokgalo, wait-a-bit tree.
mokgamiwa, one who is strangled or choked.
mokgano, milestone, beacon, boundary post.
mokgaoletši, one who intercepts.
mokgaolo, partition.
mokgaritswana, lizard.
mokgathatšhemo, tiller of new soil.
mokgathi, hoer of new soil.
mokgatli, one who throws stones.
mokgatlo, association, guild.
mokgatša, food for pigs.
mokgayo, medicine for witchcraft.
mokgekolo, n., old woman.
mokgekolwana, little old woman.
mokgeledi, watermark.
mokgelogi, one who goes astray, heretic.
mokgeloši, one who causes others to stray.
mokgethegi, chosen one.
mokgethi, one who chooses or selects.
mokgetho, choice, manner of choosing.
mokgethwa, choosen one, holy person.
mokgi, one who plucks, picks (fruit, etc.), draws water.
mokgoba, variety of tree, "dikbasboom", passage, lane, street.
mokgobi, reproacher.
mokgobo, heap, stack, pile.
mokgobo, reproach.
mokgodi, one who clears a place.
mokgodiši, one who persuades.
mokgogopha, variety of euphorbia tree.
mokgohlane, cold, influenza.

mokgokgoma, oesophagus, Adam's apple.
mokgokgothelo, thatch that is dressed (finished off) well.
mokgokgothi, the core of the mealie stalk.
mokgokološa, descent.
mokgoko, band, bond, hinge, handle.
mokgoladitho, anatomist.
mokgolokwane, rejoicing, shouts of joy (of women).
mokgolwa, one who is satisfied or persuaded.
mokgomana, nobleman, chief's relative.
mokgomaredi, follower, adherent.
mokgoni, one who is able to do, expert.
mokgonyana, son-in-law.
mokgopa, hide, skin, leather.
mokgopamiši, one who bends or makes crooked.
mokgope, must.
mokgope, mealie cob, calabash.
mokgopedi, one who asks, beggar.
mokgopha, Euphorbia.
mokgophi, one who smears.
mokgopho, smearing of the floor (with cow dung).
mokgopiši, one who causes others to stumble.
mokgopodile, stink-bug.
mokgopu, calabash.
mokgori, glutton, one who clears a place.
mokgoro, legging, ring/string of beads round the neck.
mokgokgoro, "kanniedood", tree.
mokgoropo, aloe (tree).
mokgoši, alarm, din, advertisement; **go hlaba** –, give alarm, broadcast, advertise.
mokgotha, street, path, track.
mokgothadi, courageous person.
mokgothatši, one who encourages.
mokgothi, pumpkin stalk, tendril.
mokgotleledi, one who perseveres.
mokgotse, brother-in-law, sister-in-law, beloved one, friend.
mokgotse, thread made of fibres.
mokgwa, variety of thorn-tree, "knoppiesdoring".
mokgwagetšo, crochet-work.
mokgwakgauswi, short cut method.
mokgwara, shin-guard, legging, gaiter.
mokgwaripa, variety of thornbush, "knoppiesdoring".
mokgwatha, lane.
mokgwatumo, fashion.
mokhansele, councillor.
mokhino, person without teeth.
mokhoro, abundance of food.
mokhuba, wild pear (tree).
mokhubo, navel.
mokhukhuni, one who crawls, one who stalks.
mokhukhuno, crawling, stalking.
mokhunamedi, one who kneels to, worshipper.
mokhunami, one who kneels down.
mokhungwane, Kaffir-tree.
mokhure, castor-oil plant, "Datura".
mokhurumetši, one who covers or puts a lid on.
mokhuša, dried or dehydrated vegetables.
mokhuti, hide-and-seek.
mokhutši, one who rests.
mokhutšiši, giver of rest.
Mokibelo, Saturday.
mokiti, bitter melon.
moko, marrow, kernel, pith.
mokodutlo, anything slanting.
mokojaba, guava (tree).
mokoko, domestic cock.
mokokolome, cock.
mokokoropo, huge, crooked.
mokokotlo, back, spine, ridge of a house.
mokokwana, cockerel.
mokola, nose-bleeding.
mokolo, spine, ridge of a house.

mokolobetši, one who baptizes.
mokolobetšwa, one who is baptized.
mokoloko, string (of things), single file.
mokoloni, colonist.
mokolonyane, black-jacks.
mokoloti, debtor; – **wa,** creditor.
mokoma, witch-doctor.
mokome, the great physician or doctor.
mokomokomo, gooseberry (tree).
mokone, pupa, chrysalis, cocoon.
mokonya, steep descent, slope, incline.
mokopa, mamba.
mokopanyi, one who unites.
mokopotšo, dart, (needlework).
mokoro, a canoe.
mokotami, one who sits on his haunches.
mokotedi, one who drives away a calf while the other is milking.
mokoti, hole, mine, niche.
mokotla, bag; – **na,** small bag.
mokoto, thick/bully (person).
Mokriste, Christian.
mokubana, summer-house, a shelter in the lands, shanty.
mokubati, one who walks proudly.
mokubego, smoke screen, a cloud of smoke to guide someone.
mokuki, one who (lifts) raises.
mokukiši, assistant lifter.
mokukutlwana, the vein of a leaf.
mokunya, medium (for spirits).
mokuru, pigeon, sweetheart.
mokuruetšo, the second month of a baby.
mokurukuru, hustle.
mokutukutu, hustle, bustle.
mokutwana, hut.
mokwabelo, setting, mounting.
mokwadikwadi, Cape chestnut.
mokwatšhego, one who lacks a tasty morsel.
mokweri, one who mocks.
mokwi, hearer, listener.
mola, there, yonder, while.
mola, line, row, current in a river.
molaadimo, beam.
molaba, runner, creeper, rank.
molaba, snare, trap.
moladi, one who lies down, the **motoma** (tree).
molaedi, one who orders or commands.
molaeletši, one who (entrusts) sends a message.
molaelo, order, instruction.
molaetša, message, errand.
molaetši, one who sends a message.
molagare, diameter.
molagodimo, rainbow, galaxy.
molahlegi, lost person.
molahli, one who throws away.
molahliwa, reprobate, lost one, rejected one.
molahlwa, rejected one, reprobate.
molakaposo, postmaster.
molakatši, one who wishes.
molaki, manager, caretaker.
molala, neck.
molala, plain.
molala, Milky Way, variety of palm-tree.
molalahlageng, human bones found lying about.
molakwaetši, devil's thorn.
molalatladi, rainbow.
molaledi, one who lies in wait or in ambush, trap.
molalediwa, guest, one for whom an ambush (trap) is set, one who is invited.
molaletšo, invitation.
molamo, brother-in-law, sister-in-law.
molamo, stick, knobkerrie.
molao, law, commandment.
molaodi, commander.
molaodimo, hanger, rack, beam.
molaokakanywa, bill.
molaolo, management.

molaomogolo, ġolden rule.
molaotheo, constitution.
molapo, valley, river-bed.
molase, molasses.
molata, servant, stranger, layman.
molatedi, follower, attendant.
molato, guilt, debt, transgression.
molatodi, denier, gainsayer.
molatogadi, big transgression.
molatša, cold porridge.
molawana, regulation.
molebadi, one who forgets, forgetful person.
molebeledi, onlooker, watcher, guard.
molebelelo, way of looking.
molebi, aimer, one who aims at.
molebo, runner, tendril, rank.
moledi, wet-nurse, foster-mother.
molefša, payee.
molefetši, avenger.
molefi, one who defrays or pays.
molefiši, one who (fines) exacts payment.
molekane, mate, an equal in age.
molekanetši, moderator.
molekanyi, one who measures.
molekanyo, comparison.
molekgetho, receiver of revenue, tax-collector.
moleki, one who tempts, attempts or tries plaits.
molekinyane, khaki-weed.
moleko, temptation, trial.
molekodi, supervisor.
molekule, molecule.
molekwa, probationer, one who is tempted.
moleleki, one who drives away, who expels.
molelekiši, pursuer.
molelekwa, pursued person.
molemadi, one who is accustomed to.
molemedi, one who ploughs for another.
molemelwa, landlord, the one for whom is ploughed.
molemi, one who ploughs, hoes or cultivates, ploughman, husbandman.
molemiši, extension officer.
molemo, ploughing, cultivation.
molemogi, observer.
molengwa, spoilt child.
molepelepe, a long row (chain) of things.
molephera, leper.
molepi, observer, astronomer.
molepo, grass rope, a loop.
moletašaka, Cape wagtail.
molete, a hole, a pit, a dungeon.
moleti, watchman, keeper, herd.
moletlo, a feast.
moletša, see **moletši.**
moletši, one who rings a bell or plays an instrument.
moliberale, liberal.
mollelwa, one who is much in demand.
molli, one who (cries) complains.
mollo, a cry.
mollo, fire, witch-weed; – **wana,** small fire.
mollwane, boundary.
molobi, mediator.
molodi, melody, tune, whistle, song of a bird.
mologa, species of thorn-tree.
mologi, one who plaits or weaves.
mologo, knitting, weaving.
moloi, witch, wizard.
molokafatši, one who makes righteous.
molokeloke, long row of things.
moloki, good or righteous person.
molokiši, one who mends, repairs.
moloko, relation, family, relative.
molokollwa, redeemed, liberated person.
molokolodi, deliver, liberator.
molokologi, one who is liberated, free man.
molokoloko, single file.

molomatsebe, secret informer, whisperer.
molomegi, scarifier, cupper.
molomegwa, one who is scarified, or cupped.
molomi, one who bites.
molomo, mouth, lip, beak, spout.
molomodi, one who weans a child.
molomomoso, pistol, revolver.
molongwa, one who is bitten.
molongwana, small mouth.
molopabadimo, intercessor, one who prays to the spirits of the ancestors.
molope, widow-bird, red bishop-bird.
molopodi, redeemer.
molora, ash, ashes.
molori, dreamer.
moloto o swele, the die is cast.
molotšana, wicked person.
molotšwana, little tune.
molwedi, champion.
moma, hold in the mouth.
momagana, coalesce.
momagano, coalescence.
momaretša, glue together.
momeno, fold, hem.
mometša, swallow, put into the mouth.
mometšo, throat.
momilione, millionaire.
momodi, gooseberry.
momohla, to-day.
momori, gooseberry.
mompshafatši, reformer.
mona, suck.
mona, go round, turn.
mona, here; n., envy.
monagani, thinker.
monagano, thought, a thinking.
monamane, species of tree.
monamedi, mounter, one who mounts.
monamodi, one who separates.
monamoledi, deliverer, rescuer.
monamune, citrus tree, orange tree.
mon'ang, mosquito.
Monasare, Nazarene.
Monasire, Nazirite.
monate, nice taste of food, sweetness; adj., nice, pleasant.
monatla, leg of a fowl or bird.
monato, wild lilac.
monawa, bean-stalk, legume.
mone, weakness of the eyes in children; neg., does not suck/turn.
monego, osmosis.
monei, a giver, donor, red ivory (tree).
moneneri, tramp.
monepanaledi, astronomer.
monepi, marksman, good shot.
moneri, mister, missionary.
monešapula, rain-maker.
mong, master, lord, owner.
mong, adj., one, other.
monga, crack, little opening, cleft.
mongadi, sulky person.
mongalogi, deserter.
mongana, species of mimosa.
monganeng, W.C.
mongena, S.A. beech.
mongetsane, atlas (spine).
mongongoregi, grumbler.
mongongorego, grumbling, murmur.
mongpolasa, owner of a farm.
mongthipa, owner of a knife.
mongwadi, writer, author.
mongwadiši, assistant writer.
mongwalakholomong, columnist.
mongwaledi, one who writes for or to, secretary.
mongwalo, manner (way) of writing, orthography.
mongwe, another, one, other.
mongwegi, deserter, runaway.
monitoro, monitor.
monkane, mate, equal; – **gadi;** female companion.
monkgane, Mexican marigold.
monkgo, smell, odour.
monko, odour, perfume.
monna, man, husband.

monnago, your younger brother.
monnagwe, younger brother (of a brother) younger sister (of a sister).
monnake, my younger brother.
monnamogolo, big man.
monnatena, rascal, rogue.
monnatia, a man in his prime.
monne, has sucked.
monni, one who sits, inhabitant.
mono, here.
mono, finger, digit.
monoka, suck.
monokane, wild fig-tree.
monoketša, take one by one.
monoki, one who flavours.
monokiša, cause to suck.
monoko, resin-tree, resin-bush.
monola, humidity, moisture.
monongwaga, this year.
monono, fatness, fertility.
monontšha, something that causes fatness, fertiliser.
monope, widow-bird.
monopi, leech.
monopoli, monopoly.
monošetši, irrigator.
monoši, one who gives to drink.
monotlo, talon, shin, leg, toe (of a bird); – **wana,** small toe.
monoto, the leg of a locust, the spur of a cock, soap-stone, schist.
monotswane, sugar-bird, sunbird.
monthati, my friend.
monti, a dancer, Jumping-Jack; **go tšea** –, to step out and dance single.
montima, the one who refuses or denies me.
montiredi, the person who works for me, my servant.
montlhoi, my enemy.
montshepetša, he who (causes) helps me to walk.
monwana, finger.
monwabjalwa, winebibber.
monwi, drinker.
monya, cause to suck.
monyadi, bridegroom.
monyadiwa, bride.
monyakgahla, limestone, chalk.
monyaki, seeker.
monyako, door; see: **(mojako).**
monyaku, spinach.
monyakwa, person wanted.
monyalwa, bride.
monyamane, dusk.
monyana, black-jacks.
monyana, younger brother of a brother, younger sister of a sister; also: **monyanana.**
monyana, girl.
monyanana, younger brother or sister; see: **monyana.**
monyane, younger, small (person).
monyanya, feast, festival, fete.
monyaredi, one who peeps, who looks into.
monyatšegi, despised person.
monyatši, one who despises or belittles.
monye, dial. for **mong,** owner.
monyefodi, blasphemer, reviler.
monyemotsana, headman.
monyena, S.A. Beech. "boekenhout".
moo, there.
moo, id. be (bright) shining.
moobu, wasp; – **putšana,** hornet.
moodi, sweep, howling of a dog.
moodu, howling of a dog.
moohli, spinner.
mooka, species of small honey-bee which has no sting.
mooka, white thorn-tree, "soetdoring", Karroo-thorn.
mookámedi, overseer, head, superior.
mookelwa, patient.
mookga, crop sprung up from the previous sowing.
mookgi, the one who takes fire.
mookgo, tear.
mookgopo, the (aloe) euphorbia.
mooki, nurse.

mooko, measles (in human beings).
mooko, nursing of the sick.
mookola, nose-bleeding.
moolo, howl(ing) of a dog.
moološi, winnower, broadcaster.
moomani, (moomanyi), one who (scolds) curses.
moomo, shin-bone, shank.
moopa, barren woman.
moopa, stinging nettle.
moopana, barren woman.
moopedi, singer.
moopi, one who claps his hands or applauds.
moopšane, variety of wild grape.
moopu, bat, oar.
moori, one who basks or warms himself.
mootiša, medicine for slimming.
mootledi, the driver of a team.
mootlelwana, pup.
mootli, striker.
mootlo, way of bringing up or rearing.
mootlwa, thorn, quill.
mopaki, witness, baker.
mopalema, palm-tree.
mopani, turpentine-tree, terebinth.
mopaserite, Spanish reed, rattan.
mopateletši, false witness.
mopateletšwa, one accused falsely.
mopati, one who hides.
mopatriareka, patriarch.
mopeleto, spelling.
mophadišani, competitor.
mophaene, pine, fir.
mophakiši, one who hastens.
mophaphadikota, wood-pecker.
mophato, class, thorn-tree.
mophedi, survivor, living being.
mophediši, one who causes or helps to live.
mophegišani, competitor.
mopheki, one who bars an entrance.
mophekodi, doctor, healer.
mophekwana, cross-bar.
mophemedi, protector.
mophemi, one who dodges or acts in self-defence.
mophenšenwa, pensioner.
mophethegi, a perfect one.
mophethi, accomplisher.
mophetho, the finishing-off, end, brim.
mophoki, one who drinks.
mophoko, gorge.
mophologi, one who is saved.
mophološi, rescuer, saver, redeemer.
mophološwa, one who is saved.
mophomi, deceiver.
mophomodi, one who rests.
mophonyokgi, the one that has broken loose or escaped.
mophoši, one who throws or makes a mistake.
mophumi, one who breaks or smashes.
mophunyi, one who pierces.
mophuthi, folder.
mopomi, one who cuts.
moponyi, one who shuts his eyes.
mopopoliri, poplar.
mopopotlo, ridge, stroke, file.
moporofeta, prophet.
mopotlaki, a fast person.
mopotologo, the going round.
moprista, priest.
moprofesa, professor.
moprofeta, prophet.
moprotestanta, protestant.
mopšane, small variety of honeybee.
mopšhatli, smasher, breaker.
mopulukomo, eucalyptus tree.
mopupetši, one who covers or closes up.
moputsi, rewarder.
moputso, reward.
moraba, skin bag for charms, doctor's bag; **go khunolla** –, doctor's fee.
morabana, pouch.
morabele, insurgent, rebel.
moradia, cheat, fraud, deceiver.

moradu, an old animal.
morafe, race, tribe, society.
morafi, one who takes honey from a hive.
moragi, one who kicks, kicker.
morago, afterwards, behind, after.
moragonyana, a little backwards, a short while afterwards.
moragwanyana, some time after.
moraka, cattle-range.
morakapele, first-born, first-fruits.
moraki, driver of animals.
morako, stone wall.
moraloko, play game, manner of playing.
morarela, detour, roundabout-way, secret place.
morati, lover, fan.
moretlwanoka, willow-tree.
morokapula, rainmaker.
moroki, one who sews.
moroko, sewing.
moroko, bran, husks.
morokola, awl, bit, poker.
morokolo, dung of sheep, goats or game.
morokolo, num-num, (Carissa arduina).
morokotšo, milk left in the udder for the calf, commission.
morola, Citrullis colocynthis, bitter apple.
morola, ash, ashes.
morolana, the small bitter apple plant.
morole, manure, farmyard manure.
morole, heifer, contemporary.
morolwane, syringa.
morolwaseeta, one who has his shoe pulled off.
moromedi, one who sends for.
moromi, one who sends, sender.
moromiwa, messenger.
morongwa, angel.
moropa, drum.
moropana, timbrel, nave, hub.
moropo, muzzle, nozzle, nostril.
moropola, awl.
moropotlane, gooseberry plant.
morora, ash.
morori, one who grunts.
mororo, roaring, bellowing.
mororomi, one who trembles.
mororwane, crowned plover.
morota, hump.
moroto, S.A. teak, "kiaat".
moroto, urine, semen.
moroto, species of spinach.
morotoga, slope, incline, uphill.
moruba, a game like draughts or chess.
morudi, smith, farrier, tinker.
morufana, nave, hub.
morui, possessor, rich person.
moruka, collar, necklace, bangle.
morula, tree whose fruit is used for making beer, (Sclerocarya caffra).
marula, wooden milk-pail, bucket.
morulana, a shrub used for medicine.
morulane, ear-wax, cerumen.
morulatšhipi, metalworker.
moruledi, one who thatches.
morulela, thatch (the grass).
morulelo, thatch, thatching.
morumo, seam, rhyme.
morumodi, provoker.
morumokwano, rhyme.
morunyorunyo, peristalsis.
moruo, possession, riches.
moruswi, dish, basin, crucible, jar.
morutabana, teacher, governess.
morutegi, educated person.
moruti, a minister, a preacher, missionary, (teacher).
morutiši, assistant teacher.
morutiwa, pupil, student, disciple, scholar.
morutlo, calabash for beer, calabash with a handle.
morutwa, learner, student, pupil; – **na,** scholar.
morwa, a son; – **gwe,** his/her son.

morwadi, bearer, carrier.
morwadi, daughter.
morwadiake, my daughter.
morwadie, his or her daughter.
morwaka, my son.
morwake, my son.
morwakgoši, prince.
morwaladibetša, armour-bearer.
morwalela, a flood.
morwalo, load, burden, freight.
morwalwana, small burden.
Morwana, Bushman.
morwanope, fowl.
morwarra, brother.
morwarra, cousin, father's brother's children.
morwarre, brother, cousin.
morwawe, his, her son.
morwedi, daughter; – **agwe,** his/her daughter.
morwetsana, girl, damsel, little daughter.
mošaa, vagabond, rogue.
mošabašaba, sandy-soil, long affair, sand.
mosabele, karee tree.
mošabi, trader.
mošabo, commerce.
mosadi, a woman; – **wa batho,** poor woman; - **mogolo,** old woman; – – **mosatšana,** little woman; – **mosadigadi,** big woman.
mosadusei, Sudducee.
mosaekolotši, psychologist.
mosagi, sawyer.
mosago, saw-mill.
mosako, ring, (boxing), prize-ring.
mošala-a-dutše, sluggard.
mošalalapeng, last child in a family.
mošaledi, the one who remains.
Mosamaria, Samaritan.
mosamelo, pillow, cushion.
mosamo, pillow, cushion.
mosangwana, small pillow.
mošaparegi, poor person, pauper.
mosara, (mosari), syringa tree, lilac tree.
Mosarwa, a Bushman.
mošaša, hut made of branches, small branch, twig, stick.
mošate, capital, the chief's kraal (village).
mosatšana, little woman.
mose, dress for girls, skin apron.
mose, crusher, pestle, pounder.
Moše, Moses.
moše, side or bank of a river; - **ola (mošola),** on the other side; – **ono (mošono),** on this side.
mosebe, arrow, spear.
mosebi, backbiter, slanderer.
mosedere, cedar-tree (or) wood.
mosedi, buyer of food or grain.
mosegare, noon, at noon, late in the morning; – **o mogolo,** twelve o'clock.
Mosegamanye, May.
mosegi, one who cuts, tailor.
mosego, laughter, cutting, cut.
mošegofatši, one who blesses, benedictor.
mosegwaohloga, whale.
mosehla, acacia "huilbos", yellow colour, layman.
mosehle, species of acacia, "huilbos".
mosehlo, (mark of) an incision, devil's thorn, frieze.
moseka, species of grass.
mosekamo, slant, inclination.
mosekaseko, criticism.
moseke, mosque.
mosekiši, prosecutor.
mosekišwa, accused.
mosela, tail, suffix, freshman.
mosela, trench.
Moselamose, Moslem.
moselape, dog (archaic).
moselaphala, species of thorn-tree, "slapdoring, oudoring".
moselapše, monster.
mosele, furrow, ditch, trench.

mošele, stranger, alien, foreigner.
mošelešele, the bush-bustard, "boskorhaan".
moselesele, sickle-bush.
moseme, mat.
mosemo, mat.
mosenate, senator.
moseneke, crisis.
mosentšhi, accessory (to crime).
mosenyi, culprit, destroyer, malefactor.
mosenyiši, abettor accomplice.
moseo, the other side, the farther end, opposite the door.
mosepedi, walker, traveller; – **šani,** companion.
mosepelo, travelling, journey, walk.
mosesane, fine, thin.
mosese, thin.
mosese, woman's skin covering; **go bona** –, to menstruate.
mosesele, sickle-bush.
mosetata, mustard.
mosetere, mustard.
mosetlo, crushed mealie meal.
moseto, strip.
moseto, carving, engraving, chamfer.
mosetsana, girl.
mosetšhi, pick-pocket.
Moshe, Moses.
mošiani, competitor in a race, runner.
mosibihla, mimosa.
mošidi, gunpowder, soot, charcoal, wild plum-tree, grinder.
mošifa, tendon, muscle.
mošii, winner in a race, fugitive.
mošikalekgoši, chief's righthandman.
mošikannoši, solitary person.
mošikanoka, species of tree growing on river banks.
mošikaro, the carrying, burden.
mošilabelo, karee tree.
mošimane, boy, small boy.
mošimanyana, small boy, baby boy.
mosinene, garter-snake.
mošireletši, protector, defender, guardian.
mošitatlou, species of wild asparagus plant.
mošitaphala, earwig, centipede.
mošitši, one who (prevents) disables.
mošito, sound of footsteps, metre, poetic measure.
mošitollo, scansion.
mošitši, black-jacks.
moso, to-morrow; **ka** –, in future.
mošogi, skin-dresser, tanner.
mosokologi, converted one.
mošola, opposite bank, adv., on the other side.
mošomedi, servant.
mošomi, worker, labourer; – **ka** – **nna,** colleague.
mošomiši, user.
mošomo, labour, work.
mošono, this side (of a riverbank, etc.).
mosoro, beer.
mošoro, fierce (person).
mosoro, dog, term of abuse.
mososo, "sandvaalbos", species of tree.
Mosotho, a Mosuto.
mošulafatši, one who makes a thing tasteless or disgusting.
mošunkwane, aromatic shrub, Lantana caffra, herb, medicine.
mošupa, seven.
mošupatsela, guide, manual.
mošupetši, one who points out.
mošupi, one who points at.
mošupo, the way of pointing.
Mošupulogo, Monday.
mosusumetši, one who pushes.
mošuthi, one who moves aside.
mošuthiši, one who removes.
moswa, nephew, niece, odour.
moswana, to-morrow, in the morning.
mošwana, mimosa.
moswane, morning.

mošwang, the contents of an animal's stomach, chyme.
mošwanyana, mimosa-bush.
moswara, holder of, – **selepe,** bodyguard of the chief, armour bearer; – **teu,** leader of the team; – **marapo,** master of ceremonies.
moswaredi, regent, substitute.
moswari, holder, catcher.
moswaso, joke.
moswe, meercat.
mošwelešwele, bush-bustard.
mošweu, white man, European.
moswiri, lemon tree.
motabo, ashes of certain plants added to snuff, mixture.
matabodi, one who tears.
motaga, kaolin, lime, chalk.
motagwa, drunkard.
motaka, streak, whitewash, chalk.
motakalala, crayon.
motala, old person.
motala, green, blue.
motalane, hemp.
motapa, soft porridge.
motatane, climber, creeper.
motato, wire, telegram.
motekatekana, milksop, tiny tot.
motelele, long (person).
motepa, soft porridge.
motete, anus.
moteteselo, trembling, shivering.
mothadi, swimmer, drawer, designer, draughtsman.
mothadiši, sailor.
mothaetši, listener.
mothakgalo, joy, mirth.
mothaladi, stripe, streak, line, row.
mothalo, line, the drawing of a line or furrow.
mothalokhutlo, dotted line.
mothama, cheek.
mothamo, capacity.
mothapalalo (mothathapalalo), contour.
mothape, a runner, tendril, stalk.
motheetši, listener.
mothei, founder, trapper.
mothekgi, supporter.
motheo, foundation, basis, chassis.
motheogi, one who descends.
mothepa, girl, young woman, virgin.
motherebinte, turpentine-tree.
mothetši, deceiver.
mothibalebaleng, fielder.
mothibedi, preventer, one who (stops) bars.
mothibi, one who stops or prevents.
mothinya, change of direction.
mothinyi, swerver, diver, herdsman returning home.
mothipologa, slope, descent.
mothitho, churning, butter-milk.
motho, human being, person; – **wa batho,** poor fellow, – **fela,** layman.
mothobe, beestings, colostrum, yolk.
mothobi, one who emigrates.
mothobolliši, coach.
mothofatšo, personification.
mothomi, beginner.
mothomiši, starter.
mothopabatho, kidnapper, the devil.
mothopa, hut, kitchen.
mothopedi, robber.
mothopelwa, one who is robbed.
mothopi, robber, abductor, kidnapper.
mothopo, robbing, robbery.
mothopo, fountain, spring, bud, sprout, source.
mothothi, transport rider.
mothoto, basket.
mothotwana, small basket.
mothubi, breaker.
mothubo, forced labour (for chief).
mothudi, smith, founder, shoemaker.
mothuladieta, cobbler.
mothunyi, shot, marksman.
mothuši, helper.
mothwadi, hirer, lessee.
mothwalwa, hireling.

mothwanakgopana, pygmy, midget, pigmy.
moti, beeswax, pitch.
motiakone, deacon.
motii, striker.
motiišetši, one who perseveres.
motiiši, one who strengthens.
motikinyane, khaki-weed, Mexican marigold.
motikone, deacon.
motilatilane, sorrel.
motimedi, strayed, lost (person).
motimi, one who deprives, or extinguishes.
motingwa, one who is deprived.
motlabi, one who surprises people.
motlabiwa, one who is surprised.
motlabo, concubine, adulterer.
motlae, joke, nickname.
motlaišegi, worried, pursued, pestered person.
motlaiši, one who teases, worries or torments.
motlakgomo, tree-snake.
motlaišwa, tormented person.
motlalamaswi, species of Euphorbia.
motlalei, blabber, accuser, tell-tale.
motlalepula, one whose visit coincides with rain, bringer of rain.
motlalo, abundance; **go bjetše** – thickly sown.
motlamaganyi, one who binds together.
motlametli, guardian, trustee.
motlamo, binding, bandage.
motlamolodi, one who (unbinds) sets free.
motlamiwa, prisoner.
motlang, stalk, shrub, runner.
motlanyi, typist.
motlanyo, type, typing.
motlapa, foolish (lazy) person.
motlapatlapa, fool idiot.
motlapele, first-comer.
motlatšetši, supporter, one who assists in filling up.
motlatši, reserve.
motlišantle, importer.
motliši, bringer, one who brings.
motlodi, transgressor.
motlodiwa, anointed person.
motlogedi, one who (forsakes) lets alone.
motlogi, one who departs.
motlogolo, grand child, descendant.
motloki, engraver.
motlopi, shepherd's tree, "Capparis albitrunca".
motlopo, hair dressed in the shape of a tortoise shell.
motlotlegi, honourable person, Excellency.
motlotši, one who anoints or smears.
motlotšiwa, (motlotšwa), anointed person.
motlwae, custom, habit.
moto, part below the anus of an ox.
motobatobi, restless person.
motogo, sour porridge, **(mageu).**
motolo, species of thorntree, rush.
motoloki, interpreter.
motološi, melter, founder, smelter.
motopi, finder, lifter.
motopo, oval, oval-shaped.
motoropo, townsman, villager.
mototolo, elevation, mound.
motša, apron-string.
motsana, small village.
motsaro, butter-milk.
motšatša, rectum.
motse, village, town.
motse, Acacia arabica.
motšeani, one who gets married.
motšeatšeani, drudge, bungler, stick-in-the-mud.
motsebalegi, acquaintance, famous person.
motsebatemo, agriculturist.
motsebegi, notorious person.
motsebi, one who knows.
motšega, earthenware pot.
motsene, leech.

motsenedi, intruder.
motseno, entrance, way of entering.
motsera, stinkwood.
motseta, messenger, (attache) ambassador.
motsetaphala, earwig, poisonous centipede.
motsetaphethi, plenipotentiary.
motsetere, wattle.
motšewa, bride.
motšhabedi, refugee.
motšhabi, runaway, fugitive, one who fears.
motšhabo, flight.
Motšhaena, Chinese.
motšhaki, n., guest, visitor.
motšhato, bridal; wedding.
motšhatšhwana, news.
motshedi, one who crosses, who goes over or through.
motšhedi, ratepayer, taxpayer, one who pours in.
motšhediši, tax-collector, receiver of revenue.
motshediši, comforter, consoler.
motšheledi, cup-bearer, butler.
motšhelo, tax, revenue.
motšhene, machine.
motshepegi, trustworthy person, trusted one.
motshepiši, one who promises.
motshepiwa, trustworthy person, trusted one.
motshetsheti, one who trots, trotter.
motšhidi, wild plum-tree, **la** –, hot day.
motšhitšhi, swarm, swarm of bees or insects.
motšhogi, one who is frightened.
motšhošetši, terrorist.
motšhoši, one who frightens.
motsila, rectum, descending colon.
motšipi, one who pinches.
motšitla, bulrush, poker.
motšitlo, sprig.
motso, unit.
motsodi, fountain.
motšofe, old person.
motšoko, snuff, tobacco.
motsomi, hunter.
motsošampherefere, rebel, instigator.
motsoši, one who wakens, who raises up.
motsoti, one who worries, one who dislikes.
motsoto, worry.
motsotso, moment, minute, while.
motsotswana, second.
motšu, arrow.
motsubi, smoker.
motsula, root out, pull out.
motswadi, parent.
motšwafi, sluggard, lazy person.
motswakanyi, one who mixes.
motswaki, one who mixes things.
motswako, mixture, solution.
motswala, cousin; **motswalake,** my cousin; **motswalagwe,** his (her) cousin.
motswalabana, one who begets children.
motswalabo(na), their cousins.
motswalle, friend.
motswalwapele, first-born.
motšwana, parent who has no son.
motswapitswapi, the willow-tree.
motswikinyo, ringing, wagging, jingling.
motswiri, a click, leadwood (tree).
motu, pitch, beeswax.
mouba, a pair of bellows.
moubelo, blast-furnace.
moumo, a species of the wild figtree.
moupo, charm for the driving away of birds or insects, antidote.
mouta, mould, fungus, mildew.
mouwane, fog, mist.
mouwe, there, yonder.
mowa, Cape ash.
moya, air, breath, wind, spirit; – **o mobe,** evil spirit; – **o hlabošang,** fresh air; – **wa naga,** clime, climate.

Moya-ɔ-Mokgethwa, Holy Spirit.
moyi, one who goes, goer.
moyo, baobab tree.
mpa, belly, switch, rod, the middle, a strip of blue sky between two clouds.
mpabalela, take care of me.
mpabane, vitriol, blue copper sulphate.
mpakubu, sjambok.
mpala, count me.
mpalela, be too difficult for me.
mpana, ear of corn; – **palega,** overfilled belly.
mpaola, an old tin used as a heater by the Bantu, brazier.
mpara, – **towe,** fool, ass, dunce.
mpata, oppress me.
mpati, left; **la –,** left hand.
mpatladika, wide.
mpe, bad, wicked.
mpea, place me.
mpefala, become bad; **mpefatša,** to make bad.
mpefediša, anger me.
mpefelelwa, become cross with me.
mpega, report me.
mpekenene, small boy.
mpepetla, flat, open.
mpepu (mpepula), carry me on the back.
mpetha, beat me, give me a hiding.
mpethile, beaten me, given me a hiding.
mpeye, pipe; **go leša ngwana** –, to feed a baby.
mpha, give to me.
mphafa, sweet grass.
mphagana, pullet, young hen.
mphago, provisions for the road.
mphahla, to blind me, to injure my eye.
mphaila, assegai with a broad blade.
mphaka, a knife, mealie cob.
mphapahlogo, crown.
mphapantšhi, instigator, one who incites.
mphaphati, flat.
mpharafara, surround me.
mpharana, dwarf.
mpharatšhwene, the dew-berry, four-corners.
mpharwane, lizard.
mphatlalatšane, Venus as morning star.
mphato, class of pupils.
mphatša, fissure, split, cleft.
mphaya, fig-tree, see: **mofeie.**
mphe, give me!
mpheane, tell-tale, gossip.
mphegwana, clothes-hanger.
mphekwa, lizard.
mphela, the end.
mpheleletša, end my life.
mpheng, handle.
mphenya, overcome me, conquer me.
mphenyanašilo, bully, hoodlum.
mphepa, feed me.
mpherefere, riot, rebellion, quarrel, fracas.
mpheretlhakana, mixed, motley.
mpheta, pass me, surpass me.
mphetša, five.
mphikela, a cold, influenza.
mphiri, bangle.
mphiri o kgatla, when all goes well.
mphišetša (dikgomo), look after my cattle.
mpho, gift, present; – ! fy, pooh!
mphofela, drizzle.
mphofutšo, perspiration, sweat.
mphogo, millet.
mphoka, weeds, an ear of corn that has no grain in it, camelthorn, tare.
mphokhu, blind person.
mpholo, poison.
mphoma, cave.
mphufutšo, perspiration, sweat, – **wa mpša,** in vain.
mphukudi, ghost.

mpilobilo, mixture, confusion, a motley crowd.
mpiripitlana, short and fat (boy).
mpiripitšana, a fat little boy.
mpo, go re –, start, jump away.
mpo, but, rather; n., fowl-tick.
mpodile, stink-bug.
mpogohlo, left hand.
mpogošo, left hand.
mpoifa, fear me.
mpokopoki, large, anything big.
mpotegela, be faithful to me.
mpotoko, big, strong.
mpotša, tell me.
mpša, dog.
mpsha, new; – **-mpsha,** brand new.
mpshafala, become new, become reformed.
mpshafalo, reformation.
mpshafatša, renew, reform, renovate.
mpshafatšo, renewal, reformation, renovation.
mpšhe, ostrich.
mpšhe, sugar-cane.
mpshi, milk food, porridge made of flour and milk.
mpshikela, a cold, influenza.
mpshinami, stingy person.
mpshiri, bangle.
muma, hold in the mouth, put into the mouth.
mumula, uproot.
muši, smoke.
musiamo, museum.
mušimeetse, steam.
myekga, eat into (like cancer).
myemyela, smile.

N

na, have, has.
na, interrogative particle.
na, with, together with.
na, rain, leak (leak used only of a house or shelter); **nela,** to rain for.
naase, today, to-day.
naba, stretch, the legs, prosper, grow along the ground, extend, creep, (of plants).
nabalala, lie out-stretched.
nabele, navel (orange).
nabo, with him (them).
nae, with him (her).
naetrotšene, nitrogen.
naga, country, land.
nagadimo, high veld.
nagagare, middle veld.
nagana, think, meditate.
nagašireletšwa, protectorate.
nagatlase, low veld.
nageng, rural.
nago, with you.
naila, walk gently, softly.
nailwe, soaked.
naka, horn, flute, hooter, v., select.
Naka, name of a star appearing at the commencement of winter.
nakalala, ot lie outstretched, stand astride.
nakedi, polecat.
nako, time, hour; – **efe le efe,** whenever.
nakola, tire, exhaust.
nakolane, tadpole.
nakotse, what-d'ye-call- him (it).
nala, nail.
nala, red and white (male); fem., **nalana,** (animal).
nalamodu, root-cap.
naledi, star; – **ya mosela,** comet.
nalete, needle.
naletšana, asterisk.
nalo, with it.
nama, (and) then.
nama, extend, spread out, gain ground, stretch out.
nama, flesh, meat.
namafalo, incarnation.
namagadi, female (animal).

namakgomo, beef.
namalala, lie, stretched out.
namalatša, cause to lie stretched out; sew with big stitches.
namane, calf, species of edible berry.
name, and then, afterwards.
namela, mount, ride, climb.
namelela (godimo), climb to the top.
nametša, cause to mount, lift on to, give a lift.
namola, help, rescue, intervene.
namolela, aid, rescue; **namolelo,** aid, liberation.
namolo, intervention, deliverance.
namologa, rise.
namolola, raise.
namoneiti, lemonade.
namune, orange.
nana, young, tender, **mosegare** a –, broad daylight.
nana, thake –, group of young girls.
nanabela, stalk, reach out, extend to.
nanabetša, stalk, cause to extend.
nanabologa, rise (slowly).
nanaila, walk slowly and proudly.
nanakela, walk slowly.
nanana, very small, very tender.
nane, legend.
nanedi, star.
nanengneng, always, for ever.
nanetša, stalk, take by surprise.
nang, having that which, which has.
nanganela, enter slowly (as a thorn).
nankhono, to-day.
nanoga, get up.
nonoša, cause to rise up.
nanya, walk slowly.
nao, foot; – **sekwere,** square foot.
napa, moreoever, and then, then.
nape, then; **napile,** then.
nare, buffalo.
nariki, mandarin.
naso, a black animal (male); **naswana,** black cow.
naso, with it.
natefa, be or become nice or palatable.
natefela, be interesting.
natha, be fat, fast or quick.
natla, laminate, flatten, beat out.
natlafala, become strong, (brave), manly.
natšo, with them.
natswa, female buffalo, buffalo cow.
nawa, a bean; – **morare,** runner-bean.
nawana, go ja – **tša borwa,** tread on one's heels.
nawatlou, broad-bean.
naye, with him or her.
nayo, with it.
nca-nca, exclam. of pity, sorry!
ne, aux. verb, was, be in the habit of.
nea, give.
neanya, arrange.
nebi, otter; **-ya lewatle,** seal.
neela, give to, hand over to.
neelo, dedication.
neka, walk stealthily.
nekeletša, approach stealthily.
nekethifi, negative.
nela, rain on or for.
nele, has rained.
nene, few, small, little, wee bit.
neneka, balance, do carefully, walk slowly, do mildly.
neneketša, handle carefully, walk gently.
neng, when? **le go iša neng,** never; **neng le neng,** any time.
neo, gift, talent, present.
nepa, hit, aim, strike.
nepagalo, precision, correctness, accuracy.
nepiša, correct.
nepišo, correction.
nepo, precision, accuracy, truth.
neša, cause to rain.
netefala, become true, be proved;
netefatša, make true, prove.
netha, soak, wet, leak.
New-Zealand, New Zealand.

nga, direction; **go re** –, strike.
ngaati, second stomach of a ruminant.
ngadiša, cause to sulk/refuse.
ngaka, doctor, medical practitioner, herbalist; – **ya diruiwa,** veterinary surgeon; – **ya mahlo,** oculist, eye specialist, optician; – **ya meno,** dentist.
ngala, sulk, ignore, refuse.
ngaloga, run away, desert.
ngamela, close up, stick on.
ngamola, resist, discourage.
nganga, contest, stretch, dispute; – **bala,** refuse.
ngangabela, be obstinate or stretched; – **tše,** rebelled, resisted.
ngapa, scratch, claw.
ngapo, scratching, clawing.
ngata, sheaf, bundle.
ngata, tie, fasten a napkin.
ngata, v., strike, beat, box.
ngatela, tie for, fasten a napkin or crupper.
ngatha, hoof.
ngatha, share, break off a piece.
ngathola, bite off a piece.
ngaya, chop off, sever, cut short, pass through.
nge, rad., **re** –, chop off, be silent.
ngena, sever, cut through.
ngolo, spotted.
ngongorega, grumble, grouse, murmer; – **ela,** complain against.
ngope, ditch, issue of blood, scurvy.
ngotla, strike dead.
ngunanguna, fret, murmer.
ngwadiša, enrol, cause to write, dictate to; – **wa,** be registered.
ngwaga, year.
ngwagamolele, leap-year.
ngwagola, last year.
ngwaii, silence; **re** –, be silent.
ngwako, house, homestead.
ngwala, write, draw; – **ngwalola,** copy.
ngwale, girl undergoing the rites of initiation.
ngwalediša, trace (on carbon).
ngwaledišo, carbon paper.
ngwalolla, transcribe.
ngwampo, tampan.
ngwana, child, infant; – **wa batho,** poor child.
ngwanabo, his (her) brother, sister.
ngwanayana, a girl.
ngwaneno, your relation.
ngwanešo, our relation, my brother.
ngwanešwane, relative, beloved one.
ngwang, weeds, tare.
ngwapa, scratch.
ngwapša, be scratched.
ngwapo, scratching, scratch.
ngwatha, break off a piece, share.
ngwathaganya, ngwathagantšha, break into bits.
ngwathela, share; – **na,** ration out.
ngwaya, scratch.
ngwe, one, some.
ngwedi, moonlight.
ngwee, cry.
ngwega, vanish, abscond, play truant.
ngwetši, bride, daughter-in-law.
nibijara, New Year.
nka, I can or may; pft., **nkile,** I happened to; adv., as; like.
nkabe, if only.
nkabela, dedicate to me, contribute to me.
nkadima, reflex., lend me.
nkagela, build for me.
nkane, still for all.
nkano, I may.
nke! please! if you please!, do.
nkeme tseleng, stand in my way.
nkego, as if, such as.
nkepiša, deserted portion of an ant-hill, v., cause me to dig.
nketela, visit me.
nkga, smell, stink; **go** – **sebodu,** be very lazy.

nkgahla, please me.
nkgahlanetša, meet me.
nkgaka, reflex., puzzle me, slip my memory.
nkgaogele, have mercy on me.
nkgaola, cut me off, excommunicate me.
nkgašana, little, crown.
nkgari, shell, peel.
nkgela, pluck (draw) for me.
nkgelana, fragment, remnant.
nkgerebetlana, fragment.
nkgerula, glance at me.
nkgetheng, candidate.
nkgetho, piece.
nkgo, water-pitcher, earthenware pot.
nkgoba, bark at me.
nkgodiša, honour me.
nkgokolo, n., circle, ball; adj., round.
nkgomiša, cause me to (turn back) return.
nkgopola, think of me.
nkgopotša, remind me.
nkgotswana, monwana –, a finger that scrapes out (steals)
nkgwai, peg, hook.
nkgwe, white-backed animal.
nkhakhane, cat, fur, boa.
nkho-ke-nang, food for the wolves.
nkhokho, id., nothing.
nkhokhororo, hard.
nkhono, (na-), up to now.
nkhunyana, pup.
nkhwela, die for me.
nkhwibiletša, (mahlo), cast an angry look at me.
nkhwile, dead animal.
nkile, I once, I happened to.
nkimela, be or become too heavy for me.
nkimolla, unburden me.
nko, nose, nostril, protuberance; **taba e se nang** –, pointless affair, **tshehla e ntšha** –, sunrise.
nko, go letša wa –, be glad about.
nko le molomo, sworn friends.
nkobiša, cause me to make a mistake.
nkofatša, nasalise, nazalise.
nkofatšo, nasalisation, (-z-).
nkoka, nurse me.
nkokoropo, crooked and bulky.
nkokoto, strong boy, top dog.
nkokwane, go tia –, strike the nail on the head.
nku, sheep.
nkubula, snatch me away, snatch away from me.
nkutollelago, what reveals to me.
nkwe, tiger.
nkwela, fall on me, sense for me, feel for me; – **bohloko,** have pity on me.
nkwetše godimo, has fallen on me.
nna, pron., I.
nna, v., sit, dwell, inhabit; – **fase,** sit down; aux. v., to keep on.
nna; re ka – ra, we may also.
nnake, a pet name, a term of endearment.
nnako, refuse.
nnana, sit or stand close together.
nnang, to say no, to refuse.
nnanyana, group of small girls.
nne, adj., four.
nneetše, given to me.
nnela, wait for, sit for.
nnete, truth, verity.
nngangabelela, resist me.
nngau, re –, mew.
nngele, left.
ngwaya, scratch me.
nngwe, one.
nnipi, nib.
nniša, cause to sit or occupy.
nnonnodi, dab's mine!
noša, give me to drink.
nnoši, alone.
nnoto, nought, naught, zero.
nnyatša, despise (scorn) me.
nnyo, vagina.
no, just, only.
nobi, otter.
noga, ooze, divine, trickle.

noga, snake, serpent; **noga e khwibidu,** dysentery.
nogameetsana, earth-worm.
noga-ya-teng, tape-worm, taenia.
nogo, who even/just.
noka, hip.
noka, river.
noka, season, salt, embalm.
Noka-ntsho, Orange River.
nokela, to put in, insert.
noketša, pour water on the hands, separate cattle into companies for drinking.
noko, porcupine.
noko, joint, portion between two joints, internode, inch.
noko, spice.
noko, syllable; – **-ntši,** poly-syllable; – **-pedi,** dis(s)yllabic; – **ngwe,** monosyllable.
nokola, pick up one by one.
nokolla, break up in syllables.
nola moko, discourage.
nolega, melt; – **moko,** lose hope.
nolo, easy, soft.
nolofala, become easy, soft or tender; **nolofatša,** make easy or tender, facilitate.
nolofatši, facility.
nomo, trotter that is eaten first, introduction, the leader of a swarm of locusts.
nomoro, number.
nona, grow fat.
nona, make damp.
none, blesbuck.
nonela, spread fat or water on a thing.
nonetša, sprinkle, anoint.
nonetšo, sprinkling, anointing.
nonetšwa, be anointed.
nong, vulture, big bird.
nongkhudugi, migratory bird, bird of passage.
nongosela, be in anguish, penetrating pain.
nonnodi, surprise.
nonnori, surprise.
nonoba, walk slowly, spread.
nonofatša, fertilise, fertilize.
nontšha, fatten, fertilise, enrich.
nontšho, fertilisation, fattening.
nonwane, fable, fairy-tale, a story chanted.
nonyana, bird.
nonyana, coquette.
nopa, peck, knock, crack (as a whip).
nopa, sucker.
nopela, dip the finger into, (to taste).
nopola, pick up, pick up one by one.
noša, cause to drink.
nose, honey-bee; – **tona,** drone.
nošetša, water, irrigate.
nošetšo, irrigation.
noši, alone; **ka** – automatic.
nota, pound by hammering.
note, note.
notla, make small or thin, narrow.
notlega, wax cold, abate, flag.
notlela, lock.
notlolla, v.t., unlock.
noto, hammer, mallet.
notokota, mallet, wooden hammer.
notswa, dip into, dip the finger into.
notwana, small hammer.
nowa, be drunk.
nta, louse.
ntahla, cast me out or away.
ntahle, backhand.
ntamolane, deliverer.
ntane, scab; **ra** –, dip inspector.
ntano, then, afterwards.
ntanya, grasp me firmly.
ntapiša, tire or weary me out.
ntapološa, refresh me.
ntasteri, industry.
ntatauwane, dragon.
ntatela, follow me.
nteba, come in my direction.
ntebala, forget me.
ntebelela, look at me.
nteile, beaten me.

nteka, try me.
ntekile, tried/tested me.
ntekeletšana, tassel.
ntelela, cry for me.
ntepa, skirt.
nthapelela, pray for me.
nthathanyana, fragment.
nthe; ka –, but, however, yet, still.
ntheetša, listen to me.
nthekela, buy from me.
nthetelego, round.
ntho, sore, thing, wound.
ntho, mankind.
nthoba, small hole.
nthoga, curse me; – **kela,** curse for me.
nthopa, rob me.
nthwala, carry me; – **lela,** carry for me.
nthwanthwaletša, return lost property, search for lost property.
nthweša, help me to carry (a burden), put a load on me.
ntiiša, strengthen me.
ntitia, beat me, strike me.
ntlafatša, beautify.
ntlatla, flat, basket.
ntle, outside; – **le molao,** unlawfully;, **ka – ga,** without; adj., beautiful, fine, pretty, handsome.
ntlha, end, point, primary.
ntlhanogela, turn away from me.
ntlhohlola, disturb me.
ntlhora, peak, top.
ntlhoriša, worry me.
ntlhwa, termite, white-ant.
ntlo, house, hut.
ntlwana, small house.
ntobiša, cause me to suffer a loss.
ntoma, bite me; – **tsebe,** tell me a secret.
ntoo, adj., one; adv., and then.
ntoto, penis.
ntotoma, pile.
ntotomana, heap, mound.
ntotompane, five-stones; adj., puffed up.
ntša, eat (rob) me.
ntsane, aux. verb, still.
ntsatsarapa, tall and slender.
ntse, aux. v., ind., continued action.
ntše, sa –, still.
ntsena ganong, interrupt me.
ntšha, take out, pay, extract, remove from, discharge, minus.
ntsha, duiker; **ntshane,** small duiker, young of a duiker.
ntshasametša, (ntshaseletša), set the dogs after me.
ntshebela, inform me secretly.
ntshega, laugh at me.
ntsheleka, disgust me.
ntšhi, fly, brink of a river, shore, edge, eye-lash, eye-brow; adj., many, much.
ntšhidila, massage me.
ntšhiša, cause to (pay), take out.
ntšhitše, has taken out.
ntsho, boiled water given to infants.
ntsho, n., sugar-cane, sweet-reed; adj., black, dark colour; **e** –, black ox or bull.
ntshofala, become black, dark or sad;
ntshofalo, a becoming black, darkening, black-out.
ntshofatša, blacken, darken.
ntshogošo, left; **la-,** left hand.
ntšhomiša, use me, cause me to work; – **šetša,** use me for.
ntshothwane, third stomach of a ruminant.
ntšhu, eagle, hawk.
ntšhuhla, tuft, hassock, bunch.
ntšhupa, point at me.
ntšhupetša, point something out to me.
ntšhupeletša, point at me with an idea of doing me harm.
ntshwara, catch/hold me.
ntshwarela, forgive me.
ntshwarele, do forgive me!

ntshwe, be out (of a game).
ntshwere gampe, treated me badly.
ntši, n., fly; adj., much, many.
ntšifala, multiply, – **tša,** cause to increase.
ntšifatšo, multiplication.
ntsobokwana, goatee, something protruding.
ntsupulo, grimace, rounded lips.
ntswekantswe, literal.
ntswetša, be out, forfeit one's turn (at a game).
ntudiša, cause me to sit/live.
ntwa, war, battle, fight; – **dumela,** bellicose.
ntwantšha, combat me, oppose me.
nwa, drink.
nwela, drink (for) at.
nwele, has drunk.
nweletša, cause to sink.
nwiša, cause to drink.
nya, (nyala), go to stool, have a motion.
nya, re –, disappear.
nyaba, sparkle, frolic; **nyaba-nyaba,** swarm, teem with; id., throw down.
nyabanyabetša, cause to shine.
nyabea, mix food.
nyabela, feast, itch, defile.
nyabola, melt.
nyadiša, cause to marry, marry.
nyaka, seek, desire, want; adv., nearly, – **go,** almost; – **nyaka,** seek here and there.
nyakalala, rejoice, be glad.
nyakalalo, gladness, rejoicing.
nyakega, be necessary.
nyakego, necessity.
nyakgahla, mildew, blight.
nyakurela, peep into.
nyala, marry, give the dowry; **nyalwa,** get married (of a girl); pft., **nyetšwe,** married.
nyalano, fusion.
nyama, be sorry, be sad.
nyamalala, scatter.
nyamalela, vanish.
nyamela, be sad over.
nyamo, pity, sorrow, sadness.
nyamoga, melt.
nyamolotša, blister.
nyane, small, little, minor.
nyanya, suck.
nyaoga, melt.
nyapoga, be revealed.
nyapola, spot.
nyapolla, snatch away.
nyaragana, little buttocks (hind quarters).
nyarela, peep.
nyaroga, get startled.
nyatša, despise, belittle, treat with disdain.
nyatšega, be (despised) despicable.
nyatši, paramour, concubine.
nyatšo, belittling, despising.
nyauma, swarm, teem with.
nyedi, twinkle, riddle.
nyefa, be loose, hang down.
nyefiša, caus., tie (hold) loosely.
nyefola, blaspheme, revile, curse.
nyehla, become loose, hang down.
nyela, go to stool excrete; **nyediša,** cause to go to stool, give a hiding.
nyelela, vanish, disappear; **nyeletša,** cause to disappear.
nyeloga, become visible suddenly.
nyemoga, smile.
nyemuka, smear with much fat.
nyenya, despise, disdain.
nyenyane, very small, little.
nyenyefala, become small.
nyenyefatša, make small or little, diminish.
nyenyefatšo, diminutive, belittling.
nyenyetša, whisper, walk silently.
nyepo, riddle.
nyepola, discover, find out, solve.
nyetše, has married; – **we,** be married.
nyeuma, swarm, teem with.

nyoba, sweet-reed, have sexual intercourse.
nyoga, rise, cross a river.
nyoka, stir.
nyokologa, progress slowly.
nyollo, raising up.
nyologela, ascend.
nyooko, bile.
nyopa, barren woman; v., tighten, twist.
nyoretšwe, thirst for.
nyorilwe, be thirsty.
nyorwa, be thirsty.
nyurastenia, neurastenie.
nywaga, years.
nywako, houses.
nywala, give marriage cattle (dowry).
nywanywa, smile.
nywenywa, swarm, teem with.
nywenywela, smile.

O

o, (concord), you.
oba, bend down, hook, make a mistake.
obama, bend down to, straighten.
obamela, worship, bow down to.
obega, become (bent) bowed down.
obelela, incline towards.
obeletša, reach out.
oboga, peel off.
obola, peel off, pare, rind.
odinansi, ordinance.
ofe, which, what; – le –, any.
ohla, twist, spin.
ohle, all.
ohoo! oh!
oka, nurse.
oka, draw near, entice.
okama, look over, supervise, lean over.
okamela, be above, lean over.
okane, organ.
okeletša, add to, increase.
okese, orchestra.
oketša, supplement, add to.
oketšega, become added to.
okga, carry fire.
okgola, gather up.
oko, pen, kennel, sty, cage.
okobala, subside, abate.
okobatša, cause to subside, heal.
okola, skim, take the upper part.
okologa, recover.
okomela, look down upon.
Okotobore, October.
okotša, do superficially.
oksigene, oxygen.
oksitšene, oxygen.
ola, dem., yonder.
ola, v., gather up, brush, stroke.
oleala, gather up with the hands.
oli, oil.
ologa, roll down, dismount.
ološa, winnow, broadcast; – **kgotala,** give alarm.
oma, become dry.
oma, aim a blow at, pretend to strike; – **ka hlogo,** nod the head, hint at.
omana, curse, swear.
omanya, cause to scold.
omelega, ferment, be leavened.
omela, dry up.
omelela, become completely dry.
omfolopo, envelope.
omi, re –, be very dry.
omiša, cause to dry.
omoša, make warm.
ona, wear out, snore; pron. they, them.
onala, become old or worn out (of things).
onorobaki, waistcoat.
onoroko, petticoat.
onse, ounce.
onto, oven.
ontshe, ounce.
opa, strike, knock, throb, ache; –

diatla, clap the hands, applaud; – **mokgoši,** give alarm.
opafala, become barren or sterile.
opfatša, sterilise.
opaopa, pulsate, knock, beat.
opereišene, operation.
opereita, operate.
opedişa, cause to sing, conduct; **moopediši,** conductor.
opela, sing, clap for.
opša, (ke hlogo), have headache.
ora, – letšatši, bask in the sun; – **mollo,** warm oneself at fire.
orela, bear, endure, bide.
oretša, fumigate, smoke.
orikele, auricle.
orolosi, watch.
ortela, order.
osemose, osmosis.
ota, become thin, meagre, lean; **otiša,** cause to be lean.
otelela, pursue, chase, persuade.
otla, rear, punish, ruminate, feed; **otlela,** punish for; **otlwa,** be punished, **otliša,** cause/help to punish.
otlolla, stretch out, straighten.
otlologa, become stretched out, become straight; **-ile,** be straight.
otša, hiss.
otsela, slumber.
otsi, re –, slumber.
otswa, commit adultery.
outse, oats.
owasese, oasis.
owe! shame, fie! fy(e)!

P

pa, re –, crack.
paajana, fair, passable, tolerable.
paala, (paale), true, genuine.
pabalego, conservation.
pabalelo, care, oversight, safe-keeping.
paballo, conservation, keeping, trust.
pabe, roasted maize, pop-corn.
pabilione, pavilion.
pabo, bitterness.
padi, novel.
padile, be impossible, failed.
padiša, be obstructive, cause to fail.
padišo, reader, reading book.
paente, pint; – **pedi,** quart.
paesekele, bicycle.
paesekopo, bioscope.
paesepe, biceps.
pafo, bath.
pagolola, dethrone.
paka, bake, pack, pile up; witness; n., suit of clothes, period; – **ilwego,** which is baked.
pakana, interval.
pakane, beacon.
pak'eno, at present, nowadays.
paki, witness.
pakteria, bacteria.
pakwa, be baked.
pala, a scald, upright (pole), be impossible, fail.
palabalo, prattle.
palakana, scatter.
palakantšha, scatter.
palakanya, broadcast.
palakata, appear suddenly.
palamente, parliament.
palamonwana, ring.
pale, legend.
palediša, prevent.
palega, crack, chap.
palego, cracking.
palei, E., ballet.
palela, be impossible.
palelo, lath.
palelwa, fail.
Palestina, Palestine.
palo, reading, counting, number.
palogare, average.
palokadimo, borrowing figure.

palopalo, statistics.
palophatlo, fraction.
palophokotšwa, minuend.
palotlalo, whole number.
palune, ballon.
pamfolete, pamphlet.
pampara, bumper.
pampiri, paper.
pampiridikwerana, squared paper.
pampiritšhelete, note.
pana, harness.
panana, banana.
pane, a pan, frying-pan.
panele, panel.
paneng, bea –, pledge, pawn.
panka, bench, desk, bank.
pankarea, pancreas.
pankoroto, bankrupt.
panorama, panorama.
panta, mortgage, pawn.
panya, blink, twinkle.
papa, father.
papadi, game, play, sport.
papadišo, dramatisation.
papage, his or her father.
papago, your father.
papalase, hangover, horrors, delirium.
papanyo, correlation.
papatla, flat; n., chart.
papatletša, flatten.
papatšo, commerce, trade.
papetlanako, time chart.
papetlanoto, modulator.
papetlega, be flattened.
papetliša, flatten.
papetšo, comparison.
papisi, bots.
papišo, comparison, simile.
papolo, crucifixion.
paputla, grope, feel your way.
para, bar, pub.
parabatše, devil's thorn.
parafene, paraffin.
paraka, fallow.
paralala, become stiff or erect.
paralatša, make stiff or erect.
paralelokerama, parallelogram.
parametša, stretch forth.
parapariša, cause to run.
parašutu, parachute.
parometa(ra), barometer.
parone, baron.
pasa, bass, pass, passport; v., fit well, suit.
pasara, bazaar.
Paseka, Easter.
pasela, present, gift.
paseporoto (pasepoto), passport.
pata, main road.
pata, oppress, conceal, hide, cheat.
patagana, be close together, be in straits, be compressed.
pataganya, compress, marry more than one wife.
patametšo, approximation.
patanyi, vice.
patega, be concealable.
patego, plasteing, plaster.
patela, pay, swoop, attack by surprise.
pateletša, accuse falsely, oppress.
paterone, pattern, bullet.
patikela, drive into a corner.
patile, boroko, fast asleep.
patiša, squeeze, oppress.
patla, stick.
patlapatla, re –! run (away).
patlelo, see: **lepatlelo.**
pato, spattle, act of hiding.
patoga, slope, mountain-side.
patolo, anvil, whetstone.
patologana, be parted, be separated.
patologanya, pull asunder, separate.
patšane, tick.
patše, hemp, dagga.
pe, re –! be full.
pea, clay-pipe.
peakanyo, arrangement, classification.
peanyo, arrangement, classification.
peba, mouse, rat.
pedi, two.
pedifatša, duplicate.

pedifatšo, duplicating, duplication.
pedi-tharong, two thirds.
pee, id., beautiful, flash.
peelano, condition, wager, stake; **go bea** –, give security.
peeletšo, betrothal, security.
peelo, a putting down for.
peetla, cobra.
pefelo, wrath.
pegelo, a report on.
pegi, report.
pego, notice, report.
pegosemmušo, official notice.
peipi, pipe.
peišano, race.
pejana, a little to the fore, a bit earlier or sooner.
peita, spray, inject.
peke, pick.
pekebene, penguin.
pekenene, small boy.
pekentšha, cause to shine, reflect.
pekenya, cause to shine, brandish, flash, reflect.
pekenyi, reflector.
pekwa, hawk.
pela, Native piano, musical instrument.
pelá, quick, quickly.
péla, rock-rabbit, coney.
pelaelo, doubt, anxiety, grievance.
pelaetšo, cause of doubt or grievance.
pelapela, quickly, very fast/quick.
pele, front, initial, ahead, formerly, first, forward.
pelego, confinement, birth.
pelejara, bell-jar.
peleng, at first.
pelepele, far ahead, the very first, long ago.
pelešа, beast of burden.
pelešo, load, burden.
peleta, spell.
peleto, spelling.
pelita, pleat.
pelo, boiling.
pelo, heart, pitch, core, gist; **wa** –, be satisfied; – **nolo,** kind, meek; – **telele,** patient.
pelwana, embryo, small heart.
pena, turn up, lift the hind quarters.
penama, bend the back upwards.
penapena, hop, rejoice, show off.
penapenane, flying-ant.
pene, pen.
peni, penny.
penka, turn up, show off.
penola, bend far up.
penta, paint.
pente, n., paint.
Pentekoste, Pentecost.
pentšu, banjo.
penya, wriggle, throw down.
penyana, wrestle.
penyano, wrestling.
penyeka, writhe.
peo, placing, putting, coronation.
peolane, swallow.
peolwane, swallow.
pepa, carry a child on one's back.
pepenene, evident, clear, open.
pepentšha, expose, reveal.
pepere, pepper.
pepesine, pepsin.
pepetla, flattened.
pepetletša, drive a herd or team carefully.
pepula, carry a child on one's back.
pera, be timid, ripe.
pere, horse.
perebela, button, bolt.
perekisi, peach.
perela, pearl.
perema, be afraid, fear.
peremetšha, broadcast, extend or push out the horns.
perepetša, drive forward.
perimita, perimiter.
pering, bearing.
perinki, saucer.
peri-peri, beriberi.
perr, re –! be red, be red with blood.

pešana, foal, – **e tshadi,** filly; – **e tona,** colt.
pese, bus.
pešo, roasting.
peta, squeeze, dig.
petala, petal.
pete, beetroot.
peteri, battery.
peterolo, petrol.
petho, beating, hiding.
petiole, petiole.
petla, stick out, be purulent, roll down, cobra.
petlabje, sculpture.
petlega, run down.
petleka, be open, extend, be wide.
petleke, open, wide, manifest.
petlo, adze, carpentry, chisel.
petloša, open wide.
petlwana, chisel.
peto, rape.
petola, open, expose.
petša, bet.
petšhana, foal, young horse.
petšhe, badge.
petšo, throwing.
peu, seed.
pewa, a sign or mark.
pewana, small seed.
pha, re –! be nice.
phadile, has (surpassed) won.
phadima, shine, glitter; **go a** –! there is a feast; – **ela,** shine upon.
phadimo, glittering, lustre.
phadimoga, lose gloss, shy.
phadimola, remove the lustre or gloss.
phadiša, cause to (surpass) win.
phadišana, compete.
phadišano, competition.
phae, pie.
phaela, give a side blow, remove with a sweep of the hand, sidestep.
phaeneapole, pineapple.
phaente, pint.
phaephe, pipe.
phafa, calabash, gourd.
phafana, gourd.
phafatlo, deliriousness.
phafoga, wake (up).
phafoša, wake, waken, arouse.
phaga, wild-cat, skin cap.
phagamego, raised, elevated or lifted.
phagamiša, raise, lift, uplift.
phagamišo, elevation, uplifting.
phagamo, elevation.
phago, bee-hive, hole in a treetrunk.
phahla, pack up; remove; gap; **thiba** –, fill a gap.
phahlo, luggage, obstruction in the eye.
phahlolla, unload.
phaila, wander about, drag the feet.
phaka, hasten, hurry.
phaka, eat quickly, bolt.
phakabarwa, assegai.
phakgama, wake up.
phakgamiša, waken, raise, elevate.
phakiša, make haste, hurry.
phako, wall plate.
phála, impala, red buck, trumpet.
p̂hala, conquer, beat; – **wa,** be overcome.
phaladi, scattering, dispersion, migration.
phalafala, sable antelope, trumpet.
phalago, surpassing, excellent.
phalala, run (away), flee, rescue.
phalalela, rush to, hasten to.
phalalo, migration.
phalang, surpassing.
phalo, adze, scraping, hollow in a tree-trunk (containing water).
phalola, clean shave, n., a reed flute.
phalolo, escape.
phamoga, be snatched away, deviate.
phamola, snatch away, pluck out.
phamolo, snatching away.
phamoša, cause to turn off.
phamphabodiba, big pool of water.
phanakela, hurry, haste away.
phanka, panga.

phankga, full big; **mollo wa –,** big, fire.
phanya, burst, crack.
phaolla, empty out.
phaolo, castration.
phaologa, give a different version of.
phapala, young she-goat.
phapang, dispute, quarrel, difference.
phapano, opposite, quarrel, difference.
phapantšho, characteristic.
phapha, chop, flutter, flit, flap.
phaphadikota, wood-pecker.
phaphama, wake-up.
phaphamala, float, drift.
phaphamela, flutter, fly up to.
phaphapha, windmill.
phaphara, jump up.
phaphaša, hatch.
phaphasela, flutter, flap, vibrate.
phaphatha, pat, caress, stroke.
phaphathi, flat; n., plaque.
phaphela, take a short-cut, dodge.
phaphi, tla –, head off.
phaphula, stray, wander, be stupid.
phapogelo, deviation.
phapošana, tributary, side room.
phapoše, room.
phapoši, side room, a place of rest.
phapošibodulelo, parlour.
phapošitulelo, parlour.
phara, accuse falsely, plaster, stick on, patch, besmear; go across.
phara, cucumber.
pharalala, squat down, spread.
pharama, lie down flat, squat down, **– ela sa ruri,** break down entirely.
pharela, stick on.
pharelankong, lizard.
pharihla, run, crawl fast.
pharodipataka, criticism.
pharoga, split, crack.
pharola, split.
pharologantšho, characteristic.
pharologanyo, difference, characteristic.
pharuma, hop about, seek in vain.
phasa, bring a sacrifice to the ancestral spirits, pass.
phaša, cut short, interrupt.
Phasifika, Pacific Ocean.
phasola, hit, strike.
phaswa, black and white (male).
phaswana, black and white (female).
phata, mountain-pass, stick, pole, skin blanket, bed.
phate, stick, pole, skin blanket.
phathakgа, carry something under the arm, grip.
phathankgana, wrestle, caper, struggle.
phathi, party.
phatla, forehead, brow.
phatlaa, re –, scatter.
phatlalala, scatter, disperse.
phatlalatša, scatter, disperse, broadcast; adv., openly, publicly.
phatlalatšo, dispersion, scattering.
phatloga, burst open, split, crack.
phatlogo, crack, burst, cleft.
phatlola, split, cleave.
phato, digging, burrowing, scratching.
Phato, August.
phatodi, bugle made of horn.
phatša, splinter, splint; v., lance scarify.
phatša, sterile cow, barren animal.
phaya, push aside, open a book.
phedile, has lived, has survived.
phediša, cause to live, let live, keep.
phedišano, neighbourliness, human relations, friendship.
phedišo, cancellation, ending.
phedišwa, be sustained, made to live.
phefadu, dark brown m. animal.
phefo, wind, cold; **– hlabošang,** fresh air.
phega, compete.
phegelela, compete for, strive for, persevere, do your best.
phegelelo, competition, perseverance.
phegelo, sigh, sighing.
phegišana, compete.

phegišano, competition.
phehlee, easy, comfortable.
phehli, whitlow, (stalk) borer.
phejane, last/youngest child.
pheka, bar a gate, close a gateway.
phekagana, lie across.
phekama, lie across, slant, be oblique.
phekelwa, be barred for/against.
pheketša, bar, obstruct.
phekga, deny, argue, contradict.
phekgo, turn somersault.
phekgola, turn somersault, roll over.
pheko, (cross) bar, charm, amulet.
phekola, conjure, throw bones, diagnose.
phela, live, survive, be alive.
phelakadingwe, parasite.
phelela ganong, live from hand to mouth.
phelegetšo, accompanying.
phelephethe, sly/cunning person.
phelеši, bridesmaid.
pheletšo, end, consequence, fate.
pheleu, wether.
phema, avoid, ward off, avert, prevent.
phemega, be defended.
phemela, ward off, defend.
phemelo, defence.
phemete, permit.
phemo, a warding off, an escape.
phenale, phenalethi, penalty (football).
phenkgišano, competition.
phenkwine, penguin.
phensele, pencil.
phenšene, pension.
phenthihouse, pantihose.
phenyadingwe, victor, conqueror.
phenyo, victory, conquest.
phepa, dodge.
phepe, white clay.
phepela, rejoice, dance.
phepha, dodge, avoid.
phepheletšo, instigation.
phepheng, scorpion.
phepheula, flutter, flit, flap.
phepo, feeding.
phepompe, malnutrition.
phera, narrow place; **tšwa ka** –, have a narrow escape, suffer from leprosy.
pherefere, pepper, chilli.
pherehlo, stirring.
pherekana, quarrel, be distorted.
pherekano, disturbance, disorder.
phereketša, trip, cause to stumble.
Pherekgong, January.
pheriebene, peri-urban.
pherogo, nausea.
phešelele, re – rush into.
phesente, percentage.
pheta, bead, necklace; – **ya thaga,** jewel, gem (in a crown).
pheta, report, finish, relate, turn.
phetela, end off, tell everything.
pheteletšo, hyperbole.
phetetšo, a passing on to, infection.
phetha, finish, accomplish, complete, decide, perform.
phethagatša, fulfil, fulfilment.
phethego, accomplishment.
phethego, perfection.
phethela, perform for, complete for.
phetho, finish, decision.
phetho, re –, roll over.
phethola, roll over, turn over, change.
phetholo, a turning over, a change.
phethonkga, roll over.
phethwa, be performed/completed.
phetla, wind, twist.
phetlega, sprain.
phetloga, unwind.
pheto, a passing, surpassing.
phetogo, change, turning over, metamorphosis.
phetokgolla, turn or roll over.
phetolo, reply, change, translation, interpretation.
phetonkga, roll over, turn somersault.
phetonkgo, turning somersault.
phetošadibjalo, crop rotation.
phetošo, change, amendment.

phetše, has lived.
phetšo, end.
pheu, re –, blow.
phifadu = phefadu.
phifalo, darkening, eclipse.
phihlo, arrival.
phihlo, secret, something hidden.
phikoko, peacock.
philetšhate, pilchard.
phima, extinguish.
phimola, wipe, wipe out, erase.
phinyo, penis.
phiri, hyena, wolf; –, n., bad beer.
phirima, set, become dark.
phirimálelwa, be overtaken by night, be benighted.
phirimane, evening.
phišana, small – (young of) hyena/wolf.
phišego, urge, desire.
phišo, heat.
phiswa, dark brown male animal.
phiswana, small vessel, brown female.
phitwa, water-buck.
phoa, become blistered.
phobela, dent; v., fall in, become dented.
phodišo, a healing.
phofo, flight, jump.
phogo, crown on the head, fontanelle.
phogo, champion.
phohla, fall in, sink, poke.
phohlela, sink, subside, go down.
phohu, eland; **phohwana,** small eland.
phoka, dew, smell; **go welwa ke –,** be fortunate be favoured; **tsarogile –,** clever person.
phoka, sip something hot, restrain.
phokafalo, dewpoint.
phokelo, sprinkling.
phokgo, top dog, leader.
phoko, he-goat.
phoko, act of sprinkling (medicine), blowing of the wind.
phokodišo, cause of weakness.
phokoletšo, rebate, discount.
phokolo, weakness, hardship.
phokotšo, diminishing, diminutive, lessening.
phokwana, young he-goat.
pholaka, spark-plug.
pholiša, v., polish.
pholiši, (pholitšhi), polish.
pholletša, pass through.
pholo, ox, a large male animal.
pholo, threshing.
pholo, recovery, cooling, parade.
pholofolo (phoofolo), animal, game.
phologa, escape, be saved or rescued.
phologo, salvation, deliverance, descending, survival.
phololetša, pierce.
phološa, redeem, save, deliver.
phološo, saving, salvation.
pholotšo, abortion (of an animal).
phomo, graphite.
phomola, rest, take leave.
phomolo, rest.
phona, miss, fail to attend.
phonkgela, plunge into, precipitate.
phonkgelela, venture into, plunge into.
phonyokga, escape from danger, break away.
phonyokgo, escape, breaking away.
phoofolo, wild game, animal.
phooko, he-goat.
phopha, drop (as a liquid).
phophi, a drop.
phophĭsa, secrete, slaver, drivel.
phopho, pawpaw.
phophola, grope.
phopholego, texture.
phopholetša, grope, ponder over, caress.
phophoma, bubble, rise.
phophotha, plead, pat, caress.
phophotha, apologise, ask for pardon.
phori, false, wilt, mildew; **go tšhela – mahlong,** deceive.
phoro, deceit.
phorogela, fall in.

phorogohlo, sparrow.
phoroketša, speak fluently.
phorometša, pour out a liquid.
phororo, water-fall, rapid, cascade.
phoša, miss, throw, guess, – **gala,** fail.
phošagetšego, wrong.
phošeditše, wronged.
phošetša, commit a wrong against, wrong.
phosithifi, positive.
phošo, mistake, fault, error, a throw.
phošolla, correct an error.
phošollo, correction.
photha, twist, wind, twine.
phothokgiša, turn, upside-down.
phothoma, treat medically, seize.
photla, shell ground-nuts, pod.
phoulo, pole.
phu, re –, smell badly.
Phubjane, June.
phudifudi, wild-duck.
phudufudu, steenbuck.
phuduwe (phuduwe-e-e)! time! (in play).
pfufudi, steam.
phufulelo, transpiration.
phuhla, re –, flop down.
phuhlama, fall down, collapse.
phukubje, jackal, silver jackal.
phukhuphukhu, re – flapping.
phula, pierce, strike water, pioneer.
phulamatšibogo, pioneer, the van.
phularo, a rota.
phulawatle, tide.
phuleletša, pierce.
phuleletšago, piercing.
phulo, grazing, plucking, pasture.
phuma, break, spill, let out secrets.
phumega, be breakable.
phumola, dust, wipe, erase.
phumula, erase, wipe.
phunya, pierce, strike water.
phunyeditše, bored a hole for.
phuo, mole.
phupha, float in the air, attack.
Phuphu, July.
phuphu, head-dress, eyelid.
phuphuma, bubble, foam, froth.
phuphura, chew, gnaw, masticate.
phuphusela, flutter, flap.
phuphuthela, apologise.
phupu, eyelid, tomb.
phura, gnaw.
phure, fraud, deceit.
phurela, burst open (like popcorn).
phuru, re –, jump up.
phurulla, unroll, unfold.
phurulola, unroll, unfold.
phuruma, hop, jump up.
phurumela, jump at.
phuša, wean (an animal).
phušetša, cover with soil, cover up, bury.
phušiša, wean.
phušoga, see: **phušuga.**
phušola, demolish; – **wa,** be demolished.
phušolla, demolish, excavate.
phušuga, be broken or demolished.
phušula, demolish, break (dig) up.
phušullo, demolishing.
phutla, fold, gather, assemble.
phuthagana, twist.
phuthegela, gather, for.
phuthego, assembly, congregation, gathering.
phuthela, wrap in/for.
phutholla, unfold, spread out.
phuti, duiker, concubine.
phuting, sweets, pudding.
phutlula, shell, reveal.
phutšana, young of a duiker.
piana, piano.
pidinya, beat the drum, to drum.
pikiniki, picnic.
pikitla, rub (the eyes).
pikitlo, friction, rubbing.
piletša, something that will bring evil.
piletšo, dictation.
pilo, scorched earth, a big black spot.
pilwana, small black spot.
pina, song, dance.

pinagare, pivot.
pinathabo, carol.
ping, South African black-bird.
ping!, beware!
pinka, ping.
pinki, pink.
pino, dance, dancing.
pinya, squeeze, pinch.
pinyeletša, pinch, press, wrench.
pipa, cover up.
pipelo, indigestion.
pipelwa, (– ke disego), choke with laughter.
pipetša, keep secret hide, twist a statement.
pipitla, hide, keep secret.
pipitlela, keep secret.
pipololo, uncovering.
pipitlanyana, short.
pirretša, hurl.
pitika, roll over.
pitikama, roll over and over.
pitla, squeeze, press.
pitlagano, narrowness.
pitlega, be or become narrow.
pitlego, narrowing.
pitša, pot, saucepan.
pitšana, small pot.
pitsi, zebra, uncircumcised man.
pitšo, call, assembly, calling, meeting, trade, occupation.
pitšopalo, numeration.
pitšori, time! (in games).
pitwa, water-buck.
plastiki, plastic.
pleistere, plaster.
poba, horse-fly.
pobela, shrink, lie low.
pobodi, moaning, grumbling.
pobolo, moaning.
podile, stink-bug.
podilekgwana, lady-bird.
podiša, rotten fruit.
podišo, cause of rotting or decaying.
podišwa, compost.
poeletšamedumo, alliteration.
poeletšo, repetition.
poelo, return, profit; – **-morago,** a going backward.
pofo, bondage, binding.
pogo, trunk (of an elephant) proboscis.
poifo, fear.
poka, haunt.
pokano, gathering, camp.
pokolo, donkey.
pola, thrash, thresh; n., sand-apple.
polaka, spark-plug: cf. **pholaka.**
polamere, plumber.
polanka, plank, board.
polantere, planter.
polao, murder, slaughter, illtreatment.
polasa, farm.
polase, farm.
polatefomo, platform.
poledišano, discussion, dialogue.
poleisetera, plaster.
polela, the sting (of an insect).
polelo, language, speech, report.
polelopegelo, indirect speech.
politekeniki, polytechnical.
politi, pleat.
politiki, politics; adj., political.
polo, ball, football, penis.
polo, thrashing-stick, flail.
poloa, gather (in sewing).
poloi, gathering, pleat.
polokego, safety.
polokelo, place of safety, treasury, storehouse, safe.
poloko, burying, burial, safety, salvation, conservation.
Polokwane, Pietersburg.
polomeetse, iguana.
polotše, circumcision.
polousele, blue.
poma, cut off, snuff a candle, prune.
pomaganya, cut to pieces.
pomo, bomb; **thea-,** mine a bomb.
pompa, pump.
pompala, loiter, idle.
pompi, pump, pipe.

pompo, pump.
pompom, (pompong), sweet(s).
pona, dry up, fade, wither.
ponagalo, appearance.
ponagatšo, revelation.
ponapona, be naked.
ponase, bonus.
ponego, perspective.
pongwa, be cut off, be pruned.
pono, sight, view, vision.
ponoka, go about naked.
ponopono, nakedness.
ponto, pound (£ or lb.)
pontšheng, openly, publicly.
pontšho, show, sign, exhibition.
ponya, wink, blink.
ponyane, red finch.
ponyo, twinkling, winking, blinking, **ka – ya leihlo,** on the spot.
ponyolla, open the eyes.
ponyologa, open the eyes.
poo, bull, male animal; – **ya lenala,** a tuft of grass for drawing water, a wee bit, **re** –, fart.
poomootlwa, butcher-bird, shrike.
popego, formation, build, stature.
popelo, ovary.
popi, doll, poppy, womb.
popo, formation, moulding.
popoduma, muttering, grumbling.
popojane, monkey wrench.
popollo, decomposition, unmoulding.
popomala, idle.
popponono, stink-bug.
popopolelo, grammar.
poporomente, pepermint.
popose, pawpaw.
popotela, obdurate person.
popotlakala, leaf-shaped.
poraka, small dog, cur; v., cultivate in the winter, fallow.
poraki, small dog.
poraše, brush.
poreimi, plum
poreisi, price.
poriki, brake.
poromete (poromiti), permit.
porompi, quid.
porosola, brush.
porosolo, brush.
porotla, roar.
poroto, plate.
posa, to post.
poso, post; **posong,** post office.
pota, go round, dent, press in.
potana, (potane), calf of the leg.
potasiamo, potassium.
potego, fidelity, faith.
potla, pocket.
potla, bellow, roar, belch.
potlaka, hurry, hasten.
potlakela, hasten (to) for.
potlakiša, accelerate.
potlako, haste, hurry.
potlana, small.
poto, pot.
potoka, gather.
potokana, be prevented.
potologa, go round.
potololá, beat out dents.
potološa, cause to go round.
potoloto, pencil.
potongwane, biceps, calf (of the leg).
potoro, butter.
potsa, badly cooked porridge.
potšišo, question, interrogation.
potuma, doze, slumber; – **iša,** make drowsy.
potwana, small pot.
poubala, petal.
poudi, hair-dress, coiffure.
poula, speak ill of.
pounama, lip.
powana, small/young bull.
praebete, private.
praemasetofo, primus-stove.
prairi, prairie.
profesa, profesara, professor.
profeta, prophesy.
protea, protea.
protoplasma, protoplasm.
protosoa, protozoa.

pšalo, planting.
pšalollo, transplanting.
pšere, pear.
pšha, dry out.
pšhapšha (diatla), applaud, clap on the hands, salute.
pšhamoga, come off.
pšhatla, break, smash.
pšhatlaganya, smash up.
pšhatlega, fragile, break: **pšhatlegile,** broken.
pšhega, purge, have diarrhoea.
pšhemoga, come loose, come off.
pshikologa, roll over.
pshikologo, rolling over.
pshinya, emit a wind, fart.
pshinyo, penis.
pshio, kidney.
pshirimane, dusk, sunset.
pšoo, be bright, snow-white.
puane, skin-cap, fur-cap.
pudi, goat, ring-worm, pellagra, – **ya tsela,** rumour.
pududu, grey, hoary.
pudula, bubble, puff, inflated bladder.
pudulelo, inflation.
pudutša, ring-worm.
pudutšwana, a roan animal.
pue, blister, bubble.
puku, book; – **ntšu,** dictionary.
pula, rain; – **e a na,** it rains or is raining; –! exclam., Good luck! Hail! Hurrah!
puladibati, cutlets give to old men.
pulelo, opening for.
pulo, opening.
puno, harvest, product.
punwana, by-product.
pupa, cover; **pupolla,** uncover.
pupetša, cover, stifle.
pupetšo, covering.
pududu, species of wild fruit.
puputla, drive cattle.
puputla, blow, drive a team, plead.
purapura, clock, gown.
purepura, purple.
puruma, roar, threathen.
purupuru, larynx.
puruputša, collect remnants, search.
purutla, roar.
pušano, democracy.
pušanoši, autocracy.
pušetšo, giving back, restoration, compensation.
pušo, reign, government.
pušompe, misgovernment.
pušotharo, triumvirate.
putetša, fill the mouth.
puti, boot (car).
putla, place across, pass through, run through; cross-cut, cut one's way through; – **iša,** cause to pass through; **go re** –! sit down quickly.
putlaputla, criss-cross.
putšane, kid.
putselo, remuneration.
putswa, n., old man; adj., grey.
putšwetšo, aspiration.
putuka, rummage, search.
putula, search.
putulana, wrestle, struggle.
putuputu, re –! rush hither and thither.
puwe, blister, bubble.

R

ra, father (of).
ra, refer to.
raba, rubber.
rabadia, head of a circumcision school.
rabela, rise against the government, rebel.
rabele, rebel, insurgent.
raborolo, revolver.
radeisi, radish.
radia, cheat, deceive, defraud, rob.
radiatla, artist.
radietere, radiator.

radifeisi, boxer.
radikgwa, forester.
radikgwakgwa, scab inspector.
radikgomo, cattle-farmer.
radiloro, dreamer.
radimilione, multimillionnarie.
radimpe, person with a fair round belly.
radinkgwa, baker.
radinku, sheep-farmer.
radio, radio.
radiokramo, radiogram.
radiswikiri, grocer.
raditaba, chairman.
raditšhelete, cashier.
rae, rye.
rafa, delve, take out honey.
rafentlele, scent.
rafia, raffia.
rafunya, wallow, burrow.
raga, kick.
ragela, wean, drive to the pasture and leave alone.
Ragodimodimo, Most High.
ragoga, jump up, run fast.
raka, drive away, forestall, precede; n., cupboard.
rakadiša, chase, cause to (help to) drive away.
rakalala, stand astride, arrive simultaneously from different directions.
rakanela, meet at, surround.
rake, come first, do first.
radẹkiša, pursue, chase.
radedišwa, be chased.
rakelwa, be driven off to.
rakete, racquet, racket.
rakgadi, father's younger sister or her husband.
rakgolo, grandfather.
rakgoloago, your grandfather.
rakhefi, café keeper.
rakhulong, noisy robinchat.
rakrosari, grocer.
ralala, wander, tramp.
ralebenkele, shopkeeper.
ralehufane, jealous man.
raletlotlo, financier.
raloka, play, romp.
ralokiša, play with.
raloša, cause to play.
ramaaka, arrant liar, arch-liar.
ramaatla, father of strength.
Ramaatlaohle, Almighty, Allpowerful.
ramaesela, ant-lion.
ramaesele, ant-lion.
ramaphelo, health-officer.
ramapolase, owner of farms.
ramapuku, librarian.
ramarungwane, colly, coly.
ramatlotlo, treasurer, financier.
ramatswele, boxer.
rammotoro, owner of a motorcar.
ramodula, anther.
ramogolo, father's elder brother.
ramohlagase, electrician.
ramolao, law-agent.
ramotokwane, dwarf.
ramotse, headman.
rampa, somebody with a big belly.
rampašane, (ramphešane), sandal.
ranankele, ranunculus.
rangwane, uncle, father's younger brother.
ranta, rand (coin).
rao, re –, stand up suddenly.
raoga, start, stand up suddenly.
raopa, call, invite.
rapa, commandeer, call up, collect.
rapalala, lie outstretched, be stretched across.
rapalatša, stretch across.
rapama, recline, lie on the side, go down (the sun).
rapame, horizontal.
rapela, pray, plead, beseech.
rapolitiki, politician.
raporoto, report.
rara, entwine, entangle, (dial., father).
rarabana, get entangled; **rarabolla,**

disentangle; **rarabologa,** become unravelled.
raragane(go), twisted.
rarakanya, confuse.
raramologa, become unravelled.
rarana, become entangled or twisted together; **raranya,** v.t., entwine.
rarankana, mix up, confuse.
rarega, twisted.
rarela, twist, wind, wander in speech; **go** –, around, all round.
raro, three.
rarolla, unwind.
raša, shed leaves.
rasehlare, tree-dweller.
raselete, regional director.
rasiti, receipt.
ratente, tent-dweller.
rata, love, like, wish, will.
rateise, radish.
ratha, jump from one stone to the other, split wood, strike.
ratharatha, chatter, talk ambiguously.
ratharathela, plead.
rathela, cross (e.g., a river).
ratiša, endear.
ratšhaka, gladiator.
ratshekišo, attorney-general.
ratswala, father-in-law; – **go,** your father-in-law of.
ratswale, father-in-law.
re, say, intend.
re, when; **e tla** –, when, it will happen.
re, we, us.
rea, give a name.
rea, set a trap; catch fish.
realo, say thus.
redimoga, slip, slide.
redimoša, cause to slip; slippery.
reeletša, listen to.
reetša, listen to.
reetša, listen, hearken.
reiša, help to set a trap.
reisi, rice.
reisisi, races.
reka, buy.
rekela, buy for.
rekereke, shaky, elastic, rickety.
reketla, waver, be elastic.
rekiša, self; – **itše,** has sold; – **išitšwe,** has been sold; – **šetša,** to someone else sell on behalf of.
rekolla, redeem, ransom.
rekoto, record, document.
rektoro, rector.
reledišа, cause to slip.
relela, slide, slip.
rema, chop, hew, curdle.
rena, lord, domineer, we, us.
reng, ring (circuit).
reng, ring (circuit).
reng, why? what do you way?
rengwa, be chopped.
renkalase, cobra (snake).
renne, satiated, glutted.
reolola, change a name.
Repabliki, Republic.
repha, be loose, be lame, slacken.
rephile, palsied, paralised, slackened.
rera, preach, plan, plot.
rerela, decide in favour of; – **lela,** speak up for, favour.
rereša, speak the truth.
rerišana, discuss.
reta, praise, recite.
retela, be of no avail, harden.
retelega, turn round.
reteletša, trench, dig around.
retetše, be of no avail, hardened.
retha, brandish.
retharetha, vibrate.
rethefala, b. smooth; – **tša,** smoothing; – **tše,** b. smooth.
retoga, turn round.
retologa, turn round.
retolola, turn round.
retološa, cause to turn round.
rewa, be called or named.
riba, nod.
ribama, lie face downward.
ribariba, nod the head.

ribega, turn upside-down; – **taba,** cover up an affair.
ribolla, discover, uncover.
rifi, reef.
ripa, cut off; – **ile,** has cut off; – **ilwe,** be cut off.
ripaganya, cut into pieces.
ripitla, massacre.
ripša, be cut, be servered.
rita, churn.
ritela, iron, smoothen.
ritetše, smoothened, ironed, plastered; – **we,** be smoothened.
ritša, slide.
roba, break, smash.
robadiša, put to sleep.
robaganya, break into pieces.
robagantše, broke, has broken into pieces.
robala, sleep, lie down; – **le,** have sexual intercourse.
robalana, have sexual intercourse.
robatša, cause to lie down, put to sleep; – **mmutla,** feign, deceive.
robedi, eight.
robega, break, be broken.
robja, be broken.
robong, nine.
roboto, robot.
roga, swear, use bad language.
rogaka, swear, blaspheme; – **ilwego,** cursed, damned.
roka, sew, stitch.
rokela, sew for; **rokelela,** sew on.
rokama, jut out, stand out, be elevated.
rokga, break(off).
roko, dress for women.
rokotša, suck, draw milk.
rokwa, be sewn or stitched.
rola, uncover, remove, a burden.
rolo, roll.
roma, send; **romela,** send to; **rongwa,** be sent; **-elela,** contribute.
roma, demoralise, have a bad influence on.
romeletša, incite, send by opportunity, send someone else to.
rona, spoil, be unbecoming, fit badly.
ronega, be unsuitable, spoil.
roomane, fist.
ropa, commence, start (a game), rob.
ropefala, become a ruin; **ropefatša,** destroy utterly.
ropoga, appear.
ropola, lacerate, cut open, beat.
ropologa, swell.
ropotla, beat with a stick.
rora, roar, speak angrily.
rorarora, keep on roaring.
rorela, burn to ashes.
roroma, tremble, fear.
roromela, tremble.
roša, cause to take off.
rota, pass water; **go rotela dikobo,** bed wetting.
rotha, drop, drip.
rothiša, secrete, dribble.
rothola, be cold.
rothotha, beat mercilessly, fall as hail.
roto, male baboon (leader).
rotoga, rise, ascend, become visible.
rotola, show up; – **mahlo,** make big eyes.
rotoletša, feed much.
rotore, rotor.
rotoša, cause to rise or ascend.
rotwe, top-dog, male baboon.
rra, father, my father.
rua, earn, possess, own, rear.
rufa, reward, unveil, receive gifts.
rugby, rugby.
rula, smelt iron, revive, bring to life.
rulagana, be in order.
rulaganya, organise, organize, set in order, tabulate.
rulega, malleable, be (forged) welded.
rulela, thatch.
ruma, hem, finish off, rhyme, put a trimming on the edge of something.
rumola, provoke, be aggressive.
runa, kill vermin between the nails.

runya, move underground, throb, raise up.
runyarunya, move up and down.
rupa, go through the initiation ceremonies, suffer, rush in great numbers.
rupiša, initiate, discipline.
rupula, puff up, make a skin supple.
ruri, truly, certainly, verily.
ruruga, swell.
rurruša, cause to swell.
rusa, rust.
ruta, teach, preach.
rutha, swim, blow hard.
ruthela, gain heat, become warm.
ruthela, subside, abate.
ruthetša, heat, warm up.
ruthetše, be snug warm.
ruthufala, get hot, become heated.
rutla, pull down, tear off, raze.
rutlolla, demolish, pull down, cast/tear down; – **wa,** be broken/cast down.
rutlolola, cast down.
rutlumoga, start, jump up, be torn asunder.
rwadiša, cause (help) to carry/bear.
rwaetša, devour.
rwala, carry, bear, wear.
rwalela, gather wood, carry for or to.
rwaletšwe, carried away.
rwele, carry/carrying, hold.
rweša, emburden.
rwešwa, be emburdened, be lifted on to.

S

sa, poss, concord (particle), belonging to.
sa, like, in the way of.
sa, adv., still, yet; – with the negative, no longer, not; – **le,** while.
sa, clear, dawn, disappear.
sa! go re – E! tally-ho! set a dog after, catch him!
šaba, trade, barter, buy here and there.
sabanna, savannah.
sabalala, scatter.
Sabata, (-tha) The Sabbath, day of rest.
sabohloko, gall-bladder.
sabole, sword.
sadi, (suffix), feminine, female.
šadiša, cause to remain, reserve, leave over, – **šetša,** leave for.
saena, endorse, sign your name.
saense, science.
Saeprose, Cyprus.
šaetša, be negligent, blunder, be (rash) careless.
safari, safari.
saga, n., v., saw.
šaile, be insufficient.
sakatuku, handkerchief.
šako, (sako), area, district, compound.
šala, stay, remain; – **ne morago,** followed each other.
sala, saddle.
sale, saddle.
šalela, remain.
saletša, v., saddle.
salolla, unsaddle.
sama, rest the head.
samadikwe, dizziness, giddiness.
samela, place a pillow for.
samengwaga, perennial.
samente, cement.
sammaletee, simultaneous.
samme, relative, kin, brother.
samorago, the placenta (of a woman).
samphiše, tea or coffee.
samporele, umbrella.
samprele, umbrella.
sangwaga, annual.
šanka, straddle, limp; – **iša,** cause to straddle.
santlhoko, gall-bladder, gallsickness.

santše, still, yet.
šaparega, be in need, be poor.
šapha, strike, chop.
šapharega, be poor.
šapho, chopper, smithy, blacksmith's shop.
šaphunya, beat.
šarakana, mixed, confused.
sarasara, drip, drop.
saratine, sardine.
šarelwa, get faint, become lean.
saseletša, to set dogs at.
šašetša, sprinkle.
sasetša, set dogs at.
šataka, walk proudly.
šate, hurrah, hurray; **re** –, rejoice.
Sathane, Satan.
šatoga, change colour, bleach.
šatoša, change.
satšhene, sergeant.
savanna, savannah.
šaya, want, miss, lack.
se, neg., not.
šea, here they are.
seabelo, portion given.
seabo, subsidy, portion.
seagi, good builder, famous builder.
seahlama, stupid person, idiot.
seako, ear of corn.
seala, plume, tassel; **rweša** –, praise.
sealamedi, incubator.
seamuši, mammal.
seano, totem, object of veneration.
seanyi, suckling.
seaparankwe, chief.
seaparo, dress, clothing.
Searabia, Arabian.
searolo, quotient.
seatišo, product.
seatla, hand, assistant; – **kobong,** bribery, corruption.
seba, speak (evil) of, backbite, whisper evil of.
šeba, dem., here they are.
šeba, flavour, relish, eat as a titbit.
sebabo, itch, ulcer.
sebabole, sulphur.
sebaka, space of time, distance, occasion, chance, room, space, mediator.
sebakatšatši, cicada, Christmas-bee.
sebalamakgolo, turnpike-gate.
sebalwa, reading matter.
sebana, whisper.
sebapola, peg.
sebara, brother-in-law.
sebata, carnivorous animal, beast of prey; – **kgomo,** lion.
sebatana, beast of prey.
sebato, spattle.
sebe, sin.
sebeba, medicine bag.
sebeeletšo, pillion.
sebeelwa, something put aside for.
sebefedi, short-temperedness.
šebega, be eaten as a titbit.
sebegi, reporter of fame.
sebego, tribute, offering.
sebeka, cutlet, chop.
sebela, whisper (to), tell secretly.
sebele, personal(ly), self.
sebeo, stand, charm, candlestick.
šebešebe, peace, comfort.
sebešo, hearth, fire-place.
sebetani, wrestler.
sebete, liver, courage.
sebetli, carpenter of fame.
sebetša, weapon, arm.
šebetša, give a relish to.
sebeubeu, sternum, solar plexus.
sebiletšwa, the reason for being called.
sebino, dancer of fame.
sebino, totem.
sebipo, coverning.
sebja, dish, wife.
sebjalebjale, modern.
sebjalo, plant.
sebjana, mug, dish, vessel, adj., childlike.
sebjanatsopa, earthenware pot.
sebo, fortress, rampart.

seboa, threshing floor.
seboba, glad-fly, horse-fly, bluebottle.
sebodu, lazy person, sluggard, decay.
sebofiwa, prisoner.
sebofo, band, binder.
sebogedi, spectator.
sebogo, sight.
sebogodi, guard, watch.
seboi, baobab tree.
seboka, gathering, assembly.
seboko, worm.
sebolai, killer, murderer.
sebolang, organic.
sebolayakhunkhwane, insecticide.
seboledi, orator, maxim.
seboloki, keeper, protector.
sebontšhi, symptom.
sebopega, form, nature, shape; **wa** –, handsome.
sebudula, bladder.
sebušakapatla, tyrant.
sebutšwetšwa, aspirate.
šedi, care, here they are.
sediba, fountain, well, source.
sedika, curcumference, presbytery.
sedikadikwe, circle.
sedikiši, radius.
sediko, circle.
šedile, there they are.
sedimo, sacrificial animal (for idols).
šedio, there they are.
sediredi, agent.
sedirelwa, indirect object.
sediri, agent, expert, subject.
sedirišwa, instrument, agent.
sedirwa, object, direct object.
sediša, cause (help) to cross over, console.
seditsi, tuft, tassel.
sedukuduku, whirlwind, tornado.
sedulagae, one who stays at home.
seduledi, long waiting.
sedulo, a seat.
sedumaedi, anything making a thundering noise, a young lion, a meteor, tornado.
sedumedi, Christian belief.
sedupe, sedupi, diviner, magician.
seedi, light.
seela, liquid, discharge.
seelapula, rain-gauge.
seelo, measure.
seema, proverb, saying.
seemakamaoto, tall and well-built person.
seemo, standing, rank, nature.
seenywa, fruit.
seepamabitla, digger of graves.
seeta, shoe, boot, part of a plough.
seetša, light; **nyana,** little light.
seetse, back, of the head, occiput.
sefa, sift.
šefa, here it is, here you are.
sefabatho, generous person, altruist.
sefadi, scraper.
sefaga, necklace.
sefago, a vessel for drawing water.
sefahla, duet.
sefahlego, (sefahlogo), forehead, face, visage; **go senya** –, frown.
sefaka, forearm.
sefakana, ulna.
sefako, hail.
sefala, scaffolding, corn-bin, granary.
sefale, fihla le –, arrive in time.
sefalo, shard, scraper.
sefamakhura, accelerator.
sefane, surname.
sefanteu, strap (for tying the legs of a cow).
sefapahlogo, binder, crown, headdress.
Sefapane, Southern Cross.
sefapano, cross.
sefara, fork of a tree, shoot.
sefaro, lap, cob, shoot.
sefata, mountain pass, peg, cutting.
sefatodi, cut (lengthwise).
sefe, which; – **le** –, any, each.
sefebe, whore, prostitute.
sefega, chest.
sefegwana, clothes-hanger.

sefehlelo, churn.
sefeko, passage entrance.
sefela, hymn.
sefelathabo, carol.
sefelenyane, night-adder.
sefena, snout, muzzle.
sefenenyane, night-adder.
sefepi, whip.
sefero, passage, entrance, porch.
sefeufeu, windmill.
sefifi, carcase.
sefihlolo, breakfast.
sefinkisi, sphinx.
sefo, safe, sieve, strainer.
sefofanawatle, sea-plane.
sefofane, aeroplane.
sefofi, animal that flies.
sefofo, whirr-whirr, whirling toy.
sefofu, blind person or animal.
sefoka, flag, the tuft of a tail, symbol.
sefolakorong, threshing-machine, sheller.
sefolo, spattle for threshing.
sefolotšana, stillborn.
sefolotšane, abortive animal, stillborn.
sefororo, shrew.
sefoterata, wire-netting.
sefoto, bangle made of beads.
sefu, trap, snare.
sefudi, wild-duck, small species of locust.
sefudifudi, wild-duck.
sega, laugh, cut.
segadi, brave, bold or forward person.
segadikane, bigamy, quarrel.
segadikelo, frying-pan.
segae, civil.
segafa, mad person.
segagabi, reptile, creeping animal.
segagabo, their language, their custom.
segagane, measles, frost.
segageno, your language, your customs.
segagešo, our language, our customs.
segakanya, cut up, slice.
segalanko, nose-band.
segalo, accent, pitch, tone.
šegama, lose hope, become disheartened, be sad.
seganetšwa, something that is forbidden.
seganka, necklace, swagger.
segaswa, patch, rag.
segaswi, mad person.
segateledi, nightmare.
segatelo, wine-press.
segelela, carve, cut up.
segetla, shoulder-blade.
segiša, cause to laugh, ridicule.
segišago, ridiculous.
sego, calabash; **kgopela – sa meetse,** propose to a girl, **e** –, which is not.
segodišantšu, megaphone.
segoeledi, announcer.
šegofala, be blessed.
šegofatša, bless, consecrate.
segofiši, purgative.
segohlane, grater.
segokgo, spider.
segoko, spider.
segokolodi, millipede.
segola, lair, nest.
segole, cripple, deformed.
segole, slip-knot, loop, thong.
segolo, great, large, much; – **thata,** the most important.
segologolo, ancient, orthodox.
segopatsela, bull-doser.
segopo, dustpan, shovel.
segopodi, thinker.
segopodišo, reminder, memorial.
segopolo, remembrance.
segopolwa, abstract.
segopopuwe, mixture of boiled beans and porridge.
segopotšo, reminder, remembrance.
segoši, royal, kingly; **opa** –, royal salute.
segotetši, lighter, dynamo.
segotlo, backyard, court.

segotšane, species of hawk.
segwaba, insolent person.
segwagwa, frog, toad.
segwagwarapane, lizard.
segwahla, invalid, wreck, drudge.
segwai, methylated spirits.
segwana, small calabash.
segwanti, one who walks with a proud step.
segwapa, bundle of dried meat, biltong.
segwara, buffer (state).
segwaragwara, quail.
segwe, plot, intrigue.
segwebakabofêbê (segwebakamarago), prostitute.
segwegwe, frog, toad.
segwele, loop, bridoon.
segwera, friendship.
segwere, carrot, edible root.
segwete, edible root, bulb.
segwetšane, small yellow hawk.
sehebehebe, whispering.
Seheberu, pertaining to the Hebrews; the Hebrew language.
seheitene, heathenism.
sehla, cut with a string or wire, make a groove.
sehla, yellow, tawny, grey.
sehla, season.
sehlaba, sandy soil, plateau.
sehlabahlaba, terrace.
sehlabamagotlo, thistle.
seblabelo, sacrifice, offering.
sehlabi, pain.
sehlafala, become yellow or envious.
sehlaga, (bird's) nest.
sehlagala, rug, old clothes.
sehlagana, nest, pigeon-hole.
sehlagiši, generator.
sehlaka, hut, cabin.
sehlakahlaka, island.
sehlalefi, clever person.
sehlaletši, nursery-rhyme.
sehlalogantši, semantics.
sehlamo, apparatus.
sehlankana, habits of young men.
sehlano, five shillings.
sehlapelo, bath, basin, tub.
sehlare, tree, medicine.
sehlarekenywa, fruit-tree.
sehlašana, shrub.
sehlatšišo, emetic.
sehlee, re –, be yellow, faded or grey.
sehlefala, become yellow or faded.
sehlega, be indented.
sehloa, pinnacle.
sehlodimare, lla –, wail.
sehlogo, cruelty.
sehlogo, heading, title.
sehlokolathapo, gin (cotton).
sehlokomedi, caretaker.
sehlola, outcast, one held in taboo, prostitute.
sehlomamabone, lampstand.
sehlolwa, creature, thing created.
sehlomo, candlestick, stand, medal.
sehlong, small variety of (hedgehog) porcupine.
sehlongwa, appendix, annexure, suffix.
sehlopha, group, troop, company, drove.
sehlora, squirrel, plume, tassel, prize.
sehlotlola, bad character.
sehlotša, lame person, cripple.
sehlwamoriting, one who sits in the shade.
sehlwaseeme, statue.
sehuba, chest, cough, cold; – **se segolo,** tuberculosis, phthisis.
sehumula, gasp.
sehupaenke, fountain-pen.
sehuswana, goat or sheep.
sehuswane, goat or sheep.
sehutla, hump, hunch, hunchback.
sehwirihwiri, deceiver, cheat, fraud.
sei, silk.
seidibatši, drug.
seikgakanyo, mask.
seikokotlelo, crutch.
seila, taboo, hartred, dread.

seila, sail.
seinodi, kingfisher.
seipato, pretext, subterfuge, camouflage.
seipipo, veil, covering.
seipone, mirror, looking-glass.
seipuši, self-governor.
seišamadi, artery.
Seisimane, English (language).
seithati, egotist, dandy.
seitshwari, respectable, well-behaved person.
seiwane, epilepsy.
sejabana, elbow-bone.
sejagobe, glutton.
sejakane, Christian (-like).
sejakwane, door-frame.
sejanama, carnivore.
sejato, greedy person, miser.
sejedi, pest.
sejelo, crop, table.
seji, one who eats much, pest.
sejo, food.
sejokgolo, staple food.
sejosemela, plant food.
seka, semblance, sham, appearance, like.
seka, try a case, judge.
seka, become clear, pure, or clean.
seka, sign, token, emblem, idiom, position.
sekae, ke –? which language is it?
sekaelo, pattern.
sekafoko, phrase.
sekaku, ulcer.
sekala, balance, pair or scales, scale, ploughshore.
sekalata, scarlet.
sekama, be slanting, incline, slope.
sekamela, sit in the sun; be inclined towards.
sekamiša, influence, incline.
sekamišwa, be influenced.
sekamo, comb.
sekamodi, (sekamodu), rhizome.
sekanama, mushroom.
sekapalophatlo, improper fraction.
sekaseka, criticise.
sekata, rag.
sekatumanoši, semi-vowel.
sekayo, mincing machine.
sekebeka, brigand, highwayman.
sekega, be or become pure.
sekeekee, sega –, laugh heartily.
sekela, sickle.
sekele, sickle.
sekeletša, cut in a circle, cut round.
sekelfere, dandruff.
sekene, ship, boat.
sekerete, cigarette.
sekero, (a pair of) sciccors, shears.
sekerosenke, plate-shears.
sekete, tousand.
sekete, a pound.
sekete, what-d'ye-call-it.
seketša, economise, retrench.
seketswana, small boat.
sekga, space, period, distance.
sekgabane, decoration.
sekgabetla, scale.
sekgabišo, ornament.
sekgaga, bulb (of a plant).
sekgala, space.
sekgalabjana, little old man.
sekgalabje, old man, like an old man, pertaining to an old man.
sekgalaka, eczema.
sekgalela, noon, midday.
sekgao, division, section.
sekgapa, zither, stringed musical instrument, bow.
sekgapetla, scale.
sekgatla, hilt of a knife.
sekgauswi, vicinity, nearness.
sekgawana, small division.
sekgelana, piece, bit, small rag.
sekgepetla, scale, shard.
sekgero, person without teeth.
sekgethwa, holy.
sekgoba, space, gap, area; adj., slavish.

sekgobana, small hole/opening or gap.
sekgogo, like a fowl; **go tsorama** –, to perch like a fowl.
sekgohlwana, young child, little fellow.
sekgonyo, lock, bolt.
sekgonyollo, key.
sekgopha, aloe, sisal.
sekgopi, dregs, offence.
sekgopišo, stumbling-block.
sekgoši, back part of the head.
sekgothi, back part of the head.
sekgotlelwa, mixture of porridge and milk.
sekgotlo, poker.
sekgotse, friendship.
sekgoto, rump, chine.
Sekgowa, Afrikaans, European civilisation.
sekgwa, jungle, forest.
sekgwakgwa, epilepsy.
sekgwama, purse, petty cash.
sekgwari, neat person.
sekgwebakamarago, prostitute.
sekgwekgwe, gizzard.
sekhafo, plane.
sekhu, ambush, trap, elbow.
sekhuba, chest, breast, cold; – **se segolo,** consumption, phthisis.
sekhukhu, insect, moss.
sekhukhune, a stealthy creeper.
sekhulare, circular.
sekhumula, sob.
sekhurumelo, lid.
sekhutamoya, suffocation.
sekhutlo, angle, termination.
sekhwama, purse.
sekhwękhwe, gizzard.
sekhwi, this.
sekila, gizzard.
sekiša, summon, sue, charge.
seko, sense-organ.
sekobo, ugly person.
sekobonyane, smallpox.
sekodi, spot, vice, blemish, defect.
sekoka, invalid.
sekokotla, hero, hardy person.
sekolo, school.
sekolobotane, head over heels.
sekolokotele, cotton-reel.
sekološa, cut round, plough leaving patches.
sekoloto, debt.
sekomakomane, silence.
sekomana, secret.
sekomanakomana, silence.
sekomanyana, a game.
sekome, roast corn.
sekontiri, tar.
sekontshe, scone.
sekopelo, brooch, hoe, piece of broken pot.
sekopo, shovel.
sekotlelo, basin, dish.
sekotlelopulugu, disc-plough.
sekotšho, check (material.)
sekripola, scribbler.
Sekriste, Christianity, Christian.
sekudumetša, sudorific.
sekuki, elevator, crane.
sekurufi, crew.
sekutara, scooter.
sekutu, stump, boil, abscess.
sekutwana, little stump; **gama kgomo** –, milk a cow without a calf.
sekwala, neat person.
sekwapi, peel, shell, bark.
sekwaše, squash.
sekwatelo, a stick for driving away a calf.
sekwato, see: **sekwatelo.**
sekwele, gentleman.
sekwelemi, spoil-sport, wet-blanket.
sekwere, square.
sekwerefutu, square foot.
sekwerejarata, square yard.
sekwerenoko, square inch.
sekwi, hiding place, sense-organ.
sela, hunt for food, buy food.
sela, cross, ford a stream pass over.
sela, se-class, that yonder.

selabe, (selabi), fly, any little thing in the eye.
selaganya, jump across.
selagapale, abattoir.
selageng, butcher's shop.
selai, lettuce, slice.
selalaporo, sleeper.
selalelo, supper, evening meal; – **se se Kgethwa,** Sacrament of the Lord's Supper, holy communion.
selamoledi, intercessor, redeemer.
selamolelwa, redeemed.
selao, lair, harbour.
selaodi, one who uses divining bones.
selaolane, pupa.
selapološi, stimulant.
selara, cellar.
selata, slavish, slavishly.
sele, bo-, ga-, softly, slowly.
šele, here it is.
šele, foreign, different, strange.
sele, cell, sale.
selebana, go ba –, be in sight.
selebaneng, opposite to.
selebeši, memory.
seledu, chin, beard.
selee, oval.
selefa, remuneration, pay, compensation.
selefo, fine.
selega, (can) be crossed, fordable.
selegae, civil.
selei, sledge.
seleiti, slate.
seleka, be naughty, worry, annoy; – **ile,** annoyed.
selekanyi, an instrument for measuring.
selekanyo, measurement, measure.
selekega, be worried.
selela, cross over to.
selela, buy food for.
selema, crooked horns, outstretched horns.
Selemela, the constellation of the Pleiades.
selemo, spring, early summer.
šeleng, shilling.
šeleo, dem., there it is.
selepe, axe.
selepere, slipper.
selepšana, small axe, hatchet.
selešo, poison.
selete, region.
seletši, good musician.
seletšo, musical instrument.
seletswana, small axe.
selewa, something edible.
sellallane, cry-baby.
sello, cry, lament, complaint; – **sa go (felegetša mohu) biletša dira malaong,** tattoo.
selo, thing.
seloba, tribute.
seloga, bubble up, simmer.
selogelo, (selogi), loom.
seloka, stick-grass.
seloko, loam.
selomi, a thing that bites, gripes, vermin.
selopi, sugar-bird.
selopo, trunk.
selopo, pillow-case.
selwanatsoko, an unnamed thing.
selwelwa, cause of strife.
selwi, fighter.
sema, consider, innovate.
semakatšo, wonder.
semamatletšo, sticking-plaster.
semana, beehive in a rock.
semangmang, so and so, a certain person.
sematla, pancake.
sematlafatši, tonic, stimulant, index, exponent.
sematlane, fast messenger.
semela, plant.
semelo, character, nature, instinct.
semene, semen.
semenya, curvature (spinal), ditch, donga.
semetlana, half a bottle of brandy.

semmejana, bust-bodice.
semmutlana, small hare.
semodimo, godly, divine.
semosebe, arrow-shaped.
semotho, human.
semoti, bush-baby.
semotšhene, mechanical.
semotwane, boiled grain and beans.
sempara, slang.
semphekgo, ka –, vice versa.
sempotobotwane, blindman's buff.
semumaleboto, telephone.
semumu, mute, dumb person.
šena, show one's teeth, be angry.
šena, – go, when, after.
sena, dem., this.
senagangwa, abstract.
senakangwedi, glow-worm, fire-fly.
senamelwa, vehicle, carriage.
senama, a small variety of frog.
senanatswii, a tree-frog.
senate, senate.
senatla, hero, brave and strong person.
sene, quartet(te).
senei, slice.
senene, slight, little, bit.
senepe, snap.
seng, not, otherwise.
seng, adj., one, other; – **le seng,** every one, everything.
seng, – sa bona, among themselves.
sengaka, medical certificate.
sengalo, relapse, bruise.
sengamelo, clasp.
senganga, obstinate person, one who likes to contradict.
sengange, obstinate person.
sengangela, obstinate, foolhardy person.
sengejane, left-handed person.
sengetse, back of the head.
sengwa, be considered.
sengwadi, famous writer.
sengwalwa, manuscript.
senka, search, look for, seek.
senkane, friendship.
Senkatawana, Boy of Sotho legend.
senke, zinc, galvanised iron.
senkgane, Mexican marigold, khaki-bush.
senkgankgane, khaki-bush.
senkgwa, bread.
senkhu, big flat bush.
senkwakwara, species of locust, "reënsprinkaan".
senna, manliness; adj., manly.
sennasegolo, iron on top of a house.
senno, seat.
seno, drink, beverage.
seno, just, after, as soon as.
senoga, be revealed, become manifest.
senoge, diviner, enchanter.
senoko, incense, perfume, internode.
senokwane, fraud, rogue.
senola, reveal, bring to light.
senomorula, wood-pecker.
senono, stalk near the ear (of corn).
senonwane, fabulous.
senopodi, person elect.
senoša, cause to reveal.
senotagi, alcoholic drink.
senotlelo, key.
sente, cent, perfume.
sentebale, forget-me-not.
senthulwane, waves that come rolling along, hornless cow.
sentikereiti, centigrade.
sentimetara, centimetre.
sentseretsere, cricket (the insect).
sentshwe, boil, carbuncle.
senwabolopi, sugar-bird, sunbird, honey-sucker.
senwana, thimble.
senwedi, bog, mudhole, diver.
senwelo, drinking vessel, cup.
senya, spoil, destory, damage; – **dipolelo,** scold, curse; – **hlegere,** trial and error.
senyakwa, demand.
senyalo, stain, wrinkle.
senyane, small; num, adj., nine.

senye, bladder.
senyedimi, rayon.
senyega, become bad, be spoiled.
senyegelwa, suffer a loss.
seo, dem., that.
seojana, small ant-hill.
seoka, champion, a large powerful animal.
seokgo, spider.
seokgola, elbow.
seokobatši, narcotic.
seokodiba, lake country abouding in water.
seokolela, heartburn.
seolo, antheap.
seološo, winnowing machine.
seorelo, incense.
seota, big animal.
seotli, ruminant.
seotlo, symbol, (heap of stones).
seotsela, sleepy person.
seotswa, a lewd woman, adulteress.
šeowe, dem., there it is.
sepaapaa, lizard, blue-headed lizard.
sepaketi, spaghetti.
sepalaka, splint.
sepale, sepal.
sepalete, pin.
sepapetla, flat thing.
sepataganyi, clip, clamp.
sepate, clip.
sepatšhe, wallet.
sepe, tšea ka –, trip.
sepediša, cause to walk, walk quickly, give reins to passions; – **ana,** walk together.
sepediša, – **bonokwane,** swindle, cheat; – **bošokašaka,** be proud, headstrong; – **bokgekema,** be wilful.
sepeke, bacon.
sepela, walk, roam, travel.
sepele, spelling, spelling book.
sepete, spade.
sepetlele, hospital.
sepeu, spore, embryo.
sephaka, forearm.
sephanta, fool-hardy person.
sephaphapha, windmill.
sephara, wide, broad.
sephedi, living thing.
sephemo, shield, breast-shield.
sephetho, result.
sephiri, secret, secret place.
sephohla, group.
sephoko, leader at a dance, wordy person, calabash.
sephoromootlwa, butcher-bird.
sephotlwa, pod.
sephumolo, duster, towel.
sephutha, parcel.
sephuthelo, wrapper.
sepikiri, nail.
sepinasi, spinach.
sepiniše, spinach.
sepipetše, cover, covering.
sepitša, partiality, bias.
sepoko, ghost.
sepoo, pertaining to a bull.
sepoomootlwa, butcher-bird.
seporing, spring.
seporo, railway.
sepšhatlapšhatlane, chicken-pox.
sera, troop, army.
sera, boil, simmer, teem with flies.
serafe, tribal.
serafime, seraphim.
seragamabje, catapult.
serakalala, one who stands firm.
serakamafelo, penultimate.
serakela, first-born.
serala, scaffold, platform in the lands, stage.
seralwa, drawing.
serantlatla, many huts.
serapa, small garden, graveyard.
serapo, oar.
serathana, tiny tot.
serati, lover.
seratlatla, many huts, big village.
sereba, sterile ewe.
seregana, autumn.
serekelele, extensive, big.

erekereke, jelly, sauce.
eremo, chopping, anything chopped off; **go ya seremong,** going to the end.
erena, lordly, sovereignty.
ereo, trap.
erepudi, step, stair.
eretala, raw material.
erethe, heel; – **sejasekgothi,** flee.
erethe, inferior wife of a polygamist.
eretla, pula ya –, deluge.
eretlo, madness.
eretlwe, convulsion.
ereto, poem, recitation, praisename.
eretse, clay, mud.
eriba, protruding forehead, bank, overhanging rock.
eripa, part, half; – **sa gare,** half; – **sa mmolelo,** part of speech; – **sa bone,** quarter.
eripadikota, instrument for cutting trees.
eripagare sa iri, half an hour.
eripairi, half an hour.
eripathale, pair of pliers.
erithene, quarterly return.
erithi = **seriti,** personality; **ntšha** –, humiliate.
eriti, personality, shadow, ghost.
eroba, stick, big stick.
eroba, hole, hollow, nest, stick.
erobalela, accommodation.
robe, hen's nest, fold, kraal.
erobele, sparrow.
erokamelo, peak, elevation.
rokola, calamus, a medicinal herb.
rokolo, bud, excreta of a goat.
rokolo, small garden, vegetable garden.
rokolo, a herb used as a purgative or for whooping-cough.
rolane, yellow colour, small variety of bitter-apple (solanaceae).
role, heifer.
rolo, bush-buck.

Seroma, pertaining to the Roman Church.
seroma, gym, gymnastic costume.
seromo, something desirable.
serope, buttock, thigh, second wife of a chief.
seropela, tee (golf); base (basefall).
serota, brackish soil.
serota, the hump of an ox.
seroto, basket, measure, yield, price.
seroto, industrious person, diligent person.
serotobolo, dome.
serotswana, small thigh.
serotwana, small basket.
serre, children of one father.
serua, rotten egg.
seruiwa, domestic animal.
serumula, torch, fire-brand.
serumulane, disturber of peace.
serunya, mole (animal.)
serurubele, butterfly, moth.
serurugi, swelling.
seruthufatši (seruthetši), heater.
serutwa, subject.
seruthwane, spring.
seša, stump, a projecting root.
sesa, move along, drag, swim, continue until day-break.
sesaboleng, inorganic.
sesadi, pertaining to a woman, feminine.
sešalagae, one who remains at home.
sešana, stump; – **sa basadi,** women's secret.
sešane, see: **sešana.**
sesasedi, whirlwind.
sešate, royal, protocol.
sese, thin, fine.
sese, here it is.
sešeba = **sešebo.**
sešebo, relish, titbit, tasty morsel.
sesedi, stalk-borer.
sesefalo, a growing thin.
sesegi, cutworm.
sešego, large grain-basket, elevator.

sešegwana, small basket.
seseka, crossing of the legs; **fera** –, cross the legs.
sesela, trail, pass over, scud, run about (as a dog on a scent).
selele, Cape badger, rattle.
seselela, go in search of.
sesella, loiter.
sesenyi, sinner, waster, pest, criminal.
sesepe, (sešepe), soap.
sesepedi, ring-worm.
šešerekanya (maoto), cross the legs, upset.
sesesedi, whirlwind.
sešimane, (sty of the eye), boyish.
seširaphefo, wind-break.
sešireletšo, protection, shelter, curtain.
seširo, covering, veil, curtain, blind.
seso, black.
sešo, aux. v., not yet, our(s).
sešo, ulcer, abcess, tumour, boil.
sešoba, full bulging bag.
sesohlo, cud, chew.
sesola, share, portion (of food dished up).
sašomi, artisan, craftsman.
sesolana, titbit, tasty morsel.
sesolo, bye (cricket).
sešoro, se-class, cruel, fierce.
Sesotho, Suto language, customs, etc.
sesothwana, omasum, manyplies.
sešu, dropping of a cow, dung.
sešuana, n., orphan; adj., like an orphan.
sešunkwane, aromatic shrub.
sešupanako, watch, clock.
sešupatsela, signpost.
sešupetšo, specimen.
sešupo, sign, indicator, pointer, testimony, specimen.
seswai, n., branch for extinguishing fire, sod; num. adj., eight.
seswantšho, photo, portrait, image, parable, **modimo wa** –, idol.
seta, carve, cut into.
setaele, style.
setafo, material.
setafonote, staff-notation.
setagi(ši), drug.
setagwa, drunkard.
setala, steel, stable; adj., indigenous, old.
setarata, street.
sete, set.
setee, unanimous, one, as one; **retha** –, be in step.
seteisele, starch.
seteišene, station, railway-station; – **sa mohlagase,** power-station.
setekeng, in pursuit.
seteletele, terrace.
Setemmere, September.
setempe, stamp.
setena, brick.
setene, stand, plot.
setepa, skin worm by women, skin-apron.
setepe, steppe.
seterata, street.
setereke, district.
sethabišabanna, beer.
sethaka, friendship, uniform.
sethakga, neat person, artist, gentleman.
sethala, scaffold, stage.
sethalamola, ruler.
sethalamoyeng, glider.
sethaledi, stylus.
sethalo, plain (of a building), drawing.
sethalwa, figure, drawing.
sethalwathalwa, sketch.
sethata, solid.
sethebe, mat place under the grinding stone.
sethekgo, support, banister.
sethekhu, hiccup, hiccoughs.
sethibatsela, barricade, roadblock.
sethibelo, barrier, stopper.
sethibo, stopper, cork.

sethiko, a uniting against, a concentrated effort.
sethitho, perspiration, sweat.
setho, human, human nature.
setho, limb, member, organ.
sethobolo, ash-heap.
sethobošo, brooch, safety-pin.
ethogothogo, moisture, sweat.
ethojana, young female animal, small heifer.
ethokgolo, talisman, knucklebone, grave of a chief.
ethokgwa, forest, bush.
ethole, heifer.
etholo, deaf (person).
ethopa, pig-sty.
ethopša, captive.
ethosa, the Xhosa language, customs, etc.
ethosana, shawl.
ethotho, idiot, dunce.
ethotswala, reproductive organ.
ethubaki, bomber.
ethudi, smith, a smith of fame.
ethulo, tool.
ethunya, gun.
ethwahla, press-stud.
etilo, sidestepping, avoiding.
etimamabone, lamp snuffer.
timamollo, fire-extinguisher, the principal wife of a chief.
timela, train, engine, locomotive.
tla, stamp, beat, pound.
tlaela, fool.
tlamafatši, index.
tlamo, resolution, decree.
tlankana, (setlankane), slip, counterfoil.
tlanyi, typewriter.
tlapele, ring-worn.
tlatla (setlatle), fool.
tlatlana, bag, basket.
tlatlabje, bustard.
tlela, v., anchor.
tlemo, binding, contract.
tlišamadi, vein.
setlišampholo, virus.
setlogo, origin.
setlogolo, grandchild.
setlolo, ointment, salve.
setlwaedi, custom.
setlošwa, minuend.
setofo, stove.
Setoitšhi, German.
setološi, solvent.
setološwa, solution.
setolotolo, Jewish-harp.
setongwane, share.
setontolo, stringed musical instrument.
setopamonwana, charm to prevent theft.
setopo, dead body, corpse.
setopo, stop sign.
setopša, boiled beans and fat.
setoropo, strap.
setoto, dead body, corpse.
setša, pay attention to, pardon.
setša, have mercy, pity, give seed to.
setšaba, hole, burrow.
šetše, aux. v., already; remained.
setšeamoyeng, receiver (radio).
setsekana, rag, tatter.
setsebi, one who knows.
setšema, project.
setsebitsebi, authority.
setseretsere, cricket.
setsetse, species of wild-cat.
setsha, site.
setšhaba, nation, tribe, people.
setšhabelo, refuge.
setšhelete, coin.
setšhelo, container.
setšhep(h)i, well-dressed person, dandy.
setšhoša, fright; **go rwala** –, frighten.
setsiba, crupper, drawer worn by men, patch; **bana ba** –, children of one father; – **sa bošoboro,** foreskin.
setšidifatši, refrigerator.
setšo, origin.
setsomi, hunter of fame.

setsopa, China (ware), porcelain.
setšu, elbow.
setšwa, be favoured.
setšwabadi, blister.
setswako, mixture.
setswalelo, stopper, lid, gate.
setswalle, friendship.
setswata, scar, stain, spot.
setswatswa, neat person.
setsweletšo, product.
Setswetla, the Venda (language) customs.
setswetši, (place of) confinement.
setu, silence; adj., silent.
setudi, cow which gives little milk.
setulo, chair, seat.
setumo, reputation, fame, notoriety.
setupamuši, (setupišamuši), chimney.
setutukanta, hem, binding.
seupo, preventive, insectifuge.
seuši, stumbling-block.
seuta, something mouldy, bad or rotten.
sewa, epidemic.
sewainara, alarm clock.
sewelabatho, faith.
sewelo, change, hap, coincidence.
sewelwa, incident.
sewewe, someone who talks nonsense.
seyamaleng, food.
seyantlo, custom by which a man marries his deceased wife's sister, step.
šia, leave behind, outrun, fear.
šiana, run, race.
šiba, cover up a hole, plug.
šiba, here they are.
šibolla, (šibula), remove, open up.
šidila, iron, polish, scour, rub.
šidilla, exercise.
šiela, leave for.
šielana, take turns in doing, leave to one another.
sihla, fall down, slide down.
šiiša, frighten.
šiišago, frightening.
šika, go parallel with, go along.
šikara, bear, carry, sling over the shoulders: **šikere,** has slung over the shoulders.
sikara, cigar.
sikarete, cigarette.
šikarolla, lay down a burden.
šikinya, shake, propose.
šikiša, cause to go along, help along.
šila, grind, digest.
silibera (silifera), silver.
silibo, silvo.
silika, (siliki), silk.
silikosese, silicosis.
siling, ceiling.
silintere, cylinder.
šilofala, become foolish.
šilofatša, confound, make foolish.
šimega, be roasted on a spit.
šimela, roast meat on a spit.
šimolla, begin.
sinagoge, synagogue.
šinama, close the mouth.
sinki, sink.
šinoga, stand aside, make way.
sinonime, synonym.
šinyalala, pull faces.
šiphula, crumble, walk in wet sand.
šipola, smoothen a clay-pot.
šira, shade, obscure one's view.
sirapu, syrup.
širega, be or become shaded.
širela, insure, hide, screen; **šireleditšwego,** protected.
šireletša, screen, defend, shield.
šireletšago, protecting.
široga, stand aside, move.
širogela, move to, retire to.
širologa, become (uncovered) unveiled.
šiša, give much milk, spout out, be moved; – **pelo,** sigh.
šišibala, be quiet, shudder.
šišimala, be silent, be afraid, shudder
šišimiša, cause to shudder.
šišimoga, coy, shudder, be startled.

šišimoša, startle, cause to shudder, frighten.
šišingwa, be shaken, be proposed.
šišinya, shake, propose.
šišinyega, tremble, vibrate.
šišinyetšwa, be nominated for.
sistere, sister, nun.
šita, be too difficult, for, be impossible, surpass your strength.
šitana, quarrel, argue.
šitanya, cause to (quarrel) disagree.
site, seat.
šitega, be (unable) impossible.
sitere, zither.
sitere, watering-can.
šitiša, prevent, impede, hamper.
itša, rad., cut, give.
itwa, be unable.
iwa, be outrun.
o, black.
o, here he is, here she is.
oba, pinch.
obane, forst; **ka** –, early.
obela, go under, set, disappear.
obelela, go under completely.
obeletše, be deeper than/submerged.
oboka, arrest.
odiša, cause to reprimand.
oga, cure skins, make supple.
ogo, truant; **roba** –, play truant.
ohla, break through, slip through, tresspass.
ohla, chew; – **taba,** discuss an affair.
ohlola, take a child off the back.
ohlomela, fall into, walk through grass, bushes or reeds.
oka, shock, twist.
oka, drive (cattle), stir, move.
okela, screw, tighten, fasten.
okela, have pity on, be merciful or lenient to; **šokelwa,** be pardoned.
okolla, turn (back), convert.
okologa, be converted, turn round.
okwa, be in labour; – **ke mala,** suffer from a pain in the stomach, colic.
sola, reprimand, scold, blame; **itshola,** blame oneself.
sola, serve up, dish up: **solela,** serve up for.
sola, cast the skin or the winter hair, polish, brush.
šola(a), there he (she) is.
solanka, while, meanwhile.
šole, there he (she) is.
solega, reprehensible.
solela, serve up for.
solfa, solfa.
solloro, garet, loft.
solo, solo.
sologa, flow out.
Solomone, Solomon.
solotera, solder, forge, weld.
šoma, labour, work; **šomela boroko,** work without pay; – **etše,** has worked for.
soma, tell, introduce, hem, accuse.
someng, decimal.
šomiša, use; – **wa,** be used; – **etša,** use for; **šomišetšwa,** be used for.
somo, seam, hem.
sona, it.
sonata, sonata.
šongwa, be worked, be laboured.
šono, here he (she) is.
sonopolomo, sunflower, helianthus.
sonta, become immune; **sontiša,** v., render immune, immunise.
šoo, time! (in games).
sootho, adj., dark brown.
šopa, twist, apply a tourniquet.
šopha, twist.
sopo, soup.
sora, sip, drink.
šoro, cruel, violent.
šorofalela, become angry with.
šoro(k)gohlo, id., **go wa** –, collapse, fall in.
sorokisi, circus.
soromela, sleep in the porch (entrance).

šošobana, (šošoba), frown, becomes wrinkled, shrink, creased; **šošobanya,** caus., frown, wrinkle; – **tsebe,** turn a deaf ear.
sosopane, saucepan.
sota, soda.
sotela, come near, approach; **sotetša,** caus., bring near.
šothi, shorts.
šotla, mock, tease.
šotolela, turn the back on, turn away from.
šotše, has dished up.
souso, gravy, sauce.
soutile, be immune.
soutiša, immunise.
soya, (dinawa), soya beans.
speaker, speaker.
spikara, speaker.
šuduba, rub between the thumb and the forefinger, take a pinch.
šuhla, encroach, destroy, lay waste.
sukumetša, push, shove.
šukunyetša, hide.
šulafala, become tasteless or unpleasant.
šulela, render tasteless.
šunya, flee into a forest, slip in; – **nko,** turn up one's nose, sneer at.
šunyalala, sneer at, turn up one's nose.
šunyama, be exhausted.
šunyula, bribe.
šupa, point at, indicate with the finger.
šupeletša, threaten.
šupetša, demonstrate, point out.
suphafosofate, super phosphate.
šupiša, demonstrate.
šupolla, bring forth something hidden.
šupologa, jump out of bed.
šuputša, grovel, wallow.
šušubana, see: **šošobana.**
šušumetša, push, urge.
šutela, move nearer.
šutha, draw aside, get out of the way; **šuthelela,** make room for. **šuthela,** move up, shift; **šuthiša,** cause to draw aside, postpone.
šutša, puff, simmer, bubble.
šutšologa, blow off, despair.
sutu, suit.
sutukheisi, suitcase.
sutuoli, salad oil.
swa, burn, be destroyed by fire.
šwa, be sleepy.
swaba, be sad, fade, frown; **swabiša,** cause to be sad, grieve.
swaela, mark or brand for, set apart for.
sweatša, give a portion to.
šwahla, make a rustling noise, break through.
šwahlane, twilight, dusk.
šwahlela, attack, break through, invade.
swai, file.
swaiša, divide the haul between the hunters.
šwalalana, be scattered.
šwalalanya, scatter, disperse, destroy.
šwalane, twilight, dusk.
swalo, go re –, pass quickly.
swana, look like, resemble, be alike.
swana, a black cow, black.
swanela, be fitting, be in order, be suitable; – **wa ke,** have to.
swanelago, fitting.
swanetše, ought to, must, shall.
swantšha, compare, liken, portray.
swantšha, photograph, make a portrait or a picture, paint or draw.
swanyane, rumour.
šwapašwapela, wrap up.
swara, (swere), hold, take hold of, seize, capture; – **gabotse,** take care of.
swaragana, be in contact.
swaraganya, join together.
swarela, forgive.
swarelala, hold tight.

swariša, cause to take hold of, assist, aid, help to do.
swaswa, jest, joke or sport.
šwašwamolla, pull out.
swatela, approach.
swatetša, bring near.
swaya, mark, brand, **tsebe,** prick the ear.
swele, deliberately on purpose, wilful; **go sepediša** –, be petulant.
swele, has burnt.
swenya, turn up one's nose, sneer at.
swere, has seized.
šwetašweta, hide, dodge, take shelter.
šwetše, lost.
šweu, white.
šweufala, become white.
šweufatša, whiten, bleach.
swiela, sweep, lose.
swii, rad., **go re** –, be very black, sleep tight.
swikiri, sugar.
swina, have a good crop or harvest.
swine, – **hle,** serves you right.
swinya, dive, eat secretly.
swiri, lemon.
Switzerland, Switzerland.

T

ta, go re –! end off, finish.
taamane, diamond; – **pewa,** diamond, deposit.
Taamane, Kimberley.
taba, matter, affair, business.
taba, jump across, mix snuff.
tabataba, theme.
tabe, go re –, to jump over, jump up.
tabela, walk across a beam, rope-dancing, tight-rope walking.
tabenakele, tabernacle.
taboga, to jump (over), fun fast.
tabola, hit, tear off, pass quickly, snatch.
tabolo, tearing, rent.
tadi, mouse.
tadiletša, (mahlo), stare at.
teake, dike, dyke.
taele, dial.
taelano, farewell.
taelo, order, instruction, charge, command.
taemane, diamond.
taenamo, dynamo.
taepitsi, diabetes.
taerea, diarrhoea.
taese, dice.
tafola, table.
taga, shine, glitter, intoxicate.
tagafala, tagafara, summon, subpoena.
tagafatša, glorify.
tagi, alcohol.
tagilwe, be drunk.
tagwa, be intoxicated.
tahlegelo, loss.
tahlego, perdition, ruin, loss, doom.
tahlo, loss, forsaking, rejection.
taitai, (tsebe ya –**),** a deaf ear.
taka, white-wash; mortar.
takaletšo, wishing for.
takataketša, (mahlo), look about.
takatšego, desirability.
takatšo, wish, longing, desire.
taki, crayon.
takumela, flare up.
t'ala, old.
ta'la, green, blue, raw.
talafetšego, antiquated.
talane, unripe Kaffir-corn.
talee, be very green (blue).
talelo, an ambush, a stratagem.
talente, talent.
taletšo, invitation.
tama, go re –, to greet.
tamalala, persevere, go straight on.
tamiša, pay tribute, bribe, greet, draw lots.
tamoga, stretch.
tamola, squeeze out, stretch out.

tamolla, stretch out.
tamolo, deliverance, liberation, rescue.
tampa, abundantly.
tampa, crush, walk slowly.
tampela, play, hop.
tampelele, hopscotch.
tanamaete, dynamite.
tangwa, go letša –, curse (with a click of the tongue).
tanka, tank.
tantela, wind (up or round).
tantšha, cause to grip, grasp.
tantšwe, be caught, be trapped.
tanya, catch, tighten, put in a vice, grip, trap.
tanyolla, free.
tao, commandment, precept, rule.
tao, lair.
taodišo, essay, composition, expounding, narrative.
taodišophelo, biography.
taola, knuckle-bone (such as used by witch-doctors).
taolelo, mandate, predestination.
taolo, command, authority, control, order.
taologa, melt.
taolophulo, control of pasturage.
taong, outside.
tapa, become insipid.
tapeiti, carpet.
tapetilwe, made listless.
tapile, be tasteless.
tapišego, weariness.
tapišo, fatigue.
tapo, weariness, exhaustion.
tapola, potato.
tapologo, rest.
tapološo, refreshment, resting.
tasalala, stretch, lie, outstretched.
taselpomo, shaft, pole of a cart.
tata, father; **tatago,** your father; **tatabo,** their father.
tata, wind.
tatagana, clasp, embrace.
tatag(w)e, his (her) father.
tataila, learn to walk.
tataiša, (– tsebe), train the ear.
tataišo, training.
tatamolebo, tendril.
tatamologa, stretch.
tatamoloko, wart.
tatampua, blister.
tatasela, tremble.
tate, father.
tatela, wind (round), bandage.
tatelanonako, chronological order.
tatelano ya mabaka, sequence of tenses.
tatelo, following.
tatetša, wind, spin.
tatolla, unwind.
tatolo, denial.
tau, lion; **tawana,** lion cub; – **gadi,** lioness; – **tona,** male lion (praises of a chief); **go swara – ka mariri,** catch the bull by the horns.
te, tena or **teng,** adj., naughty.
te, id., nice.
teana, strike against each other, clash.
teba, be deep, sink.
teba (dikgeru), make the teeth chatter.
teba (lwala), sharpen a millstone.
tebalelo, forgiveness, pardon.
tebalo, forgetfulness, omission, a forgetting.
tebela, strike, jib, discolour.
tebelelo, expectation.
tebelo, watch, care.
tebetebe, midst.
tebo, aim, purpose, grindstone.
tebogelo, congratulations.
tebogo, thanksgiving, gratitude.
tedu, beard, whisker.
tee, one.
tefa, be nice; n., payment.
tefelabodulo, (house) rent.
tefelanaga, land tax.
tefelo, ransom, payment; **–pele,** imprest.
tefelomorwalo, rate of freight.

tefelotshenyegelo, payment of compensation.
tefetšo, recompense, revenge, retribution.
tefišo, a fine.
tefo, price, payment, paying.
tega, drop, fall.
tege, dough.
teigi, harness.
teka, lay the table.
tekanawatle, sea-level.
tekanelo, orderly, regular.
tekano, sufficient.
tekanyetšo, estimate, balance, copy.
tekanyo, moderation, rate, measure.
tekema, stagger, totter.
tekemela, stagger.
tekesela, swagger reel.
tekesetša, sling.
teketli, pendulum.
tekisi, taxi.
tekniki, (thekniki), technical.
teko, a trial, an effort, temptation.
tekolla, remove dishes.
tekolo, inspection, cognisance.
teku, swing.
tekumela, swing.
tela, give up, renounce.
tele, a neat person, dandy.
teledimo, poisonous tulip.
telefišo, lengthening.
teleko, expulsion, exile.
telele, long, tall, high.
telo, a cry, a bleat.
telo, renouncement, a giving up.
tema, draw lots.
tema, paragraph, plot, passage.
temalo, habit, custom.
temana, verse.
tematheto, stanza.
temekiša, conjugate.
temekišo, conjugation.
temepedi, two-faced person.
temo, agriculture.
temogo, observation, recognition.
temokrasi, democracy.
temoši, signal.
temošo, warning.
tempa, frank, put on a stamp.
tempele, temple.
tena, (tenne), tire out, disgust, be repugnant to.
tenega, become tired out, become disgusted.
teng, inside.
tengkhwibidu (tengkhubedu), dysentery.
tennwe, b. disgusted/tired.
tenola, expand (the chest), bend backwards.
tenta, make supple, sun slowly.
tente, tent.
tentega, be made supple.
tentera, tender.
tentere, n., tender.
teori, theory.
tepa, skirt, gather much.
tepe, bird-lime; adj., soft, sticky.
tepelela, become discouraged, tired.
tepo, turn off or away.
tepoga, turn aside.
tepogela, turn off to.
terama, drama.
teramo, drum (tin).
terapi, therapy.
terase, terrace.
terebe, grape.
tereka, to iron.
terekere, tractor.
terempe, tram.
terentšhe, bridoon, loop-strap.
terepenteine, turpentine.
terila, drill.
terofolo, trowel.
terompeta, trumpet.
terone, throne.
teronko, gaol, prison.
teseke, desk.
teselepomo, pole of a wagon or cart, shaft.
teselo, pardon, forgiveness.
tesetšo, pardon.

tesimale, dicimal.
tesimetara, decimetre.
Testamente ya Kgale, the Old Testament; – **e Mpsha,** the New Testament.
teta, surround, encircle, emit.
teteana, be dense, compact.
teteano, density.
tetelo, delay, expectation.
tetema, shake, tremble.
tetemetša, cause to tremble.
tetesela, tremble.
tetlego, prosperity.
teu, a rope for leading a team.
teye, tea.
thaabe, hiccough.
thaba, mountain.
thaba, be glad, rejoice, be cheerful.
thabamollo, volcano.
thabe, a branch, tributary, subordinate clause.
thabela, rejoice over.
thabile, be glad or healthy.
thabiša, entertain.
thabo, joy, pleasure.
thaele, tile.
thaetlele, title.
thaetša, listen.
thai, riddle, tie.
thaka, v. choose first.
thaka, mate, companion:– **e kwagdi,** young folk. – **e tshesane,** young folk, tiny tots.
thaka, gland, pip, runner, rank, **-ya leihlo,** eyeball.
thaka banna, exclam., good gracious!
thakadu, ant-bear.
thakanela, meet halfway, hurry to.
thakanelo, meeting place.
thakangwaga, first-fruit.
thakelelo, siege.
thakga, neat, do well, purify.
thakgafala, become neat.
thakgafatša, adorn, decorate, trim.
thakgala, be glad; **thakgetše,** be glad, rejcice.
thakgalo, joy.
thakgegilego, neat.
thakgiša, trim, cleanse, decorate.
thako, expulsion.
thakone, black-finch.
thala, draw (a line), swim, sketch, sail, navigate.
thala, freckle, rope.
thalabanya, cycle, travel.
thalabodiba, whirligig.
thaladi, dash.
thalasediko, pair of compasses.
thalathala, sketch.
thalela, smear medicine on walls to prevent witchcraft.
thalo, fruit of the wait-a-while tree.
thaloki, player, actor.
thaloko, game, play.
thama, cheek; – **tša mokhukhuša,** rosy cheeks.
thamaga, red and white (ox).
thamagana, red and white cow.
thankga, smudge, smear with (grease) fat, walk swinging one's arms and legs; n., difficulty.
thangwana, little cheek.
thantholola, unravel.
thantšeng, tricky, clever.
thanya, porride made of milk and mealie meal.
thanya, shoot up, become clever, recover.
thaoga, snap, break.
thaola, break, tear.
thaotšwe, be torn.
thapa, become tame, wet or trained.
thapa, side, flank.
thapalalo, contour.
thapama, afternoon.
thapedi, petition.
thapelelo, intercession.
thapelo, prayer, prayers.
thapiša, moisten, drill.
thapišo, drill.
thapo, stalk, cord, kernel.
thapola, suffer, long for snuff.

thapolla, exercise.
thapollo, n., exercise.
tharamologo, elasticity.
thari, a skin for carrying infants, cradle.
tharo, three.
tharong, (tee-), third.
tharollo, solution (of a problem).
thata, adj., hard, difficult.
thatafala, become hardened.
thatafalelwa, tolerate, endure.
thatafalo, hardening.
thatafatša, harden.
thatafatšo, hardening.
thatafišwa, be hampered/made difficult.
thatana, little stick.
thatego, loveableness.
thathamologa, unravel, feel refreshed.
thathankga, struggle,
thato, will, desire, liking, love.
thea, found, call after, lay the foundation; – **tsebe,** prick the ear.
theba, butt, stab.
thebatheba, throb, flick, twitch.
thebe, shield.
thebele, medicine bag.
thebetha, twitch (of the eye).
thebola, booty.
thedi, pose, a standing on one knee.
thedimoga, slip, slide.
thedimoša, slippery.
thedіša, drive cattle slowly.
theeleditše, listened to.
theeletša, listen to.
theeletšwa, be named after, be listened to.
theepe, Cape pig-weed.
theetša, listen.
thei, thermometer.
theipi, tape measure.
thekeletša, balance a pot on the head.
thekesela, stagger.
thekethe, ticket.
thekga, support, stay, prop.
thekgo, support, stay.
thekgwana, snuff-box
thekišo, sale.
theki, price, handle.
thekofase, bargain.
thekokhiro, hire-purchase.
thela, pour, do homage, scatter.
thele, udder.
theledіša, smoothen, make slippery.
thelefomo, telephone.
thelela, slip, be slippery.
thelelo, slipping.
theieskopo, (thelesekopo), telescope.
theletša, smoothen, soften.
thella, slip, glide.
thello, slip(ping), mistake.
thelo, an outpour, a mould.
thema, curdle.
themiša, cause to curdle.
themo, cutting, chopping, a disease of children (sores on the neck).
themometara, thermometer.
themometa, thermometer.
themperetšha, temperature.
thena, v., prune, smoothen a stick.
theneketšo, nursery rhyme.
thenela, prune for, straighten for.
thenisi, tennis.
theng (hleng), by the side of.
thengwana, chisel.
thenkgolla, be upset (of a trap).
theni, be upset, topple.
thenoga, topple over.
thenola, upset, turn upside-down or, inside-out.
thenwa, be pruned.
thenya, bump, knock against.
theo, basis, basic, establishment, fundamental.
theoga, go down, descend.
theogelego, di sa – , troublous.
theola, descend.
theolelo, discount.
theolla, undo a trap.
theoša, lower.
theošetša, reduce (the price) for.
thepe, tap, pig-weed (Cape).

thepela, stir porridge, scoop.
thepentaene, turpentine.
therapi, therapy.
therei, tray.
therengwa, apoplexy.
therese, terrace.
therešo, truth.
therišano, consultation.
thero, planning, sermon.
theta, go round, tatoo, clear, roll down.
thetebudi, circular wall.
thetemotse, circular wall, (round a village).
thetha, roam, go round, roll.
thethekga, support.
thethengwane, little stick.
thetho, apron.
thetlwa, four-corners, (Grewia occidentalis).
theto, praises, poetry.
thetogale, epic poem.
thetša, deceive, knock over, push slightly, stumble, trip, swindle, stumble.
thetšana, fight, quarrel.
thetšo, deceit, fraud.
thetšwa, be tripped.
thiba, stop, prevent, shut.
thibela, prevent, halt.
thibama, slumber.
thibasela, slumber, nod when sleepy.
thibedi, notch, obstruction.
thibela, prevent, close, stop.
thibelago, stopping, preventive; – **moya,** air-tight.
thibelela, stop completely, corner.
thibelo, prevention, obstruction.
thibetše, prevented.
thibolla, open, remove a stopper.
thibollo, opening, uncorking.
thika, unite against, join hands in attack, surround.
thiko, uniting against, surrounding, concentrated effort.
thimola, sneeze.
thini, tin, can.
thintha, dust, shake off.
thinya, swerve, dive, bend, dodge, kneel, dislocate.
thinyega, become (sprained) dislocated.
thinyego, sprain.
thinyetša, (matolo), bend knees.
thipa, knife.
thipane, the one who does the operations at a circumcision school.
thipitlo, massacre.
thipo, ban(ning), cutting.
thiša, postpone.
thiswana, little basin, small vessel.
thite, new unploughed soil.
thiteletšo, smoothening.
thitelo, flat-iron, smoothening stone, grinder.
thitha, churn.
thitikwane, sacred plant.
thito, stem, stubble, principal clause.
thitomodu, underground stem.
tho, id., **re** –, fall, drip.
thoba, flee, prick, elope.
thobalo, sleep.
thobane, stick, cane.
thobe, fruit of **morobe,** tree.
thobegi, splinting, setting an arm or a leg.
thobego, fracture, break, setting of a fracture.
thobela, chief, salutation.
thobo, breaking, harvest, flight, beer.
thobola, peck, bite.
thobollo, exercise.
thogako, (thogo), swearing, curse, condemnation.
thogo, curse.
thogorogo, dirt, rubbish, swearing.
thojane, heifer, initiated girl, appointed time.
thoka, stick, knobkerrie.
thoka, to drink beer.
thokga, break (off), pluck.
thokgaganya, break to pieces.

thokgama, be upright.
thokgamiša, cause to stand (or be) upright.
thokgamo, uprightness.
thokgega, break.
thokgola, bone or bead used by a witch-doctor, talisman.
thokgosela, have fits, shiver.
thoko, n., side; adv., aside; **ma** –, surroundings, sides.
thoko, sewing.
thoko, he-goat.
thokolo, dung of goats or buck, fruit of the **morolo** tree.
thokwa, fawn-coloured.
thola, bitter apple, hire.
thola, be silent, become silent, become clear (of water), find.
tholla, pour out.
tho'lo, koodoo, kudu.
tholo, taking off, unloading, unburdening.
tholo, silence, adopting, find.
thologa, be upset, come down.
thololo, column, pillar.
thoma, begin, start.
thomaratšoka, butcher-bird.
thomiša, cause (help) to begin.
thomo, sending, mission.
thomo, black and white male animal, piano.
thongwana, black and white cow.
thonkga, injure a wound, hurt.
tholpa, plunder, capture, prey; n., secret.
thopela, confiscate.
thopelo, confiscation.
thopo, plunder, spoil.
thopola, spring up, ooze out, sprout.
thopollo, recapture, reclamation.
thopša, be robbed, be captured.
thoro, roar(ing), grain.
thoromo, trembling.
thosoga, appear suddenly.
thosola, syphilis.
thota, mound, hill, the hump of an ox.
thotha, carry, transport.
thotha, dip porridge in gravy.
thothela, transport for/to; – **elwa,** be transported to/for.
thothella, gather, collect.
thothi, drop.
thotho, transport.
thothobetša, clear a way, pierce, stab, pin.
thothomela, shiver, tremble.
thothomelo, trembling.
thothometša, cause to tremble.
thothometšo, cause of trembling or fear.
thothonkgana, sound made by a travelling wagon.
thoto, goods, luggage, load, pack.
thotobolo, ash-heap.
thotofala, become stupid.
thotogelo, ascension.
thotse, pip, seed of pumpkin or melon.
thotšhe, torch.
thotwana, little luggage.
thuana, small egg, first or last egg, bad egg.
thuba, smash, pierce, break down.
thubagana, be cracked or broken.
thubaganya, break, smash.
thubakanya, smash.
thubako, bombardment.
thubalatšwa, be destroyed.
thubega, break.
thubula, prick.
thudi, a room under the verandah.
thuhla, break down.
thukunya, shake hands.
thula, butt, forge, strike, mend, prepare; – **na,** clash, collide.
thulagano, clash, clashing.
thulaganyo, arrangement, tabulation.
thulama, incline, lie, descend.
thulamela, lodge, stay at.
thulamo, incline, lying.

thulela, make a road for.
thulu, (thulusi), tool.
thuma, pulverise.
thuma, grind fine, crush, stone.
thunkg(w)ane, bully.
thuntha, swim.
thunthela, swim.
thuntšha, raise (dust) smoke, fire, shoot.
thuntshwane, mushroom.
thunya, shoot, raise dust or smoke, blossom, throb.
thuo, possession; – **ya diruiwa,** animal-husbandry.
thupa, stick, cane, switch.
thupana, cutting.
thupela, be beautiful, clean or neat.
thupišo, discipline.
thupurupu, fine dust.
thuputla, fine dust (sand).
thuri, small animal kept in hiding for witchcraft.
thurugo, swelling.
thuša, help, assist; – **thuto,** teaching aid.
thušago, useful.
thušega, be assisted, recover.
thušo, help, assistance, use, aid; – **ya potlako,** first-aid, aid; – **pele,** first-aid.
thutabodumedi, religious instruction.
thutabogae, civics.
thutafase, geography.
thutapopego, philology.
thutatlhago, nature study.
thutatumelo, doctrine.
thutelo, training.
thutha, swim.
thuthufalo, warming up.
thuthafatšo, heating.
thuthupa, pop.
thuthupe, popcorn.
thuthuša, hatch.
thutišo, exercise (school).
thutlo, jerk.
thuto, teaching, lesson, doctrine, education.
thutse, baboon's tail.
thutswana, cutting, slip, little stick.
thutšwe, is struck.
thwa, id., **re** –, snap.
thwa(a)di, winner, champion.
thwagadima, position of danger, charm.
thwakga, fowl tick, tampan.
thwala, pick up, find, hire, employ; n., parcel, load; **thwetše,** hired.
thwalo, load, burden, employment, transport.
thwanyane, cleverness.
thwapa, scoop up.
thwaša, emerge anew.
thwathwaša, hatch.
thwe, go –, it is said.
thwetho, rotation.
thwethwa, hop, trot; – **ela,** hop towards.
thwethwiša, push a wheelbarrow.
thwetše, hired.
thwetšego, which has hired.
thwewa, be honoured.
thwii, straight, genuine, nice; **ema** –, stand plumb.
tia, beat; – **motato,** telephone; – **kgati,** skip.
tia, become strong; – **dihlaya,** look for something to eat.
tiba, stamp with the foot, thump, rumble.
tidiša, cause to avoid.
tiego, delay.
tiela, get strong for, beat for; – **gare,** hem in.
tiila, play, frolic.
tiile, be strong, firm or fixed.
tiilo, wandering about, roaming, need.
tiiša, strengthen, persevere, tighten.
tiišo, seal, tightening, strengthening.
tiišolla, destabilise.
tikologo, surroundings, going round.

tikološo, turning.
tila, strike the ground with the foot, avoid, side-step, dance.
tilo, spotted,
tilo, plastering, smearing.
tilodi, spotted.
tima, extinguish.
tima, deprive of, withhold from, dilute.
timana, be stingy.
time, re –, perish, be extinguished.
timega, become extinguished.
timela, get lost, disappear, wander.
timelela, vanish.
timelelo, loss.
timeletše, has disappeared for/completely.
timelo, loss, ruin.
timetša, lose.
timi, thyme.
timola, allay, assauge.
ting, sour porridge.
tintela, wind round.
tio, beat, blow, firmness.
tipa, to dip.
tipe, dip,
tipi, dip.
tiploma, diploma.
tipola, cut, sever.
tira, active voice.
tiragalo, event, happening, episode, incident.
tiragatšo, dramatisation.
tirelo, service, devotion.
tiri, grease, tar.
tiribola, dribble.
tirišo, use, usage.
tiro, deed, function, task.
tiro, predicate.
tiroatla, craftmanship.
tirokgabo, work of art.
tirollo, undoing.
tiroposo, postal service.
tirotherwa, scheme, project.
tirwa, passive voice.
tisele, diesel.
tišo, herding, care, watch.
tita, withold an opinion.
titelo, delay.
titeo, beating.
titela, brew beer.
titipa, find abundantly.
titsi, mane, hair of the tail.
tla, come, shall, will.
tlaa, come!
tla(a)bje, se llwe ke –, a thing has vanished.
tlhaba, surprise, perplex.
tlabarase, slovenly writing.
tlabega, be surprised, perplexed or confused.
tlabego, surprise.
tlabja, be surprised.
tlaboga, get scorched.
tlabola, scorch, singe.
tlabolla, render happy.
tladi, lightning, thunderbolt; **–mothwana,** the supposed practice of a witch-doctor to kill his enemies by lightning.
tladika, speak at random.
tladiša, fill.
tladitše, has filled.
tladiwa, be filled.
tlaela, mock, jest, baffle.
tlaila, sing (speak) badly.
tlaiša, worry, pester, annoy.
tlaišega, be worried.
tlaišego, worry, torture.
tlaišo, passion, torture.
tlaka, white (spot), collar.
tlakala, le –, leaf.
tlala, famine, hunger.
tlala, (tletše), be full; – **dimpa,** become angry.
tlala, rejoice, dance for joy.
tlalea, accuse, report.
tlalela, be in distress/need; **tlalelwa,** be in distress/tribulation, panic.
tlalela, become full for; – **tlala,** altogether full.
tlaleletša, fulfil, fill up, add to.

tlaleletši, adjunct.
tlaleletšo, enlargement, fulfilment.
tlalelo, trouble, distress, anxiety.
tlaletša, fill for, replenish.
tlaletšo, supplement.
tlaletšwe, be in distress.
tlama, bind, gird, tie; **itlama,** gird oneself.
tlamagano, confederation.
tlami, hyphen.
tlamo, tie, binding.
tlamollo, unbinding.
tlantla, bite here and there, beat often, crush.
tlapa, fart, become tasteless; **o tla –,** mind you!
tlapakgerere, crab.
tlapalala, become lazy.
tlaparalla, granite.
tlapatla, patter.
tlapiriganya, crush, trample on.
tlaralala, stand astride (straddlelegged), lie outstretched.
tlaraletše, stand legs apart.
tla re, e –, as soon as.
tlarea, fumble.
tlareo, deliriousness, delirium.
tlaruma, speak nonsense, talk rot, wander.
tlase, under, down, below.
tlatša, fill, complete, supplement.
tlatšo, filling, completing.
tle, be in the habit of.
tle, may.
tlekeetša, pamper, spoil.
tlekesela, stagger, tremble, shudder.
tlela, bring along, bring to come for.
tleloko, bell, clock.
tlema, bind, tie, harness.
tlemagano, confederation.
tlemegile, b. bound.
tlemo, bond, bondage.
tlemologa, become unbound, become free.
tlenya, yelp.
tlepotša, scratch with the nails.
tlere, re –, be very red.
tlerebana, tear to pieces.
tlerebanya, chop to pieces.
tlerefala, become red.
tleroga, become torn.
tlerola, tear.
tletlolo, elevation.
tletše, be full, has come for.
Tlhabane, Rustenburg.
tlhabano, fight, battle.
tlhabo, stab, stitch, slaughter.
tlhabogo, improvement, change.
tlhabollo, improvement.
tlhabošego, nice taste.
tlhabošo, raising of the voice, improvement.
tlhaelo, lack, want.
tlhagišo, presentation.
tlhago, origin, nature.
tlhagolo, weeding.
tlhahlotiro, subject study.
tlhaka, mark, asterisk, letter, roof; **– ya leihlo,** eyeball.
tlhakakgolo, capital letter.
tlhakanaselo, (tlhakanatshelo), cosmopolitan.
tlhakanelo, communal.
tlhakano, mixture.
tlhakanya, brisket.
tlhakanyane, small letter.
tlhakanyo, mixing, adding, combination.
tlhakgama, pellagra.
tlhako, hoof.
tlhakodišo, saving, rescue.
tlhakolane, fruit of **mohlakolane.**
tlhakolo, wiping, cleaning.
tlhalalo, joy, rejoicing.
tlhalano, divorce.
tlhale, thread.
tlhalefetšo, fraud, deceit.
tlhalefo, wisdom, knowledge.
tlhalo, divorce, a putting away.
tlhalošišo, definiton.
tlhalošo, explanation.
tlhame, secretary bird.

tlhamo, decoration, invention, composition.
tlhano, five.
tlhanogelo, departure from, deviation.
tlhanogo, change, (in plan or purpose) revelation.
tlhanolelo, ka –, vice versa.
tlhanolo, a turning inside out, a changing of sides.
tlhaodi, qualificative.
tlhaolo, selection, distinction.
tlhaologanyo, notion, idea, understanding, conception, intelligence.
tlhapholo, dilution.
tlhaphollo, reclamation.
tlhapo, washing, bathing.
tlhasedi, ray of light.
tlháselo, attack, raid.
tlhathollo, explanation.
tlhatlagano, pile, stack.
tlhatlamano, succession, one on top of the other.
tlhatlamo, sequence.
tlhatlamollo, removal of layers, demolishing.
tlhatlamuši, thick, black smoke, fumes.
tlhatlogelo, ascending, ascension.
tlhatlogo, rising, going up.
tlhatšo, vomiting, washing.
tlhenkge, id., sit easy, sit flat on the ground.
tlhobaelo, worry.
tlhogobo, despairing.
tlhobolo, nakedness, stripping.
tlhobolo, quiver, gun.
tlhodi, spy, mung bean.
tlhodiego, worry.
tlhodio, annoyance.
tlhogo, sprouting.
tlhogonolo, blessing.
tlhogonolofatšo, blessing.
tlhohleletšo, encouragement, excitement.
tlhohlo, challenge.
tlhohlomišo, research, investigation.
tlhohloro, dusting.
tlhoi, spite.
tlhoka, chaff.
tlhokafalo, want, lack.
tlhokego, want.
tlhoko, care, want.
tlhoko, nipple of a breast.
tlhokofalo, sorrow, grief.
tlhokofatšo, torture, torment.
tlhokofele, wart.
tlhokomelo, care, attention.
tlhokomologo, disregard, indifference.
tlhokwa, grass used for thatching.
tlholego, origin, creation, nature, defeat.
tlholo, overpowering, defeat.
tlholo, creation, creating, red hare.
tlhologelo, yearning, longing, desire.
tlhomaganyo, joining, adding to, junction, connection.
tlhomamišo, fixing, ratification, constitution.
tlhomamo, firmness.
tlhomarelo, persecution.
tlhomeletšo, adding to.
tlhomesetšo, affix.
tlhomogelo, compassion, mercy.
tlhomogo, sadness.
tlhomolo, extraction, sadness.
tlhompho, respect, regard, honour, courtesy.
tlhomphollo, disrespect.
tlhonamo, sulking.
tlhono, scraping.
tlhophego, bother, annoyance.
tlhophišo, classification, composition.
tlhorego, worry.
tlhorišo, persecution.
tlhotlo, straining, filtering.
tlhotlwa, strained beer.
tlhotse, dry skin fixed on to the bottom of a basket.
tlhotšo, limping.
tlhoyano, hatred, enmity.
tlhwekišaoma, dry-cleaning.

tlhwekišo, purification, cleaning.
tlhweko, purity, cleanliness.
tlhwelemadi, blood-poisoning.
tlima, choke.
tliša, bring.
tlobaka, splash.
tlobatloba, falling of rain.
tlobja, re –, fall into the water.
tloga, leave, depart; straightway, thereupon, leave together, aux., would.
tlogela, leave, let alone, refrain from, abandon; **lela,** leave for.
tloka, preen, engrave.
tlokela, engrave for.
tlokoma, froth up.
tlokosetša, rock, lull, hush (a baby).
tlokwane, mushroom.
Tlokwe, Potchefstroom.
tlola, anoint, smear.
tlola, jump (over), exaggerate, tresspass; – **melora,** small breasts of young girls.
tlolatlola, hop, bounce.
tlolo, jumping, trespass, unction.
tlompu, re –, plunge.
tloo, ground-nut, monkey-nut, peanut.
tloomake, ground-nut.
tloomarapo, n., 'n jugo bean.
tlopa, decorate the hair, hop.
tlopela, overdo, pour out everything.
tlopo, crest, hair pattern.
tloro, prickly pear.
tloša, take away; – **bodutu,** entertain.
tlošabodutu, hobby.
tlošitšwe, be removed.
tlošo, removal, subtraction.
tlosolo, syphilis.
tlotla, honour, **tlotlega,** be praiseworthy.
tlotlego, honour, excellency.
tlotliša, recommend.
tlotlo, courtesy.
tlotlologa, become dishonoured.
tlotlologo, dishonour, disgrace.
tlotlomela, stand on one's toes, be exalted; **tlotlometša,** raise.
tlotlontšu, vocabulary.
tlotša, anoint, smear with.
tlotšo, anointing.
tlou, elephant.
tlwaela, be accustomed, be acquainted with.
tlwaelo, custom, habit.
tlwaetšego, familiar.
tlwaologa, unlearn a habit, become unaccustomed.
to, re –! be quite alone.
tobatoba, go from one house to the other.
tobekane, mixed up.
tobekanya, muddle up.
tobeletšo, stress.
tobetša, dent in, stress.
tobetšo, accent.
tobetšwi, drawing-pin.
tobo, tribute.
tobola, peck, pick, bite as a snake.
todi, juice, nectar, white or yolk of an egg.
togamaano, plan, device.
togo, plaiting, weaving.
toile, doily, doyley.
Toitši, Germany.
toka, cut strips (of biltong), grind.
toka, right, righteousness.
tokaetša, balance on the head.
tokafalo, becoming right, righteous.
tokafatšo, justification.
tokela, cut tripe for.
tokelo, right, duty.
tokišetšo, preparation for.
tokišo, arranging, preparation.
toko, righteousness, justice.
tokollo, deliverance, emancipation, liberation.
tokologanyo, conjugation.
tokologo, liberty, deliverance, libertaion; **ka** –, candid, unabashed.
tokomane, ground-nut.
tokumente, document.

tola, spring hare.
tologa, melt, dissolve.
toloka, interpret.
toloki, interpreter, cotton reel.
tološa, melt, dissolve.
tološo, melting, solution.
tolotolo, sjambok.
tomano, biting one another; – **ya ditsebe,** a telling of secrets to one another.
tomatoma, roll over, turn somersault, tumble, walk on one's hands.
tomeletšo, ka –, on purpose.
tominione, dominion.
tomkraga, jack.
tomo, bridle.
tomo, biting, bite.
tomogo, be pulled out.
tomola, uproot, pull out; – **mahlo,** give an angry look; – **etše mahlo,** give an angry look.
tompa, splash.
tompala, splash, plop.
tompu, sound (thing falling into the water).
tona, male, masculine.
tona, officer, general, minister of the cabinet.
tonama, bend, bow.
tone, ton.
tonikete, tourniquet.
tonka, drum, empty tin.
tonki, donkey.
tonoga, be exposed.
tonya, be cold; – **etša,** give the cold shoulder.
too, re –, be cold.
too, (toyo), witchcraft.
topa, pick up, find; – **tša fase,** needy, impecunious.
topalala, stand upright.
topela, get saturated, be warmed up.
topeletša, add fluid to.
topi, percussion cap, detonator.
topisi, percussion cap, detonator.
topo, request, prayer.
topola, protrude.
topolla, redemption, redeeming.
topologo, redemption.
topopeu, endosperm.
tora, tower.
toro, dream.
toro, prickly-pear.
toropo, town, dorp; **fala,** urbanize; – **falo,** urbanisation.
tosa, pull tight.
totelwa, have erection of the penis/sexual desire.
totoba, walk totteringly.
totobala, expand, lie stretched out, be evident.
totobetše, be clear.
totoma, heap, mound, hill.
toula, beat mercilessly.
toulo, towel.
touta, repeat continually, reiterate, pound.
touto, repeating continually, reiteration.
toutšo, grindstone, whetstone.
towe, naughty.
tsaama, lay eggs (of a locust).
tšaka, battle-axe.
tsaka, re –, spit between one's teeth.
tšale, rug, shawl.
tšama, aux., v., express continuity.
tsamaya, (dial.) go, walk, march.
tšapa, weariness, tiredness.
tsapola, beat, bubble, foam.
tsaroga, jump up, shoot up.
tsarogile, (phoka), be smart.
tsarola, tear, gush out.
tše, dem., these.
tšea, (tšere), take, take on, marry; – **kgang,** argue, debate; **tšeana,** marry; – **tšie,** take heed.
tšeano, marriage.
tseba, know.
tseba, jealousy, covetousness.
tsebafa, be covetous, stingy.
tsebagala, be known, **tsebagatša,** proclaim.

tsebalega, be well-known, famous.
tsebe, ear; **loma** –, tell a secret.
tsebe, ear-mark of a child born in the open
tsebiša, inform, notify.
tsebonyana, a little knowledge.
tsee, re –, be lonely or quiet.
tšeela, take from, deprive of.
tšeela pele, proceed.
tšeelana mello, border on, adjoin.
tsefa, be beautiful, fine; – **ela,** pleasing to.
tšeiša, cause to take.
tšeka, veer, change direction.
tšela, dem., those yonder.
tsela, road, way, path, manner, scheme, **tsejana,** small road.
tseladijo, alimentary canal.
tselamadi, blood vessel.
tsema, peg, plant in the soil.
tsema, (medu), take root.
tsena, enter, – **fase,** go to the roof of, exert; – **ganong,** interrupt.
tsenela, penetrate; **go** –, a custom by which a man, after his wife's death, marries her sister.
tseneletšwe, penetrated.
tšenereitara, generator.
tseno, entering, entrance.
tšeno, dem., these.
tsentšha, put in, cause to enter; – **dinala fase,** exert, strive hard.
tsenya, put in, cause to enter; – **wa,** be brought in.
tšeo, the taking, consumption.
tšeo, (tšeowe), dem., those.
tšeometri, geometry.
tsepalala, stand upright.
tsepama, stand upright.
tsepame, vertical.
tsepamela, be fixed upon.
tseparela, cling to.
tsepelela, gaze at, stare at.
tsepelelo, a staring at.
tšere, has taken (to wife).
tseremetša, spout, squirt, jet.
tšerwe ke phefo, be blown away.
tserr, id., be hot.
tšešo, (tša gešo), belonging to us.
tsetamela, pin to.
tsetela, cutlet.
tsetla, sob, chip, shard, groan.
tsetlola, cut into slices.
tsetolla, dig out, unearth, take down.
tsetsekwane, tiptoe.
tsetsela, walk on tiptoe.
tsetsela, sob, cry whine.
tsetsema, glow.
tsetsemetša, stick/plunge into.
tsetsepela, stand firm.
tšhaba, flee, run away.
tšhaba, fear, be afraid of, terrified.
tšhabega, be dreadful, terrible.
tšhabela, flee to, escape to.
tšhabelela, run hard towards.
tšhabeša, make haste.
tšhabo, fight, fear, fleeing.
tšhabo, trade.
tshadi, feminine, female.
Tshaena, China.
tshaeno, signature.
tšhaile, time to stop work.
tšhaiša, cause to stop work, dismiss.
tšhakga, rattle, glide through, throw divining bones, pass through.
tšhalelo, backlog.
tshamelo, pillowing.
tšhaparego, poverty.
tshaphila, learn how to milk, milk without success.
tšharakano, chaos.
tsharatshara, drizzle.
tshasa, smear, rub with fat.
tšhatšha, hunting-spider; **re** –! appear suddenly.
tšhatšha, tassel of a mealie plant.
tšhatšhamela, burn.
tšhatšhane, tassel.
Tšhatšhe, Anglican Church.
tšheba, bo –, jealousy, envy.
tshebi, backbiter, reporter.
tshebotšo, warning.

tshediša, console, conaoie, sympathise with, confort.
tšhediša, collect revenue; **motšhediši,** receiver of revenue.
tshedišega, be comforted.
tshedišo, condonation, pity.
tshefo, filtration.
tshega, striped, (red and white).
tshegetša, prop, support.
tshegetšo, prop, support.
tshegišo, humour.
tshego, laughter, cut, cutting.
tšhego, lack of meat, want.
tšhegofalo, being blessed.
tšhegofatšo, blessing.
tshehla, yellow, poor; n., the sun; – **ge e ntšha nko,** dawn.
tshehlana, beer, belle.
tshehlo, devil's thorn.
tshehlwa, devil's thorn.
tsheka, grass-bangle.
tšheka, check.
tshekamo, slant(ing), slope.
tshekatsheko, criticism.
tšheke, cheque.
tshekegi, pure, true; **thuto** –, true doctrine.
tsheketšo, rationing.
tshekga, strike fire.
tshekge, grey, fawn.
tshekgetša, support, prop, uphold, adjust.
tshekgoga, turn over, turn somersault.
tshekišano, lawsuit.
tshekišo, lawsuit.
tsheko, lawsuit, court action.
tshela, cross (over), ford, contravene.
tshelane, cat-o'-nine-tails.
tshelau, weather.
tshele, quarrel, dispute.
tšhelete, money; – **iana,** a little money.
tšheletša, irrigate, water.
tshelo, hunting for food, buying of food.
tšhelo, pouring in, libation.
tshelo, crossing.
tšhelolla, exhume, excavate.
tšhemo, field, graden, poughed land.
tšhenane, bull-dog.
tshenogo, exposure, visibility.
tshenolo, revelation.
tšhentšha, change (money).
tšhentšhi, change.
tšhentšhišo, exchange.
tshenyegelo, expense, damage.
tshenyego, damage, destruction.
tshenyo, spoiling, destruction.
tshenyoina, slander.
tsheola, early rain.
tshepa, (tshepha), trust, hope, rely on; **tshepega,** be reliable.
tšhepa, dress well.
tshepe, stag, hind.
tshepedišo, course, process.
tshepego, faithfulness.
tshepelo, journey, walk.
tshepetšo, process.
tšhepha, dress well.
tshephe, springbuck.
tšhepile, neatly dressed.
tshepiša, promise.
tshepišo, n. promise.
tshepo, hope, trust, confidence.
tšheri, cherry.
tšherimolla, make the hair stand on end.
tshesane, thin, fine, slender.
tshese, thin, fine, slender; **thaka e** –, young folk.
tšhese, cheese.
tšhesi, chassis.
tshetaditho, anatomy.
tshetla, chip.
tshetlana, piece, chip.
tshetledi, anchor.
tshetlega, rest on.
tshetlego, prop, stay.
tshetlo, honey-guide.
tshetlo, stamping, beating, crusher.
tšhiano, race.
tšhibollo, scraping off, invertion.

tšhidi, stone of the wild plum.
tšhidillo, exercise.
tšhidilo, ironing, rubbing.
tšhielano, turn.
tšhifi, shift.
tšhii, re –! feel pain.
tšhika, sinew, lineage, generation; – **nnoši,** hermit.
tšhikagare, midrib (of a leaf).
tšhikalala, demonstrate, be stubborn.
tšhikamadi, blood-vessel.
tšhikaro, carrying, rest.
tšhikidi, bug.
tšhikwana, jug, milk vessel.
tšhila, dirt, filth, impurity.
tšhilafaditše, has soiled.
tšhilafala, become dirty, stain, soil; – **letše,** be unclean for.
tšhilafatša, dirty, stain, soil; **fetše,** be unclean.
tšhilego, digestion.
tšhilegompe, indigestion.
tšhilo, upper millstone, grinding (stone), mill.
tšhima, beans and samp cooked together.
tšhimane, group of small boys.
tšhimele, chimney.
tšhimologo, beginning.
tšhipa, wild-cat, genet.
tšhiphilego, cheap.
tšhipi, iron, flat iron, tin, bell, metal.
tšhipo, spring hare.
tšhireletšo, protection; **lefase la** –, protectorate.
tšhirelo, protection, screen.
tšhirahlaka, ceiling.
tšhirr, re –, be hot.
tšhisele, chisel.
tšhisepere, buckle, clasp.
tšhišimogo, awe, fear.
tšhišinyego, shaking, trembling.
tšhišinyo, shaking, proposal, motion.
tšhiširi, bug.
tšhitampholo, antidote.
tšhitano, quarrel.
tšhite, bee-bread.
tšhitego, inability.
tšhitere, watering-can.
tšhiti, isolation.
tšhitišaphero, antiseptic, disinfectant.
tšhitišo, obstacle, cause of failure.
tšhito, incapability, incapacity.
tšhitšhiboya, hairy grub.
tšhitšhidi, bug.
tšhitšhii, pain, worry, sorrow.
tšhitšhila, brisket, walk with effort.
tšhitswana, small piece of iron, tin, bell.
tšhiwana, orphan; – **eng,** orphanage.
tšhoga, get a fright, be startled, aux.v., per chance.
tšhogile, be frightened.
tshohlo, cud.
tšhoko, chalk.
tšhokolete, chocolate.
tshokologo, conversion.
tshole, tuberworm.
tšholla, pour out, shed.
tsholo, serving or dishing up.
tsholo, scolding, reprimand.
tšholo, fat of goats.
tšholobano, disorder.
tšhologa, spill, purge, overflow.
tšhologa, pour out.
tšhologo, outpour(ing), shedding, purging.
tšholotše, has shed.
tshomatshoma, drizzle.
tšhomo, work(ing).
tšhona, lack clothes.
tšhonna, exclam., oh! Dear me!
tšhonne, lack clothes.
tshontišo, immunisation.
tšhopha, twist, wind; – **ega,** be dislocated.
tshopolla, unwind.
tšhoša, spear, sword, lance,
tšhošetša, frighten, intimidate.
tšhošetšo, intimidation.
tšhoši, species of ant.
tšhošo, terror, alarm, fright.

tšhošobanyo, frowning.
tšhošwane, small variety of black ant.
tšhotha, twist, turn.
tshotshoma, perspire (especially on the nose); – **go,** greasy.
tshotšo, fat on the kidneys, suet, tallow.
tshoutišo, immunisation.
tšhuana, orphan, chicken.
tšhuba, set to fire, burn, light.
tšhuduba, poker, awl, meddlesome person.
tšhuhla, tuft (of grass).
tšhukudu, rhinoceros.
tshukumetšo, pushing.
tšhula, evil.
tšhulafatšo, becoming tasteless.
tšhulafatšo, rendering tasteless.
tšhuma, burn, light, kindle.
tšhumane-ya-gampedi, train.
tšhumatšhumega, do the round.
tšhumilwego, been burnt.
tshumu, white-faced male animal; **tshungwana,** adj., fem. of **tshumu.**
tšhupa, index., pointer, weevil, calender.
tšhupakhutlo, compass.
tšhupaletlole, account (bank).
tšhupamolato, account, bill.
tšhupanako, watch, clock.
tšhupane, concordance, index.
tšhupaphefo, weathercock.
tšhupatefo, receipt.
tšhupatlotlomoela, current account.
tšhupatlotlopolokelo, savings account.
tšhupetšo, indication, showing to, manifestation.
tšhupišo, demonstration.
tšhupo, proof, evidence, sign, example.
tšhupša, hornless or polled cattle.
tšhuputeki, test-tube.
tšhušumetšo, pushing, inciting.
tšhuthišo, removal, transfer.
tšhutla, tuft of grass.
tshwa, spit, expectorate, emit.
tšhwaane, frost.
tshwaetšanollo, dissmilation.
tshwaetšo, commission.
tšhwahlelo, attack.
tshwamoga, be extracted.
tshwamola, extract.
tšhwana, needle, pod of the mimosa.
tšhwane, frost.
Tshwane, Pretoria.
tshwanelo, duty, right, decency.
tshwano, image, analogy.
tshwantšhišo, likening, analogy.
tshwao, mark.
tshwaragano, contract, coherence, connection.
tshwarelano, forgiving one another.
tshwarelo, forgiveness.
tshwarišano, mutual assistance, cooperation.
tshwarišo, assistance.
tshwaro, seizure.
tshwaso, fishing, joking.
tshwayo, earmark, brand.
tshwedi, burn; **nkga** –, to smell a rat.
tshwee, id., be naked.
tshwela, tuber-worm, mite, hairy **moth; – mare,** spit, expectorate; – **tshwela,** drizzle.
tshwele, tuber-worm, mite, hairy moth.
tshwele! exclam., Time! (in games).
tšhwene, baboon.
tšhweng, baboon, man killed in action.
tshwenya, worry, vex, trouble, annoy, pester.
tšhwenyane, small baboon.
tshwenyega, be worried, distressed; – **ile,** be upset.
tshwenyego, trouble, worry, annoyance.
tshwetshwetha, trot.
tšhweu, white.
tshwiša, wean.

tšibafa, be stingy, niggardly.
tšibidikanya, tickle.
tšiboga, be roused.
tšibola, do for the first time.
tšididi, cold.
tšidifala, become cold.
tšie, locust; **go tšea** –, take heed.
tšielane, relay, do in turn.
tsika, pick on.
tsikana, fight at close quarters.
tsikanya, cause to come to grips.
tsike, (tsikele), a game of darts.
tsikiditla, tickle.
tsikiditlane, spur.
tsikinya, shake, wobble, tickle.
tsikinyo, shaking, proposal.
tsikiri, go letša –, make money jingle.
tsikitla, tickle, poke, gnash the teeth.
tsinkela, investigate thoroughly.
tsinya, cry, yelp, squeak.
tšipa, pinch, take a pinch of, nip.
tšipalala, stand upright.
tšipise, gypsum.
tšipola, startle, rouse.
tsirikanya, cause to jingle.
tsirinya, ring, tinkle.
tširoga, wake up.
tširoša, push aside, waken.
tšiša, bring, ooze, trickle, show the teeth.
tšitla, scatter, beat.
tšitlana, fight.
tšitlano, scattering, fight.
tšitlanya, scatter, cause to flee.
tšitšiboša, (tšitšibuša), revive, rouse, stimulate.
tšitšimoga, trill, move.
tšitširpa, giant.
tšo, just.
tsobe, stack, hay-stack.
tsodiela, perch.
tšofa, old (person or animal).
tšofala, age, grow old; pft. **tšofetše,** be old.
tsoga, wake (up), get up, rise; – **maatla,** get strong or violent; axu. v., and then.
tsogela, rise for, rise early, rise against; **maatla,** rebel, revolt.
tsogo, rising, getting up.
tšo(go), just.
tsogo, le –, arm, foreleg, inferior wife; – **le-kobong,** a bribe.
tsogwana, little arm, a person with a deformed arm, quarter-evil.
tšohle, all, every.
tšoka, wag the tail.
tsokama, perch, squat.
tsokame, perched, squatted.
tsokotla, roan; **tsokotlana,** female roan animal.
tsokotša, rinse, agitate.
tsokotšega, be rinsed or agitated.
tsokotsoko, re –, shake.
tšuile, has condemned.
tšola, take off one's trousers, undress; **tšódiša,** cause or help to undress.
tšolobano, disorder.
tsoma, hunt, look for, seek.
tšona, they, them.
tsongwa, be hunted.
tsopa, clay.
tsopola, quote.
tsopolo, quotation.
tsorama, perch, squat.
tsorame, seated.
tsoro, noble person, gentleman, steadfast, tidy.
tsororo, re –, gush out.
tšorr, re –, come down in showers.
tsošo, raising.
tsošološa, rebuild, rebuilt; – **itše,** has rebuilt.
tsota, be discontented, annoy.
tsotsi, hooligan; 50 kg mealie meal.
tsoto, discontentment.
tsotsometša, stick/plunge into.
tšua, condemn.
tšuana, chicken.
tšuba, take snuff.

tšubunya, rinse.
tšubutla, blow (as the wind) agitate, shake.
tšuile, has condemned.
tšukunya, rinse.
tšuo, condemnation.
tsupela, stick in (under).
tsupolla, project, protrude.
tsupula, project, protrude.
tsuputla, poke.
tsurutla, gush out.
tšušu, cockroach.
tšutla, blow as the wind, storm.
tšutšutla, drive, blow.
tšwa, go out, leave; aux. v., just.
tswabola, incise, beat.
tswadiša, cause to breed.
tšwafa, be lazy.
tswaing, salt-pan, salt-factory.
tšwaka, mix.
tswako, mixture.
tswala, matrix of an animal.
tswala, (tswetše), give birth to beget, bear, breed.
tswalelela, lock up.
tswalelelo, compound interest.
tswaleletšwe, be locked up, b. encaged.
tswalo, begetting, birth, interest (on money).
tswantšhanyo, simile.
tswapoga, lose colour/taste, fade.
tšwara, dress, put on clothes.
tswea, busy-body, quarrelsome person.
tswebera, stab.
tswediša, cause to go (out) forth.
tswee, id., be nice.
tšwela, go out to, progress; – **pele,** proceed, progress, advance, become civilised.
tšwelela, come forward, appear.
tšwelopele, progress.
tswenya, pull faces, turn up one's nose.
tswetla, white skin trimming, the edge of a kaross.
tswetše, has given birth to.
tšwetše pele, proceeded, advanced.
tswetši, a cow that has recently (just) calved.
tswetswe, fresh.
tswikinya, jingle, ring, wag the tail.
tswinya, pull face, turn up one's nose, be disgusted, squeak, chirp.
tswitswitla, drive a herd of cattle.
tu, re –, be silent.
tuba, stamp, beat, thump.
tudueletšo, shouts of joy.
tuduetšo, a shout of gladness.
tuka, catch fire, flame, burn; – **bogale,** become angry.
tuku, cloth, kerchief.
tula, stamp, crush, crack (a nut).
tulafatšano, cross-pollination.
tulafatšo, pollination.
tulatula, brown sugar.
tulo, session, seat, domicile.
tulosomeng, decimal place.
tuma, become known or famous, make a hit; **tumiša,** boast of, advertise, praise.
tumadipou, bilabial consonant.
tumammogo, consonant.
tumammogoino, dental consonant.
tumammogothu, explosive consonant.
tumathwee, aspirated.
thumadumo, murmur.
tumedišo, salutation, greeting.
tumelano, accord, agreement.
tumelelo, consent, approval.
tumelo, approval, consent.
tumelwana, superstition.
tumiša, make known, praise.
tumišega, be praiseworthy, laudable.
tumišo, praise, reputation, fame.
tumo, fame, reputation, rumbling.
tuntela, swim.
tupa, rise (as smoke from a chimney), pass through.
tupunya, rise, shoot up (of smoke).
tuputupu, rising of smoke.
tura, be expensive.

tutela, become hot, fester.
tutetša, heat, cause to fester.
tutubolla, open (eyes).
tutuetša, urge, encourage, hurry.
tutuma, be inflamed.
tutumologa, break out, become erupted.
tuu, re –, be silent, be quiet.
tuulala, be silent.
twaa, re –, be clear, be white, shine.
twadiša mokgoši, raise alarm, give alarm.
twanelo, a fight over, casus belli.
twantšho, resistance.
twantwadi, species of small green locust.
twatši, disease germ.
twelo, cause of strife, a fight for, aid.
tweša, instigator, agitator.
twetšidinta, typhus fever.
twetšisewa, epidemic.
twetšiswikiri, diabetes.

U

uba, snatch (away).
ubuga, be snatched away.
ubula, blow hard, storm, snatch away.
Udi, The Crocodile River.
ukama, hint on, look down upon.
ukamela, look down, keep an eye on.
umaka, mention, hint.
unya, peep out and draw back again, appear and disappear at intervals.
unyetša, hide.
upa, protect, drive away birds or evil spirits.
upolola, undo the effects of the charms.
upša, but.
uraniamo, uranium.
uša, cause to fall, cast down, drop.
uta, hide; **utolla,** reveal.
uta, become mouldy, mould.
utama, hide, lie low, be hid.
uthautha, oppress.
utla, v.t., snatch away, pull down.
utolla, reveal.
utša, hide the milk as a cow for her calf.
utswa, steal, thieve.
uwee, id., **go re** –, be fast asleep.

V

vaniša, varnish.
vaniši, varnish.
veto, veto.
vitamine, vitamin.

W

wa, like, just, as.
wa, (wele), fall to the ground; **wela,** fall on, in, for; – **tsela,** journey.
walatša, pour down, fall in torrents (as the rain).
wašara, washer.
wata, watt.
watšhe, watch.
we, o –, Shame!
weditše, has been through the initiation school, has caused to fall in.
wela, fall into, meet accidentally, come upon accidentally; – **fase,** fall on the ground; **kgwahlana,** be deserted.
wena, you.
weno, thine, yours.
wetara, weather.
wetša, send to the circumcision school.
wetše, has fallen into.
wiša, cause to fall, throw down, drop.
wo, this, this one.
wohle, all, the whole of.
wokhwi, this one.

wola, that one (mo-class).
wona, it.
woo, that one.
wouwe, that one.

Y

ya, poss, concord.
ya, pron., it.
ye, relative concord.
ye, dem., pron., or adj., this.
yekhwi, dem., this one.
yela, that one.
yena, pron., he, she, him, her.
yeo, dem., that one.
yo, dem., this one.
yona, pron., it.
yono, dem., this one, this person.
yoo, dem., that one that person.
yunibesiti, university.

Z

zipi, zip-fastener.
zoo, zoo (zoological garden).
zwii, rad., whizz.

ENGLISH – N. SOTHO

A

aback, morago; **taken** –, maketše.
abandon, lahla, tlogela, lesa.
abase, goboša, kokobetša.
abash, hlabiša, dihlong, makatša.
abate, kokobela, khula.
abattoir, selagapale, selageng.
abbreviate, khutsofatša.
abbreviation, khutsofatšo.
abdicate, tlogela, lesetša (bogoši).
abdomen, mpa, dimpa.
abduct, gapa, thopa; **abduction,** kgapo, thopo.
abet, hlohletše, kgothatša.
abhor, hloya, ila, gafa.
abhorrent, ilega; **be** –, befa.
abide, lala, hlwa.
ability, go kgona, maatla, bokgoni.
abject, nyatšegang.
ablaze, tuka, swa.
able, kgonang.
abnegate, latola, itatola, **abnegation,** boitatolo.
abnormal, sa tlwaelegago.
abode, legae, bodulo.
abolish, fediša, lesetša.
abominable, mpe; – **person,** kgwara.
aboriginal, ntlha, pele mathomo.
aborigene, semelefa.
abort, folotša, senyegelwa.
abortion, pholotšo, tshenyegelo, kgomelo tseleng.
abound, ata, nyeuma, nyakgahla.
about, prep., ka, ka ga; adv., **go** –, dikologa.
above, godimo.
abrasion, khumogo, ngapo.
abrasive, segohlo.
abreast, bapile.
abridge, khutsofatša; – **ed** khutsofaditšwego.
abroad, kua ntle.
abrogate, fediša, laolola.
abruptly, gatee; ka phomela.
abscess, sešo, sekaku, sekutu.
abscond, nyamela, ngwega, thoba.
absence, tlhokego, tlhokagalo.
absent, hlokafala, hlokega.
absolute, noši, nepagetšego.
absolution, kgololo, boitshwarelo.
absolve, golola, lokolla.
absorb, metša, hupa, mona.
abstain, ila, itima, lesa, tela.
abstinence, boitimo, boitelo, kilo.
abstract, naganwago, gopolwago.
absurd, e botlaela, segišang.
abundance, botlalo, bontši.
abundant, atileng, ntši.
abuse, senya, gobola, kgobogo.
abyss, bodiba, sekoti.
Abyssinia, Abesinia.
acacia, mogohlo, akasia.
academic, wa thuto.
accede, dumela, ineela.
accelerate, akgofiša, tsoša lebelo.
accent, n., tobetšo, – *uate,* tiiša.
accept, amogela, tšea; **be – ed,** amogelwa.
acceptable, dumelega, lebošega.
access, tumelelo ya go tsena, patamelo, ntšifalo.
accessory, adj., gotee le, n., modirišani, mosenyiši.
accident, kotsi.
acclaim, reta, tumiša.
acclimatisation, tlwaelo, go sonta.
acclimatise, tlwaela, tlwaetša.
accommodate, fa malao.
accommodation, marobalo.
accompany, felegetša, felesetša.
accomplice, mosenyiši, mosentšhi, mothuši, motlatši.
accomplish, phetha, fetša.
accord, kwana, fa, nea; n., kwano.
accordance, tumelelo.
according, ka mokgwa wa, ka (ga).
accost, bolediša, dumediša.
account, tšhupamolato, tšhupaletlotlo; – **ing officer,** mohlankedi, mohlakiši.

accrue, oketša, eketšega.
accumulate, kgobela, kgoboketša.
accuracy, go nepa, nepo.
accurate, nepegilego.
accursed, rogakilweng, rogilweng.
accusation, tlaleo, pego.
accuse, latofatša, bega, bea molato; – **falsely,** phara ka maaka, pateletša.
accused, mosekišwa, mmegiwa.
accuser, mmegi, mosekiši.
accustom, lemala, lematša, tlwaetša, **–ed,** tlwaetše.
ace, thwadi.
ache, bohloko; bolawa ke; **toothache,** mohlagare; **stomach** –; longwa ke ka teng (mala).
achieve, phetha, dira, kgona.
acid, esiti, bodila.
acidity, bodila, go baba.
acknowledge, ipolela, dumela¯araba.
acme, sehloa, ntlha.
acne, dišo, dikemola.
acquaint, tsebiša, bolela, bega.
acquaintance, motsebalegi, motswalle.
acquiesce, dumela, kgotlelela, itumela, ineela; **acquiescence,** tumelo, boineelo.
acquire, hwetša, bona, reka, rua; – **riches,** huma.
acquisition, thuo, theko.
acquisitiveness, boithuelo.
acquit, lokolla, lesetša.
acquittal, tokolla, lesetša.
acre, akere, tema.
acrid, bogale, bohla, galaka.
acrobat, mojakati, motudi.
across, rapalala, rapalega, mošola, putla, fapana; **come** –, gahlana.
act, šoma, dira; **to play,** bapala, raloka.
acting, dirago, emelago, swarelago.
action, tiro, lesolo.
active, mafolofolo, dirago, šomago, mahlahla, matšato.
active voice, tira.
activity, tiro, mafolofolo.
actor, thaloki, modiri.
actual, ya nnete, ya sebele, kgokgo.
acute, bogale, **clever,** bohlale.
adage, seema.
adamant, tiilego.
Adam's apple, kgologolo.
adapt, amantšha, lekanya, itokišetša.
adaptable, amantšhega, lokelago.
adaptation, kamantšho.
add, hlakanya; – **to,** oketša, eketša.
adder, noga; **puff** –, marabe.
addict, ineela, lemalala.
addition, tlhakanyo, koketšo, kokeletšo – **al,** oketšago, hlatlagelago.
address, v., bolela le; n., atrese.
adenoids, ditšhweleša, tša nko, diatenoite.
adept, sekgoni, setsebi.
adequate, lekana.
adhere, kgomarela, momagana, mamarela.
adherent, n., mogomaredi, adj., gomarelago.
adhesion, kgomarelo.
adhesive, gomarelang, tanyago.
adieu, dumediša, šalang.
adjacent, bapileng, mabapi.
adjectival clause, thabehlaodi.
adjective, lehlaodi.
adjoin, oketša, neana mellwane.
adjourn, šuthiša nako, thinya, phatlalatša.
adjudge, ahlola.
adjunct, tlaletši, koketšo.
adjure, antšha, rapela, eniša.
adjust, lokiša, beakanya, bofa – **clothes,** tshekgetša.
adjustment, tokišo, peakanyo.
administer, laola, sepediša; buša.
administration, taolo, pušo.
administrative, laolago, tshepedišo;
administrator, molaodi, mmušakarolo.
admirable, kgahlegago.
admiration, tumišo, kgahlego.

admire, makalela, bogela.
admissible, dumelega, dumeletšwe.
admission, tumelelo, tumelo, boipolelo, go ipona molato.
admit, dumela, amogela, tsenya; **a fault,** ipona **molato.**
admonish, sola, kgala.
admonishment, temošo, kgalo.
adolescent, yo mofsa.
adolescence, bofsa.
adopt, amogela; **a child,** godiša.
adoration, go khunamela (Modimo), lerato, tlhompho.
adore, khunamela.
adorn, (oneself), ikgabiša, hlama, thakga; – **another,** kgabiša, hlophiša, thakgafatša.
adrenalin, atenaline.
adult, mogolo, motho yo a godileng, monna, mosadi.
adulterate, senya, hwirihwitša, tswaka.
adulterer, seotswa.
adulteress, seotswa.
adultery, bootswa.
advance, ya pele, tšwela pele.
advance, tšwelopele, tlhabologo.
advantage, mohola, thušo.
adventure, bohlagahlaga.
adventurer, moleki, mohlagahlagi.
adverb, lehlathi.
adversary, lenaba, moganetši; – **in competition,** mophegišani.
adverse, bothata, lwantšhago.
adversity, tlalelo, mathata.
advertise, hlaba, mokgoši, tsebiša.
advertisement, tsebišo, pego.
advice, keletšo, kgakololo, temošo.
advise, eletša, gakolola, lemoša; – **secretly,** loma tsebe.
advocate, v. bolelela; – n.; mmoleledi.
adze, n., petlo, petlwana; v.t., betla.
aerial, sa moya; **view,** tebosenong.
aerodrome, boemelafofane.
aeronaut, moetamoyeng, moetasebakeng.
aeroplane, sefofane.
aesthetic, temogišišo ya bokgabo.
afar, kgakala, kgole.
affability, botho.
affable, yo botho.
affair, taba.
affect, ama, tutuetša, ikaketša, itiriša.
affection, lerato.
affectionate, rategago, rategang.
affiance, peelelano; **(a man),** beelela; **(a woman),** beelediwa.
affiance, n., peeletšo; v., holofetša.
affidavit, kenelwa.
affiliate, tswalanya.
affirm, tiiša.
affirmative, dumelang, dumelago.
affix, n., tlhomesetšo, v., hlomela, hlomesetša, kgoma(retša).
afflict, hlokofatša, tlaiša, tshwenya.
affliction, tlhokofatšo, mahlomola.
affluence, khumo, letlotlo, mahumo, mokhoro.
affluent, nokakeledi, elelago.
afford, nea, fa enywa.
affricate, tumagwaša.
affront, rumola, goboša.
afoot, ka maoto, ka dinao.
afore, pele.
afraid, tšhoga, tšhaba.
afresh, gape, lefsa, bofsa.
Afrikaner, Leafrikanere, Leburu.
Afrikaans, Seafrikanse, Seburu.
after, morago; šen'o, šena go.
after, not long –, go se go ye kae.
afterbirth, mohlana, sa morago.
afternoon, mathapama, ka meriti.
afterwards, (ka) morago, ntoo, kgona go; **a short while** –, moragonyana.
again, gape, la bobedi, ka bofsa.
against, lwantšha, gana, maleba le.
agape, ahlame(go).
age, nywaga, mohla, lebaka; **be of** –, godile.
aged, tšofala; **be** –, tšofetše.
aged person, motšofe; – **man,** mokgalabje; **woman,** mokgekolo.

agenda, lenanethero.
agent, agente, sediri, morekišetši.
agglomerate, bokanya; n., kgobokanyo.
aggrandise, godiša.
aggravate, befiša.
aggregate, kakaretšo.
aggress, hlasela.
aggression, tlhaselo.
aggressive, be –, rumola.
aghast, tšhogile.
agility, matšato, lebelo, bobebe.
agitate, ferekanya, hlohleletša, tsokotša.
agitation, pherekanyo, moferefere, khuduego.
agitator, moferekanyi, mohlohleletši, tweša.
ago, kgale, **long ago,** kgalekgale, **a short time ago,** maloba.
agonise, tlaiša.
agony, tlalelo, mahloko, mahlomola.
agree, kwana, lakana, dumela.
agreeable, kwanago, kgahlišang.
agreement, kwano, tumelano.
agriculture, bolemi, temo.
ahead, pele; **go –,** tšwela pele, **keep –,** beša.
aid, n., thušo; v., thuša.
ail, babja, lwala, kwa bohloko.
ailment, bolwetši, bohloko, phokolo, go fišafiša.
aim, v., oma, lebanya; leka; n., boikemišetšo, tebanyo.
air, moya; **fresh –,** moya o hlabošang; **tune,** molodi; **sky,** leratadi.
air, v., anega.
aircraft, sefofane.
airport, boemelafofane.
air-pressure, kgatelelo ya moya.
ajar, butšwego.
akin, leloko, lešika.
alabaster, alabastere.
alacrity, bofefo, lebelo.
alarm, n., mokgoši, letšhogo; v., hlaba mokgoši; – **-clock,** (alamo) sewainara.
alas, jo! aowii!
albeit, le ge.
albino, lešwefe.
album, albamo, pukupokanyo.
albumen, maregerege a lee.
alcohol, alkoholo, tagi, twatwatwa; **alcoholic drink,** senotagi.
alert, phafogileng, mafolofolo.
algae, algae, dimelameetseng.
alias, ke tsela ye nngwe.
alibi, prove an –, itatola.
alien, moeng, moditšhaba.
alight, fologa, theoga, dula.
align, tsepanya.
alike, swana(go).
alive, phela, phelago.
alkali, alkale, serota.
all, ka moka, ohle; **not at all,** le gannyane.
allay, timola, kokobetša, khutšiša.
allege, re, anegela.
allegory, seswantšho.
allegro, allegro, ka mafolofolo.
alleviate, fokotša (bogale).
alley, sefero, mokgothana.
alliance, kgwerano, tshwaragano.
alligator, kwena.
alliteration, poeletšamedumo.
allocate, abela, bea, šupa felo, aba.
allocation, kabo.
allot, abela, arolela; – **a task,** kobolela.
allotment, kabelo, karolelo.
allow, dumelela, dumela, fa; lesa.
allowance, tefo, moputso, putseletšo.
allude, ama, bolela ka.
allure, goka, goketša.
allusion, kamo, polelo.
ally, modirišani, mogwera.
almanac, alemanaka, kalentara.
Almighty, yo Maatlaohle, yo Maatlakamoka.
almost, nyakile go; lekgatheng la.

alms, neo, dikatšo, dikabelo; **give** –, hlallela, abela.
aloe, sekgopha, mokgopha.
aloft, godimo, kua godimo.
alone, nnoši, noši.
along, bapilego, go ya le, go ipata, gotee le.
aloof, ka thoko, kgakala.
aloud, ka maatla; **speak** –, phagamiša lentšu, hlaboša.
alphabet, alfabeta, a.b.c.
already, šetše, se.
also, gape, le gona; **aux. verb.,** bile; **conj.,** le.
altar, altare, aletare.
alter, v., fetola; v.i., fetoga.
alteration, phetolo, phetogo.
altercation, phapang, kgang.
alterate, hlatlolana, šielana.
alternately, ka go šielana.
alternatively, ka tlhatlolano, tšhielano.
altitude, bogodimo, bophagamo.
alto, labobedi, alto.
altogether, gotee, mmogo, ka moka.
alum, alone.
aluminium, aluminiamo.
always, ka mehla, matšatši ohle.
am, ke.
amalgamate, hlakanya, kopanya, v.i., hlakana, kopana.
amalgamation, kopano.
amass, phutha, kgobokanya, gobelana, kgobela.
amaze, makatša, gakantšha; makala.
Amazon (River), Amazone.
ambassador, motseta.
ambiguously, ka temepedi.
ambition, phišego.
amble, šankašanka, eta.
ambulance, ampolose.
ambush, n., talelo, sekhu; sefi; v., lalela.
ameliorate, fefola, timola, kaonefatša.
amend, lokiša, fetoša.
amends, tefo, moputso.
amendment, tokišo, phetošo.
amiable, rategang.
amidst, (amid), gare ga magareng a.
amino acid, aminoesiti.
amiss, foša, ka phošo.
amity, kgwerano, tlwaelano.
ammonia, amonia.
ammunition, dibetša.
amnesty, tokollo.
amoeba, amoeba.
among, gare ga.
amorous, ratago, ya lerato.
amount, bokalo, kgoboko, palo; – **to,** fihlago.
amphibia, amfipia.
ample, lekanego, ntši, ikadilego, katologilego.
amplify, godiša, oketša; **-ier,** n., segodiši.
amputate, kgaola letsogo, kgakgamolla, (leoto), – **in the joint,** lokolla; **–d,** kgaogile setho.
amulet, pheko.
amuse, segiša, bapadiša.
anaemia, tlhokamadi, anemia.
anaesthetic, seokobatši, kidifatši, kadibatši.
analogous, swanago.
analogy, tshwantšho, tshwano.
analyse, hlopholla, fetleka.
analysis, molokollo, tlhophollo, phetleko.
anatomy, kgoladitho, anatomi.
ancestor, n., mogologolo, – **s,** bagologolo, borakgolokhukhu.
anchor, tshetledi, ankora, v., setlela.
ancient, bogologolo.
and, gomme, le, mme.
andante, ka neneketšo, andante.
anew, lefsa, ka bofsa.
angel, morongwa.
anger, pefelo.
angle, (se) khutlo, sekhutlo: **right** khutlotsepa; **tri** –, khutlotharo.
Anglican church, Tšhatšhi.
angora goat, lesaeboko.

angry, befetšwego, galefileng; **be; become** –, galefa, befelwa; gakala.
anguish, tlalelo.
angular, sa dikhutlo.
animal, phoofolo, **carnivorous** –, sebata; – **husbandry,** borui; **small –s,** diphoofotswana.
animate, phediša, kgothatša, phelago.
animosity, lehloyo.
anise, anise.
ankle, kokoilane, kgwele, kgokgoilane.
annex, hlomaganya, thopa, ngwako wa kgohlagano.
annexation, thopo.
annihilate, fediša, gegera.
annotate, ngwala tlhalošo.
announce, tsebiša, bega, kwatša.
announcement, tsebišo, pego.
announcer, mogaši, motsebiši, mmegi.
annoy, tshwenya, lapiša; **-ed,** sekekile.
annoyance, tapišo, matshwenyego.
annual, ka ngwaga, sa ngwaga, – **rings,** masehlongwaga.
annually, ka mengwaga, ka nywaga.
annul, fediša.
annunciate, tsebiša, bega.
annuciation, tsebišo, pego.
anoint, tlola, tlotša, nonetša; **be –ed,** nonetšwa.
another, e mong, yo mong, šele nngwe.
answer, araba, fetola; n., karabo, phetolo.
ant, tšhošane, lenyonyo, lekeke **(termite),** mohlwa.
antagonism, lehloyo.
antagonist, lenaba, molohlanyi; **–ic,** lohlanyago.
Antarctic, antatiki.
ant-bear, thakadu.
ant-eater, thakadu; **the scaly ant-eater,** kgaga, kgwara.
antecedent, leetetši, letlapele, adj., etetšago.
antelope, phoofolo, phalafala, kgama.
antennae, dinakana.
antenuptial, pele ga lenyalo.
anterior, pele, tlago pele.
ant-heap, seolo.
anther, anthere, ramodula.
ant-hill, seolo.
anthem, kopelo, sefela.
anthology, puku ya direto.
anthracite, malahla.
anthropology, anthoropolotši.
antibody, twantšhi.
anticipate, letela, hutša.
anti-clockwise, mpogošong.
antics, makatika, metlae.
antidote, moupo, tšhitišampholo.
antipathy, lehloyo.
antiquarian, motsebatšakgale.
antique, segologolo, sa kgale, **antiquity,** bogolo.
antiseptic, tšhitišaphero, šitišago phero.
anti-serum, sethibelabohloko.
antithesis, kganetši.
anti-toxin, twantšhi.
antonym, lelatodi.
anus, mogwete, motete, anuse.
anvil, senatlelo.
anxiety, tlalelo, pelaelo, tlhodiego.
anxious, belabelega, fišega, belaela.
any, ngwe, mang le mang, eng le eng, nngwe, ofe le ofe.
anybody, mang le mang.
anyhow, le ge go le bjalo.
anything, eng le eng, se sengwe le se sengwe.
anyway, le ge go le bjalo.
anywhere, kae le kae.
aorta, aota.
apace, ka pela, ka lebelo.
apart, ka thoko.
apartment, phapoši.
apathetic, sa hlokomelego, se nago taba.
apathy, tlhokomologo.
ape, kgabo.
ape, v., etšiša, ekiša.

aperture, lešoba, sekgoba.
apex, ntlha; hlatlana, photwana.
aphis, ntadimela.
apologise, phophotha, phuphuthela, kgopela tshwarelo.
apology, phophoto, phuphuthelo.
apoplexy, apopleksi.
apostle, maopostola.
apostrophe, lenalana.
appal, tšhoša, boifiša.
apparatus, sehlamo, diaparata.
apparel, n., diaparo, dikobo, v., tšwara, apara, apeša.
apparent, bonagalang, ka ponalo.
apparently, ekete.
apparition, sepoko, seriti.
appeal, rapela, ipiletša, boipiletšo.
appear, hlaga, bonagala iponagatša.
appearance, ponagalo, sebopego.
appease, homotša, fepeletša; – **hunger,** fora tlala, **be appeased,** khoše.
appendix, mametletšo, lelana.
appetising, kganyogišago.
appetite, kganyoga dijo.
applaud, opa magoswi, opa diatla.
applause, magoswi, diatla!
apple, apola.
appliance, sedirišwa.
applicable, ama(na)go.
applicant, mokgopedi.
application, kgopelo, kopo.
applied, dirišitšwego.
apply, kgopela; – **to,** šomiša, diriša.
appoint, bea, hloma.
appointment, peo, peano.
apportion, aba, abela.
apposition, tlhomeletšo, koketšo, kemelano.
appreciate, leboga, thabela, bona kholo.
appreciation, tebogo, ponakholo.
apprehend, swara, tšhaba.
apprehension, tshwaro, temogo.
apprentice, morutwatiro, mothapišwa; – **ship,** borutwatiro.
apprise, bega.
approach, tsela, tlhakego, patamelo; batamela, hlaka.
appropriate, tšea, adj., lebaneng, lebanego, v., amoga, gapa; hlaola.
approval, tumelelo.
approve, dumelela, emela.
approximate, batametša, kgaufsi, lekanyetša, batamelago.
approximately, ka go batamela, ka tekanyetšo.
approximation, patametšo, tekanyetšo.
apricot, apolekose; **-tree,** moapolekose.
April, Moranang, Aporele.
apron, thetho, –.
apt, lokela, swanela, sekamela.
aquarium, akwareamo.
Arab, Moarabia; **Arabic figure,** palo ya Searabia.
arable, lemega(go).
arable land, naga ya temelo.
arbiter, moahlodi.
arbitrary, ka boithatelo.
arbitrate, ahlola.
arbitrator, molaki, referi, mokgaolakgang.
arbitrary, ka boithatelo.
arbour, poriele.
arc, sekabora.
arch, sekabora, kokoropo.
archaeology, akhiolotši.
archaic, segologolo.
archer, mmetši.
archipelago, lewatle la dihlakahlaka.
architecture, thutaboagi.
archive(s), bokgobadingwalo.
arctic, atiki.
ardent, fišega, fišegago.
ardour, phišego, mafolofolo.
arduous, thata.
are, are.
area, area, sekgoba.
arena, arena, bohlabanelo.
argue, ganetša, ganela, tšea kgang.
argument, kgang, taba.

arid, omeletšeng.
aridity, komelelo.
arise, tsoga, emelela; rotoga.
aristocracy, bokgomana.
aristocrat, mokgomana.
arithmetic, dipalo, thutapalo.
ark, areka.
arm, letsogo, v., hlomela.
armadillo, kgaga, kgwara.
armament, dibetša.
armed force, bahlabani.
armlet, leseka.
armour, ditlhamo, diaparo tša (tšhipi) phemelo; – **bearer,** morwaladibetša.
armpit, lehwafa, lekgwafi.
arms, dibetša, matsogo.
army, sera, dira; – **worm,** mogokong.
aroma, monko.
aromatic, nkgago bose.
around, dika, dikologa, go rarela.
arouse, tsoša, phafoša.
arrange, beakanya, rulaganya.
arraign, bega, bea molato.
array, lokiša, beakanya.
arrears, melato (mašaledi), mašokotšo.
arrest, swara, emiša.
arrival, kgorogo, go fihla.
arrive, fihla, tla; goroga; – **d home,** gorogile.
arrogance, boikgantšho, boikgodišo, makoko.
arrow, mosebe; – **shaped,** nkamosebe.
arsenic, aseniki.
arson, tšhumo, go tšhuma.
art, bokgabo; **arts,** dikgabo.
artery, seišamadi.
artesian well, mothopo.
artful, ya masene, ya bohlale; ya bohwirihwiri.
article, selo.
artillery, dibetšakgolo, dikanono.
artisan, sešomi.
artist, sekgabiši, radiatla.
as, bjalo ka, ka ga.
asbestos, asbestose, marela.
ascend, rotoga, namela, hlatloga.
ascension, thotogelo, tlhatlogo.
ascent, tlhatlogo, thotogelo.
ascertain, nyakišiša, botšiša.
ascribe, neela, bea (beêla) molato.
ash, molora.
ashamed, dihlong, ntšela, gagabiša mahlo.
ash-heap, thotobolo.
ash-pan, seolelamelora.
aside, thoko, ka thoko; **turn** –, fapoga, phamoga, hlanoga.
ask, kgopela, lopa; – **a question,** botšiša.
askance, look –, gerula.
asleep, robala, potuma, otsela.
aspect, tebo, ponagalo, lekala.
asperity, bogale, bošoro.
asperse, pateletša, fokela.
aspersion, pateletšo, phokelo.
asphalt, asfale.
aspirate, sebutšwetšwa, v., butšwetša.
aspirated, (consonant), tumathwee.
aspiration, putšwetšo.
aspire, duma, fišega; buša moya.
assail, hlasela, rotogela.
assassin, mmolai.
assassinate, bolaya.
assassination, polao.
assault, n., tlhaselo, v., hlasela, gobatša.
assegai, lerumo, phaka barwa.
assemble, phutha, kgoboketša; kgobokana, kgobokanya, beakanya.
assembly, phuthego, pitšo.
assent, v., dumela, n., tumelo.
assert, tiiša.
assess, lekanya, tšhediša.
assessor, n., molekanyi, motšhediši, wa lekgetho.
assets, letlotlo.
assign, bea, beela, arolela, šupa; – **ed to,** aroletšwe.
assimilate, huetša.
assimilation, khuetšano.

assit, thuša, swariša.
assistance, thušo, tshwarišo.
assistant, mothuši, moswariši.
associate, tlwaelana; n., mogwera.
association, kopano, mokgatlo.
assort, hlophiša, hlaola.
assorted, hlophilwego, hlaotšwego.
assuage, kokobetša, fefola, homotša.
assume, tšea, ithloma, ikgodiša, bona gore.
assure, holofetša, tiiša.
Assyria, Asiria.
asterisk, naletšana, sehlorana.
astern, ka sa nthago, morago.
asthma, asema, sehuba sa leatla, asma.
astonish, makala, makatša, tlabega.
astonishment, makalo, tlabego.
astound, makatša, gagolo.
astray, timela, lahlega, **lead** –, timetša.
astride, stand –, rakalala, tlaralala.
astigmatic, astikmatiki.
astigmatism, astikmatiki.
astronaut, moetasebakeng.
astronomer, monepadinaledi.
astronomy, bonepadinaledi.
astute, bohlale, mahlajana hlalefile.
asunder, kgaoganego, aroganego, **tear** –, kgaola, aroganya, kgaoganya.
asylum, botšhabelo, digafing.
at, ka, fa, kua, ga.
atheist, moganetšamodimo; **atheism,** boganetšamodimo.
athlete, sebapadi, moatletiki; **athletic sports,** dipapadi, atletiki.
Atlantic, Atlantika.
atlas, atlase.
atmosphere, atemosfere, lefaufau, moya.
atom, atomo; – **ic, bomb,** pomo ya atomo.
atomic energy, maatla a atomo.
atone, lefa, boelanya.
atrocity, bošoro.
attach, kgomaganya, kopanya, hlomela.
attaché, motseta.
attack, hlasela, n., tlhaselo.
attain, rua, bona, fihlela, hwetša.
attempt, leka, n., teko.
attend, go ba gona, hlokomela.
attendance, tseno, tlhokomelo.
attendant, modiredi, mohlokomedi, hlokomelago, šetšago.
attention, tlhokomelo, šedi.
attentive, hlokomelang, thaetšago.
attest, hlatsela, paka.
attestation, bohlatse, bopaki.
attire, apara; apeša; n., diaparo, dikobo.
attitude, mokgwa, boitshwaro, maikutlo, moya; **have** –, gopola.
attorney, ramolao; – **general,** ratshekišo.
attract, goka, goketša, goga, gogela, kgahliša.
attractive, kgahlišago, botse, bogegago.
attribute, bohlaodi, lehlaodi.
auction, fantisi.
auctioneer, mofantisi.
audacious, sa tšhabeng, sa boifeng, betile pelo.
audaciously, ka go se tšhabe.
audible, kwagalago, kwala.
audience, batheetši, bareetši.
auditory, mohlakiši; – **canal,** lešoba la tsebe.
auger bit, borwana.
augment, katološa, godiša, oketša.
augmentation, katološo, koketšo.
augmentative, katološo, oketšago.
augur, senoge; v., laola, hlola.
augury, n., bonoge, tlholo.
August, Agostose, Phato.
aunt, mother's elder sister, mmamogolo; – **younger sister,** mmane; **father's sister,** rakgadi.
auricle, orikele.
auspicious, mahlatse.

austere, thata.
Australia, Australia.
authentic, ya (nnete) kgonthe.
author, modiri, mothomi, mongwadi; **–ised,** dumeletšwe.
authority, setsebitsebi, motsebi, pušo, taolo; mmušo, maatla.
autobiography, biotaodišaphelo.
autocracy, pušanoši.
autocrat, mmušanoši.
automatic, itirišago.
autonomic, ipušago, itaolago.
autopsy, tlhahlobo ya setopo.
autumn, seregana.
auxiliary, thušang, thušago, mothuši.
auxiliary, v., lethuši.
avail, thuša, hola; – **able,** hwetšegago.
avarice, megabaru.
avenge, lefetša, itefetša.
avenger, molefetši, moitefetši.
avenue, mokgothana.
average, palogare.
aversion, tlhoyo, lehloyo; **to have** –, ngala.
avert, phema, fapoša, thiba.
aviation, bofofane.
aviator, mofofane.
avid, duma, fišega.
avocado, abokato.
avoid, široga, ila, phema.
avow, dumela, ipolela.
avowal, tumelo, boipolelo.
await, lebelela, emela, letela.
awake or awaken, tsoša, tsoga, phafoga.
award, nea, ahlolela.
aware, lemoga; lemoša.
awe, poifo, tlhompho.
awful, tšhabegang, boifišang, befago.
awhile, motsotsonyana, lebakanyana.
awkward, šulafetšeng, befago.
awkwardness, tšhulafalo, bobe.
awl, morokola, elese, moropola.
ax(e), selepe; **small** – seletswana; **axe-head,** bogale.
axiom, seema, nnete.
axis, ase.
axle, ase.
aye, ee
aye, go sa feleng.
azure, botala bja legodimo.

B

babala, babala, leotša.
babble, v., bolabola, ratharatha, n., polabolo, palabalo.
babe, lesea, mbua.
Babel, Babele.
babies, masea.
baboon, tšhwene.
baby, lesea.
babyhood, bosea.
Babylon, Babilonia.
baby powder, puere ya masea.
bachelor, kgope.
back, mokokotlo, mokolo; **hunch** –, lehutlo, **lie on,** kanama, kwaela, **set up,** kokoropa; **turn,** fulara; **bend,** inama, v., **to** –, emela, –, morago; – **stitch,** mohlabomorago.
backbite, seba.
backbiter, mosebi.
backbone, mokokotlo.
backfire, thunya.
background, boithekgo.
backhand, ntahle.
backing, kemelo.
backlog, tšhalelo.
backslide, thelela morago.
backwards, morago, ka sa nthago.
backyard, mafuri.
bacon, sepeke.
bacteria, pakteria.
bacteriology, paktereolotši.
bad, mpe, be –, v., **become,** bola.
badger, sesele.
badly, gampe; **suit** –, rona.
badness, bobe.
baffle, gakantšha, makatša.

bag, mokotla, kgetsi; **medicine –,** moraba; v., tsenya, kokomoga.
baggage, thoto, phahlo.
bagpipe, nakaserabana.
bail, peile.
bait, phepišo, segoketšo, v. jeletša.
bake, paka; is – **d,** pakilwe.
baker, radinkgwa, mopaki.
baking-powder, lerojana la go paka.
balance, sekala, mašaledi, papetšo, go lekana, tekanyetšo, tokaetšo; v., lekanya, bapetša, lekanetša; – **on the head,** tokaetša; – **d diet,** dijotekanywa.
balcony, mathudidimo.
bald, lefatla, hlobegile meriri.
bale, ngata.
balk, palela, ila.
ball, bolo, nkgokolo, polo.
ballet, palei.
balloon, palune, sebudula.
balm, borekhu bjo bo alafago, setlolo.
bamboo, pampu.
ban, roga, iletša, lahla.
banana, panana.
band, (se)tlamo, lepanta; mphato; lekoko, sehlopha sa baletši.
bandage, mmofo, motlamelelo, pantetši; v., bofa, tlemelela.
bandit, lerabele, senokwane.
bangle, mphiri, leseka; – **of beads,** moruka.
banish, lahla, leleka, raka.
banishment, tahlo, teleko, thako.
banjo, pentšu.
bane, bosenyi.
bank, panka, leriba, lebopo, khwiti; – **balance,** tšheletepankeng.
banking account, tšhupaletlotlo.
bankrupt, pankoroto.
bankruptcy, pankoroto, go wa.
banner, sefoka, motutu, segokobjane.
banquet, monyanya, mokete.
Bantu authority, Boipušo bja Bathobaso.
Bantu, Bathobaso, Babaso, Baswana; – **affairs commissioner,** Komsasa, Komosasa.
baobab tree, seboi, moyo.
baptise, (baptize), kolobetša.
baptist, mokolobetši.
baptism, kolobetšo.
bar, v., pheka, tswalela, gana; n., para, lepheko.
barb, nkgwai, kobi.
barbarian, motala, lelaeta; – **rism,** botala, bolaeta.
barbecue, lešimelo, sebešo.
barbed, ya meetlwa.
barber, mmeodi, mokuti.
bare, hlobotšeng; v., hlobodiša, – **land,** lekwala; **lay –,** khupolola.
bare-faced, hlokago dihlong.
bare-footed, rotšego dieta.
bare-headed, sepela ka hlogo.
barge, seketswana.
bargain, thekofase.
baritone, paritone.
bark, matswamati, lekwati, sekgamathi.
bark, bogola, goba.
barley, garase.
barn, polokelo, leoba, setala.
barnyard, lapa, mafuri.
barometer, parometa, parometara.
baron, parone.
barrage, letamo.
barrel, faki; **of a gun,** lopo, molomo.
barren, person, moopa; **animal,** moreba, sereba, ngope; – **land,** lekwala, adj., opafetšego.
barrenness, boopa, boreba.
barricade, n., sebo; v., pheka, thibela.
barrier, thibedi, pheko, lepheko.
barrow, kiribane.
barter, v.t., bapatša; n., papatšo.
base, n., bofase, letlase, motheo, bogato, sematlafatšwa; – **s,** mabogato.
baseness, bošula.

bashful, boi, dihlong.
basic, theo, ya motheo, – **slag,** manyedi.
basin, sebjana, sekotlelo, sehlapelo, molapo; – **s,** dikotlelo, dibjana.
basis, theo.
bask, ora letšatši, sekamela.
basket, seroto; – **ball,** kgwele ya diatla.
bass, labone, pasa, kodu; **sing** –, korotla, – **drum,** sekgokolo.
bassoon, pasune.
bastard, lepastere.
Basutoland, Lesotho.
bat, mmankgagane, mmopu, moopu; v., opa.
batch, sehlopha.
bath, pafo.
bath-room, bohlapelo.
bathe, hlapa.
baton, molangwana.
battalion, sekgao, sekwata, dira.
batter, thubaka, thubaganya.
battery, peteri, dikanono.
battle, tlhabano; **ready for** –, itlhametše ntwa.
battle-axe, tšhaka, magagana.
battle-field, bohlabanelo.
battlement, sebo, lerako.
bawl, goa, potla.
bay, kou; adj., khunou, khunwana.
bay, bogola, goba.
bazaar, pasara.
be, ba, baa.
beach, lebopo, moseko, khwiti.
beacon, pakane, mokolokotwane.
bead, pheta; v., kgaka, hlahlela.
beading plane, sekhafomokolo.
beak, molomo.
beam, v., kganya, phadima, n., kota, kwata, teselepomo, lehlasedi.
bean, nawa; **bean-stalk,** monawa.
bear, rwala, šikara; tswala, belega; – **fruit,** enywa, bea; – **suffer,** kgotlelela; n., bere.
beard, leledu, maledu, ditedu; **a goat's,** seledu.
bearer, morwadi, mmelegi.
bearing, pering.
beast, phoofolo; – **of prey,** sebata, sebatana.
beat, betha, (i)tia, otla, opa, tea, kgokgotha; ratha, thula (tšhipi), pidinya, batola; n., mošito, morethetho.
beat, conquer, fenya; **overcome,** pala, šita; **be beaten,** fentšwe, šitilwe; – **out,** potolla, kobolla.
beating, kotlo, petho, dikgati.
beautiful, adj., botse; adv. **be** –, lebelelega; **become,** –, tsefala, ntlefala; **make** –, tsefatša, ntlefatša.
beautify, kgabiša, thakgafatša, tsefatša, ntlafatša.
beauty, botse, bothakga.
because, ka gobane; – **of,** ka baka la.
Bechuanaland, Botswana.
beckon, bitša ka seatla, lekanyetša.
become, tla ba; swanela, fetoga.
bed, malao, bolao, moalo, phate; – **linen,** mašela a malao.
bed-clothes, n., mealo, diphate.
bedding, ditao, malao; – **wetting,** go rotela dikobo.
bedroom, marobalelo, phapoši.
bee, nose; – **-bread,** tšhite.
beef, pifi, namakgomo.
bee-farmer, moruadinose.
beehive, phago.
bee line, thwii.
beer, bjalwa.
beetle, khunkhwana, khunkhwane.
beetroot, pete.
befall, wela godimo, diragalela.
befit, swanela, lekana.
before, pele.
beforehand, ka pele, e sa ba, ešo, sešo.
beg, kgopela, lopa, rapela.
beget, tswala, belega.
beggar, mokgopedi.

beggarly, nyatšegang, humanegileng.
begin, thoma, v.i., thomega.
beginning, mathomo.
beginner, mothomi, mothei.
begone! sepela! tloga!
beguile, fora thetša.
beguiler, mofori, mothetši.
behalf, bakeng sa.
behave, itshwara, ipuša, ipea.
behaviour, mokgwa, boitshwaro.
behead, kgaola hlogo.
behind, morago; **follow** –, šala morago, latela.
behold, bona, lebelela.
being, n., sebopiwa; **a living** –, sephedi; v., le.
belch, kgeba, tshwa.
belief, tumelo.
believe, dumela, holofela.
believer, modumedi.
bell, tšhipi, tleloko; **jar,** pelejara.
belladonna (plant), morola; **fruit of** –, thola.
belle (of the ball), mmamokgadi, tshehlana.
bellicose, ntwadumela, ratago ntwa.
belligerent, mohlabani.
bellow, lla, bopa, potla.
bellows, mouba, sebutšwelo.
belly, mpa, dimpa.
beloved, moratiwa, moratwi; **to be** –, ratega.
below, fase, tlase.
belt, lepanta, mmofo, setlemo.
belted, e tshega (m.), e tshegana (fem.).
bemoan, lla, llela.
bench, panka, senno; – **the court,** lekgotla; –**es,** dipanka.
bend, koba, fera, kgopamiša; – **down,** oba, inama, khunama; – **up,** pena; **bend as a hook,** mena; – **down low,** kodumela, kotimela; – **in, inwards,** kudupana; **head,** kgothula hlogo.
beneath, fase, tlase.
benediction, tšhegofatšo.
benedicted, mošegofatšwa.
benefactor, mogaugedi, mothuši.
benefit, thuša, hola; n., thušo, mohola.
benevolence, botho.
benighted, phirimelwa, phirimalelwa.
benign, botho.
bent, kgopo, kgopameng, koropanego.
benumbed, swarwa ke bogašu, bolawa ke phefo.
bequeath, šiela motho (leruo) lefa.
bequest, lefa, nkhwa, bohwa.
bereave, hula, hlakola, thopa.
beret, perete.
berry, kenywa, kenywana.
beseech, rapela.
beset, thika, rakelela.
beside, hleng ga, ka thoko, ipatile.
besides, ka ntle ga, gape, godimo ga.
besiege, rakelela, thika dikanetša,
best, kaonekaone, bokaone, phadišago, **do** – **best,** phegelela, katana, – **man,** mofelegetši wa monyadi.
bestial, sekasebata.
bestir, phakiša, akgofa.
bestow, fa, nea.
bet, tšea kgang, phea kgang, beelana.
betray, eka.
betrayal, keko.
betroth, beeletša.
betrothal, peeletšo.
betrothed, mmeeletšwa.
better, kaone, bokaone.
between, gare ga.
beverage, seno.
bewail, lla, llela, hloboga.
beware, bona! tšhaba, ping! hlokomela!, – **of,** itoteng.
bewilder, gakantšha, gakanega.
bewildered, gakanegile.
bewilderment, kgakanego.
bewitch, loya, upa, loa.
bewitcher, moloi.

beyond, mošola, moše, feta, fetiša, tlola(go).
bias, sepitša, tshekamo.
Bible, Bibele.
biceps, paesepe.
bicycle, leotwana, paesekela.
bid, re;
bide, kgotlelela, letela.
biennial, sengwagapedi.
big, -golo, kgolo; **so big,** – kaaka, kana, kaka; **how big,** e kakang.
bigamist, nyetše segadikane.
bigger, feta ka bogolo.
bilabial, tumadipou.
bile, nyooko.
bill, molomo, tšhupamolato, molaokakanywa.
billow, lephoto.
biltong, segwapa.
bind, bofa, tlema; golega.
binding, mophetho.
biography, taodišophelo, taodišetšo.
biology, thutaphedi, payolotši.
bioscope, paesekopo.
bird, nonyana; **young of a** –, lefotwana.
birdlime, bolepo, boletswa, tepe.
birth, pelego, tswalo, matswalo; v., tswala, belega.
birthday, letšatši la matswalo.
bishop, mopišopo; – **bird,** mmanoke, mmamonotswana; – **birds,** bommanoke.
bit, nyenyane, nthathana, n., mogala.
bitch, mpša e tshadi.
bite, loma, koma, kobola, **(snake),** kopa.
bitter, e babang; **be** –, baba, galaka.
bitterly, gabohloko.
bitterness, go baba, go galaka.
black, -so, ntsho, – **people,** babaso; **blacken,** ntshofala, fifatša, tshofatša; – **power, movement,** mokgatlo wa black power.
black consciousness, boitemogo bja bathobaso.
blackness, boso.
black-out, phifatšo, phifalo.
blacksmith, mothudi.
black-jack, mošitši, mokolonyane.
bladder, senye, sebudula.
blade, legare, bogale; – **of grass,** lenono.
blame, sola, bea molato, tomela.
blameless, se na molato.
blanch, šweufala, šweufatša.
blanket, kobo; **cotton** –, lepai.
blaspheme, nyefola, hlapaola, roga.
blasphemy, nyefolo, thogako.
blast, tšubutla, tšutla, ubula.
blaze, tuka; **a** –, letswatha.
bleach, šweufatša.
bleak, tšididi, tonya, tshehla.
bleat, lla.
bleed, tšwa madi.
blemish, sekodi, bosodi.
blend, tswakanya, tsenana.
bless, šegofatša, hlogonolofatša.
blessing, lešego, lehlogonolo.
blight, boori, nyakgahla.
blighter, mošaa.
blind, foufatša, fahla; v.i., foufala, pompala; – **person,** sefofu.
blindfold, bofa (khupetša) mahlo.
blindman's buff, sempotobotwana.
blindness, bofofu.
blink, ponya.
bliss, boiketlo, bomadimatle.
blister, lephone, letšwabadi; v., nyamolotša; – **s,** maphone.
blithe, thabileng, thabilego.
block, legong, kutu.
block-head, lešilo, sethoto.
blood, madi; **boiled** –, bobete; – **circulation,** tshepelo ya madi; – **poisoning,** tlhwelemadi; – **-stained,** thankgetše madi, mpholomadi, toyamadi. **white** –, leditšhweu; **red** –, ledikhubedu.
bloodshed, polao, tšhollo ya madi.
bloom, thunya, khukhuša, palega, atlega.

blossom, thunya, khukhuša, palega.
blot, šilafatša; n., sekodi; – **out,** phumola, phimola.
blouhaak, mongana.
blow, kotlo; v.t. budulala, budula; – **the fire,** butšwetša; v.i. **as the wind,** foka; – **hard,** tšutla, tšubutla, ubula; – **as bellows,** ubela; – **a trumpet,** letša phalafala; – **out the candle,** tima lebone; **give a side blow,** phaela; – **n away,** tšerwe ke phefo.
blubber, lla.
bludgeon, thoka, patla.
blue, tala, putswa, botala bja legodimo; **washing** –, polousela, v., lousela.
bluegum, mopulukomo.
blues, lepelela, kganya.
bluff, fora, foretša.
blunder, foša, šaetša, n., phošo.
blunt, kubegile.
blur, senya, dira sekodi.
blush, hubala, khukhuša.
bluster, bopa, hlaba lešata; n., popo, lešata.
boa-constrictor, hlware.
boar, kolobe e tona (ya naga).
board, papetla, phaphathi, lekgotla, lepolanka; tafola; dijo v., fepa.
boarding-house, kgorogelabaeti.
boast, ikgantšha, ikgodiša, itumiša.
boaster, moikgantšhi, moikgodiši.
boat, sekepe, seketswana, mokoro.
bobbin, kadi, sehlora.
bobby, lephodisa.
bode, hlola.
bodice, semmejana.
bodily-shape, sebele.
bodkin, nalete, tlhabišo.
body, mmele; **individual,** motho; **a collection,** sehlopha, lešaba.
body-guard, baletakgoši.
boekenhout, mongena.
bog, mohlaka.
bogey, bogy, sethotsela, setšhošo.
boil, v.i. bela, kgakgatha; v.t., bediša, apea; v.i. **boil up,** biloga; – **over,** falala; – **sore,** sekaku, sekutu; **boiling point,** bobelo.
boiled grain, dikgobe.
boiler, ketlele, sebelelo, poilara.
boisterous, hlaga; – **wind,** tšutlang, ubulang.
bold, bogale; – **man,** mogale; – **person,** segadi.
boldness, bogale.
bolster, mosamo, mosamelo.
bolt, kopela, kgonya, phaka, kwametša, tšhaba, hlanoša dinao; n., pautu, sekgonyo.
bomb, pomo; **mine a bomb,** thea pomo.
bombardment, thubako.
bomber, sethubaki.
bond, pofo, tlamo, kgwerano.
bondage, bohlanka, bolata.
bone, lešapo, lerapo.
bonfire, mollo wa moletlo.
bonnet, kapi.
boom, v., duma, kiritla; **prosper,** atlega; n., modumo, katlego.
boon, thušo, neo, mpho; v., thuša.
boot, seeta.
booth, ngwakwana, sehlaka, phapošana.
bootlegger, kwefa.
booty, kgapo, thopo, khulo.
boonze, nwa bjalwa.
border, mollwane, mellwane, leši morumo.
border, v., ruma, soma.
bore, bora, lapiša, tena; n., boro.
boredom, tapišo, go tena, bodutu.
bore-hole, sediba sa go borelwa, petse.
border, phehli.
born, tswalwa, tswetšwe, belegwa, belegwe.
borough, motse.
borrow, adima.
borrowing, kadimo; – **figure,** palokadimo.

bosom, sehuba, sefega.
boss, laola, rena, buša; (n.) molaodi, morena, baasa.
botany, pothani, thutadimela.
both, bobedi.
bother, tshwenya, lapiša, n., matshwenyego, tlalelo.
bottle, lepotlelo, botlolo.
bottom, bofase, botlase.
bough, lekala.
boulder, leswika.
bounce, tola, fofa.
bound, ya, ela, tlola, fofa; n., tlolo, mollwane.
boundary, mollwane, mmotwana.
bounteous, botho, tlopelago.
bountifully, gagolo, ka botlalo.
bounty, neo, mpho, kgaugelo.
bouquet, ngatanamatšoba.
bow, v., inama, obama; – **down to,** obamela, n., bora, segole, kinamo, kobamo, sekgapa tumedišo; – **legged,** digoro.
bowel, lela; **large** –, ngati; **lower** –, telele.
bowels, mala.
bowl, n., moruswi, mogopo, sego; v., poula.
bowler, mopoudi.
box, n., lepokisi, letlole, lekese; v.t., tia ka matswele.
boxer, ramatswele, radifeisi.
boxing-ring, mosako.
boy, mošimane.
boycott, ila, poikhota; boikota; n., poikhoto.
brace, bobedi; v.t. tshegetša; –, n., omoselaga, kobi, sekgwego.
bracelet, leseka; **copper** –, mpshiri.
braces, kruspane.
bracken, mmalewaneng.
bracket, kobi, nkgwai, lešakana.
brackish, letswai; – **soil,** serota, lenyaphiri.
brag, ikgantšha, ikgodiša, kgantšha.
braid, mologo, leetse; v., loga, phetha.
brain, bjoko.
brake, poriki; **-s,** diporiki; **apply the** –, bofa (di)poriki.
bramble, monokotswai.
bran, moroko.
branch, n., lekala, thabe, lešika, leloko; v., arogana, iphara; **a forked** –, maphata, maphaga; – **ed root,** modukala; **small** –, mošaša.
brand, v.t., fiša, swaya; n., leswao, serumola, tšhoša, bosodi.
brandish, kgatikanya, retha.
brand-new, mpshampsha.
brandy, poranabeine, poranti.
brass, porase.
brasso, poraso.
brave, adj., senatla, bogale; – **man,** mogale; v., hlohla, beta pelo.
bravery, bonatla, bogale.
bravado, boikgodišo, thumolo.
brawl, moferefere, tshele; v., ferekanya.
bray, lla, šoga, setla.
braze, solotera, thatafatša.
brazier, mpaola.
Brazil, Brazile.
breach, kgaolo, thubego, tlolo ya molao.
bread, borotho, senkgwa.
breadth, bophara.
break, roba, thuba, robaganya, phuma, pšhatla; – **off,** rokga, thokga; n., khutšo.
break, a law, tlola; – **off a branch,** phamola; – **off a joint,** lokolola; – **off a twig,** kgetla; – **off a bit, as food,** ngwatha; – **down, as a house,** rutla, rutlola; **as a wall,** phušolla; – **in, as animals,** tlwaetša; – **as water against a rock,** kgaphasela; **break through,** – šwahla; – **into,** phula; – **of day,** bosa, masa; – **into,** phunya (phula) ngwako; – **up a home,** phuma lapa; **break neck,** kotsi;

(voice) kotofalo; – **into bits,** ngwathaganya.
breakers, maphoto.
breakfast, sefihlolo; v., fihlola.
breast, sefega, kgara, sebuba, leumo; **a woman's** –, letswele, lebele.
breastbone, of an ox, bokwana; – **of a sheep,** sefega.
breath, moya; **be out of** –, fegelwa; **recover** –, hupologa; **keep** –, khupela moya.
breathing-space, bokhutšwana.
breather, bokhutšwana; **breathing,** khemo.
breeches, borokgo.
breed, mohuta, n., lešika; v., tswala, tswadiša, rua.
breeze, phefo.
brew, apea bjalwa, dira bjalwa, hlakanya.
bribe, reka, loba.
bribery, seatla kokong, šinolo.
brick, setena.
bricklayer, meselane.
bridal, monyanya wa tšeano.
bride, ngwetši, monyadiwa, motšewa.
bridegroom, monyadi.
bridesmaid, moetšana, mofelegetši wa ngwetši, pheleši.
bridge, n., moratho, leporogo, – **of the nose,** mmopo.
bridle, tomo, mogala; v., tsenya tomo, laola.
brief, adj., khutšwana, kopana, n., lengwalonyana, taetšo.
briefly, ka bokopana, ka bokhutšwana.
bright, phadima(ng), kganyang, bohlale, seleng.
brighten, phadimiša, ediša, kgantšha.
brim, morumo; **of a hat,** lepeno, lemeno.
brimstone, sebabole.
brine, meetse a letswai, meokgo.
bring, tliša, tla le, tlela; – **back,** buša; – **up,** godiša; – **home,** gorośa, – **out, something,** ntšha.
brink, ntšhi, leši, khwiti.
brisk, mafolofolo, hlaga, phafogiiego.
brisket, tlhakanya.
bristle, boditsi, porosolo.
Britain, Britain, Engelane.
broad, phaphathi, petleke, ahlamego, bophara.
broadcast, phatlalatša, gaša.
broil, gadika, beša; n., kgang, moferefere.
broke, pankoroto, tšhonne, hlaetšwe.
brooch, sethobošo, tlhabišo.
brood, n., lešika, matswinyane; v., alama.
brook, n., nokana, molatswana; v., kgotlelela.
broom, leswielo.
broth, mothotho.
brother, morwarra, mogolo, moratho, ngwanešo.
brother-in-law, mogwe, mogwa, sebara, molamo.
brow, phatla, ntšhikgolo.
brown, phifadu, phefadu; sotho.
browse, fula, phura.
bruise, letšwabadi; v.t., tetetša, tlapirigana.
brunt, boima.
brush, n., porosolo; v.t., porosola.
brutal, šoro.
brutality, sehlogo.
brute, yo šoro (yo sehlogo), sebata.
bubble, puwe, pudula, sebudula; v.i., biloga, kgakgatha.
buck, phoofolo; v., kgana, tlola.
buckle, kgokedi, tšhisepere, sekopela; ngomela, kopela.
bud, v., khukhuša, thunya; n., lehloma.
budget, tekanyetšo.
buff, serolane, sehla.
buffalo, nare.
buffer, segwara, segora.
buffet, tuba, thula.

bug, n., tšhitšhidi, tšitširi.
bugbear, setšhošetši.
bugle, phalafala, phala, perompeta.
build, aga.
builder, moagi.
building, moago, kago.
building material, dikago.
bulb, segwere, sekgaga, kotolana.
bulge, totoma, mohlopa.
bulk, bontši, botlalo.
bulky, kgolo.
bull, poo; **small/young** –, powana.
bullet, kolo.
bullfrog, letlametlo.
bullock, pholo; **pack** –, lekaba.
bully, mphenyanašilo, nkgwete.
bulrush, lekgaga, motsitla.
bulwark, sebo.
bump, khutla, thula.
bunch, sešoba, lešihla, lerose, ngata, kgola, ntšhuhla.
bundle, v., phuthela; n., sešoba; ngata.
bungle, fora, šaetša.
bunion, phone, v., letšwabele.
bunk, ngwega, roba sogo; n., malao.
bunkum, ditšie badimo.
buoyant, gogolago, phaphamago, thabilego, mafolofolo.
bur(r), mogoma, letadi.
burden, n., morwalo, phahlo, boima, v.t., imela, beleša.
bureau, biro.
burglar, lehodu.
burial, poloko, phihlo, kepelo.
burly, koto, wa lešata, golo.
burn, swa, fiša, tuka, tšhuma, babola, babela; **been burnt,** tšhumilwe.
burner, lebone, lampi.
burning, phišego, phišo.
burrow, rafunya, epa; n., molete.
burst, palega, phatloga, pharoga.
bury, boloka, epela, fihla.
bus, pese; – **halt,** boemapese.
bush, sethokgwa, sekgwa, sehlahla.
bush-baby, sebota.
bush-buck, serolo, tšhošo.
Bushman, Morwana.
bushveld, dikgweng.
business, kgwebo, ditaba; – **centre,** tulokgwebo.
bustle, mokurukuru, khuduego.
busy, dira, itapiša, swaregile.
busy-body, modubadubi, moithapodi.
but, upša, eupša, fela.
butcher, radinama; – **'s shop,** selageng, leselaga.
butcher-bird, sepoomootlwa, sephoromootlwa, letšoka.
butt, thula, khutla, theba.
butter, seredi.
butterfly, serurubele.
butter-milk, motsaro.
buttock, lerago, lešago.
button, n., konope, konopi; v., konopela; **sew on a** –, rokelela konopi.
buy, reka.
buyer, moreki.
buzz, boba, bobola, duma.
by, ka, ke, ga, fa, go.
by-law, molawana.

C

cab, thekisi.
cabbage, kole, khabetšhe.
cabin, phapoši, lephephe, mohlahlana.
cabinet, kabinete, letlole.
cabinet-maker, mmetli.
cable, mogala, v.t., romela mogala; – **gram,** mogalawatle.
cacao, khoukhou.
cackle, v., kgerekgetša, lla; n., sello.
cactus, sekamotorofeie.
cad, kgwara.
cadet, kadete.
cafe, khefi; – **keeper,** rakhefi.
cage, serobe, oko, hoko lešakana.

cake, kukisi, kuku, khekhe.
calabash, sego, kgapa, phafa.
calamity, kotsi, tlalelo.
calcium, kal(a)siamo.
calculate, bala, akanya, humana.
calendar, tšhupamabaka, almanaka, kalentara, khalenta.
calender, tšhupa.
calf, namane, lebotlana; **of leg,** potongwane.
call, bitša, goetletša, etela.
callipers, kedi, tekantšhi.
callous, se nang kgaugelo.
callus, phone.
calm, homola, homotša.
calorie, kalori.
calumny, tshebo, pateletšo.
calve, tswala.
Calvinism, Secalvine.
calyx, kalekisi.
camel, kamela.
camel-thorn, mogohlo, mokola, mphoka.
camera, khamera; **sit in –,** sekiša ka kobong.
camouflage, seipato.
camp, campa, hloma mešaša; **– ed,** kampile.
campaign, tlhabano, v., hlabana.
can, aux., v., ka; **tin –**; kane, boleke, lekanti, **– not,** palelwa, šitwa.
Canaan, Kanana.
Canada, Kanada.
canal, mokero, kanale.
canary, kanari.
cancel, khansela.
cancer, kankere, mofetši.
candid, botegago.
candidate, nkgetheng, moikemiši, mohlahlobiwa.
candle, kerese, lebone.
candlestick, sehlomo, polakere.
cane, rotwane, nyoba, ntsho; **stick,** kgati, thupa; v., otla.
canine, sempša, **– tooth,** polai.
cannibal, ledimo, lekgema.
canoe, mokoro.
canon, kanono.
cantankerous, ya mereba, ya kgang ya kgapa.
cantaloupe, sespansepeke.
canter, kata.
canvas, seila.
canvass, goketša.
cap, kuane, mmese, kepisi; **knee –,** khuru.
capable, kgona; aux., v., ka.
capacity, mothamo, boteng.
cape, kapa, hlohlo.
Cape Town, Kapa.
caper, phathankgana, kgana.
capital, mošate; tlhakakgolo; letlotlo, kapetlele.
capitalism, bokapitale.
capitulate, ineela, tela.
caprice, bokadikadi, matepe.
capriciousness, matepe.
capricorn, molatšatši wa kheprikone.
capsize, thenkgolla.
captain, kapotene, tona, molaodi.
captive, lethopša, mogolegwa; v., **be taken –,** golegwa.
captivity, bothopša, tlhahlelo.
capture, thopa, swara.
car, mmotoro, motoro.
caravan, karabane, molokoloko.
carbohydrates, khapohaetrete.
carbon, khapone, **– dioxide,** khaponetaok(o)saete, **– monoxide,** khaponemonoksaete.
carbonate, khaponate.
carbuncle, n., sentshuri, lethopa, kwatši.
carburettor, khabareita.
carcass, setopo, setoto.
cardboard, papetla, khatepoto, **– box,** khatepokisi.
card(s), karata, dikarata.
cardinal, ye kgolo.
care, pelaelo, tlalelo, pabalelo, tlhokomelo, v., hlokomela; **– for,** baballa.

career, boiphedišo; v., kitimela kua le kua, ralala.
careful, hlokomelang, hlokomelang gabotse, šedi gabotse.
careless, sa hlokomeleng, šaetšago.
caress, phaphatha, fepeletša, ola, fotša.
caretaker, mohlokomedi, moleti.
cargo, thoto, phahlo.
carnal, senama.
carnivore, sebata, sejanama.
carol, pina, sefela, kopelothabo.
carpenter, mmetli.
carpentry, bobetli.
carpet, tapeiti, khapete, sealwa.
carriage, kariki, koloi.
carrier, morwadi, mothothi, kheriana.
carrion, nama e bodileng, setoto.
carrot, segwere, segwete, borotlolo.
carry, rwala, šikara, thotha, gokara, duta; – **me,** nthwala.
carrying-poles, mapara.
cart, n., kariki.
cartilage, sekalešetla, lehihiri, – **rings,** mesehlo ya sekalešetla.
cartography, go thala dimapa.
cartoon, seswantšho sa go kwera.
cartridge, kolo, paterone.
cart-wright, mothulakoloi.
carve, seta, betla.
carver, moseti, **(knife),** thipapeko.
cascade, phororo, moelo, bontš(h)i.
case, taba; lekase, tsheko, lekga.
cash, tšhelete, kheše.
cash book, ngwalelamatlotlo.
cashier, raditšhelete, mmalatšhelete.
cask, faki.
cast, betša; lahla; – **the skin,** sola; **off,** ruma; – **down,** rutlolla.
castaway, molahlegi.
caste, thokolwana.
castigate, otla.
castle, sebo.
castor-oil, kasteroli; – **plant,** mokhura, (mokhure).
castrate, fagola.
casual, ka sewelo.
cat, katse; **wild** –, phaga; **musk** –, tšhipa; – **o'nine-tails,** tshelane.
catalogue, kataloko.
cataract, phororo, lera la mahlo, ledutšwe.
catarrh, mokgohlane.
catastrophe, kotsi.
catch, swara, rea, tanya.
catechism, katekisema.
category, kgoro.
cater, fepa, šomela; – **er,** mofepi.
caterpillar, seboko.
cattle, kgomo, dikgomo.
caucus, khokhase, sedutu.
cauldron, pitša, ketlele e kgolo.
cauliflower, kholifolawa.
causative, lediriši.
cause, sebak(w)a, lebaka.
causeway, setarata, moratho.
caustic, lomago, bogale; – **soda,** sota.
caution, (v.), sebotša, eletša, (n.), keletšo, tlhokomelo.
cautiously, ka tlhokomelo.
cave, legaga, mphoma, v., hlokomela! pasopa! ping!
cavern, legaga, mphoma.
cavity, sekoti, phago.
caw, lla; n., sello sa legokobu.
cease, fela, tlogela.
cedar (tree), mosedere.
cede, tela, gafela.
ceiling, siling, tšhirahlaka.
celebrate, bina.
celebrity, tumo.
celibacy, bokgope, bosoga.
celibate, wa kgope, lefetwa.
cell, sele.
cellar, leobo, selara, kelere.
cello, tšhelo.
Celsius, Celsius.
cement, samente.
cemetery, serapa.
cenotaph, leswika la kgopotšo.
censor, sensara; n., sensoro.
censure, kgalemela, omanya, sola.

census, palo ya batho.
cent, sente.
centenary, ngwagakgolo.
centigrade, sentikereiti.
centimetre, sentimetara.
centipede, lesokolodi, legokolodi.
Central Africa, Afrika-Gare.
centre, (bo)gare; – **bit,** borwanagare.
century, kgolo, ngwagakgolo.
cereals, dithoro, mabele.
ceremony, thlokomelo ya mokgwa, tirelo, mosepelo.
certain, -ngwe, itšeng; – **person,** mokete; – **thing,** sekete; – **truly,** nnete.
certainly, ka kgonthe, ka nnete, ruri.
certainty, nnete, therešo.
certificate, lengwalo la bohlatse.
certify, paka, tiiša.
cessation, kemišo, tlogelo, bofelo.
cession, tlogelo, telo.
chafe, gohla, kgobola.
chaff, moko, lefela, v., swaswa.
chain, ketane, tšhaene; v., golega.
chair, setulo.
chairman, modulasetulo, raditaba.
chalk, tšhoko, motaka, motaga.
challenge, hlohla; n., tlhohlo.
chamber, kamora, phapoši.
chameleon, leobu.
chamfer, moseto.
champion, thwadi, nkgwete, molwedi, phinere.
chance, sewelo, sebaka, mahlatse.
chancellor, hlogotona, mokanseliri.
chandler, morekiši.
change, phetogo, phetolo; tšhentšhi; v., fetola, tšhentšha, šatoša.
channel, mokero, kanale.
chant, kopelo; v. opela.
chaos, modubadubo, tšharakano, mpilobilo.
chap, monga, legotšane, moesa.
chapel, kapele.
chaperon, mofelegetši.
chaplain, moruti wa dira, kapelane.
chapter, kgaolo.
char, fiša, modiro lapeng.
character, semelo, mokgwa, moanegwa.
characteristic, pharologantšho, mokgwa.
characterise, phara, dipataka.
charcoal, magala, mošidi.
charge, tatofatšo, peo ya molato, tlhokomelo, tlhaselo, v., bea molato, laela, hlasela; – **a battery,** tlatša, **put in** – **of,** laelela.
charge-office, tšhatšofisi.
charger, pere (pitsi) ya mašole.
chariot, koloi (ya ntwa).
charity, lerato.
charm, pheko, moupo, toyo, v., kgahliša, loya.
charming, kgahlišang, kgahlišago.
chart, papetla; – **er,** lengwalo la tumelelo.
chase, leleka, raka, rakediša.
chasm, legaga, sekoti.
chassis, tšhesi, motheo.
chaste, sekegileng, hlwekilego, thakgafetšego.
chastise, otla, betha, (i)tia.
chat, kgang, v., swara kgang, boledišana.
chattels, thoto.
chatter, bolabola, bobola.
chatterbox, mmalabadi.
cheap, tšhipiša, tšhipile, fokotša theko.
cheat, n., mothetši, sehwirihwiri; v., fora, hlalefetša, hwirihwitša.
check, v., tšheka, n., sekotšho, tšheko.
chekk, lerama, thama; – **bone,** rapothama.
cheekiness, kgang, mereba.
cheer, n., thaba, ditlatse; v., thabiša, kgothatša.
cheerful, thabileng, thabilego.
cheese, kase, tšheše.
chemical, khemikhale, adj., sekhemise.

chemist, rakhemise.
cheque, tšheke.
cherry, tšheri.
chess, moruba wa sekgowa, tšheše.
chest, sehuba, kgara, letlole.
chew, sohla, hlahuna; – **the cud,** otla.
chicken, tswiana, tšhuana.
chicken-pox, mabora, sepšatlapšatlane.
chide, kgalema, omanya.
chief, n., kgoši; adj., kgolo, golo.
chilblain, magotšane.
child, ngwana.
child-birth, pelego.
childhood, bjana.
childish, bjana.
childless, se nang bana.
childlike, bokangwana.
chimney, tšhimele, setupišamuši.
chin, seledu.
China, Tšhaena, China.
Chinese, Motšhaena.
chink, monga, letlere, tšhelete.
chip, lefatša, tšhipisi, tshetlana.
chirp, lla, tswirinya, tswinya.
chisel, tšhisele, petlo; v., betla.
chloroform, seidibatši, klorefomo.
chlorophyll, klorofile, setalafatši.
chocolate, tšhokolete.
choice, kgetho.
choir, khwaere.
choke, kgama, tlima, beta.
choked, betwa, kgangwa; – **with laughter,** pipelwa ke disego; – **by food,** balelwa.
choking, kgamo, peto.
cholera, kholera.
choose, kgetha, hlaola.
choose first, raka, thaka.
chop, phapha, rema, kgabela; n., kgotswana.
chopper, selepe.
chopping, themo.
choral music, mogobo.
chord, thapo, kodukwana.
chorus, mogobelo.
chosen, mokgethiwa; **be** –, kgethwa.
Christ, Kriste.
christen, kolobetša.
Christian, Mokriste.
Christianity, Bokriste.
Christian name, n., lebitšo, leina.
Christmas, Krisemose.
Christmas-bee, sebakatšatši.
chromatic, (sa) notonyane, kheromatiki.
chronic, gogago, sa feleng, medilego.
chronicles, histori.
chronologically, ka tatelano, tlhatlamano.
chrysalis, mokone.
chuck, foša, lahla.
chuckle, sega.
chum, mogwera, monkane.
chunk, segoba.
church, kereke.
church-council, lekgotla la kereke; – **district,** sedika.
church-member, setho sa kereke.
church-warden, moletšatšhipi, moletakereke.
churn, kara, fehla.
cigar, sikara.
cigarette, sekerete, sikarete; – **s,** disekerete.
cinder, legala, mošidi, melora.
cinderella, mmamelora.
cinema, paesekopo.
circle, sediko, ntikodiko, sedikadikwe.
circuit, tikologo, – **court,** kgotlatshepedi.
circular, sekhulare, lengwalophatlalatšwa.
circulate, dikološa, potološa.
circulation, tikologo, tikološo.
circumcise, bolotša, rupiša, wetša, rupa.
circumcision, lebollo.
circumference, sedika.
circumflex, kapi.
circumscribe, laodiša, bea mellwane.
circumspect, tsarogilego, bohlale.

circumspection, tsarogo, bohlale.
circumstance, boemo, lebaka, maemo.
circumstantial, ya sewelo, ekeletšago, oketšago, laetšago.
circumvent, fora, hlalefetša.
circus, sorokisi, serekisi.
cistern, tanka, thini.
citizen, moikarabedi, moagi.
citizenship, boikarabedi, thutaboagi.
city, motse, motsemogolo, toropo.
civil, segae, selegae, hlomphegago; – **servant,** mohlanka wa mmušo.
civilise, hlabologa; **civilised,** hlabologileng.
civilisation, tlhabologo.
claim, baka, bakiša, ikabetše, seka; n., mmako, kleime.
claimant, mmedi, mmaki, moseki.
clamber, namela ka thata.
clammy, bošidi.
clamour, mokgoši, mogoo, goeletša.
clamp, sepatišo, sepatišetšo, sekurufi.
clan, lešika, leloko, mohlobo.
clang, tsirima, tsidima, lla.
clap, opa (magoswi).
clarification, tlhalošo, tlhathollo.
clarify, hlaloša, hlatholla.
clarinet, klarinete.
clash, thulana, n., thulano.
clasp, kgwaetša, ngamela, hupara, tatagana; n., sekgoge.
class, legoro, mphato, sehlopha, klase; – **room,** klasekamore.
classic, klasiki.
classify, hlopha.
classification, tlhopho.
classroom, klasekamore.
clatter, thanya.
clause, thabe, temana, lefokwana.
clavicle, kgetlane.
claw, monotlo, monatla, leroo, borofa, nkgwai; v., swara, ngapa; – **hammer,** notwanamanakana.
clay, letsopa.
clay-pot, moeta, nkgo.
clean, hlwekilego, thakgafetše, hlwekiša.
cleanliness, tlhweko, bothakga.
cleanse, hlwekiša, thakgafatša, hlatswa.
cleansing, tlhwekišo, tlhapišo, thakgafatšo.
cleanness, tlhweko, bothakga.
clear, selego, sekilego, pepeneneng, kwagalago, molaleng.
clear, tekolla, kgola, tloša, – **the table,** tekolla.
clearly, gabotse.
clearness, tlhweko, go kwagala.
cleave, beka, pharola, fatola, aroganya; – **to,** kgomarela.
cleft, monga, lefaro, sefata, karoganyo.
clemency, kgaugelo, botho.
clement, kgaugelo, gaugelago.
clench, swara, pinyeletša, tiiša; – **the first,** huna letswele.
clergyman, moruti.
clerk, klereke, tlelereke, mapalane.
clever, hlalefile, thantše.
cleverness, bohlale.
click, thathapa, n., lentha, lera.
client, mogomaredi, kliente, modirelwa.
cliff, legaga.
climate, klimate.
climatic, – **zone,** legaroklimate.
climax, sehloa.
climb, namela, hlatlola.
climbing (plant), morarane.
clinch, pinyeletša, swara.
cling, kgomarela, mamarela – **to,** itshwarelela.
clinic, kliniki.
clink, tsidima, tsirima.
clip, kota, poma, pataganya; n., sepate, sepatišetswana.
cloak, n., kobo; v., apeša; pata, uta.
clock, tšhupanako, orlosi.
clockwise, ka mmagojeng.
clod, lekote, lekwate.

clog, fara, pata, kgoramela.
close, tswalela, khurumetša, pipa, thiba; – **come,** batamela; adj., hupelanago, kgauswi.
closet, boithomelo.
clot, lehlwele.
cloth, lešela.
clothe, apara, tšwara, apeša.
clothes, diaparo.
cloud, leru; – **-burst,** matlakadibe.
clout, phasola.
cloven, maphata; – **-hoofed,** ditlhako tša mapharo.
cloy, kgoriša.
club, molamo, thoka, mokgatlo.
clubfoot, segole, radinawana.
cluck, kokoretša.
clue, mohlala, tšhupo.
clump, sehlopha.
clumsily, ka boatla.
clumsiness, boatla.
clumsy, boatla, botlogole.
cluster, sehlopha, lešihla, kgola, lerose; v., phuthega, kgobokana.
clutch, swara, kudupana, n., klatše, tlelatšhe.
clutter, magašagaša, lešata.
coach, koloyana.
coach, mothobolliši, motlwaetši; – **ing,** tlwaetšo, thapišo.
coal, lelahla, malahla; **live** –, legala.
coalesce, momagana.
coalescence, momagano.
coalition government, mmušo wa pušišano.
coarse, makgwakgwa, magwata, magwaše.
coast, lebopo.
coat, baki, kobo; – **of arms,** sefoka.
coat-hanger, mphegwana, hengara.
coax, fepeletša, rapela, opeletša.
cob, sefara, pere ya go namelwa.
cobble, roka dieta.
cobbler, morokadieta, mothuladieta.
cobra, peetla, renkalase.
cobweb, bolepa, bobi, bolepo.
cock, mogogonope, mokoko.
cock-crow, ge dikgogo di lla.
cock-eyed, moihlwe, leanago.
cockle, kgetla, kgapetla.
cockle, leolo.
cockroach, lefene, lefele.
cocky, makokwana.
cocoa, khoukhou.
cocoanut, khokhonate.
cocopans, dikgampane.
cocoon, sekgopana.
cod, hlapi, koto, v., hlalefetša.
coddle, hleka, phaphatha.
code, molao, tsela.
codling-moth, mmotoapole.
codliver-oil, makhura a sebete sa hlapi.
co-education, go rutwa gotee.
coerce, gapeletša.
coffee, kofi.
coffin, lekase (la setopo).
cog, khokho.
cogent, kgodišago, gapeletšago.
cogitate, gopola, akanya.
cognate, leloko la.
cognisance, tsebo.
cognition, tsebo, temogo.
cognize, lemoga.
cohabit, robala le, phela le.
co-heir, mojalefa le.
cohere, kgomagana, amana, ya le.
coherence, kgomagano, kamano, go ya le.
cohesion, kamano, kgomagano.
cohort, sekgao, sehlopha sa bahlabani.
coil, khoile, legaro.
coin, n., (se)tšhelete; v., bopa (tšhelete).
coincide, welana.
coincidence, sewelo, diwelana, mawelakgahlano.
coir, kwaere.
cold, phefo, botšididi, mpshikela, mokhohlane, maruru, tonya; **become** –, fola.

coldness, botšididi.
colic, kgadikego; **have –,** gadikega.
collaborate, dirišana.
collapse, wa, phohlela, burama, phuhlama.
collar, kholoro, sekgapa; swara (ka molala).
collar-bone, kgetlane.
colleague, mošomi-ka-nna.
collect, kgobokanya, bokanya, koleka.
collection, kgobokanyo, sehlopha, koleke.
college, kholetšha, lekgotla.
collide, thulana.
colliery, malahleng.
collision, thulano.
colloquial, sekamehla, segae.
colon, khutlwana, kgorwana, lelakgolo.
colonel, kolonele, koronele.
colonise, hloma koloni.
colonist, mokoloni.
colony, koloni.
colour, mmala, **many colours,** mebalabala.
Coloured (person), Wammala; **– s.,** Bammala.
colour-fast, mmala o sa galogeng.
colouring, sefammala.
colour scheme, thulaganyomebala.
colt, pešana, petšhana e tona.
column, kholomo.
columnist, mongwalakholomong.
comb, sekamo, kamo; v., kama.
combat, lwantšha; n., ntwa, tlhabano.
combination, kopanyo, tlhakanyo.
combine, kopanya, hlakanya.
combustible, tšhumega, tuka (go).
combustion, tšhumo, go tuka.
come, tla; **– back,** boa; **– back home,** goroga; **– near,** batamela; **– from, out,** tšwa; **– to pass,** diragala.
comedy, (papadi ya) metlae.
comeliness, botse.
comely, botse; **– woman,** lehlagamonna.
comer, motli, mofihli.
comet, naledi ya mosela, khomete.
comfort, n., khomotšo, boiketlo, matshedišo, v.t., homotša, tshediša, sediša.
comfortable, sa boiketlo.
comforter, mohomotši, motshediši, mosediši.
comic, segišang, segišago.
coming, go tla.
comma, feelwane, fegelwana.
command, n., taolo, v., laola.
commandant, molaodi, komotanta, **– -general,** komotantatona.
commandeer, epa dira, rapa dira.
commander, molaodi.
commandment, molao.
commando, sera.
commemorate, bina, gopola.
commence, thoma.
commend, tumiša, laeletša, neela; **– oneself,** ikgafela.
comment, swayaswaya, phara dipataka; n., tshwayotshwayo.
commerce, papatšo, kgwebo.
commercial, (traveller), mmapatši.
commission, tshwaetšo, morokotšo.
commissioner, komsasa; **– of oaths,** moeniši.
commit, neela, dira.
committee, komiti.
commodity, phahlo.
common, ya ka mehla, **– wealth,** kgweranaditšhaba.
commotion, khuduego, moferefere.
communal, kopanelo, mmogo.
communicate, neelana, bega.
communication, tsebišano, kominikasi.
communion, kopano, Selalelo se se Kgethwa.
communism, bokominisi.
communist, mokominisi.
community, setšhaba, morafe.
compact, kgohlaganego, teteaneng.
companion, mogwera, thaka; monkane; motswalle; **– ship,**

bogwera; **female** –, monkanegadi.
company, khamphani, komponi, setlamo, mokgatlo, sekgao, sera.
comparable, bapetšwago le, lekanywago le, bapetšega.
comparatively, ka papetšo.
compare, bapetša, lekanya, bapiša.
comparison, papišo, tekanyo, tshwantšho.
compass, khamphase, tšhupakhutlo, kompase.
compasses, pair of –, thalasediko.
compassion, kgaugelo, kwelobohloko.
compatible, kgonega, ka kopanwa.
compatriot, moagišani.
compel, gapeletša.
compensate, bušetša.
compensation, pušetšo.
compete, phadišana, phegišana.
competent, kgona, kgonago.
competition, phadišano, phegišano.
competitor, mophadišani, mophegišani.
compile, kgobokanya, hlopha, bokela, kgoboketša.
complacent, iketlile (go).
complain, belaela, ngongorega.
complainer, complainant, mmelaedi, molli, mmegi.
complaint, ngongorego, pelaelo.
complement, v., tlaleletša, n., tlaleletšo.
complete, tletšeng, phethegileng; v., phetha, fetša.
completely, ka go phetha, ka go fela.
completion, phetho, bofelo, mophetho.
complex, rananego, – **sentence,** lefokofokwana.
complexion, mmala (wa sefahlego).
complexity, tharano.
complicate, thatafatša, rarana.
complicated, rarane(go).
compliment, lakaletša mahlogonolo rweša, diala; n., diala.
complicity, tirišano, kabelo.
complimentary, godišago, retago.
comply, ineela, dumela.
component, setho.
compose, hlophiša, hlama, hlaka; – **d,** hlamil(w)e.
composite, hlakanego – **number,** palobopša.
composition, taodišo, tlhamo, tlhophišo, – **of soil,** popomobu.
compost, podišwa.
compound, v., hlakanya, boka, n., tlhakantšhetšo, kompo.
comprehend, hlaologanya, kwišiša.
comprehensible, kwagala(go), kwišišega.
comprehension, tlhaologanyo, kwišišo.
compress, pitlela, patiša, gatelela.
compression, kgatelelo.
compressor, segatedi.
compromise, v., kwana; n., kwano.
compulsion, kgapeletšo.
compulsory, gapeletšago.
compute, bala, lekanyetša.
comrade, thaka, mogwera.
comradeship, sethaka, bogwera, setswalle.
concave, kgampi, sekoti, semenya.
conceal, pipetša, fihla, uta.
concede, dumela, ineela.
conceit, boikgodišo, boikgantšho.
conceited, ikgantšha(go), ikgogomošago.
conceive, kwišiša, ithwala, ingwa.
concentrate, hlokomedišiša.
cencentrates, metswakotii.
concentration, tlhokomedišišo.
concentric, segaresetee.
concept, kgopolo.
conception, boithwalo, kgopolo.
concern, taba, modiro, pelaelo; – **ing,** ka ga, amanago.
concert, khonsata, kwana, lekanyetša, n., kwano.
concertina, korosetina.
concession, teseletšano, tumelo, neo.
conciliate, boelanya; **conciliation,** kagišo, poelano.

concise, kopana, akaretšago, ka bokopana.
conclude, akanya, phetha.
conclusion, kakanyo, bofelo, kakaretšo, makgaolakgang.
concoct, akanya, lekanyetša šaetša.
concoction, kakanyo, tšhaetšo.
concord, kwano, lekgokedi.
concordance, tšhupane.
concourse, kgeregelo, phalalelo.
concrete, sa popego, khonkriti.
concubine, phuti, motlabo, nyatši.
concur, dumelana, kwana.
concurrence, kwamo, tumellano.
concurrent, sammaletee, kwanago.
concussion, kgahlametšo (ya bjoko).
condemn, tšua, ahlola, tšwa, sola.
condemned, tšwilwego.
condemnation, kahlolo, tšuo.
condensation, themo, phokafalo.
condense, patiša, akadibetša, akaretša, kgahla, thema.
condescend, ikokobetša.
condition, maemo, popego, peelano, mokgwa.
condole, hlobogela, sediša.
condolence, kwelobohloko, sello.
condonation, tshedišo, tesetšo.
condone, sediša, fetiša, lesetša.
conduce, iša go.
conducive, thušago, direlago.
conduct, boitshwaro; v., opediša, sepediša.
conduction, tshepedišo.
conductor, malokwane, moopediši, kontae.
conduit, mosele, mokero.
cone, khouni.
confectionary, dibosabosane.
confederacy, kgwerano, kopano.
confederate, n., thaka; v., dira kwano, dira kgwerano.
confederation, tlemagano, kgwerano.
confer, nea, rerišana, laela.
conference, therišano, poledišano, komferensi.
confess, ipona molato, dumela, ipobola; – **ion,** boipobolo.
confide, bota, tshepa, holofela.
confidence, potego, tshepo, kholofelo.
confident, tshepa(go), holofetšego.
confidential, ka potego, ka kholofelo, ya sephiri, thopeng.
configuration, sebopego, beela mollwane.
confinement, pelego, thibelo, kgolego.
confirm, tiiša, hlatsela, hlomamiša.
confirmation, tiišetšo, tiišo, tlhomamišo, kamogelo.
confiscate, amoga, thopela.
confiscation, kamogo, thopelo.
conflagration, malakabe, mollo o mogolo.
conflict, tlhabano, ntwa, phapang.
confluence, magahlano, dikgatlo, kgahlano.
conform, kwana, ineela.
conformation, kwano, popego.
conformity, kwano, tshwano.
confound, gakantšha, tlaba.
confounded, gakantšhitše, tlabile, mafee!
confuse, gakantšha, rarakanya.
confusion, kgakanego, tšharakano.
congenital, ya tlhago, abetšwego.
congested, v.i., **to be** –, betagana, kitlagana, patagana.
congestion, kitlagano, patagano.
conglomerate, bokana, kgobokana, kgopa.
congratulate, lebogela, lakaletša mahlogonolo.
congregate, kgobokana, phuthega.
congregation, phuthego, kgobokano.
congress, pitšo, kgobokano.
conjecture, v., hloma, gopola; n., tlhomo, kgopolo, kakanyo.
conjugate, temekiša.
conjugation, temekišo.
conjunction, lekopanyi.
conjunction, kopano, tlhakano.

conjunctive, lekopanyi; adj., kopanyago.
conjure, loya, upa.
conjuring, toyo, kupo.
conjurer, moloi, moupi, sedupe.
connect, kopanya, bofaganya.
connected with, amana(go), mabapi le.
connection, kopanyo, kopano, leloko, mabapi le.
connective, lekopanyi.
connexion, see: **connection.**
conquer, fenya, hlola.
conqueror, mofenyi, mohlodi.
conquest, phenyo.
conscience, letswalo.
conscious, ikutlwa, kwa, tseba lemogago, kwago.
consciousness, boikutlo, temogo.
consecrate, thakga, kgetha, kgakola, kgethafatša, šegofatša.
consecration, thakgafatšo, kgethafatšo, tšhegofatšo, kgakolo.
consecutive, hlatlamanago.
consecutively, ka tlhatlamano.
consensus, kwano.
consent, n., tumelo, tumelelo; v., dumela, dumelela, kwana.
consequence, pheletšo, mafelo, malatelo.
consequently, bjale, ka baka leo.
conservation, poloko, paballo.
conserve, boloka, babalela.
consider, akanya, nagana, eleletša, sema.
considerable, golo, kgolo.
considerate, hlokomelago.
consideration, keleletšo.
considering, ka ge, kganthe.
consign, gafela, romela, neela.
consignee, moamogedi.
consist, go ba gona, bopilwe (hlophilwe) ka, ema.
consistency, kgotlelelo, phegelelo, tielelo.
consistent, kgotlelelago, kwanago le, tiileng.
consistently, ka kgotlelelo.
consistory, konsistori.
consolation, khomotšo, tshedišo.
console, homotša, sediša.
consolidate, tiiša, teefatša.
consolidation, teefatšo, tiišetšo.
consonant, tumammogo.
consort, mogwera, thaka, mogatša; v., felegetša, gwerana le.
conspicuous, pepeneneng, bonagalang.
conspicuously, pepeneneng.
conspiracy, borukhuhli.
conspirator, morukhuhli.
conspire, rukhuhla, rera.
constable, lephodisa.
constant, tillego, sa feleng.
constantly, ka mehla yohle.
constellation, sehlopha sa dinaledi.
consternation, lešašanošano, tšhogo, tlalelo, kgakanego.
constipate, bipela.
constipated, bipetšwe.
constipation, pipelo.
constitute, hloma, thea.
constitution, molaotheo, tlhomo.
constituency, tikologo ya kgetho.
constrain, gapeletša, swara, thiba.
constraint, kgapeletšo, thibelo.
constriction, kgamo, khunyetšo.
construct, bopa, aga.
construction, kago, popego.
construe, hlatholla, kopanya.
consul, motseta, khonsolo.
consult, rerišana.
consultation, therišano.
consultee, morerišani.
consulting, rerišanago.
consumable, dirišegago, lewago.
consume, ja, fediša.
consumer, moji, mošomiši.
consummate, phetha, fetša, tlatša.
consummation, phetho.
consumption, sehuba se segolo, tšhomišo, tšeo.
contact, kopano, kgahlano, kamano.
contagious, fetelago.

contain, na le, rwala.
container, setšhelo.
contaminate, tšhilafatša; – **tion,** tšhilafatšo.
contemplate, gopola, akanya.
contemporary, thaka.
contempt, nyatšo.
contemptible, nyatšega.
contemptuous, nyatšago.
contend, ganetša, phega.
content, diteng, kgotso, iketlile.
contention, go baka, kgang.
contentious, phegegago.
contentment, khutšo, boiketlo, kgotso.
contents, mateng, dikagare, mothamo.
contest, phegišano, kgang, tshele.
context, kamano, maloka le.
contiguous, neanago mellwane, batametšego.
continent, lefasana, kontinente, karolofase.
continual, ya ka mehla, sa feleng, gapegape.
continually, ka mehla.
continue, iša pele, šala, dula, nna.
continuity, bosafeleng, go iša, tšwelelo.
continuous, tšwelelago; – **tense,** lebakaletšweledi.
contort, šokanya, phetla, kgopamiša.
contortion, kgopamišo, tšhokanyo, phetlo.
contour, thapalalo, – **line,** motathapalalo.
contraband, phahlo ya kgogotšo, papatšo ya setsetse.
contract, kontraka, tlamano; v., hunyela, kwana, dira kontraka.
contraction, khunyelo, khunyetšo.
contradict, ganetša, **contradiction,** kganetšo.
contrary, fapanang, malatola.
contrast, phapano, pharologanyo, v., fapanya.
contravention, go senya, tlolo.
contribute, thuša, nea, diriša.
contribution, neo, kabelo, thušo.
contrite, hlomogago, nyamago.
contrition, tlhomogo, manyami.
contrivance, maano, sedirišwa, tlhamo.
contrive, loga maano.
control, v., laola; n., taolo; – **measures,** ditaolo, tsamaišo.
controller, molaodi.
controversy, kgang, kganetšo.
controvert, ganetša, tšea kgang.
conundrum, nyepo, thai.
convalesce, fola; – **nce,** pholo.
convene, kgobokanya, epa pitšo.
convener, moepapitšo.
convenience, boiketlo, tokelo, nolofatšo.
convenient, loketšego, nolofatšago.
convention, tlwaelo, kgwerano, kopano.
conversation, poledišano, kgang, polelo.
converse, boledišana, bolela.
conversion, tshokologo, phetogo.
convert, mosokologi; v., fetola, sokolla.
convex, lehutlana, semmotwana, sethotana, khutlologile.
convey, rwala, thotha, bega.
conveyance, koloi, senamelwa.
convict, mogolegwa, mmofiwa; v., ahlola.
conviction, kahlolo, kgopolo, tumelo, bonwe molato.
convince, kgodiša, fenya ka polelo.
convocation, phuthego, pitšo.
convolute, ikgara, rara.
convoy, v., felegetša; n., mofelegetši, phelegetšo.
convulsion, seretlwe, lešintlwana.
con(e)y, pela, tšhenene, tlholo.
coo, kuruetšo.
cooing, kuruetšo.
cook, v., apea; n., moapei.
cookery, kapeo.
cooking, kapeo, moapeo.

cool, tšididi, fodiša, tšidifatša, fola; – **room,** botšidifatšo.
coolie, lekula.
coop, faki.
co-operate, dirišana, thušana.
co-operation, tirišano, koporasi.
co-ordinate, lekanya, bapiša, kopanya, lekanago.
co-ordination, kopanyo, kgotlaganyo.
coot, sefudi, kgogomeetse.
cop, lephodisa, v., swara.
cope, katana, phegišana.
copper, koporo; – **plate,** ratibatša, papetla koporo.
copious, ntši, kudu.
copula, seleba.
copulate, kopana, robala le, gwela; – **ion,** kopano.
copulate, v.t., kopanya, bofa, tlema.
copulative, kopanyago, n., leba; – **formative,** lebopileba.
copy, kopiša, etšiša, ngwalolla; n., tekanyetšo, ketšišo, kopi; – **right,** tokelo ya ngwalollo.
coquette, seaka.
coral, khorala.
cord, mogala, thapo.
corded, bofilwego.
cordial, kgahlišago, thabišago, botho.
cordially, ka lethabo, botho.
cordon, sediko, sedikadikwe, thakelelo.
corduroy, forbele.
core, pelo, bogare, thapo.
cork, poropo, v., thiba.
cork-screw, kgogaporopo.
corm, segwere.
corn, tšhela letswai, noka, korong.
cornea, khonea, leapešaleihlo.
corned-beef, pifi, namabolekana.
corner, sekhutlo, khona, huku; **round the** –, morareleng.
corner, thibelela, kgesa.
corner-stone, letlapa la sekhutlo.
cornet, koronete.
corn-flour, folouru.
cornflower, letšobakorong.
cornice, lebalelo.
coronation, peo ya kgoši.
corporate, tlemanego.
corpse, setopo.
correct, nepilego, lokiša, koreka.
correction, tokišo, nepišo.
correlate, bapanya, nyalanya.
correlation, nyalanyo, papanyo.
correspond, swana, ngwadišana.
correspondent, mongwadišani, mongwaledi.
corresponding, swanago.
corroborate, tiiša.
corroboration, tiišo.
corrode, lewa ke makgalwa, rusa.
corrosive, jago.
corrugated, potegileng.
corrupt, bodiša, senya.
corruption, go bola, go senya ga.
corset, khosete, postoroko.
cosmopolitan, tlhakanasele.
cosset, nnake, moratiwa, hleka.
cost, theko, tshenyegelo, v., tura, (ja) bokae.
costing, kakanyatshenyegelo.
costume, khosetšhumo.
cottage, ngwakwana, thutsana, mohlahlana.
cotton, garane, lešela, leokodi – **-wool,** wulu.
couch, n., bolao, mpete, v., robala.
cough, v., gohlola; n., sehuba.
council, lekgotla, khansele.
councillor, mokhansele, mokgomana.
counsel, n., mmoleledi, keletšo, morero; v., eletša, rerišana.
count, bala, palo.
countenance, n., sefahlogo; v., emela.
counter, fapanya, fediša, lwantšha, n., khaontara; – **sink,** borwanakatološi.
counterfeit, v., etšiša; n., ketšišo.
counterfoil, setlankana.

countermand, laelolla, khansela, fediša.
countless, sa balweng, sa balwego.
country, naga, lefase, lešoka.
country, setereke, selete.
coup, kgapo, – **d'etat,** go gapa bogoši/mmušo.
couple, n., bobedi, mmedi; v., hlomaganya, kopanya.
couplet, sereto.
courage, sebete, bogale.
courageous, yo bogale, senatla.
course, khoso, tšhiano, tsela, boyo, moela, tshepelo, tatelano, thuto, lebelo, v., ela, šiana, tsoma; dijo, tsholelwa, latela.
court, lekgotla, khoto; v., loša, ferea, beka; – **-case,** tsheko; – **-room,** kgoro.
courteous, hlomphago.
courtesy, tlhompho.
courtyard, lapa, segotla.
court-martial, lekgotla la ntwa.
cousin, motswala, kgaitšedi.
cove, kou, sekabora, thota, moesa.
covenant, kgwerano, kwano.
cover, n., sekhurumelo, seširo; sepipetše, v., khurumela, bipa; – **totally,** aparela.
covering, seširo, sekhurumelo, seaparo, sebipo, phutha, sepipetšo.
covert, bokhutelo, botšhabelo, seširelo, kutamong, sephiri.
covertly, ka sephiri, thopeng.
covet, duma, lakatša, ikganyogela, kganyoga.
covetousness, megabaru.
cow, n., kgomo e (ya) tshadi; kgomogadi; v., tšhošetša.
coward, lefšega.
cowardice, bofšega, boi.
coy, tšhabang, ntšela.
crab, tlapakgerere.
crack, n., monga, lenga, letlere; v., palega, thanya.
cracker, krekere.
crackle, thanya, re thu.
cracklings, dikgadika.
cradle, thari.
craft, maano, tiroatla, bohwirihwiri, mošomo, seketswana.
craftsman, motsebatiroatla, sešomi.
craftsmanship, botsebatiroatla.
crafty, hwirihwitšago, ya maano.
crag, legaga, lewa, leswika.
cram, gatella, ithuta.
cramp, bogašu, sepatišetšo.
crane, mogolodi, sekuki; – **fly,** leponono.
cranial, ya legata.
cranium, legata.
crank, šopa, dikološa, mona.
crankshaft, kerenke.
crash, thulana, wa, robega.
crate, letlole.
crater, molomo wa bolokano.
cravat, thai.
crave, hlologelwa, duma, rapela.
craw, sejelo.
crawl, abula, gogoba, gopa ka mpa.
crayon, motakalala, krayone.
craze, bogafa, botlamara.
crazy, gafago.
creak, v., gwaša, tsirima, lla; n., kgwašo.
cream, lebebe, setlolo, seredi.
creamery, mabebeng.
creamy, sekalebebe.
crease, šošobanya, menagana, n., lešošo.
create, hlola, bopa.
creation, tlholo, popo.
creator, mohlodi, mmopi.
creature, sebopiwa, sephedi.
creche, khretšhe, ngwako wa bana.
credentials, lengwalo la (bohlatse) tumelo.
credible, tshepega, botega.
credit, n., khodi, tumelo, tshepo, tumišo, v., bota, holofela.

creditable, botega, tshepega.
creditor, mokolotiwa.
credulous, dumelago tšohle.
creed, tumelo.
creek, kounyana.
creep, abula, gagaba, rara.
creeper, mohuhumedi, moabudi, senami, serapo.
creeping thing, segagabi, segopi.
creeps, šišimoša.
cremate, fiša (setopo).
crescendo, tlhatlogo.
crescent, golago, eketšago, balamago.
crest, letlopo, sehloa, tlopo.
crevice, monga.
crew, sehlopha sa bathadiši.
crib, n., legopo, thari; v., ngwalolla, kopiša.
cricket, khrikhete, krikete, mamokgadi, senseretsere.
cried, llile,
crime, bosenyi, molato, tlolo.
criminal, sesenyi, mosenyi, monyemolato, motlodi.
crimson, bohubedu, karmosene.
cringe, obama, hleka, ithapeletša, ithapelela.
crinkle, šošobanya, šošobana.
cripple, segole, sehlotša, v., hlotšiša, golofatša, šitša.
crippleness, bogole.
crisis, moseneke, bogomo.
criterion, selekanyo.
critic, mosekaseki.
criticise, sekaseka.
criticism, tshekatsheko.
croak, lla.
crochet, n., mokgwagetšo, korašo; v., kgwagetša, koraša.
crock, thuba, roba, gobatša; n., sebjana.
crockery, dibjana, dibja.
crocodile, kwena.
croft, serapa.
crone, mokgekolo, setšofatšana,
crony, mogwera, thaka.
crook, sehwirihwiri, leswena, moradia.
crooked, kgopameng, kgopo.
crookedness, bokgopo, bokoropana.
crop, puno, thobo, sejelo, v., buna, roba.
cross, sefapano, befetšwe, fapana; – **over,** tshela, sela.
crossbar, lepheko, draghoute,
cross-examine, botšišiša.
cross-eyed, leana.
crossing, letšibogo, kgahlanong.
cross-legged, fera.
crossness, go befelwa, pefelo.
cross-question, botšišiša, sekiša.
cross-section, boputlo.
crouch, boba, batalala, khukhuna.
croucher, sebataladi, mokhukhuni.
crow, legokobu, legukubu; lla.
crowbar, kepi, kofutu.
crowd, n., lešaba, bontši, v., kgobokana.
crown, n., kgare, mofapahlogo; – **of a watermelon,** kgokgola; – **of the head,** phogo; – v.t., rweša kgare, bewa bogoši.
crucial, makgaola, kgaolago.
crucifix, seswantšho sa sefapano.
crucifixion, papalo.
crucify, bapola.
crude, tala, hlaelago, makgwakgwa, gorofo.
cruel, šoro, sehlogo.
cruelty, bošoro.
cruise, leeto go yo hlola, sepela ka sekepe sa go hlola.
crumb, lerathana.
crumble, foforega, nyelela.
crumpet, kokisi.
crusade, bohlabanedi.
crusader, mohlabanedi.
cruse, moruswi, sedibela.
crush, pšhatla, setla, pitlaganya.
crust, legogo.
crustation, bogogo, legogo.

crutch, seikokotlelo, lehlotlo.
cry, sello, mollo, mogoo; v., lla, goeletša.
cry-baby, sellallane, sellane.
crystal, kristale, legakwa.
crystallisation, kgahlo.
cub, ledinyane; **a lion's** –, tawana, **leopard's** –, lengwana; **a tiger's** –, nkwane; **a wolf's** –, phišana.
cube, kube, taese, daese.
cubic, kubiki.
cubic measure, tekanyokubiki.
cud, mootlo.
cuddle, ola, phaphatha.
cudgel, n., molamo, thobane, thoka; v.t., itia, setla, tula, betha.
cuff, khafo, mophethotsogo, kotlo, titio; v., itia, betha, tlelapa, phasola.
cull, phuta, kgetha.
culpability, molato.
culpable, molato, otlega, solega.
culpable homicide, polaokotsi.
culprit, mosenyi.
cultivate, lema, hlagola, aga.
cultivator, molemi, mobjadi, mohlagodi.
culture, setho.
culvert, leporogwana, khalbete.
cumber, imela, tshwenya.
cumbersome, imelago, imelang.
cumbrous, šitšago, tshwenyago.
cumulate, kgobela, kgobokanya.
cunning, maano, thetšo, hlalefileng, bohlale, bophelephethe.
cup, senwelo, komiki, phafana; v., lomega.
cupboard, raka, lekase, khapoto.
cur, mpša, sekebeka, leswena.
curable, fodišega, ka fodišwang.
curate, morutiši, moruti.
curator, motlamegi, mohlokomedi.
curb, swara, kakatlela, thiba.
curd, n., makgahla, dithata; v., themiša.
curdle, themiša.
cure, v.t., fodiša, alafa; n., phodišo, kalafo.
cure skins, šoga.
curious, go duma go tseba, bofeane, phišegotsebo.
curl, leetse, mogaro, gara.
currants, makwapi a diterebe.
current, moela.
curriculum, lenanethuto.
curry, kheri; v., šoga, betha, porosola.
curse, v., omanya, rogaka, roga; hlolela, n., komanyo, thogako, mahlapa.
cursed, rogakilwego.
curser, moomanyi, mothikito.
curt, kopana.
curtail, fokotša, poma, khutsofatša,
curtain, seširo, garateine, sešireletšo.
curtsey, curtsy, go thinya khuru.
curve, momenyamo, kgogoropo, kgopamo.
cushin, mosamelo, mosamo; v., samela.
custard, khastate.
custody, tlhokomelo, bofepi, pabalelo, kgolego.
custom, mokgwa, tlwaelo, setlwaedi.
customer, morekedi, khastamo.
customs, lekgetho, khastamo.
cut, sega, ripa, poma, rema.
cuticle, lera, letlalogapi.
cutlery, dithipa, disegi, dingwathi.
cutlet, sebeko sa nama.
cutting, thupana, moepo, sefata, lehloma.
cutting (excavation), sefata.
cutworm, sebokosegi.
cycle, leboyo.
cyclone, ledimo, saeklone.
cylinder, silintere.
cylindrical, silintere, sesilintere.
cymbal, simpale.
cynic, nyatša mathabo, mošun
cypress, mosiprese.
Cyprus, Saeprose.

D

dab, kgwatha, kgwatša, kgotla; n., kgwatšo, kgotla, sekodi.
dabble, tlapuletša, kolobiša, bera, šašetša.
dad, tate, rra, tata!
dagga, patše, lebake, matekwane, (di)mau.
dagger, thipa.
dahlia, dahlia.
daily, ka matšatši, ka mehla, ya mehleng.
dainty, sešebo; hlabošegang, metšegago.
dairy, lebeseng, maswing – **cow,** mmofu, kgomo ya maswi; – **farming,** bogami; – **produce,** dimaswi.
daisy, teisi.
dale, moedi, molapo.
dam, letamo, ageletša, tama.
damage, tshenyego, tshenyo; v., senya; -s, tshenyegelo; **suffer,** loba, senyegelwa.
damn, rogaka.
damp, bošidi; **damping,** fokela, šašetša.
damsel, morwetšana, kgarebe.
dance, bina, gobela, tantsha, n., mogobelo, pina, koša.
dancer, mmini.
dandruff, sekelefere, lehlono.
dandy, sethakga, setswatswa, setšhephi.
danger, kotsi, tsietsi.
dangerous, nago le kotsi.
dangle, lepelela, kgaphasa.
dapper, mafolofolo.
dare, beta pelo, leka.
daring, sa boifeng, betago pelo.
dark, so, ntsho, leswiswi, bošego.
darken, fifala, fifatša.
darkness, leswiswi, boso.
darling, nnake, moratiwa.
darn, roka, thiba.
dart, n., mosebe, motšu, mokopotšo; v., tlolela pele, betša.
dash, pšhatla, phuma, thula; n., thaladi; – **to the ground,** digela fase.
date, tšatšikgwedi, lebaka, tatlele; – **s,** ditatlele.
daub, phara.
daughter, morwadi, morwedi.
daugther-in-law, ngwetši.
daunt, tšhoša.
dauntless, bogale, sa tšhabego.
David, Dafida.
dawdle, diega.
dawn, masa, mahube, v., sa
day, letšatši, mosegare.
daybreak, masa, mahwibi.
day-labourer, molefšakaletšatši.
day-star, naledi ya masa.
daze, idibatša, idibanya.
dazzle, fahla.
deacon, motiakone, motikone, modiredi, mohlanka.
dead, hwileng, mohu, ithobaletše,
dead-house, makota.
deadlock, padile, paletšwe, šitilwe.
deaf, foafoa, ša kwego; – **-and-dumb,** semumu; – **person,** sefoa, setholo.
deafen, thiba tsebe.
deafness, bofoa, botholo.
deaf-mute, semumu.
deal, dira, bapatša, aba; n., kabelo.
dealer, mogwebi, mmapatši, morekiši.
dean, motikone, molapo.
dear, rategang, tura.
dearth, bohlokwa.
death, lehu.
debar, thibela.
debate, v., tšea kgang; n., kgang.
debauch, fapoša, kgeloša.
debauchee, sehlola.
debauchery, bohlola, bohlotlolo.
debility, bofokodi, phokolo.
debit, kolotiša; n., molato.
debonair, thabišago, botho.
debris, matladika, marope.

debt, molato, sekoloto.
debtor, mokoloti, monyemolato.
debut, tlhagothomo, tšwelothomo.
decade, lesome la mengwaga.
decadence, konalo, poelomorago.
decametre, tekametara.
decamp, ngwega, khuduga.
decant, tšholla.
decapitate, kgaola hlogo.
decay, v., bola, onala, n., polo konalo.
decease, n., lehu, mohu; v., hwa, hlokafala, timela.
deceased, mohu.
deceit, thetšo, phoro.
deceitful, bohwirihwiri, bonokwane, thetšago, forang.
deceive, foraforetša, fora, hlalefetša, thetša, hwirihwitša, lahletša.
deceiver, sehwirihwiri, senokwane.
December, Disemere, Manthole.
decency, tlhompho, boitshwaro, go loka.
decent, botho, lokilego.
deception, thetšo, phoro.
decide, phetha, ahlola.
deciduous, hlohloregang.
decimal, tesimale someng.
decimal fraction, palophatlotesimale.
decimalization, tshomefišo.
decimal point, khutlosomeng.
decision, phetho, kahlolo.
deck, apeša, kgabiša; n., teke.
declaration, pego, taodišo.
declare, re, bega, tsebiša.
decline, gana, rapama, lepelela.
declivity, thulamo, motheogo.
decompose, bola, tologa, bopologa, bopolla.
decomposition, go bola, tologo, polo.
decorate, kgabiša.
decoration, kgabišo, mokgabo.
decorative, kgabišago.
decorous, bothakga, botse.
decoy, fapoša, fora.
decrease, fokotša, fokotšega; n., phokotšo.
decree, molao, taelo.
decrepit, tšofetšego, fedilego.
decry, kgalema, nyatša.
dedicate, abela, neela.
dedication, kabelo, neelo, go ineela.
deduce, phetha.
deduct, fokotša, tloša.
deduction, tlošo, phokotšo.
deed, tiro, tokumente.
deeds-office, kantoro ya ditokumente, bongwadišo bja bong.
deem, hloma, gopola.
deep, tebileng, bodiba.
deepen, tebiša, epa.
deer, phoofolo, kgama, tshepe.
deface, senya, nyeletša.
defamation, tshenyoina, kgobošo.
defame, goboša, senya.
default, hlokomologa, senya, n., bobomotša, tlhaelo.
defeat, n., phenyo; v., fenya, fediša.
defect, sengalo, sekodi, phošo, bosodi.
defence, phemelo, tšhireletšo, tlhabanelo.
defend, phemela, šireletša, emela.
defendant, mosekišwa, mophemedi.
defender, mophemedi, mošireletši.
defer, šuthiša, diegiša.
deference, kgodišo, tlhompho.
defiance, tlhohlo, nyatšo, thumolo.
deficiency, bohlokwa, tlhaelo.
deficient, hlaelago, – **verb,** lehlaedi.
defile, tšhilafatša, senya, goboša, kgotlela.
defilement, tšhilafatšo, kgobošo.
defiler, motšhilafatši, mogoboši.
define, bea mellwane, hlatholla.
definition, tlhalošišo, tlhathollo.
deflect, fapoga, fapoša.
deflection, phapogo, phapošo.
deform, golofatša.
deformed, golofetše; – **person,** segole.
deformity, bogole.

defraud, hlalefetša, fora.
defray, lefa.
deft, thakgafetše.
deftness, bothakga, botswatswa.
defunct, hwilego, mohu.
defy, nyatša, rumola, hlohla.
degenerate, senyega; – **ion,** tshenyego, kgobogo.
degrade, kokobetša, tlotlolla.
degree, kgato, tikree.
deign, sema, ipha, sebaka.
deity, bomodimo, modimo.
dejected, nyemile moko.
delay, diega; diegiša, n., tiego.
delectable, bose, natefago.
delegate, moromelwa, moromiwa; v., roma, romela.
delete, tloša, ntšha.
deliberate, akanya, rera.
deliberation, kakanyo, morero.
delicacy, sešebo, sa bose.
delicate, boleta.
delicious, bose, mohlodi, monate.
delight, n., lethabo, nyakallo, kgahlego; v., kgahla, thabiša.
delighted, kgalemetše, thabile.
delightful, kgahlišago.
delirious, tlarea, fafatla.
delirium, tlareo, phafatlo; – **tremens,** papalase, diorisi.
deliver, phološa, neela.
deliverance, phološo.
deliverer, mophološi, mogolodi.
delivery boy, moišaphahlo.
dell, molatswana.
delta, teltha, manwaneng.
delude, fora, hlalefetša.
deluge, meetsefula, lefula, matlorotloro.
delve, epa.
demand, nyako, pelo; v., nyaka, bela.
demean, itshwara, kokobetša.
demeanour, boitshwaro, mokgwa.
demented, gafago, tlatlago, segafi.
demerit, molato, tlhaelo, phošo.
democracy, pušano, temokrasi.
demolish, senya, phušolla, fediša, phušola, kgereša.
demon, diabolose, motemone.
demonstrate, laetša, šupetša.
demonstration, taetšo, tšhupetšo.
demonstrative pronoun, lešupi.
demoralise, senya mekgwa.
demur, dikadika, belaela; n., tikadiko, pelaelo.
den, legolo.
denial, tatolo, kganetšo.
denizen, moagi, modudi.
denominate, rea, thea, leina, bitša.
denomination, theo, tšhupetšo, bokereke, borei, tekanyo.
denominative verb, letšwaineng.
denominator, lerei, selekanyo.
denote, bontšha, šupa.
denounce, sola, bega, kgala.
dense, kitlane(go), nnane, kitlagane.
density, kitlano, teteano.
dent, phobela, kuba.
dental, sa meno, – **consonant,** tumammogo -inong.
dentate, ya meno.
dentist, rameno, ngaka ya meno.
denudation, kgothego, kgorego.
denude, hlobola, gora, bipolla.
deny, latola, ganetša.
deodorant, polayamonkgo.
deodorise, bolaya monkgo.
depart, tloga, sepela.
department, kgoro.
departmental, ya kgoro.
depend, bota, holofela, tshepha; – **upon,** ikholofetša, ikanya.
dependable, botega.
depict, swantšha, ngwala.
deplete, fokotša, fediša.
deplore, nyama, belaela.
depopulate, khuduša.
depopulation, khudušo.
deport, raka, leleka, khuduša.
depose, ntšha tirong, pagolola.
deposit, bea, boloka pankeng, n., mogogolwa, dipositi, peeletšo.

deposit slip, setlankana sa poloko.
depot, bobolokelo.
deprave, senyega, befa.
depraved, senyegile, befile.
deprecate, lwantšha, gana.
depreciate, onala, nyatša.
depreciation, konalo, nyatšo.
depredate, thopa, hlakola, senya.
depredation, thopo, tshenyo, tlhakolo.
depredator, mothopi, mohlakodi mosenyi.
depress, gatella, hlomoša pelo.
depression, kgatello, tšhaparego, tšhayo.
deprive, amoga, hlokiša; thopa, hlakola.
depth, botebo.
deputation, baromiwa.
deputy, motlatši, motseta, moromiwa.
derange, ferekanya, gakantšha, gafiša.
derelict, tlogetšwego, lahlilwego.
deride, sega, kwera.
derision, ditshego, disego.
derivation, botšo, setšo.
derivative, letšo.
derive, tšwa, bona.
derived-verb, lediriletšo.
derrick, sekuki.
descend, fologa, theoga.
descendant, motlogolo, setlogolo, leloko.
descent, go theoga, thulamo, botšo.
describe, laodiša, hlaloša, thala.
description, taodišo, tlhalošo.
descriptive, lehlaloši.
desecrate, goboša, tlotlolla, senya.
desert, v., tlogela, ngwega; **be – ed,** lahlwa, wela kgwahlana.
desert, leganata.
deserter, mongwegi.
deserve, lebanwa ke, swanelwa ke.
deserving, swanetšwego.
design, morero, moakanyetšo, tshwantšho; v., rera, akanyetša, swantšha.
designate, lebiša, šupa, swaya, aba.
desirable, nyakega, rategа.
desire, kganyogo, thato, v., rata, gaba, duma, ikganyogela.
desist, tlogela, lesa.
desk, teseke, panka.
desolate, bodutu, tlogetšwego.
despair, v., holofologa, hloboga; n., kholofologo, tlhobogo.
despairer, mohlobogi.
despatch, romela, roma, bolaya.
desperate, tlaletšwe, holofologa, go ba tlalelong, gakanegile.
despicable, nyatšega.
despise, nyatša.
despoil, senya, thopa.
despond, nyema moko, hloboga.
despot, nkgogo, nkgwete.
dessert, tlhatswapelo, phuting.
destabilise, šarakanya.
destination, tebo, boyo, taelelo.
destine, lebiša, laelela, romela.
destiny, tebo, tlholelo, boyo.
destitute, hlaetšwe, hlokago.
destroy, senya, fediša, šwalalenya, bolaya.
destroyer, mosenyi, mofediši.
destructible, senyega.
destruction, tshenyo, tahlego, timelo, phedišo.
detach, lokolla.
detachment, mphato, sekgao.
detail, in –, ka bophara, ka botlalo; **– ed,** tletšego.
detain, diegiša, golega, thibela.
detect, hwetša, kgesa; **– or,** sehumani.
detective, lefokisi, letšeka.
detention, tiego, kgolego.
deter, thiba, tšhoša.
detergent, sehlwekiši.
deteriorate, senyega, boela, morago, bola.
determination, tiišo, kgotlelelo.
determine, tiiša, phetha, laetša, rera.
detest, ila, hloya.
dethrone, pagolola.
detonator, topi.

detour, morarela.
detract, tloša, pateletša, nyatša.
detraction, tlošo, nyatšo, tshebo.
detriment, tshenyego, tobo, tahlego.
devastate, senya, fediša, šwalalalanya
devastation, tshenyo, tšhwalalanyo, phedišo.
develop, tšwela pele, gola, godiša.
development, tšwelopele, kgodišo.
deviate, fapoga, kgeloga, hlanoga.
deviation, phapogo, tlhanogo, tepogo.
device, maano, seema, togamaano.
devil, diabolo, Sathane; – **ish,** bodiabolo.
devise, loga maano.
devious, raranago, manyokenyoke.
devoid, hlokago.
devote, (i)neela, swaela.
devoted, ratago, ineelang.
devotion, boineelo, kobamelo, boikgafo, tirelo;
devour, rwaetša, gagola, metša, laila.
devout, boifago Modimo.
dew, phoka.
dewlap, lebodu, kodu.
dexterity, bokgoni, botswiriri.
diabetes, taepitisi, twetšiswikiri.
diabolic, wa moya o mobe.
diacritic, leswao.
diagnose, pheka, laola, rekola.
diagonal, leputla.
diagram, tshwantšho.
dial, taela, taele.
dialect, mmolelo.
dialogue, poledišano.
diameter, molagare, kgaolagare.
diamond, taemane, taamane.
diaphragm, letswalo.
diarrhoea, letšhologo, letšhollo, taerea.
diary, pukutšatši.
dice, taese, bola.
dictate, biletša.
dictation, piletšo.
dictator, mmušanoši.
dictionary, pukuntšu.
didactic, rutago.
die, hwa, hlokafala
die, bola; taese; **the – is cast,** moloto o swele.
died, hwile, hlokafetše.
diet, dijo, sejo.
differ, fapana.
difference, phapano.
different, šele, fapanago.
difficult, thata, boima.
difficulty, bothata, matshwenyego, tlalelo, boima.
diffidence, bobotlana, boikokobetšo.
diffident, yo boi, ikokobetšago.
diffuse, gaša, phatlalatša, tšholla.
diffusion, phatlalatšo, tšhollo, kgašanyo.
dig, epa.
digest, šila, otla; n., kakaretšo.
digestion, tšhilego.
digger, moepi,
digging, kepo; – **s,** meepo.
digit, mono, monwana.
dignify, godiša, tlotla.
dignity, tlhompho, motlotlegi.
digress, fapoga, kgeloga, hlanoga.
dikomporomae, swings.
dilate, namalatša, katološa, lelefatša, taologa.
dilatory, tšwafago, diegago.
dilemma, tlalelo.
diligence, mafolofolo, boroto.
diligent, mafolofolo.
diligently, ka mafolofolo.
dilute, hlaphola.
dim, lerothwane, letobo; otofatša, fifatša.
dimension, tekanyo, bogolo.
diminish, fokotša, nyenyefatša.
diminutive, nyenyefatšo, nyenyane.
dimple, sekhutinyana, sesegišabaeng; – **s,** disegišabaeng.
din, lešata, thuthušane.
dine, ja.
dingy, leswiswi, ditšhila.
dinner, letena, matena.

dip, ina, tipa; n., tipe, botipelo, tipelo.
diphtheria, difeteria, dišotšhweu.
diphthong, tumopedi.
diplomacy, maano.
diploma, tiploma.
diplomat, ramaano, motseta.
dire, boifiša, boifišang.
direct, laola, lebanya, lebanego; – **towards,** lebiša.
direct object, sedirwa.
direct speech, poleloseboledi.
direction, nnga, thoko, taetšo, taolo.
director, molaodi.
dirge, sello.
dirt, tšhila, ditšhila.
dirty, ditšhila, tšhilafatša.
disable, palediša, golofatša, gwahlafatša.
disadvantage, tlalelo, tlhaelo, poelamorago.
disagree, fapana, sa kwane, ganetšana.
disagreeable, mpe; galakišago, šulafala, šulafetše, go se kwane.
disagreement, phapano, kgang.
disappear, hunyela, nyamela, ngwega, fela, nyelela, gohlomela.
disappoint, swabiša, nyamiša; **fail,** hlaela.
disapprove, gana, se dumele, se rate.
disarm, amoga dibetša, **disarmament,** kamogadibetša.
disarrange, šašarakanya, gakantšha, ferekanya.
disaster, kotsi.
disbelieve, holofologa, belaela.
disc, papetlasediko.
discard, lahla.
discern, lemoga, kgetha.
discerner, molemogi.
discernment, temogo, pharologanyo.
discharge, ntšha, lokolla, thunya, phetha, fela maatla, fokotšega.
disciple, morutiwa.
discipline, thupišo, boitišo.
disclaim, ganetša, gana, latola, itatola.
disclose, utlolla, bolela, bula, bololla.
discolour, galola, šatoga.
discomfit, ferehla, šitiša, palediša.
discomfiture, tlalelo, tšhitego, phenyo.
discomfort, tlalelo, kgakanego, bothata, phokolo, go se iketle.
disconcerted, gakanegile, tšhogile, belaela, tlaletšwe.
disconnect, bofolla, akolla, aroganya.
disconsolate, hlobogilego.
discontent, ngongorego, kgalalo.
discontinue, tlogela, lesa, lahla.
discord, tšhaetšo, phapang.
discount, phokoletšo, theolelo.
discourage, belaetša, nyemiša pelo, nola moko.
discouragement, pelaetšo, tšhošo.
discourse, kgang, poledišano; v., boledišana.
discover, bona, hwetša, ribolla.
discoverer, moribolli, mohumani.
discovery, khumano.
discredit, hlabiša dihlong, belaela, n., dihlong, pelaelo.
discreet, hlalefilego, bohlale.
discrepancy, phapano.
discretion, tlhaologanyo, tlhokomelo, tlhalefo, bobabaledi.
discriminate, hlaola, kgetholla.
discuss, boledišana, tšea kgang, rerišana.
discussion, kgang, poledišano, therišano.
disdain, v., nyatša, galala; n., lenyatšo, kgalalo.
disease, bolwetši, bohloko; – **germs,** ditwatši.
disembark, fologa (fološa) sekepeng.
disengage, lokolla, bofolla.
disentangle, rarolla, bofolla.
disfigure, senya, golofatša.
disgrace, n., dihlong, manyami, tlhomphollo; v., hlabiša dihlong.
disgraceful, hlabišang dihlong.

disguise, ikgakanya, pata.
disgust, feroša sebete, tena, šulafatša, – **ing,** tenago.
dish, sebjana, sejo, – **cloth,** fatuku.
disharmony, tšhitano, go se kwane.
dishearten, tšhoša, nyemiša pelo.
dishonest, sa botegego, se tshepege.
dishonesty, go se botege.
dishonour, tlhomphollo, tlotlollo; v., hlompholla, hlabiša dihlong, kgotlela, nyatša.
disinfect, upa, hlwekiša.
disinfectant, moupo, sehlwekiši.
disinherit, amoga nkhwa (lefa); ruolola.
disjoin, lokolla, kopolla.
dislike, se rate, hloya, ila.
dislocate, thinyega, phetlega.
dislocation, thinyego, phetlego.
disloyal, sa botege/botegele sa tshepegeng.
disloyalty, go se botegele.
dismay, belaetša, n., pelaetšo.
dismember, kgaola ditho, thubaka.
dismiss, phatlalatša, aloša, –ed, phatlaladitše.
dismount, fologa, theoga.
disobedience, go se kwe; kganano.
disobedient, sa kweng, ganago go kwa.
disobey, sa kwe, gana, hlokomologa.
disorder, tlhakantšuku, tšhašarakan(y)o, moferefere.
disorganise, šašarakanya.
disown, latola, gana.
disparage, nyatša, leša dihlong.
disparity, phapano.
dispatch, roma, tšhabeša, fofotša.
dispel, leleka, phatlalatša.
dispensary, khemisi.
dispensation, tebalebo, kabelo, tšhayo.
dispersal, phatlalatšo, kgašo.
disperse, phatlalatša, gaša, phatlalala.
dispersion, kgašo, phatlalalo, tšitlano.
dispirit, fediša pelo, tšhoša, belaetša, nyemiša moko.
displace, tloša, bea bakeng sa.
display, v., ikgantšha, bontšha; n., pontšho.
displease, šulafatša, kgopiša.
disposal, telo, taolo, thekišo, tahlo, kabo.
dispose, tela, lahla, rulaganya, aba rekiša.
disposition, mokgwa, tshekamelo.
dispossess, amoga.
dispute, kgang, kganetšano; v., ganetšana, swara kgang.
disqualify, ntšhwetša, tšwa.
disquiet, khuduego, tšhoša.
disregard, nyatša, hlokomologa.
disrepute, solega, nyatšega.
disreputable, nyatšegang.
disrespect, nyatša.
disruption, thubego.
dissatisfy, belaetša, ngongoregiša.
dissect, hlahlamolla, phakologanya, kgola ditho.
dissemble, ikaketša.
dissembler, moikaketši.
dissembling, boikaketšo.
disseminate, gaša peu, phatlalatša.
dissension, phapang, tšhitano.
dissent, gana, ikaroganya.
dissimulation, boikgakanyo, boipato.
dissipate, senya, phatlalatša.
dissipation, phatlalatšo, tshenyo.
dissociate, tlogela, ikaroganya, lokolla, aroganya.
dissolve, nyaoga, nyaoša, phatlalatša.
distance, sebaka, bokgole; v., katoga.
distant, kgole, kgakala.
distaste, tena, ila, šulafalela.
distemper, bolwetši, motaka, v., penta.
distend, otlolla, gagamatša, buduloga.
distension, kotlollo, pudulogo.
distil, tisitila; – **lation,** tisitilo.
distinct, bonalago, fapanago.
distinction, pharologanyo, tlhaolo.
distinctly, gabotse.

distinguish, hlaola, lemoga, bontšha phapang.
distinguished, hlaotšwego, hlomphegago.
distort, kgopamiša, šokanya.
distract, hlokomološa, gakantšha.
distraction, kgakantšho, matshwenyego.
distress, kgakanego, tlalelo; **be in –,** tlaletšwe; – **ed,** tshwenyega.
distribute, aba, abela.
distribution, kabo, kabelo.
district, selete, setereke.
distrust, belaela; pelaelo.
disturb, tshwenya, ferehla.
disturbance, khuduego, pherehlo.
ditch, lengope, mokero.
divan, sofa, rospanka.
dive, thinya, sobela, swinya.
diver, moswinyi, mothinyi.
diverge, fapoga, arogana, kgeloga.
divergence, karogano.
divers, ngwe le ngwe, ntši.
diverse, fapanago, šele.
diversify, fapantšha, fapanya.
diversity, phapano, pharologano.
divert, fapoša, sokološa, tepoša.
divide, arola, aba.
dividend, karolwa, karolo.
divination, taolo, bonoge.
divine, n., moruti; adj., sa Modimo, semodimo; v., laola, profeta.
diviner, senoge, sedupi, lephale.
divining-rod, theledi.
divinity, bomodimo, Modimo.
divisibility, karolego.
division, karolo, sekgao, kgaogano.
division sign, seka sa karolo.
divisor, karodi.
divorce, v., hlala; n., tlhalo; – **d,** hladilwego.
divorcee, mohlalwa.
divulge, bololla, tsebiša, senola, utolla.
dizziness, samadikwe, matladika.
dizzy, bolawa ke samadikwe.
do, dira šoma – **as if,** itiriša; **it will –,** go lekane.
docile, rutega, tlwaetšega.
dock, boemelakepe; lepokisi la tsheko.
doctor, ngaka, **witch –,** moloi, **rain –,** moroka, v., alafa, phekola.
doctoring, bongaka, kalafo.
doctrine, thutatumelo, tumedi.
document, tokumente, lengwalo.
dodge, efoga, široga, phema.
doe, phoofolo e tshadi, tshepe.
doer, modiri, sediri.
doff, rola, hlobola.
dog, mpša, mosoro; **wild –,** lehlalerwa, letaya; **top –,** nkgwete, kgadibete.
dog, hlomarela, hlomara.
dogged, hlogothata, tiile(go).
dogma, thuto, borapedi.
doily, toile.
doing, tiro, tiragalo.
doldrums, dikhomolo.
dole, kabelo.
doleful, manyami.
doll, popi; **play with –s,** raloka mantlwantlwane.
dollar, tolara.
dolorous, manyami, nyamišago.
dolt, sethoto.
domain, selete.
dome, sethothobolo.
domestic, ya legae, mohlanka, – **animals,** diruiwa; – **quarters,** lapa.
domesticate, thapiša, tlwaetša.
domestic science, thutalegae, thutalapa.
domicile, v., dula, aga; n., gae, madulo.
dominant, koketšwa.
dominate, rena, buša.
domination, pušo, borena.
domineer, kgadibetša, laola.
dominion, tominione, mmušano bogoši.

domino, tomino.
don, apara, tšwara, rwala.
donate, fa, nea.
donation, mpho, neo.
done, dirile.
donga, lengope, leope.
donkey, esela, tonki, pokolo.
donor, mofi, monei.
doodle, thalathala.
doom, tahlego, tšuo.
door, lemati; – **way,** mojako.
door-keeper, moleti wa mojako, moletakgoro.
dormant, khutšago, robalago.
dormitory, ntlo ya marobalo.
dorsal, la mokokotlo.
dose, n., selekanyo, v., noša sehlare.
dot, n., khutlo, lerontho, v., bea dikhutlo, kgathola.
dotage, botšofadi.
dote, tšofala, thotofala, fišega.
double, gabedi, pedifatša, bobedi.
doubled, hutagane, menagane.
double-faced, ikaketšang, thetšang.
doubt, belaela, n., pelaelo.
doubtless, ka kgonthe.
dough, hlama, tege.
doughnut, kukisi, kokisi.
dour, thata, tiilego.
dove, leeba; **rock** –, leebarope.
dovetail, lomaganya, lomanya.
dower, kabelo ya mosadi.
down, tlase, fase; **go** –, fologa, theoga; **fall** –, wa, wela fase; **throw** –, wiša; **the sun is** –, letšatši le sobetše (diketše).
down, mafofaletane.
downcast, swabile, nyamile.
downfall, go wa, tahlego.
downhill, n., mothetheo, thapamo; v., **go** –, theoga, rapama.
downpour, pula e kgolo.
downright, ka kgonthe, ka nnete.
downs, molapo, melapo.
downwards, fase, tlase.
dowry, magadi, bogadi.
doze, otsela, potuma.
dozen, tosene.
draft, sehlopha (sekgao) sa banna, go goga tšhelete ka korotelo, akantšwego.
drag, goga, ega.
dragon, kgokgolodumo, ntatauwane, terakone.
dragon-fly, leponono.
drain, mosela, pšhišo; v., pšhiša, gamola.
drainage, kgamolo, kgamogo.
drake, pelepele (pidipidi) e tona, sefudi se setona.
Drakensberg, Drakensberg.
drama, terama, tiragatšo.
dramatisation, papadišo.
dramatise, bapadiša, diragatša.
drape, apeša, – **over,** kgaphetša.
draper, morekišadiaparo, morekiši wa mašela.
drapery, diaparo.
draught, kgogo, mothalo, moya.
draughts, moruba.
draughtsman, mothadi.
draw, goga, thala, tomola; – **water,** ga, kga; – **er,** mothadi.
drawer, lehlayana, laiki; – **of water,** mogi, mokgi; – **of things,** mogogi.
drawers, setsiba, lekgeswa.
drawing, seswantšho, sethalo mothalo; – **book,** pukuthalelo; – **pin,** tobetšwi.
dread, poifo, tšhogo; v., tšhaba.
dreadful, boifiša, tšhošago, tšhabega.
dream, n., toro, v., lora.
dreamer, molori.
dreary, nyamišago.
dregs, magorogoro, dintshe.
drench, noša, kolobiša.
dress, seaparo; v., apara, apeša.
dribble, rotha, rothiša.
dried, omilego; – **fruit,** makwapi; – **meat,** segwapa.
drift, n., letšibogo, ledibogo; – **wood,** magogodi; v., tlekoga, phaphama.

drill, boro, thapišo, v., nwa, phoka.
drinker, monwi.
drinking-place, bonwelo.
drip, rotha, rothela, dutla, re tho.
dripping, makhura.
drive, gapa, otlela, tsamaiša; – **away,** rakediša, raka, koba; n., mokgothana.
driver, mogapi, mootledi.
drivel, phophiša, ediša mare.
drizzel, tshwelatshwela, n., mohuhwane.
droll, segišago, makatšago.
drone, nosetona, sebodu, modumo.
drones, mabobolane.
droop, duta, lepelela,
drop, lerothodi, phophi, v., rotha, lahla.
dropsy, mamokebe.
dross, manya, ditšhila.
drought, komelelo.
drove, mohlape, sehlopha.
drown, betwa, kgangwa ke meetse.
drowsy, boroko, potuma; **make –,** potumiša.
drudge, itapiša, kodimela.
drudgery, boitapišo.
drug, seokobatši, seidibatši, setagi(ši).
drug peddler, mmapatšadiokobatši.
druggist, mokhemisi.
drum, moropa; v., letša moropa; pidinya; **–majorette,** mosetsana wa matšarete.
drummer, moletšamoropa.
drunk, boilwego, tagwa.
drunkard, setagwa.
drunkenness, botagwa.
dry, omiša, oma, omela; – **up,** pšha; – **cupping,** lomega.
dry-clean, hlwekišaoma.
dryness, komelelo.
dry-rot, polo.
dual, ka dipedi, ka babedi.
dub, rea, bitša.
dubbin, setlolo sa letlalo.
dubious, e belaetšang.
duck, lepelepele, lepidipidi, sefudi, v., phefa.
due, tshwanelo, kolotwago.
duel, ntwa ya babedi.
duet, sefahla, duet.
dug-out, mokoro, lekokgwana.
dulcet, bose, botse.
dull, e sethoto, lerotho, bodutu.
dullness, bothoto, bodutu.
duly, ka tshwanelo.
dumb, semumu; **dumbness,** n., bomumu.
dumbfounded, maketšego, gakanegile, swerwe ke kgakge.
dummy, tami, seka.
dump, laolla, lahla.
dumps, nolegile moko, nyamo.
dunce, setlaela.
dune, lerotobolo, setotomane.
dung, boloko, thokolo, masepa.
dungeon, kgolego.
duodenum, tuotenama, (lela).
dupe, thetša, fora.
duplicate, kopiša, pedifatša; n., kopi, pedifatšo.
durable, tiileng, tiilego.
duration, lebaka, nako.
dusk, šwalane, phirimane, lerotho.
dust, lerole, v., thintha, hlohlora.
duster, sephumolo.
dustpan, seolela, seolelatlakala.
dusty, lerole.
duty, tshwanelo, malokelo, mešomo.
dwarf, kgopana; – **bean,** nawantšhuthana.
dwell, aga, dula.
dweller, moagi, modudi.
dwelling, ngwako, ntlo, moago.
dwindle, kokobela, fela.
dye, mmasa; tae, v., tšhela mmasa.
dyke, leboto, taeke.
dynamite, tanamaete, tanameiti.
dynamo, taenamo, segotetši.
dynasty, bogoši.
dysentery, tengkhwibidu.

E

each, mang le mang, e mong le e mong.
eager, fišega, mafolofolo.
eagerness, phišego, mafolofolo.
eagle, ntšhu.
eaglet, lefotwana la ntšhu.
ear, tsebe; – **of corn,** seako; – **-drum,** moropanatsebe; – **-training,** go tataiša tsebe, tlwaetšatsebe; – **-wax,** morulane; – **-phone,** tsebjana.
earl, mohlomphegi, mokgomana.
early, pele, ka masa.
earn, rua, gola.
earnest, rereša, bela.
earnings, tefo, moputso.
ear-ring, lengina, mmapa.
earth, lefase, mabu.
earthen (vessel), sebjana.
earthenware, ditsopa.
earthly, sa lefase, sa lefela.
earth-nut, tloo, letokomane.
earthquake, tšhišinyego ya lefase.
earth-worm, nogameetsana.
earwig, motsetaphala.
ease, bonolo, boiketlo, bohlofo; **be at** –, iketla.
easily, gabonolo, gabohlofo.
east, bohlabatšatši, bohlabela.
Easter, Paseka.
easy, bonolo, bofefo.
eat, ja, koma.
eatable, selewa, lewa, jega.
eating-house, bojelo.
eaves, mathudi, masenamelo; – **drop,** kwela.
ebb, hunyela, fela.
ebony, eponi.
eccentric, šele, makatšago.
echo, kgalagalo, mareetšane, v., galagala, kgerekgetša.
eclipse, n., phifalo; v., fifala.
economic, ya boiphedišo, pabalelo.
economise, seketša, iphediša, kolopetša, babalela, ekonomaesa.
economy, boiphedišo, ekonomi, pabalelo.
ecstasy, tlhalalo, makalo.
eczema, sekgalaka, lekhwekhwe.
eddy, phororo, setsokotšane, dikologa.
edge, bogale, leši, mophetho, morumo; v., ruma.
edible, lewa, jega.
edict, molao, taolo.
edifice, moago, ntlo e kgolo.
edify, agiša, agelela.
edition, kgatišo.
editor, morulaganyi.
educate, ruta, godiša.
education, thuto; – **dept.,** kgoro ya thuto.
eel, kgoka.
eerie, tšhošago.
efface, phumola, hlakola, fediša.
effect, sephetho, tiro; v., phetha, dira.
effective, phethago, kgontšhago.
effects, thoto, phahlo, maruo.
effeminate, sesadi.
effervesce, biloga.
efficiency, bokgoni.
efficient, kgonang, kgonago.
effigy, seswantšho.
effluence, kelelo.
effluent, elela, elelago, tšwago.
effort, go leka, teko.
effrontery, bohlokadihlong, makgapha.
egg, lee, letšae; **bad** –, thue, serue; **shell of an** –, legapi; **sit on** –, alama.
egg-flip, senolee.
egg-shaped, selee.
egg-shell, tlapi la lee, kgopa ya lee.
egocentric, boikgopolo, boitshepo.
egoism, boithato, boitsholelo.
egoist, seithati, moithati.
egotist, seithati, moithati.
egress, phalalo, matšo.
egret, kgogobadimo.
eider, mafofaletane.

eight, seswai, borobedi; – **th,** boseswai.
eight hundred, makgoloseswai.
eighteen, lesomeseswai.
eight o'clock, iri ya boseswai.
eighty, masomeseswai.
eisteddford, phadišano, eisteddfod.
either, goba, le ga e le, e mong wa bobedi.
ejaculate, goeletša.
eject, ntšha, tshwa, lahlela ntle; – **ion,** tumota, tumata.
eke, atiša, lelefatša, oketša.
elaborate, ka boitapišo, phethegileng.
eland, phofu, phohu.
elapse, feta.
elastic, rekere, raramologa; **elasticity,** tharamologo.
elbow, setšu, sejabana, sekgono.
elder, mogolo, mogolwane.
eldest, mogolo.
elect, kgetha; n., mokgethwa.
election, kgetho.
electoral-officer, mokgethiši, mohlankedi wa kgetho.
electric current, moela wa mohlagase (mohlakase).
electrician, ramohlakase.
electricity, mohlakase, mohlagase.
elegance, botse, kgahlego, bothakga.
elegant, botse, bothakga.
elegy, sello.
element, tokollo, elemente.
elementary, ya mathomo.
elephant, tlou; **trunk of** –, mmogo.
elephantiasis, bolwetši bja go ruruga setho.
elevate, phagamiša, kuka, godiša.
elevation, bophagamo.
elevator, sešego.
eleven, lesometee.
elf, Senkatawana, Tikološi.
elicit, ntšha, utolla, hlagiša.
elide, tlogela.
eligible, hlaolega, kgethega.
eliminate, šia, lahla, tloša.
elision, tlogelo.
elite, bakgomana, bahlomphegi.
elliptical, selee.
elocution, thuto ya (go bolela gabotse) boboledi.
elongated, lelefetšego.
elope, tšhabelela monna, thoba, ngwega.
eloquent person, seboledi.
else, mongwe, nngwe, šele.
else, conj., gongwe.
elsewhere, go gong, go šele.
elucidate, hlaloša.
elucidation, tlhalošo.
elude, široga, phefa.
emanciate, ota, otiša, bopama.
emaciation, popamo.
emanate, tšwa.
emancipate, lokolla, golola.
embalm, gwamiša ka dihlare, lota.
embank, ageletša.
embark, namela sekepe, tšea leeto.
embarrass, gakantšha.
embassy, batseta.
embed, sobeletša, šitlela.
embellish, kgabiša, thakgafatša.
ember, legala.
embezzle, utswa.
embitter, galakiša, babiša.
emblem, seka.
emboss, kokobatša.
embrace, khwaparetša, gokarela.
embrocate, tlola, pikitla, tshasa.
embrocation, setlolo.
embroider, kgabiša, tsantsabetša.
embroidery, mokgabišo.
embryo, pelwana, embrio.
emend, kaonefatša, phošolla.
emerge, tšwa, hlaga, – **anew,** thwaša.
emergency, tšhoganetšo.
emetic, sehlatšišo.
emigrant, mofaladi.
emigrate, falala; – **ion,** phalalo.
eminence, bophagamo.
eminent, phagamile.
emissary, motseta, moromiwa.
emission, kgašo, kedišo, tokollo.

emolument, tefo, moputso.
emotion, khuduego.
emperor, kesara, kesare.
emphasis, tiišo, kgatelelo.
emphasize, gatelela, tiiša.
empire, mmušo.
employ, thwala, thapa, diriša, šomiša; n., modiro.
employee, moswaratiro, mothwalwa, modiredi.
employment, modiro, thwalo.
employer, mothwadi, modiriši.
empower, fa maatla, fa tokelo, matlafatša.
empty, tšholl, kgothola; re hoo, se nago selo.
emulsify, tswaka.
emulsion, emalšene.
enable, kgoniša, kgontšha.
enact, diriša, bea (hloma) molao.
enamel, enamele.
encage, tswalelela.
encamp, kampa, hloma ditente.
enchant, loya, upa.
enchantment, bodupe, boloi.
encircle, dika, dikanetša.
enclose, hlahlela, tiela gare.
enclosure, legora, lešaka.
encompass, dikanetša.
encore, poeletšo, enkhoo, v., boeletša.
encounter, v., gahlana le; n., kgahlano, tlhabano.
encourage, kgothatša, hlohleletša, tutuetša.
encouragement, kgothatšo, tlhohleletšo, tutuetšo.
encroach, šwahlela, tlola moedi, metša.
encumber, thatafatša, imela, thibela.
encumbrance, thatafatšo, morwalo, thibelo, matshwenyego.
encyclopedia, (en)saeklopedia.
end, bofelo, pheletšo, v., fela, fediša, pheta.
endanger, tsenya kotsing, kotsifatša.
endear, ratiša, eketša lerato.
endeavour, leka, kikitlela; n., teko.
endless, sa feleng.
endocrine, endokrini.
endow, nea, humiša.
endowment, neo, khumišo.
endurance, kgotlelelo, tiišetšo.
endure, kgotlelela, tiišetša.
enema, enema, peita, thulega.
enemy, lenaba.
energetic, mafolofolo.
energy, mafolofolo, maatla, enetši; – **providing,** matlafatšago.
enervate, bofiša, tšhoša.
enforce, tiiša.
enfranchise, nea bouto, lokolla.
engage, beeletša, beeletšwa, thwala.
engagement, peeletšo, setlamo, ntwa.
ngender, tswala, hlagiša.
engine, entšene, hlogo ya setimela.
engineer, moentšenere, v., rulaganya, šušumetša, – **-ing vice,** patanyi.
England, Engelane, England.
English, Seengelese, Seisimane.
Englishman, Leisimane.
engrave, tloka, seta, gaba.
enhance, oketša, godiša, phagamiša.
enigma, nyepo, thai.
enjoy, ipshina, thabela.
enjoyment, lethabo, boipshino.
enlarge, godiša, oketša; katološa.
enlargement, kgodišo, koketšo, tlaleletšo.
enlighten, bea seetšeng, eletša, bonišetša, laodiša, laetša; – **ed,** edišitšwe.
enlightement, kedišo, pudulogo.
enlightening, kedišo, keletšo, taodišo.
enlist, ngwala, ngwadiša.
enliven, phediša, thabiša, kgothatša, tutuetša, tsoša.
enmity, lehloyo, bonaba.
ennui, bodutu.
enormous, kgolo, tona.
enough, lekane, kgodišang, tennwe.
enquire, botšiša, nyakišiša.
enquirer, mmotšiši.

enquiry, potšišo, nyakišišo.
enrage, galefiša, befetša; **–d,** fufuletšwe.
enrich, humiša.
enrol, ngwadiša; – **ment,** ngwadišo, palonane.
ensemble, moka.
ensign, sefoka, seka.
enslave, hlankiša.
ensnare, rea, thea.
ensue, latela, tšwa, diragala.
ensure, tiiša, phetha, kgonthiša.
entail, phetha, tliša, dira gore, hlola.
entangle, rarana, šarakanya.
entanglement, tharano, tšharakanyo.
enter, tsena, tsenya.
enteric (fever), tengkgolo.
enterprise, morero, tiro.
entertain, tloša bodutu, thabiša.
enthusiasm, mafolofolo, phišego.
enthusiast, yo mafolofolo, seroto.
entice, gokara, goketša.
entire, ka moka, ka botlalo.
entirely, botlalo, ka moka.
entitle, bitša, fa tokelo.
entitled, loketše.
entrails, mala.
entrance, sefero, botseno, kgoro, mojako.
entreat, rapela.
entrust, gafela, neela.
entry, botseno, matseno, tlhabelelo.
entwine, logaganya, tatetša.
envelope, omfolopo.
envious, hufega, ba le mona.
environment, tikolgo.
envy, hufega, duma, botšheba.
envoy, motseta, moromiwa.
enzyme, ensime.
epic poem, thetogale.
epicure, mojatswetswetswe.
epidemic, twetšisewa.
epidermis, letlalo la ka godimo.
epileptic, mohwahwa.
epilepsy, seiwane, dikotwana, maebeebe, dithunthwane, dihwahwa.
epiglottis, lelengwana, pelopelwana.
episode, tiragalo.
epistle, lengwalo, epistola.
epoch, mohla, nako, lebaka.
epos, sereto.
Epsom, salt, Engelesouto.
equable, lekaneng.
equal, n., molekane, thaka; adj., lekanago.
equal to, ke.
equality, go lekana.
equally, ka go lekana.
equanimity, go kwana.
equate, lekanya.
equator, ekhweita, mogarafase.
equinox, tekananako.
equip, hlama.
equipment, ditlhamo, ditlabakelo, ditlabele.
equity, toka, go se hlaole.
equivalence, tekano.
equivalent, lekaneng le, lekanago.
era, lebaka, nako, mohla.
eradicate, tumolla, fediša.
eradication, tumullo, phedišo.
erase, phumola.
eraser, sephumodi.
ere, pele, ešo, e sa ba.
erect, emiša, aga, re thwii.
erosion, kgogolego, kgobogo.
erotic, sa lerato.
err, foša, timela.
errand, taetšo, molaetša.
errant, ralalago.
erratic, fetofetogago.
erratum, phošo.
error, phošo.
erroneous, phošo.
escalator, morathadiko.
escape, tšhaba, phonyokga, n., phologo.
escapade, bolotšana.
escarpment, boriba, mothepologa.
escort, felegetša; n., mofelegetši.
Eskimo, Moeskimo.
especially, gagolo, kudukudu.

espouse, beka, beelela, gokara.
espionage, bohlodi, hlodimela.
espy, bona, senka, hlola, hlodimela.
esquire, mohlomphegi.
essay, taodišo.
essence, boleng, bokgonthe, (flavour), senatefiši.
essential, tshwanelo, nyakegago.
establish, hloma, thea.
estate, bohwa, leruo, boemo.
esteem, sema, hlompha, lekanyetša; n., tekanyetšo.
estimate, lekanyetša, akanya.
estimation, kgopolo, tlhompho, tekanyetšo, kakanyo, tshemo.
estuary, molomonoka.
et cetera, bjalobjalo.
eternal, sa (feleng) felego.
eternity, bosafeleng.
ether, itere.
ethics, thuto ya maitshwaro.
ethnic, serafe.
ethnography, taodišaserafe.
ethnology, thutaserafe.
etiquette, tlhomphano, tshwanelo.
etymology, etimolotši.
eucalyptus, mopulokomo.
Eucharist, Selalelo se se Kgethwa.
eulogise, reta, tumiša.
eulogy, theto, tumišo.
eunuch, mofagolwa, moamogwabonna, kgope.
euphorbia tree, mokgopha, mohloko.
euphemism, phefolo.
Europe, Europa.
European, Moeuropa, Lekgowa.
evacuate, nya, ntšha, tloga, tšwa, tšholla.
evade, široga, phefa.
evaluate, akanyetša, bala.
evangelist, mmoledi, moebangedi.
evaporate, pšha, nwega, moyafala.
evaporation, nwego, moyafalo.
eve, mantšiboa.
even, mantšiboa; lekan(y)a; boreledi, papetla, lekelelanya.
evening, mantšiboa, šwalane.
event, tiragalo, karolwana.
eventful, golo, phelang.
eventual, mafelelo.
eventuality, tiragalo, kgonego.
eventually, mafelelong.
ever, ka mehla; kile; **for** –, go ya go ile.
evergreen, talamehleng, motalane.
everlasting, sa feleng.
evermore, ka mehla, na neng le neng.
every, mang le mang, nngwe le nngwe.
everybody, mang le mang.
everyone, mang le mang.
everywhere, kae le kae, gohle.
evict, ntšha, falatša, raka.
evidence, bohlatse, tšhupo, bopaki.
evident, bonagalago, molaleng.
evil, bobe, bokgopo, sebe.
evil-doer, modiradibe.
evince, šupa, bonagatša.
evoke, hlagiša, tsoša.
evolution, phuthollo, tlhagelelo, ebolusi.
evolve, gola, tšweletša, phuthologa.
ewe, nku e tshadi.
ewer, nkgo.
ex-, ya kgale, tšwa go.
exact, nepilego, v., gapeletša, pata.
exacting, thata, bolayago.
exactly, ruri, nepilego.
exaggerate, feteletša, okeletša.
exalt, godiša, phagamiša, tumiša.
examination, tlhahlobo.
examine, hlahloba, sekiša.
examiner, mohlahlobi.
example, mohlala, tšhupo.
exasperate, galefiša, befetšwa.
excavate, epa, epolla.
exceed, phala, feta, fetiša.
exceedingly, gagolo, ka go fetišiša.
excel, phala, feta.
excellence, botse, bose.
excellency, mohlomphegi.
excellent, phalago, phadišago.
except, tlogela, ka ntle go; ge e se.

exception, fapanago, learogi.
excess, fetago, tekanyo.
exchange, bapatša, ananya; n., papatšo, kananyo, segareng.
excise, lekgetho, motšhelo.
excite, hlohleletša, ferekanya, huduegiša.
excitement, moferefere, khuduego.
exciting, huduago.
exclaim, goeletša, hlaba mokgoši.
exclamation, mokgoši, kgotso.
exclude, šia, tlogela, kgetholla.
excommunicate, kgaola, ripa.
excrement, dilahlwa, mantle, masepa.
excretion, sentšhwa, mantle.
excruciating, tlaišago.
excursion, moratšho, leeto.
excuse, lebalela, swarela.
execute, phetha, bolaya.
executive, phethago, – **body,** khuduthamaga.
exempt, lokolla, tlogela.
exercise, itlwaetša, thapolla, hlabolla, diriša, n., tlwaetšo, thutišo.
exercise book, puku ya maitekelo.
exert, phegelela, leka, katana.
exertion, phegelelo, teko, katano.
exhale, huetša.
exhaust, lapiša, fediša, n., eksoso.
exhaustion, tapo, tapišo, phetšo.
exhibit, v., bontšha, n., pontšho, sebontšhwa.
exhibition, pontšho.
exhilarate, thabiša, tsoša, thakgatša.
exhort, kgothatša, laya.
exhortation, kgothatšo.
exhume, epolla, tšhelolla.
exile, n., teleko, tahlo; v., raka, leleka, lahla.
exist, go ba gona, phela, ba ntshe.
existence, bophelo, bontshe.
existing, phelago, lego gona.
exit, botšo, lehu.
exodus, khudugo, eksodose.
exorbitant, fetišago tekanyo.
exorcise, leleka meoya.
exotic, šele.
expand, gola, katologa.
expanse, tšhabalalo, kalego.
expansion, go gola, katologo.
expect, lebelela, holofela, letela, lebeletše.
expectation, tebelelo, kholofelo, tetelo.
expectorate, tshwa mare.
expectoration, mare, sehuba.
expedient, thušang, thušago.
expedite, akgofiša, tšweletša.
expedition, lebelo, thomeletšo, lesolo.
expel, leleka, ntšha.
expend, ntšha tšhelete.
expenses, tshenyegelo, tefo.
expenditure, tshenyegelo, dijego.
expensive, tura.
experience, boitemogelo, tlwaelo, v., itemogela.
experiment, itekela; n., maitekelo; boitekelo.
expert, sediri, setsebi.
expiate, lefela.
expiation, tefelo, poelanyo.
expiration, bofelo, mohuetšo, khemelontle.
expire, fela, huetša, hwa.
explain, hlatholla, hlaloša.
explanation, tlhathollo, tlhalošo.
explicit, kwagala, bonagala.
explode, thunya, re pa!
exploit, diriša.
exploration, tlhohlomišo.
explore, hlohlomiša, utolla.
explosion, go thunya.
explosive, sethunyi, thunyago.
exponent, hlalošago, sematlafatši.
export, gwebela, iša ntle; n., kišontle, – **goods,** diyantle.
expose, bontšha, utolla, laodiša, bonagatša.
exposition, taodišo.
expound, laodiša, hlaloša, katološa.
express, bolela, hlagiša.
expression, seka, tlhagišo, polelo.

expressive, tiišago, hlalošago.
expropriate, amoga.
expulsion, thako, teleko.
exquisite, thakgegilego, bose (botse) kudu, phadišago.
extend, naba, otlolla.
extension, nabo, koketšo, katološo.
extensive, nabilego, bophara, katološo.
extent, sebaka, botelele.
extenuate, fokotša, fefola.
exterior, bokantle; e ka ntle.
exterminate, bolaela ruri, fediša.
external, ka ntle, sa/ya ka ntle.
extinct, hwilego, fedilego.
extinguish, tima, fediša.
extol, reta, tumiša.
extort, pata, gapeletša.
extortion, kgopeletšo, patiko.
extra, koketšo, oketšago, ekesetra.
extract, kgola, tomola, hlomola.
extraction, tomolo, tlhomolo, setšo.
extraordinary, makatšang, e šele.
extravagant, senyang tšhelete.
extreme, kudukudu, fetišago, pheletšo.
extremity, bofelo, pheletšo.
extricate, phološa, ntšha.
exude, tšwa sethitho, kga.
exult, hlalala, thakgala.
eye, leihlo; v., lebelela, hlola, diša.
eyeball, thaka ya leihlo.
eyebrows, dintšhikgolo.
eyelash, ntšhi.
eyelet, leihlwana.
eyelid, phuphu.
eyes, mahlo.
eye-tooth, polai.
eye-witness, mmoni, hlatse.
eyrie, sehlaga sa ntšhu.

F

fable, nonwane.
fabricate, bopa, itlholela.
fabulous, makatšago, senonwane.
face, sefahlogo, lebana, iponela; – **to** –, lebantše difahlogo.
facetius, segišago, swaswago.
face-value, theko ya ka mehla.
facial, ya sefahlogo.
facile, bonolo, bohwefo.
facilitate, nolofatša, iketliša.
facility, kgonagatšo, nolofatši.
facilities, dinolofatši.
facing, lebanego le kgabišo, lebišitše.
facism, bofasese.
faction, lekoko, sehlopha.
factor, katišani, lebaka.
factory, feketori, faporiki.
factotum, moswaredi.
faculty, lekala la thuto.
fade, galoga, tswapoga.
faeces, mampho, mantle.
fag, lapa, lapiša, sekerete.
fag(g)ot, morwalo, ngata.
fail, palelwa, foša, phošagala, n., phošo.
failing, tlhaelo, phošo.
failure, phošo, konya, pala.
faint, idibala, sa kwagaleng, n., kidibalo.
faint-hearted, boifago, tšhabang.
fair, lokilego, paale, fantiši; – **weather,** bosa.
fairness, botshephegi.
fairy, modimotsane; mmamaphegwana, – **tale,** nonwane.
faith, tumelo; **lack of** –, bohlayatumelo.
faithful, botegang, tshepegago.
faithfully, ka potego.
faithless, sa tshepegeng.
falcon, pekwa, sepekwa.
fall, wa, wela fase; **id** –, re tho.
fallacy, maaka.
falling, go wa, theogo.
fallow, poraka, latša, kgatha.
false, ya maaka; ikaketša, fora.
falsehood, maaka, bofora.
falter, kwakwetša, dikadika.

fame, tumo, setumo.
familiar, tlwaetšego, tlwaelana le.
family, kgoro, leloko, lešika, lapa.
famine, tlala.
famish, bolawa ke tlala.
famous, tumilego, v., tuma; – **people,** batsebalegi.
fan, leselo, boditse; foka sefokišamoya; morati, mothekgi.
fanatic, segogotlo, segafi.
fanaticism, bogogotlo, bogafi.
fang, sepolai, lerofa.
fantastic, makatšago, gakgamatšang.
far, kgole.
farce, n., go swaswa, papalo, botlaela, v., noka.
fare, tefo, go sepela.
farewell, laelana, dumedišа, taelano.
farm, polasa; v., lema, rua.
farmer, rapolase, molemi.
farther, kgojana, kgakala.
fascinate, kgahliša, kganyoga.
fashion, fešene, moaparo, mokgwa; v., bopa.
fast, ikona, itima.
fast, ya lebelo, tšhabeša, **-colour,** sa galogego.
fasten, bofa, hunela.
fastener, mmofi; mmofo, sekgokedi.
fastness, lebelo.
fat, makhura; **become,** –, nona.
fatal, bolayang, bolayago.
fate, tlholelo, pheletšo, sewelabatho.
father, (r)ra, tate, tata.
father-in-law, ratswale.
fatigue, tapo.
fatness, go nona, monono.
fatten, nontšha.
fault, molato, phošo.
faulty, ya phošo.
fauna, diphoofolo, diphedi.
favour, n., kgaugelo, sepitša, mogau; v., gaugela; rerelela.
favourite, lešwalo, moratiwa, rategang.
fawn, ithapelela, phaphatha.
fear, poifo, v., boifa, tšhaba.
feast, mokete, monyanya; v., ipshina.
feat, tiro e (kgolo) maatla.
feather, lefofa.
feature, sebopego, ponego.
February, Feberware, Hlakola.
fee, tefo, moputso.
feeble, fokolang, fokolago.
feebleness, phokolo.
feed, fepa, otla.
feel, phopholetša, kwa.
feeling, maikutlo.
feelers, dinakana.
feet, dinao, maoto.
feign, itiriša, ifaketša, ikgakanya.
feint, oma, ometša.
felicitate, lakaletša mahlogonolo.
felicity, mahlatse, mahlogonolo.
feline, sekakatse.
fell, rema, uša, wiša.
fellow, mogwera, thaka
fellow man, my –, mogagešo.
fellowship, sethaka, setswalle.
felon, be, šoro; n., mosenyi.
felony, tshenyo, bokgopo.
felt, felete.
female, tshadi, namagadi.
feminine, ya tshadi.
femur, lešukhukoto.
fen, molapo, mohlaka.
fence, legora; v., agelela, ageletša.
fencing, go ageletša, – **material,** diagetlelo.
fend, phefa, phema.
ferment, bediša, bela, omela, omelega, ferekanya.
fermentation, pelo, pherekanyo.
fern, mmalewaneng, patadikgagane.
ferocious, bogale, sehlogo, šoro.
ferocity, bogale, sehlogo, bošoro.
ferret, nakedi, moswe; dupelela.
ferry, letšibogo, mokoro; sela.
fertile, nonnego, enywago.
fertilise, nontšha, ungwiša.
fertiliser, monontšha.
fertility, monono.

fervent, fišega (go).
fervour, phišego.
fester, tutela, kupela.
festival, monyanya, mokete, moletlo.
fetch, tliša, tšea.
fête, monyanya.
fetish, modingwana, moeno.
fetter, mmofo, v., bofa, golega.
feud, kgang, moferefere, phapano.
fever, letadi, matšhona; fiša, khukha, phišo.
few, sego kae, nyane, nene.
fiancee, moratiwa, mmeeletšwa.
fiasco, konya, potsa.
fibre, tlhale, tlhajana.
fickle, kalatša, dikadika, hlanama.
fiction, senonwane.
fiddle, fiolo.
fiddlesticks, ditšiebadimo.
fidelity, potego, botshepegi.
fidget, dira letope.
field, naga, tšhemo; v., thiba lebaleng, fila.
field-marshal, felemašele.
fieldsman, mothibalebaleng, mofidi.
fiend, lenaba, yo mobe.
fierce, šoro, bogale.
fierceness, bogale, bošoro.
fiery, wa/ya mollo, galefile.
fife, fifero, nakana.
fifteen, lesometlhano; – **th,** bolesometlhano.
fifth, bohlano.
fifty, masomehlano, masometlhano.
fig, feie, feige, lego, **a – tree,** mofeie, mofeige, mphaya.
fight, ntwa, tlhabano; v., lwa, hlabana.
figment, sa akanyo, ya kgopolo.
figurative speech, dika, ka dika.
figure, popego, sebopego, palo.
figure-head, legoto, seswantšho.
filament, mamodula, filamente.
filch, utswa.
filcher, lehodu.
file, feile, faele, swaila, v., feila, boloka.
file, a row, molokoloko, lethathamo; v., bopelela.
fill, tlatša, kgoriša, khoše.
filling up, n., motlatšo.
filly, pešana, e tshadi.
film, filimi, lera, letha.
filter, v., hlotla; n., mohlotlo.
filth, tšhila, matlakala.
filthy, ditšhila, tšhilafetše.
filtrate, sefa, hlotla.
filtration, tshefo, tlhotlo.
fin, sephegwana, lephegwana.
final, ya mafelelo.
finality, bofelo.
finance, tšhelete.
financial, ya letlole.
finch, thaga.
find, bona, hwetša, topa.
fine, tefišo, tshesane, botse; mathume; **a –,** selefo. v., lefiša.
finesse, maano, bohwirihwiri; v., hwirihwitša.
finger, monwana; – **-nail,** lenala.
finger-print, kgatišo ya monwana.
finger-tip, ntlha ya monwana.
finish, fetša, fediša, phetha.
finite, beetšwege mellwane.
fir, mphaene.
fire, mollo, thunya, fiša, raka, **small –,** mollwana.
fire-arm, sethunya.
fire-fly, senakangwedi.
firepan, lekopelo la magala.
fire-place, sebešo, leifo.
fire-shovel, seolela-mollo.
fire-wood, dikgong.
fireworks, dilakalaka.
firm, tiilego, tiiša, n., feme.
firmament, lefaufau, legodimo.
firmly, ka go tiiša, tiišetša, tiilego.
first, pele, ya ntlha.
first-aid, thušo ya potlako, thušopele.
first-born, leitšibulo.
first class, lokileng kudu.

first-fruits, thakangwaga.
firstling, leitšibulo, ya serake.
firstly, la mathomo, sa pele.
fish, hlapi; v., rea dihlapi.
fisherman, morei, wa·dihlapi.
fishery, boruahlapi.
fish-hook, uku, huku, nkgwai.
fist, letswele, feisi.
fit, hwa dituntwane; – **tightly,** patagana.
fit, swanela, lokela, lekana, loketše, hlama.
fits, ditotwane, dituntwane.
fitness, go tia.
fitter, morudi, mohlami, molokiši.
fittings, ditlabakelo.
five, hlano; – **hundred,** makgolohlano.
fivefold, gahlano.
fix, hloma, lokiša, lomeletša.
fix, kotsi, tlalelo; **–ed,** points, dikhutlopewa.
fixture, se se tiileng.
fizz, šutša, phokgotha, kgakgatha, šašanyega.
flabbergast, makatša, tlaba.
flabby, matepeta.
flag, n., sefoka; v., lapa, nolega.
flagrant, bonagalang gagolo, siišago.
flake, kgapetlana, kgakgapšana; – **off,** foforega.
flame, kgabo, lelakabe; **v.,** lauma
flank, lehlakore, thapa.
flannel, folene.
flannel graph, kgomaswantšho.
flap, phepheula, phaphasela.
flare, tuka, takumela, folere; – **up,** lauma.
flash, gadima, phadima.
flask, lebotlelo.
flat, phaphathi, papetla.
flat (quarters), folete.
flatly, refuse –, ganela ruri.
flatness, bopapetla.
flatten, papetliša, papatla.
flatter, phaphatha, latswa ke leleme, roriša, gegea.
flatterer, mororiši, mophaphathi, teme.
flattery, thorišo, diteme.
flatulence, go pipitlelwa.
flaunt, (i)kgantšha.
flavour, noka; n., mohlodi.
flavourless, bošula.
flaw, monga, phošo, molato.
flax, folakese, lodi.
flay, bua, tswia.
flea, letsetse, letšimane.
flee, tšhaba.
fleece, letlalo la boya; v., kuta, thopa.
fleet, lebelo, bofefo.
fleet, sehlopha sa dikepe.
flesh, nama; – **of fruit,** bojeo.
flex, mena, oba.
flexible, nolo, menega.
flicker, nyedima, kgagamela.
flight, go fofa, go tšhaba, phofo.
flimsy, sese, senyega gabonolo.
flinch, tšhaba.
fling, betša, akgela, foša.
flint, legakabje, legakwa.
flip, fofa, phepheula.
flippant, hlomphollago, bolela ditšie badimo.
flirt, v., hlohloma, kalatša, akgela, n., seaka, mmaphateng; – **with men,** goketša banna.
flit, khuduga, tšhaba.
float, v., phaphama, phupha, n., mokawe, sephaphami.
flock, n., mohlape; v., kgobokana.
flog, itia, betha, otla.
flood, n., morwalela, meetsefula; v., enela tlatša, falatša.
floor, lebato, v., uša fase, bata.
flop, phuphusela, phepheula. n, konya, potsa.
flora, dimedi, flora.
floral, samatšoba, la matšobana.
florist, ramatšoba.
flotsam, dikgogodi, magogodi.
flounce, phonkgela, akga, kadipotšana; n., setsekana.

flounder, bidikama, pitikama, foša.
flour, bupi, folouru.
flourish, atlega, šegofala, retha.
flout, kgala, nyatša, kwera.
flow, ela.
flower, n., letšoba, lebue, v., khukhuša, thunya; – **-bud,** lehlomatšoba.
flu, geripi, mokhohlane.
fluctuate, akgaakgega.
fluency, boreledi.
fluent, boreledi, bonolo, elago, seela.
fluid, meetse, seela.
fluffy, sekafofa.
fluke, mahlatse, kgopa.
flurry, ferekanya, khuduego.
flush, falatša, meetsefula, fofa, fofiša, ediša, tšhoga, kgeregela.
fluster, gakantšha, gakanya, taga.
flute, n., naka; **flutist,** n., moletši.
flutter, phuphusela, phaphasela.
flux, moelo, tološa, setološi.
fly, ntšhi, adj., hlalefile.
fly, v., fofa, tšhaba.
flying-ant, kokobele.
foal, petšhana; v., tswala.
foam, lephilo, lehulo; v., fufula.
focus, tsepelela, tebanya, nepišo, nepiša, fokase, nepo.
fodder, furu.
foe, lenaba, sera.
foetus, in early stage, madi; **about three months old,** tlhaka; **full grown (human),** senamana; **an aborted** –, sefolotšane.
fog, mouwane, kgodi, letobe.
foil, palediša, šitša; n., thini, foili.
foist, foraforetša.
fold, lešaka, mohlape, lemeno; v., mena, fera, phutha; – **hands,** kopantšha diatla.
folder, mmeni, setsekana.
foliage, matlakala.
folio, letlakala.
folk, batho; – **song,** mogobelo.
folk-lore, dinonwane.
follow, latela, šala morago; – **me,** ntatela.
follower, molata, molatedi.
following, latelago; n., balatedi, bakgomaredi.
folly, bošilo, bothotho.
foment, thoba, bediša, hlohleletša.
fond, rata, ratang, ratago.
fondle, ola, hleka, fepeletša.
foundling, nnake.
fondness, lerato.
font, sebjana sa kolobetšo.
food, sejo, dijo.
fool, n., setlaela, lešilo, v., fora, thetša.
foolhardy, ngangela, šilofetše.
foolish, šilofetše.
foolishness, bošilo, botlaela, botlatla.
foot, lenao, leoto.
football, kgwele ya maoto, futupolo.
foot-fault, phošo ya maoto.
footpath, mmila, tselana.
footprint, mohlala.
foot-soldier, lesole la maoto.
footstep, kgato, mohlala.
footwear, dieta, ditlhako.
footwork, go tshetshetha.
fop, lekako.
foppery, bokako.
for, ka baka la, bakeng sa.
forage, furu; v., sela, utswa.
forbear, lesa, n., borakgolo.
forbid, iletša, gana, thibela.
force, gapeletša; n., kgapeletšo, maatla.
forced, gapeletšwa.
forceps, matlao.
forcible, ka maatla; – **ly,** ka mmetela.
ford, n., letšibogo, v., sela; – **able,** selega.
fore, pele, kgale.
fore-arm, sefaka, sephaka.
forebode, hlola, itlholela.
forecast, akanya, hlola, profeta.
forclose, thiba.

forefather, rakgolokhukhu, rakgolo, mogologolo.
forefinger, tšhupabaloi, šupabaloi.
forehead, phatla.
foreign, šele, ya (keeng) keng.
foreigner, o šele, mošele, moeng, mofaladi.
foreman, ketapele, foromane.
foremost, (ya) sa pele, pelepele.
forenoon, mosegare.
fore-runner, ketapele, phulamadibogo.
foresee, bonela pele.
forest, sethokgwa, sekgwa.
forester, radikgwa.
forestall, raka pele.
forestry, kagodikgwa.
foretell, profeta, laola.
forever, ka mehla, bosafeleng.
forewarn, seba, sebela, sebotša.
forfeit, loba, lahlegelwa.
forge, semete, šapo, bothuding, v., thula, rula, fora.
forger, mothudi, mofori.
forgery, phoro, kutso ya leina.
forget, lebala.
forgetfulness, bolebadi.
forget-me-not, (flower) sentebale.
forgive, lebalela.
forgiveness, tebalelo, tshwarelo.
fork, foroko, maphaga, v., fara.
forked, maphata, maphaga.
forlorn, lahlilweng, tlogetšwego.
form, sebopego, v., bopa.
formal, ka molao.
formation, popo, popego.
formative, lebopi.
former, pele.
formerly, pele, kgale.
formidable, maatla, boifišago.
formula, fomula, kaelo.
formulary, fomuliri, fomoliri.
formulate, laodiša, bopa.
fornication, bootswa.
forsake, lahla, tlogela.
forswear, latola, eka.
fort, sebo.
forth, pele, tšwelela; – **coming,** tlago.
forthwith, gona bjale, semeetseng.
fortify, matlafatša, tiiša.
fortitude, bogale, bonatla.
fortnight, bekepedi.
fortess, sebo.
fortunate, mahlatse, lehlogonolo.
fortune, maruo, mahlatse, lešego.
forty, masomenne.
forward, pele, mmapalapele; v., roma.
fossil, marapo a kgale, fosili.
fossilize, onafala.
foster, tlwaetša, godiša, tlametla.
foster-father, ramotlametli.
foster-mother, mmamotlametli.
foul, ditšhila, v., tšhilafatša.
found, thea, tološa, rula.
foundation, motheo, folomente.
foundation-stone, leswika la motheo.
founder, mothei, motološi, morudi.
foundling, lethwalwane.
foundry, bobopelo.
fountain, sediba, mothopo.
fountain-pen, pene ya sehupaenke.
four, nne, – **ne,** – **-hundred,** makgolonne.
fourteen, lesomenne; – **th,** bolesomenne.
fourth, bone.
fowl, kgogo, nonyana.
fowl-run, hoko, oko.
fox, phukubje.
fraction, palophatlo.
fractious, ferekanyago, ngangago.
fracture, thobego.
fragile, robegang.
fragment, kgapetla, nthathanyana, seripana.
fragrance, monko.
frail, boleta, robegang.
frailty, boleta, bogwahla.
frame, foreime, kosene; – **s,** mahlomo.
framework, mohlako, mahlomo.
frank, molaleng, pepeneneng, (ma)kgonthe lokologileng.

frantic, galefileng.
fraternity, kagišano, botho.
fraud, thetšo, phoro, tlhalefetšo, boradia, bomenemene, mašumatho.
fray, hlarolla; n., tlhabano.
freak, selo se se makatšago.
freckled, maronthwana dipatso.
freckles, dithala, dipatso.
free, lokologileng; v., lokolla.
freedom, tokologo.
free-booter, senokwane.
freely, ka tokologo.
freeness, tokologo.
freewill, boithatelo, go ithapa, boithaopo.
freeze, kgahla, gatsela.
freezing-point, bokgahlo, kgatselo.
freight, morwalo, tefamorwalo.
French, Fora.
frenzy, bogafa.
frequent, atileng; v., etela, gantšhi.
frequently, atiša, gantši.
freckles, marothorothwana.
frescoes, makwala, makgolo.
fresh, talá, hlabošago, mpsha.
fresh air, moya o hlabošang.
freshen, mpshafatša, hlaboša.
freshman, yo mofsa.
fret, ngongorega, kgabiša, seta, kokona.
fretful, tshwenyago, lepelelago.
fricative, tumagwaša.
friction, pikitlo, kgohlano.
Friday, Labohlano.
friend, mogwera, monkane.
friendship, kgwerano, sekgotse.
frieze, moseto.
friezes, mesehlo, diseto.
frigate, sekepe sa ntwa.
fright, poifo, tšhogo, go tšhoga.
frighten, tšhoša, tšhošetša.
frightful, tšhabegang, boifišang.
frigid, tšididi; – **zone,** letšididing.
frigidity, botšididi.
frill, legabe, leši, morumo.
fringe, morumo o kgabišitšwego.
frisk, kgana, tlolaka, kalapa.
fritter, kokisi, sematlana.
frivolous, tlaela, senyago, botlaela, lefela.
fro, go tloga kua; **to and** –, kua le kua, go ya pele le morago.
frock, seaparo, purapura, roko, mosese.
frog, segwagwa, segwegwe.
frolic, thakgetše, thakgala, swaswa, dira metlae.
from, go tloga (go) ga, tšwago.
front, fa pele, bokapele.
frontier, mollwane.
frost, tšhwane, lekgwa, šobane, – **bite,** kgatselo.
froth, lephilo, mahulo.
frown, šunyalala, šošobanya.
frozen, kgahlile, gatsetše.
frugal, ngwathang.
fruit, kenywa, seenywa.
fruitsalt, letswaikenywa.
fruit-tree, mohlare wa dikenywa.
frustrate, palediša, šitiša, nolegiša moko.
fry, beša, gadika.
frying-pan, pane, segadikelo.
fuel, sebešwa, dibešwa.
fugitive, motšhabi, mofaladi.
fulfil, phetha, feleletša, phethagatša.
fulfilment, phetho, phethego.
full, tletše, tletšego; **become** –, tlala.
full-grown, godile(go).
full-stop, khutlo.
fully, ka botlalo, gagolo.
fulminate, gadima, duma, thunya.
fulness, botlalo.
fulsome, tenago, galakišago.
fumble, mpampetša.
fume, muši, v., galefa.
fumes, hlahlamuši, kgakgamuši, mekubego.
fumigate, upa, arametša, kubuetša, thuntšhetša, kueletša.
fun, lethabo, moswaso.
function, tiro, v., šoma.

fund, sekhwama, letlole.
fundament, motheo, lešago.
fundamental, ya theo.
funds, ditefo, ditšhelete, sekhwama.
funeral, poloko, phihlo.
fungus, tututšhwane, mouta, fankase.
funnel, tupamuši, mojagobedi.
funny, segiša(go), segišang.
fur, boya, nkhakhane.
furlong, ferelone.
furious, galefileng, befetšwego.
furnace, sebešo, onto, leifo.
furnish, fa, nea; – **ings,** ditlabakelo.
furniture, fenitšhara, phahlo, fenišara.
furore, mafolofolo, phišego.
furrow, mokero, foro.
further, kua pele, gape, iša pele.
furthermore, mme.
furtive, bonokwane, ka sephiri, hwirihwitšago.
fury, pefelo, kgalefo.
fuse, tološa, tologa, fiusa, n., fiuse.
fusion, tlhakatlhakanyo, motswako.
fuss, n., lešata, mokgoši, khuduego, v., hlakiša, tshwenya.
fusty, nkgago.
futile, lefela, mafela.
future, ietlang, letlago, ka moso, bokamoso.

G

gab, balabala, ratharatha, bolela.
gabble, n., palabalo; v., balabala.
gabbler, mmalabadi.
gable, lebota.
gad, ralala, kobakobana, hlahlatha.
gadabout, lekobakobane.
gad-fly, seboka.
gaff, kobi, huku, kutla.
gag, homotša, thiba molomo; n., sethibamolomo.
gage, beeletša, panta, tshepiša.
gaggle, balabala, sehlopha sa ditshadi.
gain, poelo; v., boelwa ke.
gainsay, latola, ganetša.
gainsaying, kganetšo, tatolo.
gait, mosepelo, motsamao.
galaxy, molalatladi, molagodimo.
gale, phefo, ledimo.
gall, nyooko; v., tshwenya.
gallant, bogale; n., mogale, senatla.
galleon, sekepe.
gallery, manno a ka godimo.
gallery, mokoro, khwitšhi (sekepeng).
gallivant, ralala.
gallon, gelone, galone.
gallop, kata, paraganya.
gallows, segole.
galore, ntši.
gamble, sepediša ditaese, leka.
gambol, kgana, tlolaka, kalapa.
game, papadi, thaloko, diphoofolo; – **reserve,** bošireletšo bja diphoofolo; **small** –, diphoofotšwana.
gamekeeper, moletadikgwa.
gammon, fora.
gamut, kamute, lerenoto.
gander, leganse le letona.
gang, lekoko, sehlopha.
ganger, foromane, ketapele.
gangrene, kankere, mofetši.
gangway, kgoro, sefero.
goal, kgolego, teronko.
goaler, moletakgolego.
gap, sekgoba, phahla; **fill a** –, thiba phahla.
gape, edimola.
garage, karatšhe.
garb, diaparo, mašela.
garbage, thogorogo.
garden, serapa.
Garden Route, Tselarapa.
gardener, raserapa.
gardening, temo, borapa.
gargle, n., kgakgametša, kgakgakga; v., re kgakgakga! phoroša, itsukula.

garland, kgare, mokgabo wa matšoba.
garlic, konofele.
garment, seaparo, kobo.
garner, sefala, polokelo; v., boloka, kgoboketša.
garnish, kgabiša.
garret, ntlwana ya ka godimo.
garrison, bahlabani, sera, mphato wa masole.
garrulous, maphoko, mmalabadi.
garter, kaušopanta.
gas, gase, kese.
gash, phula madi.
gasp, fegelwa, sehumula.
gastric, sa(mogodu) mpa.
gastritis, (phišo) ya mogodu.
gate, heke, eke.
gateway, kgoro, sefata, lesoro.
gather, v., phutha, kgobokanya, botha, boka; – **s,** mešošo; – **for,** phuthegela, bothegela.
gathering, kgobokano, pitšo; poloi, mošošo, sešo.
gauge, kelo, seelo, v., lekanya, ela.
gaunt, otileng, gwametšwe.
gauntlet, tlelafo, haneskunu, seatla.
gauze, sefo.
gay, thabileng, nyakaletšeng.
gaze, boga, lepa.
gazette, kuranta (ya mmušo), kgatišobaka, tsebiša semmušo.
gear, kere, dikgerekgere ditlhamo, ditlabele.
gelatine, tšelatine.
geld, fagola.
gelding, pere e fagotšweng.
gem, lebenyabje, pheta ya thakga.
gender, bong, mong.
genealogy, lešika, leloko.
general, tona, molaodi, akaretšago.
General Post Office, Posokgolo.
generally, akaretšago.
generate, tswala, hlagiša.
generator, sehlagiši, tšenereitara.
generous, go se timane, fanago, khuparollago seatla, fago kudu.
genet, tšhipa.
genial, thabišang, botho.
genital organs, mapele.
genius, sehlalefi.
genteel, hlomphegang.
gentile, moditšhaba.
gentle, nolo, botho.
gentleman, lejentelmane, yo botho.
gentleness, botho, bonolo.
gentlewoman, mohumagadi.
gently, gabotse, bosele.
genuine, kgonthe.
genus, mohuta.
geography, thutafase.
geologist, mogeologi, moithutafika.
geology, geologi, thutafika.
geometry, tšeometri, geometri.
germ, setšo, twatši.
Germany, Toitši.
germinate, mela.
germination, go mela, mmelo.
gesticulate, lekanyetša.
gesticulation, moakgo.
gesture, seka, ketšišo.
get, bona, rua; – **to,** fihla; – **at,** fihlela; – **on,** tšwela pele; – **out of the way,** tloga, široga; n., go tswala.
geyser, ketlele, poilara.
ghastly, boifišang.
ghost, sepoko, seriti.
giant, senatla, kokoto.
gibberish, (speak), bjebjera.
gibe, kwera.
giddy, samadikwe, dimokana.
giddiness, samadikwe, matladima.
gift, neo, mpho, seloba; – **of grace,** neo ya kgaugelo.
gigantic, kgolo kudu, tona.
giggle, sega.
gild, manega ka gauta.
gill, leswafohlapi.
gilt, manegile ka gauta.
gimlet, borwanatsogo.
gin, sefu, molaba, sehlokolathapo.
ginger, gemere; – **beer,** gemere.

gingerly, bosele.
ginning, tlhokolo.
giraffe, thutlwa.
gird, tlema, bofa, rakanela, garela.
girder, lepheko.
girdle, mmofo, lepanta; v., bofa.
girl, mosetsana, kgarebe.
girlhood, borwetsana, bokgarebe.
girth, mmofo.
gist, pelo, tabakgolo, tabataba.
give, fa, nea, ntšha, ineela.
given to me, nneetše.
giver, mofi, monei.
gizzard, kila, kilana, sekila, sekhwele.
glacier, moelakgapetla, klesia.
glad, thaba, nyakalala.
gladden, thabiša.
glade, sekgala, molala, lepatlelo.
gladiator, ratšhaka, ratšhoša.
gladly, ka thabo, ka nyakalalo.
gladness, lethabo, nyakalalo.
glance, n., kgerulo; v., gerula, gadima, thedimoga.
gland, thaka.
glare, kganya, phadima, tsepelela.
glass, galase; **looking** –, seipone.
glass-cutter, sesegagalese, seripagalase.
glass-jar, lefiso.
glass-ware, dibjagalase.
glaze, galesefatša, manega ka galase.
gleam, lehlasedi; kganya.
glean, budutša.
gleaning, pudutšo.
glee, lethabo, nyakalalo.
glen, molapo, molatswana.
glib, leleme la borethe, boreledi.
glide, thelela, phupha.
glider, sethalamoyeng, sephaphamamoyeng.
gliding, joint, tokollotheledi.
glimmer, kganya, phadima.
glisten, phadima.
glitter, kganya, kgagamela.
global, senkgokolo; – **method**, tselakakaretšo.
globe, nkgokolo(fase).
globular, nkgokolo, sedikadiki.
gloom, manyami, nyama, phirima.
glorified, tagafaditšwego, tumišitšwe.
glorify, reta, tumiša, godiša.
glory, tumo, letago, tumišo.
gloss, letago, phadimo, matsaka.
glossary, klosari.
glottal consonant, tumahee.
glottis, lešobakgokgokgo.
glow, kganya, hlena; **-ing coals**, magala a hlennego.
glow-worm, senakangwedi.
glucose, klukose.
glue, segomaretši, v., gomaretša.
glut, kgoriša.
glutton, sejagobe, mogori.
gluttonous, go phaka, megabaru.
gluttony, megabaru, go phaka, bojato.
gnash, tsikitlana, furanya, tsikitlanya.
gnashing, ditsikitlano, phuranyo.
gnat, montsane, selabi.
gnaw, gabura, phura, kokona.
gnome, kgopana, seema, seka.
gnu, kgokong.
go, ya, sepela.
goad, seotledi, letsolwana, kgati; v., hlaba, hloheletša, tutuetša.
goal, maleba, tebanyo, phello.
goal-keeper, radinong.
goal-posts, dipala.
goat, n., pudi; **a he** –, phoko; **a small he** –, phokwana; **a small** –, putšana.
gobble, phaka, gabura.
go-between, mmoelanyi, agente, mmoledi.
goblet, komiki, phafana, sego.
goblin, tikološi, modimotsane, sepoko.
go-cart, koloyana-kgorometšwa.
God, Modimo; **gods**, medimo; **ancestral spirits**, badimo.
goddess, modimogadi (wa mosadi).
godless, hlokago modimo, sa boifego Modimo.
godlike, semodimo.

godliness, borapedi, bodumedi.
godsend, mahlatse, lehlogonolo.
goggles, digalase, dikokolese, seširetšamahlo.
goitre, sekgokgokgo.
gold, gauta; golden, adj., ya gauta.
golf, kolofo.
golf-ball, polo ya kolofo.
golf-links, lepatlelo la kolofo.
gong, tšhipi.
gonorrhoea, tšhofela, gonorea.
good, loka, botse, lokile(go).
good-bye, gabotse, šalang.
goodness, botse, botho.
goods, thoto, diphahlo.
goodwill, kgaugelo.
goose, leganse; sethotho.
gooseberry, momodi, leropotlane.
goose-flesh, bana ba phefo.
gore, madi, v., phula, hlaba.
gorge, mogorogoro, v., metša.
gorgeous, botse kudu, manyedinyedi.
gorilla, korila.
gospel, ebangedi.
gossip, mmalabadi, mosebi, mokgotse, mpheane, v., seba.
gourd, sego, kgapa, leraka, mokopu.
gourmand, sejagobe.
gout, honyelele, nogakoto.
govern, buša, laola.
government, mmušo, goromente; – **gazette,** kuranta ya mmušo.
governor, mmušiši.
governor-general, tonatlou.
gown, purapura, kobo.
grab, gapa, swara, ubula.
grace, kgaugelo lešoko.
grade, hlophiša; n., sehlopha.
graded, hlophilwego.
gradient, motheogo, lephama, mosekamo.
gradual, bosele, ka bonya.
gradually, gasele, gabotsana.
graduate, kratšueita; n., sealoga, mokratšueiti.
graft, hlomela; n., tlhomelo.
grain, mabele, thoro; – **elevator,** sešego, sefala, – **mill,** tšhilo.
gramophone, keremafomo.
granary, sešego.
gram, kramo; pl., dikramo.
grammar, popopolelo.
grand, botse, (k)golo.
grandchild, motlogolo, setlogolwana.
grandeur, botse, bothakga.
grandfather, rakgolo, koko.
grandiose, ikgantšhago, kganyago.
grandmother, mmakgolo, koko.
granite, tlaparalla.
grant, fa, nea; thušo.
grape, terebe, morara.
graph, kerafo.
graphite, phomo, kerafite.
grapple, aka, swara, betana.
grasp, swara.
grass, bjang; mabjang; **quick** –, mohlwa, – **-eating (animal),** sejabjang.
grasshopper, tšie.
grate, rostere, lešimelo, v., gohla, kreiti, ifo.
grateful, leboga(ng).
grater, segohlo, segohlane.
gratify, kgahla, kgahliša.
gratification, kgahlišo.
gratis, fela.
gratitude, tebogo.
gratuitous, filwego fela, ithapago, fela.
gratuity, neo, mpho.
grave, lebitla, bohunamatolo; adj., kotsi, v., seta.
gravel, lekgwara, karabole.
graveyard, serapa.
gravitate, gogelwa fase, dula, nna.
gravitation, maatlakgogedi.
gravity, boima, maatlakgogedi.
gravy, moro, mareremela.
gray, putswa, pududu, kotswana.
graze, fula, fudiša.
grazing, phulo.
grazing-place, mafulo.

grease, makhura, tiri, tšhaša, tlotša; -**sy,** tshotshomago.
greasiness, tshotshomo.
great, golo, kalo, kaaka.
greatness, bogolo.
greaves, dikgadika.
Greece, Gerike.
greedily, gabura, phaka, kalametša.
greediness, bojato, megabaru.
greedy, megabaru, sejato, sejagobe.
green, tala, botala.
green beans, dinawa tše tala.
green manure, monontšhatala.
greenness, botala.
greet, dumela, dumediša.
greeting, tumedišo.
grey, pududu.
gridiron, maratetšo, rostere.
grief, manyami, maswabi.
grievance, matshwenyego, pelaelo.
grieve, nyama, swaba.
grievous, nyamišang, sehlogo.
grill, šimela, n., tšhimelwa.
grim, bogale, boifišago, šoro.
grin, šena, šunyalala.
grind, šila, loutša.
grinder, mošidi, tšhilo.
grindstone, toutšo, lwala, tšhilo.
grip, swara, n., tshwaro.
gripe, gadika, gadikega.
gristle, mogano.
groan, tsetla, dumaela, tsetsela, n., tsetselo.
grocer, rakrosari; – **ies,** dikrosari.
groom, mmabaledi wa dipere.
groove, moseto, v., gorulla.
grope, phopholetša, apaapa.
gross, koroso, koto, boima, palomoka.
ground, mabu, lefase.
groundless, hlokang nnete.
group, sehlopha, lekoko; v., boka.
grouse, ngongorega; n., leperwana.
grove, sekgwana, sethokgwana.
grovel, khukhuna, abula.
grow, mela, gola, mediša.
growl, rora, bogola, ngongorega.
grown, godile, metše.
grub, seboko, dijo; **hairy** –, tšhitšhiboya.
grudge, lehufa, lehloyo, timana; **bear** –, swara ka pelo.
gruel, motepa.
gruelling, šoro, mpe, n., kotlo.
gruesome, šiišago.
grumble, ngongorega, bobora, balabala.
grumbler, mongongoregi.
grunt, kgorotla, ngongorega.
guarantee, emela, tiišetša, karanti, beelela, beeletša.
guard, moleti; mohlapetši, v., leta, diša.
guardian, motlametli, mofepi, mohlapetši.
guava, kojaba; mokojaba.
guess, akanya; kakanyo.
guest, moeng, moeti.
guidance, taetšo, tlhahlo.
guide, hlahla, n., mohlahli.
guile, bohwirihwiri, thetšo.
guillotine, kilotine.
guilt, molato.
guilty, na le molato.
guineafowl, kgaka.
guise, ikgakanya, boikgakanyo.
guitar, katara.
gulf, kgogometšana.
gullet, mometšo.
gully, moselo, leope.
gulp, kampetša.
gum, lerinini, borekhu.
gum-tree, mopulukomo.
gun, sethunya; **shot** –, dihala.
gunner, mothunyi (wa dikanono).
gunpowder, mošidi.
gurgle, kgakgakga.
gush, thopola.
gusset, tšitlelo, kasete.
gust, phoko, tšubutlo.
gustiness, ditimo.
gusto, mafolofolo, lethabo.

gut, lela.
gutter, moselo, katara.
guttural, adj., magalagapa, modumokodu.
gym, jimi, seroma, boithobollelo.
gymnasium, boithobollelo.
gymnastics, dithobollo.
gypsum, samente, tšipise.

H

Haberdashery, nalete le garane.
habit, mokgwa, tlwaelo.
habitable, dulega, agiwa.
habitat, madulo, legae, bodulo.
habitation, ngwako, bonno.
habitual, tlwaetše(go).
habituate, tlwaetša, tlwaela.
hack, rema, touta, peke, kgabetla.
hackly, ya meseto.
hack-saw, sagatšhipi.
haemetite, letsoku.
haemorrhoids, matšala.
haft, mpheng.
hag, moloi, mokgekojana.
haggard, tšhogilego.
haggle, tsota.
hail, sefako.
hail, dumediša, tšwa.
hailstone, thoro ya sefako.
hailstorm, pula ya sefako.
hair, moriri, boya, **a** –, ntsha ya moriri.
hair-brush, sebeanyo, porosolo.
hair-root, moduboyana.
hale, gopa, iketlang.
half, seripagare, hafo.
half-caste, lepastere, lekgoba.
halfcent, hafosente.
half-time, boikhutšo, kgaotšo.
halfway, magareng, bogare; **meet** –, thakanela.
hall, holo, ngwako.
hallow, kgetha, ikgafela, ikgethela, n., mokgethwa.
hallow, raka, koba.
hallucinate, fora, loya.
halo, pitšo, kganya.
halt, ema, emiša, boemo.
halter, hal(e)tere.
haltingly, ka go emaema, hlotšago.
halve, ripa gare.
ham, namakolobe, sepeke.
Hamite, Hamite.
hamlet, motsana.
hammer, amole, noto; v., kokotela.
hammer-head, (bird), mašianoke.
hamper, thibela, tshwenya, seroto.
hampered, be –, thatafišwa.
hand, seatla, letsogo; nea.
handbook, pukukgakollo, tšhupathuto.
handcuff, bofa, šoboka, golega.
hand-drill, borotsogo.
hand-breadth, paralatšo ya seatla.
handful, morafo, legoswi.
handicap, thibela, tshwenya.
handicraft, modiro wa diatla.
handiness, thušago.
handkerchief, sakatuku.
handle, mpheng, mokgoko, theku, v., swara, rarolla.
handling, tshwaro.
hand-made, dirilwe ka seatla.
handmaid, lelata.
handsome, botse, bogegago.
hands up, emiša(ng) matsogo.
hand-work, modiro wa diatla.
handwritting, mongwalo (ka seatla).
handy, thušago, kgauswi.
handy-man, makgonatšohle.
hangar, sethopa sa difofane.
hanger, sefegwana, hangara.
hanging, lepeletšeng, go fega.
hangman, mofegi, mofegabatho.
hang-over, papalase, babalase.
hank, tlhale, lenti, garane.
hanker, duma, lakatša, fišega, kganyoga.

haphazard, šašarakane(go).
hapless, madimabe.
happen, diragala, hlagelwa; **-ed,** diregile.
happiness, lethabo, tlhalalo.
happy, thabile, thakgetše.
harangue, kgang, thero, polelo ya go foka.
harass, tshwenya, tlaiša.
harbinger, ketapele.
harbour, boloka; boemakepe letšibogo.
harbourless, hloka madulo.
hard, thata; – **palate,** magalagapa (thata), – **board,** papetlathata.
harden, thatafala, kgahla.
hardhearted, pelothata.
hardness, bothata.
hardship, bothata, mathata.
hardware, ditšhipi.
hardwood, legongtšhipi.
hardy, e maatla; senatla.
hare, mmutla.
hare-brained, gafago.
hare-lip, molomosekammutla.
harem, hareme, ngwako wa basadi ba Bohomede.
hark, ekwa, kwaa! theetša.
harlot, sefebi, seotswa.
harm, tshenyo, kotsi; senya, gobatša.
harmful, senyago, ya kotsi.
harmless, hloka kotsi.
harmonic, hamoniki.
harmony, kwano, kwanadumo.
harness, teigi; v., pana, bofa.
harp, harepa; v., letša harepa.
harpsichord, harepakhoto.
harry, senya, thopa, tlaiša.
harrow, ege, v., tlaiša, ega.
harsh, makgwakgwa, šoro, bogale.
harshness, magwaše, bošoro, lonya.
hart, kgama e tona.
hartebeest, kgama.
harvest, puno, thobo, v., buna.
has, na le.
hasp, tšhisipere, sekopelo.
haste, potlako, phakišo; phakiša.
hasten, akgofa, phakiša.
hastiness, phakišo, mafolofolo.
hat, kuane, kefa.
hatch, phaphaša, thwathwaša, tloka.
hatchet, selepe.
hate, hloya, ila; lehloyo.
hateful, hloyegą, ilega, hloišago.
hatred, lehloyo, kilo.
haughtiness, boikgogomošo.
haughty, ikgodišago; **b.** –, ikgogomoša.
haul, goga, swara, maswaiša.
haunch, letheka, serope.
haunches, sit on –, kotama, tsorama.
haunt, etela, hloriša, dula, poka, bodulo.
haunted, poka.
have, na le, rua; **to** –, go ba le, swanelwa ke.
haven, bolapologelo, kou, botšhabelo.
haversack, kanapa.
havoc, tshenyo, polao, senya.
hawk, pekwa, sepekwa.
hawker, semauši, semaušo.
hay, furu.
haze, letobe; **hazy,** leutu.
he, o, a.
head, hlogo; – **over heels,** sekolokotane, – **office,** ofisikgolo.
head, eta pele; – **off,** tla phaphi.
headache, rengwa (opša) ke hlogo.
headiness, hlogothata.
heading, hlogo, thaetlele.
headlong, ka potlako.
head-land, kapa.
headman, tona, ramotse.
headstrong, hlogo e thata, ngangela.
head-quarters, mošate.
headway, tšwelopele.
heal, fodiša, alafa.
healing, phodišo, pholo, kalafo.
health, maphelo, bophelo; – **education,** (thuta)maphelo.

health-officer, ramaphelo, mohlankedi wa maphelo.
healthy, phelago, iketile.
heap, mokgobo, thotobolo, v., kgoboketša.
hear, kwa, theetša.
hearer, mokwi.
hearing, go kwa, tsheko.
hearken, theetša.
hearsay, marbarebare, pudi ya tsela.
hearse, koloi ya ditopo; hese.
heart, pelo, bogare, garegare ga.
heart-ache, pelo e bohloko.
heart-breaking, manyami, mahlomola.
heart-burn, seokolela; – **burning,** lehufa.
heart-felt, hlomodišang.
hearth, sebešo, ifo.
heart-rending, masetlapelo, šiišago.
hearty, thabilego, ka lethabo.
heat, borutho, phišo; ruthufatša; – **wave,** lephoto la phišo.
heaten, ruthufatša.
heater, seruthufatši.
heathen, moheitene, moditšhaba.
heave, kuka, kokomoga, fegelwa.
heaven, legodimo.
heavily, ka boima; imelwa.
heaviness, boima.
heavy, boima, imela, – **soil,** mobu o nonnego; – **-weight,** boimaima.
Hebrew, Moheberu, Seheberu.
hedge, legora, v., ageletša.
hedgehog, hlong.
heed, n., tlhokomelo, v., hlokomela, šetša.
heedful, hlokomelago, šetšago.
heedless, sa hlokomeleng.
heel, serethe.
hefty, boima, koto.
he-goat, phooko.
heifer, lethologatse, sethole.
height, bogodimo, botelele.
heighten, phagamiša.
heir, mojalefa, mojabohwa.
helicopter, helikoptere.
hell, hele.
helm, heleme.
helmet, kefa, helmete.
help, thušo; v., thuša, swariša.
helper, mothuši, moswariši.
helpful, thušago.
helping, thušago, n., sesola.
helpless, palelwa, hloka thušo, tlaletšwe.
helter-skelter, lešašano.
hem, mena, n., lemeno, – **in,** tiela gare.
hematite, letsoku.
hemorrhoids, matšala.
hemp, patše.
hen, kgogo (nonyana) e tshadi.
hence, go tloga mo; ke gona.
henceforth, go tloga (bjale) mo.
herald, ketapele, mokui, mmegi.
herb, mošunkwane, setlang, motlang.
herd, modiši, mohlape; v., diša; **small** –, mohlatswana.
here, fa, mo, mono.
hereafter, morago ga mo.
hereby, ka gona.
hereditary, abelwago, abelago.
heredity, kabelo.
herein, fa teng, ka gona.
heresy, bokgelogi, tlhanogo, kgelogo.
heretic, mohlanogi, mokgelogi.
heritage, lefa, bohwa.
hermaphrodite, kgeramatona.
hermit, modulanoši.
hernia, senapa.
hero, mogale, senatla.
heroine, mogale (wa mosadi).
heroism, bonatla, bogale.
heron, kokolohutwe, moholohute.
hesitate, diega, dika-dika.
hessian, lepele, hešiene.
hessian bag, saka, lesaka, kgetsi.
heterogeneous, tlhakantšuku.
hew, rema, phapha, betla.
hiatus, hiatuse.
hibiscus, hipiskose.
hiccough, (hiccup), sethekhu, thaabe.

hid, utile, fihlile; **–den oneself,** iphihlile.
hide, uta, khutiša, fihla
hide, letlalo, mokgopa.
hide-and-seek, khudukhutle, mokhuti.
hideous, mpe, befang.
hiding, kotlo, mmetho; **give me a –,** mpetha, ntea; **given me a –,** mpethile, nteile.
hieroglyph, haeroklifi, hirotlifi.
high, telele, godimo, phagameng.
higher, phagameng; v., phagamiša.
highland, nagadimo.
high priest, moprista e mogolo.
high school, sekolo sa ka godimo.
high spirited, išega, mofolofolo.
high-tide, phulawatletletlolo.
high treason, borukhuhli bjo bogolo.
High Veld, Nagadimo.
highway, tselakgolo, pata.
hilarius, thabilego.
hill, mmoto; **– s,** meboto; **– side,** patoga.
hillock, mmotwana.
hilly, ya (dithaba) meboto.
hilt, sekgatla, mpheng.
him, yena, mo.
hind, morago; kgama (e tshadi), tshepe.
hinder, thibela, tshwenya.
hinder parts, marago.
hindmost, e ka moragorago.
Hindoo, Mohindu.
hindrance, thibelo, sekgopi.
hinge, segono; **– joint,** tokollo ya segono.
hint, keletšo; sebela, oma.
hip, noka, letheka.
hip-bone, kgwele.
hippopotamus, kubu.
hire, thwala, hira.
hireling, mothwalwa, yo a thwetšwego.
hiss, šutša, otša.
historian, mohistori.
history, ditiragalo, histori.
hit, betha, nepa, tuma; n., nepo, kotlo.
hitch, segole, lehuto, thibelo; v., bofa.
hither, keno.
hitherto, go fihla bjale.
hive, phago.
hoar, putswa, pududu.
hoard, boloka, boka, n., mokgobo.
hoarse, magwaša.
hoary, putswa.
hoax, fora, n.. phoro.
hobble, hlotša.
hobby, setlošabodutu, tlošabodutu.
hoe, mogoma, letšepe, lema, leketša, hlagola.
hog, kolobe.
hoist, phagamiša, kuka; sekuki.
hold, swara, rua, n., tshwaro.
holder, seswaro, seroto.
hole, lešoba, molete; v., phula, phunya.
holiday, makhutšo, holitei.
holiday resort, bokhutšo.
holiness. kgethego, bokgethwa.
Holland, Holane, Holland.
hollow, sekoti, kgatampi, phago; v., hura, gorulla; **– ed,** gorutšwego.
holy, kgethwa, sekgethwa; **very – thing,** sekgethwakgethwa.
home, legae, gae, madulo.
home-craft, thutalapa.
home-hygiene, maphelo a lapa.
homeless, se nang legae.
homely, bokagae, sa tlwaelo.
home-made, itiretšwego.
home-nursing, kokelagae.
homer, leebaposo.
homesick, hlologetšweng gae.
homestead, ngwako.
homeward, ka nnga gae, gae.
homicide, polao, mmolai.
homily, thero.
homing, yago gae, gorogago.
homo, motho; **– geneous,** swanago ka mehuta.
homonym, tumatshwano.
hone, loutša; n., toutšo.

honest, botegang, tshepegang.
honesty, potego, tshepego.
honey, dinose; nnake.
honey-guide, tshetlo.
honeycomb, lemapo, lemepu.
honeymoon, tšhollaboeng.
honey-sucker, senwabolopi, senopi.
honorary, hlomphegang, tlotlega.
honour, tlhompho, tumišo; v., hlompha, tumiša; – **me,** ntlhompha.
honourable, hlomphegago, motlotlegi.
hood, kuane, kapa.
hoof, tlhako, ngatha, – **ed, animal,** phoofolotlhako.
hook, kobi, nkgwai, huku; v., kgwagetša, kgweša.
hooks and eyes, dihakisi le mahlwana.
hooligan, molotšana, sekebeke, tsotsi.
hoop, hupulo, lepanta.
hoot, goa, letša naka.
hooter, naka ya mmotoro, hutere.
hop, kgana, kolokota, thwethwa.
hope, kholofelo, tshepo, v., holofela, tshepa.
hopeless, lefela, hlokang tshepo, hloboga.
hopping, go tlolatlola, – **on one leg,** go thankobela.
hopscotch, tampelele.
horde, lekoko.
horizon, bogomapono.
horizontal, rapame(go).
hormone, homone.
horn, naka, lenaka; **a cupping** –, mohlogo.
hornet, mobu, mantlhakane.
hornless, senthulo, e tšhupša.
horrible, boifišang, befago.
horrid, tšhošang.
horrify, tšhoša.
horror, poifo, bohlola, bošoro.
horse, pere, pitsi; – **latitudes,** megaranafasepitsi.
horseback, nametše pere.
horse-fly, poba.
horseman, monamedi wa pere.
horse power, maatlapere.
horticulture, temo, borapa.
hose, lethopo, kaušo, hosphaephe.
hosiery, dikaušo.
hospitable, amogela batho.
hospital, sepetlele, bookelo.
hospitality, kamogelabaeng.
host, monggae, bontši.
hostel, hostele, ngwako wa baeng.
hostess, monggadi.
hostility, lehloyo, bonaba, ntwa.
hostile, hloya(go), lwantšhago.
hot, borutho, fiša, ruthofetše, bollo; – **day,** letšatši la motšhidi.
hotbed, lekidi.
hotchpotch, setšhu(u).
hotel, hotele.
hothead, senganga.
hothouse, lekidi.
hotness, borutho, phišo.
Hottentot, Mokgothu.
hound, mpša, lephefo, hlomarela.
hour, nako, iri.
house, ntlo, ngwako; v., boloka.
house-breaking, go thuba ntlo.
housecraft, bolapa.
household, lapa, tša lapa, sa ntlo.
house-pest, sesenyi, dilomi.
housewife, mosadi wa lapa.
housing, kago ya dintlo, kageletšo.
hover, phupha, okaokela, akalala.
how, bjang; – **much,** bokae?
however, fela, ka nthe.
howl, lla, hlaba moolo.
hub, hapo, moropana, morana.
hubbub, lešata, moferefere.
hubby, mogatša, monna.
huckle, noka, letheka, morota, lehutlo.
huckster, bapatša, mmapatši, semauši.
huddle, kgobokanya, kopanya, patišana.
hue, mmala, mokgoši.
huff, šutša, pefelo, hlasela.
hug, akarela, gokara(ela).
huge, golo, tona, kgolokgolo.

hulk, mmele wa sekepe, maroulo.
hull, legapi, lekgata, kgapetla, mmele.
hum, pobolo, mogobo; v., goba, bobola.
human, sa motho, setho, botho; – **relations,** phedišano; – **being,** motho.
humane, yo botho.
humanity, ntho, botho, batho.
humble, kokobetša, ikokobetša; **has - d,** kokobeditše.
humbug, sehwirihwiri, molotšana; fora, ditšiebadimo.
humdrum, bodutu.
humerus, lešuhutsogo, lerapo la sefaka.
humid, bošidi; **humidity,** monola, bošidi.
humiliate, kokobetša, nyatša, ntšha serit(h)i.
humility, boikokobetšo.
humming, pobolo.
humour, mokgwa, tshegišo, maikutlo; dumelela.
humorous, segišang.
hump, thota, serota.
hump-backed, lehutla.
humus, humase, podišwa.
hunch, thota, serota; – **back,** lehutla.
hundred, lekgolo; – **times,** galekgolo; – **weight,** kgoima; **three –,** makgolotharo.
hunger, tlala.
hungry, bolawa ke tlala, kganyoga.
hunk, segoba.
hunt, tsoma, nyaka.
hunter, motsomi.
hurdle, lepheko, lephekwana.
hurl, foša, betša, akgela.
hurrah, šate, pula!
hurricane, ledimo, ledimogadi.
hurriedly, ka potlako.
hurry, phakiša, akgofa.
hurt, gobatša, bolaya.
husband, monna, mogatša.
husbandry, bolemi, thuo.
hush, homotša, hlokosetša.
husk, lekgapetla; v., kgokgoša, tlebola.
huskiness, makgarihla.
hustle, kgorometša, sukumetša.
hut, sehlaka, ntlwana.
hutch, letlole, serobi, oko.
hyacinth, hiasinte.
hybrid, lepastere.
hydro-electric, mohlagasemeetse.
hydrogen, haetrotšene.
hydrophobia, bogafa bja mpša.
hyena, phiri.
hygiene, maphelo, paballommele.
hygienic, ya maphelo.
hymn, sefela, kopelo.
hyperbole, pheteletšo.
hyphen, tlami.
hypocrisy, boikaketšo, boikaketšo.
hypocrite, moikaketši.
hyssop, hisopo.
hysteria, mafofonyane.
hysterics, mafofonyane.

I

I, nna, ke.
ibis, (bird), lehaahaa.
ice, lehlwa, kgapetla.
ice-cream, lebebetšididi.
idea, kgopolo, kelelelo, maano.
ideal, maikemišetšo, lokilego, kgonthe.
identical, swana, swanago.
identification, tšhupo ka monwana.
identity number, palo ya boitšhupa.
ideophone, leekiši.
idiocy, bošilo; **idiotic,** bošilo.
idiom, seka, seema.
idiosyncrasy, kogpolo ya motho a nnoši, semaka.
idiot, sethoto, lešilo.
idle, se nang modiro; lelera, itiša.
idleness, maitišo, bobodu.

idler, sebodu.
idol, modingwana, modimo o šele.
idolatry, go direla medimo e šele.
if, ge, ga, gola.
ignite, tukiša, gotetša, tšhuma.
ignition, go tšhuma, tšhumo.
ignoble, solegago, nyatšegang, bošula.
ignominious, dihlong, sekgobo.
ignorance, go se tsebe; **–t,** sa tsebego.
ignore, se šetše, hlokomologa.
iguana, polomeetse, legogomedi.
ill, bošula, bobe, bolwetši; gampe, bohloko; v., babja, lwala.
ill-bred, godišitšweng gampe.
illegal, tlolago molao.
illegitimate, – **child,** hlaba, lethwalana, ngwanakutswa.
illfated, mahlola.
illicit, sa dumelegeng.
illiterate, sa rutegang.
ill-mannered, ya mekgwa e mebe.
illness, bolwetši, bohloko.
ill-treat, swara gampe, bolaya.
illuminate, boneša, bonegela.
illumination, ponego, ponegelo.
illusion, phoro, thetšo, boiphoro.
illustrate, swantšhetša, šupiša.
illustration, seswantšho, tshwantšhetšo.
ill-will, kilo, lehloyo, bonaba.
image, seswantšho; – **s,** diswantšho (betlwa).
imagination, kakanyo, kgopolo.
imagine, gopola, rera, itlhoma.
imbecile, sethotho, lešilo.
imbibe, nwa, metša, monya.
imitate, etšiša, etša, ekiša.
imitation, kekišo, ketšišo.
imitator, moetši, moetšiši, moekiši.
immaculate, hlwekilego, hlokang, sekodi, thakgilego.
immaterial, go fo swana, se na taba.
immature, sa kang ya butšwa, tala, fsa.
immediate, bjale, ka bjako, kgauswane.
immediately, semeetseng, gona bjale, ka bjako.
immense, kgolo kudu, kgologadi.
immigrant, mofalaledi.
immigrate, falalela, khudugela.
immigration, phalalelo.
imminent, kgauswi, kotsi.
immobile, sa suthegeng, tiilego.
immobility, totobalo, totomalo.
immoderate, fetišišago, fetago, tekanyo.
immolate, hlabela.
immoral, bohlola, bohlotlolo; – **person,** sehlola, sefebe, sehlotlola.
immorality, bohlola, bofebe.
immortal, sa hweng, sa felego.
immortality, go se hwe; go se fele; bosahweng.
immovable, tiilego, se nang go šuthišwa.
immune, sontile(go), soutile(go).
immunisation, tshontišo, tshoutišo.
immunise, sontiša, soutiša.
immunity, tshouto, tshonto.
imp, Senkatana, Senkatawana, Tikološi, moesana.
impair, senya, fokodiša, ngotla, gwahlafatša.
impala, pha'la.
impale, ageletša ka legora, phula.
impart, neela, ruta, tsebiša.
impartiality, go hloka, hloka tlhao, go se kgethe.
impassable, sa selweng/selwego.
impassioned, fišega.
impatience, go fela pelo.
impatient, felang pelo.
impeach, bega, tlalea, belaela.
impeccable, sa solegego, sekegilego.
impecunious, hlokago tšhelete, topa tša fase.
impede, thibela, tshwenya.
impediment, matshwenyego, kgopišo, molato, tlhokego.

impel, gapeletša, tutuetša.
impend, hlola kotsi.
impenetrable, sa tsenelelweng.
imperative, laolago, modirišotaelo.
imperfect, sa phethegang.
imperfectly, šaetšago.
imperial, sa borena; – **ism,** boimperialeseme.
imperil, tsenya kotsing.
imperious, laolago, gapeletšago.
impersonate, itira, ipea bakeng sa.
impertinence, kgang, mereba.
impertinent, ba le kgang (mereba).
impervious, sa phulweng, sa tsenweng, sa tsenelelwego.
impetuousity, mahlagahlaga, bogale.
implacable, sa boelanywago, hlokago boikokobetšo.
implant, hloma, tsema.
implement, kgerekgere, phetha.
implicit, kwagalago, sa rego selo.
implied, sa bolelwago, akaretšago.
implore, rapela, lopa.
implosive, tumammogoteng.
imply, re, akaretša.
import, kgwebišo, ditšwantle; v., gwebisa; – **ation,** tlišontle.
importance, bogolo, boima, bohlokwa.
important, kgolo, bohlokwa.
importer, motlišintle.
importune, tshwenya, gapeletša.
impose, rweša, thetša, lefiša, laela; **a levy,** ntšhiša lekgetho.
imposition, phoro, lekgetho, morwalo.
impossible, palago.
impostor, mofori, mothetši.
imposture, bohwirihwiri, boferefere, phoro.
impotency, bofokodi.
impotent, hlokago maatla, fokolang.
impound, tsenya seketeng.
impoverish, humanegiša, hlokiša.
impracticable, sa kgonegego.
impregnable, ilago go fenywa.
impress, gatiša, tiiša.
impression, kgatišo, pobetšo, kgopolo.
imprest system, mokgwa wa tefelopele.
imprint, gatiša.
imprison, golega.
improbable, se direge, belaetšago.
improper, se nang tshwanelo.
improve, lokiša, bona bokaone, hlalefa, kaonefatša.
improvement, bokaone, tokišo, kaonefatšo, **show** –, bontšha bokaone.
improvise, hlaka, hlama, bolela semeetseng, loga leano semeetseng.
impudence, mereba, kgang.
impudent, kgang, mereba.
impugn, latola, itatola, ganetša.
impulse, tlhohleletšo, kgapeletšo, tširogo.
impulsive, putlaputla.
impulsion, kgapeletšo, tširogo.
impunity, go hloka kotlo, go hloka kotsi.
impure, ditšhila.
impurity, tšhila, selabi.
imputation, pego; tsholo.
impute, bea molato, balela.
in, ka gare, gae, **come** –, tsena.
inability, go (šitwa) palelwa.
inaccessible, sa tsenweng, sa batamelweng.
inaccuracy, phošo.
inadequate, go se lekane.
inadvertence, go se lemoge.
inadvertent, hlokomologago.
inane, e sego ya selo, e fela, rego hôô.
inanimate, e hwileng, sa pheleng.
inappropriate, sa lokelego.
inasmuch, e re ka, ka ga.
inaudible, sa kwagalego.
inaugural, šimollago, thomago.
inaugurate, kgakola, bula.
inborn, ya tlhago.
incandescent light, seetša se se tsetsemang.
incapable, šitwang, e paletšweng.

incarcerate, golega.
incarnation, namafalo.
incendiary, tšhumang.
incense, insense, dibano, seorelo, orela.
incentive, tšhušumetšo.
inception, tšhimologo, mathomo.
incessant, sa feleng.
inch, noko.
incident, sewelo, sewelwa, tiragalo, mokgwa.
incidentally, ka sewelo.
incinerate, lorela.
incise, seta.
incision, go gaya, go hlabela.
incite, hlohleletša, ferekanya.
incitement, tlhohleletšo, pherekanyo.
inciter, mohlohleletši, moferekanyi.
inclement, bothata.
incline, sekamiša, thulamiša; v., sekama, thulama.
inclined, sekametšego.
include, tsenya gare, akaretša; – **ing,** gotee le, go balwa le.
incognito, ikgakantšha.
income, moputso, puno.
incoming, tsenago.
incomparable, sa kang ya lekangwa.
incompatability, go se kwane, go se dumellane.
incompatible, sa kwanego.
incompetent, šitwang, fokolang.
incomplete, sa phethegang.
incomprehensible, sa kwagalang.
inconsistent, fapanang.
inconspicuous, sa bonagalego.
inconstant, fetogang.
inconvenience, tshwenya.
inconvenient, tshwenyang, sa lokelang.
incorporate, tsenya ka gare, akaretša.
incorrect, phošo.
incorrigible, palago.
increase, atiša, oketša, ata, koketšo.
incredible, sa dumelegeng.
increment, kokeletšo, koketšo.
incubate, alamela, alama.
incubator, sealamedi.
inculcate, gatella, tiišetša, tsenya.
inculcation, tsenyo, tiišetšo, kgatello.
incumbent, modiredi.
incur, ipiletša, gokela.
incurable, hlokang kalafo, palago; – **disease,** bolwetši bjo bo sa alafegego.
incursion, tlhaselo.
indebted, ba le molato.
indecent, sa lokang, solegago.
indecisive, dikadikago, belaelago.
indeed, ka kgonthe, ruri.
indefatigable, mafolofolo, sa lapego.
indefinite, felelago sebakeng, hlokago tiišo, sa kwagaleng.
indemnify, lefelela, bušeletša, lokolla.
indemnity, tefelelo, pušeletšo, tokollo.
indent, kuba, kobetša, otara, sehla.
independent, itaola(go); – **ce,** boitaolo.
index, tšhupane, tšhupaboteng, setlamafatši, eksponente.
Indian, Moindia.
indicate, šupa, šupetša.
indicative, šupago, modirišopego.
indicator, tšhupo, sešupo.
indict, bega, tlalea, sekiša, bea molato.
indictment, pego, tlaleo, tshekišo.
indifference, se nago taba, tlhokomologo.
indifferent, hlokomologago, itlhokomologago, sa rego selo, se nang taba.
indigence, bohloki, bohumanegi.
indigenous, sa tlhago.
indigestion, tšhilompe, pipelo.
indignant, befetšwe(ng), e galefile(ng).
indignation, kgalefo, pefelo.
indignity, nyatšo.
indirect object, sedirelwa.
indirectly, ka go rarela.
indiscreet, ya bošilo.
indiscretion, bošilo.
indiscriminate, go se hlaole, go se kgethe.

indisposed, fokola(go), lwalago.
indisposition, bolwetši, bofokodi.
indisputable, sa ganetšwego.
indistinct, sa bonagaleng gabotse.
individual, mongwe, ka noši.
indolence, bobodu, botšwafa.
indolent, tšwafa(go).
indomitable, ganang go thapišwa, palang, šayago go fenywa.
indoor, gare ga ntlo.
indorse, ngwala lebitšo, emela.
indubitable, se na pelaelo.
induce, kgodiša, kgona, fenya.
induct, tsenya, kgakola.
induction, kgakolo, tsenyo.
indulge, lesetša, lemalela, ikgafela, dumela.
indulgence, tesetšo, kgaugelo.
industrial, sa diatla, sa ntasteri.
industrious, mafolofolo; **(person)** seroto.
industry, ntasteri.
inebriate, tagilwe, letagwa.
inebriation, botagwa.
inedible, sa lewe (go).
ineffective, sa thušego, sa kgonego.
ineffectual, lefela, sa thušego.
inept, fokolang, ronago, bošilo.
inequality, go se lekane.
inert, sa itapišego, botšwa, maroulo.
inertness, bobodu.
inestimable, sa lekanyetšwago.
inexact, phošo, fošang, sa nepego.
inexcusable, sa lebalelwego.
inexhaustible, sa lapeng, sa feleng maatla.
inexorable, e thata, tiilego.
inexpectant, sa lebelelwego.
inexpensive, sa tureng, tšhipilego.
inexperience, hlokago boitemogelo, tlhokatlwaelo.
inexplicable, sa hlalošegang.
inexpressible, sa bolelwego.
infallible, sa fošeng.
infamous, bohlola, sa dihlong.
infamy, bohlola.
infancy, bosea, bjana.
infant, lesea, ngwana.
infantry, bahlabani ba maoto, díra.
infatuate, šilofatša, kganyoša.
infect, fetetša, fetela.
infectious, fetetšago.
infection, phetetšo, phetelo.
infer, re, phetha.
inferior, tlase, mohlanka.
inferiority, kgalalo, – **complex,** boinyatšo, bobotlana, botlase.
infest, tšhilafatša, tlaiša, tsenya, bolwetši.
infidel, moditšhaba, moheitene.
infidelity, tumologo, boheitene.
infinite, sa felego, se nang tekanyo, sa felelago.
infinitive (mood), modirišogo.
infirm, sa tiang, fokolang.
infirmary, bookelo, sepetlele.
inflame, gotetša, tuka.
inflamed, kekago, tukago, fišago.
inflammable, tukago.
inflammation, keko, tuko, go tuka.
inflate, budulela, budulatša.
inflation, inflasi, infleišene.
inflect, kgopamiša, kuba, mena.
inflexible, sa kubegeng.
inflict (pain), kwiša, bohloko.
influence, tutuetšo, sertiti, khuetšo.
influenza, geripi, mokhohlane, infuluensa.
influx, tšhologelo.
influx control, taolotšhologelo.
inform, tsebiša, bega.
informal, e seng ka tlwaelo.
information, tsebišo, pego.
informer, mmegi, motsebiši.
infringe, tlola molao, roba.
infuriate, galefiša, befediša.
infuse, tsenya, tšhela, phololetša.
ingenious, hlalefilego.
ingenuous, ka tokologo.
ingoing, tsenago.
ingot, setena (sa gauta), foromo.
ingrain, ya semela.

ingrained, tsemile medu.
ingratiate, ithatiša, ratiša.
ingratitude, go hloka tebogo.
ingredient, setswaki, seteng.
inhabit, dula, agile.
inhabitant, moagi, modudi.
inhale, buša moya, arubela, hema.
inherit, ja (lefa) bohwa, abelwa.
inheritance, lefa, kabelo.
inhibit, ganetša, thibela.
inimical, lwantšhago, senyago.
inimitable, sa (etšišwang) latelwago.
iniquitous, sa lokang, e kgopo.
iniquity, bokgopo, bobe.
initial, pele, thomago, tlhakapele, saena ditlhakapele/tlhakaina tša pele.
initiate, thoma, wetša, kgakola, bolla.
inject, hlabela (kurumane).
injection, kurumane, tlhabelo.
injunction, taelo.
injure, gobatša, ntšha kotsi; – **d,** gobetše.
injurious, senyago, ya kotsi.
injury, kgobalo, kgobatšo, kotsi.
injustice, go se loke, tlhokatoka.
ink, enke, – **pot,** pitšana ya enke.
inkling, kgopolo, kgopotšo.
inland, gare ga naga, nageng.
in-law, leloko la kgomo, mogwa.
inlay, manega, hlomela.
inlet, kounyana, monatlana.
inmate, moagi, moagišani.
inmost, garegare, kgabagare.
inn, kgorogelabaeng, ntlo ya baeng.
innate, ya tlhago.
inner, e ka gare.
innermost, ya ka garegare, ya kgabagareng.
innings, sebaka, lebaka.
innocence, go hloka molato, go se tsebe.
innocuous, se nang kotsi.
innovate, mpshafatša, thoma, šimolla, fetoša.
innumerable, fetang palo, nyeuma, -go, go se balege.
inoculate, hlabela, kurumane.
inoffensive, se nang (kotsi) taba.
inoperable, sa šomeng.
inopportune, sebaka se sa lokang.
inordinate, ka sewelo.
inorganic, sesaboleng.
inquest, nyakišišo ya lekgotla, tekolo.
inquire, botšiša, nyakišiša.
inquirer, monyakišiši, mmotšiši.
inquisition, nyakišišo, tshekišo, tefetšo.
inquisitive, fišegelago/nyakišišago ditaba.
insane, gafang, segafi.
insatiable, sa kgoreng; e megabaru.
inscribe, ngwala.
insect, khunkwane, sekhukhu.
insecticide, moupakhukhu, polayakhukhu.
insecure, sa tiang, nago le kotsi, belaetšago.
insensible, sa kweng.
inseparable, sa kgaoganweng.
insert, tsenya, lomela, lokela, khwamela.
inside, bogare, boteng, gare ga, dikateng, bokagare.
inside-out, (turn), hlanola.
insidious, bohwirihwiri, hwirihwitšago.
insight, selebeši, temogo, tlhaologanyo.
insignia, ditshwao, dimentlele.
insignificant, nyane, e seng ya selo.
insincere, forago, aketšago.
insipid, bošula, tapileng.
insist, tiiša, phegelela.
insolence, kgang, mereba.
insolvent, welego, pankoroto, tšhonnego.
insomnia, tlhobaelo.
inspan, pana.
inspect, hlahloba.
inspector, mohlahlobi.

inspection, tlhahlobo.
inspiration, kgothatšo, pudulelo.
inspire, kgothatša, tutuetša.
install, hloma, bea.
instance, sebaka, tšhupo.
instant, gatee, ya potlako.
instantaneous, ka potlako.
instantly, ka potlako, akgofago.
instead, bakeng sa.
instep, boraoto.
instigate, hlohleletša, ferekanya.
instil, tsenya.
instinct, tlhago.
institute, hloma, sehlongwa.
institution, molao, ngwako.
instruct, laela, ruta.
instruction, taelo, taetšo, thuto.
insructive, rutago.
instrument, sedirišwa, seletšo.
insubordination, go se kwe, lenyatšo.
insufficient, hlaelang, sa lekaneng; v., hlaela.
insult, roga (ka), omanya; n., komanyo, thogako.
insuperable, sa fengwego, ilago go fenywa.
insurance, tšhireletšo, phemelo, inšuransi.
insure, šireletša, phemela, inšura.
insurgent, rabele.
insurrection, phetogelo, pherehlo.
integer, palotlalo.
integral, botlalo.
integrate, phetha, kopanya.
integrity, potego, botlalo, tshekego, botshepegi.
intellect, kelelo, bohlale.
intelligence, bohlale, kelelo, pego.
intelligent, hlalefilego, bohlale.
intelligible, kwišišegago.
intend, ikemišetša, re, gopola.
intense, tiilego.
intensify, tiiša.
intent, phegeletšeng.
intention, maikemišetšo, kgopolo.
intentionally, ka boomo, – ikemišetša.
inter, epela, boloka, fihla.
inter, gare ga.
interaction, tsenelelano.
intercede, rapelela, boelanya, humela.
intercept, thibela, kgaoletša, swara tseleng.
intercession, khumelo.
intercessor, morapeledi, moemedi, khumedi, mmoelanyi.
interchange, bapatša, ananya.
intercom, thelefomo ya ka gare, tsebišano.
intercourse, kopano, v., kopana.
interdependence, kgolano.
interdict, v., ganela, thibela; n., kganelo, thibelo, kiletšo.
interest, tswalo, kgahlego, mašokotšo.
interesting, kgahlišago, hlabošago.
interfere, tsena gare–, tshwenya, namola, itlhakanya le, thibela.
interference, boitapišo, thibelo.
interim, sebakana, solanka.
interior, bokagare, e ka gare, e gare; n., bogare.
interjection, lelahlelwa.
interlock, swaragana, kopana.
interlude, tlhabelelogare.
intermarry, nyalelana.
intermediary, monamoledi.
intern, tsenya mo teng, golega.
internal, mo teng; – **affairs,** ditaba tša gae.
international, gare ga merafe.
interpose, tsenya ka gare, tserekanya.
interpret, toloka, fetola, hlatholla.
interpretation, tlhatholło.
interrogate, botšišiša, botšiša, opotša.
interrogation, potšišo, potšišišo.
interrogative, lehlaodipotšiši, lebotšiši.
interrupt, tsena ganong, tshwenya.
intersect, fapana, fapanya.
intersperse, tswaka, gaša.
interstice, sebakana.
intertwine, rarana, logaganya.
interval, sebaka, kgala, paka.
intervene, tsena ka gare, namola.

intervention, namolo, tseno ka gare.
interview, poledišano, kgang, v., boledišana.
intestate, ka ntle le lengwalo la nkhwa (bohwa).
intestines, mala, diretlo, dikagare.
intimacy, sekgotse, setswalle.
intimacy, kopano.
intimate, tsebiša, lemoša.
intimate, sekgotse, sephiri; n., thaka, mmotegi, a., botegago.
intimation, pego, tšhupo.
intimidate, tšhošetša.
into, mo go, ka teng, ka gare.
intolerable, sa kgotlelwego.
intolerance, go fela pelo.
intolerant, felago pelo.
intonation, segalo.
intoxicant, setagi, sebuiši.
intoxicate, tagiša, taga.
intrepid, bogale, sa boifego.
intricate, raraneng, e thata.
intrigue, maano, morero o mobe, bomenetša.
introduce, hlagiša, tsenya, bega.
introduction, matseno, tlhagišo, pego, tsebišano.
intrude, itšhubelela, tsenelela.
intuition, tsebo ka tlhago.
inundation, morwalelo wa meetse, meetsefula.
invade, hlasela, tsenelela, šwahlela.
invader, mošwahledi.
invalid, fokolago, sekoka, lwatša.
invalidate, bolaya, senya.
invaluable, (sa) bohlokwa.
invariable, sa fetogeng.
invasion, tlhaselo.
invective, thogako, mahlapa.
invent, hlaka, hlama.
invention, tlhamo, tlhako.
inventor, mohlami, mohlaki.
inventory, lenaneo (la diphahlo).
inverse proportion, kabelo ya go fapana, kabelophapano.
inversive, ledirolli.
invert, ribega, hlanola, menola.
inverted commas, ditsebjana.
invest, fa maatla, apeša, bea(fiša), tšhelete.
investigate, nyakišiša, botšišiša, kwelela.
investigation, nyakišišo, potšišišo.
investigator, mmotšiši, monyakišiši.
investment, peo ya tšhelete.
inveterate, tsemilego medu, tiilego.
invidious, ilega, befetšwe, ba le mona; – **ness,** nyatšego, sepitša.
invigorate, matlafatša, tiiša; – **or,** mmatlafatši.
invincible, sa hlolwego, sa fengwego, ila go fenywa.
invisible, sa bonagaleng, sa bonwego.
invitation, taletšo, memo.
invite, laletša, mema.
invoice, lenanetheko, lenanephelegetšo.
invoke, rapela, bitša, ipiletša.
involuntary, itaolago.
involve, tsenya, phuthela.
inward, gare.
inwards, ka gare.
iodine, ayotini, iodine.
irate, galefilego, befetšwego.
ire, kgalefo, pefelo.
Irish, – **ruling,** methalomesesane.
irksome, tshwenyago, tenago.
iron, tšhipi, aene; v., ritela, šidila; – **ore,** borale bja tšhipi.
ironic(al), ka go gegea.
irony, kgegeo.
irradiate, ediša.
irrational, se nang kelelo, bošilo.
irreconcilable, adj., se nang (poelanyo) go boelanywa.
irrefutable, se nang go ganetšwa.
irregular, arogilego, hlotšago.
irreparable, padilego.
irresistible, se nago go thibelwa.
irrespective of, ka ntle le.
irresponsible, hlokago boikarabelo.
irreverence, tlotlologo, tlhompholło.

irrigate, nošetša.
irrigation, nošetšo.
irritable, galefega, rumolega, baba; –**bility,** thumolego.
irritate, hlabahlaba, galefiša, rumola, tshwenya, hlohlontšha.
irritation, tlhabotlhabo, thumolo.
island, sehlakahlaka.
isolate, beela thoko, hlaola; –**him/her,** mmeela thoko.
isolation, peelothoko, tlhaolo.
issue, tlhagišo, setšo, phetho, tšhologo ya madi; v.i., tšwa, tšhologa.
isthmus, molalanaga, moseneke.
italics, moseka.
itch, lekhwekhwe, go hlohlona, sebabi; v., baba, hlohlona.
itching, babago, hlohlonago.
item, hlogwana.
itinerant, sepelago, etago.
itinerary, morero wa leeto.
it, wona, yona, sona, lona.
itself, by –, ka boyona/bosona/bolona/boona.
ivory, lenaka la tlou, nakatlou.
ivy, morara, aebi.

J

jab, hlaba, kgitla, jeba, thula, sega; n., jebe.
jabber, bolabola, balabala, bjebjera; –**er,** mmalabadi.
jabbering, palabalo.
jacarandah, mojakaranda.
jack, tomkraga.
jackal, phukubje.
jakass, tonki ya (poo).
jackboot, sekgwahlapa.
jacket, baki, paetši.
jackpot, jekepoto.
jade, mosadi wa seapu; v., lapiša, hwa pelo, a., tala.
jagged, makgawekgawe, dikgetlo.
jail, kgolego, teronko, v., golega.
jailer, ratšhankane, molotakgolego.
jam, jeme, jamo.
jangle, dira lešata, tsotana, tshele.
January, Janaware, Pherekgong.
Japan, Japane.
jar, lefiso, moruswi, v., lla, tsotana.
jargon, polabolo.
jaundice, bohloko bja nyooko.
jaunt, leetwana.
jaunty, thabilego.
javelin, letsolo, lerumo.
jaw, mohlagare; **jaw-bone,** lehlagare, lerapo la mohlagare.
jay, legehle, (m)papagai.
jealous, hufega, hufegela.
jealous, make –, hufegiša.
jealousy, botšheba, lehufa mona.
jean, jini.
jeer, kwera, sega, soma, n., kwero, katrolo.
jelly, borere, jeli, rekereke, v., kgahla.
jelly-fish, hlapi-jeli.
jemmy, kofutu.
jeopardise, tsenya kotsing.
jeopardy, kotsi, pitlagano.
jeremiad, sello, dillo.
jerk, ubula, rutla; n., thutlo, kubulo.
jerky, kgotlakgotla, rutlarutlago.
jersey, jesi, jeresi.
jest, swaswa, tlaela.
jester, moswaswi.
Jesus, Jesu.
jet, tshwa, tseremetša; n., jete; –**plane,** sefofane sa go tseremetša.
jetsam, magogodi.
Jew, Mojuta, Mojuda.
jewel, lebenyabje.
jewellery, dibenyabje.
jib, tebela.
jiffy, go ponya ga leihlo.
jig, motšeko.
jigsaw, sagamotšeko.
jilt, kalatšane, tswiri, nonyana, v., fora, lahla.

jingle, lla, tsirinya, tsikirimanya.
job, modiro, mmereko, mošomo, hlaba, šoma, rutla.
jobber, mošaetši, mmapatši, sehwirihwiri.
jocular, swaswago, thabile.
jog, kgarametša, thula.
johnny, moesa.
join, kopanya, lomaganya, kgomagana.
joiner, mmetli, molomaganyi.
joinery, bobetli.
joint, lekopano, kgomaganyo, lelokollo; **out of** –, tshwephoga.
joist, kota.
joke, swaswa, tlaela; moswaso.
jolity, lethabo, mokete.
jollification, lethabo.
jolly, thabile.
jolt, kgorokotša, thula, khutla.
jostle, šikinya, thula.
jot, ngwala, thala.
journal, jenale, pukutšatši.
journalism, bojenale.
journey, leeto; v., eta.
Jove, Jupitere.
jovial, thabileng.
joy, lethabo, nyakallo.
joyful, kanyakanya, thabileng.
joy-ride, leeto la lethabo.
jubilate, hlalala, nyakalala, didietša.
jubilation, lethabo.
jibulee, ngwaga wa nyakalalo.
judge, moahlodi; v., ahlola.
judgment, (judgement), kahlolo, tšuo.
judgment-day, letšatši la kahlolo.
judicial, ya bokgaolakgang.
judicious, bohlale.
jug, sebjana, senwelo, nkgo.
juggle, loya, thetša; n., thetšo, toyo.
juggler, senoge, selopi, mothetši.
juice, todi, matute, maswi.
juicy, bose.
July, Julae, Phuphu.
jumble, dubekanya, n., tlhakantšuku, thulano.
jumbo, tlou, kgolawa.
jump, tlola, fofa; n., tlolo.
jumper, motlodi, boro, seaparo.
jumpy, tšhabago, yo boi.
junction, kopano, kgahlano.
June, June, Ngwatobošego.
jungle, sethokgwa, lesodi.
junior, monyane.
jurisdiction, tokelo ya boahlodi.
jury, juri.
just, loka, fela; adv., no; **who** –, nogo.
justice, go loka, toka.
justify, lokafatša, itokafatša.
justly, ka toka.
jut, khutlola, rokama.
juvenile, yo mofsa; – **delinquency,** bosenyi bja baswa.
juxtapose, bapiša.

K

kaffir-corn, lebele, mabele(thoro).
kafir-tree, mmale, mokhungwane.
kangaroo, kankaru.
karakul, karakule.
karoo, karu.
karroo-thorn(tree), mooka.
kaross, lethebo, letata.
keel, khile.
keen, boale, mafolofolo.
keep, boloka, swara.
keeper, mmoloki, mmabaledi.
keeping, poloko, paballo.
keepsake, segopodišo.
kennel, serubi, oko.
kernel, thapo.
kettle, ketlele: – **drum,** moropana.
key, senotlolo, sekgonyollo, khii.
key-note, khiinote.
keyboard, khiipoto.
khakhi-bush, senkgankgane.
kiaat, (teak), moroto, monoto, kiata.
kick, raga ka leoto; – **me,** nthaga.
kid, putšanyane, putšane, maminana.

kidnap, thopa, utswa.
kidney, pshio; – **shaped,** sekapshio.
kikuyu grass, mohlwa wa Kikuyu.
kill, bolaya.
kilogram (kg.), kilokramo.
kilogrammes, dikilokramo.
kilolitre, kilolitara.
kilometre, kilometara.
kiln, onto.
kilt, mosese, khiba.
kin, leloko, lešika; ba leloko.
kind, mohuta, mohlobo.
kindergarten, sekolo sa malapane.
kindle, gotetša, beša, tukiša.
kindness, botho, bopelotlhomogi.
king, kgoši.
kingdom, mmušo, pušo.
kiss, katlo; v., atla; – **of live,** katlophedišo.
kitchen, morala, khitšhi, khwitšhi.
kitten, katsenyana, katsana.
klipspringer kololo, kome.
kloof, sefata, phata.
knack, mokgwa.
knapsack, kanapa.
knave, molotšana, moradia.
knavery, boradia, bolotšana.
knead, duba.
knee, letolo, khuru.
knee-cap, khurumelatolo, khurumelakhuru.
knee-halter, khina.
kneel, khunama, khubama.
knicker, borokgwana.
knife, thipa, mphaka, mmese.
knight, mogale.
knit, loganya.
knob, kgolokwane, hlogwana.
knobkerrie, molamo, thoka.
knock, opa, opaopa, thula; – **down,** digela fase.
knot, lehuto; v., swina.
know, tseba; – **by heart,** tseba ka hlogo; – **-how,** kgona, bokgoni.
knowing, bohlale, tsebago.
knowledge, tsebo.
knuckle, senoko; – **bone,** taola, kgagare.
koodoo, tholo.
korhaan, setlatlawe, mošelešele.
kraal, lešaka, motse.
krans, legaga.
Kruger National Park. Serapaphoofolo sa Kruger.

L

laager, pokano, lara.
label, setlankana, sešupo, phara setlankana.
labial consonant, tumapou.
laboratory, laporatori, laboratori.
laborious, mafolofolo, boima, bothata.
labour, modiro, mošomo, pelego; v., khubama, dira, šoma.
labour bureau, piro ya mošomo.
labourer, modiri, mošomi.
labyrinth, mararankodi.
lac, senotasetšo, moti.
lace, lokeletša, hlahlela; n., kanta, leisi.
lacerate, gagola; segaka.
lack, hloka, šaya; n., tlhokego.
lad, moesa, mošimane, mohlankana.
ladder, manamelo, llere.
laden, rwalang.
ladle, leho.
lady, mohumagadi; – **bird,** podilekgwana.
lag, diega, šala morago, raka, swara, phutha, apeša.
laggard, yo a diegang, sebodu.
lagoon, letshanatswai.
lair, bolao, letšaba.
lake, letsha.
lamb, kwana, kwanyana; v., tswala.
lame, hlotša(ng), ritsang.
lament, sello, v., lla.
lamp, lebone, lampi; – **snuffer,**

setimamabone; – **stand,** sehlomamabone.
lance, lerumo; v., phatsa.
lancet, leakgamotšana.
land, lefase, naga, temo; – **tax,** tefêlanaga.
landdrost, maseterata.
landmark, mollwane, pakane.
landowner, monyenaga, mongpolasa.
landscape, ponagalo ya naga.
land speculator, mmapatšalefase.
landward, lebanageng.
lane, mokgothana.
language, polelo; – **study,** thutapolelo; **official** –, leleme la semmušo.
languish, fokola.
lank, otileng, otilego.
lantern, kgagamela, lanteren.
lap, difaro, difarong; v., latswa; – **up water,** kgaphetša meetse (sempša).
lapse, feta, sebaka, phošo, koô.
larceny, bohodu, go utswa.
lard, makhura a kolobe.
large, golo; **become** –, gola.
larva, seboko; **(bees),** mana.
larynx, kodu, purpuru, mogolo.
lash, sefepi, sephadi; v., betha, otla.
lass, kgarebe, morwetsana.
lassitude, tapo, go lapa, go tšwafa.
lasso, kgaphetša, kgapetša; n., segwele, segole.
last, bofelo, morago, ka go fela.
last, n., llase.
last, kgwahlile, tiile.
latch, sekgonyo, perebere.
late, morago, bošego, nako e šiile.
lately, bjale, mehleng ye, maloba; tšwa go.
latent, letšego.
lateral, ya lehlakore, – **bud,** lehlomahlakore.
latex, maswi.
lath, lebalelo, palelo.
latitude, mogaranafase.
latrine, boithomelo.
latter, morago; ya bobedi, mafelelo, – **rain,** kgogolamoko; – **ly,** maloba, pakeno.
laud, reta, tumiša; n., theto, tumišo.
laudable, tumišega.
laugh, sega; – **at me,** ntshega; – **ing stock,** ditshego.
laughter, lesego.
launch, thoma, betša, tsenya meetseng.
laundry, lonteri, bohlatswetšo.
lava, manya.
lavatory, boithomelo.
lavish, safa, senya.
law, molao, tao: **be submissive to** –, laolega; **abide by** –, boloka molao; **break a** –, tlola molao; **lay down a** –, bea molao; – **and order,** molao le phedišano.
lawful, dumelelwa.
lawless, ngaloga, hloka, tao.
lawlessness, bohlokatao, mojano.
lawn, lapanabjang, lone.
lawsuit, tsheko, tshekišano.
lawyer, agente, ramolao.
lax, hlephileng, tšwafile.
laxative, segofišamala.
laxity, bolea, boriri, bobodu.
lay, bea, thea, teka, latša.
layer, llaga, tlhatlagano.
laying, peo.
layman, motho fela.
laziness, bobodu, botšwafa, bonya.
lazy, tšwafile(go), botšwa.
lead, hlahla, eta pele.
lead, (metal), loto, lota, morodi.
leader, ketapele, mohlahli, phokgo, – **ship,** boetapele.
leading, go (hlahla), eta pele; – **note,** noterathela, notešupa; – **part,** bothwadi; – **scale,** lerethito.
leaf, letlakala, lephephe; – **bud,** lehlomatlakala.
leaf-shaped, popotlakala.
league, kgolagano, kgwerano.
league, liki, lekga, leke.
leak, dutla; – **as a house,** na.

leaky, dutlang, dutlago, nago.
lean, otileng, sesane.
lean, rapama, sekama, ithekga.
leanness, go ota; boketa.
leap, tlola, fofa, taboga, n., tlolo, tabogo; – **like a frog,** phuruma; – **about as young locusts,** kopakopa, tlolatlola; – **with joy,** kalapa, tila; – **year,** ngwagamolele; – **-frog,** go selana.
learn, ithuta.
learned, rutegileng.
learning, thuto, tsebo.
leash, lebja, mogala, teu.
least, nyane; le gannyane.
leather, letlalo, mokgopa; – **goods,** thoto ya matlalo.
leave, khunollo, tumelelo, llifi.
leave, tloga, tlogela, šia; – **for,** tlogelela.
leaven, komelo, mohlabego.
leavings, mašadiša, mahlohlora, maratha.
lecture, thuto, thero, kgalemo; v., ruta, rera, kgalema.
ledge, leriba, sephakwana.
ledger, lêtša, pukukgolo, ngwalelakgolo.
leech, motsene, monopi, ngaka.
leek, diliki.
lees, makgarihla.
left, ntsogotlo, mpogošo, tshadi, ka nngeleng, la mpati.
left-hand, lanngele, lantsogošo.
left-handed pers., nngejane lempogošo.
left to right, sengeleng go ya sejeng.
leg, leoto; **hind** –, serope.
legacy, bohwa, nkhwa.
legal, ya molao; – **personality,** boikemelamolaong.
legal advice, keletšomolao.
legal adviser, moeletši, go tša molao.
legend, nonwane, mabarebare, pale.
legging, kamase.
legibility, palego, go balega.
legible, balega.
legion, mphato, sekgao sa mašole.
legislate, bea (hloma) molao.
Legislative Assembly, Palamente.
legume, monawa.
leisure, boiketlo, maitišo.
leisurely, ka boiketlo.
lemon, swiri, swirilamunu.
lemonade, namoneiti.
lend, adima.
lender, moadimi.
length, botelele, bolele.
lengthen, lelefatša, šwapola; **by adding to,** hlomaganya.
lengthwise, ka botelele.
lengthy, e teletšana.
lenient, bonolo.
lens, lense, galase e godišang.
lentis, ditlhodi.
leopard, nkwe, lepogo, lengau; **small** –, lepogonyana.
leper, molephera.
leprosy, lephera.
lesion, sekodi, kgobalo, lebadi.
less, nyenyane, fokotšegileng, tloša.
lessen, nyenyefatša, fokotša, fefola.
lesson, thuto.
lest, e se be, e se re.
let, dumelela, lesa, tlogela; – **a house,** hiriša.
lethal, bolayago.
letter, tlhaka, letere, lengwalo.
lettuce, selae, letase.
level, tekanetšo; **spirit** –, baterpase; v., lekanetša.
lever, lebara; v., matolola.
leviathan, kgokomodumo, kgolomodumo, a., kgolo, kaakatlou.
levitate, phaphamiša, akalatša.
Levite, Molefi.
levity, bohwefe.
levy, lekgetho, lebi.
lewd, bohlola, bohlotlolo.
lewdness, bohlola, bohlotlolo.
liabilities, melato, dikoloto.

liar, yo maaka, moakedi, moaketši, ramaaka.
liars, boramaaka(na).
libel, tshenyo (kgobošo) ya leina.
liberal, hlallelago, falatšago, gololago.
liberal, n., moikgololedi.
liberate, lokolla, bofolla, golola.
liberator, mogolodi, mophološi.
Liberia, Liberia.
libertine, sehlola.
liberty, tokologo, kgololego, boitumelo.
librarian, ramapuku, molaebrari.
library, laebrari, bokgobapuku.
license, laesense, tumelelo, bohlola.
licentiousness, bohlola.
lick, latswa, fenya, hlola.
lid, sekhurumelo; **eye –,** phuphu.
lie, n., maaka; v.i., aka, akela, aketša; **– down,** lala, robala; **on the side,** rapama; **– on the back,** kanama; **– on the face,** ribama; **– flat,** patlama; **– stretched out stiffly,** namalala; **– in the sun,** sekamela; **– flat so as to hide,** batalala; **– upon one another, as strata,** hlatlagana; **– late in the morning,** selwa; **– in wait for,** lalela; **– flat, of an animal,** botha; **– upon,** lala godimo; **– with a person,** lala le; **– in, after childbirth,** elama.
life, bophelo.
life cycle, lephelo.
life history, histori ya (bophelo) tlhago.
life-work, tirobophelo.
lift, kuka, emiša, matolola.
ligament, mošifa, tšhika.
ligature, bofa sebofo, mmofo.
light, seetša, lesedi; lebone, v., gotetša; thumaša, a., edilego.
light, bohwefe, bofefe; **– house,** ntloseetša; **– breeze,** phefšana.
light colour, mmala o tagilego.
light diet, sejo se bohwefe.
light rays, mahlasedi.
lighten, bonegela, ediša, fefola.
light-hearted, thabilego.
lightheavy-weight, boimaimahwefo.
lightness, bohwefe, bobebe.
lightning, legadima, tladi.
light-weight, boimafefo, boimahwefo.
like, swanang le, swanago le.
like, v., rata, kganyoga, kgahlwa ke.
likely, rategago, kgahlegago, ekete, mohlomong.
liken, swantšha, bapetša.
likewise, bjalo.
liking, lerato, thato.
lilac, perese, **-tree,** mosari.
lily, lili; **arum –,** mogaladitwe.
limb, setho.
lime, motaga, kalaka.
limestone, manyaphiri, kalaka.
limit, mollwane, kgaolang.
limited, kgaoletšwego, lekantšwego.
limp, hlotša.
limpid, sekilego, hlwekilego.
limpidity, tlhweko, tshekego.
limy, sekamotaga, sekakalaka, gomarelago.
line, mothaladi, lethale.
lineage, leloko, lešika.
linen, lene, lešela.
liner, sekepe.
linger, diega, dika-dika.
linguist, ramaleme.
liniment, setlolo.
lining, furumo ya seaparo.
link, kopanya, n., kopanyi.
linnet, hlanhlagane.
linoleum, tapeiti, lenoleamo.
linseed oil, leneoli, linsiti.
lint, pantetši, mmofo, setlamelo.
lintel, searamo, mophako, kosene.
lion, tau.
lioness, tau e tshadi.
lip, molomo, pounama.
liquefy, tološa, taolola.
liquid, seela, a., seelago.
liquidation, likwiteišene.
liquor, bjalwa.
lisp, bebenya.

list, lenaneo, lenane, bea ka dihlopha.
listen, theetša, kwa; – **to me,** ntheetša.
listener, motheetši, mokwi.
listless, lapilego, nolegilego.
listlessness, tapo, nolego.
literal, ntswekantswe, ntšukantšu.
literature, dingwalo.
litre, litara.
litter, bana ba kolobe goba mpša, matlakala.
little, nyenyane, sego kae; – **finger,** monwana o monyane, manapanyane.
live, phela, aga, dula, iphela.
lived, phetše, pheditše.
lively, mafolofolo.
liver, sebete.
livestock, diruiwa.
living, phelang, phelago; – **thing,** sephedi.
lizard, mokgaditswana, mokgaritswana.
load, morwalo, phahlo, thoto; v.t., hlahlela.
loading, foraga; – **facilities,** bolaišetšo.
loaf, senkgwa, senkgwe, borotho, lekako.
loaf, tšwafa.
loafer, motšwafi, setšwafi.
loamy soil, seloko.
loan, kadimo, v., adima.
loath, sa rateng, tšwafang, gana.
loathe, tenwa ke, šišimoga, ila, hloya.
lobe, lerethepeu, lerethe, lerephu.
lobster, kgala, tlapakgerere.
local, felo fa, sa felo fao.
local government, mmušogae, mmušotikologo.
locality, felo(mo), felo fao.
location, lokasi.
locative, lefelo; lehlathafelo.
lock, senotlelo, sekgonyo; v., notlela, kgonyela.
lock-jaw, tetanose, kgohlanyamehlagare.
locomotion, tshepelo.
locomotive, hlogo ya setimela.
locust, tšie.
locust-bird, leakabosane.
lodge, lala, bea; n., ntlo; – **an appeal,** ipiletša.
lodging-place, bonno.
loft, ntlwana ya godimo.
lofty, phagameng.
log, legong, kota.
log-book, pukutiragalo.
logic, lotšiki, kwagalo.
logical(ly), ka (tlhaloganyo) tlhatlologanyo.
logical sequence, tatelano e kwagalang.
loin, letheka.
loiter, diega, sesella, dikadika.
loiterer, modiegi, modikadiki.
lone, nnoši.
loneliness, bodutu.
lonely, lewa ke bodutu.
lonesome, lewa ke bodutu.
long, telele; – **for,** hlologelwa.
long ago, kgale.
longevity, bophelo bjo botelele.
longing, tlhologelo.
longitude, lesetafase.
look, lebelela, bona; – **forward to,** lebeletše; – **up,** lelalela godimo; – **round,** gadima; – **after,** diša; – **back,** getla; – **down, (upon),** okamela; – **up to** (respect), hlompha; **down upon (despise),** nyatša; – **like,** swana.
looking-glass, seipone.
loom, selogelo, selogi.
loop, segole, segwele.
loose, bofologile, nyefile.
loosen, golola, tlemolla.
loot, gapa, thopa; n., kgapo, thopo; – **er,** mothopedi.
lop, ripa, poma.
loquat, lokwata.
lord, morena, mong, v., rena.
Lord, Morena; **the Lord's Prayer,** thapelo ya Morena.
lordship, borena.

lorry, lori.
lose, lahla, loba, timela.
loser, molobi, mosenyegelwa.
losing, tobo, tahlo.
loss, timelo, tobo, tshenyegelo; **at a loss,** gakanegile; **irreparable –,** lehu la pitšana.
lost, timeditše, timetše.
lot, kabelo, karolo.
lots, draw –, tema; **cast –,** laola ka bola.
loud, hlabošago, dirago lešata.
loud-speaker, segodišantšu.
lounge, lontše.
louse, nta.
lovable, rategang, rategago.
love, lerato; **mutual –,** leratano; v., rata.
lover, morati; **beloved,** moratiwa.
low, fase, tlase.
lower, theoša, fološa, lepeletša.
low intonation, kgalafase.
lowland, molala, molapo, nagatlase.
lowliness, boikokobetšo, kokobelo.
low pressure, kgatelelo fase.
low-spirited, fedileng pelo.
low tide, phulawatletlase.
low tone, segalotlase.
loyal, botegela, botegang, gweranago.
loyalty, potegelo, bogwerano.
lubricate, tlotša, kirisa, logetša, tshasa.
lucern, lesereng.
luck, mahlatse lehlogonolo; **bad –,** madimabe.
lucky, mahlatse.
lucky beans, dikhungwane.
lucrative, ruišang.
lucre, khumo.
luggage, thoro, morwalo.
lukewarm, boruthwana, bololo.
lull, khomolo, homotša, robatša, hlokosetša.
lullaby, go duduetša ngwana, tuduetšo, kuruetša.
lumbago, noka.
lumber, useless things, tša lefela, tše se nang thušo; **timber,** dikgong, dikota.
lumberman, moremamere.
luminary, seetša, lebone, edišago.
luminous, kganyang, edišang.
lump, lekote, lekwate; boruruga.
lunacy, bohlanya, bogafi.
lunactic, lehlanya, segafi.
lunch, n., setshegare, lantšhe, letena.
lung, leswafo.
lung (disease), sehuba (se segolo); **in cattle,** ntaramane.
lurch, hwidinya, kadietša, thekesela.
lure, gokela, goketša, molaba.
lurid, sehla, befago.
lurk, hlola, khuta, boba, lalela.
luscious, bose, hlabošegang.
lush, beine, botagwa.
lust, kgahlego, tumo, phišego.
lustily, ka (matšato) mafolofolo.
lustre, letago, phadimo, go kganya.
lustrous, kganyang, phadimago.
lusty, mafolofolo.
lute, lute.
Lutheran, ya Luthere.
luxuriant, melang ka maatla.
luxury, matsaka, nyabalatšo.
lying, lalago, robalago; **– in wait,** talelo; **(lie),** aketšago.
lymph, lemifi.
lynx, lengau.
lyric, koša pina.

M

mabela, bogobe bja mabele.
macadamize, kontira; **-d road,** tsela ya sekontiri.
macaroni, makaroni.
machine, motšhene.
machinery, metšhene.
mackintosh, kobo ya pula.

mad, gafago, hlanya(ng); v., gafa.
madden, gafiša, hlakanya hlogo.
madman, segafi, lehlanya.
madness, go gafa, bohlanya.
madrigal, bodupe, matrikale, pinarato.
magazine, kgatišobaka, makasine.
maggot, sebokwana.
magic, bodupe, boloi.
magician, sedupe.
magistrate, maseterata, magistrata.
magnanimity, bopelokgolo.
magnanimous, pelokgolo.
magnesium, maknesiamo.
magnet, kgogedi, makenete.
magnetic field, lepatlelokgogedi.
magnetic north, leboakgogedi.
magnetic pole, phoulomakenete.
magnetism, bogogedi, bomakenete.
magnificence, letago, botse, šebešebe.
magnificent, phadišago, botse kudu.
magnify, godiša.
magnifying glass, galasekgodiši.
magnitude, bogolo.
mahogany, mohokani.
maid, ngwanenyana, kgarebe; **old –,** lefetwa.
maiden, kgarebe, morwetsana.
maidenhood, bokgarebe, boroba.
mail, poso.
mail bag, mokotla.
maim, golofatša.
main, golo, kgolo, tona.
main clause, thabekutu.
mainland, nagakgolo.
main root, modutona.
maintain, lota, tiiša, boloka.
maintenance, phepo, tshwaro, tšhireletšo, tirišo.
maize, mafela, mahea; – **stalk borer,** sebokophehli.
maize-planter, polantere ya lehea.
majestic, ya segoši.
majesty, borena, morena.
major, kgolo, majoro.
majority, bontši, bogolo.
make, dira; **create,** hlola; **-ready,** itokiša; – **kind,** mohuta.
make a bed, ala; – **a fire,** gotetša mollo.
make an effort, leka, itekela.
maker, modiri, mmopi; **creator,** mohlodi.
malady, bolwetši, bohloko.
malaria, letadi, malaria, matšhona.
Malay, Molei.
male, tona, monna, poo, roto.
malediction, thogako.
maledictory, rogakago, rogago.
malefactor, mosenyi, modirabobe.
malevolent, befago, lwanago.
malice, pefelo, bonokwane, bobe, lonya.
malicious, befetšwego, befago.
malign, senyago leina, pateletša, phara(go) ka bobe.
mallet, noto, notokota.
malnutrition, phepompe.
maltreat, tlaiša, hlokofatša, dira gampe.
mamba, mokopa.
mammal, seamuši, senyantšhi, mmamala.
man, monna, senatla; **young –,** lesogana; **old –,** mokgalabje.
manage, kgona, laola.
management, taolo.
manager, molaodi.
mandate, taolelo, taelo, tagafara.
mandoline, mantoline.
mane, moetse, seditse, mariri.
manful, senna.
manganese, mankanese.
mange, lekhewekhwe, sebabi, pabo.
manger, legopo.
mangle, gagola.
mango, manko, menko.
manhandle, tlaiša, hlokofatša.
manhater, moilabanna.
manhood, bonna.
mania, bogafa, botsenwa, botlamara.
maniac, segafi.

manifest, bonagatša, šupa.
manifestation, ponagatšo, ponagalo.
manifesto, manifese, tlhalošaboemo.
manifold, ntši.
manipulate, swara; – **tive, skill,** bokgoni.
manipulation, tshwaro.
mankind, ntho, batho.
manliness, senna, bonna.
manna, manna, leotša.
manner, mokgwa.
manners, mekgwa.
mannerism, keleketlana, mokgwana.
manoeuvre, laola, šuthiša, swaraswara, dira ka maano.
man-of-war, sekepe sa ntwa.
manor, ntlokgolo, polasa.
manpower, dira, madira.
mansion, ntlo ya morena.
manslaughter, polao.
mantelpiece, letlapa la leifo.
mantis, mmaseletswane, seremapetlo.
mantle, phuraphura, kobo, purapura.
manual, mošupatsela, adj., wa diatla; – **dextirity,** bokgoni bja diatla.
manufacture, dira, bopa, loga.
manure, morole, mmutedi.
manuscript, sengwalwa, leyakgatišong.
many, ntši; – **times,** gantši.
Maori, Maori.
map, mmapa, mmepe.
mar, senya.
maraud, thopa, hlakola.
marauder, mothopi, mohlakodi.
marble, mmabole.
march, sepela, (go) matšha.
March, Matšhe, Mopitlo.
mare, pitsi e namagadi, peregadi.
margarine, matšarine.
margin, moratho, mollwane.
Marico, Marico.
marigold, (Maxican), monkgane, senkgane.
marine, sa (tša) lewatle.
mariner, mosepetšasekepe, mokepe.
marionnette, marionete.
mark, leswao, moputso, v., swaya, putsa; **a scar,** lebadi; **miss the** –, foša; **hit the** –, nepa; **to** –, hlokomela.
marker, moswai, mongwadi.
market, mmaraka, lepatlelo, v., rekiša, bapatša.
marketing, go bapatša, thekišo.
marking gauge, selekanyi.
marksman, monepi, mmetši.
marksmanship, nepo, go nepa bonepi.
marmalade, konfeiti ya dinamune.
maroon, marunu.
marriage, lenyalo, tšeano.
marrow, moko; **vegetable** –, sephotsana.
marry, nyala, tšea; **cause to** –, nyadiša; **has -ied,** nyetše.
marsh, mohlaka.
martial, sešole.
martial law, molaontweng.
martyr, khwelatumelo, motlaišwa.
marvel, makala, kgotsa; n., makalo.
mascot, lešwalo, pheko, thokgola.
masculine, tona, bongtona.
mash, kgotla, hutšwetša, tswakanya; n., sebutšwetšwa, sekgotlelwa.
mask, seikgakanyo, segakiši.
mask, ikgakanya, ikgakantšha, gakiša.
mason, moagi, meselane.
mass, bokgolokgohla, bontši; **one** –, kgopa e tee.
massacre, thipitlo, v., ripitla.
massage, thoba, šidila; n., thobo.
massive, kgolo, boima.
mass-meeting, pitšokgolokgohla.
mast, kota ya sekepe.
master, nkgwete, mong, morena; v., fenya, thapiša, kgona.
mastery, borena, bokgoni, makgone.
masticate, hlahuna, sohla.
mastication, tlhahuno.
mastiff, mpša ya pofa.
masturbation, kgobošo ya mapele.
mat, legogwa, mmete, moseme,

mosemo, legogo; **small** –, legogwana; v., loga.
match, lehlokwa, nyalanyo, phegišano, thaka, v., lekana, lekanya.
match-box, segwahla, mankgwari.
matches, mollo, mahlokwana.
matching, nyalanyo.
matchless, fetang tekanyo.
mate, thaka, mokepe wa bobedi; v., kopanya.
material, ditlakelo, mašela, sere, materiale, sedirišwa.
materialism, bophelekakhumo.
mathematics, matesese, mathematiki.
matrimony, lenyalo.
matrix, tswala, popelo, foromo.
matron, mosadimogolo.
matter, selo, taba, molato; **(pus),** boladu.
mattock, manakisi.
mattress, matrase.
mature, godile, budule, butšwitše; v., gola, butšwa.
maturity, bogolo(ng), putšo(ng).
maw, tielo, tšelo, mogodu; nkilana.
maxim, seema.
maximum, botlalokgolo, makisimamo, makesemamo.
May, Mei, Mosegamanye.
mayor, ramotse, majoro.
maze, tharano, kgakanego; tlabo, mararankodi, v., tlaba.
me, nna.
meadow, mafulo.
meagre, otileng, hlokago, fokolang.
meal, bupi, dijo; **morning** –, sefihlolo; **evening** –, selalelo.
mealie, lehea, lefela; – **crib,** sefala; – **meal,** bupi, – **husks,** megwang.
mealie-rice, gereisi, magaela; – **stalk,** lehlaka.
mean, potlana, tlase; re; **intend,** rera, gopola; **average,** gare.
meander, menokana, rarela, lepelela.
meandering, ya manyokenyoke.
meaning, tlhalošo, kgopolo.
means, diswaro, tšhelete; **by** – **of,** ka (ga), ka thušo ya; **by no** –, le ganyenyane; **by all** –, ka kgonthe, ke sebele; **by any** –, ka mokgwa ofe le ofe.
measles, mooko; **in animals,** mabele.
measure, tekanyo, selekanyo, kelo, seelo; v., lekanya, ela, lekantšha.
measurement, tekanyo; – **of time;** tekanyanako.
measuring tape, thapotekanya, lentitekanya.
meat, nama.
meat-pie, kukunama.
mechanical, semotšhene.
meddle, itapiša, dubaduba.
meddlesome, dubadubago.
mediaeval, mehlagare.
median, gare, molagare.
mediate, boelanya, namolela.
mediation, poelanyo, namolelo.
mediator, mmoelanyi, monamoledi, moemedi.
medical, ya bongaka, ya kalafo.
medical examination, tlhahlobo ya kalafo.
medical practitioner, ngaka, moalafi.
medicinal, ya dihlare.
medicine, sehlare, mešunkwane; – **box,** lepokisana la dihlare; **sprinkle** –, upa; **burn** –, kubetša.
meditate, akanya, gopola.
meditation, kakanyo, kgopolo.
Mediterranean, naga ya gare; – **Sea,** Watlegare, Mediteraniene.
medium, dirišwago, mokunya.
medium vowel, tumanoši ya gare.
medlar (fruit), lebilo, **(tree),** mmilo.
medley, tswakano, tlhakantšuko, tswaka.
meek, pelonolo.
meekness, bopelonolo, boikokobetšo, bobotlana.
meercat, moswe, kgano.

meet, gahlana, gahlanetša; – **me,** nkgahlanetša; **come together,** kopana.
meeting, pitšo, lekgotla, kgobokano.
megaphone, segodišantšu.
melancholic, swabilego, mahlomola.
melancholy, mahlomola, maswabi.
melee, moferefere.
mellow, boleta, buduleng, bose; v., butšwa.
melodious, ya molodi, bosana.
melody, molodi.
melon, sepanspeke; **water** –, legapu.
melt, nyaoga, tologa, tološa, gadika.
member, setho, leloko, – **ship,** botho, boloko.
members, maloko, ditho.
membrane, lera, letlalwana.
memento, segopotšo, segopodišo.
memorable, swanelago go gopolwa, gopodišega.
memorandum, memorantamo, lengwalwana, pego, pukutšatši.
memorial, leswika la kgopotšo, segopodišo.
memorise, ithuta ka hlogo, gopodišiša.
memory, kelelo, kgopolo.
menace, tšhošetšo, kotsi; v., tšhošetša.
mend, lokiša, roka, thula.
mendacious, wa maaka, aketšago.
mender, mothudi, molokiši.
mendicant, mokgopedi.
mending, go lokiša, tokišo.
menial, mohlanka, modiredi.
menstruate, ikhunela, bona mosese.
menstruation, lehlapo.
mental, ya(hlogo) kgopolo.
mental arithmetic, dipalo tša (hlogo) kgopolo.
mentally deranged, gafago, fafatlago.
mental satisfaction, kgodišego moyeng.
mention, re, bolela, umaka.
mentor, moeletši.
mercenary, mohlabani yo a thwetšwego.
merchandise, diphahlo tša theko, thoto.
merchant, mmapatši, morekiši.
merciful, yo kgaugelo.
mercury, mekhuri.
mercy, kgaugelo.
mercy killing, polao ya mogau.
mere, fela; n., letsha.
merely, fo.
merge, sobeletša, tswaka, ina.
meridian, lesetafase.
merino, merino, lefarelane.
merit, tshwanelo, mohola, moputso.
merriment, lethabo, tlhalalo, thaloko.
merry, thabileng, thakgetše(go).
mess, bošaedi, tshenyego, dijo, mese, tlhakantswiki, mahlakanasela.
message, molaetša, tsebišo.
messenger, moromiwa, semamatlane.
metal, metale, tšhipi; – **work,** bothulatšhipi; – **worker,** morulatšhipi.
metamorphosis, phetogo, metamofose.
metaphor, tshwantšhišo.
mete, pakane, kelo, mollwane; v., ela, meta, abela.
meteor, sedumaedi, mitiore.
meter-reader, mokalametara.
method, mokgwa, tsela.
methodically, ka(tsela) mokgwa.
metre, metara.
metric, metriki, – **system,** mmalo wa metriki.
mettle, bogale, mafolofolo, sebete.
mew, lla.
Mexican, Momeksiko, Momexico.
Mexico, Mexico, Meksiko.
mezzo, mezzo, ka tekanyo.
mezzo-soprano, mezzosoprano.
microbe, maekropo, maekorope.
microphone, (mike), maekrofone, maekerofone.
microscope, maekrosekopo.
mid, e gare.

midday, mosegare (o mogolo).
middle, gare, bogare; – **finger,** monwanagare; – **ear,** tsebegare, – **tone,** segalogare; – **-class,** batho.
middleweight, boimagare.
middle veld, nagagare.
middling, e magareng.
midget, selabe, kgopana.
midnight, bošegogare.
midpoint, bogare, ntlhagare.
midrib, tšhikagare, kgopogare.
midriff, letswalo.
midst, bogare; magareng.
midsummer, lehlabulagare.
midwife, mmelegiši.
midwinter, maregagare.
might, maatla.
mighty, e maatla.
migrate, huduga, khuduga.
migration, khudugo.
migratory, khudugang, hudugang; **bird,** nongkhudugi.
mild, bonolo, borutho.
mildew, nyakgahla, tlhakgama, mouta.
mildness, bonolo.
mile, maele, meila.
milieu, tikologo, bogolelo.
militant, lwanago, lwišago, ratago/dumago ntwa.
military, bohlabani, bosole, bahlabani.
milk, lebese, maswi; v., gama.
milk-busch, mositlanoka.
milk-drink, seno sa maswi.
milker, mogami.
milking, kgamo; – **vessel,** kgamelo.
milk-tooth, leinobosea.
Milky Way, mola wa godimo.
mill, lwala, tšhilo; v., šila.
millenary, nywaga e sekete, mileniamo.
millepede, lesokolodi, legokolodi.
miller, mošidi.
millet, leotša, lebelebele.
milligram milikramo.
millilitre, mililitara.
millimetre, milimetara.
millenery (shop), lebenkele la dikefa.
million, milione.
millionaire, momilione.
millstone, lwala, tšhilo.
mime, papadikekišo.
mimic, mankekišane.
mimosa (tree), mošwana.
mince (minced meat), nama e (kailwego) šitšwego; **-ing machine,** sekayo.
mind, mogopolo; v., elahloko, šetša.
mindful, šetšago, hlokomelago.
mine, moepo, maene; v., epa, thea pomo.
mine prop, sethekgamoepo.
miner, moepi.
mineral, minerale; – **salts,** matswaiminerale.
mineral spring, mothopotswai.
mineral wealth, leruo la meepo.
miner's phthisis, thaesese.
minim, sekganote, minimi.
minimum, minimamo, botlalonyane.
mining industry, ntasteri ya meepo.
minister, tona, moruti, v., direla.
ministry, tirelo, boruti.
minor, nyane, monyane; – **interval,** pakanyane; – **scale,** lerenyane, lerathonyane.
minority, bonyane.
mint, minte, minti; – **plant,** kwena.
minuet, minuete.
minus, tloša, n., leswao la tlošo.
minute, motsotso.
minute, nyenyane.
minute-book, puku ya metsotso.
minutes, metsotso.
miracle, mohlolo.
mirage, diphalana tša selemo, madibolokwana.
mire, leraga, maraga, seretse.
mirror, seipone.
mirth, lethabo, nyakallo.
misadventure, kotsi, tsietsi.

misapprehend, go se kwišiše.
misbehave, itshwara gampe, senya.
misbehaviour, bosenyi, bošaedi.
miscarry, goma tseleng, folotša, thedimoga.
miscellaneous, hlakahlakanego.
mischief, bobe, bomenemene, bosenyi, go seleka, makoko.
mischief-maker, moseleki, molohlanyi.
mischievous, senyago; selekago; **(person),** sesenyi.
misconduct, go senya, bosenyi.
misdeed, tshenyo, molato.
misdirect, fošiša.
miser, sejato.
miserable, madimabe, mahlomola.
miserly, timana.
misery, bomadimabe, manyami.
misfortune, kotsi, bomadimabe.
misgive, belaetša.
misgiving, pelaelo.
misguide, kgeloša, faposa, timetša.
mishap, kotsi, tlalelo.
misinterpret, foša.
misjudge, ahlola ka phošo, foša.
mislay, lahlegelwa ke.
mislead, timetša, kgeloša, lahletša.
misogyny, go ila basadi.
misprint, phošo ya kgatišo.
miss, foša; **lack,** hloka; **come short,** hlaela; **be missing,** hlokega, sego; n., phošo, mohumagatšana.
missile, sebetša.
mission, thomo; – **station,** setase.
missionary, moruti; **society,** genosekapa.
mist, mouwane, kgodi, mogodi.
mistake, n., phošo, timelo; v., foša, timela.
mistaken, timetše.
mister, morena.
mistletoe, bolepu, bolepa boletswa.
mistress, mohumagadi; – **paramour,** nyatši, phuti.
mistrust, pelaelo; v., belaela ka.
misunderstand, go se kwišiše.
mite, tshwedi, tshwela, selwanyana, selabe.
mitigate, fokotša, fefola; **soothe,** khutšiša.
mitten, mofi.
mix, tswaka, tswakanya, hlakanya; – **up matters,** dubekanya, tobekanya; **mixed feelings,** kanyakanya; – **clay,** duba, dubakanya; **be mixed,** hlakane.
mixture, motswako, tswakano, tlhakatlhakano, tlhakantšuko, modubelo.
moan, ona, bobola, belaela, tsetla, duma; n., kono, pobolo, pelaelo.
mob. lekoko, kiti, lešaba; – **psychology,** kiti.
mobility, tšhuthego.
mock, kwera, soma; n., sesomo; **mocker,** mokweri.
mockery, sesomo, kwero.
mode, mokgwa; (mus.) mokgwatumo.
model, mmotlolo, sekao, malebela; v., bopa.
modelling, mmopo, popo; – **board,** sebopelo.
moderate, lekanetša.
moderation, tekanetšo.
moderator, molekanyetši.
modern, sebjalebjale.
modest, ikokobetšang, e ntšela, bobotlana.
modesty, boikokobetšo, masisi, bobotlana.
modify, fetola.
modulator, modulatore, papetlanoto, motšulatoro.
mohair, boya bja pudi.
Mohammedanism, Bohomede.
moist, e meetse, monola, e kolobileng, bošidi.
moisten, kolobiša; **-ed,** kolobišitšwe.
moisture, monola, bošidi.
molar, la mohlagare.
molasses, molase.
mole, serunya, phuo, khuti.

molecule, molekule.
molest, tshwenya, hlodia.
mollify, nolofatša.
molten, tologilego, tologileng.
moment, motsotso; go ponya ga leihlo.
momentuous, golo, kgolo.
monarch, kgoši.
monarchy, bogoši.
monastery, monasteri.
Monday, Mošupologo, Mantaga (A.).
monetary system, tselatšhelete.
money, tšhelete, diswaro; – **order,** orotele ya tšhelete; – **lender,** moadimiši.
monitor, mmonitha, molebeledi.
monk, moitlami, modulanoši.
monkey, kgabo; – **tricks,** bomenemene.
monkey-nut, tloo, tloomaake.
monocle, monokele.
monogamy, go nyala mosadi yo tee.
monopoly, monopoli, kgwebanoši.
monosyllabic, nokotee.
monotheism, bodimotee.
monotonous, lapišago, bodutu.
monotony, bodutu, moteno.
monsoon, monsunu.
monster, kgokomodumo, ntatauwane, selotšoko.
month, kgwedi.
monthly, ka kgwedi.
monument, segopotšo, monyumente, sephikantswe.
mood, modirišo, mokgwa; – **y,** matepe.
moon, kgwedi; **new-,** kgwedi e balamile.
moonlight, ngwedi, seetša sa kgwedi.
moor, mohlaka.
moor, v., emiša sekepe.
Moors, Bamore.
mope, hlonama, ngongorega, nyama.
moral, setho, thero, thutaboitshwaro.
morals, setho, boitshwaro.
moralising, go ruta setho.
morass, mohlaka.
morbid, fokolago, lwalago.
mordant, nyabulago.
more, fetang, gagolo, gape.
moreover, gape, le ga e le.
morgen, mmorogo.
morning, gosasa, moso, ka masa.
morning service, tirelo ya masa.
morning star, naledi ya masa, mphatlalatšane, mahlapholane.
morose, hlonameng, hlonamego.
morphology, popegopolelo.
morrow, moso, gosasa.
Morse, Morse, – **code,** tsela ya Morse.
morsel, leratha, sengwatho; **tasty** –, sešebo, sebalodi.
mortal, hwang, bolayago, hwišago, semotho, lehu.
mortality, lehu.
mortar, seretse, leraga, taka.
mortgage, beela; adimiša; n., peelo.
mortify, bolaya, tlaiša.
mortise, lomaganya, lomela; molomo.
mortuary, makota.
mosaic, dipataka.
Moses, Moshe.
Moslem, Moselamose, Leselamose.
mosque, moseke.
mosquito, monang; – **weight,** boimamonang.
moss, dikokomana, boriba.
most, gagolo, ntši.
Most High, yo Godimodimo, Ragodimodimo.
mote, thojana, lefatšana.
moth, mmoto, tshole, tshwele.
mother, mma, mme, moamuši; **your** –, mmago; **his or her** –, mmagwe.
mother-in-law, mmatswale, mogwegadi, matswale.
motherless, sešuana, bošuana.
mother-tongue, polelo ya setlogo.
motion, tšhikinyo, tšhišinyo, v., ithoma.
motionless, totobala, totomala.

motive, lebaka, kgapeletšo.
motley, mebalabala, mahlakanasela.
motorcar, mmotoro, motoro; **-s,** mebotoro; **owner of** –, rammotoro.
motorist, mootledi, monamedi wa mmotoro.
mottled, matheba, mebalabala.
motto, moano, seema.
mould, sebopelo, mouta, foromo; v., bopa.
mould-bord, poto.
moulder, mmopi, moforomi.
moulding, go (bopa) bopela, go foroma.
mound, mmoto, totoma.
mount, hlatloga, namela; fasola momaganya.
mountain, thaba; – **ridge,** mokokotlo.
mountainering, go namela thaba.
mountain-range, molokoloko.
mountain-side, letswapo, lephama.
mounted, pharilwe, momeditšwe, nametše.
mounted policeman, leisisi,lephodisa la pitsi.
mourn, lla, fifala; – **over,** llela, ilela; – **bitterly,** lla gabohloko.
mourning, sello, dillo, bofifi.
mouse, legotlo, peba, tadi.
moustache, tedu.
mouth, molomo; **inner part of** –, legano; – **of a river,** manong.
movable, šuthega.
move, šikinya, šuthiša, tloša, huduga; n., tšhutišo, – **ment,** tshepelo; – **to,** šuthela.
mow, buna.
mower, mmuni, mosegi.
much, ntši; **so** –, kalo, gaka(a)lo; **very** –, gagolo; **be too** – **for,** palela; **rahter** –, kutswane.
muck, tšhila, morele.
mucus, mamina, mamila.
mud, seretse, leraga.
muddle, v., tswaka, dubakanya, hlakanya.
muddle, tlhakantswiki, tšhašarakano.
muddy, e seretse.
muffler, mmofolara, serepe.
mudguard, mmotorosekepe.
mug, senwelo, pikiri, lebikiri.
mulberry, mmurupei.
mulch, khupetša, thibego.
mulching, go khupetša, pipo.
mule, meila, mmoula.
multimillionaire, radimilione.
multiple, katišanetšwa.
multiplicand, katišwa.
multiplication, katišo, ntšifalo.
multiplication table, lenanekatišo.
multiplier, katiši, seatiši; moatiši.
multiply, ata, ntšifala, atiša, – **by,** atiša ka.
multitude, bontši, lešaba.
mumble, bolabola.
mummy, mmami.
mups, nauwe.
munch, hlahuna, hlakuna.
municipal, ya mmasepala.
municipality, mmasepala.
mural decoration, makwala, makgwai, kgabišomaboto.
murder, polao; v., bolaya.
murderer, mmolai.
murmur, ngongorego; v., ngongorega.
murmurer, mongongoregi.
muscle, mošifa, segoba.
muscular, e maatla; – **control,** taolamešifa; – **system,** tsela ya mešifa, – **cramp,** namanakhunyedi.
muse, nagana, gopola.
museum, musiamo.
mushroom, tlokwane, tokwane, tututšwane.
music, boopedi, molodi, koša; **make or play** –, letša.
musical instrument, seletšo.
musician, moletši, masekanta; **famous** –, seletši.
musk, maseke.
musket, tlhobolo.
muslin, maseline, khase.

mussel, kgopa, kgohu; **shell of a –,** kgetla.
must, swanetše; n., mouta.
mustard, mosetata, mosetara.
muster, rapa, phutha; pitšo.
musty, utileng, utilego.
mutability, phethogo.
mutation, phethogo.
mute, semumu, seokobatsi, masepa a dinonyana.
mutilate, golofatša, kgola setho; **-ed,** kgaogilego setho.
mutineer, rabele, v., rabela.
mutiny, mpherefere, borabele.
mutter, bobola, ngongorega.
mutton, nama ya nku.
muzzle, molomo, moropo, sefena, mmogo, sebofamolomo; v., bofa molomo.
my, wa ka, ba ka, ya ka.
myopia, ponelokgauswi.
myself, nna, nnoši; **I –,** nna ka bonna.
mysterious, makatšago.
mystery, n., bosatsebjeng, lekunutu.

N

nag, pere e nyenyane, v., ngongorega.
nagana, nagana.
nagging, ngongorego.
nail, lenala; sepikiri; kokotela.
naive, sebjana, bokangwana.
naked, hlobotšeng, ponoka; **the –,** mapono.
name, leina, lebitšo, v., rea lebitšo.
namely, ke go re, ebong.
namesake, moreeledi.
naming, go thea leina.
nap, boroko, kotselo; v., potuma.
nape, sekgoši, sekgothi.
napkin, leleiri, khai, lešela.
narcotic, okobatšago, kidibatši.
narrate, laodiša, anegela.
narrative, kanegelo, taodišo.
narrow, pitlaganeng, tshesane, ngotlegago.
nasal, ya nko; – **bone,** moropo.
nasal cavity, dinko, lešoba la nko.
nasal consonant, tumammogonko.
nasalisation, nkofatšo.
nasalise, nkofatša.
nasty, mpe, befago.
nation, setšhaba, morafe.
national, ya setšhaba.
nationality, mohlobo.
national road, tselakgolo, meneroto.
native, mohlolegi.
Native, Mothomoso.
nativity, matswalo.
natural, tlholego, tlhago; – **environment,** tikologo ya tlhago.
nature, tlholego, tlhago; – **study,** thutatlhago; – **conservation,** pabalelo ya tlhago.
naughty, selekang, makoko.
nausea, pherogo, go feroga.
naval, ya dikepe; – **battle,** ntwawatleng.
nave, hapo, hapu, moropana.
navel, mokhubo, – **orange,** nabele; – **cord,** kalana.
navigate, sepetša sekepe, thala.
navigator, mothadiši, mosepetšasekepe.
navvy, mošomi.
navy, dikepe tša ntwa.
Nazirite, Monasire.
near, kgauswi.
nearly, nyakile.
nearness, bokgauswi.
neat, thakgegilego; **person,** sethakga.
neatly, ka bothakga; – **dressed,** tšhepile.
neatness, bothakga.
necessary, nyakega, hlokega.
necessity, tshwanelo, tlhokego, nyakego.
neck, molala, thamo; **-muscle,**

mogano; – **clasp,** rwala megono.
necklace, pheta.
neckring, lepetu.
nectar, manopi, bolopi.
need, sehlokwa, tlala, tlalelo; v., hloka.
needle, lemao, nalete.
needlework, boroki, moroko.
needlework-centre, borokelo.
needs, dinyakwa.
negation, kganetšo, tatolo.
negative, kganetšo, lelatodi, nekethifi.
neglect, hlokomologa, lahla; n., tlhokomologo.
negligence, bošaedi, tlhokomologo.
negligent, šaetša(go), hlokomolago.
negotiate, bapatša, rerišana.
neigh, lla; n., sello sa pere.
neighbour, moagišani.
neighbourhood, tikologo.
neighbouring, neanago mellwane.
neither, le ga e le.
nephew, moswa, setlogolo.
nerve, mothapo, mogalatšhika.
nervous, tshwenyega, tšhogile, tšhogatšhogago.
nest, sehlaga.
net, lelokwa; – **ball,** kgwele ya diatla.
nether, fase, tlase.
nett, fela, nett.
netting wire, sefoterata.
nettlerash, lekhwekhwe.
network, marangrang.
neuter, tirwega.
neutral, kemelathoko, neterale.
never, le gannyane.
nevertheless, le ga go le bjalo.
new, fsa, mpsha; **become** –, mpshafala; **make** –, mpshafatša.
newly, gona bjale.
newsagency, bophatlalatšaditaba.
news, ditaba, mehlamo.
new moon, lebalana.
news-bearer, mmegi.
news broadcast, kgošo ya ditaba.
newspaper, kuranta.
news-teller, mmoledi, mmegi.
New Zealand, New-Zealand.
next, – **to,** hleng ga; – **year,** išago; – **time,** ka moso.
nib, nnipi.
nibble, phura, kokona.
nice, bose.
niceness, bose.
nicety, sa bose.
niche, sekhutlwana, tulonyana.
nick, mosehlo, moseto; – **of time,** bonako; v., seta, sehla.
nickname, lebitšo la sesomo.
nicotine, makala, bokwai, nikotine.
niece, setlogolo, moswa.
niggard, sejato, motimani.
niggardly, timana, timanago.
night, bošego.
nightfall, šwalane, phirimane.
nightly, ka bošego/mašego.
nightmare, segateledi, sekutapoana, phofa.
nightshade, mogauwane, morolana.
nil, nnoto.
nimble, bofefo, bohwefe.
nimbus, maru a pula, marupula.
nine, senyane; **-nth,** bosenyane.
nineteen, lesomesenyane.
ninety, masomesenyane.
nipper, seripapikiri, moesa, leinothipa.
nipple, letswele, tlhoko; topi, nipole.
nippy, bogale.
nit, legae, letšae.
nitrate, naetreite.
nitrogen, naetrotšene.
no, aowa, nnako.
nobility, bakgomana.
noble, mokgomana, bokgomana.
nobleman, mokgomana.
nobody, go se motho.
nocturnal, bošego.
nod, kebiša hlogo, potuma.
nodule, lekgohlwana.
noise, lešata, lerata, modumo.
noiseless, e reng tuu.
noisiness, lešata, lerata.

noisy, dirang lešata.
nomad, mohlokašope, lebobakobane.
nominal, ka leina, e nnyane, e fase.
nominate, ikgethela, šišinya, rea lebitšo.
nomination, kgetho, tshišinyo.
non-reaistic, šayago bokgonthe.
nonsense, ditšie badimo; **speak** –, balabala.
non-white, e sego lekgowa, yo moso, wa mmala.
nook, sekhutlwana.
noon, mosegare.
noose, segole, v., rea.
nor, le ga e le.
north, leboa; – **of,** ka leboa la –.
North America, Amerika-Leboa.
north-east, leboabohlabela.
North-Pole, Phoulo ya Leboa.
north-west, leboabodikela.
nose, dupa, dupela; n., nko.
nostril, kgalanko, **-s,** dinko.
not, se, ga, ga se.
notable, šetšega, bogega, tumišega.
notate, ngwala.
notation, mongwalo(palo) note.
notch, sehla; **notched,** sehlilwego.
note, note, tsebišo, pampiritšhelete, lehlare; v., ela hloko.
noted, tumilego, tumileng.
noteworthy, šetšega, tumišega.
nothing, ga se selo, lefela.
notice, tsebišo, v., bona, hlokomela.
notification, tsebišo.
notify, tsebiša.
notion, kgopolo, mogopolo.
notoriety, (se)tumo.
notorious, tsebega ka tše mpe.
notwithstanding, le ga go le bjalo.
nought, nnoto, lefela.
noun, leina; **abstract,** leinakgopolo; **common** –, leinagohle; **proper** –, leinaina; **collective** –, leinakgoboka; **-class,** legoroina.
nourish, fepa, otla.
nourishment, phepo, dijo, kotlo.
novel, fsa, e mpsha; n., padi.
novelty, selo se sefsa.
November, Nofemere, Dibatsela.
novice, yo mofsa.
now, bjale, gona bjale.
nowadays, pak'eno, mehleng ye.
nowhere, ga go (mo) felo.
noxious, senyago, – **weed,** mphoka.
nuclear, ya nyuklea.
nucleus, nyuklea.
nude, hlobotšego, ponokago.
nuisance, letshwenyo, tapišo.
null, ya lefela.
nullify, dira lefela, fediša.
numb, rephilwego, hwilego.
number, nomoro, palo; – **whole** palotlalo; – **system,** tselapalo.
numberless, go se na palo.
numerable, e ka balwang.
numeral, lebadi; **multiple** –, lebalaka; **cardinal** –, lebalapalo; **ordinal** –, lebalatatelano; **indefinite** –, lebalafela.
numerate, bala.
numeration, palo, palobitšwa, pitšopalo.
numerator, lebadi.
numerically, ka palo.
numerical, senomoro, ka tatelano.
numerous, ntši.
nun, sesetere.
nunnery, ntlo ya bosesetere.
nuptials, bogadi, lenyalo.
nurse, mooki, mofepi; v., oka, lela.
nursery, ntlo ya masea, bomedišetšo.
nursery-rhyme, tlhaletšo, sehlaletši.
nursing-home, bookelo.
nurture, fepa, godiša.
nut, koko, mmuru; **ground** –, tloo.
nutriment, sejo, kotlo.
nutrition, kotlo, phepo.
nutritious, fepago, otlang.
nutritive, fepago, otlang.
nutshell, kgeru, letlapi.
Nylstroom, Modimolle.

O

O! mmalo, mmawee, oho!
oak, moeike; – **trees,** meeike.
oar, lehuduo, serapo, lesokwana.
oasis, owasese.
oath, keno, kano.
oatmeal, outse, bupi bja habore.
obduracy, bonganga, bohlogothata.
obdurate, ngangago.
obedience, go kwa, boikobo.
obedient, kgwang, kwago, ikokobetša ikoba.
obese, nona, nonnego.
obey, kwa theetša, ikoba.
object, selo, morero, tebo.
object, sedirwa; **indirect** –, sedirelwa.
object, gana, belaela, galala; – **ed,** ganne.
objection, kgano, kgalalo.
objectival concord, lekgokasedirwa.
objective, šele, tebo.
obligate, gapeletša, tlema.
obligatory, tlamegile, gapeletšega.
oblige, gapeletša, thuša.
obliging, thušang, thušago.
oblique, sekameng, rapameng.
obliterate, fediša, phumola.
oblivion, tebalo.
oblivious, lebalago.
oblong, (ya) motopo.
obnoxious, senyago, ilegago, lobišago.
oboe, oboi.
obscene, ditšhila, rogago.
obscure, hlokang lesedi, leswiswi, v., fifatša, pata, šira.
obsequious, ikokobetšang, sekgoba, fepeletšago.
observation, temogo, tlhokomelo.
observe, hlokomela, bona, hlompha.
observer, molemogi, mohlokomedi.
obsolete, onetšeng, talafetšeng.
obstacle, lepheko, thibelo.
obstacle race, tšhianophekwa.
obstinacy, manganga, bohlogothata.
obstinate, ngangago, v., ngangela.
obstruct, pheka, thibela, šitiša.
obstruction, thibelo, lepheko.
obtain, bona, hwetša, humana.
obtainable, hwetšagala.
obtrude, itsenya, tshwenya.
obviate, šuthiša, phema.
obvious, pepeneneng, bonagalang.
occasion, lebaka, sebaka.
occasional, ya sewelo, ya sebaka.
occasionally, ka sewelo, ka sebaka.
occult, utilego, sephiri(ng).
occupant, moagi, modudi.
occupation, modiro, mošomo.
occupy, dula (aga)go, diriša.
occur, diragala.
occurrence, tiragalo.
ocean, lewatle; – **current,** moelawatle.
ochre, letsoku; **black** –, sebilo.
octave, noteseswai.
October, Oktobore, Diphalana.
odd, makatšang, segišang.
odd number, palo ya go se lekanele.
oddment, lešaledi.
odious, hloiwago, ilegang.
odium, lehloyo.
odour, monkgo, monko; – **less,** sa nkgego.
of, wa, ba, ya, sa, ka.
off, tlogile, tlošitšwe.
offal, diretlo, mašaledi.
offence, molato, tlolo, tshenyo.
offend, tlola, senya.
offender, mosenyi, motlodi.
offer, ithaopa, neo, sehlabelo, dira/direla sehlabelo; **offer** –, intšha sehlabelo.
offering, sehlabelo.
off-handed, se nang taba, sa šetšego.
officer, tona, mohlankedi.
official, mohlankedi wa mmušo; – **language,** leleme la mmušo.
officiate, hlankela, rera.
offish, ikgogomošago.
offload, laolla, belegolola.
off-saddle, salolla.

offside, hlakorešele.
offspring, bana, leloko, setlogolo.
often, gantši; **very** –, gantšintši; **how** –, gakae?
oh! jo! aowii!
oil, oli, makhura.
oil-painting, seswantšho sa oli.
oil-stone, seloutšomakhura.
ointment, setlolo.
old, tala, tšofetšeng, v., onala, tšofala.
old age, botšofadi, boputswa.
old-fashioned, ya segologolo.
Olifants River, Lepelle.
olive, mohlware.
omen, tlholo, sešupo; **ill** –, mahlolakotsi.
omit, šia, tlogela, lesa.
omnipotent, yo maatla ka moka.
omnipresence, go ba mo gohle.
on, godimo ga, go, mo, fa, adv., **go** –, ya pele, tšwela pele; – **the way,** tseleng.
once, gatee, ka tšatši le lengwe; – **more,** gape; – **for all,** ruri; aux. v., –, kile.
one, tee, e mong, le leng, nngwe; **any** –, mang le mang; **every** –, e mongwe le e mongwe.
one-eyed, moihlwe, moihlo.
oneness, botee.
onerous, imelang, e boima.
oneself, ka boyena, ka nama, ka noši.
onion, eie, nyala.
only, fela, nnoši, ka noši.
onlooker, mmogi, molebeledi.
onomatopoeia, leekiši, leetšiši.
onset, mathomo, tlhaselo, tšhimologo.
onslaught, tlhaselo, phomegelo.
onward, pele, kua pele.
ooze, tshotshoma, dutla, kga kodumela, n., seretse.
opaque, sa edišego, sa bonagatšego.
open, bula, thibolla, raramolla, katologanya, bulegile; – **the mouth,** ahlama; – **the hand,** khuparolla; – **the eye,** budulola; – **note,** notepulwa.
open, in the –, pepeneng.
opening, phahla, kgoro, pulo, sekgoba, sekgala; – **between the teeth,** lesoro; – **in garment,** selepe, lephakga.
openly, pontšheng, phatlalatša, ka tshenolo.
open veld, legola.
opera, opera.
operate, dira; – **cut open,** bua.
operation, tshepedišo, tiro, opareišene, puo; – **theatre,** teatere ya opareišene.
operative, dirago, šomago.
operator, modiri, mosepediši, mmui.
opinion, kgopolo, mogopolo.
opponent, mmakiši, mophegišani, moganetši, lenaba.
opportune, loketšego, lokilego, bonako.
opportunities, dibaka, makga.
oppose, lwantšha, gana, ganetša; – **me,** ntwantšha.
opposite, latolago, lebaneng le, fapanang; n., lelatodi.
opposition, kganetšo, bobakapušo.
oppress, pata, tlaiša, gatelela.
oppression, tlaišo, kimetšo, kgatello, bogateledi.
oppressive, tlaišago, patago, – **air,** sekhutamoya.
oppressor, motlaiši, mopati, mogateledi.
option, kgetho, tlhaolo.
opulence, lehumo.
or, goba, le ge e le.
oracle, orakele, ngaka ya ditaola.
oral, ya molomo.
oral drill, tlwaetšo ya molomo.
orange, namune.
Orange Free State, Freistata; – **River,** Noka ya Ntsho.
orator, seboledi.
orb, kgokolwana, kgokolo.

orbit, modiko.
orchard, serapa se dikenywa.
orchestra, okese, mminotetšo.
ordain, hloma, laola, bea.
order, molao, otara, tatelano; –, bopelela, hlatlamana, **take in –,** monoketša; v.t., laola; laela; **put/set in–,** beakanya, rulaganya.
orderliness, makgethe, bothakga.
orderly, ka thulagano, ka bothakga.
ordinal numeral, lebalatatelano.
ordinance, molawana, odinansi.
ordinarily, ka mehla.
ordinary, ya ka mehla, ka tlwaelo.
ore, borale.
organ, setho, okane, kwadi; **reproductory –,** sethopelegi.
organic, sebolang, dibolang.
organisation, thulaganyo, peakanyo.
organise, beakanya, rulaganya.
organiser, mmeakanyi, morulaganyi.
organist, moletši wa okane.
organs, internal, –, dikateng, diretlo, mala; – **of speech,** ditho tša polelo.
orgy, mokete wa bjalwa.
orient, bohlabela, bohlabatšatši.
oriental, bohlabela.
orifice, molomo, lešoba.
origin, tlhago, setšo, botšo, setlogo.
original, ya(pele), mathomo.
originality, boithomelo.
originally, mathomong, tlhagong.
originate, hlagiša, thoma, thea.
Orion, Kgogamašego.
ornament, kgabišo, sekgabišo; v., kgabiša.
ornamental, kgabišago, – **tree,** sehlarekgabiši.
ornate, kgabišitšwego.
ornithology, tsebo ya dinonyana.
orphan, tšhuana, tšhiwana.
orphanage, ditšhuaneng.
orthodox, segologolo, kgonthe.
orthography, mongwalo.
oscillate, kadiela, akgaakgega, dikadika.
oscillation, kadielo, thekeselo.
ostensibly, ka go etšiša, eke.
ostentation, boikgantšho, pontšho.
ostrich, mpšhe.
other, ngwe, šele; **the – day,** maloba; **the – side,** mošola, moše.
otherwise, go se bjalo, ka mokgwa o mong.
otter, nebi.
ought, e ka kgona, swanetše.
ounce, ontshe, onse.
our, ya rena, ya gešo.
ourselves, borena; rena ka noši; **or i- prefixed to the verb, e.g., we see ourselves,** re a ipona.
oust, ntšha, tšwa, ntshwetša.
out, ntle, ka ntle; **come** – tšwa; **take –,** ntšha; **go –, as a flame,** tima; **push –,** kgorometša ntle, leleka; – **with you!** eya kua!
outbreak, tsogo, go wa, tlhago.
outcast, molelekiwa, molahlwa.
outcome, setšo, botšo; – **result,** bofelo, mafelo.
outcry, kgoelelo, sello, mogoo.
outdo, feta, fetiša, phala.
outdoor, ka ntle, kgakala.
outer, ya ka ntle, bokantle.
outfit, (clothes), diaparo, v., hlama, apeša; **outfitter,** morekišadiaparo.
outgoing, yago, tšwago.
outhouse, morala.
outing, leetwana.
outlander, moeng.
outlaw, lahla, molahlwa.
outlet, botšwelo, sentšhamoya.
outline, akaretša thalathala, legokgo, magomo.
outmost, pheletšong, e ka ntle.
outnumber, feta (ka palo).
outpace, šia, feta.
out-patient, mookelwantle.
outpost, moraka.
outrageous, šoro, kgalegago, hlabišago dihlong.
outright, gatee, ka moka, molaleng.

outrun, šia, feta.
outset, mathomong, tšhimologong.
outside, bokantle, kgakala, kua ntle, ka ntle.
outsider, moeng.
outsize, kgolo.
outskirt, mellwane, bogomo.
outspan, bofolla, golola.
outspoken, ka tokologo.
outspread, ala; nama, atlarela, hlarolola.
outstanding (event), tiragalokgolo.
outstrip, šia, feta.
outward, ntle, kua ntle.
oval, selee, ya menopo.
ovary, popelo, tswalo.
oven, onto.
over, godimo; – **against,** bolebana le.
overall, obarolo.
overbear, fenya, hlola.
overbearing, laolago, ikgogomošang.
overburden, imela, imetša.
overcast, bipa, na le maru, thibile.
overcasting, morulelo.
overcome, fenya, hlola, phala.
overcoat, jase.
overdo, iša kgole, fetišiša.
overfeed, betelela.
overflow, falala, tšhologa, kgaphatša.
over-hasty, v., potlakiša, phakiša.
overhaul, lokiša, mpshafatša.
overhead, godimo, ka (kua) godimo.
overhear, kwa, kwela.
overland, phara (phatša) naga.
overlap, hlatlagana.
overlapping, lepeletšego.
overlook, okama, hlokomologa, swarela; hlahloba.
overpower, fenya, hlola.
overrule, buša, rena.
overseas, mošola wa mawatle.
oversee, lebelela, okamela, lekola.
overseer, molebeledi, mookamedi.
oversight, tlhokomologo, phošo.
oversleep, selwa.
overstock, golelaphulo.
overtake, fihlela.
overstrain, ngangega.
overstraining, ngangego.
overthrow, menola, thenkgola; n., menolo, thenkgolo.
overture, obatore, mohlabelelo.
overturn, pitikolola, ribegetša, thenkgolla.
overwhelm, hlola, fenya.
owe, ba le molato, kolota.
owl, leribiši, makgotlo.
own, ithuela, rua; ipolela.
owner, mong.
ox, pholo; **pack** –, lekaba.
oxidation, oksitase.
oxygen, oksitšene, oksigene.
oyster, kgetla; – **shell,** legapikgetla.

P

pa, tate, r(r)a.
pace, kgato, legato.
Pacific, Phasifiki, Lewatletu.
pacify, khutšiša, homotša.
pack, thoto, phahlo, sehlopha.
package, sephutha, ngata, phahlo.
packet, pakana, sephuthana.
packing, go phutha, sephutha.
pack-ox, lekaba.
pact, kwano, kgwerano.
pad, kitela, katela, tlatša; n., mosamelwana; **writing** –, pukungwalo.
padding, tlatšo.
paddle, tlampuletša, tlapuletša.
paddle wheel, leotwanakhûduo.
paddock, kampana.
padlock, sekgonyo, seloto.
pagan, moditšhaba, moheitene.
page, letlakala, mohlanka.
pail, kgamelo, emere, bakete.
pain, bohloko, sehlabi; maswabi; v., baba, galaka; – **killer,** sebolaya-sehlabi; **inflict** –, kwiša bohloko.

painful, bohloko, babago.
painless, sa kwišeng bohloko, sa babego.
painstaking, mafolofolo.
paint, penta, pente, ferefe; v., penta, ferefa, swantšha.
painter, moferefi, mopenti, motloki, moswantšhi.
painting, seswantšho, go (ferefa) penta.
pair, bobedi, babedi, (di)pedi; – **of pincers,** tane.
palace, mošate, ntlokgolo.
palatable, bose.
palatalisation, kgalapatšo.
palate, magalapa.
pale, sehla, galogile; **paleness,** kgalogo, bosehla.
Palestine, Palestina.
pall, kobo, sekhutlane.
palm, legoswi, legofe; **spread out the palms,** akaretša, atlarela; **a – tree,** mokolana, mopalema; **the South African –,** molala.
palpable, adj., e ka phopholetšwang, bonagalang, swaregang.
palpitate, opaopa, uba, itia.
palpitation, go uba ga pelo.
palsied, rephile, ditho, reketla.
palsy, rephile ditho.
paltry, nyatšegang, hlokang mohola, nyenyane.
pamper, tleekeetša, kgoriša, lema ekelela.
pamphlet, pamfolete, pukwana.
pan, pane, mogobe.
panacea, pheko.
pancreas, pankarea.
pandemonium, lešata, pherekano, lešašano.
pane, galase ya lefastere.
panel, panele, sehlopha.
panel-beater, mopotolodi.
pang, sehlabi, bohloko.
panga, phanka, lepaka.
pangolin, kgaga, kgwara.
panic, letšhogo, lešašano, tlalelo; v., tšhoga, gakenegile, tlalelwa.
panorama, pono, ponelokgole, panorama.
pant, fegelwa, šutša.
panther, nkwe.
pantihose, phenthihouse.
pantry, lefera, polokelo ya dijo.
papa, tate, papa.
papacy, bopapa.
paper, pampiri, lephephe, kuranta.
paper-bag, mokotla wa pampiri.
paper-money, tšhelete ya mahlare.
pawpaw, phopho, popose.
parable, seswantšho.
parachute, parašutu.
parade, fola; n., mofolo, phareiti.
paradise, paradeisi.
paradox, kgakantšhano, paratokso.
paraffine, parafene.
paragraph, kgala, temana.
parallel, bapetšego, mogaranafase.
parallelogram, paralelokramo.
paralyse, hwa bogašu, repha ditho.
paralysis, repha ditho.
paramount, kgolo, segolothata.
paramour, nyatši, phuti.
paraphrase, hlaloša.
paraplegic, rephilego ditho, segole.
parasite, kgofa, phelakadingwe, boori.
parasol, samporele, sekhukhunyana.
paratroop(er), mopharašute.
parcel, phasela, sephuthana, lepakana; v., paka, arola.
parch, omelela, pona, fiša.
parched, omeletšeng, omeletšego.
parchment, letlalongwalo.
pardon, tebalelo, tshwarelo, tesetšo; – **to forgive,** swarela, setša; **beg for –,** go puputla, kgopela tshwarelo, phophotha.
pare, ebola, tlebola.
parent, motswadi, mogolo.
parenthesis, kgaretšo, mašakanabora.
Paris, Parys, Paris.

parish, phuthego.
parishioner, setho sa phuthego.
park, phaka.
parking, go phaka.
parley, boledišana.
parliament, kgotlakgolo, palamente.
parlour, kamore ya baeng, phapošitulelo.
parody, go gegea.
parole, go itlema ka keno.
parquet, lebato la mapolankana (mamatšana).
parrot, lepapagai, legehle.
parry, phema.
parsimonious, timana.
parsley, pareseli.
parsnip, segweretšhweu.
parson, moruti.
part, karolo, kgaolo; v., kgaoganya, arola; – **-time,** ya sebaka/letogo.
partake, ngwatha, ja, ipshina ka, ba le kabelo, hlakanela.
partial, hlaola.
partiality, tlhao.
participant, moabedwi, mohlakanedi, modiriši, modirišani.
participate, hlakanela, ba le kabelo, dirišana.
participial, (mood), modirišohlaodi.
particle, karolonyana, sekgawana, lerathana.
particular, itšeng, itšego.
particularly, gagolo.
particulars, ditlhalošišo.
parting, kgaogano, karogano.
partition, kgaoganyo, seširo; v., aba.
partly, ka ntlha e nngwe.
partner, modirišani, mogwebišani.
partnership, tirišano, kgwebišano.
partridge, kgwale, lehuhu, legwara.
party, phathi, lekoko.
pass, sefata, pasa; v., feta, fepa, ragela, – **through,** putla; – **by quickly,** kgabola; **cause to – through,** putliša.
pass judgement, tšua, tšwa.
passage, sefero, sekgala, phahla, tema.
passage, leeto.
passenger, monamedi.
passing, fetago, – **note,** noteketedi.
passion, phišego, tlaišego.
passionate, ka phišego.
passive, sa rego selo; **(voice),** ledirwi, tirwa.
Passover, Paseka.
passport, paseporoto.
past, fetileng; – **tense,** lefetile; **past conditional,** lefetilepeelano; **past continuous,** lefetile tšweledi; – **imperfect,** lefetilešaledi; – **perfect,** lefetilephethi; **remote perfect,** lefetilephethikgole.
paste, segomaretši; v., phara, gomaretša, momaretša.
pastel, pastele.
pasteurisation, paseterišo, pasetarišo.
pastime, maitišo, boitišo.
pastor, modiši, moruti; – **al,** bodiši.
pastry, dikukisi.
pasture, mafulo, phulo; v., fudiša.
pat, phaphatha.
patch, setsiba, segaswa; v., phara, mama.
pate, hlogo, legata.
patent, patente, phadišago, pepeneng.
paternity, borra.
path, tsela, pata, mmila.
pathetic, mahlomola.
pathology, thutabolwetši.
pathos, maswabiša.
patience, bopelotelele.
patient, iketla; **be** –, bea pelo.
patient, molwetši.
patiently, ka go iketla.
patriarch, mopatriareka, mogologolo.
patrimony, bohwa, nkhwa, lefa.
patriot, moratalabo.
patriotism, boratalabo.
patrol, patrolo, v., dikologa le.
patron, moemedi, mošireletši.
patronise, emela, šireletša, thekga.

patter, patapata.
pattern, paterone, sekaelo, mosego, makgwai, mohlala, seakanyetšo.
paucity, bobotlana, tlhaelo.
paunch, mogodu.
pauper, mohloki, mohumanegi.
pauperism, bohloki, khumanego.
pause, khutša, n., (bo)khutšwana.
pave, ala (ka matlapa), bata.
pavement, tselanathoko, tselathokwana.
pavilion, tente, pabilione, bobogelo.
paw, leroo, borofa; v., gata.
pawpaw, phopho, popose.
pawn, sebeelo; v., beela, beetša.
pay, lefa, putsa; n., tefo, moputso.
payee, molefša.
payer, molefi.
payment, tefo, moputso.
pea, erekisi, tlhodi.
peacable, ratang khutšo.
peacably, ka khutšo.
peace, khutšo, marumo fase!
peacemaker, modirakhutšo.
peach, perekisi; – **tree,** moperekisi.
peacock, p(h)ikoko.
peak, ntlha, sehloa, tlhora.
peal, modumo, sello.
peanuts, ditokomane, ditloo (make).
pear, piere, pšere; – **tree,** mopšere, mopiere.
pearl, perela.
peasant, monageng.
peat, seloko.
pebble, leswikana.
peck, loma, kobola, nopola.
pectoral, ya sehuba.
peculiar, makatšang.
peculiarity, mokgwa, semaka, pharologanyo.
pecuniary, ya tšhelete.
pedagogic, serutiši.
pedagogue, morutiši, morutabana.
pedal, petela.
pedant, mokeatseba.
peddle, bapatša, ralala.
pedestrian, mosepedi.
pedigree, lešika.
pedlar, mmapatši.
peel, ebola, kela; n., lekgata.
peep, hlodimela, hlola.
peep (chirp), tšwirinya, lla.
peep-hole, seokomelabagwe.
peepshow, pontšhohlodimelwa.
peer, molekane, thaka, mokgomana; v., tadimišiša, tsepela mahlo, lebeledišiša.
peerless, se nago tekanyo.
peevish, ngala, lepelela, bopa.
peg, semapo, kokontwane, sebapola, kokotela; – **out,** bapola.
pelican, kukara.
pell-mell, lešašanošano.
pelt, mokgapa, letlalo; v., betša.
pelvis, noka, letheka.
pen, pene, oko, lešaka; v., ngwala.
penal, otegago, otlwago.
penalise, otla, lefiša.
penalty, kotlo, phenale (football).
penance, kotlo, tefišo.
pencil, petoloto, phensele.
pendant, sefokana.
pendent, lekelelago.
pending, lekelelago.
pendulum, tekehli.
penetrate, tsena, tsenelela, phunya.
penguin, phenkwine, pekebene.
penicillin, peniseline.
peninsula, nkasehlakahlaka.
penis, lepele, ntoto, morotwana, phinyo, modiša; **have erection of –,** totelwa; – **of a bull,** polo.
penitence, boitsholo.
penitent, itsholago, nyamilego.
pennant, sefokana, folagana.
penniless, hlaetšwego, hlokago, pankoroto.
penny, peni; – **weight,** boimapeni.
pension, phenšene; – **er,** mophenšenwa.
pensive, gopolang, naganang.

pentagon, pentakono, khutlohlano, khutlotlhano.
Pentecost, Pentekoste.
penultimate, serakamafelo.
penury, tlhaelo, khumanego, tlhokego.
people, batho, setšhaba.
pep, mafolofolo.
pepper, pherefere.
peppermint, poporomente.
pepsin, pepesine.
per, ka.
perambulate, sepela, ralala.
perambulator, koloyana ya bana.
perceive, lemoga, ela hloko.
percent, phesente, kgolong.
percentage, kgolong, sephesente.
perceptible, lemogega, bonagala.
perception, temogo.
perch, tsodiela, tsorama, kotama.
percolate, hlotlega.
percussion, kotlo.
percussion band, mminotetšo, okese ya meropa.
perdition, tahlego, tshenyego.
peremptory, gapeletšega.
perennial, sanywaga, samengwaga.
perfect, phethegileng, hlamatšegileng; – **tense,** lephethi.
perfection, phethego.
perfidious, forago, menolang, ekago.
perfidy, keko, go se botege, phoro, boradia.
perforate, phunya, hlabaka, – **d,** phuntšwe.
perforce, gapeletšegile.
perform, dira, phetha; – **for,** direla, phethela.
performance, tiro, papalo.
perfume, monko, (se)nkgišamonate.
perhaps, gongwe, kgotsa, kgane.
peril, kotsi.
perilous, kotsi, šišang.
perimeter, modiko, perimeta, modika.
period, lebaka, sebaka, **have monthly period,** bona kgwedi, phetha; – **for,** direla, phethela.
periodical, ka mabaka, n., makasine, kgatišobaka.
perish, senyega, hwelela, bola.
perishable, products, dibunwa tše senyegago.
peri-urban, pheriebene.
perjure, enolla.
perjury, kenollo.
permanent, sa feleng, tiileng.
permanent tooth, leinoruri.
permanently, ka tiišetšo, ruri.
permeate, koloba, tsenelela; tswenatswena.
permissible, dumelelega, dumelelwa.
permission, tumelelo.
permit, dumelela; n., tumelelo; **be – ted,** dumeletšwe.
permutation, phetolo, phetogo.
permute, fetola.
pernicious, senyang, lobišago, mpe.
perpendicular, tsepameng, molatsepa rego thwii.
perpetrate, phetha, dira.
perpetual, sa feleng.
perpetually, ka go sa feleng.
perpetuate, tiiša.
perplex, tlaba, gakantšha, makatša.
perplexity, tlabego, kgakanego.
persecute, hlomarela, tlaiša, hlomara.
persecution, tlhomaro, tlaišo.
perseverance, kgotlelelo, phegelelo.
persevere, kgotlelela, phegelela.
persist, kgotlelela, tiišetša.
persistency, kgotlelelo, phegelelo.
persistent, go se lapišege.
person, motho; **a certain** –, mokete, **first** –, mmoledi; **second** –, mmoledišwa; **third** –, mmolelwa.
personage, motho, ntho.
personal, sa motho, ka nama.
personality, seriti, serithi, semangmang; **legal** –, boikemelamolaong.
personate, emela.
personification, mothofatša.

personnel, phesonele.
perspective, ponego.
perspicacity, temogo.
perspicious, bonagalang, kwagalang.
perspiration, kudumela, mphufutšo, sethitho.
persuade, kgodiša, otelela.
persuasion, kgodišo, kgono.
persuasiveness, maatla a go kgodiša.
pert, kgang, hlaga.
pertain, ya ka, malebana le.
pertinacity, bohlogothata, kgotlelelo.
pertinent, lokelang, swanelang.
perturb, tshwenya, belaetša.
perusal, padišišo.
peruse, badišiša, lotolotša.
pervade, tlala, tsenelela.
perverse, kgelogago, befago, ngangelago.
pervert, hlanoša, kgeloša, n., mokgelogi, motimedi.
pest, sesenyi, sejedi, lehu la sewa.
pester, tshwenya, tlaiša.
pestilence, lehulebe, leuba.
pestle, mose, v., setla.
pet, seruiwaseratwa; v., phaphatha.
petal, petala, poubala.
petition, thapedi; v., rapela, lopa.
petitioner, morapedi.
petrify, fetoga lebje, gakala, lebjefala, swikafala.
petrol, peterolo.
petroleum, peteroleamo, sepeterolo.
petrol-pump, pompi ya peterolo.
petticoat, onoroko.
petty, potlana, nyenyane, nyatšegang; – **chief,** kgošana; – **cash,** sekgwama, sekhwama.
petulant, rumolega.
petulence, thumolego, matepe, swele.
pew, sedulo, panka ya kereke.
phalanx, manakailana, mašapo a menwana.
Pharaoh, Farao.
pharisee, mofarisei, moikaketši.
pharmacy, khemisi.
pharynx, farinkisi.
phase, boemo, kgato, bobono.
pheasant, le(k)hu(k)hu, kgwale.
phenomena, diponagalo.
phenomenon, ponagalo.
philanthropist, moratabatho.
philanthropy, boratabatho.
philology, filolotši, thutapopego.
philosopher, rabohlale.
philosophy, filosofi.
phlegm, boleta, segohlola, bolepa, go tšwafa.
phonetics, thutamedumo, fonetiki.
phonic (method), tumatlhaka.
phonology, fonolotši, thutapopomedumo.
phosphate, fosfate.
phosphorus, fosforo.
photograph, seswantšho.
photosynthesis, fotosintese.
phrase, sekafoko, v., fokatša.
phrasing, phokatšo, go fokatša.
physic, kalafo, sehlare, bongaka; v., alafa.
physical, sebopego, fisiki; sa mmele, – **condition,** maemopopego; – **defect,** bogole; – **exercise,** boitšhidillo, thobollo, kotlollo.
physician, ngaka.
physics, fisika.
physiology, fisiolotši.
piano, piano, piana.
pick, peke, kgetho; v., fula, kgetha; – **up,** topa; – **a bone,** kokona; – **a quarrel,** fehla ntwa; – **one's teeth,** itukula.
pick-a-back, pepula.
pickax(e), manakisi, peke.
picket, koko(n)twane; baletadira, ditlhodi; ageletša.
pickle, boloka ka asene; **–d fish,** hlapi ya khanakhana.
pickles, pekelese.
picnic, pikiniki.
picture, seswantšho.
picturesque, bogegang.

pie, pastei, phae, tlhakantšuku.
pieblad, mebalabala.
piece, seripana, karolo; – **s,** matoka.
piecemeal, ka marathana.
pierce, phula, phunya, hlaba.
piercing, phulang, phunyang.
pietism, boikobotumelong.
piety, borapedi.
piffle, bošilo, ditšiebadimo.
pig, kolobe.
pigeon, leeba, mokuru; v., fora.
pigeon-hole, rakana.
pig-headed, sethoto, bohlogothata.
pig-iron, tšhipi ya makgwakgwa.
pigment, mmala, mmasa.
pigmy, kgopana.
pike, lerumo.
pilchard, philetšhate.
pile, ntotoma, mokgobo, v., bokanya, kgoba.
piles, matšala.
pilfer, utswa.
pilgrim, moeti.
pilgrimage, leeto la mokriste.
pill, pilisi, philisi.
pillage, thopa, phuma.
pillar, kokwane; – **of cloud,** thololo ya leru.
pillion, sebeeletšo.
pillow, mosamelo, mosamo; v., samela, sametša; – **slip,** selopo.
pilot, mofofane, mokepe.
pimple, peis, kemola.
pin, sepelete, sepalete.
pin-cushion, mosamelo wa dipalete.
pinafore, thetho.
pincers, letlao, tang.
pinch, soba, tsipa, pitlaganya.
pine, mophaene; v., nyama.
pineapple, phaeneapole.
pinion, lephego; v., tlema matsogo.
pink, pinki.
pinnacle, sehloa, ntlhora.
pint, phaente.
pioneer, mophulatsela, ketapele.
pious, boifang modimo.
pip, thotse, thaka; v., lla.
pipe, phaephe, pompi, peipi.
pipe-line, molokoloko wa dipompi.
piping, diphaephe, motswirinyo.
piracy, bohoduwatle.
pirate, lehoduwatle.
pistil, mamodula, pistile, phistili.
pistol, raboloro, serope sa kgogo.
piston, phistene.
pit, molete, petse.
pitch, motu, sekontiri; v., hloma; fifatša; foša, betša; – **(cricket),** lebalana; – **tone,** segalo; – **height,** bogodimo.
pitcher, nkgo, segwana.
piteous, swabišang, nyamišang.
pitfall, moreo, mogogotla, mošima.
pith, pelo, moko.
pithy, e maatla, nepago.
pitiable, hlomolang, masetlapelo.
pitiless, se nang kgaugelo.
pittance, tefonyana.
pituitary, lepologago.
pity, kgaugelo; v., gaugela.
pivot, pinagare, phifote.
pixy, pixie, radinakana; – **cap,** mmese wa ntlha.
place, felo, sebaka, tulo; – **of rest,** bolapologelo.
place, bea; **give – to,** šuthela; – **me,** mpea.
place holder, sethibakgala.
place of birth, botswalelo.
placenta, samorago; mohlana.
placid, homotšego, iketlilego.
placidity, boiketlo, khutšo.
placing, peo, go bea.
plague, leroborobo; matshwenyego, v., tshwenya, tlaiša.
plaid, tšale, kobo.
plain, hlokang kgabišo; **make –,** hlaloša; – **knitting,** logela gojeng.
plainly, pepeneneng, lebaleng.
plaint, pelaelo, sello, pego.
plaintiff, mmelaedi, mosekiši, mmegi, motlalei.

plaintive, belaelago.
plait, loga.
plan, maano, morero, polane, sethalo; v., thala, loga maano.
plane, khafa; sekhafo, tekanetšo.
planet, polanete, setšatši.
plank, lepolanka.
plant, semela, sebjalo, v., bjala, hloma; – **ed,** bjetše.
plantation, sethokgwa.
planter, mobjadi; polantere.
plant-food, sejosemela.
plaque, phaphathi.
plaster, poleistere; v., phara.
plasterer, mophari.
plastic, plastiki; – **art,** bokgabo bja go bopa.
plate, sejelo, poroto; v., manega.
plateau, sehlaba, polatou.
platform, sethala, polatefomo.
platter, mogopo.
plausible, kgodišang.
play, papadi, thaloko; tiragatšo; raloka, bapala, letša; – **truant,** roba sogo; – **mirthfully,** nyakalala; **player,** mmapadi, thaloki.
playful, ralokago, nyakalago.
playground, lebala la dipapadi, bobapalelo.
playmate, thaka, monkane.
plaything, sebapadišo.
playtime, nako ya go bapala, maitišo.
plea, kgopelo, thapelo.
plead, rapela, phophotha, puputla.
pleasant, thabišago, kgahlišago.
pleasantness, lethabo, bose.
please, kgahliša, thabiša; – **oneself,** ithatela; **if you** –, hle; – **to,** tsefela.
pleasing, kgahlišago, thabišago.
pleasure, lethabo, nyakalalo.
pleat, lepeliti, poloi; v., pelita.
plebeian, ya segae.
plectrum, sethankgodi.
pledge, kholofetšo; v., holofetša, panta.
plenipotentiary, segafelwa maatla – ka – moka, motsetaphethi.
plenitude, botlalo, bontši.
plenteous, e ntši.
plentiful, ntši, kgora.
pleurisy, pholoresi, ploresi.
pliability, bolea, se le meetse.
pliers, kinipitane.
plight, tlalelo; v., holofetša.
plod, katana, kata.
plot, serepe, segwe; v., rerišana; – **of ground,** setsha, tema.
plough, mogoma; v., lema.
ploughable, lemega.
ploughman, molemi.
ploughshare, sekala.
pluck, ga, fula, hloba, rutla; – **out,** gonya, tumola.
pluck, sebete, dikateng.
plug, sethibo, sepako, poropo; v., thiba, kaba, poropela.
plum, poreime; **wild** –, letšhidi.
plumb, selekalekanyi, baterepase; v., lekalekanya; **stand** –, ema thwii; – **er,** radipompo, polamere.
plume, lefofa, seala, v., kgantšha.
plump, nonneng, nonne; v., nona, phonkgetša.
plunder, khulo, thopo, v., hula, thopa, phuma.
plundering, khulo, thopo.
plunge, phonkgelela, swinya.
plural, bontši.
plurality, bontši.
plus, (hlakanya) le.
ply, momeno, llaga; v., mena; šomiša; – **wood,** kotallaga.
p.m., t.p. (thapama).
P.M., (per month), k.k., ka kgwedi.
pneumonia, nyumonia.
poach, utswa diphoofolo.
pocket, potla, mokotlana, v., tsenya potleng.
pocket-book, pukwana ya potla.
pocket-money, tšhelete ya potla.
pod, sephotlwa, tšhwana.

poem, sereto.
poet, moreti, sereti.
poetry, theto.
poignant, bohloko, bogale, hlabang.
point, ntlha, tabakgolo; **on the – of,** lekgatheng la go; v., **– at,** šupa; **– out,** šupetša, bontšha; **– of new,** tebelelo, kgopolo.
pointed, ya ntlha.
pointless, se nang taba, kubegileng.
poise, lekanya boima.
poison, mpholo, bohloko; v., leša, loya; **– ous,** ya mpholo.
poke, thula, khutla, hlaba; **– fun at,** bapala ka.
polarise, phoularisa.
pole, kota, phoulo, ntlha.
polecat, nakedi, kgophane.
polemics, dikgang, polemiki.
police, maphodisa.
policeman, lephodisa.
policy, maano, maikemišetšo, kontraka; **insurance,** kwano.
polio, polio.
polish, pholiši, pholitšhi; v., pholiša.
politeness, setho, tlhompho.
political, (ya) politiki, **– party,** phathi.
politician, mopolitiki, morerapušo.
politics, politiki.
poll, hlogo, kgetho; v., poma.
pollen, modula.
pollinate, dulafatša.
pollination, tulafatšo.
polling, go kgetha; **– station,** bokgethelo.
poll-tax, motšhelo.
pollute, tšhilafatša.
pollution, tšhilafalo, tšhilafatšo.
polygamist, e a nyetšeng segadikane (basadi ba bantši).
polygamy, go nyala (segadikane) basadi ba bantši; go pataganya.
polygon, khutlontši.
polysyllabic, nokontši.
polytheism, bodimontši.
pomade, setlolo sa meriri.
pomegranate, garanate.
pommel, totoma, hlogwana, kotolana.
pomp, kgwanto, bokgabane, boikgantšho.
pompousness, boikgantšho, bokako.
pond, bodiba, letamo.
ponder, akanya, nagana, eleletša.
ponderous, boima.
pontoon, ponto, lekawe.
pony, petšhana, pešana.
pool, bodiba, lediba, sediba.
poor, humanegileng; n., bahloki.
poor child, ngwana wa batho; **– woman,** mosadi wa batho.
pop, modumo, sello, v., thunya, thuthupa.
pop-corn, thuthupe.
pope, mopapa.
poplar, mopopoliri.
poppy, popi.
populace, batho.
popular, ratwago, nyakegago, tumilego, tsebagala(go).
popularity, tumo, go ratwa ke batho.
populate, nniša batho.
population, setšhaba, baagi.
populous, ba bantši; lešaba.
porcelain, setsopa, poseline.
porch, mathudi, kgoro.
porcupine, noko.
pore, lerobana, lešobana; v., boga, akanya.
pork, nama ya kolobe.
porous, mašobana.
porridge, boušwa, bogobe, bošwa.
port, boemakepe.
portable, e rwalegang; **– radio,** radiošikarwa.
portage, tefo ya go (thota) rwala.
portal, ya sefata.
portend, senola.
porter, molebeledi, moletakgoro.
portfolio, potofolio.
porton, kabelo, karolo.
portrait, seswantšho.
portray, swantšha.

Portuguese, Mopotokisi, Lepotokisi.
position, kemo, boemo, maemo.
positive, tiileng, samaruri, seka, nnete.
positively, ka nnete, ruri, ka sebele.
possess, rua, ba le, na le.
possession, leruo, maruo, thuo.
possessive, ruago.
possessive concord, lekgokamong.
possessor, mong.
possibility, kgonego.
possible, go ka kgonega.
possibly, e ka ba, mohlomong.
post, poso, modiro, kota; **cattle** –, moraka; **a gate** –, photo v., posa; **to place,** go bea; – **office,** poso(ng).
postage, tefo ya lengwalo; – **stamp,** setempe.
postal (order), posotere.
poster, (lengwalo la) tsebišo.
posterior, ya morago.
posterity, ditlogolo, leloko.
posthumous, tswetšwe morago ga lehu.
postman, morwalaposo.
postmark, leswao la poso.
postmaster, raposo.
post-office, posong, poso.
postpone, diega.
posts, dikota.
postscript, kokeletšo (ya lengwalo).
posture, boemo, leemo, modulo.
pot, pitša, **a clay** –, moeta.
potable, e ka nowang.
potash, potase, logo.
potassium, potasiamo.
potato, tapola.
potency, maatla.
potent, e maatla, e tiileng.
potentate, kgoši.
potential, kgonegago, – **mood,** modirišokgonego.
pot-hole, sekoti, sedibana, moletšana.
potion, seno, sehlare.
potsherd, kgapetla.
potter, mmopi; – **'s clay,** letsopa.
pottery, bobopapitša, setsopa.
pouch, mokotlana, moraba, sekhwama; v., metša.
poulterer, mmapatši wa dikgogo le maganse.
poultice, poleisetere.
poultry, dikgogo, diruiwa tša maphego.
pounce, kgoula, tlolela godimo ga; - **upon,** kgoulela; n., lero la pekwa.
pound, ponto.
pound, sekete; v., iša seketeng.
pound, setla, tula, touta; – **er,** mose.
pounding block, lehudu.
pour, tšhela, – **out,** tšholla.
pout, hlonama, tsupula.
poverty, bohloki, khumanego.
powder, puere, phaota, mošidi; – **dust,** lerojana.
powdered milk, maswilerojana.
power, maatla.
powerful, e maatla.
powerless, fokolago, hloka maatla.
pox, chicken –, mabora; **small** –, sekobonyane, segagane.
practicable, kgonegang, ka dirwang.
practical, ya tirišo, ka dirwang.
practice, tirišo, tlwaetšo; tiro, bošomelo.
practice, diriša, tlwaetša.
prairie, prairi.
praise, theto, tumišo; v., reta, tumiša.
praiseworthy, tumišega, tlotlega.
prance, tlola, kalapa.
pranks, metlae, makoko.
pray, rapela, lopa; – **for me,** nthapela.
prayer, thapelo, topo; – **book,** puku ya merapelo.
prayerful, ratang thapelo.
preach, rera, ruta.
preacher, moruti, moreri, mmoledi.
preaching, thero.
preamble, tlhagišo, pegopele.
precarious, ya kotsi, belaetšago, befago.
precaution, tlhokomelo; **take,** –, hlokomela.

precautionary, hlokomelago.
precede, tla pele, eta pele.
precedence, sa pele, sa mathomo.
precedent, mohlala.
precept, thutišo, taelo.
precinct, tikologo, mollwane.
precious, ya bohlokwa.
preciousness, bohlokwa.
precipice, legaga, lewa.
precipitate, wela (godimo), phonkgela, phakiša.
precipitation, maitsheko, potlako, pula.
precis, kakaretšo.
precise, hlokomelago, nepago.
precisely, ka kgonthe; nepago, verešago.
preciseness, tlhokomelo, nepo.
precision, nepagalo.
preclude, thibela, iletša.
precocious, butšwitšeng pele ga nako; – **child,** ngwana wa segadi, yo a thantšego.
precursor, ketapele, setlangpele.
predator, sebata.
predecessor, moetapele, ketapele.
predestinate, kgethela pele, laolela pele.
predestination, taolelo, kgethelopele, taolelopele.
predicament, tlalelo.
predicate, tiro, kanegedi.
predicative, dirago.
predict, laola; – **evil,** hlola.
prediction, taolo.
predispose, laolela pele, lokišetša, sekametša.
predominant, segolothata, laolago, hlolang, bušago.
pre-eminent, phadišago, kgolo.
preface, ketapele.
prefer, rata, kgetha, hlaola; – **able,** ratega.
preference, tlhaolo, kgetho.
prefix, hlogo.
prejudice, beba, kgetholla, sekamela, n., tlhaolo, kgethollo, tseba, mona.
pregnancy, boimana, boithwalo, kemolo.
pregnant, become –, ima, ithwala, emara, emola; **of a cat, dog or pig,** ga mpa.
prehistoric, bogologolo.
preliminary, sa mathomo, e tlang pele, ya pele; **do** –, tšea maoko.
prelude, setlapele, matseno.
premature, fošišago, boile tseleng.
premeditate, rera pele, akanya pele.
premier, tonakgolo, ya pele, sa mathomo.
premise, bea pele.
premium, moputso, tefo, poelo.
preoccupied, se nago taba, sa šetšego selo.
prepalatal consonant, tumammogogalapeng.
preparation, go itokišetša, tokišetšo, peakanyo.
preparatory, boitokišetšo.
prepare, itokiša, rulaganya, lokišetša; – **the way for,** thulela tsela; – **for,** itokišetša.
prepay, lefela pele.
preponderance, boima bjo bogolo.
preposition, letlema.
preposterous, segišago, sa tsebalegen
prerogative, tokelo.
prescribe, šupetša, kgethela, beela.
prescribed, kgethetšwego, beetšweg
prescription, taelelo, molaetša.
presence, go ba gona, bogona; **los of mind,** gakanega.
present, mpho, neo; v., fa, nea, hlagiša, bega, **to be** –, go ba g
presentable, hlagišega, bontšheg hlamatšega.
presentation, neo, tlhagišo.
presentiment, maikutlo, kholof tlholego.
present tense, lebjale.
preservation, poloko, paballo pabalelo.

preservative, bolokang.
preserve, boloka, babalela.
preserver, mmoloki, seboloki.
preside, laola, swara setula, hlahla.
president, mopresidente.
press, gatelela, šidila, katelela; – n., **a machine,** kgatišo; – **the newspaper,** kuranta; **(urge)** phegelela; **in with finger,** bobetša, kuba.
pressure, kgapeletšo, kgatelelo, itshema; – **point,** kgatego.
pressure-cooker, pitšakgatelelo.
prestige, seriti.
presumably, mohlamongwe, gongwe, ekete.
presume, ikgodiša, bona gore.
presuming, ikgogomošago, mereba.
presumption, kgopolo, boikgodišo.
presumptuous, ikgodišago, mereba.
pretence, seipato, boitirišo.
pretend, ikgakanya, itiriša, baka, itshema.
pretext, seipato, boikgakanyo.
prettiness, botse, bothakga.
pretty, botse.
prevail, fenya, hlola, buša; – **ing,** bušago, hlolago, dutšego.
prevailing, sa ruri, hlolang, fenyang.
prevalent, bušago, akaretšago.
prevaricate, aketša, bolela maaka.
prevent, thibela, šitiša; **ed**, thibetše, phemile.
prevention, thibelo.
preventive, thibelang; n., sephemo.
previous, pele; – **knowledge,** tsebo ya pele.
previously, pele.
prey, sebolawa, kgapo, thopo; **beast of** –, sebata; **to** –, thopa.
rice, theko, poreisi, seroto.
riceless, ya bohlokwa.
rice-list, lenaneroto, lenanetheko.
rick, hlaba; n., tlhabo.
rickle, mootlwa.
rickly-pear, toro, torofeie.

pride, boikgogomošo, boikgodišo, boitumišo.
priest, moprista.
priesthood, boprista.
prim, ya bothakga, kgabileng.
primary, ya pele, ya (ntlha), theo, kgolo.
primate, mopišopo e mogolo.
prime, ya ntlha; golo; – **minister,** tonakgolo; v., hlahlela; – **number,** tlhokakatišani.
primer, padišo ya pele.
primitive (custom), segologolo.
primus stove, poraemasetofo.
prince, morakgoši.
princess, morwediakgoši, kgosatšana.
principal, hlogo, khumopolokwa; – golo.
principality, naga ya kgoši, bogoši.
principally, gagolo.
principle, kutu, theo.
print, gatiša; kgatišo; **(calico),** lešela la mebala.
printer, mogatiši.
printing, kgatišo; – **press,** kgatišo.
prism, porisma.
prior, pele.
prison, kgolego, teronko.
prisoner, mogolegwa, sebofša.
privacy, thopa, sephiri, setu, phapogelo, bodutu.
private, sephiri, thopa, praebete; – **parts,** mapele; – **leave,** llifi ya praebete.
privately, thopeng, sephiring; **speak** –, sebela, loma tsebe.
private property, thuo ya mothomongwe, sa mmamongwe.
privilege, tokelo.
privy, sephiri, boithomelo.
prize, thopo, moputso, kgapo, sehlora; v., rata gagolo.
probable, e ka bago, ekete.
probably, mo gongwe, mohlomong.
probation, teko, boiteko.
probationer, molekwa, moitekedi.

probe, lehlotlo, leka, hlohlomiša, hlotla.
problem, mathata, tlalelo, marara.
problematical, se se makatšang.
procedure, tshepedišo, tsela.
proceed, iša pele, tšwela pele; – **ed,** tšwetše pele.
process, tshepetšo, – **ed, product,** sekhušwa.
procession, mokoloko; **go in –,** bopelela.
proclaim, kwatša, goelela, tsebatša, tsebagatša.
proclamation, kgoeletšo, tsebišo.
procrastinate, dikadika.
procurable, hwetšwago, humanwago.
procure, bona, hwetša, humana.
prod, kgotla.
prodigal, senyang tšhelete, lehlaswa, bohlaswa.
prodigious, kgologolo.
produce, ntšha, hagiša; n., tšweletšo; - **r,** mohlagiši, motšweletši.
product, puno, setšweletšo, seatišo, sephetho.
production, go ntšha, tšweletšo.
profane, gobośa, rogaka.
profess, ipolela, ipobola.
profession, boipobolo, boipolelo, modiro.
professor, profesa, profesara.
proficient, kgonago.
profile, molahlakore.
profit, poelo, thušo, v., thuša, hola, boela, boetša; – **by,** holega ka.
profitable, boelago, thušang, holang.
profound, ya kgonthe, tebileng.
profuse, tlopela(go), fago kudu.
progenitor, motswadi.
progeny, ditlogolo, ditlogolwana.
programme, lenaneo.
progress, tšwelopele; v., tšwela pele; – **ive,** tšwelelago.
prohibit, iletša, thibela, ganela.
prohibition, kiletšo, kganelo.
project, morero, setšema.
project, betša, rera, loga maano.
projection, protšekto.
projector, protšekta.
prolific, tswalang gagolo, enywang kudu.
prolong, telefatša, lelefatša.
promenade, sepela, mmila.
prominence, bophagamo, bogolo.
prominent, phagameng, bonagalang, tumilego, khutlotše.
promiscuous, tlhakantswiki, hlakahlakanego.
promise, kholofetšo, tshepišo, v., holofetša, tshepiša; – **d,** holofeditše.
promontory, hlogo, kapa, ntlha.
promote, tšweletša (pele), thuša.
prompt, phakišang, akgofang, kgothatša, hlohleletša, mafolofolo.
promptly, ka pela, semeetseng, gatee.
promulgate, kwatša, tsebiša.
prone, sekametše, namaletše, batalala.
pronominal form, popego ya lešala.
pronoun, lešala.
pronounce, kwagatša, utlwagatša.
pronunciation, kutlwagatšo, kwagatšo.
proof, tšhupo, bopaki.
prop, kokwane, setshegetšo; v., tshegetša, thekga.
propaganda, mokgoši; **make –,** hlaba mokgoši.
propagate, tswadiša, gaša.
propagation, tswadišo.
propel, soka, kgarametša.
propeller, lefehlo.
proper, ya kgonthe, lokilego; – **noun,** leinaina.
properly, ka tokelo, ka tshwanelo.
property, thoto, phahlo; seeng.
prophecy, profeta, porofeta.
prophet, moprofeta, moporofeta.
proportion, kabelo, tekanyetšo, v., lekanyetša.
proportionate, lekalekanego, lekaneng; v., lekanyetša.
proposal, tšhišinyo, tšhikinyo.

propose, šišinya, akanya, rera, hlagiša.
proposition, tšhišinyo, tlhagišo, go ithapa.
propound, beela pele, šišinya.
proprietor, mong.
propulsion, tshukumetšo, tšhušumetšo.
pro rata, ka go (lekana) lekanyetša.
proscribe, leleka, tšwa, ganela.
prose, kanegelo.
prosecute, sekiša, iša tshekong.
prosecutor, motšhotšhiši, motšhetšiši.
prospect, tshepo, kholofelo; v., kopola, popola.
prospector, mopopodi, mokopodi.
prosper, tswelela pele, atlega, naba, šegofala.
prosperity, lešego, katlego, tetlego.
prostitute, sefebe, seotswa, sehlola, segwebakabofêbê, segwebakamarago, kgeke.
prostitution, bofebe, bohlola, bootswa.
prostrate, namaletše.
project, šireletša, phemela.
protection, tšhireletšo, paballo.
protector, mošireletši, mmabaledi.
protectorate, nagašireletšwa.
protein, protine.
protest, ganela, belaela, n., pelaelo.
protestant, moprotestante.
protestation, kganano, kganelo, pelaelo.
prototype, mohlala.
protract, lelefatša, telefatša.
protractor, selekanyakhutlo.
protrude, rokama, khutlola.
protuberance, kutu, totoma.
proud, ikgogomoša(ng).
prove, šupa, bontšha.
provender, dijo, furu, mphago.
proverb, seema.
provide, thuša, fepa, fa, nea.
province, porofense, profense.
provision, thušo, neo, mphago.
provisional, sebakanyana, solanka.
provocation, thumolo, tlhohlo, kgopišo.
provoke, rumola, galakiša, kgoa, hlohleletša.
provoking, rumolago, galefišang, hlohlago.
prow, sehuba sa sekepe.
prowess, bonatla, bogale.
prowl, n., thopo, khulo, v., thopa, hula, khukhunetša.
proximate, ya kgauswi.
proximity, bokgauswi.
proxy, motsetaphethi, moemedi, maatla (a motsetaphethi), sebaka; maatla a go phetha.
prudence, tlhokomelo, bohlale.
prudent, hlalefile.
prune, lekwapiporeime.
prune, poma, kgotha, thena, kotela.
pruning, pomo, kgotho.
pry, nyarela, hlola, nyakišiša, sekašeka.
Psalm, Psalm, Pesaleme.
pseudonym, lebitšo la go iphihla.
pseudopodium, sekaleoto.
psychologist, mosaekholotši.
psychology, saek(h)olotši.
pub, para.
puberty, bosogana, bokgarebe, boroba.
public, batho, setšhaba, pabliki; – **holiday,** boikhutšogohle; – **property,** phahlo ya setšhaba.
publican, molekgetho, mongpara.
publication, kgatišo.
public-health, maphelo a setšhaba.
public-house, kgorogelabaeng.
public prosecuter, motšhotšhiši.
publicity, tumo, botumo.
publicly, pepeneneng, pontšheng, phatlalatša.
publish, gatiša.
publisher, mogatiši.

pudding, phuting.
puddle, modubedube, seretse.
puerile, tša (bjana) bošimane.
puff, thunya muši, kokomoga, utša.
puff-adder, marabe, letšolobolo.
pugilist, radifeisi.
pugnacious, ratago ntwa.
pull, goga, rutla, hlomola; – **down,** rutlolla; – **tight,** tosa.
puller, mogogi.
pullet, mphagana, serobana.
pulley, katrolo.
pulmonary, ya maswafo.
pulp, sohla, tula; n., sesohlo.
pulpit, prekesetulo, sethala.
pulsate, opaopa, rethetha.
pulsation, morethetho, kopaopo, thebetho.
pulse, mošito, morethetho, sephotla; v., rethetha, opaopa.
pulverise, šilaganya, thuma.
pump, pompa; n., pompi.
pumpkin, lefodi, lerotse; **seed of** –, thotse; **rind of** –, legapi; **stalk of** –, kgothi; **large green variety** –, lekatane.
pun, go bapadiša mantšu.
punch, tia, phunya; n., sephudi.
punctilious, hlokomedišiša.
punctual, ka bonako.
punctuality, bonako.
punctuate, kgathola.
punctuation, kgatholo.
punctuation mark, leswaodikga, tshwao.
puncture, lešoba; nthoba; n., phunya.
pungent, bogale.
punish, otla.
punishment, kotlo, thupa, dikgati.
puny, nyane, fokolago.
pup, mpšanyana, nkhunyana.
pupa, mokone.
pupil, morutiwa, morutwa; (eye), thaka, tlhaka.
puppet, popi.
purchase, reka, theko.
pure, sekegileng, kgonthe, bothakga; – **bred,** ya madi.
purgative, segofiši, segofišamala.
purge, hlwekiša, gofiša mala.
purification, tlhwekišo, tshekišo.
purify, hlwekiša, sekiša; – **oneself for,** itshekišetša, itlhwekišetša.
purist, e a kgethang mantšu.
purity, tlhweko.
purl, logela lengeleng, ruma.
purple, purepura, bohubedu bja bophefadu.
purport, kgopolo, tlhalošo, v., ra, re.
purpose, tebo, morero, boikemišetšo.
purposely, ka boomo.
purr, gona, kgorotla.
purse, sekhwama, sekgwama; v., šošobanya.
pursue, latela, šala morago, hlomara; **pursue,** rakediša.
pursuit, be in –, ba le setekeng; – **in,** nokela, lokela.
purvey, nea, fa; – **ance,** phepo.
pus, boladu, maladu.
push, sukumetša, kgarametša; – **down,** wiša; – **wheel-barrow,** thwethwiša.
puss(y), katse, katsana.
put, bea, betša, re; – **in,** tsenya, nokela; – **-back,** khutliša; – **on,** rwala, apara, tšwara; – **away from,** gafa; – **aside for,** beela.
put off, diega, thiša, diegiša.
putrefy, bola, tutela; v., bodiša.
putrid, bodileng, nkgago.
putty, phati, motu, moti.
puzzle, marara, malea, malepa, kgakanego; v., tlaba, gaka.
putty-knife, thipamotu.
pygmy, mponepone, sepharanyana, kgopana.
pyjamas, dipejama, ditšwarwamalaong.
pyramid, piramiti.
python, hlware.

Q

quack, kwakwaretša.
quadrangle, khutlonne.
quadruped, kotonne.
quail, khwiri.
quake, šišinyega; n., tšhišinyego.
qualification, boithutelo, thuto, dikala.
qualificative, tlhaodi.
qualificative concord, lekgokatlhaodi.
qualificative pronoun, lešalatlhaodi.
qualified, kgona(go), tseba(go).
qualify, hlaloša(go), hlaola, itokišetša.
quality, boleng, khwaliti.
quantity, bokaakang.
qualm, pherogo, letswalo.
quarantine, tswalelelo, kwarantine, kiletšo.
quarrel, phapang, tshele; v., ferekana, ya mereba, ya kgang.
quarrelsome, ferekanyago, fapanyago, ya kgagapa.
quarry, epa, moepo, lekgwara.
quarter, kotara, kwarata, karolo ya bone, kgweditharo.
quarterly, ka karolo ya bone; gane ka selemo; – **return,** serithene.
quarter of an hour, kotarairi.
quartet, sene.
quartz, kwaretšhe, legakabje.
quash, pšhatla, tima, fediša.
quaver, roromela, khwebara.
quay, kou(wana), khii.
queen, kgošigadi, mohumagadi.
queen-ant, mmantlhwa, mmampobe.
queen-bee, makome.
queenly, boka kgošigadi.
queer, makatšago, makatšang.
quell, tima, fediša, kokobetša.
quench, tima, fediša, nyorolla.
query, potšišo; v., botšiša; belaela.
quest, nyakišišo, kgopelo; v., nyaka, sekaseka.
question, potšišo; **in** –, taba-taba; **cross** –, lotolotša; – **mark,** potšišo.
questionable, belaetša(go).
quick, akgofago, ya(potlako)lebelo.
quicken, akgofiša, potlakiša, phakiša.
quickening, kakgofišo, phakišo.
quickly, ka pela, ka pele; phakiša.
quickness, potlako, phakišo.
quicksand, kwenamohlaba, tebetebe, lešikihledi.
quick-witted, tsarogilego.
quid, porompi, prompi.
quiescence, tšhišibalo, khutšo.
quiescent, e reng tuu; khutšitšeng.
quiet, e reng tuu, homotšeng; n., khomolo; v., homola, homotša.
quietly, re tuu, ka setu.
quill, lefofa, mootlwa, naka.
quilt, kobo ya mafofa.
quince, kwepere; mokwepere.
quinine, khwinine.
quinsy, tutomo ya mometso, bolwetši bja mogolo.
quintessence, sebelebele, samaruri.
quintet, khwintete, sehlano.
quit, lesetša, tloga, tela.
quite, ka kgonthe.
quiver, kgotlopo, tlhobolo; v., roromela.
quorum, karolo, khoramo.
quote, khouta, tsopola.
quotation, tlhabo ka tsopolo; – **marks,** ditsebjana.
quotient, searolo.

R

rabbi, moruti, rabi.
rabbit, mmutla; **(rock)** –, pela.
rabble, mahoohoo, dimpša, dilo.
rabid, galefileng, gafang.
rabies, bogafa bja dimpša.
race, morafe, mohlobo, mohuta, tšhiano; v., šiana, beišana, n., peišano.

racial, semorafe, ya morafe.
racial relations, phedišano ya merafe.
rack, borala, tshenyego, sefata; v., tlaiša.
racket, lešata, ipshina.
radiance, phadimo, go kganya.
radiant, phadimago, kganyago.
radiate, phadima, kganya, ediša.
radiation, kedišo.
radio, radio.
radiology, radiolotši.
radish, radeise, rateise.
radium, radiamo.
radius, sedikiši; sefaka.
raft, sephaphami, lekawe.
rafter, phate, kota.
rag, lenkgeretla, segaswa.
rage, kgalefo, pefelo; v., galefa, befelwa; – **n,** gakalela pele.
ragged, mathatha, mankgeretla.
rags, mankgeretla.
raid, tlhaselo, thopo, v., thopa, hlasela.
rail, kwera, romela, ageletša; n., seporo.
railing, kwero, legora.
railway, seporo, ditimela; – **crossing,** boselaseporo; – **station,** setitšhing, seteišene; – **line,** seporo.
raiment, seaparo, kobo.
rain, pula; **a continuous** –, modupe; **early** –, tsheola; **it is raining,** e a na; – **after harvest,** kgogolamoko; **a slight shower of** –, modutšwana; – **falling at a distance,** sephadi; **scent of** –, lefoka; **(drop),** rotha; **cease to** –, khula; – **clears away,** sa, sele; – **gauge,** kelapula.
rainbow, molalatladi.
rainfall, pula.
rainmaker, morokapula.
raise, kuka, emiša, tsoša.
raisin, rasene, lekwapi, rasenkisi.
rake, hareka.
rally, kgoboketša, boelana, bokana, kgobokana, kwera, beta pelo, thuša.
ram, kgapa, phoko; v., hlahlela, bethela, setlela, thula.
ramble, ralala, kobakobana.
rambler, mmanthaladi, lekobakobani.
rambling, thalalo.
ramification, pharo, makala.
ramify, fara(fara), dira makala.
rampart, sebo, lerako.
ranch, moraka.
ranching, peamoraka, thuadikgomo.
rancid, bodilana, e bošula.
rancour, sekgopi, lehloyo.
rand, ranta.
random, go se kgethe; **speak at** –, tladika.
range, paka, mohlwaela; v., beakanya.
rank, mola, molebo, boemo, v., beakanya, naba, nkga.
rank, bošula, gola ka kudu.
ransack, sekaseka, hula.
ransom, rekolla, lefela; n., tefelo, thekollo.
rant, ikgantšha.
ranunculus, ranankele.
rap, kokota, opaopa; n., kokoto, kopaopo.
rapacious, megabaru, ratang go (gapa) thopa.
rape, kata; n., kato.
rapid, phakišang, ka lebelo, n., – **ly,** ka lebelo.
rapid, phororo, lephotophoto, mothetheoga, mogolomelo.
rapine, kgapo, thopo, khulo.
rapt, ipshina, thaba, letša wa nko.
rapture, lethabo.
rare, bohlokwa.
rarely, ka sewelo, e sego gantši.
rascal, senokwane, sehwirihwiri.
rash, phomegela, phonkgela, šaetša; – **person,** lešaedi, lephonkgedi.
rash, mogorogo, lekhwekhwe, dibabo, welago godimo.

rashness, phomegelo, go phonkgela.
rasp, gohla; raspere, feilakgwakgwa.
rat, legotlo.
rate, tekanyo, motšhelo, lekgetho, lebelo, tswalo; v., lekanya, roga.
rate-payer, motšhedišwa, montšhalekgetho.
rather, go ena le, gagolo, ka kgonthe, upša, bokaone.
ratify, tiiša.
ratio, kabo, tekanyo.
ration, kabelo, rešene, v., abela; – **out,** ngwathelana.
rattle, setšhakgatšhakga; v., tšhakgatšhakga.
rationalise, gopodišiša.
ravage, thopa, senya; n., kgopo, tshenyo.
rave, gafa.
ravel, hlarolla, rarolla.
raven, legokobu; v., garola, hula.
ravenous, megabaru, gagolago.
ravine, mogohlogohlo, sefata.
ravish, kata, beta, thopa, thabiša, gagolo.
raw, tala.
raw material, seretala.
rawness, botala.
ray, lehlasedi.
rayon, rayone, senyedimi.
raze, phušolla, phimola.
razor, thipa ya go beola, **(blade),** legare.
reach, fihla, fihlela; – **out,** obeletša.
react, fetoga.
reaction, phetogo.
read, bala; – **silently,** bala ka setu, ipalela.
readable, balega.
reader, mmadi, padišo.
readily, ka pela, ka boithatelo.
readiness, boithatelo, mafolofolo.
reading, go bala.
readjustment, tokišo, thulaganyo.
ready, itokišeditše, lokileng, itokišitšeng; v., itokiša.
real, ruri, ya sebele, ya kgonthe, mmakgonthe.
reality, boamaruri, bommannete.
realise, bona, lemoga, phetha.
really, ruri, ka kgonthe, ka sebele.
realm, mmušo, bogoši; – **of the dead,** bodulabahu.
reap, buna, roba, sega.
reaper, mmuni, morobi, mosegi.
reaping, puno.
rear, morago; godiša, tswadiša.
rearrange, beakanya gape.
rearrangement, peakanyagape.
reason, lebaka, tlhaologanyo, akanya; phega, phegiša.
reasonable, kwalago, swanelago.
reasonably, ka tekanyo.
reasoning, kakanyo.
reassure, bea pelo, kgotsiša, kgodiša.
rebel, lerabele; motsošampherefere; v., rabela, fetogela, tsogela maatla.
rebellion, borabele, mpherefere, moferefere.
rebound, tlolela morago; n., poelomorago.
rebuff, fotlela, gana; n., kgano.
rebuild, aga lefsa, tsošološa.
rebuilt, tsošološitše.
rebuke, kgala, sola; n., tsholo.
recall, elelwa.
recede, boela morago.
receipt, rasiti, tšhupatefo.
receive, amogela.
receiver, moamogedi, seamogedi.
receiver of revenue, molekgetho.
recent, mpsha, ya bjale.
recently, gona bjale, malobanyana.
receptacle, sebjana, pitša, polokelo.
reception, kamogelo; **a bad** –, kamogelo e mpe.
recess, boikhutšo.
recipe, mohlako.
recipient, moamogedi.
reciprocal, diranago; ledirani.
reciprocate, dirana, lefetša, fana.
recital, theto, go reta.

recitation, sereto.
recite, reta.
reckless, sa šetše, šoro, bogale.
reckon, bala, gopola, lekanya, holofela.
reclaim, hlapholla, mpshafatša, phološa.
reclamation, phedišo (ya maope).
recline, sekama, khutša, kanama.
recluse, hlaotšwego, dula nnoši; n., modulannoši.
recognise, elelwa, lemoga; **–d,** dumeletšwego.
recognition, temogo, kelelo.
recoil, tšhaba, boela morago.
recollect, gopola, elelwa, kgobokanya gape.
recommend, tumiša, eletša.
recommendation, keletšo, tumišo.
recompense, lefa, n., tefo, tefeletšo.
reconcile, boelanya, boelana; – **oneself,** ipoelanya.
reconciliation, poelanyo, poelano.
record, lenanethoto; rekoto; pego; v., bega; **–ing,** kgatišo; – **library,** bokgobarekoto.
recount, anegela, laodiša.
recourse, ithuša ka, botšhabelo.
recover, bona; fola, thušega, hwetša.
recreant, mokgelogi, lefšega.
recreation, maitišo, boitapološo.
recriminate, solana, pharana.
recruit, kalatša.
rectangle, khutlonnethwi.
rectify, lokiša, phošolla.
rectitude, go loka, toka, bokgabane.
rector, hlogo.
rectum, motsila.
recumbent, khutšago, sekameng, kanameng.
recur, boelela, diragala gape.
recurrence, leboelela, maboelela.
red, hwibidu, khubedu, bohubedu.
red handed, catch –, kgesa.
redden, hwibila; hubala; – **ish,** bohubetšwana.
redeem, rekolla, phološa, golola.
redeemer, mophološi.
redemption, topollo, phološo.
rediculous, segišago.
redness, bohubedu, bohwibidu.
redouble, boeletša.
redoubt, sebo.
redress, lokiša, otlolla; n., tokišo.
Red Sea, Lewatlekhwibidu.
reduce, fokotša, iša go.
reduction, phokotšo.
redundant, šaletšeng.
reduplicate, boeletša.
red-water, morotokhwibidu, roibatere.
reed, lehlaka.
reef, rifi, lekekema, mokekema.
reel, thekesela; n., toliki, toloki.
refer, ra, umaka, šupetša.
reference, malebana (le) tšhupetšo.
reference book, puku ya tšhupetšo.
referendum, referentamo.
refine, hlwekiša.
refined, hlwekišitšwego.
refinement, tlhwekišo.
refinery, bohlwekišetšo.
reflect, bekenya, bonagatša, akanya, šupa.
reflection, kgadimolo, sešupo, kgopolo.
reflector, pekenyi, sekgantšhi.
reflex action, khunanoši, refolekisi.
reform, mpshafatša, mpshafala.
reformation, mpshafatšo.
reformer, mompshafatši.
refractory, ngangago, ganago.
refrain, tlhabeletšo; ila, tlogela.
refresh, lapološa, kgatholla; – **ing,** lapološago.
refreshment, tapološo.
refrigerate, tšidifatša.
refrigeration, tšidifatšo.
refrigerator, setšidifatši.
refuge, botšhabelo, setšhabelo.
refugee, motšhabi, motšhabedi.
refund, bušetša, pušeletšo.

refusal, tatolo, kgano, kganetšo.
refuse, gana; **–d,** ganne.
refuse, matlakala, dithole; – **hole,** molete wa matlakala.
refutable, ganetšega.
refute, ganetša.
regain, bona gape, hwetša, – **consciousness,** hlabolaga, idibologa.
regal, segoši, serena.
regale, amogela, kamogelo, mokete.
regalia, diswao (ditlhamo) tša kgoši.
regard, hlokomela, hlompha; n., tlhokomelo.
regarding, malebana.
regenerate, mpshafatša.
regent, bušago, moemedi wa kgoši, mmušiši.
regiment, mphato, imphi.
region, selete, tikologo.
regional news, ditaba tša tikologo.
register, rejistara, ngwadiša.
regret, manyami; v., nyama.
regrowth, maidi.
regular, lekanetšego, ka melao ya ka mehla.
regularly, ka tekanelo, ka mehla.
regulate, lokiša, sepetša ka molao.
regulation, molawana.
rehabilitate, tsošološa.
reign, mmušo, pušo; v., buša, laola.
rein, –s, marapo.
reinforcement, tiišo, tlaleletšo, matlafatšo.
reiterate, boeletša.
reject, gana, lahla, galala; – **ed,** hlaswitše, hlanogetše.
rejection, tahlo, kgano.
rejoice, thaba, nyakalala.
rejoicing, nyakalalo, thabo.
rejoin, kopanya fetola.
rejoinder, phetolo, karabo.
rejuvenate, mpshafatša.
relapse, wela, boela morago.
relate, anegela, bega.
related, amana, leloko le tee, tswalane.
relation, leloko, taodišo.
relative, leloko, ba–, amanago, leamanyi.
relative clause, thabekamanyi.
relative concord, lekgokaleamanyi.
relax, itiša, iketla, nyefa.
relay, neeletšana.
release, lokolla; n., tokollo.
relevant, lebaneng, lebanego.
reliable, botegago, botegang.
reliance, kholofelo.
relief, phološo, thušo, popego.
relieve, thuša, lokolla.
religion, bodumedi.
religious, bodumedi, dumelago.
relinquish, tlogela, lesa.
relish, sebalodi, bose, sešebo; v., rata, latswega, natefiša.
reluctance, go se rate, go tšwafa, kgano.
rely, bota, holofela; – **on,** ikanya.
remain, šala, šalela, lala, nna, šiwa, hlwa.
remainder, mašalela, mašaledi.
remaining, tše šetšego, mašalela.
remains, šetšeng, mašalela, setopo.
remand, pušetšo, tiego, supetša.
remark, re; n., phoko, temošo.
remarkable, makatšang, tumišegang.
remedial, fodišago, pheko, thušago.
remedy, sehlare, kalafo, thušo; v., alafa, lokiša.
remember, gopola, elelwa.
remembrance, kgopolo, segopotšo.
remind, gopotša, gakolla.
reminiscence, kgopolo.
remission, tebalelo, tesetšo.
remit, swarela, lesetša.
remittance, tefo.
remnant, lešaledi, mašaledi, mašalela.
remonstrance, kganano, kgalo, pelaelo.
remonstrate, belaela, kgala.
remorse, manyami, boitsholo.
remorseful, itsholago.
remorseless, hlokago kgaugelo, šoro.

remote, kgakala, gole, kgole.
remoteness, bogole, bokgole, kgale.
removal, tlošo, tšhuthišo, khudugo, khudušo.
remove, šuthiša, tloša khuduša; **–d,** tlošitšwe.
remunerate, lefa, putsela, bušetša.
remuneration, tefo, pušetšo.
rend, gagola, garola.
render, nea, fa, gafela.
renew, mpshafatša, boeletša.
renounce, gafa, lesa, tela.
renovate, mpshafatša, swafatša.
renown, tumo, tlotlišo.
rent, khiro, rente; kgagolo, v., garoga, hira.
repair, lokiša, roka; n., tokišo.
repartee, go gegea, phetolo.
repast, dijo, monyanya.
repay, lefela, lefetša, bušetša.
repeal, fediša.
repeat, boeletša.
repeatedly, gantši, kgafetša, leboelela.
repel, leleka, raka, fenya, gafa.
repellent, seraki.
repent, nyama, itshola.
repentance, boitsholo, go nyama.
repertoire, repetoa, lenanemmino.
repetition, poeletšo.
repine, ngongorega, belaela, nyama.
replace, bea bakeng sa, mpshafatša.
replacement, peobakeng.
replenish, tlaletša, ekeletša.
replete, tletše, khoše, tenne.
repletion, botlalo, mokhoro.
replica, kopi, ketšišo, tshwantšho.
reply, araba, fetola; n., karabo, phetolo; – **paid,** karabo e lefilwe.
report, pego, raporoto; bega.
repose, lapologa, khutša, robala, n., khutšo; – **ful,** khutšago, homotšego.
reprehensible, solega.
represent, emela; bontšha.
representation, kemelo, pontšho, pelaelo.
representative, moemedi.
repress, thiba, thibela.
reprieve, diegiša kotlo, fega, gaugela.
reprimand, kgala, sola; n., kgalo, tsholo.
reprint, gatiša gape.
reprisal, go itefetša.
reproach, sola, kgala; n., tsholo.
reprobate, sehlola, molahlwa; v., tšwa, lahla.
reproduce, bušološa, itswala.
reproduction, pušološo, tswalo.
reproof, kgalemelo, tsholo.
reprove, v.t., kgalemela, kgala, omanya.
reptile, segagabi, noga.
republic, repabliki.
republican, morepabliki.
repudiate, latola, lahla, gana.
repugnance, go galala, pherogo, kilo.
repugnant, ilego, ferogago.
repulse, leleka, hlola.
reputation, tumo, botumo.
repute, tumo.
request, kgopela, lopa; n., kgopelo.
require, nyaka, hloka.
requirement, tlhokego, senyakwa, nyako, tshwanelo.
requisition, kgopelo, nyako.
requital, pušetšo, tefetšo.
requite, lefetša, bušetša.
rescue, phološa; n., phološo; **come to** –, phalala, phalalela.
research, nyakišišo.
resemblance, tshwano.
resent, hloya, ila; – **ful,** befega.
resentment, sekgopi, kilo.
reserve, šiela, boloka, beela; n., motlatsi.
reserved, beetšwe, ipoetše.
reservoir, letamo.
reside, aga, dula, nna.
residence, legae, ngwako.
resident, modudi, moagi.
residue, mašalela, mašaledi.
resign, tšwa, tela, itokolla, tlogela.
resignation, boitokollo.

resin, serekhu.
resist, iphemela, lwantšha; – **me,** nngangabelela.
resistance, twantšho, kgano, boitamolelo.
resisted, ngangabetše.
resolute, itlamileng, tiileng.
resolution, sephetho, setlamo.
resolve, itlama, setlamo.
resonance, tumo, kgalagadišo.
resonant, dumang, dumago.
resort, tšhabela, ithuša ka.
resound, galagala, kgerekgetša, duma.
resourceful, maano, hlalefile.
respect, tlhompho; v., hlompha.
respectability, tlhomphego.
respectful, hlomphegang.
respectively, ka tatelano.
respiration, khemo, go buša moya.
respite, khutšisa; n., khutšo.
respond, araba, fetola.
responsible, ikarabela, laolwa ke.
responsibility, boikarabelo.
rest, khutšo, v., khutša; **give –,** khutšiša.
rest, mašalela, mašaledi; – **ed,** ikhuditše.
restitution, pušetšo.
restive, ngalago, bohlogathata, ganago.
restless, kobakoba, huduega, hloka khutšo.
restoration, pušetšo.
restore, bušetša, tsoša.
restrain, thibela, šegela; iletša,
restraint, kganelo, thibelo.
restrict, kgaoletša, thibela.
result, sephetho, bofelo, poelo.
resume, thoma sefsa, akaretša, boela.
resurrect, tsoša.
resurrection, tsogo.
resuscitate, tsošološa, rudiša.
resuscitation, tsošološo.
retail, kgwebjana.
retain, swara, boloka, gana le.
retaliate, iphetetša, itefeletša, itefetša.
retard, diegiša.
retardation, tiegišo, titelo.
reticence, khomolo.
retina, retina.
retinue, balata.
retire, tlogela modiro, tšhaba, ya go khutša.
retort, karabo e nepagetšeng, v., araba.
retract, gogela morago.
retreat, boela, morago, tšhaba, katakata.
retribution, tefetšo, pušetšo.
retrieve, buša, bona, boelwa.
retrograde, boela morago.
retrospect, go lebelela morago.
return, boa, buša.
reveal, utolla, senola; – **to me,** nkutollela.
revel, ipshina, hlalala.
revelation, kutollo.
revenge, tefetšo.
revenue, lekgetho, ditseno, motšhelo.
revere, godiša, hlompha.
reverence, kgodišo, tlhompho.
reversal, tirollo, phetogo, phetolo.
reverse, fetola, bušetša, morago, dirolla.
reversive, ledirolli.
revert, boela, khutiela.
review, lekola, hlahloba; n., tekolo.
revile, nyefola, kgala, roga.
revise, boeletša, fetola, lokiša.
revision, poelelo, poeletšo, phetolo.
revival, tsošološo, tsogo, tšitšibogo **(of courage),** letsošo, kilogo.
revive, tsoga, tsošološa, tsoša, hlabolla.
revoke, fediša, latola.
revolt, tsogela, rabela, hlanogela; n., mpherefere, borabele, tsogelo.
revolution, tsogelo, borabele, tikologo, tikološo.
revolutionary, moferekanyi, ferekanyago.
revolve, dikologa.

revolver, raborolo, raboloro.
reward, moputso, tefo; v., lefa.
rhebuck, letlabo.
rhetoric, makgethepolelo.
rheumatism, bonyelele.
rhinoceros, tšhukudu.
rhubarb, rupapo.
rhyme, morumokwano, theneketšo.
rhythm, mošito, moretheto.
rhythmic, ka morethetho.
rib, kgopo, thapa.
ribbing, sekgopo.
ribbon, lenti, lente.
rice, reisi, reise.
rich, humile; **(person),** mohumi.
riches, mahumo, maruo.
richets, ragitise (bolwetši).
rickety, kgolokgothega.
rid, tloša, phološa.
riddle, thai, nyepo.
ride, namela, reila.
rider, monamedi.
ridge, mopopotlo, mokokotlo.
ridicule, kwera; n., kwero, ditshego.
ridiculous, segišago; **make -self-,** itshegiša.
rife, laolago, tletšego.
riff-raff, digobogi, dihlola.
rifle, sethunya; v., hlakola.
rift, lefaro, lefato.
rift-valley, moedi, lefato.
rig, kgabiša.
right, toka, tokelo; lokileng; – **hand,** mmagoje, la go ja; v., lokiša; – **turn,** la ga ja reto!
righteous, lokilego, lokileng; – **person,** moloki; **the** –, baloki.
rigid, tiileng, thata, gwalaletšego.
rill, nokana.
rim, leši, foreime, khwiti.
rind, legape, lekgapetla.
rinderpest, khukhama matšhona.
ring, palamonwana, sediko, reng; **an ear** –, lengena; v., tsidima, lla, letša.
ringleader, ketapele, nkgwete.
ringworm, pudutša, dipudi.
rinse, tsokotša, hlatswa.
riot, mpherefere, moferefere.
rip, gagola, fatša.
ripe, butšwitšeng, buduleng; v., butšwa; **be** –, budule.
ripen, butšwiša, butšwa.
rise, hlaba, tsoga, emelela, rotoga.
risk, phonkgela, beta pelo, leka; n., kotsi.
rite, tirelo; mokgwa, bogwera, bjale.
ritual, tirelo.
rival, mophegišani.
rivalry, phegišano.
river, noka.
rivet, ribete.
road, tsela, pata; – **barrier,** lephekatsela; – **side,** tsela(na) ya ka thoko.
road-map, mmapatsela.
road-safety, polokego tseleng.
road-sign, tšhupatsela.
roam, ralala, goloma, kobakobana.
roan, thamaga, nala.
roar, rora, duma.
roast, gadika, beša; – **ed,** gadikile.
rob, hlakola, utswa, thopa.
robber, lehodu, mohlakodi, mothopedi.
robbery, bohodu, tlhakolo.
robe, phuraphura, kobo, v., apeša.
robinchat (noisy), rakhulong, bjalapeu.
robot, ropoto.
robust, tiileng, maatla.
rock, leswika, letlapa.
rock, hlokosetša, ebesela.
rockery, rokhari, sepapana sa matlapa.
rocket, mosebe wa mollo.
rock-pigeon, leebarope.
rock-rabbit, pela.
rod, kgati, thupa, mogwane; – **for measuring,** phatatekanyi.
rodent, kokoni.
rogue, senokwane, molotšana.
roll, pitika, kgokologa, thetha, phuta;

rolo, sephutho, palongwalwa, mogaro.
roller (dough), mpidikane.
romance, taba ya lerato; okeletša.
Rome, Roma.
romp, raloka.
romper, gempeborokgwana.
rondavel, rontabola.
roof, tlhaka, thulelo, rulela; – **material,** marulelo.
rook, legokobu.
room, phapoši, kamora; **make – for,** šuthelela.
roomy, katologilego, kgolo.
roost, kotama, robala.
root, modu, segwere; **take –,** tsema medu; – **up,** tumola.
rope, mogala, thapo.
rose, rosi.
rot, bola.
rotate, dikologa, dikološa, fetoša.
rotation, tikologo, tikološo, thwetho.
rotation (crops), phetošo ya dibjalo; **(grazing)** phetošo ja phulo.
rotten, bodileng, bodilego.
rough, makgwakgwa, magwaše.
rough estimate, tekanyetšo.
rough sketch, sethalwathalwa.
roughage, makgarea, digwaši.
round, kgokolo, sediko; **go –,** dikologa; – – **way,** morarela.
roundabout, ka go potologa.
roundness, bodiko.
rouse, tsoša, kgothatša.
rout, tshwalalanyo, tshele; v., šwalalanya.
route, tsela.
routine, mokgwa, sekamehla.
rove, ralala, kobakobana.
rover, mmanthaladi, lekobakobane.
row, molokoloko, mothaladi, mola; v., hudua.
row, moferefere.
rowdy, lešata.
royal, segoši, ya kgosi, serena, sešate.
rub, pikitla, gohla, tshasa.
rubber, raba, rapa.
rubbish, matlakala, ditšhila, thogorogo.
rubbish heap, thotobolo.
ruby, legakadima.
rudder, sekurufi, lephegwana.
ruddy, hubedu.
rude, se nang boitshwaro, yo makgakga.
rue, lla, golola, swaba.
ruffian, senokwane.
ruffle, fapanya, ferekanya.
rug, phate, tšale.
rugged, makgawekgawe.
ruin, lerope, lešope; v., phušola, senya, ropefatša; n., tshenyego, tahlego.
ruins, arope, mašope.
rule, mmušo, molao; v., buša, laola, thala mola.
ruler, mmuši, kgoši, sethalamola.
rumble, duma, kurutla.
ruminate, otla, nagana.
ruminant, seotli, kotlane.
rummage, dupelela, nyakišiša.
rumour, pudiyatsela, mabarebare.
rump, sekgoto.
rumple, šošobanya, menaganya.
run, kitima, ela; n., hoko, oko. – **through,** putla.
runner, mokitimi.
runner (plant), molebo, morara(no), **(cloth),** šelaserapo.
running, go kitima, go šiana.
runway, bothwethwelo.
rupture, kgaogano, thobego.
rural, ya naga, nageng; – **area,** magaeng, dipolaseng.
rush, kitima; kgorogela.
rush, lehlakanoka, kgorogelo.
rushing, maphakaphaka.
rusk, paskeiti, pisekite,
rust, ruse, makgalwa, boori, v., rusa.
rustic, ya naga, mampara.
rustle, mogwaša; v., gwaša.
rusty, lewa ke makgalwa.

ruthless, šoro, hlokang mogau.
ruthlessness, bošoro.
rye, rae, rogo.

S

Sabbath, Sabata, sabatha.
sable-antelope, phalafala.
sabotage, sabotasi.
sabre, sabole, tšhoša.
sack, mokotla, saka, kgetsi; v., phuma, raka.
sackcloth, (lešela la) saka.
sacrament, sakramente.
sacred, kgethegileng.
sacrifice, sehlabelo; v., direla sehlabelo, hlabela, tela.
sacrilege, goboša (senya) tše kgethwa.
sad, manyami, swabileng; v., swaba, nyama.
sadden, swabiša, nyamiša.
saddle, sala, sale; v., sala, saletša.
sadness, n., manyami, maswabi.
safari, safari.
safe, bolokegileng; polokelo.
safeguard, tšhireletšo, v., šireletša.
safety, boiphemelo, polokego.
safety-pin, sethobošo.
saffron, e tshehla.
sagacious, hlalefileng.
sagacity, tlhalefo.
sage, mohlalefi; adj., hlalefileng.
sago, sago.
sail, seila; v., sesa, thala.
sailor, mothadiši.
saint, mokgethwa.
sake, ka baka la; **for goodness** –, mmalo!
salad, selai.
salary, tefo, moputso, v., lefa.
sale, thekišo, fantisi.
salesman, morekiši.
salient, bonagalang.
saline, letswai.
saliva, mare.
sallow, sehla, galogile.
sally, go tšwa.
saloon, kamora, salono.
salt, letswai; v., noka.
salpetre, salepetere.
salubrious, hlabošang, phedišang.
salutary, phedišang, thušang.
salutation, tumedišo.
salute, dumediša, n., tumedišo.
salvation, polokego, phološo.
salve, setlolo.
same, swana, sa le sona.
samp, lekokoro, setampa.
sample, ngwatha; n., sešupo.
sanctification, kgethego, kgethwafalo.
sanctified, kgethegileng.
sanction, tumelelo, tiišo, dumelela.
sanctity, kgethego, tlhweko.
sanctuary, felo mo go kgethwa, botšhabelo.
sand, mohlaba, lešabašaba.
sandal, mphašane, ramphašane.
sandapple tree, mmola.
sandwich, sangwetšhi.
sandy soil, sehlaba.
sane, hlalefilego.
sanguine, holofelago, fišegago.
sanitary, ya maphelo, hlwekilego.
sanitation, tlhwekišo, sanitasi.
sap, maswi, matute.
sapling, sehlašana.
sarcasm, kodutlo, tshotlo.
sardine, saratine.
sash, lepanta, – **cramp,** sepataganyi.
Satan, Sathane.
satellite, satelite.
satiate, kgoriša, khoriša.
satire, kwero, sesomo.
satisfaction, kgodišego, kgotsofalo.
satisfy, kgodiša, khoriša, itumela kgotsofala; –**ied,** kgotšwe.
saturate, koloba, kolobiša.
saturation, go koloba.
Saturday, Mokibelo.
sauce, souso, moro.

saucepan, pitša, sosopane, kastrolo.
saucer, piring, moriswana.
saucy, mereba, ikgantšhago.
sausage, boroso.
savage, (wa)sehlogo, šoro, befile.
save, phološa, boloka.
saving, phološo, ka ntle go.
savings, tšhelete e bolokilweng.
savings account, tšhupatlotlopolokelo.
saviour, mophološi, mmoloki.
savour, mohlodi, bose.
savoury, bose, sebalodi.
saw, saga; – **yer,** mosagi.
saxophone, seksafone.
say, re, bolela.
saying, polelo, seema.
scab, ntane, lekhwekhwe.
scabbard, kgatla, kgotlopo.
scabies, lekhwekhwe, ntane.
scaffold, sethala.
scaffolding, sethala.
scald, babola, fiša; n., pala.
scale, sekala, kgapetla, legapi, v., namela, kala; – **insect,** ntasekgapi.
scalp, legata, letlalo la hlogo.
scamp, sehwirihwiri, senokwane.
scamper, kitima.
scan, šitolla, nyakišiša.
scandal, sekgopišo, go seba.
scansion, mošitollo.
scant, sesane, nyenyane, hlaetšego.
scar, lebadi, mokhubo.
scarce, hlokega, bohlokwa.
scarecely, ka gonyane, ka thata.
scarcity, bohlokwa.
scare, tšhoša, tšhabiša.
scarecrow, setšhoša, setšhoši.
scarf, serepe, sekhafo.
scarify, gaya, phatša, segasega.
scarlet, sekalata.
scarlet fever, letadi la sekalata.
scatter, gaša, phatlalala, – **ed,** phatlaladitše.
scene, tema,˙felo, pono.
scent, monko, bodupo, sente, senkgišamonate; v., dupa, dupelela.
sceptre, thobane ya kgoši, pušo.
scheme, merero, maano, tlhakatiro; v., loga maano, rera, hlaka tiro.
scholar, morutiwa, morutegi, morutwana.
school, sekolo; v., ruta; – **board,** lekgotla la sekolo.
schoolmistress, morutạbana, morutišigadi.
science, saense, thutamahlale.
scientist, setsebi, ramahlale.
scissors, sekero.
scoff, sega, kwera, n., dijo.
scold, omanya, roga.
scone, sekontshe.
scoop, gaba, fala, fata; – **up water,** kgapšakgapša.
scope, sebaka, morero.
scorch, babola, tlabola.
scorched, omelela, pona; – **earth,** pilo.
score, sekoro, masomepedi, palo; v., kora, noša, bala dintlha.
scorn, lenyatšo; v., nyatša.
scorpion, phepheng.
scoundrel, sehwirihwiri.
scour, fogohla, gohla, koropa.
scrouge, kotlo; v., otla.
scout, tlhodi; v., hlola.
scramble, katana, namela.
scrap, setsekana, thathana; v., lahla; – **heap,** thotobolo.
scrape, fala, olela, gora; – **coals from fire,** gokola.
scraper, segopi, sefadi, phalo.
scratch, ngwaya, ngapa, kgwarinya.
scrawl, hlahlafinya.
scream, goa, goeletša, lla.
screech, lla, meketša.
screen, seširo, tšhireletšo; v., šira, širela.
screw, sekurufi, sekurufu, v., kurufela; – **driver,** setšhophakurufu.
scribble, kgwarinya.
scribbler, sekgwarinyetšo, sekripola.
scribe, mongwadi, mongwaledi.
script, mogatišo.

Scriptures, Mangwalo a Makgethwa.
scroll, sekorolo.
scrub, mehlašana; – **cattle,** mekgerane; v., koropa, gohla.
scruple, dikadika, belaela.
scrupulous, hlokomelago.
scrutinise, nyakišiša, latišiša.
scuffle, katana, n., katano.
scull, hudua, soka; n., lesokwana.
scullery, bohlatswabjana.
sculptor, mmetlabje, mmetladiswantšho.
sculpture, petlabje.
scum, lephilo, maphoko, ditšhila.
scurvy, sekabi.
scythe, sekele, sega.
sea, lewatle.
sea-breeze, phefšanawatle.
seal, setempe, tiišo, v., tema, tempa, tiiša; n., nebi ya lewatle.
sea-level, tekanawatle.
sea-lion (Cape), nebi ya lewatle.
seam, moroko.
seaman, mothadiši, molewatle.
sear, babola.
search, nyakišiša, nyaka.
seashore, lebopo.
season, sehla; v., noka.
seat, senno, sedulo; site; v., nniša, dudiša.
seaweed, bjangwatle, bolele.
secede, arogana, ikgaoganya.
secession, karogano.
seclude, hlaola, ikgaoganya.
second, ya bobedi, motsotswana, motlatši; – **person,** mmoledišwa.
secondary, ya bobedi; – **school,** sekontari.
secrecy, sephiri.
secret, sephiri, koma, lekunutu; – **thoughts,** dithopa; **tell** –, loma tsebe, sebela; **tell me** –, ntoma tsebe.
secretary, mongwaledi, rakgoro.
secretary-bird, tlhame, (hlame).
secretly, thopeng, sephiring.
sect, bahlanogi.
section, karolo.
secundus, moswaredi.
secure, lota, lotegilego, bolokegile.
security, poloko, toto, peeletšo; **give as** –, beeletša.
sedate, okobetšego, iketlileng.
sedative, seokobatši.
sediment, maitsheko, ditubi, mobutuledi.
sedition, pherekanyo, twantšhamolao, moferefere.
seduce, fapoša, kgeloša.
seducer, mofapoši.
see, bona,; – **for oneself,** iponela.
seed, peu, thaka; **small** –, pewana.
seed-bed, sethopo, seloto.
seedling, mpšanyana.
seek, nyaka, nyakišiša, – **in vain,** pharuma.
seem, bonagala, ekete.
seeming, bonagalang.
seer, mmoni, senoge.
seesaw, letantse.
seethe, bela.
segment, mosehlwana.
seize, swara, gapa.
seldom, ka sewelo, e sego gantši.
select, kgetha, hlaola.
selection, kgetho, tlhaolo.
self, nnoši, ka noši; **I myself,** bonna.
self-accusation, go itshola.
self-assertion, boikgodišo.
self-conceit, boikgogomošo.
self-confidence, boitshepo, boipoto.
self-conscious, go ikgopola, go se itebale; – **ness,** boitemogo.
self-contempt, boinyatšo.
self-control, boitaolo, boipušo, boitshwaro.
self-deception, boiphoro.
self-defence, go itšhireletša, go iphemela, boiphemelo.
self-esteem, boitlhompho, boikgantšho.
self-evident, go molaleng.

self-government, boipušo.
self-help, go ithuša.
selfish, timana, jela ka thoko.
selfishness, bojato, go timana.
self-knowledge, boitsebo.
self-love, go ithata.
self-made, boitiro, itirilego, itiretšego, sa maitirelo.
self-murder, go ipolaya.
self-pollination, boitulafatšo.
self-portrait, boitshwantšho.
self-possession, boithuo.
self-praise, boitheto.
self-preservation, boipoloko.
self-reliance, boitshepo.
self-respect, boitlhompho.
self-restraint, boipušo.
self-sacrifice, boineelo, boikgafelo, go itira sehlabelo.
self-sufficiency, boitekanelo.
self-will, go ngangela, bohlogothata.
sell, rekiša, bapatša; – **oneself,** ithekiša; – **on behalf of,** rekišetša.
seller, morekiši, mmapatši.
selling price, thekišo.
semantic, hlaologanyago.
semblance, ponagalo, sebopego.
semen, peu, motoro, matšhedi.
semi, seripa.
semi-circular, sedikohalofo, sedikoripa.
semi-colon, khutlwana.
semi-vowel, sekatumanoši.
senate, senate.
senator, mosenate.
send, roma, romela.
senile, tšofetšeng.
senility, botšofadi.
senior, mogolo.
sensation, maikutlo, khuduego.
sensational, gathwafatšago.
sense-organ, seko.
senses, dikutlo, dikwi.
sensible, hlalefileng.
sensitive, e utlwang, kwang.
sentence, lefoko, kahlolo; v., ahlola, kweba.
sentinel, mohlapetši.
separable, arolega.
separate, aroganya, kgaoganya.
separatoin, kgaoganyo, tlhalo.
separator, romoro, sentšhalebebe.
sepia, sepia.
September, Setemere, Lewedi.
septic, bodišang.
septic tank, tanka ya kelelatšhila.
sepulchre, lebitla.
sequel, hlatlamanago.
sequence, tatelano, tlhatlamano.
sequestrate, amoga.
sequestrator, maomogi.
serenade, serenate.
serene, sekileng, okobetšeng.
serenity, tshekego, tšhišimalo.
serf, mohlanka.
serial, kuranta, latelanang, tiragatšo, dikgao; – **number,** nomoro ya tlhatlamano.
series, tlhatlamano.
serious, kotsi.
sermon, thero, thuto.
serpent, noga.
serum, seramo.
serval, koti.
servant, mohlanka, modiredi, mošomedi.
serve, direla, solela, lokela, šomela, thuša; – **you right,** swine hle; – **with drink,** hlaba ka morutlo.
service, tirelo; – **for the chief,** bothokgo.
serviceable, thušang.
servile, ya bohlanka.
servitude, bohlanka.
session, tulo, tulelo.
set, bea, hloma; – **the sun,** dikela; – **aside,** tlogela; – **upon, as dogs,** saseletša; – **a tune,** hlabeletša; – **out,** wela tsela; – **table,** teka.
set, sehlopha, maano, sete, sehlaga.
set-back, tšhitišo.

settle, dula, fediša, ikagela, itudiša, dulela sa ruri.
settlement, boikagelo, phetho.
settler, mofalaledi.
seven, šupago, šupa; – **hundred,** makgološupa.
seventeen, lesomešupa.
seventh, ya bošupa.
seventy, masomešupa.
sever, kgaola, poma, ripa, **be –ed,** ripša.
several, ntšinyana; – **people,** ba bantšinyana.
severe, thata, šoro, bogale.
severity, bothata, bogale, bošoro.
sew, roka.
sewage, tšhila, mantle.
sewerage, kelelatšhila, kelatšhila.
sewer, mokero wa ditšhila.
sewing machine, motšhene wa go roka.
sex, bong, mong, keng; sekese; **have sexual desire,** totelwa.
sextant, sekesetanta, sekstanta.
sextet, setshela.
sexton, molebeledi wa kereke.
sexual intercourse, robala le, kopano, robalana.
sexual organs, (male), lepele; **female,** ditlase, nnyo.
shabby, mankgeretla.
shackle, bofa, kgweša.
shade, moriti, seširo; v., šira; – **the eyes,** bea mekganya.
shadow, moriti.
shady, moriti(ng).
shaft, teselepomo, taselpomo, mpheng, theku, mosebe; **mine –,** mokoti.
shake, šišinya, thothomela.
shaky, fokolago, thothomelago.
shale, letsopatlapa.
shall, tla, tlo.
shallow, sa išego.
sham, kekišo, phoro, v., fora, ekiša.
shamble, thekesela, hlaphuhla.
shame, dihlong; – **on you,** mafee.
shamefaced, sefahlogo sa dihlong.
shameful, mahlabišadihlong.
shamelessness, ho hloka dihlong.
shank, mo(o)mo, lenotlo.
shanty, mokubana; – **village,** masakana.
shape, popego, sebopego; v., bopa.
shapeless, se nang sebopego.
shapely, hlamatšegile.
share, kabelo, karolo, sekala, sekara; v., arola, kgwaetša, abela.
shark, šaka.
sharp, bogale, hlalefile.
sharpen, lootša, loutša, batola.
sharpness, bogale.
shatter, pšhatla, robaka.
shave, beola; – **hair,** kota; – **oneself,** ipeola.
shawl, tšale, tšajana, sethosana.
she, o, e, yena.
sheaf, ngata, segola.
shear, kuta, kota.
shears, sekero.
sheath, kgatla, segatla.
shed, polokelo, leobo; v., – **(blood),** tšholla madi; – **(tears),** lla; – **(leaves),** raša; **has –,** tšholotše.
sheep, nku, dinku.
sheep-fold, lešaka.
sheet, lakane, letlakala, lesenke.
shelf, lehlaya, borala, raka.
shell, kgapetla, legapi, kolo; v., ebola, kgokgoša, photla.
shelter, tšhireletšo, mošaša; v., šireletša.
shelve, beela, diegiša, fega.
shepherd, modiši; v., diša.
sheriff, motsetelakgoro, moromiwa wa lekgotla.
shield, thebe, kotse; v., phemela.
shifting spanner, sepanerešutišwa.
shimmer, phadima, kganya.
shin, moomo, – **-bone,** moomo, lenotlo.
shine, kganya, nyedima; phadimo.
shining, phadimo, go kganya.

ship, sekepe.
shipwreck, thubego, tshenyego ya sekepe.
shirk, roba sogo; tšwafa.
shirt, gempe; – **opening,** selepe.
shiver, thothomela, roromela; n., thothomelo.
shivering, mothothomelo.
shoal, sehlopha.
shock, šoko, letšhogo; v., tšhoša.
shoe, seeta; **put on** –, rwala; – **-maker,** moroki wa dieta.
shoot, lehlogedi, v., hloga, thunya.
shooting, go thunya.
shop, lebenkele, seroto, v., reka; – **assistant,** morekišiši, – **keeper,** ralebenkele.
shopping, go reka, theko; – **bag,** mokotlana.
shore, lebopo, leši, mošiko.
short, kopana, – **(person),** mpharanyana; **come** –, hlaela; **take a** – **cut,** tla phaphi, putla.
shortcoming, tlhaelo, tšhito.
shortly, mankgapela.
shortness, bokopana.
shorts, gomela, šothi.
short story, palenyane.
shot, dihala; petšo.
shoulder, legetla; – **of meat,** letsogo.
shoulder-blade, segetla.
shout, goa, goeletša.
shove, sukumetša, kgorometša, šuthiša.
shovel, sekopo, šofolo.
show, bontšha, laetša; – **off,** ikgantšha; n., pontšho; – **n,** laeditše.
shower, pula, mohuhwana, pulana.
shred, nkgeretlana.
shrew, mmalešatana, sefororo.
shrewd, hlalefileng.
shriek, lla, meketša, duduetša.
shrill, sello se bogale, lešata.
shrine, altare, felo mo go kgethwa.
shrink, hunyela, gogega, boela; v., hunyetša, šošobana.
shrivel, šošobana, pona.
shroud, lešela la mohu; v., bipa.
shrub, mohlašana, mohlahla, **(edible),** morogo.
shrug, khutlola magetla.
shudder, roromela, šišimoga; **cause to** –, didimoša.
shun, ila, širogela, tšhaba.
shut, tswalela, thiba.
shutter, setswalelo.
shuttle, seetana.
shy, ntšela, dihlong.
shyness, dihlong.
sick, lwala, babja; – **person,** molwetši.
sickle, sekele, sekela.
sickle-thorn, moselesele.
sickness, bolwetši, bohloko.
side, lehlakore, thoko; **to** – **step,** tila, phepha, phefa.
sideways, ka lekeke, ka thoko.
siege, thakelelo; v., rakalela.
sieve, mohlotlo, sefe; v., sefa.
sift, sefa, hlotla, nyakišiša.
sigh, fegelwa, gona.
sight, go bona, mahlo, pono.
sign, tšhupetšo, tšhupo, leswao, seka; v., saena.
signal, temoši, v., šupetša, bitša ka letsogo.
signature, tshaeno.
signet, sekani, leswao.
significance, tlhalošo, bogolo.
signify, re, tsebiša.
signpost, sešupatsela.
silage, botelo, furukepelwa.
silence, khomolo, setu, sekomana.
silhouette, n., seriti, v., ritifatša.
silk, silika.
silkworm, sebokesei.
silliness, bothoto, bošilo.
silly, sethotho, lešilo.
silo, letlolo, v., furufatša.
silt, mobutšhaledi.
silver, silibera, silifera.

similar, swana.
similarity, ka go swana.
simile, seswantšho, papišo, tshwantšhanyo.
simmer, kgabakgaba.
simple, nolo; bošilo.
simple interest, tswalonolo.
simple sentence, lefokonolo, lefokonngwe.
simpleton, lešilo, sethotho.
simplicity, bonolo.
simplify, nolofatša.
simply, fela.
simulate, etšiša, ekiša.
simultaneous, mmogo, sammaletee.
sin, sebe, dibe; v., dira dibe.
since, e sa le, go tloga.
sincere, ya kgonthe, ya nnete.
sincerely, ka kgonthe, ruri.
sincerity, makgonthe.
sinew, lešika, mošifa.
sinewy, e maatla.
sinful, dirang dibe.
sing, opela, bina, lla; – **ing,** go bina, go opela.
singe, babola, tlabola.
singer, moopedi, mmini.
single, tee, nnoši; kgope; – **(out),** hlaola.
singly, ka noši.
singular, botee, makatšang.
sinister, boifišago, mpe.
sink, sobelela, kgohlomela, kokobela; **cause to–,** nweletša n., sinki, lephlapelo.
sinless, se nang sebe.
sinner, modiradibe.
sip, sora, phoka, hupa.
sir, morena.
sire, (r)ra, rakgolo, v., tswala.
sisal, kgopha.
sister, of a man, kgaitšedi; **of a woman,** ngwanabo; **a girl's elder** –, mogolo; **a girl's younger** –, monagwe; **his younger** –, kgaetšediagwe.
sister-in-law, mogadibo.
sisters, bokgaetšedi.
sit, dula, nna, tsorama.
sitting-place, bodulo, bonno.
sitting-room, phapošitulelo.
situated, dutšeng.
situation, maemo, bodulo.
six, boselela, tshela; – **hundred,** makgolotshela.
sixfold, gaselela.
sixteen, lesometshela.
sixth, ya boselela; **one,** teetsheleng.
sixty, masometshela.
sizable, kgolwanyane.
size, bogolo, saese, nomoro.
sjambok, mpakubu.
skate, relela.
skein, mogaro.
skeleton, marapo (matšapo) a mmele.
sketch, marapo (mašapo) a mmele.
sketch, tshwantšho, sethalwathalwa, seswantšho; v., swantšha, thalathala.
ski, thedimoga.
skiff, seketswana.
skill, botsebi, bokgoni.
skilled, tsebang, kgonang.
skim, okola.
skimmed milk, motsaro.
skimp, timana.
skin, letlalo, mokgopa; v., bua.
skinny, otileng.
skinflint, sejato, ngame.
skip, tlola, tshela (kgati), kalapa.
skipper, motsamaiši wa sekepe.
skipping-rope, kgati, thapo ya tshelampa.
skirmish, pupurutlano, go ngapana.
skirt, malethekana, mosese, roko; v., šika le.
skittles, mohwidinyane.
skull, legata.
sky, legodimo, leratadimo.
sky-scraper, ntlomalekeleke.
slab, letlapa.
slack, nyefilego, repha, hlephileng, tšwafa.

slacken, hlephiša, hlepha, nyefiša, nyefa, repha.
slake, tima lenyora.
slam, betha, tia.
slander, seba, pateletša; n., tshebo, pateletšo.
slang, sempara.
slant, sekama, thulama, n., tshekamo, letswapo.
slanting, sekameng.
slap, phasola, phaphatha, bata.
slash, hlatha, tia, ripa.
slate, letlapa, seleiti.
slaughter, hlaba, bolaya; n., polao.
slave, lekgoba, lethopša.
slaver, phophiša, ediša mare.
slavery, bokgoba, bothopša.
slavishly, sekgoba.
slay, bolaya, hlaba.
sledge, selei.
sledge hammer, noto.
sleek, boreledi, phadimago.
sleep, boroko, robala.
sleeper, morobadi.
sleepiness, boroko.
sleeping, go robala.
sleeping-chamber, borobalo.
sleeping-place, boalo.
sleeping-sickness, borokwane.
sleepless, khidiega; **b.** –, hlobaela.
sleeplessness, malaomabe, khidiego.
sleepy, swerve ke boroko, potuma.
sleet, lehlwapula.
sleeve, letsogo la seaparo.
sleigh, selei.
sleight, botswiri, bokgoni, phoro, bohwirihwiri.
slender, sesane, otile.
slenderness, bosese.
slice, ntsetlwana, sengwatho, senei, v., beka, tsetlola.
slide, thelela, thedimoga.
slight, sesane, ganyenyane, v., nyatša, galala.
slightly, ka gonyane.
slim, sese; hlalefile, ota.
slime, boleta, seretse.
sling, lešelathekgo, seragamabje; v., betša; – **over the shoulder,** šikara.
slink, ngwega, thoba.
slip, thelela, ritša; n., thupana; – **through,** šohla; – **away,** ngwega, thoba; – **the memory,** gaka; – **off,** tshwamoga; – **into,** khukhunela.
slipper, mamphašane, selipera.
slippery, boreledi, thelelang; **render** –, thelediša.
slit, lephakga.
sloop, sekepe.
slop, meetse a ditšhila.
slope, tshekamo; v., sekama.
sloping, go sekama.
sloping ground, motheoga.
sloppy, e seretse.
sloth, bobodu, botšwa.
slothful, tšwafang, lonya.
slouch, lepeletša, lepelela.
slough, letlapi, v., sola.
sloven, lešaedi.
slovenly, ka go šaetša.
slow, nanya, bosele, iketla, nanakela.
slowly, ka lelelo, gasele.
slowness, bosele, bonya.
sludge, seretse.
slug, kgopa, sebodu v., betha.
sluggard, sebodu.
sluggish, tšwafa.
sluice, mokero.
slum, masakeng, makubeng.
slumber, otsela; n., kotselo.
slump, go hlepha.
slur, tšhilafatša, feta, fela; n., sekodi, tsholo, bora.
slush, seretse.
slushy, seretse.
slut, lešaedi.
sly, bohwirihwiri.
smack, betha; n., kotlo.
small, nyane.
smallness, bonyane.
small (of the back), noka.
smallpox, sekobonyane.

smart, hlalefilego, baba, tšhephile.
smash, pšhatla, phuma, robaganya.
smear, dila, kgopha, tlola, tshasa.
smell, monkgo; moswa; v., nkga, dupa.
smelt, tološa, rula.
smelting-furnace, sebešo sa go tološa.
smile, nywanywa, bososela.
smite, otla, tia, bolaya.
smith, mothudi, morudi.
smithy, šapo.
smock, roboka.
smocking, thoboko.
smoke, muši; v., goga, thunya.
smoking, gogago (thunyago) muši.
smooth, boreledi; v., ritela; – **ened,** ritetše.
smooth-tongued, leleme la borethe; **(person),** seboledi.
smother, betwa.
smudge, tšhilafatša, kgamathela.
smuggle, gogotša, kwefa.
smuggling, kgogotšo, go kwefa.
smut, sekodi; tšhilafatša.
smutty, ditšhila.
snack, sesolana, dijonyana.
snuffle, terentshe.
snail, kgohu, kgopa.
snake, noga.
snake-bite, go longwa ke noga.
snap, kgaola, loma, thunya, swantšha, re thwa.
snare, sefu, v., thea, rea.
snarl, rora; n., mororo.
snatch, ubula.
sneak, sehwirihwiri; v., huhumela.
sneer, šunyalala.
sneeze, ethimola.
sniffing, mešutšo.
snivel, hlwephetša mamina, lla.
sniveller, sellallane.
snob, kgwara, legwane.
snooze, otsela, potuma.
snore, gona, kurutla, letša magalagapa.
snort, letša dinko.
snout, sefena; – **beetle,** tšhupa.
snow, lehlwa, kapoko.
snow-white, re (twaa) moo, pšoo.
snub, kgalemela, sola.
snuff, motšoko, fola, v., goga, tšuba; – **a candle,** poma.
snuff-box, thekgwana.
snuffers (pair of), ditlao.
snug, ruthetše.
so, bjalo; **it is** –, go bjalo; **and** –, ka gona.
soak, ena, ina, koloba, kolobiša.
soap, sesepe, sešepe.
soapstone, monato, mothumoka.
sober, hlabologileng.
soccer, kgwele ya maoto, futupolo.
sociability, kagišano, leago.
social, monyanya.
socialism, kabelano, leago, bosošiale.
social life, phedišano, kagišano.
social security, boikago; – **studies,** thutaleago.
social welfare, tšweletšaleago.
social worker, modirelaleago.
society, leloko, kopano, mokgatlo.
sock, kaušo, sokisi.
socket, sekoti, pitšana, nkgotlotswane.
sod, lekwate.
soft, boleta, bonolo, borume; **little** –, boletiana.
soft-ball, polonolo.
soften, nolofatša, nolofala, theletša, letefatša.
soft-heartedness, bopelohlomogi.
softly, gabonolo, gasele.
softness, boleta, bonolo.
soil, mabu, mmu; **poor** –, lehwafa.
soil, tšhilafatša; – **ed,** tšhilafaditšе.
sojourn, hlwa, dula, lala, bohlwelo.
solace, homotša; n., tshedišo, khomotšo.
solar, ya letšatši.
solar system, setšatši.
solder, solotera; – **ing,** tsholotero.
soldier, mohlabani, sera, lesole.

sole, nnoši, noši.
solely, fela, ka noši.
solemn, ya kgonthe, nnete.
solfa, solfa.
solicit, kgopela.
solicitor, agente.
solicitude, tlhokomelo.
solid, thata, tiileng; n., sethata.
solidify, thatafala, kgahla.
solitary, nnoši, bodutu.
solitude, bodutu.
solo, solo.
soloist, moopedinoši.
Solomon, Solomone.
solstice, seremotšatši.
soluble, tološega, nyaogega.
solution, tlhalošo, setološwa, tharollo.
solvable, tološega, hlalošega.
solvability, go tološega, hlalošega.
solvability, go ba le diswaro.
solve, hlaloša, rarolla, tologa.
solvent, setološi, setološa.
sombre, so, leswiswi, nyamile.
some, ngwe.
somebody, mongwe, mokete, semangmang.
somehow, ka mokgwa o mongwe.
someone, mongwe, mokete.
somersault, sekolokotane; v., kolokota.
something, se sengwe, sekete.
sometimes, ka mabaka, ka dinako tše dingwe.
somewhat, ka go nyane.
somewhere, bokete, felo gongwe.
somnambulist, mosepela-a-robetše.
son, morwa, mošimane; **my** –, morwaka.
sonata, sonata.
song, kopelo, pina, koša; – **a hymn,** sefela; **a war** –, koma; **a bird's** –, molodi.
son-in-law, mogwe, mogwa, mokgonyana.
sonnet, sonete.
sonny, mošimanyana.
sonorous, molodi.
soon, mankgapela, ka pela; **as – as,** seno.
soot, mošidi.
sooth, nnete; **for** –, ka kgonthe.
soothe, okobatša, homotša, fodiša.
soothsayer, senoge.
sooty, e mošidi.
sop, sopo; v., ina.
sophisticate, fora, thanya, hwirihwitša, **–d,** thantše.
sorcerer, moloi.
sorcery, boloi, too, bophale.
sordid, bolotšana, bošula.
sore, sešo, bohloko; v., baba.
sorrow, manyami, mahlomola.
sorry, nyamile, maswabi.
sort, mohuta, v., hlaola.
sortie, tšhwahlelo.
sot, letagwa.
soul, moya, bophelo, motho, sebopiwa.
sound, modumo, – **film,** filimi ya Medumo.
sound, hlotla, hlaba mokgosi, letša.
sound, fodilego, tiilego, iketlile.
soup, sopo.
sour, baba, bodila, bohla.
source, mothopo, mohlodi.
sourness, bodila, go baba.
south, borwa.
South Africa, Afrika-Borwa.
south-east, borwabohlabela.
southpole, phoulo ya borwa.
souvenir, segopotšo, segopotši.
sovereign, boipušo, kgoši.
sovereignty, boipušo.
sow, bjala, gaša; **–n,** gašwa, gašitše.
sower, mobjadi.
space, sebaka, phahla, lebala.
spacecraft, sephatšamaru.
spacing, katologanyo.
spacious, sebaka se segolo.
spade, garafo, sepete, **small** –, garaswana.
spaghetti, sepaketi.

span, sepane, paralatšo; v., paralatša.
spangle, phadima.
spank, betha, otla.
spanner, sepanere.
spare, boloka, swarela; šadiša.
spare wheel, leotwanadutwa.
sparingly, ka gonyane.
spark, thaa, hlase; v., thanya.
spark plug, pholaka ya hlase.
sparkle, kganya, bekenya.
sparrow, phorogohlo.
spasm, bogašu, leswethe.
spate, lefulo, phalalo.
spatter, fafatša.
spawn, mae a hlapi; v., bea mae.
speak, bolela; – **up for,** rerelela.
speaker, mmoledi, – **in parliament,** spikara, speaker.
spear, lerumo, tšhosa; v., hlaba.
spear-shaped, selerumo.
special, itšego, itšeng, kgethilwego.
specialist, matwetwe, komang ka nna.
species, mohuta, leloko, mohlobo.
specific, itšego, hlomameng.
specification, molaetša.
specify, šupa, laetša.
specimen, sešupo, mohlala.
speck, sekodi, letheba, tlhaka.
speckled, maronthwana.
spectacle, segakgamalelo.
spectacles, dipeketsana, digalase, diporele.
spectator, mmogi, molebeledi.
spectre, seriti, sethotsela.
speculate, bapatša.
speculation, kakanyo, papatšo.
speculator, moreka-a-rekiša.
speech, polelo.
speechless, hloka polelo.
speed, lebelo, bjako.
speedily, ka (pela) lebelo.
speedy, phakišang, akgofang.
spell, peleta, re, kgagamalo.
spell, boloi.
spelling, (mo)peleto.
spelt, leotša.
spend, ntšha tšhelete, senya.
spendthrift, sesenyi.
spent, lapile, fedile.
sperm, peu.
spew, tshwa, hlatša.
sphere, kgolokwe, tikologo.
spherical, nkgokolo.
sphinx, sefinkisi.
spice, dinoko.
spider, segoko, segokgo.
spider's-web, bobi, letata, bolepu.
spike, sepikiri, v., hlaba.
spill, phuma, falatša, tšholla.
spin, ohla, rara.
spinach, sepiniše, morogo, sepinasi.
spinal cord, mookolela, mongetsane; – **column,** mokokotlo.
spindle, selogo.
spine, mokokotlo.
spinster, kgarebe, lefetwa.
spiral, morara, rarago.
spire, sehloa, tora.
spirit, moya; **departed spiritis,** badimo; – **a ghost,** seriti, sepoko; **ardour,** maatla; **the Holy spirit,** Moya o Mokgethwa; – **level,** baterepase; **evil** –, lelopo.
spirited, mahlahlo, mafolofolo.
spiritual, ya moya, semoya.
spit, tshwa, tshwela (mare).
spite, lehloyo.
spittle, mare.
splash, tla(m)puletša, gaša, hlaphuhla.
spleen, lebete.
splendid, kganyago, botse kudu, bogegago.
splendour, botse, letago.
splice, pharola.
splint, sepalaka.
splinter, lefatša, lehlokwana.
split, pharola, fatša.
spoil, senya, hleka, lemala; n., dithebola, maswaiša.
spoiler, mosenyi, mothopi.
spoke, sepeke; – **shave,** sefefapeke.
spokesman, mmoledi.

sponge, sepontšhe.
sponsor, moemedi.
spontaneous, ka noši.
spook, seriti, sepoko.
spool, toliki, toloki, kgaro.
spoon, leho, lehwana.
spoor, mohlala; v., lata.
sporadic, ka sewelo.
sportsman, radipapadi.
sportsmanship, setho sa thaloko.
sport, papadi, thaloko.
spot, sekodi, letheba, setswata, felo; **on the** –, ka ponyo ya leihlo.
spouse, mogatša.
spout, molomo wa ketlele; v., tseremetša, tsupulotša, tshwa.
sprain, thinyega; n., thinyego.
sprawl, ikotlolla, phathakgana.
spray, lehulo, lehlare; v. gaša.
spread, gaša, phatlalatša, fetetša, nama; – **out,** anega, ala, tsharolola.
sprig, lehlogedi, thupana, lehlare, motšitlo.
spring, selemo, seruthwane, tlolo, seporing, mothopo; v., mela, tlola.
springbuck, tshephe.
spring-hare, tšhipa, tola, kušu.
sprinkle, šašetša, bera, foka, gasa.
sprout, hloga, n., lehlogedi.
spruce, tšhepha, tšhephile(go).
spume, lehulo, lephilo.
spunk, hlase, mafolofolo.
spur, letsolwane, v., kgothatša.
spurious, ya phoro, ya maaka.
spurn, nyatša, galala.
spurt, tseremetšo.
spy, tlhodi, tshebi; v., hlola.
spy-glass, thelesekopo.
squabble, ferekana, fapana; n., tshele.
squadron, sekgao.
squalid, ditšhila, befago.
squall, lla, goa; sello; phoko ya phefo.
squander, senya, forosetša.
square, sekwere.
squash, leraka, pitla, v., pšhatla.
sqaut, kotama, tsorama.
squatter, mokotami, mokoloni.
squeak, lla, tswinya, motswinyo.
squeamish, ferošago, ferogago.
squeeze, pitla, gama.
squint, leana.
squirrel, sehlora.
squirt, tshwa, tseremetša.
stab, hlaba.
stabilise, tiiša.
stability, go tia.
stable, setala, tiileng; v., hlahlela.
stack, mokgobo, sehlopha; v., kgobela, hlopha.
staff, lepara, setafo.
staff, badirišani, bašomišani.
stag, tshepe.
stage, sethala, kgato; – **fright,** mahlomašiabatho.
stagger, thekesela, makatša, gakgamatša.
stagnant, emego, emeng.
staid, tiileng, tiilego.
stain, sekodi, motako, bosodi, setaki, v., tšhilafatša, mara.
stained glass, galase ya mebala.
stair, manamelo.
stake, tšea kgang, n., phate, kabelo.
stale, utileng, tapileng, bošula, senyegileng.
stalk, lehlaka, lenono; lehlokwa, molebo; v.i. khukhunetša; – **borer,** seseti, sebokophehli.
stallion, poo ya pere.
stalwart, e maatla, e bogale, mmotegi.
stammer, kgamakgametša, koakoetša, kwakwetša.
stamp, setempe, v., tula, setla, kuba.
stand, ema; – **up,** emelela; – **together,** emelana.
stand, be made to –, emišwa.
standard, boemo, mphato, sefoka, ya theo.
standardise, lekanetša.
standing, emeng; boemo.
stanza, tematheto.
staple food, sejokgolo.

star, naledi.
starch, seteisele, v., teisela.
stare, lebelela, boga, tsepelela.
start, thoma.
startle, tšhoša.
starvation, tlala.
starve, bopama, ikona dijo.
state, boemo.
state, mmušo, naga, v., re.
statement, taodišo, polelo.
statesman, mokgomana.
station, seteišene.
stationary, emego.
stationery, dingwalelo.
statistics, (di)palopalo.
stative verb, ledirami.
statue, leswika la kgopotšo, sehlwaseeme.
stature, bogolo, boemo.
status, boemo.
statute, molao.
staunch, tiileng, botegago.
stave, phate, thalonote.
stay, dula, lala, hlwa, thiba, thekga.
stays, bostoroko.
stead, legato; **in – of,** bakeng sa.
steadfast, tiileng, go se lapišege, sa šikinyege.
steadfastness, go tia.
steady, tiileng, iketlilego; v., tiiša.
steak, nama ya kgomo.
steal, utswa.
stealthy, ka sephiri, kutamong.
steam, mušimeetse, phufudi.
steamer, sekepe sa mušimeetse, sefufutši.
steel, setala, v., thatafatša, tiiša.
steep, ina.
steep hill, mokonya.
steeple, sehloa, tora.
ster, poo.
stem, kutu, thito, lehlokwa; v., thibela.
stench, go nka.
step, kgato, v., gata; **– brother,** wa rra wa lapa le lengwe.
sterile, nyopileng; – **cow,** moopa.
sterilisation, kopafatšo, tlhwekišo.
sterilise, hlwekiša, opafatša.
sterling, ya kgonthe, ya nnete.
stern, bogale, tiileng.
stern, marago a sekepe.
sternness, bothata.
stethoscope, mankgwanyane.
stew, setšhuu, mokhuša; v., khuša.
stick, patla, kgati, thupa, lepara, mošaša, mogwane; v., kgomarela, hlaba.
stick/plunge into, tsetsemetša, tsotsometša.
sticking-plaster, semamatletšo.
sticky, kgomarelang.
stiff, gwagwaletše, hlamaletše.
stiffen, gwagwalatša.
stifle, kgama.
stigma, mmamodula, setikima.
stile, moratho.
still, sa, ntše; v., homola, homotša.
stillborn, lefolotšana, sefolotšana.
stillness, khutšo, khomolo.
stimulant, sematlafatši, setsoši.
stimulate, tsoša, hlaboša.
stimulation, tsošo, tlhabollo.
sting, lebolela, polela; v., loma.
stingy, timana, kuna, tsebafa.
stink, nkga.
stint, homola, bea mellwane.
stipulate, laetša, šupa.
stipulation, molaetša.
stir, hudua, hlohleletša.
stitch, mohlabo; v., roka.
stock, lešika, diruiwa, phahlo, adj., tala, v., rua; **small** –, dihuswane.
stockade, sebo, lefao, lešaka.
stock-breeder, morui wa diruiwa.
stock-farming, thuo.
stocking, kaušo.
stoke, bešetša.
stoep, mathudi.
stoke, gotetša, bešetša.
stoker, mogotetši.
stolid, tšwafago, sethotho.

stomach, mogodu, mpa.
stomach-ache, lewa ke mala, gadikega.
stone, leswika, letlapa, lebje; – **carving,** petloswika; – **a kernel,** thotse; **a millstone,** lwala, tšhilo; – **age,** bogolokhukhu.
stone, thuma, kgatla.
stool, setulo, senno, mantle; v., ithoma; – **as corn,** fara.
stoop, inama, hutlalala.
stop, thiba, emiša, ema; n., sekhutlo, – **sign,** setopo; – **ped,** eme.
stoppage, thibelo.
stopper, sethibo.
storage, poloko, polokelo.
store, lebenkele, polokelo; v., boloka.
storehouse, polokelo.
store-keeper, ralebenkele.
stork, leakabosane, mogolodi.
storm, ledimo, moferefere; v., hlasela.
story, kanegelo, taba.
stout, e maatla, **(person),** senatla.
stouthearted, bogale, **(person),** mogale.
stoutness, bonatla.
stove, setofo.
stow, boloka.
straddle, šanka.
straggle, ralala, fapoga.
straggler, mmanthaladi, lekobakobane.
straight, reng thwi, otlologile, lokileng; – **line,** mothalothwi.
straighten, otlolla.
strain, lapišago, n., tapišo, ngangego.
strait, pitlaganeng, sese; **sea** –, mosela.
straiten, pitlaganya.
strand, lebopo, tlhale, lethale; – **ed, cotton,** tlhale ye e ohlilwego.
strange, keeng, šele.
stranger, moeng.
strangle, v., kgama, beta; – **d,** betilwe; **b. strangled,** kgamilwe.
strangulation, kgango.
strap, lerapo, lebja; v., bofa.
stratosphere, setratosfere.
strategy, maano.
stratum, llaga ya lefase, lelalano, stratum.
straw, lehlaka; dirite.
stray, timela, lahlega.
streak, mothaladi; v., thala.
stream, nokana, moela.
street, setarata, mokgotha.
strength, maatla.
strengthen, tiiša, fa maatla; – **ing,** tiišo.
stress, tobeletšo, kgateletšo; v., tiišetša, tobeletša.
stretch, otolla, bapola, nganga.
stretcher, leako.
strew, gaša.
strict, tlhoko.
strictly, ka tlhoko.
stride, kgato, legato.
strife, kgang, phapang.
strike, tia, opa, kgwarinya, gana go dira, teraeka; – **him/her,** mmetha; – **repeatedly,** mmethaganya.
striking, makatšang.
string, thapo, senare.
stringent, tiileng.
strip, hlobola, khumola, khupolola, moseto.
stripe, mothaladi, moreto.
striped, mereto.
strive, katana, phegelela; – **hard,** tsentšha dinala fase.
striving, katano, phegelelo.
stroke, mothalo, titeo; v., ola, phaphatha; – **of luck,** lešoto, mahlatse.
stroll, sepela.
strong, tiileng, maatla; **become** –, matlafala.
stronghold, sebo.
strongly, ka maatla.
strop, loutša.
structure, moago, popego, sebopego.
struggle, katana, n., katano, thagarago.
strut, gwanta, hubaka, gobata.

stubble, motlang.
stubborn, ngangelago.
stubbornness, bonganga.
stud, konope, mohlape.
student, morutiwa, moithuti.
studio, phapoši.
study, ithuta, thuto.
stuff, kitela, aketša, n., lešela, diphahlo.
stuffiness, khupelano.
stuffy, sekhutamoya.
stumble, kgopša, thetšwa, thetša.
stumbling-block, sekgopišo.
stump, thito, kutu, seša, lekgonogedi; – **finger,** lefonokwane.
stun, idibanya.
stunt, bomenemene.
stunted, kgopana.
stupefy, šilofala, idibatša.
stupendous, makatšang.
stupid, sethoto, lešilo.
stupidity, bošilo, bothotho.
stupor, kidibalo, makalo.
sturdy, e maatla.
stutter, kgamakgametša, kwakwetša.
stutterer, mokgamakgametši.
sty, oko, lešaka, hoko ya kolobe, sennyane.
sty, sešimanyana, pikitla, sennyane.
style, mokgwa, lenono, setaele.
stylish, botse, sebjalebjale.
stylus, pene.
sauve, botho, bonolo.
suavity, botho, bonolo.
subdivide, ngwathaganya.
subdivision, ngwathaganyo.
subdue, fenya, hlola.
subdued, homotšeng, kokobetšeng.
subconscious mind,meriti ya kgopolo.
subject, molata, modiri, sediri, serutwa, thuto; v., ikoba, fenya.
subject study, tlhahlotiro.
subjection, kokobetšo, boikobo.
subjective, (sa) sediri.
subjugate, fenya, ineela.
subjugation, phenyo, kokobetšo.
subjunctive mood, modirišogore.
sublime, phagameng.
submarine, tlase ga lewatle.
submerge, ina, sobeletša; **–d,** sobeletše.
submission, boineelo, boikokobetšo, peelopele, go kwa.
submissive, ineelago, ikokobetšago.
submit, ikgafela, beela pele.
subordinate, hlankiša, obamiša; n., molata, monyane, mohlanka.
subordinate clause, thabenyana.
subordination, boikokobetšo, bonyane (gram.).
subpoena, biletša tshekong, tagafala.
subsecton, tema, karolwana.
subsequent, latelang.
subside, kokobela, homola, khula.
subsidiary, thušang, oketšang.
subsidy, seabo, thušo.
subsist, phela.
subsistence, go phediša.
subsoil, mobutlase.
substance, selo, ntho.
substandard, mphatwana.
substantial, kgonthe, kgolo, tiileng.
substantiate, phetha, hlatsela, tiiša.
substitute, bea bakeng sa; n., moemedi, kemedi.
subterfuge, seipato.
subterranean, tlase ga mmu.
subtle, hlalefile, bohwirihwiri.
subtract, ntšha, tloša.
subtraction, go tloša, tlošo.
subtropical, (sa)nngamolatšatši, sa thokomolatšatši.
suburb, legoro.
subversion, thenkgolla, thenola.
subway, bohuhumelo.
succeed, kgona, latela(na), atlega.
success, katlego, mahlatse.
succession, tlhatlamano, mokoloko.
successive, latelanago.
successor, mohlatlami, mojalefa.
succour, thuša, n., thušo.
succulent, sebalemeetse.

succumb, hlolwa, ineela, šitwa, timela, hwa.
such, bjalo, nka, n., – **and** – **person,** semangmang, mokete; – **and** – **a thing,** sekete; – **and** – **a place,** bokete.
suck, anya, monoka, mona, nyanya.
sucker, momoni, lehlogedi, semomono, semamaela.
suckle, amuša, anyesa.
suckling, lesea.
sudden, phakišang, e lebelo.
suddenly, mankgapela, ka potlako, gateetee.
suddenness, kakgofo.
sue, sekiša, tagafala.
suer, mosekiši.
suet, lekhura, lemipi, lebipi.
suffer, kgotlelela, tlaišega, kwa bohloko, dumelela, hlokofala; – **the consequence,** šikara kotlo.
sufferings, mahloko, mathata.
suffice, go lekana.
sufficient, lekaneng; **be** –, enela.
suffix, mosela.
suffocate, kgama, beta.
suffocation, kgango, sekhutamoya.
sugar, swikiri.
suffrage, tokelo ya go bouta.
sugar-bird, mmanotswane.
sugar-cane, mmoba, nyoba.
suggest, hlagiša, šikinya.
suggestion, tšhikinyo, kakanyetšo.
suicide, go ipolaya, boipolai.
suit, sutu, paka, tsheko; v., lebana, swanela.
suitable, lebaneng, loketšeng, swanetšego.
suitcase, sutukheisi.
suite, sete; **lounge** –, sete ya lontše.
suitor, mološi, moferei.
sulk, ngala, bopa; **cause to** –, ngadiša.
sulkiness, go ngala.
sulky, ngalang.
sullen, ngalang.
sully, senya, tšhilafatša, fetetša.
sulphates, salefate.
sulphur, sebabole.
sultana, salatana.
sultry, betago.
sum, tlhakano, palo, kopano, tšhelete, v., hlakanya.
summarily, ka boripana.
summarise, akaretša.
summary, kakaretšo.
summation, tlhakanyo.
summer, lehlabula; – **house,** mokubana.
summit, hlora, sehloa, ntlha.
summon, sekiša; biletša, epa.
summons, tagafala.
sumptuous, nyabalatšago, bohlokwa.
sun, letšatši.
sunbeam, lehlasedi.
sun-bonnet, kapi.
Sunday, Sontaga, Lamodimo.
sunder, aroganya, kgaoganya.
sundown, ka phirimane, mantšiboa.
sundowner, diphafana tša bošego.
sundried, kwapilego, makwapi.
sundries, dilwana, diphahlwana.
sundry, nngwe le nngwe.
sunflower, sonopolomo.
sunken, sobeletše.
sunlight, (seetša sa) letšatši.
sunny, e kganyang, borutho.
sunrise, go hlaba ga letšatši, ge le hlaba.
sunset, phirimane, phirmatšatši.
sunshine, kidibatšotšatši.
sup, lalela, ja selalelo.
superannuate, fa phenšene.
superb, botsebotse, phadišišago.
superficial, sa tseneleleng, se nang botebo.
superintendent, mookamedi.
superior, sa godimo, phalang, fetang.
superlative, kgolo kudu, fetišišago.
supernatural, mohlolo.
supersede, tloša, ema bakeng sa.
superstition, tumelwana, tumelakhwele, tumelathoko.

supervise, hlokomela, okamela.
supervision, tlhokomelo, kokamelo.
supervisor, mohlahlobedi, molekodi.
supper, selalelo.
supplant, hlalefetša.
supple, boleta, bonolo.
supplement, oketša, n., koketšo.
supplementary, oketšago.
suppleness, boleta.
supplicant, mokgopedi, morapedi.
supplicate, rapela, rapelela.
supplication, kgopelo, thapelo.
supplies, phepo, diphahlo.
supply, setša, fepa; n., phepo, phahlo.
support, thekga, thuša, n., thušo; – **oneself,** iphediša.
supporter, moemedi, mothuši.
suppose, hloma, gopola.
supposing, ge eba, hloma eke.
suppress, gatella, pitla.
suppurate, tšwa boladu.
suppuration, pikihla.
supremacy, bogolo.
supreme, kgolo, phagameng.
Supreme Court, Kgotlakgolo.
sure, ya nnete; tiile, ka kgonthe.
surety, moemedi; peelo.
surf, maphoto, lešulo.
surface, sefahlego, sefatla, bokagodimo; v., gohla, khafa.
surfeit, imetša, tena, phaka n., khoro.
surge, lephoto.
surgeon, ngaka, rathipane.
surgery, bobui, bongaka.
surly, ngalang.
surmise, gopola; n., kgopolo.
surmount, fenya, feta.
surname, sefane.
surpass, feta, phala; – **ing,** phalang, fetang.
surplus, mašalela, pheteledi.
surprise, tlaba, makatša; n., nonnodi, nonnori, makalo.
surrender, ineela; neela, tela, gafela.
surround, dika, rakanela; – **ing,** tikologo.
survey, lekola, lekanyetsa.
surveyor, molekanyetši.
survivial, bophelo, phologo.
survive, phela, phologa.
survivors, mašaledi, mašaletšana.
susceptibility, tšhabello, peko, tsenego.
susceptible, tsenega, utlwega.
suspect, gonona.
suspend, lekeletša, fega, kgaola, emiša.
suspended sentence, kahlolo ye e fegilwego.
suspense, tikadiko, pelaelo.
suspension, kemišo, v., sekgoatša, phego.
suspicion, pelaelo, maseme.
suspicious, belaešega; **make** –, gonontšha; **become** –, gonona.
sustain, phediša, thekga, kgotlelela.
sustenance, phepho.
swab, semoni, phumola, omiša.
swaddle, phutha.
swagger, ikgantšha, šankašanka.
swallow, metša.
swallow, peolane.
swamp, mohlaka, tebetebe.
swarm, motšhitšhi; v., nyeuma.
swarthy, ntsho.
swat, bolaya.
sway, ebela, akgaakga, buša.
Swaziland, Swatseng, Swaziland.
swear, ena, roga.
swearing, mahlapa, go roga.
sweat, kudumela, sethitho, mphufutšo.
sweep, swiela.
sweeper, moswiedi.
sweet, bose, lekere, monamonane.
sweetcorn, trimane, mahea.
sweeten, natefiša; – **the mouth,** lokotša.
sweetheart, nnake, moratiwa.
sweet-oil, sutuoli.
sweet-pea, letšobaseereki.
sweet-potato, morepa, potata.

sweets, malekere, dipompong.
sweetness, bose, monate.
swell, ruruga, kokomoga.
swelling, serurugi.
swerve, thinya, fapoga.
swift, phakišago.
swiftly, ka (lebelo) bjako.
swiftness, lebelo.
swill, tsokotša, nwa, tšhela.
swim, rutha, thala, thutha.
swimmer, moruthi, mosesi, mothadi.
swindle, thetša, hlalefetša.
swindler, mohlalefetši, mothetši, sehwirihwiri.
swine, kolobe.
swing, teku, mankadile, komporomae; v., akgaakga, hwindinya, akga.
swingle, swengele.
swirl, tsokotša, rara, ferehla.
swish, betha, tšutla, gwaša, tswikinya.
switch, thupa, mpa, kopanya.
Switzerland, Switzerland.
swoon, idibana, samadikwe.
sword, sabole, tšhoša.
sycamore, mogo.
syllable, noko.
symbol, seka, sešupo; – **ise,** swantšha.
symmetric(al), lekanetšego.
symmetry, go lekana, go swana.
sympathise, kwela bohloko.
sympathy, matshedišo, kwelobohloko.
symphony, simfone, tumammogo.
symptom, seka, sešupo.
synagogue, sinagoge.
synod, sinote.
synonym, sinonime, lehlalošetšagotee.
syntax, popafoko.
synthesis, tlemaganyo ya mafoko.
syphilis, thosola, tlosolo.
syringa, morolwane.
syringe, setšhelo, kurumane.
syrup, kgotla-o-mone, sirapu, todi.
system, mokgwa, tsela.
systematically, ka peakanyo.

T

taaibos, mogoriri.
tabernacle, tabenakele.
table, tafola, bojelo.
table-cloth, tafoletuku.
table-land, sehlaba, polatou.
tablet, phaphathi.
table-ware, dibjana.
taboo, seila.
tabulate, hlopha.
taciturn, reng tuu; homolang.
tack, sepikiri.
tacking, tlhabego.
tact, bohlale, maano.
tactics, maano.
tadpole, kuduntsane, nakolane..
tail, mosela; – **end,** ntlha.
tailor, moroko, mosegi.
taint, mmala, kodi, v., senya.
take, tšea; – **to,** iša; – **from,** amoga; – **accept,** amogela; – **hold of,** swara; – **by force,** amoga, gapa; – **out,** ntšha; **away,** tloša; – **out of the water,** inola; – **fire,** akgela; – **out a thorn,** hlomola; – **out an eye,** gonya; – **off, hat or shoes,** rola; – **off a garment,** apola, tšola; – **off a pot from the fire,** hlatlola; – **a temperature,** ela themperetšha; – **stock,** bala phahlo; – **a wife,** tšea, nyala; – **heed,** hlokomela; – **place,** diragala; – **to,** rata; – **root,** tsema medu; – **breath,** buša moya, khutša; – **in,** fora; – **down,** fegolla; **-n out,** ntšhitše.
taken, be – up, letša wa nko.
take notes, ngwala dintlha.
taking, rategang.
takings, diswaro, tšhelete, diamogelwa.
tale, nonwane.
talent, neo, talenta.
talisman, pheko.
talk, bolela; polelo, bega, boledišana;

poledišano; – **ative pers.,** mmolabodi.
talker, mmoledi.
tall, telele, kgolo.
tallness, botelele, bolele.
tallow, makhura.
talon, lerofa, lenala, lenotlo.
tambookie (grass), mašiši.
tambour, moropa.
tambourine, moropana.
tame, tlwaetšeng, thapileng, nolo; v., thapiša, tlwaetša; – **er,** mothapiši.
tampan, thwakga, lekudula.
tamper, hwirihwitša, dubaduba, itsenya tabeng tša ba bangwe.
tan, šoga.
tang, mohlodi, modumo, ntlha.
tangent, mothalokgoma.
tangled, rarega, raraneng.
tank, tanka.
tankard, kgapa, phafa, moeta.
tanner, mošogi.
tantalize, konketša, kgantšhetša.
tantamount, lekanago.
tap, thepe, pompi, v., kokota.
tape, lenti, theipi.
tape-measure, lentitekanyo.
taper, lebone; – **ed,** ya ntšotšo.
tapestry, diala.
tape-worm, nogana ya mala, noga ya teng, khumela.
taproot, modutona.
tar, tiri, sekontiri; v., kontira.
tarantula, mmantlo, selaledi.
tardy, diega, tšwafago.
target, tebo, tebanyo.
tariff, lekgetho.
tarnish, senya, tšhilafatša.
tarpaulin, seila.
tarry, diega, leta.
tarsal, lenakaila, thasala.
tart, kukisi; bodilana.
tartar, tatara, segomarelameno.
tartaric acid, thathariki.
task, tiro, modiro.
tassel, lešaphu, kukutana, seala, sehlora.
taste, mohlodi; v., kwa, latswa.
tasteful, bose, kwalang.
tasteless, bošula, tapilego, bohla.
tasty, natefago, latswega, bose.
tatter, lenkgeretla; v., gagola.
tattle, polabolo, v.i., bolabola.
tattler, mmalabadi, mosebi.
tattoo, gaya; – **oneself,** itshwaya maswao.
tattoo, sello sa go (felegetša mohu) biletša dira malaong.
taunt, befediša, kwera, rumola.
tavern, para.
tax, lekgetho, motšhelo; v., tšhediša.
taxation, lekgetho, motšhelo.
tax-collector, wa lekgetho, molekgetho, motšhediši.
taxi, tekisi, kolointefe, thekisi.
tea, teye, foofo.
teach, ruta.
teacher, morutiši.
teaching, thuto.
teaching-aids, dithušathuto.
teacup, komiki, senwelo.
teak, morotho.
team, sepane.
team-work, tirišano, tšhomišano.
teapot, pitšana ya teye.
tear, mookgo, mogokgo, keledi.
tear, letlere; v., tlerola, gagola; thaola.
tease, kwera, tshwenya, hlohla.
tea-spoon, lehwana.
teat, letswele.
technical, thekniki.
technique, botsebi, thekniki.
tedious, lapišago.
tedium, bodutu, tapišo.
teem, nyeuma.
teeming, nyeumang.
teens, bosogana, bofsa.
teeth, meno; **show the** –, šena meno.
telegram, thelekramo, motato, mogala.

telegraph, thelekrafo, v., romela motato.
telephone, thelefomo; v., itea motato.
telescope, thelesekopo.
teleprinter, motšhene wa theleke.
television, thelebišene.
tell, bolela, bega; – **him/her,** mmotša.
teller, mmoledi, mmegi.
tell-tale, tshebi, mpheane.
temerity, bogale.
temper, tswaka, fefola, pefelo.
temperament, mokgwa, sebopego.
temperance, boitimo.
temperate, ya/sa magareng, thempereiti.
temperature, themperetšha.
tempest, ledimo.
temple, tempele; – **of the head,** lešula.
tempo, lebelo, mmetela, nako, tempo.
temporary, lebakanyana.
tempt, leka.
temptation, moleko, teko.
tempter, moleki.
ten, lesome.
ten thousand, diketesome.
tenable, phemega, swarega.
tenacious, phegelelang, thata.
tenant, modudi, mohiri.
tend, diša, lebela, oka.
tendency, mokgwanyana, tshekamelo.
tender, tentere, boruma; v., tentera.
tender-hearted, pelonolo.
tenderness, bonolo, botho, borume.
tendon, mošifa, tšhika.
tendril, tatamolebo, morapo.
tenement, bodulo, madulo, ngwako.
tenfold, galesome.
tennis, thenisi.
tenor, tinoro, laboraro.
tens, masome.
tense, lebaka.
tense, gagametšeng, ngangilwego.
tension, kgagamalo, manganga.
tent, tente.
tenth, tee someng.
term, lereo, kotara.
terminate, fediša, phetha; – **ing,** ya mafelelo.
termination, phedišo.
terminology, mareo.
terminus, mafelelo, bofelo.
termite, mohlwa, lekeke.
terrace, therese, terase, sehlabahlaba, seteletele.
terracotta, ya letsopa.
terrapin, pshinyaleraga.
terrestrial, sa lefase.
terrible, boifišang, šoro, tšhabega.
terribly, o šoro.
terrific, boifišang, tšhošago.
terrified, boifa, roromela, tšhogile, tšhaba.
terrify, boifiša, tšhoša.
territory, nagadilete.
terror, go tšhoga, poifo.
terrorise, tšhošetša.
terrorist, motšhošetši.
terror-stricken, tšhogile.
terse, akaretšago, bokopana.
test, molekwana, teko; v., leka; – **me,** nteka.
testament, lengwalo la (nkhwa) testamente.
Testament, Testamente; **the Old –,** Testamente e Tala; **the New –,** Testamente e Mpsha.
testicle, lerete.
testify, hlatsela, hlatsetša, paka.
testimonial, lengwalo la bohlatse.
testimony, bohlatse, bopaki.
test-tube, tšhuputeki.
tetanus, tetanose, kgohlanyomehlagare.
tether, mmofo.
text, taba, thuto, diteng.
textbook, puku ya kgakollo.
textile, logilweng, dilogwa.
testure, phopholego.
than, go ena le.
thank, leboga.
thankful, thabela, leboga.
thank-offering, sehlabelo sa tebogo.

thanksgiving, tebogo.
thanks, malebogo, tebogo.
that, yoo, woo, seo, yeo; gore, gobane.
thatch, rulela; n., marulelo.
thaw, tologa.
theatre, paesekopo.
thee, wena, o.
theft, go utswa, bohodu.
their, bona, gabo, tšona, yona, **preceded by the poss. particle.**
them, ba, e, di, bona, yona, tšona.
theme, taba, tabataba, maleba.
themselves, bona ka noši, tšona ka noši.
then, ke moka/gona, ka fao, mohlang woo; **so then,** gee.
thence, gona.
theology, thutatumelo, teologi.
theorem, tsela, sekgolwa, theorema.
theoretical, ya teori.
theory, teori.
therapy, t(h)erapi, phekolo, kalafo.
there, kua, moo, mola.
thereby, ka gona.
therefore, ka baka leo, ke gona.
therefrom, go tloga moo.
thereof, go fihla moo.
thereupon, bjale, kgona go, napa.
thermometer, themometa, thei.
thermostat, selaolathempheretšha.
these, ba, tše, a, ye.
thesis, thesisi, kakanyotherwa.
they, ba, di, e.
thick, koto, teteaneng.
thicken, kgahla, themiša, kotofatša.
thickhead, setlaela.
thickness, bokoto.
thickset, teteaneng, koto.
thief, lehodu.
thieve, utswa, hlakola.
thigh, noka, serope.
thimble, fengere, senwana.
thin, sese, e meetse, otile.
thin out, fokotša.
thine, ya gago.
thing, selo, ntho.
think, gopola, akanya.
thinness, bosesane, popamo, go ota.
third, ya boraro, tee tharong.
third person, mmolelwa.
thirst, lenyora, mogau; v., nyorwa, nyorelwa.
thirsty, be –, nyorilwe.
thirteen, lesometharo.
thirty, masome a mararo, masometharo.
this, yo, wo, le, se, bjo, go.
thistle, lešeše, šitlwane, mantlalekgeru.
thither, kua, fao, gona.
thong, lebja, kgole, mogala.
thorax, sebuba, sefega.
thorn, mootlwa; **devil's** –, tshehlo.
thron-tree, sehlare sa meetlwa.
thorny, e meetlwa.
thorough, phethegileng, botlalo.
thoroughfare, tsela.
those, bao, yeo, tšeo, ao.
thou, wena, o.
though, le ga, le ge.
thought, kgopolo, kakanyo, kelelelo.
thoughtful, gopolang, hlokomelang; –**ness,** tlhokomelo, šedi.
thoughtless, sa gopoleng, hlokomolago.
thousand, sekete; – **s,** dikete.
thousand and one, kete le tee.
thousand and ten, kete le some.
thousand one hundred and eleven, kete le kgolo-some-tee.
thrash, (thresh), fola, betha, matla.
thrashing, pholo, petho.
thread, garane, tlhale, gare, v., folella.
threadbare, onetše, hlobotše.
threat, tšhošetšo.
threaten, šupeletša, tšhošetša.
three, tharo, diraro.
threefold, gararo.
three hundred, makgolotharo.
thresh, fola, matla.
threshing, pholo.

threshold, serepudi, mogato.
thrice, gararo.
thrift, pabalelo, tsheketšo, boipolokelo.
thrifty, bolokang, seketšago.
thrive, atlega, tšwela pele.
thriving, katlego.
throat, mogolo.
throb, opa, runya.
throne, thereone, terone, sedulo sa bogoši.
throng, bontši, kiti, v., bokanela, katelelo, nyeuma.
throttle, kgama, beta; n., kgologolo, b. – **d,** kgamilwe.
through, ka, ke.
throughout, ka gohle.
throw, foša, betša, lahla.
thrower, mmetši, mofoši.
thrust, kgorometša, hlaba.
thud, go opa.
thumb, mankgogoropo, monotona; **hold -s,** hupile dinala.
thump, tula.
thunder, modumo; v., duma.
thunderbolt, tladi.
thunderstorm, pula ya ditladi, matlakadibe.
Thursday, Labone.
thus, bjalo, ka mokgwa wo.
thwart, thibela, ganetša.
thyme, timi.
thyroid gland, thaka ya kgokgokgo.
thyself, wena ka noši.
tibia, moomo.
tick, kgofa, patšane.
ticket, thekethe; – **examiner,** mokgatladithekethe.
tickle, tsikiditla.
tide, phulawatle, thaete.
tidings, mehlamo.
tidiness, bothakga.
tidy, ka bothakga.
tie, bofa, tlema; n., thai; **to** –, lekalekana; swina.
tiger, nkwe; – **bush-cat,** koti.
tiger-cat, lepogo, phaga.
tight, tiileng.
tighten, tiiša, swineletša; **-ing,** tiišo.
tight-fitting, swinelago.
tile, thaele, mmopa.
till, lema, go fihla; n., lehlayana.
tilt, sekametša, pipa.
timber legong, kota
time, lebaka, nako, mohla; **short** –, motsotsonyana, lebakanyana; **in** - ka bonako; **some** – **ago,** maloba; **from that** –, go tloga moo; **at the present** –, bjale; – **card,** papetlanako; – **keeper,** moswaranako, ranako; **a time,** lekga, **times,** gamakga.
time! pitšori; šoo!
timely, lebaka la gona.
time-table, tšhupadipaka.
timid, e boi, dihlong.
timidity, boi, poifo.
timorous, e boi, e tšhabang.
tin, boleke, thini.
tinder, konu, twala.
tinge, taka, tsenya mmala.
tinker, mothudi wa dibjana.
tinkle, tsirinya, tsidima.
tinned, ya maleke; – **beef,** namabolekana; – **fish,** hlapibolekana.
tint, mmalanyana.
tiny, nyenyane.
tip, ntlha, boditse.
tipple, nwa bjalwa.
tipsy, boilwe, tagilwe.
tiptoe, tantabela.
tire, lapa, lapiša.
tiresome, lapišang.
tissue, tlhalenama; – **paper,** pampišanathume.
tit, se senyane.
titanic, kgolo kudu.
titbit, sešeba, sebalodi, sesolana.
tithe, karolo ya lesome, –, lekgetho.
title, thaetlele.
titter, sega, segasega.

titivate, kgabiša, ikgabiša.
tittle-tattle, go bolabola.
to, go.
toad, segwagwa, segwegwe.
toast, šimela, beša, lakaletša lehlogonolo; n., senkgwabešwa.
tobacco, motšoko, fola.
tobacconist, ramotšoko, radifola.
today, lehono, momohla.
toddler, maminana, mapimpane; **-s,** bomaminana, bomapimpane.
to-do, khuduego.
toe, monwana wa leoto; – **of a bird,** monotlo.
together, (ga)mmogo, gotee; – **with,** le.
toil, modiro; v., dira ka maatla.
toilet, boithomelo, toilete.
token, sešupo, tšhupo, seka., segopotšo.
tolerable, kaone, paale.
tolerance, tumelelo, kgotlelelo.
tolerate, kgotlelela, thatafalelwa.
toll, lekgetho; v., letša tšhipi.
tomahawk, tšhaka.
tomato, tamati.
tomb, lebitla, phupu.
tombstone, letlapa la lebitla.
tomcat, katse ya poo.
tomfool, setlaela.
tommy, lesole.
tommy rot, ditšiebadimo.
tomorrow, gosasa, ka moso.
ton, tone, tono.
tone, segalo, modumo.
tongs, letlao, kinipitane, ditlao.
tongue, leleme, polelo.
tonic, sematlafatši, (mus.) notetheo; – **solfa,** ditlhakanote.
tonnage, kelo ka ditone.
tonsil, thaka.
too, le, gape; – **much,** fetiša.
tool, thulu, geresekapa, thulusi.
tooth, leino; pl. meno; – **-brush,** porosolo ya meno.
toothed, ya meno, reketšwe.
tooth pick, sefatameno.
top, bogodimo, godimo; n., mankwanyane.
topic, taba, sererwa.
topmost, ya ka godimo.
topple, wa, thenoga.
top-soil, mobugodimo.
topsyturvy, sekolokotane, go kolokota, hlanogile.
torch, serumola, thotšhi.
torment, hlokofatša, tshwenya.
tormentor, mohlokofatši, motshwenyi.
torn, kgeigile; – **clothes,** mankgeretla; **be asunder,** kgakgamotšwe.
tornado, mamohlake, ledimo, mamogašwa.
torpedo, topedo.
torpid, hlamaletšeng.
torrent, lefulo.
torrid, fišang, borutho; – **zone,** legaro la phišo.
tortoise, khudu, mohudu.
tortuous, kgopameng, manyokenyoke, e kgopo.
torture, hlokofatša.
toss, akgela, dira matengwa.
total, ka moka, ohle, palomoka; v., hlakanya.
totem, seano, mmino.
totter, thekema, thekesela.
touch, kgwatha, ama, kgoma, neana bokoti; – **line,** mollwane.
touching, hlomodišang, godimo ga, huduegišang, mabapi le.
touchy, huduega, tukang bogale, rumolega.
tough, thata, tiileng.
toughen, thatafatša, tiiša.
tour, leeto; v., eta.
tourist, moeti, mosepedi.
tourniquet, tonikete, v., tsirimetša.
tow, kgole; v., goga.
toward(s), go, mo go.
towel, hantuku, toulo.
tower, tora, sehloa, – **above,** rokamela.

town, motse, toropo.
town clerk, tona ya motse.
town council, lekgotla la motse.
town hall, ntlokgolo ya motse.
townsfolk, baagi ba motse.
townsman, moagi wa motse, motoropo.
toxic, mpholo, bohloko.
toy, sebapadišwa; bapala, raloka.
trace, mohlala; v., lota, thala.
traceable, lotega, thalega.
trachea, mogolo, kgôkgôma.
track, mohlala, tsela; v., lota.
tract, mohlala, tsela; v., lota.
tract, selete, pukunyana.
tractability, bonolo.
tractable, bonolo, rutega.
tractor, terekere, torotoro.
trade, kgwebo, papatšo, mošomo, v., bapatša, kalokana.
trade mark, leswao la kgwebo.
trader, mmapatši, mogwebi.
tradesman, mmapatši.
trade wind, matlišakgwebo.
tradition, mabarebare, tlwaelo, moetlo.
traditional, tša bagolo, mokgwa wa kgale, ya semelo, tlwaelo.
traffic, therafiki; – **jam,** sephethephethe.
traffic-inspector, molaoladithwethwi, mohlankedi wa therafiki.
tragedy, mahlomola, manyami, masetlapelo.
tragic, mahlomola, manyami.
trail, mogoga, mohlala; v., goga.
trailer, koloigogwa.
train, setimela, terene, tataiša, ruta.
trainer, mothobodiši.
training, tataišo, thutelo.
trait, mokgwa.
traitor, moeki.
tram, terempe.
tramp, sekobakobane, v., gata, ralala.
trample, gataka, gatelela.
trance, sekakidibalo, sekatoro.
tranquil, iketlilego, khutšitšego, homolago.
tranquility, khutšo, boiketlo.
tranquillise, khutšiša, homotša.
transact, rerišana, phetha, kwana.
transaction, kgwebo, kwano.
transcend, feta, phala, phadiša.
transcendency, go feta, go phala.
transcribe, ngwalolla.
transcriber, mongwalodi.
transcription, ngwalollo.
transfer, šuthiša, tšhuthišo; **(needlew.)** kopolla; – **to,** fetišetša.
transferable, šuthišega.
transfer pattern, patrone ya phetišetšo.
transfiguration, tagafatšo, phetogo.
transfix, hlaba, phunya.
transform, fetoga, fetola.
transgress, tlola molao, senya, oba.
transgression, tlolo, molato, tshenyo, karogo.
transgressions, dikarogo.
transgressor, motlodi, mosenyi, moarogi.
transient, e fetang.
transition, phetogo ya segalo, thathelo, teransišene.
transitive, – **verb,** lefetedi.
translate, fetolela.
translation, phetolelo.
translator, mofetoledi, toloki.
transmission, tshepedišo, phetetšo, thomelo.
transmit, romela, fetišetša, fetetša.
transmitter, sefetišetši.
transmutation, phetogo.
transparent, bonagatša(ng).
transpiration, phufulelo.
transpire, kudumela, kwala, fufulelwa.
transplant, bjalolla; n., pšalollo.
transport, rwala, thotha, n., thotho, thwalo; – **to/for,** thothela.
transportation, thotho.
transpose, fapanya, fetola.

transposition, phetolo, phapanyo.
transverse, phuleletšago, phatša, sela; n., lepheko.
trap, sefu, molaba, v., thea.
trapper, morei, mothei.
trappings, dikgabišo.
trash, ditšiebadimo.
travail, katana, lapiša; n., mašoko.
travel, eta, sepela; n., leeto, mosepelo.
traveller, moeti, mosepedi.
travelling, mosepelo, leeto; – **companion,** mosepedišani.
travelling-expenses, tefo ya maoto.
traverse, phuleletšago, fapanego.
trawl, lelokwagogwa, rea dihlapi.
tray, therei, sekenkeporoto, tshelwana.
treacherous, boradia, ekago.
treachery, boradia, bonokwane, keko.
treacle, kgotla-o-mone.
tread, gata; n., kgato.
treason, keko, boikepi.
treasure, lehumo, letlotlo; v., boloka.
treasurer, ramatlotlo.
treasury, polokelo.
treat, amogela gabotse, dira, šoma.
treatment, tshwaro; **bad** –, tshwaro e mpe; **medical** –, kalafo, phekolo.
treaty, kwano, kgwerano.
treble, gararo; trebele, v., atiša gararo.
tree, sehlare, more.
trek, huduga, falala; n., khudugo, phalalo.
tremble, roromela, tetema.
tremendous, boifišang, kgolo kudu.
tremor, tšhišinyego.
tremulous, šišinyegang.
trench, mokero, v., epa.
trenchant, segago, bogale.
trenching, moepelo.
trespass, tlola, senya, oba, (ikobela) molato; n., molato.
trespasser, motlodi, mosenyi.
tress, leetse, kgaro.
trial, teko, tsheko, maitekelo; **public** –, go sekišwa phatlalatša.
triangle, khutlotharo, (mus). traenkele.
triangular, sa / ya khutlotharo.
tribal, ya setšhaba.
tribe, setšhaba, kgoro.
tribesman, mosetšhaba.
tribulation, tlalelo, tlaišego, mathata.
tribunal, lekgotla.
tributary, nokakeledi.
tribute, diloba, sebego.
trick, bomenemene, thetšo; v., thetša, swaswa; sephiri.
trickery, bomenemene, bohwirihwiri.
trickle, rothela, dutla.
tricky, forago, hlalefetšago.
tried, lekilwego; lekile; – **me,** ntekile.
trifle, selwana.
trifling, lefela.
trill, šikinya, duduetša.
trim, hlama, kgabiša, poma.
trimmer, mokgabiši, mohlami.
trimming, kgabišo.
Trinity, Boraro (bja Modimo).
trio, seraro, batho ba bararo, trio.
trip, n., leeto, v., kgopa, phereketša.
tripe, legata, diretlo.
triple, diraro, gararo.
tripod, masego, moratetšo.
triumph, phenyo, fenya; – **ant** fenyago.
triumvirate, pušotharo.
trivial, difefe.
trombone, terompone.
troop, mohlape, sehlopha, dira.
troop-carrier, thwaladira.
troops, dira, bahlabani.
trophy, sefoka.
tropic, molatšatši; – **al,** ya molatšatši.
Tropic of Cancer, Molatšatši wa Khansere.
Tropic of Capricorn, Molatšatši wa Kheperikone.
tropics, melatšatši.

trot, tshetshetha, kata, hlehla; n., mokato.
trouble, molato, tlalelo, mathata, mehlako; v., tshwenya, hlakiša.
troubler, motshwenyi.
troublesome, tshwenyang, lapišang.
trough, mogopo, sejelo.
trounce, betha, otla; – **ing,** petho.
troupe, sehlopha, lekoko, koša.
trousers, borokgo; **long** –, tšhologa; **short** –, gomela; **threequarter** –, kgasebakeng.
trowel, torofolo, trofele.
truant, mongwegi, **play** –, ngwega, roba sogo.
truce, khutšwana, lethopo.
truck, papatšo, letorokisi, koloi; v., laiša, bapatša.
truculence, bošoro, bogale, bolaeta.
truculent, šoro, laetago.
trudge, fokola, hlotša.
true, nnete, kgonthe.
true-love, nnake, moratiwa.
truly, ruri, ka kgonthe.
trump, thetša; šitiša, n., trompeta.
trumpet, porompeta, trompeta, lepapata.
trumpeter, moletši wa trompeta.
truncheon, molamo, lepara.
trundle, leotwana, toliki.
trunk, letlole, kutu, sebelebele.
truss, sehlopha, sephutha, v., bofa.
trust, tshepo, trasete, v., bota.
trusted, tshepegang, botegang.
trustee, motshepiwa, mohlapetši, mohlokomedi.
trustful, botegang, tshepegang.
trustfulness, botshepegi, potego.
truth, therešo, nnete, kgonthe.
try, leka, ahlola; – **me,** n̂teka.
tsetse-fly, ntšitsetse.
T-square, T-sekwere.
tub, faki.
tube, tšhupu, lethopo, pompo.
tuber, semodu, segwere.
tuberculosis, sehuba se segolo, mafahla, T.B., thiibii.
tuck, šunyetša, phutha, mošunyetšo.
Tuesday, Labobedi.
tuft, tšhutla, tlopo, boditse.
tug, goga, kgogo, sekepekgogi.
tuition, thuto.
tulip, teledimo.
tumble, wa, tomatoma.
tumour, sešo.
tumult, moferefere, lešata.
tundra, mohlakatšididi.
tune, molodi, tšhuni.
tunnel, tonele, thanele.
turban, mmese.
turbid, seretse, bilogileng.
turbulent, mokurukuru, sephethephethe, ferekanago!
turf, letsopa, mokato(ng).
turkey, kalakune.
turmoil, lešata, moferefere.
turn, dikološa, dikologa, mona; – **direction,** fapoga, tepoga; – **round,** sokologa, fulara; – **back,** boa; – **upside-down,** ribega; – **from side to side,** bidikama; – **a corner,** khona; – **twist,** šopa; – **away from,** hlanogela, **-ed away from,** hlanogetše; – **against,** melela dinaka.
turncoat, mohlanogi.
turnip, thenipi, rapa.
turnpike-gate, heke ya go mona, sebala-makgolo.
turpentine, thepentaene, terepenteine.
turret, toranyana.
turtle, pšhinyaleraga, v. **turn** –, kolokota.
turtle-dove, leeba, leeba-kgorwana.
tusk, lenaka la tlou.
tutor, moruti.
twang, go letša nko.
tweezers, sepato.
twelve, lesomepedi.
twenty, masome a mabedi, masomepedi.
twice, gabedi.

twig, mošaša, lehlare, lekalana, thabjana, mahlare.
twilight, phirimane, šwalane, lerotho.
twine, thapo, v., bofa, tlema.
twinge, soba, pitla; n., sehlabi.
twinkle, pekenya, phadima, ponya.
twinkling, go ponya ga leihlo.
twins, mafahla.
twirl, dikologa, mona.
twist, šopha, ohla, rara; – **bit,** borwanarara; **ed,** raragane(go).
twitch, thebetha.
two, bedi, pedi; **dimensional,** tekanyopedi.
two thirds, peditharong.
type, mohuta, v., tlanya, thaepa.
typhoid, tengkgolo.
typhoon, ledimo, thaefune.
typhus, tifuse, lenta, tswetšidinta.
typical, ya mohuta, swanang le.
typify, swantšha, šupa.
typist, mothaepi, motlanyi.
typographer, mogatiši.
typographical error, phošo ya kgatišo.
typography, tsebo (thuto) ya kgatišo.
tyrannic(al), šoro.
tyranny, bobušakapatla, pušo e šoro.
tyrant, sebušakapatla.
tyre, lepanta, thaere, – **gaiter,** keitara; – **pressure,** kgatelelo/pudulogo ya thaere.

U

ubiquitous, go ba ka gohle.
udder, thele, mokaka.
ugliness, go befa.
ugly, befa, – **person,** sekobo.
ulcer, sešo, **a syphilitic** –, thosola.
ulcerate, tšwa boladu.
ultimate, ya mafelelo.
ultimatum, kepantwa.
ultimo, fetileng.
ultra, fetago tekanyo, ultra.
umbilical, – **cord,** kala, kalana.
umbrage, moriti, kgopišo.
umbrella, samporele, sekhukhu.
umpire, malokwane, moahlodi.
unable, paletšweng, šitilwego.
unacceptable, sa amogelwego.
unaccustomed, sa tlwaelwago.
unacquianted, hlokago tsebo.
unanimity, kwano.
unanswerable, hlokago phetolo.
unarmed, sa itlhamang, se nang dibetša.
unassuming, ikokobeditšego.
unattended, nnoši.
unattractive, befang, befago.
unauthorised, ka ntle go tumelelo.
unavoidable, se nang go phengwa.
unaware, unawares, itebetše.
unbecoming, sa swanelago.
unbelief, go se dumele.
unbiased, se nang kgetholo.
unbind, bofolla, tlemolla.
unblemished, hlwekile, se nang sekodi.
unbolt, kgonyolla.
unborn, sa bago ya tswalwa.
unbosom, ipobola.
unbridled, hlokago boitshwaro.
unbuckle, konopolla.
unbutton, v., konopolla, bofolla.
uncertain, belaetšang; **to be** –, belaela.
unchangeability, go se fetoge.
uncharted, sa bewago mmepeng.
unchecked, itaolang, lokologileng.
uncircumcised, – **person,** lešoboro.
uncle, malome, ramogolo, rangwane.
uncombed (hair), mahlafarara.
uncomfortable, sa iketleng.
uncommon, ya bohlokwa.
uncommunicative, reng tuu.
uncompromising, fadileng.
unconcern, tlhokomologo.
unconditional, fela.
unconscious, idibetšego, itebetšego; – **state,** kidibalo.

unconstitutional, ka ntle ga molao.
uncontrollable, sa laolegego.
uncooked, e tala.
uncork, thibolla.
uncover, khurumolla, rola.
uncultured, hlokago setho.
undaunted, sa boifego, sa tšhabeng.
undecided, dikadikang, belaelang.
under, fase, tlase; **pass** –, huhumela.
underdone, tala.
underestimate, nyatša.
underhand, hlalefetšago, hwirihwitša.
underline, thala ka tlase.
undermine, epa, senyetša, lobiša.
underneath, fase, tlase.
underrate, nyatša.
understand, kwišiša, lemoga.
understanding, kwišišo, temogo, kwano.
understood, it is –, go a kwala.
undertake, ikemišetša, ithapa.
undertaker, moepedi, ramakase.
undesirable, sa nyakegeng, e ganwang.
undetermined, belaelang, dikadikang.
undo, dirolla, fediša.
undone, dirolotšwe, fedišitšwe.
undoubted, se nang pelaelo, ka kgonthe.
undress, apola, hlobola.
undulating, maphotophoto.
unduly, ka mokgwa o sa lokang.
undying, sa feleng, sa hweng.
unearth, epolla, utolla.
uneasiness, go tshwenyega, pelaelo.
uneasy, belaela, tshwenyega.
unemployed, se nago modiro.
unequal, sa lekanelego.
uneven, maphotophoto, sa lekanelago, makgwakgwa.
unexpected, sa kago ya lebelelwa, sewelo.
unexpired, sa kago ya fela.
unfair, sa lokang.
unfaithful, sa botegeng.
unfamiliar, šele; – **person,** moeng.
unfasten, bofolla, tlemolla.
unfit, ronang, sa lokago.
unfold, menolla, phurolla.
unforseen, ya sewelo, sa lebelelwago.
unfortunate, madimabe, manyami.
ungainly, marolo, sa hlamatšegego.
unglazed, sa phadimišwago/galasefatšwago.
ungodly, ilago Modimo.
ungovernable, sa laolweng.
unhappiness, manyami.
unhappy, nyamile,
unhealthy, fokolang.
unholy, bokgopo.
unification, kopano.
uniform, semphato, yunifomo, swanago.
uniformity, go swana, tshwano.
unify, kopanya.
unilingual, polelotee.
unimaginative, se nang kgopolo.
unimportant, difefe, e sego ya selo.
uninhabited, marope, lešoka.
unintentional, sego ka boomo; – **ly,** sego ka boomo.
uninvited, sa kang ya laletšwa.
union, kopano, kwano.
unique, e nngwe fela, nnoši, šayago tshwano.
unison, moloditee, kwano, kodutee; – **reading,** palammogo.
unit, motšo, botee.
unit of measure, seelo, kelo.
unite, kopanya.
united, kopantšwego, kopanego.
United Nations, Kopano ya Ditšhaba.
universe, leratadima; **unversal,** mo gohle.
university, yunibesiti.
unkempt, mahlafarara.
unkind, se nang botho.
unknown, šele.
unlawful, ka ntle go molao.
unless, ge e se.
unlike, fapanang, sa swanego.
unload, rola, laolla, belegolla.

unlock, notlolla, kopolla.
unlucky, madimabe, hloka lešego.
unmanageable, pala.
unmarried, sa nyalang, sa nyalwang; – **woman,** kgarebe, lefetwa; – **man,** kgope, lesogana.
unnecessary, ya lefela, sa nyakegeng.
unpack, pakolla, phahlolla.
unpaid, sa lefšago.
unparalleled, fetang tekanyo.
unpick, rarolla, thatholla.
unpleasant, sa kgahlišeng; – **taste,** bošula.
unplug, thibolla.
unprofitable, se nang thušo, lefela.
unqualified, sa kgonego, sa lokelago, se na tokelo.
unravel, hlaramolla, rarolla.
unreasonable, hlokago kgopolo.
unrefined, sa hlwekišwago.
unrest, khuduego, moferefere.
unripe, tala.
unroll, phurolla.
unruly, ya kgang, sa laolwego.
unsafe, ya kotsi.
unscrew, kurufolla, nyopolla.
unscrupulous, hwilego pelo.
unseen, sa bonweng.
unselfish, hlokago mona.
unserviceable, se nang thušo.
unsettled, ferekaneng.
unsex, fagola.
unsightly, befang, befago, šišimišago.
unskilled, boatla, bošaedi.
unsuitable, ronang.
unstable, akgaakgega, šišinyega.
untamed, hlaga.
untidiness, bošaedi, bohlaswa.
untidy, mahlafarara, sa hlwekago, bošaedi.
untie, bofolla, lokolla.
until, go fihlela, go iša go.
untimely, e sego ka nako.
untiring, go se lapišege.
unto, go.
untrue, ya maaka, se nang nnete.
untrustworthy, sa botegeng.
untruth, maaka.
unveil, širolla, bipolla.
unwanted, se nyakege.
unwell, fokolago, lwalang, babjang.
unwilling, ganang, ganago.
unwillingness, go gana.
unwise, botlaela; – **person,** setlaela.
unwittingly, ka go sa tsebe.
unworthy, sa swanelago.
unwrap, phutholla, phurolla.
unyielding, tiileng, fadileng.
up, godimo; **get** –! tsoga! **all** –, go fedile; **stand –,** nanoga, emelela, ema; **time is** –, nako e fetile; **make** –, kgabiša; – **to now,** go fihla bjale, **cheer** –, thaba.
upbraid, kgalema, kgalemela.
up-country, nagatletlolo.
upheave, phagamiša.
uphill, thata; **go** –, rotoga, namela.
uphold, tshėgetša, tsetlamiša, thekga.
upon, godimo ga, mo go.
upper, ya godimo; – **arm,** lešukhutsogo.
uppermost, e godimodimo.
upright, thwi, tsepame.
upright, stand –, topalala; **be** –, thokgama.
uprightness, go loka, bokgabane.
uproar, moferefere, lešata.
uproot, tomola, kakapolla.
upset, gakantšha, ferekanya; **be –,** gakanegile, tshwenyegile.
upside-down, turn –, thenola, ribega.
up to date, go se šalele.
upwards, godimo.
uranium, uraniamo.
urban, ya motse,
urbane, mekgwa e mebotse, tlhompho.
urbanisation, toropofatšo, toropofalo.
urbanise, toropofala, toropofatša.
urge, kgothatša, phišego, ťutuetša.
urgency, potlako, kakgofo.
urgent, ya potlako, gapeletšago.

urinate, hlapologa, rota.
urine, mohlapologo, moroto, mohlapo.
urn, pitša, moeta.
us, rena, re.
usage, mohola, mokgwa, tlwaelo.
use, mohola, thušo diriša, šomiša.
use me, ntšhomiša.
useful, na le mohola, thuša.
useless, se nang (mohola) thušo.
usher, tsenya, bega.
usual, ya ka mehla; – **ly,** ka mehla.
usurp, gapa, amoga.
usury, go jela batho.
utensils, dikgerekgere.
utilise, diriša.
utility, thušo, mohola, kholo.
utmost, go fetišiša.
utter, phethegileng, bolela maaka.
utterance, polelo.
utterly, ruri.
uttermost, ruri, ya kgole.
uvula, lelengwana.

V

Vaal River, Lekwe.
vacancy, sebaka, sekgala, sekgoba.
vacate, tšwa, tlogela, tloga.
vacation, khutšo.
vaccinate, enta, hlabela.
vaccination, kento.
vaccine, kenti.
vacillate, dikadika, kadiela.
vacuum, kgarokgaro, sebaka, rego hoo.
vagabond, mmanthaladi, moleleri, moneneri.
vagary, bolotšana.
vagina, nnyo, ditlase.
vagrant, ralalang; n., moleleri.
vague, sa kwagaleng.
vain, ikgantšhang.
vainglory, boikgantšho.
vale, molapo, moedi.
valet, mohlanka, v., hlankela.
valiance, bogale.
valiant, bogale.
valid, lokileng, ya kgonthe, maatla; theilwego.
valley, molapo, moedi.
valour, bogale, bonatla.
valuable, ya bohlokwa, ya mohola.
valuation, tekanyo ya theko.
value, mohola, theko; v., sema.
valueless, lefela, se nang mohola.
valve, belefe.
vampire, senwamadi.
van, koloi, ba pele.
vandal, mosenyi.
vadalism, go senya (fela) ka boomo.
vane, taetšaphefo.
vanish, hunyela, ngwega, timelela.
vanity, boikgantšho, lefela.
vanquish, fenya.
vaporise, moyafatša.
vapour, moyameetse.
variable, fetogang, fapanang.
variableness, go (fetoga) fapana.
variance, phapano.
variant, fapanang, lefapantšhi.
variation, phapano.
varicose, rurugileng, – **vein,** tšhikakoto.
varied, ya mehutahuta.
variegated, ya mebalabala.
variety, mehutahuta, mohuta.
various, fapanang.
varnish, baniši; v., baniša.
vary, fapana, fapanya.
vase, sebjanatsopa.
vassal, molata, mohlanka.
vast, kgolo.
vault, tlola, fofa; n., legaga.
vaunt, ikgodiša.
veal, nama ya namane.
veer, tšeka, fapoga, monamona.
vegetarian, seja-(moja) merogo.

vegetable, morogo; – **garden,** serapa sa merogo.
vegetate, mela.
vegetation, dimela.
vehemently, ka bogale.
vehicle, koloi, senamelwa.
veil, lešira, seširo; v., šira.
vein, setlišamadi.
veld, naga; – **fire,** mollo wa hlaga, - **sore,** sešo.
venerable, hlomphegang.
venerate, bina, hlompha.
veneration, tlhompho, moeno.
venereal, – **disease,** thosola.
vengeance, tefetšo.
venison, nama ya phoofolo.
venom, bohloko, mpholo, bogale.
vent, lešoba, botšo.
ventilate, tsenya moya.
ventilation, tsenyomoya.
venture, phonkgelela, beta pelo.
venue, felo, bokopanelo.
Venus, Mphatlalatšane, Sefalabogogo.
veracious, ya nnete.
veracity, nnete, kgonthe.
veranda(h), mathudi.
verb, lediri; – **prefix,** hlogolediri.
verbal, ka molomo.
verbal concord, lekgokalediri.
verbal noun, leinago.
verbatim, ntšu ka ntšu.
verdant, tal'a.
verdict, khalolo, themo.
verge, mollwane, ntšhi, nyaka go, v., sekamela.
verify, tiiša, bontšha nnete, leka.
veritable, ya nnete.
verity, nnete.
vermiculite, bemikulaete.
vermilion, bohwibidu.
vermin, dilomi, dilo.
versatile, fetogang; – **person,** kalatšane.
verse, temana, sereto.
versed, tlwaetšeng.
versifier, moreti.
versify, reta.
version, phetolo, tlhalošo; taodišo.
versus, lwantšhago, ganetšago.
vertebra, mokolo; – **l,** ya mokokotlo.
vertical, tsepameng, thwi.
verve, kgothatlo, mafolofolo.
very, gagolo, ruri.
versper, mantšiboa, phirimane.
verspers, thapelo ya mantšiboa.
vessel, mothapo, sebjana, sekepe.
vest, penegempe; v., apeša.
vestibule, molomo, phapoši.
vestige, mohlala.
vestry, konsistori.
veteran, mogale, kadija, mogolo.
veterinary surgeon, ngaka ya diruiwa.
veto, veto, kotelo.
vex, gakantšha, tlaba.
vexation, tlabego.
vibrate, šikinya, thothomela.
vicar, moruti, moemedi, sebaka.
vicarage, ngwako wa baruti.
vicarious, legatong la.
vice, patanyi, bohlola.
viceroy, kgošana.
vice versa, semphekgo, tlhanolelo.
vicinity, tikologo.
vicious, mpe, šoro, bogale.
vicissitude, phetophetogo.
victim, sebolawa, namanyana wee!
victor, mofenyi, mpuru.
Victoria Falls, Diphororo tša Victoria.
victory, phenyo.
victuals, dijo, mphago.
vie, phegišana.
view, pono, v., lebelela.
vigil, go phakgama.
vigilant, phafogileng.
vigorous, maatla.
vile, mpe, bolotšana.
village, motse, toropo, **-r,** motoropo.
villain, senokwane, molotšana.
vindicate, lokafatša, hlapa ka.
vindication, tokafatšo, boikarabelo.
vindictive, itefeletšago, itefetšago.

vine, moterebe, morara; **wild –,** mopšana.
vinegar, asene, binika.
vineyard, serapa sa (merara) meterebe.
vintage, puno ya diterebe.
viola, fiolo.
violate, senya, tlola, beta.
violence, maatla, kgapeľetšo.
violent, ka maatla, befileng, šoro.
violin, fiolo.
violoncelloo, fiolotšhelo.
viper, marabe, noga.
virgin, kgarebe.
virile, senna.
virtue, bothakga, mohola, bokgabane, maatla.
virtuous, ya kgabane.
virulent, befileng, bogale, bohloko.
virus, birase.
visage, sefahlogo.
viscous, tanyago.
visibility, ponagalo.
visible, bonagala.
vision, pono.
visit, etela; – **ing,** ketelo; – **me,** nketela.
visitor, moeng.
visual, ya pono.
visualise, gopola, bona eke.
vital, ya bophelo.
vitality, mafolofolo.
vitamin, vitamine, sematlafatši.
vitiate, senya, tšhilafatša.
viticulture, pšalo ya meterebe.
vivacity, mafolofolo.
vivid, bonagala, kwagala.
vixen, phukubje e tshadi, mmalešatana.
viz, ke go re.
vlei, mohlaka, moedi.
vocabulary, tlotlontšu.
vocal cord, lerakodu; – **exercise,** tlwaetšantšu.
vocalist, moopedi.
vocation, pitšetšo; – **al,** ya pitšetšo, – **al training,** thutišotiro.
vociferate, dira lešata, goa.
vogue, mokgwa.
void, hlokago, se nang selo, rego hoo; n., sebaka.
voice, lentšu, kodu; **soft –,** lentšwana.
volatile, phakišago, tšhabago.
volcano, bolkano, thabamollo.
Volksraad, Palamente.
volley, bataola, thalamoyeng.
volt, boloto.
volume, bolumo.
voluntary, ithapago, ka boithatelo.
voluntarily, ka go kgahlega.
volunteer, moithapi, v., ithapa.
vomit, hlatša; n., mahlatša; **cause to –,** hlatšiša.
Voortrekker, Leforotrekere.
voracity, megabaru.
vortex, phororo, pherello.
vote, bouta; n., bouto; **casting –,** kgetho ya makgaolakgang.
voter, mmouti.
voting, go bouta.
vouch, tiiša, hlatsela, paka.
voucher, setlankana.
vouchsafe, dumela.
vow, keno; v., ena; **-ed,** enne.
vowel, tumanoši.
voyage, leetowatle.
vulgar, nyatšegang.
vulgar fraction, palophatlo.
vulture, lenong, letlaka.

W

wad, sethibo.
waddle, thekesela, tlakasela.
wade, sela.
waft, moyanyana, v., pheretla, phaphama.
wag, tswikinya.

wage, tefo, moputšo; – **war,** lwa.
wager, phea (tšea) kgang.
wages, tefo, moputso.
wagtail, moletašaka, mokgoronyane.
wail, lla, tsetla.
wailing, sello.
waist, letheka; – **band,** lepanta.
waistcoat, onorobaki.
wait, leta, emela, bea pelo.
waiter, mohlanka.
wake, tsoga, phafoga, tsoša.
waken, tsoša, phafoša.
walk, sepela, eta; – **slowly,** nanya; – **together,** sepedišana; **strut,** gwanta; – **in single file,** bopelela; – **round,** dikologa; – **with a stick,** hlotlela; – **on the hands,** tomatoma; **walk with effort,** kgosoka, tšhitšhila. n., tshepelo, mosepelo; – **proudly,** gwataka, gobata.
walker, mosepedi.
walking-stick, lehlotlo, patla.
wall, leboto, lemoto.
wall-chart, papetlaboto.
wallet, sepatšhe.
wall-map, mmapa wa lebotong.
wallow, rafunya, bidikama.
wall-paintings, makwala.
wall-plug, poropo ya leboto.
walnut, thamane.
waltz, bina, balasa.
wand, thupa.
wander, kobakobana, ralala; – **stray,** timela; – **in search of food,** sela; – **be delirious,** fafatla.
wanderer, lekobakobane, moraladi.
wandering, kobakobano, thalalo, timelo.
wane, fela, fokola; – **the moon wanes,** ya tshofing.
want, rata, nyaka, hloka; n., tlhaelo.
war, ntwa, v., lwa; – – **cry,** mogobo, mokgoši wa ntwa.
warble, opela, tswirinya; n., kopelo.
ward, kamora, šireletša; – **off,** phema.
warden, molebeledi, mohlapetši.
warder, moletakgolego.
wardrobe, letlole, lekase, wotropo.
ware, sa theko, diphahlo.
warehouse, ntlophahlo, lebenkele.
warfare, ntwa, tlhabano.
warm, borutho, v., ora, ruthufatša, ikomoša; **be-,** ruthetše.
warmth, borutho, phišo.
warm weather, bosorutho.
warn, sebotša, lemoša.
warning, temošo, tshebotšo.
warp, kgopamiša.
warrant, tagafala; v., fa (maatla), karanti.
warranty, peeletšo, karanti.
warrior, mohlabani, sera.
war-ship, sekepe sa ntwa.
wart, tlhokofele, kakana.
wary, hlokomelago.
wash, hlatswa; – **oneself,** hlapa; – **someone else,** hlapiša; – **for,** hlatswetša.
wash-basin, lehlapelo, lešapelo.
wash-cloth, baselapi.
washing, tlhatso, mašela (a go hlatswa).
wasp, mobu, moruthwana.
waste, matlakala, marathana; v., senya; – **dump,** thotobolo; – **basket,** sekgobaditlakala.
wasteful, senyago.
wastefulness, bosenyi.
waster, mosenyi.
watch, lebelela, šetša, diša; n., molebeledi, tšhupanako, orolosi, watšhe.
watchful, hlọkomelang.
watchword, seema, seka, moeno.
water, meetse; v., nošetša; **to pass** –, rota, hlapologa.
waterbuck, kwele, pitwa.
waterfall, phororo, photophoto.
water-furrow, mokero, foro.
water-level, baterepase, selekantšhi.
water-melon, legapu.
waterproof, thibelago meetse.

watershed, phatolameetse.
water-supply, (phepo ya) meetse.
watery, e meetse, e tepe.
watt, wata.
wattle (tree), motsetere, mofere.
wave, lephoto; v., kgatikanya, oba; – **the head,** šišinya hlogo.
wax, tsina, motu; morulane; v., gola; – **coating,** tulelamotu.
way, tsela, mokgwa; **make** –, šuthela.
waylay, lalela.
way-mark, sešupatsela.
wayside, hleng ga tsela.
wayward, hlogothata, ngangago.
we, re, rena.
weak, fokolang.
weaken, fokodiša.
weakness, bofokodi.
weal, katlego, lehlogonolo.
weal and woe, lešego le dillo.
wealth, humile.
wean, tshweša, lomolla, phuša.
weapon, sebetša, lerumo.
wear, apere, rwele; – **out,** onala, jega, senyega; **worn,** jegilwe(go).
wearied, lapile.
weariness, tapo.
wearisome, lapiša, lapišang.
weary, lapiša, tshwenya.
weasel, kgano.
weather, boso, wetara; – **bureau,** piro ya boso.
weather-chart, papetlaboso.
weave, loga; **–r,** mologi.
web, letata, bobi, bolepu.
wed, nyala, tšea, tšeana.
wedding, lenyalo.
wedge, tshetlelo, sethami, phatša, v., setlela, thamiša; – **shaped,** sekaphatša.
wedlock, lenyalo, tšeano.
Wednesday, Laboraro.
wee, nyenyane, nana.
weed, sekoro, ngwang, mofero, v., hlagola.
week, beke; – **-end,** mphelabeke.
weekly, ka beke, kgatišobeke.
weep, lla, seka meokgo.
weeping, sello; – **willow,** mogokare.
weevil, tšhupa.
weft, sebalelo.
weigh, kala, ela, bega (A).
weight, boima, sekadi; v., imitša; n; keloboima.
weighty, e boima.
weir, letamo.
weird, makatšago, boifišang; moloi.
welcome, thabelwang, v., amogela ka thabo.
weld, ngomanya, momaganya.
welfare, katlego, kagišo.
well, sediba, petse; v., iketlile, lokile; **be** –, phela gabotse; **wish** –, lakaletša mahlogonolo; **very** –, gabotsebotse.
well-behaved, yo botho, itshwarago setho.
well-being, boiketlo.
well-bred, e lokileng, yo mekgwa e mebotse.
well-formed, hlamatšegile.
wellnigh, nyakile.
well off, humile.
welter, bidikama, ipitika.
wench, kgarebe.
wend, ya, sepela.
west, bodikela.
westerly, ka bophirima, bodikela.
western, bophirimela.
wet, meetse kolobileng; v., kolobiša; – **blanket,** sekwelemi, mosenyalethabo.
wether, tshelau.
whale, mosegwaohloga, leruarua.
what, eng, ofe, bafe, dife.
whatever, eng le eng.
wheat, korong.
wheat-land, tšhemo ya korong.
wheel, leotwana, lebele.
wheelbarrow, kiribane; lepara.
wheeze,sehumula, sekhumula.

whelp, ledinyana, mpšanyana, nkhunyana.
when, neng? leng?
when, ga, ge, mohla, e tla re.
whence, go tšwa kae.
whenever, e tla re, neng le neng, nako efe le efe.
where? kae? go kae?
where, gona, moo; – **there is,** mo go bago/lego.
whereabouts, kae?
whereabouts, bodulo, felo fa.
whereas, ka ga, conj., kganthe, athe.
whereby, ka gona.
wherefore, ka baka la eng?
whereupon, ya ba gona.
wherever, mo gohle, kae le kae.
whet, loutša.
whether, goba.
whetstone, toutšo, tootšo.
whey, hloa.
which, rel, pron., yo, le, ye, se, ba, a, tše, etc.; inter pron., ofe, bafe, efe, sefe.
while, mola, solanka, ge, ga, e tla re, ya re, sa le.
whimper, tsetsela.
whimsical, makatšago.
whine, lla, n., sello.
whip, sefepi, sephadi; v., otla, betha.
whip-lash, foroslaga, foroselaga.
whipping, kotlo.
whirl, ferella, tšokotša.
whirlpool, dibapherehlwa.
whirlwind, setšokotšane, sesasedi, sedingwadingwane.
whirr-whirr, sefofo.
whisk, feta ka pele; hwidinya.
whiskers, ditedu, maledu.
whisper, sebela nyenyetša, loma tsebe.
whistle, letša molodi, tswirinya; – **for it,** iponela; n., molodi.
white, tšhweu, šweu, re twa! re moo.
white ant, mohlwa.
whiteness, bošweu.
whitewash, taka.
whither? kae? – **away?** go iwa kae?
whitlow, phehli.
whittle, tlokotla.
whizz, bobola.
who? mang? plur., bomang? rel. pron., e, yo, ba, ya, le, a.
whole, ohle, moka; – **number,** palotlalo.
wholesaler, holosele.
wholesome, lokileng, phedišang.
wholly, ka go fela, gohle.
whom, yena yo, yo a.
whomsoever, mang le mang.
whoop, mogoo, mokgoši; v., goa, bitša.
whooping-cough, lethakgo, kotokoto, kgookgoo.
whore, seotswa, sefebi.
why, ka baka la eng?
wick, thapo ya lebone, thodi, pete.
wickedly, gampe.
wickedness, bobe, bokgopo.
wide, petleke, sephara, -phara.
widen, pharalatša, ahlamiša, katoša.
widow, mohlologadi wa mosadi.
widower, mohlologadi wa monna.
widowhood, bohlologadi.
widow-bird, mmanoke.
width, bophara.
wield, kgatikanya.
wife, mosadi, mogatša; **inferior–,** mogadingwana.
wild, hlaga, phoofolo, sebata; – **fig tree,** moumo, mogo.
wildebeest, kgokong.
wilderness, lešoka.
wildness, bohlaga.
wile, bomenemene, boradia.
wilful, swele, boomo.
wilfulness, boomo.
will, thato, testamente; v., rata; **aux.,** tla.
willing, dumela(go).
will-o'-the-wisp, mollo wa badimo, mokebe.
willow, moduwane, motswapi-tswapi

mogakare, moretlwanoka(ne).
win, fenya, hlola, rua.
wince, tšhaba, šišimoga, hunyela.
wind, phefo; – **belt,** selete sa phefo; – **break,** seširaphefo, lefaaphefo.
wind, waena, tata, nyopa.
windfall, mahlatse.
windmill, sefeufeu, phaphapha.
window, lefastere.
windpipe, mogolo, kgokgokgo.
windscreen, seširaphefo.
windward, ka phefong.
wine, beine, – **press,** kgatakelelo ya diterebe.
wine-bibber, setagwa.
wine-making, thitabeine.
winepress, segatelo.
wing, lephego; – **ed creatures,** boramaphegwana.
wink, ponya, nyemotsa.
winner, tšhia, mofenyi.
winning, kgahlišang, fenyago.
winter, marega.
wipe, hlakola, omiša, phaila.
wire, lethale, terata, motato; v., tia mogala; – **gauze,** sefeterata.
wireless, seyalemoya, radio.
wiry, e maatla, tiileng.
wisdom, bohlale; – **tooth,** leino la bogolo.
wise, bohlale, hlalefileng, hlalefile; – **men,** babohlale.
wise, mokgwa.
wisely, ka bohlale.
wish, lakatša, rata; n., takatšo.
wish, – **luck,** lakaletša mahlogonolo.
wisp, sephuthana, thotana.
wistful, hlologetšeng.
wit, tlhaologanyo, kelelo, bohlale; **be at** – **'s end,** gakanega, tlabega.
witch, moloi (wa mosadi).
witchcraft, boloi.
witch-doctor, keatseba, ngaka.
with, le, ka.
withdraw, katologa, hunyela, tloša, ntšha, goga (tšhelete), gomiša.
wither, pona, omelela.
withhold, thiba, ganela, tima.
within, ka gare.
without, ka ntle (go), hloka.
withstand, ganela, ganetša.
witness, hlatse; paki; bohlatse; v., hlatsela, bona; – **-box** bohlatsetšo.
wittingly, ka boomo.
wizard, moloi, sedupe.
woe, bomadimabe.
woeful, madimabe, manyami.
wolf, phiri.
wolfskin, letlalo la phiri.
woman, mosadi; **old** –, mokgekolo.
womanhood, bosadi, sesadi.
womankind, tshadi, basadi.
womanly, sesadi.
womb, popelo, tswala.
wonder, makala, tlabega; n., mohlolo.
wonderful, tlabegang, makatšang.
wondrous, makatšang.
won't gana, ganela, re nnako!
woo, loša, ferea, fepeletša.
wood, legong, sethokgwa, kota; – carving, petlo; – **en,** sa kwata; **small piece of** –, legonyana-; **much** –, magong.
wooden, ya legong.
woodland, sethokgwa.
woof, sebalelo.
woodwork, (thuta) petlo.
wool, boya, wulu.
word, lentšu, polelo; **small** –, lentšwana; **brief** –, polelwana.
work, modiro, mošomo; v., dira, šoma; – **for,** šomela, – **book,** puku ya mošomo.
worker, modiri, mošomi.
workman, motsebatiroatla.
workmanship, bokgwari.
work of art, bošomelo, bolokišetšo.
world, lefase.
wordly, salefase, sa lefela.
worm, seboko, lešotša.
worry, tshwenya, tlaiša.

worse, befago; **grow** –, keka.
worship, direla, rapela, khunamela; **totem,** bina, ena, hlompha.
worshipper, morapedi; mmini.
worst, e mpe ka go fetišiša; v., fenya, hlola.
worth, theko, tshwanelo, mohola; – **how much?** ja bokae?
worthless, se nang mohola, ya lefela.
worthy, lokelwang ke, lebanego.
wound, ntho; v., gobatša, phula madi.
wrangle, moferefere, phapang; v., tsoša moferefere.
wrap, phutha, phuthela, swapaswapela.
wrapper, sephuthelo.
wrath, bogale, kgalefo.
wrathful, galefa; galefiša.
wreak, itefeletša, lefeletša.
wreath, kgare, keranse.
wreathe, loga, šopha.
wreck, senya, robega; n., thobego.
wrecker, mosenyi; – **of,** moroba –.-
wrench, rutla, amoga; n., popojane.
wrestle, penyana, betana, katana.
wrestling, kadipotšano, katano, penyano, phethonkgano.
wretch, molahlegi; **poor** –!, ngwana wa batho?
wretched, yo madimabe, (wa) batho.
wretchedness, bomadimabe.
wriggle, penya, solopana.
wriggling, leswete.
wring, gamola, šopa, lokolla.
wrinkle, lešošo.
wrinkled, maolo, šošobagane.
wrist, lenakaila.
writ, taelo ya go thopa.
write, ngwala.
writer, mongwadi.
writhe, imeneka, inyoka.
writing, lengwalo, mongwalo.
wrong, phošo, bobe.
wrong, v., foša, phoša; – **against,** phošetša.
wronged, phošeditše.
wrought iron, tshipithulega.

X

X-ray, X-rei, mahlasedi a X.
xylophone, silofone.
xylose, saelose.

Y

yacht, seketswana.
yam, yamo.
yard, lapa; **back** –, mafuri, segotlo.
yard, jarata, kgato.
yarn, tlhale, metlae, nonwane.
yawn, edimola.
ye, le, lena.
year, ngwaga; **this** –, lenyaga; **next** –, išago; **last** –, ngwagola.
yearly, ka mengwaga.
yearn, hlologelwa, fišega.
yearning, tlhologelo, phišego.
yeast, komelo, tlhabego.
yell, goa, goeletša.
yellow, sehla, serolane, modipa.
yellowness, bosehla.
yelp, tlenya, lla.
yeoman, molemi.
yes, e, ee.
yesterday, maabane; **day before** –, maloba.
yet, sa lego, anthe; **not** –, ešo.
yield, tswala, ntšha, enywa, ineela; n., puno.
yoke, joko; v., pana, bofa; n., sekgela sa legetla.
yolk, mothobe.
yon, yola, bale, wola, yela.
yonder, fale, mola.
yore, kgale, bogologolo.
you, o, wena; pl. le, lena; **as an object,** go.
young, mpsha, fsa; – **girl,** kgarebe; –

man, lesogana; – **est child,** phejane.
youngster, motekatekana, sekgohlwana.
your(s), sa gago, sa lena.
youth, bosogana, bokgarebe, bofsa, babafsa.
youthfulness, bofsa.
Yuletide, nako ya Krisemose.

Z

zeal, phišego, phegelelo.
zealous, fišegang.
zebra, pitsi (ya naga).
zenith, ntlha ya godimo.
zephyr, phefo e tshesane.
zero, nnoto.
zest, phišego, mahlodi, tatso.
zigzag, letswedintsweke, manyokenyoke, v., tswedikana.
zinc, senke.
zip, zipi.
zither, sekgapa.
zone, legaro.
zoo, zoo, serapa sa diphoofolo.
Zululand, kwa Zulu.